NEW ENGLAND GENESIS

A Trilogy

CLINT HULL

Paperback ISBN: 978-1-64718-611-1
Hardcover ISBN: 978-1-64718-612-8
Epub ISBN: 978-1-64718-613-5
Mobi ISBN: 978-1-64718-614-2

Published by BookLocker.com, Inc., St. Petersburg, Florida.

The characters and events in this book are fictitious. Any similarity to real persons, living or dead, is coincidental and not intended by the author.

Printed on acid-free paper.

BookLocker.com, Inc.
2020

Library of Congress Cataloging in Publication Data
Hull, Clint
New England Genesis by Clint Hull
Library of Congress Control Number: 2020909167

Also by Clint Hull

Occupying Powers
A Novel of World War II and the Occupation of Japan

Author's Note

The three novels that compose *New England Genesis* depict that period in history from the founding of the Massachusetts Colony through Queen Anne's War as seen through the eyes of three generations of an immigrant family. The first novel, *New England Dreams*, is based on the life of the Reverend Joseph Hull, an Anglican minister who brought his congregation of 115 souls to Weymouth in 1635. The second novel, *New England Wakes*, deals with Joseph's son Tristram and his involvement with the first Quakers to arrive in Boston in 1656. *New England Rising*, the third novel, covers the lives and times of Tristram's sons Joseph and John, starting with King Philip's War in 1675 and ending with the death of Joseph in 1720. This first century in New England history evolved from a dream, or rather a variety of dreams. A gradual awakening to the realities of the Great Migration led inexorably to a rising dissatisfaction with and resistance to foreign rule. Hence the genesis of my title for this trilogy.

Clint Hull
Yarmouth Port, Massachusetts, 2020

Acknowledgments

New England Dreams had its origin in my father's attempt to write a biography of his immigrant ancestor, Reverend Joseph Hull. In the 1930s Dad covered Newport County in Rhode Island for the Historical Records Survey of the Works Progress Administration. In that capacity he gathered considerable information about his subject. His notes, which I inherited on his death, provided a basis for my novel. Unveiled at the annual meeting of the Hull Family Association in 2010, it received modest acclaim.

I had no intention of penning a sequel; but at the urging of Phyllis Hughes, the HFA genealogist, I embarked upon a follow-up novel about Joseph's eldest son Tristram. She provided me with relevant information on the subject. *New England Wakes* is more a generational sequel, for the action takes place while Joseph is still alive. It was completed in 2015.

New England Rising was my idea. I am a descendant of Tristram's younger son John, who settled in Jamestown, Rhode Island, where I grew up. Since John's brother Joseph settled across the bay in Kings Town, it seemed logical and necessary to include him in the novel. Phyllis Hughes was again generous in her support of my project.

I'm also grateful to all the readers who commented on these novels prior to publication. A special note of appreciation goes to my wife for her continued love and emotional support during many years of writing.

Contents

NEW ENGLAND DREAMS

A Novel Based on the Life of
Reverend Joseph Hull

One

"Am I now a stranger in the church where I was baptized?"
(Crewkerne, Somerset, 1629)

Joseph Hull trod the well-worn path through the graveyard beside St. Bartholomew's Church in Crewkerne. The morning sun warmed his cheeks, but a cool westerly breeze heralded the early advent of winter. To dispel his wintry thoughts, he summoned up memories of his childhood – of hiding among the headstones and roaming the hills beyond the church. But his mind reverted always to a darkened bedroom where his mother lay ill. while his father sought to resign himself to a death that appeared to be imminent. Hull had come to Crewkerne, riding the thirty miles from St. Giles church in Northleigh where he was rector, to offer what solace he could to his father and possibly to bury his mother.

She was seventy-eight and had borne nine or ten children, but half of them died at birth or shortly thereafter. Only two of her sons were still alive. His older brother George lived in Crewkerne with his wife and five children. Another brother William, a minister like himself, had died two years earlier at Colyton in Devon, leaving only his wife. Hull had served as curate under William after he graduated from Oxford and before he became rector of St. Giles. Strange that such a large family should be diminished so soon. He thought of his

3

wife Anne and their five children, and wondered if the same fate would befall them. At thirty-four, he stood six feet tall and could walk for hours without tiring. Yet he well knew that a man's condition was subject to rapid and unexpected change.

As he neared the entrance to the church, he saw a man clad in dark clerical garb like his own. The man was dwarfed by the twin castellated towers of yellow stone that flanked a large stained glass window set into the massive arch above the door. Yet Hull recognized the shock of wind-tossed reddish hair as belonging to a former classmate at St. Mary Hall. They had been ordained priests together. That was ten years ago

"Warham!" he cried. "What brings you to Crewkerne?"

"I thought I might find you at the church," Warham said,. "I need a favor." His words were soft spoken, almost conspiratorial.

"I'm staying with my parents," Hull said. "But what is it you need?"

Warham raised his head and spoke with more confidence. "I want to speak at a church service."

"Ask the wardens for permission. You know the rules."

"It's not that simple. Two years ago I was suspended as a lecturer in this church. I was fortunate enough to obtain a post in another diocese."

Hull studied his friend closely. Since their ordination at St. Mary Church in Silverton, they had met on several occasions; but he knew little about Warham's current circumstances or intentions, and he was troubled by his words and by the anxious look in his gray eyes.

"Why were you suspended?" he asked.

"The chancellor of the diocese, a man named Duck, charged me with repeating a sermon in my home for my family and a few friends."

"That's hardly sufficient cause for suspension."

"Duck had an eye on me. He said I used unauthorized prayers, and that I questioned the propriety of certain games in the *Book of Sports*."

"And were those charges true?"

Warham bowed his head again, as if he expected a reprimand. "I suppose so. But the games are contrary to God's command to keep holy the Sabbath, and we all stray on occasion from the authorized text."

Hull readily admitted to that fault. In his estimation William Laud, now Bishop of London, was overly zealous in his efforts to enforce strict conformity with the *Book of Common Prayer*. Granted that bishops were obliged to stem a rising tide of Puritanism, but they gained little by penalizing ministers for minor infractions of the rules. Such rigidity would only swell the ranks of nonconformists and dissenters. He was fortunate in that his own parish in Northleigh was under the diocese of Exeter, where Bishop Hall was more lenient about such matters.

"So what do you want me to do?" he asked.

"Arrange for a service," Warham said. "You were born and baptized in Crewkerne. The wardens will listen to you."

"What is it you want to say?"

"I've decided to emigrate to New England, and I'd like to bid farewell to my friends in Crewkerne. Nothing like a sermon." He seemed about to continue, but thought better of it.

"And you think, if I vouch for you, they'll give you a license."

Warham waved his hands dismissively. "Never mind the license. If you conduct the service, you can allow me to say a few words."

Hull remained dubious. "That sounds rather underhanded," he said to gain time. "I've thought of going to New England myself, but I have a comfortable living at St. Giles and a family to consider."

Warham raised his eyebrows in surprise. "Why would you want to emigrate?" he asked.

"Some years ago I spoke of it with Sir Ferdinando Gorges. He was in charge of the Plymouth fort at the time. I think he still is."

"How do you come to know Gorges?" Warham interrupted.

Hull detected a note of wariness, even apprehension, in his friend's voice. "My father had some business dealings with the family. When I was a curate in Colyton, his son Robert invited me down to Plymouth to view the fort. He sent Robert to New England to set up a colony at a spot called Wessaguscus, but it failed to take root. Gorges was convinced that England's future prosperity is closely linked to colonization."

"Are you still in contact with him?"

"I last saw him three years ago. It was shortly after Robert died. He seemed interested in my future and offered to help me in any way he could. I think he was looking for someone to fill the void left by his son."

"Then you'll talk to the wardens?"

"I'm conducting a prayer service this evening for the sick and dying," Hull said. "I'll consider your request."

* * *

Hull was surprised at the number of parishioners who had gathered in the chapel for the prayer vigil. Was his family held in such high esteem, or had Warham spread the word about the service?

Following the opening prayer and a brief homily on how to benefit from adversity, he introduced Warham as, "A man well known to you, who wishes to ask for your prayers as he embarks upon a new life in a far off land." Satisfied that he had effectively limited the scope of Warham's remarks, he surrendered the pulpit to his friend.

Warham began by speaking of his plan to sail from Plymouth in the spring. "Everyone agrees that the Church of England is in need of reform," he went on, "yet it seems incapable of meaningful change from within. New England offers us a fresh frontier, an alternative to the separatism that is rife in our land, an opportunity to establish a new colony with a more enlightened form of worship."

A murmur of disapproval spread among the gathering. Two men rose and slipped out of the chapel. Hull's hands gripped the edge of his seat, and he started to get up. His instinct told him he should end the service at once; but Warham's next words were more reassuring, and he settled back in his chair.

"I come to thank you for your past kindness, to ask for your prayers on the journey I am about to undertake, and to bid you farewell. If anyone here feels moved to accompany me, you can speak to me after the service."

Hull was on his feet as Warham finished speaking, but on his way to the pulpit he decided to restrain his anger. Any criticism of his friend's remarks would add to the unease that had gripped the audience. He recited an authorized prayer and concluded the service.

As people were filing out of the chapel, he confronted Warham. "I had no idea you intended to recruit followers for the Puritan cause. You place me in an awkward position."

"I'm sorry you feel that way. I said what all men know to be true."

"You had better leave before the rector arrives."

"I'll be gone long before he can file a report," Warham said.

"I was thinking of myself. I have a mother to attend in Crewkerne."

"I'm sorry," Warham said as he gathered up his cloak. "I should have considered that." He left quickly by a side door.

As Hull passed the baptismal font on his way out, he was confronted by the rector, a tall imposing man in his fifties. His clothing was in disarray, having been hastily donned; and his breath was labored. The rector was not a close friend, but their relationship thus far had been amicable.

"Where is John Warham?" he demanded. Righteous anger was writ large across his florid face.

"He left after the service," Hull replied.

"He has been forbidden to preach in this diocese. I hold the wardens responsible for granting him permission."

"I allowed him to speak," Hull said calmly. If he couldn't placate the rector, he could at least give Warham more time to escape. "He told me he wanted to say good-bye to people he knew and had grown to love. I saw no harm in that."

Suddenly aware of the state of his attire, the rector straightened his collar and fastened a button on his shirt. This done, he drew himself up to his full height and vented his displeasure on Hull. "I find no record of a license for the service this evening?"

"I spoke privately to one of the wardens."

"Then you were extended a courtesy, and you abused it. Neither you nor Warham is registered in the *Book of Strange Preachers*."

Hull rested his hands on the square stone font. He felt the anger rising within him and had to fight to control his words. "Am I now a stranger in the church where I was baptized?"

"That's neither here nor there," the rector said. "I am obliged to report this incident to the Spiritual Court of the diocese. Granted, yours is the lesser offense; but I'll see to it that Warham is excommunicated."

"His remarks may have lacked discretion, but he has the interest of the Church at heart." Hull was surprised to hear himself defending Warham. He recognized that his anger was directed not at the rector but at the restrictive regulations imposed by the church hierarchy. Such rules were not new, but until now they had not weighed directly upon him.

"I doubt that the bishop will agree with you. Loyalty is too often a mask worn by separatists. Warham appears to be well along that road."

"Banishment is hardly an effective remedy for someone planning to leave the country," Hull said with a bitter laugh.

"Perhaps not," the rector said, "but it puts an obstacle in his path."

"The Church is much better served by men devoted to removing obstacles," Hull replied.

The rector turned away from him in disgust. "I shall put your opinion in my report to Bishop Curle."

"Do what you must," Hull said. "My duty is at my mother's bedside."

Two

"Reasonable men can always find a middle way."
(Northleigh and Exeter, Devon, 1631)

Hull normally spoke to his brother George only when he visited his parents in Crewkerne. Helping their father manage the family property kept George fully occupied. To find him at the door of the rectory in Northleigh was a singular event that boded no good. Hull invited him in, and he greeted Anne in a distracted manner. His tanned face and rough clothing confirmed his connection to the soil. He looked distraught.

"Shall I fix tea?" Anne asked, setting aside the apron she was sewing.

"Perhaps after we talk," Hull said, leading George toward the office.

"They slit Leighton's nose and cut off his ears," George said when the door was shut. "As if that weren't enough, they branded *SS* on his forehead, for sower of sedition, and sentenced him to life in prison."

Hull read the indignation in his brother's normally mild blue eyes, and he recognized the nervous twitch in his cheek. The case of Alexander Leighton was a frequent topic of conversation, even in the remote hamlet of Northleigh. Hull had followed the events surrounding Leighton with considerable interest, for they bore upon restricted expression of thought, whether in writing or speech. Leighton had studied medicine at St. Andrew's and Leiden. Twice barred from practicing in Scotland, he went to Holland, where he published a pamphlet titled *An Appeal to the Parliament: Zion's Plea Against Prelacy*, an attack on Anglican bishops as tools of the Antichrist. Upon his return he was censured in Star Chamber and confined at Newgate. While awaiting sentence, he was placed in irons in an unheated cell exposed to the rain and snow and denied visits by his wife and friends. Hull had not read the *Appeal*, but the nature and severity of the sentence struck him as barbarous. Yet George's announcement didn't correspond with his own knowledge of the case.

"I heard that Leighton escaped from prison before his sentence could be carried out," he said. It was more a question than a statement.

"He was captured as he tried to leave the country," George muttered, keeping his voice down lest he alarm Anne and the children in the next room. "How can you go on preaching, when such punishments are meted out in the name of God and religion?"

"What would you have me do, resign?" Hull asked. "My resignation would have no effect on the events in London, whereas my continuance as a minister may preserve a semblance of reason and moderation in the Church."

"Do what you think is right," George said. "For my part, I can no longer remain in England when the courts condone – nay, embrace – such torture for matters of conscience."

"Where will you go?"

"Massachusetts. I plan to join John Warham. He has a church in Dorchester near Boston."

"If you're in New England, who will help father harvest the crops?"

"He can manage on his own. I need to get away from this madness."

"Madness is indeed rife," Hull agreed, "but it resides largely in London. If it should spread to Devon, I may well decide to join you."

"That would be fine indeed," George said.

"You must write and tell me what you find in New England," Hull said as he led George out to where the family was gathered for dinner.

"We're having lamb stew," Anne said, motioning toward a place at the table, "and you're welcome to stay the night."

"I must get back," George said. "Perhaps another time."

"Are we going to New England?" Joanna asked as the door closed behind him, a note of eagerness in her voice.

Joanna was eleven and their firstborn child, her name a combination of his own and that of his wife. Hull glanced at Anne. She had stopped stirring the stew and was regarding him apprehensively.

"I trust it won't come to that," he said, "but I share George's concern and wish him well."

Reassured by his words, she resumed cooking; but Joanna's face registered her disappointment.

* * *

The variegated colors of autumn were giving way to winter's dull mantle as Hull crossed the glebe field that lay between the rectory and St. Giles parish church in Northleigh. His thoughts too were brown and gray, and the steep path seemed to mirror his life and his future prospects.

Pausing in the middle of the field, he looked about. Come spring, the poor of the parish would once again plant vegetables in this earth; and Anne would tend her garden next to the rectory, though how she found time with six children in the house was a mystery to him. It was good for a man to maintain his kinship with the soil.

As a young man he had viewed the ministry as a walk in the English countryside, a walk strewn with minor obstacles but for the most part level and pleasant. He saw himself as a rector, a spiritual leader respected by his congregation, and as a husband and father, a provider honored and loved by his family. He had assumed all those roles; but the lines of this picture had now blurred, and the road ahead was no longer clear and unencumbered.

Puritans and nonconformists contributed to the general unrest and confusion of the time, yet he refused to place the blame entirely on them. He was amenable to modifications in church practice; but the church hierarchy, following the lead of Bishop Laud, were uncompromising in their resistance to change. Hope for a meeting of minds, a common ground, faded with each new directive from London. Whether or not he wore a white surplice over his cassock was of no consequence, and whether the altar was made of wood or stone had little bearing upon salvation. Laud's concern for such trappings only obscured the substance of the Anglican faith.

In Northleigh he had been shielded thus far from such controversies. But rumor had it that the bishop of Exeter had been summoned to London to answer to charges of Calvinist tendencies and leniency toward Puritans. The news made him apprehensive about his own future. Having run afoul of church rules in Crewkerne, he foresaw a day when Laud's arm would extend to every pulpit in England and render the role of a minister meaningless.

Standing as if rooted, he looked up at the square tower of St. Giles. It loomed castle like above the hedgerows, imparting a sense of security – but also of beleaguerment. Twenty miles to the west was a tower twice as high, the cathedral of St. Peter in Exeter. He resolved to journey there to seek guidance and to voice his support for Bishop Hall. Far better to seize upon events at the outset than to wait until they caught him up.

* * *

Reining in his horse, Hull gazed down upon the walled city of Exeter. The city was protected by a castle on the north, by the river Exe on the south. A canal brought great sailing ships to the quays, and a dozen churches served as a spiritual conduit to bring God's word to the populace. Dwarfing the surrounding buildings were the massive guild hall and the lofty cathedral with its Norman towers, flying buttresses, and pinnacles. He had long regarded it as a testament to the faith of its makers. Current pieties paled in comparison.

His goal now in sight, he nudged his steed into motion, allowing the animal to set its own pace. He passed through the west gate and stopped, as was his custom on visits to the city, at the shop of a printer and book seller. The proprietor, a young and curly haired man named Barrows, pointed out several new additions to his stock, among them a volume of the *Occasional Meditations* for which Bishop Hall was justly famous.

Hull tucked the book under his arm and moved on to a table where a number of pamphlets overlapped each another. They had paper covers and four to a dozen pages of text. Most of them dealt with religious subjects. He examined each one with care. At the rear of the table, half hidden under another pamphlet, he found a copy of *Zion's Plea Against Prelacy*, the pamphlet that had cost Leighton his ears and landed him in jail. He glanced about to make sure he and Barrows were alone in the shop before opening it.

"I found this on your table," he told the book seller. "You run a great risk by displaying it openly."

"I thought I had disposed of it," Barrows said in feigned alarm. "I shall burn the cursed thing at once. Unless you wish to take it off my hands."

Hull was about to decline, but reconsidered. To counter the spread of Puritan influence, he must be able to recognize the face of the enemy. "If that will keep you from claiming that you intend to burn it," he said.

Barrows laughed. "I should know better than to lie to a minister."

Hull took out his purse to pay for the two items.

"No charge for the pamphlet," Barrows said. "You likely saved my ears. Give my regards to the bishop when you see him."

* * *

On entering the cathedral, Hull was humbled as always by the fan-like Gothic arches that supported the lofty nave, and by the centuries-old stained glass in the massive east window. He paused to look at the minstrels' gallery and its carving of twelve angels playing various instruments, then traversed the choir and turned right at the bishop's throne. Skirting the main altar, he knelt down in the Lady Chapel to pray.

He too was heir to a tradition of faith made manifest in works. Should he preserve the old or seek to create something new either here in Devon or in a new land? Puritan efforts to establish a model for church reform in the colonies seemed petty when compared to the vastness of Exeter cathedral. Perhaps one day someone would erect an edifice such as this in the wilderness of New England. A dream worth his consideration!

Passing through the south transept, he crossed to the adjoining chapter house and took a seat in the oak-paneled anteroom. He had been there often, but always at the bishop's behest. He hadn't come now to complain or to question. He wanted to know how Bishop Hall viewed current conditions in the Church. As an assistant ushered him into the book-lined study that served as the diocesan office, he wondered if the bishop too had a dream.

Bishop Joseph Hall rose to greet him. A tall slender man in his late fifties, he had a prominent forehead. His gray eyes were set into cavernous sockets separated by a long aquiline nose. He wore a straight black robe and red skullcap. An amulet resembling a sea shell hung from a gold chain under his neatly trimmed white beard. He looked more like an Oxford don than a prelate of the Church of England.

"Well, Joseph, have you come to replace me?" he asked. "Our names are so similar that few would notice the difference."

It was a standing joke between them. "I'm not yet prepared to do that, your Excellency," Hull said in mock seriousness. "I have come out of concern for my own future and that of the Church."

"The Church's future is quite predictable," the bishop said, motioning him to sit down. "William Laud will be appointed Archbishop of Canterbury. He is already acting in that capacity. He will redouble his efforts to achieve uniformity through strict adherence to traditional church forms and practices. Puritans will feel even more alienated and accuse him of popery. Who can say how it will all end? But you spoke of your future. Are you dissatisfied with your post at St. Giles?"

"Not at all, but I am troubled. Your summons to London is of great concern. I'm mindful of what happened to Leighton. A minister must be free to preach and hold services without fear of incurring Laud's wrath."

"My writings are hardly comparable to Leighton's," the bishop said, waving his hand in a gesture of dismissal. "But all that aside, this isn't the first time I've had to kneel before Laud." He leafed through the papers on his desk. Finding what he sought, he held the sheet up close to his face.

"Let me read you something. It's from a sermon I delivered several weeks ago in London." He cleared his throat, as if he were about to address his flock in the cathedral. "Tradition has its proper place in the Church, but it cannot be allowed to usurp the role of scripture. Substance must not give way to circumstance. For truth resides in differences. As gold is buried in dross, or wheat amongst chaff, the world in which we live is a commingling of truth and falsehood. It is God's work, not ours, to separate them."

"How did Bishop Laud respond to that?" Hull asked.

"Laud and I may differ about certain policies and rituals, but we agree on matters of church unity. However, within that unity a variety of customs can be accommodated. Better to swallow a ceremony than rend a church."

Hull wondered whether this last piece of wisdom was in the sermon or fresh out of the bishop's mind. "Do you see some hope of reconciliation, or at least compromise, with the Puritan reformers?"

"Reasonable men can always find a middle way," the bishop said.

"What about John Winthrop? Do you consider him reasonable?"

The bishop frowned. "Winthrop proclaims his loyalty to Church and Crown; but now that he has a royal charter for Massachusetts, I fear that his hubris will take him in a different direction. Pride is the downfall of many a good man. Even bishops are not exempt from such temptation."

Although the reference was to Laud, Hull knew it was also meant as an admonition for himself. He thought of the pamphlet secreted in his saddle bag next to the bishop's *Meditations*. "It's a human weakness," he granted.

"Why this concern with Winthrop and Puritans?" the bishop asked. "Do you have a mind to emigrate to New England?"

"If I did, it would be in the cause of church unity and not without a congregation loyal to the Church of England."

The bishop walked to the window and stood looking out. "I cannot recommend such a move," he said. "You have a family to consider. Besides, the Massachusetts Colony has suffered through a hard winter and has little chance of success. Yet the idea of dispatching Anglican ministers to New England may appeal to Laud and the King. It would caution the colonists to remain loyal and help to ensure that Winthrop keeps his promise."

"Too many ministers might create the same situation we have here in England," Hull said. "But a few loyal churchmen who are open to diversity of opinion and receptive to change might do some good."

The bishop turned to face Hull. "And do you see yourself as such a man?" he asked.

"I'm not yet sure. It warrants serious reflection."

"May God guide you and direct your decision," the bishop said.

* * *

Rather than moving Hull to develop his idea, the bishop's halfhearted approval had a calming effect on him. If Bishop Hall could cope with Laud's growing influence and maintain an independent spirit, surely he could do the same within his own limited sphere. And the bishop was right. He had a wife and children to consider.

After reading the pamphlet given to him by Barrows, he had to agree that Leighton's condemnation of the hierarchy was too extreme. Yet he could not condone the punishment that had been meted out. He regarded sedition as a crime against civil authority. Religious offenses should be treated as heresy. The slitting of noses and branding of cheeks were tactics reminiscent of the inquisition. Heretics too were reasonable men who could be brought by argument to see their error. If not, excommunication was a more suitable remedy. Yet heresy often bordered upon sedition by stirring up the populace to rebellion, and Hull was glad he didn't have to make such judgments.

Such was his frame of mind when, several weeks later, he answered a knock and found Barrows cowering on his doorstep. The book seller wore a coat but no hat. His curly hair was wild from the wind and weather. Fear and anxiety had replaced the smile he displayed at their last meeting.

"May I come in for a moment?" he whispered, as if he were afraid to offend the howling gale.

"Of course," Hull said. "I'll have my son tend to your horse."

"I travel on foot," Barrows said. "A horse is difficult to conceal."

"Then come and warm yourself by the fire. Are you hungry?"

Barrows entered the great room of the rectory, where he stood, coat still on, his back to the fireplace. "I don't want to trouble you or your wife."

"I'll have Anne fix something for you," Hull said. "We can talk in private after you've eaten."

The book seller's fears appeared undiminished after the meal as they sat in the office where Hull counseled his parishioners. "I gather that you're fleeing from something," he said. "Did the authorities find another seditious pamphlet in your shop?"

"Worse than that. The type was all set and ready for printing. I was upstairs when they broke in, so I had time to slip out by the back door. Last night I took shelter in a barn."

"You can sleep here tonight," Hull said. "But where are you going? Won't your family be worried about you?"

"I have no family to concern me, and no destination. It's all so sudden. Someone must have told the authorities what I was doing. I meant no harm by it. It was just another opinion on a religious controversy."

"Who was it that broke in? Someone from the diocese?"

"I didn't stop to see who it was, but I suspect it was the constable. He has orders from London to keep an eye on Bishop Hall. Seems that some of the bishop's writings are suspect in the eyes of the Church."

"Is he involved in your plight?" Hull asked.

"No, except perhaps by association. These days one never knows."

"Have you thought of booking passage on a ship bound for New England? There must be opportunities for a printer in the colonies."

"I have thought of that. I don't have much choice, if I want to keep my ears. I hope I'm not placing you or your family in any danger."

"I'm sure no one witnessed your arrival," Hull said. "Now you must get some rest. You'll want to be on your way before daybreak. You may well find a ship that's ready to sail in Plymouth."

"That seems reasonable," Barrows said.

* * *

Hull rose early the next morning; and Anne made porridge for Barrows before he crept off into the darkness, leaving Hull to face the fact that dissent would no longer be tolerated anywhere in England. If Bishop Hall was under surveillance, other ministers in the diocese might also be suspect. Indeed, he might soon find himself on such a list; for he too was willing to compromise on matters of church reform, to bend the rules if the situation warranted. The incident in Crewkerne had doubtless been recorded and passed along the ecclesiastical chain of authority. Now he was guilty as well of abetting the escape of a fugitive and possessing seditious literature.

He would be wise to burn the pamphlet. If Barrows had recorded the transaction, it would not be found in his possession. Yet the idea of burning a book pained him. He would be destroying what someone else had built – the mansion of another's mind. But the safety of Anne and the children was more important. That night when all were asleep, he tore the incriminating pamphlet into a dozen pieces and threw them one by one upon the smoldering ashes in the fireplace. But the bright flames failed to dispel the dark thoughts that had taken possession of his soul.

Concerned about Barrows' fate, Hull asked a townsman who was going to Plymouth to inquire into the book seller's whereabouts. The man brought back sobering news. Barrows had been apprehended boarding a ship bound for New England. He was arrested, tried, and sentenced to what had become the customary punishment for sedition. During his questioning, he had steadfastly refused to implicate anyone else. The man reported this last piece of information with a knowing look, as if he were quite certain that Hull would be interested.

Stunned by the realization that a single word from Barrows would have sealed his own fate, Hull saw that he had to make a choice. He could either adjust his thinking to conform to directives from London or add his voice to the growing chorus of dissent. Or he might heed the advice he had given to Barrows and go to New England.

The prospect of emigrating aroused his restless spirit, but what effect would such a move have on his family? The children would likely regard it as an adventure. Anne was prone to accede to his wishes, yet he wanted to know how she really felt before he took any action. Her wholehearted cooperation was essential in coping with the rigors and challenges of a sea voyage and life in the colonies.

He broached the subject cautiously one evening after the children were asleep. Anne sat by the fireplace knitting a woolen scarf for Joanna. Her dark brown hair covered much of the shawl that was draped about her shoulders. The light from the fire accentuated the creases alongside her eyes and on her forehead, a consequence of giving birth to six children. In all other respects she was as young and strong as on the day he married her.

"We wouldn't go there alone." he assured her. He stood with his back to the fire, hands clasped behind him. "I'll have to gather a congregation for my church in the wilderness. It may take a year to do that and to secure a ship."

"When will we leave St. Giles?" Anne had ceased knitting. The two needles formed a cross on her lap. She regarded him warily.

Hull frowned. Rather than express her opinion of his idea, she chose already to treat it as an accomplished fact. "I can't possibly recruit enough people here in Northleigh, but I know some farmers near Crewkerne who may be willing to emigrate. Bishop Laud's influence is much more oppressive in Somerset."

"Then you're set to oppose Bishop Laud."

"Not openly. I simply want to escape his jurisdiction."

"Please don't be angry with me, Joseph; but were I not your wife, I should require a much better reason to go to New England than dissatisfaction with Bishop Laud. And how are tenant farmers to pay for their passage?"

Her comments surprised and disturbed him. He had assumed that the congregation he recruited would share his own motivation and vision of the Church. It hadn't occurred to him that he might have to offer them a different incentive in order to persuade them to follow him.

"That can be worked out later," he said with growing respect for her opinion. "But I want to know how you feel about such a move. Speak for yourself, not as my wife."

"I cannot so easily separate one from the other," Anne said, casting her eyes down shyly in the manner that had won his heart over a decade ago. "The thought of moving so far away frightens me. We've been comfortable here in Northleigh, and I should hate to leave. But if Bishop Hall agrees that your ministry lies elsewhere, I am content to abide by his decision."

"Nothing has been decided. If such a move frightens you, I'll say no more about it."

"Tell me what we may expect to find there in New England," Anne said. "Once I've grown accustomed to the idea, it won't seem quite so frightening."

Hull bent down and kissed her. "It won't happen straightaway," he said. "You'll have ample time to prepare yourself and the children. I can make some inquiries in Somerset. Then we'll decide how best to proceed."

His inquiries in Crewkerne, Batcombe, and Broadway aroused a fair amount of interest but few firm commitments. Some farmers expressed their doubts as to his own dedication to the plan. They were waiting for him to take some definitive action before they made up their minds. He would have to give up his post in Northleigh and devote himself fully to planning a future in New England. Three months after broaching the idea, he told his wife they would have to relocate to Somerset. Anne reacted with calm resignation to the announcement, as if she had been expecting it. Yet he could see, as she prepared for the move, that it was hard for her to relinquish the home she had created for him, the home where her six children were born. On more than one occasion he found her standing in the middle of a room lost in reverie, and he imagined he could read her thoughts.

Hull soon realized that it would be equally difficult for him to give up his position as rector of St. Giles. When at last all was ready, he preached a farewell sermon to the loyal congregation he had served for twelve years. After the service Anne took the children back to the rectory, while he shook hands with his parishioners. The partings were painful, often tearful as well. When all had left, he stood alone in the chancel of the stone church he had come to regard as his province. Kneeling, he prayed to God for some sign that he had made the right decision.

When he was done, he made a circuit of the nave and north aisle. The morning sun shining through the stained glass brought the carved bench ends to life with color. He paused to look up at St. Peter with his key and St. Paul with his sword He would need both authority and courage to preach in New England. Climbing up in the tower, he looked out over the plain that sloped gently southeastward to the sea. In all his years at Northleigh little had changed. He considered ringing the bells to announce that an era was coming to an end, but decided against it. No one in the village would understand.

Back on the ground, he strolled through the old graveyard on the south side of the church. He had buried many of Northleigh's residents there. But the dead had nothing to say to him, and he set out toward the rectory. Half way across the glebe field he noticed Joanna running toward him.

"Mother doesn't feel well," she called out as she drew closer, "but she said not to worry. She's going to have another baby."

Hull looked up at the sky. Surely this was the sign he sought, a new life to match his own new beginning. Smiling at Joanna, he quickened his pace. He wanted to hear the good news directly from Anne.

Three

"I need your advice."

(Ashton Court and Batcombe, Somerset, 1632)

Hull surrendered the reins of his mare to the liveried groom at Ashton Court, the ancestral seat of the Smyth family and the current residence of Sir Ferdinando Gorges.

"Take good care of her," he said.

"She's in good hands, sir," the groom replied.

It was Hull's first visit to Ashton Court. Sir Ferdinando had resigned his command at Plymouth fort and married Lady Elizabeth Smyth, his fourth wife. He was over sixty, and Hull assumed he had married a rich widow in order to pursue his own interest in colonization. But that was not the reason for his visit to Gorges. After resigning his post as rector at Northleigh, he had moved to Batcombe in Somerset and set about recruiting a congregation. But it was more difficult than he expected to convince people that they should emigrate to New England. Undaunted, he placed his future in God's hands – which didn't prevent him from acting in his own interest.

The yellow stone facade of Ashton Court extended a good seven rods to the right of a central three-story tower. A longer wing to the left was under construction. He was ushered into the vaulted hall, where fluted stone pillars flared out at the summit to form an arched ceiling. Their effect on him was oppressive. Unaccustomed to the trappings of wealth, he was apprehensive about his reception. Would Gorges even remember him? Would he recall the offer of patronage he had made so many years ago?

* * *

"Reverend Joseph Hull to see you."

Sir Ferdinando Gorges set aside the leather-bound volume on recent explorations of the American continent. "Show him in," he said in a voice accustomed to command.

His gaze swept the mahogany paneling, the green velvet drapes, the bookshelves that extended from floor to ceiling. The library was his domain, yet his pride of possession was tempered by an awareness that he was merely a tenant at Ashton Court. Thomas Smyth, his stepson, was heir to the Smyth estate. His own modest holdings at Birdscombe lay several miles to the west.

At the library window Gorges gazed upon the verdant meadows stretching eastward to the Avon River and the bustling port of Bristol. In his brief letter requesting an audience, Hull had expressed a wish to start life anew. Gorges knew from experience that fresh starts usually involved a sum of money. He recalled his first meeting with Hull at Plymouth fort. They had strolled on the ramparts, and Hull had agreed with him that colonies were vital to the future prosperity of England. His dreams of colonization had been disrupted by Winthrop and his Massachusetts Bay Colony, but he was adjusting to this new challenge. He now had the means and a plan for governing New England.

"Thank you for granting me this audience."

Startled out of his reverie, Gorges turned to greet his visitor. Hull's face was open and cheerful, but he had lost weight. A dark suit hung loosely on his slender frame, and he clutched his hat in his left hand. Suddenly aware of his own girth, Gorges resumed his seat at the desk. "I trust you and your family are well," he said, motioning his visitor to take a seat.

Glancing about the richly appointed library, Hull wondered how this infusion of wealth might have affected the character of the man he had met in Plymouth. Most of what he knew about Gorges was gleaned from talks with his son Robert. Knighted by the Earl of Essex for his military service at Rouen, Sir Ferdinando was elected to Parliament in 1593 and assumed command of Plymouth fort soon after. He was imprisoned for his association with Essex's plot to kidnap the Queen, but was pardoned and restored to his post upon King James' accession to the throne. His interest in New England, which dated from 1607 with the Popham colony, culminated in the settlement at Wessaguscus. "If you had been there," he confided after Robert's death, "he might have succeeded." Hull had never asked him for a favor. Now, noting the elegant clothes of the portly and rather pompous personage who presided at Ashton Court, he feared this latest marriage had altered Sir Ferdinando's vision and outlook on life.

"We're expecting our seventh child," he said.

"I heard you are no longer at Northleigh."

Hull set his hat on the parquet floor beside his chair and launched into a description of his plans to emigrate to New England and the actions he had taken thus far to achieve that goal. His voice became animated as he spoke, and he gestured with his hands and arms to emphasize his points.

Gorges listened patiently. "So you're here to ask for help in financing this venture," he said when Hull was finished. There had been no mention of money, but he knew the game.

Hull shook his head. "I've come because I need your advice," he said

Gorges uttered an audible sigh of relief. Leaning back in his chair, he folded his hands across his vest. "What appears as good advice today may prove to be bad tomorrow. Why do you want to go to New England?"

"A more moderate voice is needed in these religious disputes," Hull said. He was glad to be answering questions rather than stating his case. "A congregation that adheres to Anglican principles will provide an alternative to Puritan influence in the colonies. At least, that is my hope."

"Winthrop appears to have scant interest in moderation," Gorges said. "But I don't mean to discourage you. How can I help?"

"When I left Northleigh, I had a clear vision of what I needed to do; but I'm finding it difficult to recruit the right people. Most men who are dissatisfied with the Church tend to support the Puritan cause. If I enlist their support, I shall have to convert my own congregation."

"You need more time to gather your company," Gorges said. "I see no insurmountable problem in that."

"It's not simply a question of time. Anglicans, even those who harbor nonconformist sentiments, are reluctant to leave England for purely religious reasons. My vision has little appeal for them."

Gorges reflected a moment. "You must think in terms of a colony rather than a congregation. Men work six days a week. They pray but one."

"I'm a minister. What else can I offer them."

"You can offer them land! In New England a man plants vegetables and gathers wood on his own property. His labors benefit his own family. I know of no greater incentive. But you'll need men with a range of skills, if your colony is to survive. A carpenter is of more use than a vestryman." He allowed Hull to absorb this advice before taking a new tack. "How do you propose to finance this colony of yours?"

"Families will pay for their passage and contribute whatever they can toward the general provisions," Hull said. "I have some money of my own to make up any difference."

"You should contact a cattle dealer before you go and take some with you. You'll find a ready market for them in New England."

"I'm a minister," Hull said indignantly. "I deal in souls, not cattle."

Gorges brushed the comment aside. "There's a dealer in Broadway named Standerwick. You can mention my name."

Hull didn't argue. Having grown up on a farm, he was familiar with cattle; but all that was behind him "I have one other concern," he said, leaning forward in his chair. "My older brother George emigrated to Massachusetts a year ago, and he writes that the sentiment there is independent if not actually separatist. I fear my reception may not be very cordial."

"That will depend largely on where you plan to settle."

"I have Wessaguscus in mind."

"I thought as much," Gorges said with a sigh. Clergymen tended to be naive, a malady connected to their calling. "Your brother is right. Winthrop has placed his company and his charter beyond easy reach of royal authority. He proclaims his loyalty to the

King, yet he seems bent on making the colony autonomous – an endeavor that is certain to fail. In Wessaguscus you will be subject to his influence and control."

"But my goals are spiritual, not political," Hull objected.

"It has become difficult to distinguish between the two," Gorges said. "To emigrate, you must now take an oath, acknowledging the supremacy of the King and Church. Any talk of moderation will be interpreted as sympathy for the Puritan cause."

"Some changes advocated by the Puritans are warranted," Hull said, "but they can't be achieved by separation. As for myself, I can function only as a minister of the Church of England."

Reassured, Gorges sought for a way to mesh Hull's vision with his own efforts to govern New England. "How many families are you planning to take with you?" he asked.

"At least twenty. Thus far, I've enlisted four, in addition to my own."

"And do you have Church approval?"

"I've spoken to Bishop Hall in Exeter," Hull said, "but I'm acting on my own initiative. I haven't sought Laud's blessing, nor do I need it."

"Hear me out. I have little enthusiasm for Laud's attempts to enforce conformity; yet his appointment as Archbishop of Canterbury is imminent. He'll have the ear of the King and may prove a valuable ally." Although he trusted his visitor, Gorges chose his words with care. "I have it on good report that the Privy Council is setting up a committee to investigate the origin of the Massachusetts charter. Once that charter is rescinded, I hope to persuade the King to name a Lord Governor for all of New England."

From the way Gorges savored the title, it was clear what name he had in mind. Hull saw some advantage to himself in such a development. "But how would a governor exercise control at such a distance?" he asked.

Gorges did not hesitate. "I propose to divide New England into nine provinces. The Lord Governor would oversee these provinces, aided by a chancellor, a treasurer, a marshal, a bishop, an admiral."

"Your proposal includes a bishop!" Hull interrupted.

Gorges smiled at the sudden show of interest. Did Hull aspire to such eminence? "I should have sent a bishop along with Robert to Wessaguscus. My son had enthusiasm, but he was ill prepared to deal with the authorities in Plymouth, let alone the rigors of a New England winter."

"Robert did the best he could," Hull said.

"Still, if he had succeeded, we would have a general governor there today; and I wouldn't have to contend with men like Winthrop."

"Are you no longer interested in the Maine province?" Hull asked, recalling their earlier conversation in Plymouth.

Gorges emitted a loud snort. "My fellow West Countrymen were eager to fish and trade with the natives but loath to pay for the privilege. They have no concern for England's future glory, and they care naught about the need to guard our colonies against incursions by the French and the Dutch. Still, if you decide to go to Maine, I can make some arrangements."

"Can Winthrop stop me from settling in Wessaguscus?"

"I think not. His position is tenuous. He dare not incur the enmity of Laud and the Church. Besides, the Council for New

England, of which I am still a member, has a valid claim to the whole territory."

"I thank you for your time," Hull said, rising to leave.

"I can look into getting you a vessel," Gorges said as he saw Hull to the door. "Twenty families, you said."

* * *

Following Gorges' advice, Hull made steady progress in recruiting his colony. Men who had listened politely as he spoke of a place where spiritual growth could not be stifled by arbitrary rulings from the church hierarchy, now leaned forward to hear more about free land and other economic benefits to be derived from a move to New England. Listening to them express their dreams of building a house, cutting wood, planting crops, and raising animals on land they could call their own, Hull saw that this colony would possess a life and a mind of its own. His followers saw him only as their minister, a man who had a particular role to play in the success of their venture. It was his church, but it was their colony.

Before the winter set in, ten families totaling sixty souls had agreed to emigrate. Most were tenant farmers, men accustomed to hard work who had the various skills needed to tame the wilderness. Gorges sent word that a ship would be available in the spring. With that in mind, Hull pressed forward, confident that he and his congregation would be ready to leave when the date arrived. Anne entered into the spirit of the undertaking; though her pregnancy forced her to stay close to home. He told her of each family that agreed to join his company, hoping to take her mind off her confinement.

But he was troubled by his own mother's experience. Her second-born son, also named Joseph, had died shortly after birth; and another child had failed to survive the first year.

"You've already borne six children," he said to reassure her and himself. "You just need to rest."

"Don't worry," Anne said. "I'll be ready to travel by spring."

Her labor was prolonged and difficult, and the old midwife spent many hours at her bedside. They named the child Dorothy; but after giving birth, Anne developed chills and a high fever. Hull hired a wet nurse for the baby and summoned a doctor.

"There's nothing more I can do," the doctor said after he examined Anne. "We can only pray that the fever breaks."

Hull expected the verdict, yet it was still a shock. He knew well the perils associated with childbirth. With no ministerial duties to occupy him, he stayed by Anne's side, applying cold compresses to her burning forehead, talking to her by day, praying over her at night. He struggled to appear cheerful in front of the children, who were ever present; but alone at night he gave vent to his anxiety, mingling tears with his prayers.

Toward morning on the eighth day after the baby was born, Anne died of childbed fever. Hull sat alone at her bedside until daybreak, holding her cold hand and staring off into space. For the first time since he was ordained, he was unable to pray. Anne's death banished all other thoughts. Without a wife his plan to emigrate was shattered, his future uncertain. He felt lost, like a ship adrift without a rudder. It seemed that God had abandoned him.

The children's voices roused him to an awareness that his life must go on. He broke the news to them, then watched as they filed past the bed on which Anne lay. The faces of the three youngest –

Griselda, Elizabeth, and Temperance – were sober and uncomprehending. Tristram and Joseph fought to hold back their tears as they reached out to touch the hands folded upon her chest. Joanna lingered after the others were ushered out in the care of the wet nurse, then knelt and wept uncontrollably, her face buried in the bed clothes. Hull touched her shoulder; and she turned to him, sobbing against his chest.

"What are we going to do?" she asked.

"We can talk about that later," Hull said.

He placed Anne in her coffin, helped dig her grave, and made daily visits to the cemetery. Kneeling on the hard earth, he knew he had buried more than his wife. His dream of emigrating to New England was interred with her. His chief concern now was the welfare of his children, especially his newborn daughter. He knew his situation was not unique. Women often died in childbirth, and he had counseled many a bereaved husband and father to look for another wife. Yet his love for Anne was not so easily set aside.

Joanna, who was thirteen, sought to console him. "We can still go to New England. I can cook and care for the children and keep the house clean, so you'll have plenty of time to work on your sermons."

Her narrow face rounded into a smile, and her dark eyes gleamed with anticipation and pride. She had clearly given the matter a good deal of thought. Hull was touched by her youthful enthusiasm.

"I can't leave England right now," he said, pressing her slender body to his chest. "God has other plans for me."

"What are they?" she asked.

"I'm not sure yet. We must pray to Him to show us the way."

"I pray every night for you and for mother."

"I know you do. I'll find a housekeeper, but I depend on you to assist her with the children. Joseph can help too. I'll speak to him about it."

"Joseph's not much good about the house," Joanna said. Her tone was accepting rather than judgmental. "You should speak to Tristram."

Hull had to chuckle at her astute assessment of her brothers. Joseph, his second-born child, tended to resist routine, preferring to fend for himself. But Tristram, who was next in line, exhibited a genuine involvement in the welfare of the family. "As you wish," he told her. "You're in charge."

Joanna laughed as she ran off to break the news to her brother.

Like many things in this life, Hull reflected, children were both a blessing and a sorrow. But another woman might consider seven of them too much of a burden. He would leave that too in God's hands.

Four

"I have a ship!"
(Broadway, Somerset, 1633-1635)

Despite her brave offer, Joanna was still too young to assume the full responsibility of a housekeeper. Hull had visited a number of tenant farmers in the area while recruiting his congregation for New England and dealing in cattle to finance his venture. He often took the younger children with him on these visits, hoping to ease the burden on his pregnant wife. One of the farmers had a daughter named Agnes, who offered to mind the children while Hull spoke with her father. Her face was rather plain, but she had an engaging manner. He finished his business and was preparing to leave, when his five-year-old daughter Elizabeth asked, "Can we come back and see Agnes again?" His response was noncommittal. No need to tell her he would not be coming back because the farmer had no money to buy his cattle.

But this time he was on a different mission. Agnes greeted him at the door of the cottage and escorted him to the field where her father was tilling the soil. She said she remembered him and inquired about the children by name. She seemed at ease in his presence. He found her more attractive than on his previous visit. Her auburn hair was tied back, exposing a deeply freckled face; and her body seemed to have filled out a bit. She had recently celebrated her twenty-third birthday, a fact she made known to him on the walk. She appeared quite capable of organizing his household with warmth and affection – qualities his children needed most.

The farmer stopped tilling and heard him out. "I guess I can manage without Agnes for a couple of months until you get back on your feet," he said after some deliberation. "But it's her decision."

"I'll pay her a fair wage," Hull assured him, "and I'll see to it that you get a heifer as your part of the bargain."

"In that case, I can guarantee she'll say yes," the farmer said.

Hull was glad to hear that Agnes had served in a similar capacity on previous occasions. So it was arranged for her to move into the cottage at Batcombe. He took Joseph and Tristram into his room, making a place for Agnes near the girls. Elizabeth was delighted to see her once again, while Temperance was tolerant. Joanna was more reserved, and Hull thought he detected a trace of jealousy in her grudging approval. The two boys accepted Agnes without comment, much as if a new piece of furniture had arrived. As for Hull, his initial satisfaction with her work gradually gave way to the realization that he might one day ask this competent young woman to be his wife. For now he continued his daily visits to Anne's grave.

Having restored some order to his household, Hull dispatched a message to Gorges, detailing his circumstances and change in plans. Sir Ferdinando expressed his sympathy and offered some advice. "You needn't give up your dream of one day emigrating to New England. There will always be another ship. It's the same as finding another wife. As you know, I've had some experience in that line. But a word of caution. Take care not to frighten her at the outset.

Present yourself as a minister and a widower who needs a mother for his children. Time enough to talk of emigrating after you're married."

The advice sounded like common sense, but Hull regarded it as a bit devious. It was also irrelevant. Anne's death was a sure sign that God's plan for him did not involve a voyage to New England. Nor could he claim the title of minister, since he held no office in the Church. To remedy that problem, he accepted an appointment as officiating curate at St. Aldhelm in Broadway. It was a demotion after his years as a rector, but it kept him in Somerset. That reinforced Gorges' view that his setback was temporary, yet Hull was convinced that his future lay in England.

Once more a clergyman, he began to think seriously of filling the void in his life brought about by Anne's death. His children needed a mother, and he wasn't prepared to spend the rest of his life alone and celibate. A minister without a wife lacked authority – like a church without a pulpit. Human love was but a pale reflection of the divine; nonetheless, it was a gift to be sought, nurtured, and cherished. Man was not made to enter heaven alone.

Agnes had willingly stayed on beyond the two months of their original agreement. The children all liked her and were accustomed to seeing her around. Even Joanna seemed to have accepted her as an integral part of the household. Hull's relationship with Agnes was formal, as befitted a housekeeper; yet he took pleasure in her company, and he admired the sprightly manner in which she went about her duties. On her part she appeared to enjoy his talk at table, while maintaining a discreet distance, physical as well as emotional. Still, it was safe to assume that a woman her age would welcome a proposal of marriage.

With this in mind Hull set out to seek her father's approval. He found the farmer in the barn feeding the heifer delivered to him as part of the deal for Agnes. When informed of the bargain he had made, she had replied, "I never realized I was worth so much." They both laughed heartily, but his affection for her was stirred.

Her father displayed no surprise at his proposal. "What does she have to say about it?" he asked as he resumed feeding the livestock.

"I have yet to speak to her," Hull said. "I wanted your consent first."

"As is right and proper. But it's her decision."

"Then I have your permission to proceed?"

Pausing in his chores, the farmer looked his prospective son-in-law up and down. "If Agnes wants to marry you," he declared, "she'll do it with or without my permission. But for what it's worth, you have my blessing."

* * *

Hull waited until the next evening to tell Agnes about his talk with her father. The weather was pleasant, and he invited her to join him for a walk into Broadway, half a mile distant. As they passed by the thirteenth century church with its dual nave and its square crenellated tower, Hull ventured to take her hand. She appeared mildly surprised, but made no effort to withdraw it. They spoke as usual of household matters and of each of the children in turn. Her keen insight into their characters amazed him. In her eyes they were not just children to be fed and cared for, but seven individuals with different needs and dreams. It was one of her more endearing qualities.

They paused to look up at Roche castle, an ancient entrenchment on the brow of Blackdown hill, while Hull sought for the right words to convey his needs and his feelings for her. He had to avoid any hint of condescension. She must feel free to accept or reject his offer, as her heart dictated. Not until they reached Everys almshouse – a high wall hid the poor men housed therein from their view – did he fasten upon a proper way to proceed.

"Are you content with your employment?" he asked.

"The surroundings are pleasant, and I'm very fond of the children."

"Would you consider staying on permanently, not as a housekeeper but as my wife?"

He stopped in the middle of the road and released her hand, while his eyes searched her face for some sign of acceptance. Her expression had become suddenly serious, even a bit stern.

"I never thought of marrying a man Father's age, and a minister to boot," she said. "I don't get to church very much. Not that I'm against it, but Mother has been sick lately, and there's a lot of work to do on the farm." She smiled demurely, as if she were pleading with him to overlook what she obviously regarded as a minor fault.

"I understand," Hull said. Impressed by her frank innocence, he wanted to tell her about his past trials and his dreams for the future; but he felt it advisable to concentrate on his present status. "I'll soon be forty. I'm in good health, and I can give you a good home. I need a woman I can love and cherish, as well as a mother for my children. Does the prospect of raising seven young ones with more to come, God willing, frighten you?"

"I've had a lot of experience looking after my brothers and sisters," Agnes said, "but you haven't said anything about your plans for the future."

"What do you mean?" Hull stammered, surprised by the question.

Agnes looked down at her hands, which were clasped in front of her. "Will you remain here in Broadway, or will you seek a permanent post somewhere elsewhere?"

"That depends in part on you," Hull replied with evident relief. "As my wife, you shall have an equal voice in determining the course of our life together."

Agnes raised her head, and a warm smile lit her freckled face. "I'm trying to picture myself as a minister's wife in a village not too far from here."

"I shall do my best to obtain such a position."

"Joanna told me you used to be a rector in Devon," Agnes said, her demeanor once again serious. "Why did you leave?"

Hull seldom spoke of New England since Anne's death, and he could safely assume that Agnes was unaware of his efforts to recruit a colony. He was free to equivocate, as Gorges advised. Yet her frankness disarmed him and ruled out any attempt at deception. He sought to answer her honestly without causing her undue alarm.

"I left Northleigh because the restrictions imposed by the church hierarchy had made my position as a minister untenable. I considered emigrating to New England; but my wife's death made that impossible. So you see me now, a curate selling cattle to feed his children."

"And are the restrictions of which you speak still unbearable?"

"They've become somewhat less onerous. The King and Archbishop Laud have other concerns at the moment."

"I'll need a bit of time to consider your proposal," Agnes said. "I want to talk to my parents before I give you an answer."

"That is perfectly reasonable," Hull said.

He took her hand again as they continued their walk. It felt warmer and softer than when she was simply his housekeeper. He knew without any doubt that he was prepared to love this practical unassuming girl for as long a time as God granted them together. It troubled him that he had glossed over his efforts to recruit a colony; but he had replied honestly to her questions and concerns. No need to tell her more than she wanted to know.

A week later Agnes agreed to become his wife. Joanna accepted the news stoically; but he sensed that his daughter felt she had failed him.

"The children listen to you," he said to reassure her. "I depend on you to help them accept Agnes as their mother."

"And what happens when they do?" she asked, a trace of bitterness in her voice. "Will I become one of them again?"

"No," Hull said. "At that point I'll give you another assignment."

* * *

Agnes quickly assumed her role as mother and wife. Hull was well pleased with the comforts she provided him and with the manner in which she made Joanna her aide and confidante. His quest for a more permanent post as rector bore no fruit. Meanwhile, his dissatisfaction with conditions in the Church received additional nourishment.

"I did hope that, as archbishop, Laud might adopt a conciliatory approach to the divisions in the Church," he told Agnes on their evening walk, which was becoming a ritual. "Yet his treatment of Prynne in Star Chamber harks back to the torture meted out to Alexander Leighton."

"He's doing some good," Agnes replied. "You said he's concerned about the welfare of tenant farmers like my father."

She seldom spoke ill of people – an admirable trait in a wife. "True," he said, "but I suspect his motives. He also allowed the wakes and revels to go on; but closing them would have antagonized the King, who had published his own *Book of Sports*. And his opposition to enclosures, though it benefits the poor, is designed to prevent further encroachments by the country squires on Church lands. His true goal is restoration to the Church of all property seized after the dissolution of the monasteries."

"But an archbishop ought to concern himself with the welfare of the Church," Agnes said. "You seem to blame him for doing his duty."

"I blame him for suppressing any opposition through torture, fines, or imprisonment. His focus at the moment is on those men who attract public attention. But mark my words. The day will come when every minister in England will fear to preach, lest his words offend Archbishop Laud."

"What will you do when that day arrives?"

"I'll follow the example of Bishop Hall in Exeter. He says what he thinks, while recognizing and defending the authority of the Church to require him to answer for his opinions. I disagree with certain measures Laud has adopted to enforce conformity; but I support the Church of England and the established prelacy."

"Will that keep you out of trouble?"

"I sincerely hope so," Hull said.

That summer and well into the fall he carried out his duties at St. Aldhelm, careful to give the diocesan authorities no cause for concern. When he was summoned to Ashton Court for an audience with Gorges, he felt certain that it was related to his plan to emigrate. Yet he was happy in his marriage and reasonably content in his post as curate. He had no desire to resurrect his dream.

* * *

The journey on horseback was arduous, and Hull decided to spend the night with a colleague in Bristol, arriving at Ashton Court the next day fresh and well rested. Gorges received him in the library as before, but remained seated behind his desk.

His failure to rise at Hull's entrance was not out of a lack of courtesy. It was due rather to his preoccupation with a longstanding dream that was soon to be fulfilled. As he motioned Hull to take a seat, his thoughts were on the assurances he had received from the highest circles in London that he was soon to be named Governor General of New England. He thought also of a ship being built in Scotland, a ship that would enable him to take possession of his domain. He would require a sizeable company of soldiers to enforce his authority, but he had also stressed to Archbishop Laud the need for a body of clergymen loyal to the Church of England. That was where Hull fit in. His plan to settle in Wessaguscus, which Gorges had considered foolhardy at first, was now much more attractive; for it would plant an Anglican minister at the heart of a colony whose loyalty to the Church and Crown was suspect. It might prove helpful to establish a point of contact within the enemy camp. He had no doubt but that Winthrop intended to make the Massachusetts Colony virtually autonomous. It was his duty to forestall that intention.

He looked at Hull, who sat fingering his hat. "I congratulate you on your marriage," he began. "Now that your life is back to normal, have you given any further thought to settling in Wessaguscus?"

Hull met his gaze without flinching. "My life now is as a curate at St. Aldhelm in Broadway. I have no other thoughts."

"What have you told the families who agreed to sail with you?"

"That my plans are postponed indefinitely. I've had no contact with any of them since I married Agnes."

"But you're still in Somerset and in the cattle business."

Hull knew what Gorges was saying. He had not contacted Bishop Hall, nor had he tried to secure a post in the diocese of Exeter. His dream of emigrating might be dormant, but it was not dead. Yet that realization did not alter his decision.

"Agnes is at home in Somerset," he said, "and I have no desire to emigrate."

"I summoned you here today to tell you that a ship is available to transport you and your colony to Massachusetts. But if you're content to remain in England, I shall pursue the matter no further."

Gorges leaned back in his chair, and Hull noted that the last button on his embroidered vest was unfastened. This sign of burgeoning prosperity made him wary of Sir Ferdinando's motives, even as he strove to suppress a sudden resurgence of his own enthusiasm. Was the move to New England in God's plan for him after all? The opportunity was there to grasp, yet he held back, waiting for Gorges to continue. When he was silent, Hull decided that he owed it to himself and to Agnes to get more information.

"Only a fool is unwilling to change his situation in life for the better," Hull said, leaning forward in his chair.

Gorges smiled. "Quite true. My prospects have also improved of late. I won't go into the details. Suffice it to say that if certain matters develop as I hope, I may soon be able to provide some tangible support for your mission."

"What do you want me to do?" Hull asked.

"You need only pursue your dream," Gorges said. "It would be best to give no indication at present that you have my support."

"But how do you benefit from all this? Am I to report to you on conditions in Massachusetts?"

Gorges placed his arms on the desk. "Your presence will remind Winthrop that he remains subject to the Church and Crown, and that he must abide by the terms of his charter. As for reporting, I leave that to you. I don't expect you to be a spy."

"But I shall represent the Church of England."

"Not officially. Archbishop Laud need know nothing of this. I'm sure he would approve; but he might consider my action premature."

Hull rubbed the palms of his hands on his knees, an action that often helped him to think more clearly. "I fear my family will feel isolated in a colony populated by Puritans."

"You won't be alone for long," Gorges said, "and it may prove advantageous to be first on the scene."

"When would you expect me to leave?" Hull asked.

"The ship will be available in the spring. Since your plans were well advanced when your wife died, you'll have ample time to prepare."

"I don't deny that you have rekindled my interest in New England," Hull said, "but Agnes is unaware of my previous plans. I must discuss it with her before I can give you an answer."

"By all means," Gorges said with satisfaction. Rising from his chair, he escorted Hull to the door. "Tell her New England has more to offer than the post at St. Aldhelm or anything Bishop Hall may have for you in Devon."

Hull rode off, his mind occupied with visions of a church and a home in Massachusetts. With the support of Gorges, his future prospects were all but guaranteed. He could hardly wait to break the news to Agnes.

* * *

"I have a ship!" Hull burst out upon entering the house.

"What need have you for a ship?" Agnes asked in bewilderment. She sank down on a bench by the hearth. Her clenched hands rested on her gray skirt, and her labored breathing was noticeable under her bodice.

He froze, his coat dangling by one sleeve from his broad shoulder. Enwrapped in his dreams, he had forgotten that she remained ignorant of his plans. "I can explain everything," he said.

Hanging the coat on a peg, he sat beside her and took her hand. He spoke at length of his reasons for emigrating, his earlier efforts to gather a congregation, and the assurances Gorges had given him.

"The offer came as a surprise," he concluded. "I put all that out of my mind when Anne died. I thought Gorges had done the same."

Agnes withdrew her hand and regarded him accusingly. "What you propose is an entirely new way of life. You should have told me about these plans before I married you."

Hull winced at her blunt honesty – a trait he had found endearing, even admirable, when he first met her. "All my plans appeared dead at that time, and I didn't want to cause you needless concern."

"Now as your wife I'm duty bound to follow where you lead."

"I speak not of obligation. I want to know what is in your heart."

"My heart is in turmoil," Agnes said, her voice more gentle. "I have never traveled farther afield than Bristol. And Massachusetts has become a haven for dissenters. Are you sure we'll be welcome there?"

Hull sensed that she had forgiven him, that she was already thinking of their future. "I shall tend to my own congregation and cause no problems for the local authorities. Besides, I have a right to settle there, and Governor Winthrop is still subject to the laws of England."

"Won't you need Bishop Pierce's approval?"

Hull frowned. As Bishop of Bath and Wells, Pierce was a staunch disciple of Archbishop Laud and a zealous enforcer of his regulations. He had prohibited any repetition of sermons on Sunday evening because it detracted from the revels. And he forbade catechizing on church liturgy, directing clergy to adhere strictly to the *Book of Common Prayer*. Hull regarded these rules as an affront to his calling as a minister. If he could no longer sermonize as he saw fit within the bounds of approved doctrine, then he was simply a puppet responding to the pull of the hierarchy. With the support of clergymen like Pierce, Archbishop Laud would soon control what was spoken from every pulpit throughout the land.

"Pierce has no reason to object," he assured his wife. "I shall not join the ranks of preachers who hide their identities in order to emigrate. If I cannot go as a minister of the Church of England, I will not embark."

"When does your ship sail?" Agnes asked.

"Early next spring, from Weymouth."

"Then I have time to get used to the idea."

"If you have any doubts, I can tell Gorges I'm not ready."

Agnes smiled as she took his hand. "You may not get another ship. Go and gather your colony. Come spring, I'll be ready."

A sob escaped Hull as he embraced her. She hadn't said that she was sorry she married him, but her questions and her comments vexed his spirit. He resolved to be more open with her in the future.

* * *

Having previously recruited a number of families in Batcombe, Hull concentrated his efforts around Broadway. He promised people free land, the opportunity to profit from their own labors, and a church free of unwarranted restrictions. Though he had some success, he soon recognized that he must devote all his time to recruitment and preparations for the trip if he wanted to sail in the spring. Giving up his post as curate would only make his task more difficult. He knew from past experience that to gather a congregation, he had to be a minister in good standing. Then it occurred to him that he might combine the two activities by accepting offers to preach in other towns, while he spoke to families who showed some interest in emigrating. Such itinerant preaching was against regulations; but he had only five months to gather his colony, and it would take that long for word of his activities to reach the ears of Bishop Pierce.

"I'm going with you," Agnes announced one day as he prepared to leave the rectory on one of these preaching engagements. "Joanna can mind the children."

"Whatever for?" Hull asked. "It's bitter cold outside."

"You talk only to the husband. After you're gone, his wife convinces him to stay where he is. If I speak to the wife and the children while you talk with the man, we may have more success."

Hull hugged her. "I thank God for sending me the right woman to help me carry out His work."

Heedless of rules, he preached wherever he could muster an audience, seeking to recruit people when the service was over. Before winter was out, he was charged with attending a visitation in Chard without permission and with telling people in Glastonbury that a judgment hung heavy over the land and would fall first on the clergy. His explanation – that nonconformists and dissenters were the underlying cause of this judgment and equally subject to it – appeared to satisfy Church authorities for a time. But when he continued to hold services in nearby towns, he was cited for preaching without a proper license and summoned to appear in diocesan court. Ignoring the summons, Hull gave up his post and moved his family to Weymouth, where his ship awaited him.

"What will you do now?" Agnes asked when he got word that he had been excommunicated. "You can't sail if you're not in good standing in the Church."

"I can do what Warham did when he was banished," Hull replied. "I'll get reinstated in another diocese. Bishop Hall will vouch for me."

Five

"He mustn't think his soul is inferior."
(Weymouth, Dorset, and on the *Welcome*, 1635)

Hull had enlisted over a hundred persons, ranging in age from one year to sixty and including tailors, chandlers, joiners, husbandmen, weavers, and coopers. Heeding Gorges' advice, he softened his requirement for church membership in order to assemble a colony that was self-sufficient. Singly or in family groups they gathered in Weymouth. Hull's household was by far the largest. In addition to his wife and his seven children, he had acquired three indentured servants – two men and a woman.

Provisioning for the sea voyage and for the settlement in Wessaguscus occupied his days. He acquired all the wood and metal tools that merchants in Weymouth assured him were essential for such a venture. Since they spoke from long experience, he took heed of their advice, purchasing locks and fetters, a hand vice, share, coulter, wood hook, wimble with piercer bits, fish hooks and lines, hoes, pitchforks, whip and hand saws, shovels, spades, files, hammers, augers, chisels, broad and pickaxes, gimlets, froes, hatchets, bellows, scoop, great pail, ladder, plow, cart, wheelbarrow, axletree, and lantern. He also had to arrange for the loading and feeding of half a dozen head of cattle.

Agnes assisted him in buying meal, malt, oatmeal, beef, pickled pork, bacon, peas, grits, oil, butter, cheese, vinegar, aqua vitae, mustard seed, and salt. She selected hats, shirts, a waistcoat, suits of cloth, frieze, and canvas, a sea cape of coarse cloth, Irish stockings, handkerchiefs, shoes, boots, canvas for sheets, and a coarse rug. She purchased necessary household utensils – an iron pot, greater and lesser kettles of copper, a frying pan, spit, gridiron, brass mortar, skillet, and curry combs. And she met with other wives, encouraging them and lending whatever assistance they needed.

"We'll have some thirty children aboard," she observed a week before they were due to sail.

"A good sign that the colony will take root and prosper," Hull said.

At this point in his preparations he was visited by a man named Seton, whom he had first met as a student at Oxford. After graduation, while Hull pursued his path as a minister, Seton had cast about in London for a goal that matched his talents. He embarked on a series of ventures designed to improve his lot and his station, but with no lasting success. Hull had lost contact with him over time and was surprised to find him at the door.

"I hear that you're preparing to sail to New England, I thought you were still in Northleigh."

"And I thought you were still in London," Hull replied, ushering him into the small cottage where the family was staying.

While Agnes fixed tea, he had a chance to study his friend. Time had been unkind to Seton. His brown wavy hair, prominent cheekbones, and square chiseled chin had attracted the women in his youth. But some illness had ravished the robust figure he cut at Oxford, and he relied now upon good manners and grooming to recommend him – or so it appeared to Hull.

"Are you in Weymouth on business or for your health?" he asked.

"Either one would be most welcome," Seton said. "I have become a stranger to both estates. But what made you decide to leave England?"

Hull described his own past - the death of his wife, his remarriage, his dissatisfaction with Laud's edicts, and his plans to emigrate. Set on's gaze lingered on Joanna as she served the tea. She stood an inch taller than Agnes. Her luminous blue eyes and ruddy unblemished complexion complemented a mild but confident manner. Noting Set on's interest, Hull realized his daughter was becoming a woman and would soon be eligible for marriage.

"Am I to conclude that you have become a Puritan?" Seton asked.

"Not at all," Hull said. "I go as a minister of the Church of England."

After tea he suggested a visit to the docks. "I need to check on some cargo. The *Welcome* has made several voyages to the American colonies and is thoroughly seaworthy. You can have a look at her, if you like."

"It would be fine indeed to start afresh in a new land," Seton said as they walked to the harbor.

"I'd be glad to have you in my company."

Seton brushed the suggestion aside. "Is your wife also eager for this venture?" he asked. "It seems a large undertaking for a young woman."

"She had a few reservations at first, but seems to have embraced the idea."

"And the children? They must be sorry to leave England behind."

"Joanna is looking forward to a new life in the colonies. The younger ones regard it simply as an adventure."

Aboard the *Welcome* Seton asked about the accommodations and the length of the voyage. Hull showed him the cramped quarters below deck and hinted at the hardships associated with a month or more at sea. "We sail in three days," he concluded. "Let me know if you decide to join us."

"Opportunity must be grasped when it is offered," Seton said. "You may count me as one of your colony, but I can contribute no more than my passage. I have sustained a recent reversal of fortune."

"Souls are more important than money," Hull replied.

Agnes was less enthusiastic when informed of Seton's decision. "He never once took his eyes off Joanna," she said.

"She's of an age when men are going to notice her," Hull said. "But other matters are far more pressing. I'll deal with that issue, if it arises."

On the 20th of March, 1635, the *Welcome* set sail from Weymouth, bound for New England. Heading the list of 106 colonists were:

"1 JOSEPH HALL of Somerset a Ministr aged 40 year

2 AGNIS HALL his Wife aged 25 yr

3 JOANE HALL his daught aged 15 Yeare

4 JOSEPH HALL his sonne aged 13 Yeare

5 TRISTRAM his son aged 11 Yeare

6 ELIZABETH HALL his daughtr aged 7 Yeare
7 TEMPERANCE his daughtr aged 7 Yeare
8 GRISSELL HALL his daughtr aged 5 Yeare
9 DOROTHY HALL his daughtr aged 3 Yeare
10 JUDETH FRENCH his s'vamt aged 20 Yeare
11 JOHN WOOD his s'vaunt aged 20 Yeare
12 ROBT DABYN his s'vamt aged 28 Yeare"

Hull noticed the vagrant spellings, but made no effort to correct them. His mind entertained a fleeting picture of Bishop Hall in all his episcopal finery boarding a ship bound for New England.

* * *

Seton stood at the rail looking out to sea and wondering why he had ever agreed to embark on such a mad endeavor – a sentiment quite prevalent among the other passengers after a week of rough weather and widespread seasickness. The fresh air revived his spirits, and he moved forward to be out of the wind. Standing in the lea of the forecastle, he overheard a man and a woman engaged in a heated conversation. He recognized the voice of Hull's maidservant, Judith French. As their talk went on, he realized the man was John Wood, another servant. They were hidden from his view, but he pictured the tall, muscular Wood looking down upon petite, full-bosomed Judith. The maid's words carried clearly, but he had to strain to catch Wood's response.

"Say what you like, Miss Joanna will never love the likes of you!"

"We'll see about that. She treats me nice and decent."

"Nice and decent ain't the same as love. You just wait and see what happens when the pastor finds out."

"It was him that put the idea in my head. He was sayin' how we all need to work together in this place we're goin' to, 'cause we're all the same in God's eyes. That means I'm just as good as anyone else."

"If goin' to the county jail and servin' seven years 'denture for stealin' sheep makes you as good as Miss Joanna, I'm fit for the pastor's wife."

"I'm goin' to make my mark any way I can."

"You're thinkin' if you marry Miss Joanna, the pastor will take you out of 'denture. Well I'm tellin' you, that peach ain't ripe for pickin' – not by you or nobody else."

"Just stay out of my way, woman!"

Seton forgot about his queasy stomach as a simple plan took shape in his head. He needed a helpmate where they were going, and he resolved to use what he was hearing to his own advantage.

* * *

As Hull moved easily along the heaving deck, hands clasped behind his back, head bowed against the wind, he noticed Seton standing by the rail. "The sea air is a good tonic," he said.

Seton nodded. "Tween decks I feel every motion of the ship in the pit of my belly. I'll sleep topside tonight if the weather permits."

"Many aboard would prefer to be back in England," Hull said.

"Any dry land would be welcome," Seton said. "Not that I regret my decision to sail with you. I look forward to some stroke of fortune that will change my life and render my past failures irrelevant."

"A new life comes from hard work rather than a stroke of fortune," Hull said.

"A man must follow his own path," Seton countered. "How are your wife and the children bearing up?"

"Agnes has been feeling rather poorly. Joanna is caring for the girls. The two boys like to pretend they're part of the crew."

"Joanna is an attractive and capable young woman," Seton said. "Small wonder that men like John Wood are drawn to her."

"Why do you say that?" Hull asked, steadying himself on the rail.

Seton described the exchange he had just overheard. Instead of growing angry, Hull seemed increasingly calm. "Have you no concern for your daughter?" Seton asked. "Wood is an indentured servant."

"We're all equal before God," Hull said.

"Someone should assure Joanna she needn't worry about finding a husband. A young woman needs such reassurance. Otherwise, she may surrender her heart to the first suitor."

"How is it you know so much about young women?"

"I have a daughter in London. I do what I can for her, even though I never married her mother."

Hull refrained from asking how he proposed to care for the girl when he arrived in New England. "Joanna had a lot of responsibility after her mother died. She's quite mature for her age."

"Still, she ought to know of Wood's interest," Seton persisted. "I'll gladly speak to her, with your permission. An outside opinion often carries more weight than parental admonitions."

Hull made a dismissive motion with his hand. "I'll mention it to my wife," he said.

He found Agnes resting in the cabin they shared with the two youngest girls. The other children were housed 'tween decks with the rest of the colony. "Seton inquired about your health," he announced from the door.

"I appreciate his concern," she replied coolly.

"What is it about Seton that you dislike?"

"I can't help but feel that he has some hidden motive behind his words and his actions."

Hull sat on the edge of her bunk. "Seton told me that John Wood is attracted to Joanna. He asked for my permission to speak to her about love and marriage. He says she's more apt to take advice from an outsider."

"What did you say to him?"

"That I wanted to get your opinion."

"Why don't you just speak to Wood?"

"The matter is not so simple," Hull said. "He mustn't think his soul is inferior – that he is any less worthy of salvation for being a servant. If I were to forbid him to love Joanna, I would be acting contrary to my own teachings. I must trust her to make the right decision."

"And what is that?" Agnes asked, giving him a stern look She wanted no part in such moral niceties. Servants were duty bound to obey their masters. Their souls were not at issue in such a matter.

Hull met her gaze without flinching. "I trust Joanna to do what her heart dictates. It would do no harm for Seton to talk with her. In the meantime, I'll keep close watch on Wood's actions."

"Let me speak to her first," Agnes declared in a voice that brooked no opposition. "I suspect Mr. Seton may want to plead his own case."

"I saw no sign of that," Hull said, "but I'll watch him as well."

* * *

The cramped and smelly quarters 'tween decks made Agnes sick, so she waited until Joanna came by the cabin before telling her about Wood's interest in her. "Did you know he was imprisoned for stealing sheep?" she asked to cap off her words of caution.

"Yes, I know," Joanna replied. She had busied herself making up the bunk bed and seemed hardly to be listening. "It's only natural for a man to seek his freedom any way he can."

Her reply wasn't what Agnes expected. "Your pity for an unfortunate person is commendable, but you're not obliged to feel affection for him."

Setting down the pillow she was fluffing, Joanna turned to face her stepmother. "Did Father ask you to speak to me?"

"No, it was my idea," Agnes said, taking her hand. "I don't want to see you hurt. Has Mr. Seton said anything about this?"

"He warned me to be on my guard against Wood."

Agnes suppressed her anger against Seton for preempting her. "What else did he have to say?"

"That I was still very young and needn't worry about finding a husband. I asked him why he was telling me this. He said he had Father's permission to speak to me and that he was only interested in my welfare."

"And what did you say?"

"I told him my heart is my own concern."

"I'm glad you didn't encourage him."

"He seems nice enough. Is there something wrong with him?"

"I suspect that, old as he is, he may want to marry you himself."

"You married an older man," Joanna reminded her. "But I've given little thought to marriage, to one man or another."

"That's all for the good."

Fearing she had made matters worse, Agnes adopted a new tack. "Perhaps we can turn Wood's attention to someone else, someone more suitable and within easy reach."

"Whom do you mean?" Joanna asked.

"Judith French. I'm sure she's drawn to him. We need only devise a scheme that will make him aware of her interest."

Joanna's eyes sparkled. "You mean a plot to bring them together? That should brighten up this tedious voyage."

"Let me think about it," Agnes said. "We'll talk again tomorrow."

Joanna turned to leave the cabin. "Tell Father he needn't worry about me," she called back from the doorway.

Agnes was left to reconsider her opinion of Seton. Older men were inclined to be more gentle and considerate. She would have liked to add less demanding; but her own marriage was proof to the contrary. Joseph seemed determined to make her pregnant by the end of the voyage. She determined to reserve judgment until she knew a bit more about Seton and his intentions.

* * *

With the advent of calm seas Hull held Bible classes on deck, as much to distract his followers from their cramped conditions, the monotony of the dried food and foul water, the pervading stench below deck, as to minister to their spiritual welfare. John Wood seized upon the opportunity to make Joanna notice him. As soon as she settled herself on the deck, he took a seat right in front of her. He sat perfectly still without turning to look at her, yet hoping all the while that she might acknowledge his presence in some way. He suspected that the pastor and his wife had an eye on him; but he didn't care. He felt secure in his newly assumed role as a student of the Bible.

This scene was repeated daily with no reaction from Joanna. Then one morning, seated in his chosen place, Wood was aware of a new sensation. Her foot was exerting ever so slight a pressure on his backside. The minister was rambling on about the *Book of Job*, saying how everyone aboard the ship was akin to Job, having been stripped of past, possessions, and the comforts of home. He assured them, if they remained steadfast in their devotion to God, they could overcome the trials that lay ahead and attain a more prosperous future.

Wood's body tensed as he waited to see whether or not she would withdraw her foot. But the pressure continued, and the sermon on Job faded to a background murmur as he pondered his next move. The contact appeared to be intentional, yet it might be simply an accident. He leaned back, increasing the pressure just enough to express his gratitude, while affording her a chance to pull away. Much to his delight, she did not withdraw her foot. He even fancied she was moving it to rub his back.

His one thought was to sustain or increase the contact. If she was sending him a message, some response was in order. If she took offense, he could claim that he fell asleep. It was a common reaction to the minister's lectures.

Closing his eyes, he allowed his body to sink backward until his head rested in her lap. She shifted her leg a bit, as if she wanted to make him more comfortable. For some minutes he was content to bask in the scent of her warm body. The ship had no facilities for bathing, yet he was intoxicated with the mingled odor of sweat, stale food, and children. Then he was struck by the thought that she too might be asleep and unaware of his head in her lap. As if in response to his fear, Wood felt her fingers move tenderly through his unruly hair. Overjoyed at this proof of affection, he opened his eyes and gazed up into the face of Judith French.

* * *

From his post at the rail Seton watched as Wood took his seat in front of Joanna, as Agnes whispered something to Judith French, and as the servant changed places with Joanna. His grip on the rail tightened as he waited to see what would happen next. His future hung on the outcome of this farce. He expected Wood to leap to his feet and rush off. Then he could take credit for alerting Joanna to her danger. But Wood did not move. The initial look of surprise on his face modulated to contentment and relief. He had obviously decided to accept what was offered to him. Seton turned away in disgust.

The next day he noted that both Judith and Wood had lost interest in the Bible. To his mind, Hull's refusal to chastise his servant was a refusal to face adversity. Seton took pride in his own readiness to confront his foes. So far it had availed him naught but relocations, often precipitous and nocturnal. With his future in the balance, he resolved to make a final attempt to secure a fair measure of happiness for himself.

The *Welcome* was nearing the coast of New England , and Seton and Hull stood side by side at the rail, scanning the western horizon for the first sight of land. "What will you do when we reach Boston?" Seton asked.

"First of all, I must get permission from the authorities to settle in Wessaguscus," Hull said. "That may take several weeks."

"Where do we stay in the meantime?"

"Master Chapel has agreed to let us remain on his ship while he picks up cargo in Dorchester for the return voyage. My brother George resides there, and he can help us find suitable lodgings onshore. I trust you will stay with the company."

"That depends on whether or not I can find a wife," Seton said.

Hull shifted his gaze from the future that awaited him to this more proximate concern. Was Agnes right after all? Was Seton about to ask him for permission to marry Joanna? "You're quite right," he said hesitantly. "To survive and prosper in the colonies, a man needs a good woman at his side. Do you have someone in mind?"

Seton continued to look out to sea. "My expectations aren't as high as they used to be," he said. "Judith French would suit me fine."

"My servant girl?" Hull asked, unable to conceal his surprise.

"She seems to be attracted to John Wood," Seton went on, "but I'm sure she'll be receptive to a better offer. By releasing her into my custody now, you'll be sparing yourself some problems later on."

Hull frowned. "I'm depending on Judith to help Agnes care for the household and the children when we get to Wessaguscus."

"You said that we're all equal before God," Seton said, shifting his gaze to regard Hull. "Surely that applies to Judith as well."

To escape the trap that was set to close on him, Hull responded with the only argument that came readily to mind. "Her salvation is not at issue. As holder of her bond, I am responsible for her material welfare; and in my judgment her interest is better served by remaining in my employ."

"You mean your interest," Seton said.

"Both, in this instance," Hull said.

"In that case," Seton said, "I shall seek out fresh opportunities when we arrive in Boston. Something will turn up. It always does."

Six

"Why are you here?"
(Boston, Massachusetts Bay Colony, 1635)

"Boston at last!" Hull cried exultantly as he rowed toward shore. Behind him in Rendell's Cove the *Welcome* lay at anchor. On a hill to the north the vanes of a windmill turned in a light breeze off the water. The ramparts of a fort were visible to the south. Was England the enemy against whom the colonists felt compelled to defend themselves? But his mind did not dwell for long upon that thought. His business was to place a petition to set down at Wessaguscus before the General Court. With this goal clearly in view, he docked his boat and set off to find the court clerk.

His course took him away from the docks and into the narrow dirt streets, still muddy from a recent rainfall. Looking about him, he strove to appreciate how much the settlers had accomplished in the past five years, subduing an inclination to compare what he saw with towns in England. The meetinghouse on what was termed King Street struck him as suitably grand when compared to the neighboring houses. Built of wood, it had a large chimney at one end and a thatched roof. The area in front was set aside as a market; but it was late in the day, and few merchants were about.

Continuing on past the prison, he turned left, as Master Chapel had directed him. At the next corner, opposite the schoolhouse and burial ground, he came upon a wood-framed dwelling with a single end chimney covered in clay. Facing the street were a batten entrance door and a small window with diamond-shaped panes. The homes in Devon and Somerset were no larger, but they were stone and had an aura of permanence. With the exception of a few buildings near the harbor, Boston struck him as a makeshift defense against the Indians and the wilderness, something that would serve until a more impressive city could be erected.

With no great expectation as to what he would find, Hull knocked on the door. A middle-aged man, slightly bent from his labors, ushered him into the single great room. At the fireplace a stout woman was stirring soup in an iron pot. Three children squatted nearby, waiting for the evening meal. The furnishings included a table on which the family Bible lay open, an armchair, several joint stools, a spinning wheel, and a frame bed folded against the wall opposite the fire. A crude wooden ladder led up to the loft where the children slept. He doubted that Agnes would be content in such a house, and resolved to provide her with a more elegant dwelling.

"The court meets again the first week in July," the clerk said. "I'll see to it that your petition is on the docket."

"That's two months off," Hull said. "I have a hundred men, women, and children who need to settle there before it's too late to plant a crop."

The clerk's face became solemn. "I'm sorry, but that's all I can do."

"Is there anyone who can help speed their decision?"

"You might talk to John Winthrop. He's no longer governor, but he may be able to assist you."

Declining an offer to stay for supper, Hull made his way back to the ship. News of the delay caused some grumbling among his followers, but he could offer them scant hope of more immediate action.

* * *

Winthrop sighed as his visitor was announced. "Another minister!" he muttered. "I hope this Hull is not a purist like Roger Williams."

A small man in his late forties, Winthrop had a broad forehead, arched eyebrows, and a long pointed nose. A heavy tapering beard accentuated the length of his face. Rising from the table that served as his desk, he walked to the door of his study – a modest yet well appointed room on the ground floor of his home in Boston. Unlike its neighbors, the house had two stories. He regarded this not as ostentation, but as an indication of God's approval.

Hull's demeanor on entering was assured, even a little arrogant. Winthrop knew the look. Williams had it whenever he came before the assistants to defend his opposition to oaths for men who were not church members. He had declared – on that occasion or a later one – that a man who was justified should not pray with an unjustified person, not even his own wife. Winthrop had refuted those errors, but now the congregation at Salem had chosen Williams as their pastor. Some clergymen were founts of vexation. It was well that they were barred from holding public office and had but an unofficial role in the government of the colony.

"You come in a good season," he said when his visitor was seated. "I trust you have experienced no undue hardship since your arrival."

"Thank you for your concern," Hull said, "but I anticipated some hardships in coming to New England and have placed my future and that of my congregation in God's hands."

Winthrop nodded. "It is only thanks to God's providence that we have survived these past five winters. I pray the worst ordeals are behind us."

As if in response to his prayer, the pungent aroma of venison stew wafted from the adjoining room. He had renounced the pleasures of the hunt in order to mortify his flesh, though some wits claimed that his poor marksmanship diminished the value of his sacrifice. Yet man had a right, nay an obligation, to partake of God's bounty, provided he didn't become a slave to his belly.

"Your wife is a good cook," Hull observed.

"I'll give her your compliments. Is your family with you?"

"I have seven children and a new wife on the ship. My first wife died shortly before I left England."

"I deeply regret your loss," Winthrop said, "but I'm glad God sent you another good woman in her place."

How would he fare if Margaret were to die? No doubt he would marry again for the children's sake. He felt a surge of sympathy for Hull; but he reminded himself that his concern was with ideas, not sentiments.

"Are you acquainted with Roger Williams?" he asked.

"His brother-in-law is a passenger on the *Welcome*," Hull said, "but I know Mr. Williams only by reputation."

Winthrop recovered quickly from his surprise. "Williams would have it that any breach of the commandments that define our relationship with God is beyond the province of civil authority and can be punished only if the peace has been disturbed. What do you make of his opinion?"

Hull sensed he was being tested. He could ill afford to antagonize the most influential man in the colony. Yet he was not one to dissimulate. "It is at variance with recent efforts by the King and Archbishop Laud to strengthen the bond between the Church and the Throne."

"And do you support their efforts?" Winthrop asked.

Hull shrugged. "I'm an ordained minister of the Church of England," he replied. "I have little choice in the matter."

"That may well be; but I came to Massachusetts to create a church that is free of the trammels of papacy, a church that is true to its original purpose, a church that will serve as a beacon to guide others to a truer and more meaningful union with God. Are you opposed to that undertaking?"

Hull fingered his hat thoughtfully. Winthrop's support for his petition might well hinge on his reply to this question. He gave due consideration to his response. "I respect your purpose, but you've set yourself a difficult task. As for myself, I've come to New England to place myself beyond the reach of church authorities."

"I don't understand you, sir," Winthrop said. "If you weren't sent by Archbishop Laud, why are you here?"

"I seek a place to set down where I can minister to my followers without interference. I've filed a petition with the clerk, but waiting two months for the General Court to meet will cause us great hardship. I was told that you might be able to help us."

Winthrop regarded Hull as if he were trying to read his mind. "There is little I can do," he said at last. "The Court will not be hurried in such matters. Besides, John Haynes is now governor."

His words were tinged with regret. He had served four terms in that capacity, but the colonists were wary of any further extension. No doubt they feared the establishment of another ruling class comparable to the nobility in England. Winthrop hoped one day soon to resume the reins of government. It would make his task much easier.

When Hull was silent, he asked, "Where is it you wish to set down?"

"My patron has recommended that I settle in Wessaguscus."

"And who is your patron?"

"Sir Ferdinando Gorges." Hull's statement was seemingly without guile.

Winthrop frowned. In his eyes Gorges was a royalist adventurer whose goal was to govern New England, a man who posed a greater threat than Laud. Surely Hull must realize that such a claim of patronage could only work to his detriment – or were his words a thinly veiled threat?

"How comes Gorges to be your patron?"

Hull sensed from the cautious tone of Winthrop's question that he had regained a measure of control. Yet he was loath to press his advantage, save by implication. "I met him perhaps fifteen years ago, before he sent his son Robert to establish a settlement on these shores. When I decided to emigrate, I turned to him for guidance. He helped me to obtain a ship."

It sounded innocent; yet in matters related to Gorges, Winthrop had good reason for caution. "I've had recent word that your patron is building a ship and gathering soldiers in order to establish his authority once he is appointed general governor of New England. I also hear that Archbishop Laud is recruiting an army of Anglican clerics to be sent to the colonies." He watched his visitor closely for a reaction, but detected no sign of embarrassment.

"I know nothing about ships or armies," Hull said truthfully. Gorges had spoken to him of the pending appointment, but had remained silent as to his plans to exercise control over the colonies. Hull saw now the wisdom of that silence.

The minister's quick response and the sincerity in his voice allayed Winthrop's fears. "I'm inclined to believe you. At any rate, Wessaguscus can hardly be considered fertile soil for the seeds of Anglicanism."

Hull thought it best not to argue that point. "I just want to set up a community that will grow and prosper," he said. "I have no other desire."

"You must realize," Winthrop said gravely, "that to extend your ministry, you will need the approval of the Assembly of Ministers."

Hull's features darkened, and he started to rise. Realizing that he had to maintain his composure, he settled back in his chair.

"With all respect to the assembly," he said, struggling to be polite, "as an ordained minister, I require no further authorization to preach to anyone who will listen."

"That opinion will win you scant support in the General Court," Winthrop shot back.

"Surely the laws of England apply equally in her colonies," Hull said.

Winthrop's fingers drummed on the table before him. Perhaps he had underestimated this minister. He had no wish to appear disloyal to the Crown, and he could ill afford to draw undue attention to himself. Despite Hull's assurances, his ties to Gorges struck Winthrop as ominous. The best solution was to isolate Hull and his colony in a place remote from Boston. Wessaguscus served that purpose reasonably well.

Yet his penchant for disputation would not be denied. "Are you opposed to our congregational form of church government?" he asked.

Hull reflected for a moment. He was not prepared to eliminate the hierarchy; but, given his situation, congregational principles might benefit his leadership. "Not at all," he said. "Indeed, I rely on it to protect my church from the outside interference I experienced in England. But I must say that your Assembly of Ministers sounds very much like a hierarchy."

Winthrop smiled at the manner in which Hull was able to combine acceptance with criticism. But his conciliatory thoughts soon gave way to a vision of a great fleet plying its way across the Atlantic bearing hundreds of soldiers and scores of Anglican clerics, all under the command of Gorges. He decided to strike a bargain.

"When the Court meets in July," he said, "Williams is again on the agenda. He may aid your cause. The deputies will be too confounded by his scruples and rhetoric to take heed of Wessaguscus. I'll support your petition, if you in turn will agree to abide by our rules."

Hull realized that he had to subdue his pride for the sake of his followers. "Insofar as my conscience permits," he promised.

Winthrop was content. With Hull exiled to the wilderness south of Boston, he could attend to the real threat – the prospect of Gorges as the royal governor. But first he must savor Margaret's venison stew.

* * *

Early in June the *Welcome* made port in Dorchester. Hull's colony had been quartered aboard the ship since their arrival, passing the time with trips ashore for provisions and to stretch their legs, while waiting for the next session of the General Court. Hull had his brother George's assurance that arrangements could be made for the colony on land. The ship docked in the Neponset River, which washed the southern shore of the town. From the deck Hull could see the cod fishery and grist mill. Upstream a new bridge spanned the river. As he stepped ashore, Hull longed to see a familiar face in this land he was prepared to call his home.

At the center of town a score of simple dwellings, much like those in Boston, surrounded the fort and the meetinghouse. Vegetables sprouted in the gardens, and sunflowers were in bloom. The fertility of the soil inspired Hull with confidence that the land at Wessaguscus would be equally fruitful. But the crops had to be planted first, and he relied on his brother for help.

From the size of his house, George appeared to be one of the more prosperous residents of Dorchester. His wife Thomasine answered the door, and several of the children came forward to greet their uncle. Hull was surprised and pleased to find John Warham also on hand. The three men sat on the front porch that George was in the process of building.

"Dorchester appears to be quite orderly and according to plan," Hull said as he sipped the hard cider Thomasine had served them. "Boston struck me as being rather haphazard."

George's eyes lingered upon the neighboring houses, as if to confirm that assessment. His ruddy face was deeply tanned, and he had put on weight since leaving England. "We're ahead of Boston in many respects," he said. "Our town government is a model for several other communities."

"George is a deputy to the General Court," Warham said. "We both feel that the towns should have a greater voice in those laws that concern the whole colony."

Hull studied his college friend. Warham too had changed since their parting in England. His red hair was still unruly; but he seemed more assured, more at peace with himself. His gray eyes looked inward, reflecting his soul, as well as outward upon the world. He was clearly a man with a dream and a purpose.

"It's a slow process," George said. "The colony is governed by an inner circle of assistants and adjutants, men who are chiefly interested in the creation and preservation of a model reformed church."

"I trust that as a deputy you'll endorse my petition to set down in Wessaguscus," Hull said. "I've been assured of Winthrop's support."

"Then you should have no problem," George said. "But why a place like Wessaguscus? It's not even a plantation, just trappers and old comers who were there before Winthrop arrived."

"I won't disturb them," Hull said. "I have my own congregation, which they're welcome to join."

Warham got up and planted himself squarely in front of Hull. "You are no longer in England, " he stated. "Church membership here is limited to those who are justified, and only church members can become freemen and vote. Take care whom you make welcome."

"Only God can know if a man is justified," Hull said, setting down his cider. "My church is open to anyone who desires to be saved. Do you see that as a problem when I get to Wessaguscus?"

"People here are much given to complain," Warham said, "and the position of a minister is tenuous at best."

"A group of people from Dorchester are relocating to Windsor in the Connecticut Colony," George said as he refilled his brother's cup. "Warham and I have agreed to join them."

"I don't understand," Hull said, surprised by this announcement. "You appear to be well settled here."

"The boundaries of Dorchester are set. I need more land on which to raise crops and graze my cattle."

Hull turned to Warham. "But you have an obligation to minister to the families who came with you from England."

"Most of those families are going to Windsor. As their pastor, I must abide by their decision."

"Have you no reasons of your own?"

"Indeed I do. Winthrop is convinced that his band of Puritans has a covenant with the Almighty – like that between God and the Israelites – and that any breach of their contract will incur the wrath of Heaven. He is determined to apply his beliefs to the government of the entire colony."

"The assistants are more concerned with issues of morality and religion than the welfare of the populace," George said. "You can save yourself a good deal of grief by coming with us."

"He's right. You must join us," Warham said.

"I promised Winthrop that we would keep to ourselves and not trouble anyone," Hull said. "I trust the assistants will leave us in peace. My chief concern now is getting settled before it's too late to plant a crop."

"Then I wouldn't wait for the Court to rule on your petition," George said. "They'll be more apt to grant permission if you're already there."

"That may be true," Hull said, "but first I must find lodging ashore for those who came with me."

"I can arrange for temporary quarters in the fort," George said, "and I'll put you in touch with a man named John Bursley. He came here ten years ago and now lives in Wessaguscus. He has a ship big enough to carry your provisions, but most of your colony will have to get there by land. I'll dispatch a messenger to find out when his ship is available."

* * *

"This is all so primitive," Agnes said when she saw the site Hull had selected. "We must do everything ourselves: build houses, clear more land, plant gardens, and who knows what else."

"We have a score of able-bodied men eager to do the work" Hull said. "The Indians are friendly, and old comers like Bursley are ready to help."

His brave words masked his own disappointment. Wessaguscus was as George had described it – isolated dwellings owned by hunters and trappers, remnants of the colony Robert Gorges had sought to establish twelve years earlier. Their crude houses were made of logs, the roofs thatched with coarse grass found along the shore. The shell of a church, built by Sorrell or his successor Barnard, was too small to accommodate Hull's congregation; but he anticipated the day when a new meetinghouse would become the focal point of the town. Meanwhile, the settlers built their cabins – a great room and a loft – and planted the seeds they had brought with them in plots of land already cleared by the Indians.

So it happened that Hull and his followers were already settled in their new surroundings when the General Court met in July. After that meeting Winthrop noted in his journal, "At this same session Mr. Hull, a minister in England, and twenty-one families were granted permission to set down at Wessaguscus, which was established as a plantation."

In August, some two months after their arrival in Wessaguscus, they experienced a storm like none they had ever seen. High winds snapped or uprooted hundreds of trees and blew roofs off the newly built houses. A surge of water from the sea flooded low-lying portions of the settlement. People took what shelter they could find and prayed to God for deliverance. A lunar eclipse that followed only added to their fears. Those who kept journals labeled the storm as a hurricane. Others simply shook their heads in astonishment and set about to repair the damage.

"Even nature is against us," Agnes said.

"The storm was a test of our will," Hull replied. "You'll feel differently as the town develops. And with the help of Joseph and Tristram and the servants, I'll soon have a new roof over your head. In our present circumstances, seven children are a blessing."

"It will soon be eight," Agnes said, placing a hand on her stomach.

Hull's face beamed as he embraced her. "I see this as evidence that God has shed His grace and His blessings upon our colony."

Seven

"I shall continue to serve."
(Weymouth, Massachusetts Colony, 1635-1637)

That autumn Wessaguscus was established as the town of Weymouth. Hull took the oath of freeman and was installed as the authorized minister of the Weymouth church. And during the winter Agnes delivered her firstborn child – a son whom they named Hopewell. Both town and church continued to grow throughout the spring and summer, attracting remnants of the Gorges colony, Puritans who had no place else to worship, separatists from Plymouth, and men of no sect whatsoever. Hull welcomed all who attended his services, even an occasional Indian. While honoring the law of the colony that church membership was limited to those who were saved, Hull justified his actions by insisting that some provision must be made for those in transition. He recognized that, to the Puritan mind, the elect were chosen by God and that salvation was a free gift rather than a goal to be achieved; yet his reason and training as a minister persuaded him that a man's good deeds were not without merit, regardless of his religious affiliation. He realized that this opinion would, as Winthrop warned, get him in trouble; but he was unaware that storm clouds of another nature had begun to gather.

"Why is Mr. Jenner preaching in your church?" Agnes asked.

It was late summer, a year after their arrival in Weymouth, and she sat across the rude table from him in their simply furnished cabin. Joanna was by the fireplace mending a smock for her sister Elizabeth, while with her foot she rocked a cradle where the baby rested peacefully. The other children were in the loft, presumably asleep.

"He was invited to preach by a group of men who don't like the way I conduct services," Hull said. The matter was uppermost in his thoughts, but he had hoped it might not trouble his family. "It seems I'm not enough of a Puritan for them."

"Will you attend his service?"

Hull shook his head. "I don't want people to think that I endorse his views, nor that I'm afraid to let him express them. I prefer to wait and see what impression he makes on the congregation."

"But who is he?" Agnes persisted. "Where does he come from?"

"According to Bursley, he hails from the east of England and is newly arrived in the colony. He has a church in Roxbury. No doubt he was recommended by the authorities in Boston."

"Will he try to establish a church in Weymouth?"

"To do that, he would have to get approval from the Assembly of Ministers," Hull said, adopting a cheerful note lest Agnes be forced to share his concern. "That seems unlikely. They just rejected the petition of a congregation in Dorchester – those who remained when Warham left – because not enough members could demonstrate they were among the elect. Those who invited Jenner to come here may have the same problem."

"But he could try to take over your church," Agnes said.

"Would we have to leave Weymouth if he did take over?" Joanna broke in.

"That is unlikely," Hull replied. "My church rests on a firm foundation, and my followers constitute a majority of the congregation."

The women seemed satisfied with this declaration, but Hull could not dispel a persistent fear that events might take a less favorable course. That spring the newly erected town of Weymouth had sent Bursley and John Upham as deputies to the General Court in Boston. Upham, who was one of Hull's company, reported on his return that Winthrop regarded Weymouth as "a hotbed of episcopacy."

They were walking the short distance from the meetinghouse to their homes. "I'm not surprised," Hull said. "Before we arrived, the settlers who were already here were torn between the Puritans in Boston and separatists in Plymouth. Both sides were bent on rooting out the Anglican forms of religion planted by Robert Gorges and his colony. That's one reason I chose to settle in Wessaguscus."

Upham appeared to ponder this statement. "If that's the case, why did Winthrop allow us to set down here?"

Hull stifled a chuckle. "I let him think Sir Ferdinando was my patron. He could ill afford to provoke the authorities in England. Besides, he wasn't governor at the time, so his power was somewhat limited."

"It still is," Upham said. "Vane seems to have a firm grip on the reins of government. But that didn't stop Winthrop from trying to prevent me from being seated as a deputy."

"I fear that I'm responsible for Winthrop's displeasure," Hull said. They had reached Upham's house, which was one of the largest in town.

"That may be," Upham said, "but he never mentioned your name."

Hull knew why he was in disfavor. From the outset he had made welcome all who chose to attend his services. He did not proclaim such inclusiveness from the pulpit, but he turned no one away. This offended the Puritan element in town and was reported to both the church and civil authorities in Boston. Another minister was their response. Recalling his promise to Winthrop, Hull decided to let Jenner make his case.

* * *

Hunched over with his head pulled down, Tristram felt like a turtle withdrawing into its shell. When his father conducted the service, the whole family sat in the second pew. But today Tristram was far back near the door.

"Have you lost your senses, listening to that man?" Agnes would surely scold him when he got home. "He's only here to stir up trouble. What will your father say when he finds out?"

Tristram assured himself that he was simply a spy and not a traitor. His parents' recent talk about Mr. Jenner had carried up to the loft, where he lay awake. When he asked Joanna about it the next day, she agreed that he should attend the service and report back to his father. He had never listened to a Puritan minister, and he didn't understand why Mr. Jenner was preaching in Weymouth. If people were dissatisfied with his father's sermons, they need only speak to him, and he would do whatever was right and fair.

"You're much too young to worry about such things," Agnes would say. He liked Agnes, except when she treated him as a child. He was twelve years old; and he knew the area around Weymouth better than anyone else in the family, except maybe his father. When he grew up, he wanted to sail the ocean like Master Bursley – or maybe apprentice to a carpenter like his brother Joseph.

Everyone rose as Mr. Jenner entered. He was short and rather stout, with sideburns but no beard. His eyes darted from face to face but settled on no one in particular. Tristram waited for him to speak. "Don't judge a man by his looks," his father had impressed upon him. "Hear what he has to say."

After a prayer and a reading from scripture, Mr. Jenner mounted the pulpit. "I thank all present for inviting me to preach in Weymouth," he began. "I come here not to sow seeds of discord, but in a true spirit of reconciliation and harmony. I come to hear your concerns and address your spiritual needs – needs that Mr. Hull seems to have neglected."

Tristram snorted. He and his brother had helped build that pulpit, and Mr. Jenner had better take care what he said from it. The man in front of him turned and gave him a severe look. Tristram sought to catch Mr. Jenner's eye as he launched into his sermon, but the minister's gaze and his words floated above the assembly like so many butterflies. "Flutterbys," his sister Elizabeth called them. Whenever his father preached, Tristram felt that each word was aimed directly at him. Maybe that was what made Puritan ministers different. They scattered their words over the congregation, instead of aiming them at any one person. According to his father, Puritans were good people who were looking for some sign that would mark them as one of God's chosen few. Tristram was content to be among the many who were uncertain of their fate.

Mr. Jenner was talking about being justified, and about people he called the elect. Tristram squirmed in his seat. He had no permission to be there from his father or Agnes. Did that mean he was not one of those elect? When the sermon ended and Mr. Jenner turned his back briefly to the congregation, he slipped out of the building and ran home.

* * *

Hull leaned against the woodpile as he listened to his son's account of the church service and his impression of Jenner. "How many were there?" he asked when Tristram had finished.

"Maybe half as many as on Sunday."

"And were they pleased with what he had to say?"

"They listened to him, but he never really looked at them. He seemed somehow separated. I don't expect he'll be here for long."

Hull smiled at this assessment. "There's more to it than that, but I'm glad to have your opinion of Mr. Jenner."

"Then you're not angry at me for going there without telling you?"

"No. And I'll tell Agnes not to scold you."

He watched as Tristram departed carrying an armful of firewood. The boy took after him in that he was inclined to wonder and worry. His older son was content to work and eat, letting others make the decisions. Joseph would have an easier life.

In the weeks that followed, the gravity of the situation became more apparent as the Assembly of Ministers and the magistrates espoused the cause of Jenner. Hull had few friends in either circle.

Most of those who had come with him from England remained loyal; yet the dissident faction was gaining support, and Jenner stayed in Weymouth.

"I blame myself for opening my church to outsiders," Hull confided to Agnes as they lay in bed. "Yet I could hardly do otherwise. I hoped to win back those who were disaffected with the Church of England, but I've managed only to swell their ranks."

"Your duty is to your own followers," she replied. "You're not responsible for what other people do or say."

He touched her arm. "I shall never abandon my congregation. A minister who has no church is like a carpenter without tools."

Agnes took his hand, and he kissed her. She came into his arms, intent on granting him the solace God had bestowed on married couples.

* * *

In his free time Tristram liked to explore the surrounding countryside, and he often took his sister Elizabeth along on these excursions. She was two years younger than Temperance, but more resourceful and fearless by nature. On one occasion they had encountered two Indians deep in the forest. Tristram had learned a few words in their language. While he was debating what to say, Beth offered them the sweet cakes which Agnes had packed. The Indians studied the strange food before eating it, then led the way to a patch of the sweetest blackberries he had ever tasted.

When Joanna said their father might have to give up his church and leave Weymouth, Tristram set out to find another place where the family could settle. His father often spoke of Hingham, which bordered Weymouth on the east, and of a minister named Peter

Hobart. He didn't reveal his destination to Beth, but she readily agreed to accompany him.

Starting from King's Cove, they stuck to the shoreline. It was not the most direct route; but he had been that way before, and he didn't want to meet anyone who might ask about his mission. They passed Great Hill, then struck inland. From a hilltop he made out a neck of land and two mounds that looked like islands but were really part of the mainland. They passed through woods of white oak, pine, and cedar. Wild turkeys, pheasants, and quail took flight at their approach. Tristram had heard tales of moose, wolves, wildcats, and bear, but he kept these to himself lest he alarm Beth. Still, he proceeded with caution, keeping an eye out for larger game, and was relieved when they met only a red fox, two deer, and a porcupine.

Regaining the shore, they paused to rest and to eat. On their right was the mouth of a stream that formed the border between Hingham and Weymouth. Satisfied with their progress and confident that they were now safe, Tristram embarked on a gory tale of treachery and slaughter associated with Paddock's Island, pointing it out to Beth as he spoke.

"But that happened long before we got here," he assured her, "and the men who died were all Frenchmen."

"Why were the Indians angry at them?" she asked.

"They were defending their territory. There used to be thousands of Indians hereabouts. Only a few hundred are left."

"What happened to the rest?"

"A plague killed them. Those who lived thought the gods were punishing them for killing the Frenchmen. That's one reason why the English settlers got a warm welcome."

"You're making it all up," Beth said gleefully.

"I am not. I heard it from lots of people, and Father says it's true."

"Well, I'm glad the Indians are our friends now," Beth said, turning her attention to the cornbread Agnes had baked.

Pied teals and gulls wheeled overhead, anticipating the scraps. A hedgehog peeped out from under a bush, then scurried off. When they had finished their meal, Tristram followed the stream to a place where they could cross. There was a ferry farther inland, but the ferryman would want to know why they were going to Hingham.

"'ll get my clothes wet," Beth objected, staring at the water.

"Take them off," Tristram said as he heeded his own advice.

They forded the stream, reaching Hingham early in the afternoon. Here too the homes were constructed of logs and had thatched roofs; but they were closer together than in Weymouth and appeared to be clustered around a large building, which Tristram took to be the meetinghouse.

"Mr. Hobart will answer our questions," he said, making straight for the building. "We'll be home before it gets dark."

"What do we want to know?" Beth asked as she hurried after him.

"What it's like to live in Hingham."

A ladder was propped against the face of the building to the left of the entrance. A thin wiry man was making repairs to one of the shutters. They stood watching until he noticed them.

"I'm Peter Hobart," he said. "What can I do for you?"

Tristram gave their names. "We came to find out all about Hingham."

Hobart let out a hearty laugh from his belly. Tristram distrusted men whose laughter was only in their heads. They had something to hide.

"And what do you propose to do with that information?" Hobart asked as he came down from the ladder.

"My father may need it, if he has to leave Weymouth."

"Is your father Joseph Hull?"

Tristram nodded, while Beth grinned broadly.

"I've had good reports of him," Hobart said. "I'm sorry that things aren't working out as he hoped."

"Are you a Puritan minister like Mr. Jenner?" Beth asked.

Hobart smiled. "I confess to being a Puritan, but my views are quite different from Mr. Jenner's." He turned again to Tristram. "If your father decides to move, tell him to contact me. Hingham is a good place to live."

"Your church is a lot bigger than ours," Tristram said.

"Come along. I'll show you inside." Hobart led the way, pointing out a hand-carved pulpit he had brought with him from England.

As Tristram was examining it and comparing it to his own crude handiwork in Weymouth, he heard Beth ask, "Why are there no pictures?"

"The building serves also as a courthouse and a fort," Hobart said. "We use it to store grain and powder, and sometimes as a stable."

Again outside, Tristram turned as if to leave, but Beth hung back. "Please, may I have some water?" she asked.

"Of course. My home is right over there." Hobart pointed it out.

"Why are the houses here so close together?" Tristram asked as he tried to keep pace with Hobart. Beth lagged behind.

"So people will be near the fort in case of trouble."

"Are you afraid of the Indians?" Beth asked, hurrying to catch up.

Hobart laughed again. "Not at all. They attend my services. But the authorities in Boston say we shouldn't live more than half a mile from the fort. A minister must follow the rules – as much as possible."

As they reached Hobart's house, several children ran out to greet them, followed closely by his wife, Elizabeth. She hovered over Tristram and Beth in a motherly fashion, listening as they described their home in Weymouth; but she didn't ask whether their parents knew where they were. Tristram was grateful to her for that. Much to his surprise, Beth simply sipped her water; whereas at home she gulped it down. He asked her about it when they had broken away from the hospitality afforded by the minister's wife.

"I wanted to see where Mr. Hobart lived," she said.

"That was smart. I like it here in Hingham."

"Mrs. Hobart seems very nice." Beth had no further comment.

They returned by a broad trail that led over Great Hill, arriving home late for the evening meal. Agnes was accustomed to their expeditions.

"What great adventures did you two have today?" she asked.

"We hiked along the shore toward Hingham," Tristram said.

His half truth appeared to satisfy her.

* * *

When he had finished eating, it was Hull's custom to walk about the town. He claimed it aided his digestion. He normally went alone, stopping frequently to speak to any members of his congregation whom he chanced to meet. So he was somewhat surprised when Tristram offered to join him. He listened calmly to his son's account of the trip to Hingham. He didn't ask why they went. He knew the answer.

"I'm glad Hobart is hospitably inclined," he said when Tristram was done, "but your mission is premature. I'm not ready to leave Weymouth."

"Mr. Hobart seems like a good man," Tristram said. "Much better than Mr. Jenner. And Mrs. Hobart makes good biscuits."

Children were inclined to seize upon simple solutions to complex problems, Hull reflected. A move to Hingham would be an admission of defeat. Still, with a rival minister in town, his living had been reduced. A day might come when he would be obliged to find another place and some other means to support his family. It would do no harm to acquire a piece of land in Hingham as a precaution. But he kept that thought to himself, lest he alarm Agnes and the children.

A secondary allotment of land was made in Weymouth, and eighteen acres were set off for Jenner. Hull received fifty-four acres, but he took scant comfort in that. Jenner continued to gain support among the townspeople; whereas his own popularity, based on attendance at services, was on the wane. To add to his discomfort, Upham's fears were borne out at the fall session of the General Court. He and Bursley were sent home, while Read and Walton were seated. Both belonged to the party that supported Jenner. Winthrop's hand in the proceedings was all too visible.

Bursley had become a frequent visitor to the Hull household. His voyages up and down the coast kept him in touch with ship masters from abroad; and during his term on the General Court he made a number of useful contacts, both business and political. Hull depended on him for the latest news from Boston and from England. They would retire to the relative privacy of a log bench that Hull had erected alongside the front entrance to his cabin. There Bursley would smoke his pipe, while Hull traced geometric patterns in the dirt at his feet.

"Read informed the court that Upham is your close friend and voice," Bursley reported on this occasion, "and that I represent those who came over with the Gorges party. All fairness went out the window."

"So I have no appeal in Boston if Jenner and his followers take over my church," Hull said.

"You might make friends with the Indians," Bursley said. "They gave Roger Williams a refuge when he was cast out in mid-winter."

"I'm in no danger of being banished," Hull said, certain that Bursley was joking.

"The point is, you have to provide for yourself and your family."

"I know the gospel admonition," Hull said. "I've contacted Peter Hobart and acquired some land in Hingham. But don't let on to Agnes. I don't want her to think our situation is more serious than it actually is."

Bursley knocked out the ash from his pipe against the heel of his boot. "Hingham is still Massachusetts. The Plymouth Colony is looking for settlers. There you'd be free of Winthrop and the assistants."

"I refuse to abandon those I brought with me," Hull said. "From Hingham I can still minister to them. But I pray it won't come to that."

"I hope you're right," Bursley said, tucking the pipe in his pocket.

* * *

Though Hull was polite when he encountered Jenner on the street, he seethed inwardly at the prospect of surrendering all he had built with his own hands. He watched as his congregation drifted inexorably toward his rival. Meanwhile, Read and Walton mustered support for Jenner in Boston. The deputies and magistrates would adjudicate any disputes in the Weymouth church. The situation called for direct intervention. He must fight to hold on to what he had. He decided to face the opposition and gauge its strength.

Jenner seemed surprised to see Hull sitting in the front pew. His voice quavered as he recited the opening prayers, but he quickly regained his composure. When the time came for the sermon, his hands grasped the edge of the pulpit to steady himself. His gaze brushed over Hull as he spoke.

"Please join with me in giving thanks to God for the blessings He has bestowed on us. First I want to welcome Mr. Hull, who has chosen to visit us today. I trust he will be satisfied."

"I'm hardly a visitor," Hull said, his voice loud and strong. "I'm the designated pastor of this church." He was on his feet now, his eyes flashing. "I know every one of you by name, and you know me. Are you here to weigh Mr. Jenner's words against my own? Or have you now become so hungry for spiritual nourishment that you must attend two services?"

"This is neither the time nor the place for such questions," Jenner said in a firm voice. "Please sit down and allow me to continue."

Several men seconded the plea, but Hull ignored them as he stepped into the aisle and turned to face the congregation. "I disagree. What better way to arrive at an informed judgment than to hear what each of us has to say on the issues that divide us?"

"Some issues are not open to our private judgment," Jenner said. "My words reflect the considered opinion of the Assembly of Ministers and of the magistrates in Boston."

"Opinion, nonetheless," Hull said. "I weigh my words carefully in my heart before I utter them. Unlike Mr. Jenner, I'm not content to convey to you the thoughts and decisions of other men who place their own interests above the established doctrine of the Church."

"Apparently, you feel that the Church has no need for reform," Jenner declared. He had stepped down from the pulpit and stood now on a level with Hull. "If that is your position, you have no place in this colony." His words provoked a murmur of approval among those assembled.

"I accept all essential doctrines," Hull said, raising his voice to be heard, "but I reject certain practices mandated by those in power to serve their private interests. Church and state are as closely united here as in England. Winthrop and the magistrates seem bent on instituting much the same system they came to New England to escape."

"Enough!" Jenner cried. "I must ask you to leave."

"It is indeed enough!" Hull shouted above the clamor of voices. "The time has come for you to choose a minister who serves your needs."

Having delivered his ultimatum, he stalked out. He paused briefly to study the faces of the wardens stationed at the door, looking for some sign of approval; but they were expressionless.

* * *

"The congregation has chosen Jenner!" Hull announced, bursting into the great room of his cabin. "I've been expelled from my own church!"

Agnes stopped nursing the baby. She sat quietly, her head bowed. Tristram waited eagerly for his next words. Joseph seemed withdrawn. The younger children just stared at him. Joanna was the first to speak.

"Can he just come in and take over?"

Hull removed his coat and tossed it on a bench. "With no bishop to rule on such matters, the congregation can choose whichever minister they prefer. My supporters are no longer in the majority."

"Can't you appeal to the Assembly of Ministers?" Agnes asked.

"They support Jenner and will be glad to be rid of me."

"What will you do?" Joanna asked.

Slumping into a seat at the table, Hull rested his head on his hands as if he were praying. Several minutes of silence ensued before he spoke again.

"I've already made provisions for our future. I own some land in Hingham, and I have good reason to believe we'll be welcome there."

"We're moving to Hingham!" Tristram cried with evident satisfaction. Joanna and Agnes both scowled at him.

"Not, however, as a minister," Hull continued. "That would be a poor way to repay Peter Hobart for his hospitality."

"But you can't give up your ministry," Agnes objected.

"Jenner's victory is not complete," Hull said, giving her a fond look. "I shall continue to serve those in my congregation who remain loyal to me."

"But how will we live in Hingham?" Agnes asked. "What will you do?"

Hull expected the question. "I can sell cattle to those who are newly arrived in the colony. I have connections with a dealer in Somerset. I'll arrange at once for a shipment."

Agnes smiled. "That's what you were doing when first I met you."

Hull regarded his wife with some surprise. Was she offering him support, or were her motives more selfish? "It won't make us rich," he said, "but it will put food on the table."

* * *

Some days later Joanna encountered Mr. Jenner at the church. She had gone there to fetch a book for her father. As she was about to leave, she saw the minister approaching. She could easily have slipped out at the side, but a stubborn streak in her nature made her stay where she was. She wouldn't speak to him, just nod to show him she had a right to be there. She had nothing against him as a man. He was her father's rival, and she saw him solely in that light.

Jenner essayed a smile when he spotted her. "I trust your parents are well, Miss Joanna," he said.

She detected a note of condescension in his voice, as though he were addressing a child. Tristram said his sermons were like that –

that he looked down upon the congregation as so many obedient children. In her father's eyes, everyone was on the same level. She distrusted people who were puffed up with their own worth. All men were poor in God's eyes. So her father said.

"They're quite well, considering they may have to leave Weymouth." She was surprised by her words, but had no desire to take them back.

"You mustn't blame me for that," Jenner said. "Your father brought it upon himself. I simply heeded the call of those in his congregation who were disaffected."

He was still patronizing her, justifying his actions. "I trust you have the proper remedy for their disaffection," she said as she brushed by him.

Jenner muttered a reply, but she didn't stop to listen.

* * *

Hull's hands gripped the pulpit his sons had made as he surveyed what remained of his congregation. Some forty or fifty men, women, and children had gathered to hear his farewell sermon. His topic was Christ's departure from His home district of Judea, where the populace regarded Him simply as a carpenter's son; and he cited the maxim that a prophet is devoid of honor in his own country. With that behind him, he allowed his gaze to linger on his wife and children in the second pew before continuing.

"More than a year ago we set down in Weymouth and built this church to the greater glory of God. With His blessing we prospered. But it now appears that a majority of church members want Mr. Jenner as their pastor. In consequence, my position as your minister has become untenable." He raised his hands to quiet a murmur of objection. "In order to avoid further dissension, I have decided to move to Hingham. But I am also mindful of my obligation to meet the spiritual needs of all those who sailed with me from England. You may rest assured that I shall continue to serve as your minister. Some of you have offered your homes for that purpose. I am deeply grateful. Even though I feel obliged to relocate, I shall remain in your midst – and, I hope, in your minds and hearts."

With that Hull stepped down and left the church. The murmur of voices grew as his loyal followers absorbed the full import of his remarks. Mingling with those who gathered outside the church, he was convinced that his parting words had been well received.

But one man had a different opinion. "You ought to stay and fight for what is rightfully yours," he said.

"Even if the people should turn against Jenner," Hull replied, "another minister will come to take his place. A majority of the congregation no longer supports me, and I have to look out for my family."

"It looks to me like you're running away," the man muttered as he walked off.

At home Agnes quickly reconciled herself to the move. To mitigate Joanna's lack of enthusiasm, Hull promised to take her along when he held services in Weymouth Young Joseph accepted the change without question, while Tristram and Elizabeth took full credit for discovering their new home in Hingham.

Eight

"You have no status."

(Hingham, Massachusetts Colony, 1637-1639)

Hull moved his family to Hingham early that winter. He had made no special provision for the move, and only the beneficence of Hobart sustained them with some degree of comfort until their new home was ready. Hobart was from East Anglia and a Cambridge man. Even though Hull was a west countryman and an Oxford graduate, they discovered that they had much in common. Hobart was a congregationalist, but he was critical of the form of church governance fostered by the authorities in Boston. He placed no restrictions on church membership; and his congregation included nearly everyone in Hingham. His service consisted of a catechism lesson, the singing of psalms, prayers and a sermon, an occasional baptism, and monthly communion. Men sat on the left, women and children on the right. Another sermon and prayers came after lunch.

Recognizing that the success of the Hingham church stood in sharp contrast with his failure in Weymouth, Hull was obliged to wonder what he had done wrong. He took comfort in ministering to those followers who had remained loyal. Each week he rode the eight miles to Weymouth on horseback. His services in Upham's home were much shorter than Hobart's. He told himself it was a temporary trial, yet it galled him that he no longer had a church to call his own.

Jenner's popularity declined after Hull's departure; and it wasn't long before a group of parishioners made up largely of new settlers invited Robert Lenthall, a minister who had served them in England, to preach in Weymouth. But Winthrop forbade Lenthall's ordination. All this was reported to Hull by Bursley or by Upham, who was once again a deputy to the General Court. Hull saw no advantage for himself in this confusion. He could only watch, while preaching to his small band of followers.

Hobart was equally well informed about the actions of the General Court, and he passed on to Hull the latest news from Boston. The Lords Commissioners in England were again demanding that the patent issued to the Massachusetts Bay Colony by King Charles be returned, but Winthrop continued to stall.

"If I were in Winthrop's place," Hobart said one evening as they sat by the fire in the modest cabin he called the rectory, "I would stop making excuses. Further delay will only hasten the imposition of a royal governor. The King has expressed his intention to name Sir Ferdinando Gorges to that post. But the great ship he was building broke in half at launch, and Gorges no longer has sufficient resources to exercise real control in New England. Still, you may benefit from his appointment."

Hull sipped the hot cider that Hobart's wife had kindly provided. "Not here in Massachusetts," he said. "The renewed threat of a royal governor will only help Winthrop and the assistants to establish their Puritan theocracy. Anyone who ventures to voice support or approval for the Church of England is deemed a heretic."

"The General Court is beginning to make its voice heard," Hobart said. "You should become a deputy."

"As a minister, I'm prohibited from serving in that capacity," Hull said. "Besides, Winthrop would surely block my appointment."

"Winthrop will shy away from any action that may offend Gorges," Hobart countered. "And in Hingham you're just a freeman."

"But the people in Hingham hardly know me, and I have little experience in such matters. I fear I should make a very poor deputy."

"At least consider it," Hobart said. "We need more men in Boston with independent vision."

* * *

Anne Hutchinson was a major topic of conversation that winter and into the spring. She had arrived in the colony with her husband and eleven children a year before Hull settled in Wessaguscus. Her weekly religious discussion groups for women in Boston were so popular that she had arranged for a second meeting open also to men. Henry Vane, who was then governor, attended these sessions. But when Vane returned to England and Winthrop was again in office, she ran afoul of civil and religious authorities for her antinomian opinions – that the moral law is of no use or obligation, because faith alone is necessary for salvation. Particularly repugnant to them was her assertion that she was certain she was among God's elect. Summoned to appear before the General Court in November, she was convicted of heresy. Her banishment was delayed, because she was again with child. But in the spring of 1638 she was excommunicated by the church at Boston and ordered to leave at once. Thirty families went with her, settling in Portsmouth on the island of Aquidneck in Narragansett Bay.

"Williams, then Wheelwright, and now Mrs. Hutchinson!" Hobart said as he and Hull crossed the muddy training field where the Hingham militia held its weekly drills. A light rain was falling, and their soggy great coats were heavy from long exposure to the weather. "Anyone who dares challenge the powers in Boston is banished. Though I have some difficulty feeling charitably inclined toward a woman who regards most ministers as emissaries of Satan."

"She used that term to describe ministers who doubt the dispensation and efficacy of grace as proclaimed in the gospels," Hull said. "Your preaching extends God's grace to all who hear and heed your words. Even I feel quite comfortable listening to you."

"The inclusiveness of which you speak would hardly identify me as one of the elect in her eyes. What do you make of her claim that she can recognize those who are saved – as if the seal of faith is on their foreheads?"

"We are judged by our works as well as our faith," Hull said.

"Then Mrs. Hutchinson would consign us both to hellfire." They had reached the edge of the field, and Hobart stopped to scrape mud from his boots. "But I admire her courage and her intellect. Her responses at the trial made Winthrop appear rather foolish. In the end she convicted herself."

Hull nodded. "Her principal offense was her gender. But I'm surprised to hear you defend her."

"I don't defend her; but I distrust men like Winthrop who presume to judge others while arrogating absolute power unto themselves."

"I thought you regarded Winthrop as a man of vision," Hull said.

"I endorse his vision for Church reform, not the manner in which he governs the colony. Massachusetts is greater than Boston. Have you given any further thought to serving as a deputy?"

"I'm still considering it," Hull replied.

* * *

At home Hull sought to balance his responsibilities to his family with his calling as a minister. Having promised Hobart that he wouldn't preach in Hingham, he confined his sermonizing to services in Weymouth. The cattle business was proving profitable, and Agnes had ordered some English furniture for the cabin. He took pleasure in gratifying her need for material comfort. For the moment his own salvation was planted in the field of commerce. He was simply waiting for God to water that seed – or to reveal an alternate plan.

"I've been invited to preach in Salem," he told Agnes one day upon his return from the harbor. "They may have a post for me."

Agnes ceased stirring the soup kettle. Wiping her hands on her apron, she approached the chair where Hull sat and placed a hand on his shoulder. "We're happy here and settled," she said calmly. "You'll only be courting trouble in Salem. You know what happened to Mr. Williams."

Hull put his hand over hers. "My ministry differs greatly from that of Roger Williams. Besides, the church in Salem has reconciled with Boston."

"And what happens if they decide they don't want you?"

"I'll tend to my cattle and become a deputy to the General Court in Boston, as Hobart suggests. But I won't surrender my status as a minister."

"You have no status," Agnes told him. "You slip into Weymouth on Sundays and hold services for a handful of people. Would moving to Salem change all that?"

"It's too soon to speak of moving," Hull said. "But I can at least see what Salem has to offer me."

Agnes withdrew her hand and came around to face him. "A move back to England would suit me better," she declared.

Hull stared at her in surprise. Were her words a reaction to the news of the moment, or had this sentiment been building for some time? She looked down, as if ashamed of her outburst, but made no apology.

"I must go wherever God leads me," he said.

"Then I pray He leads you to the General Court," Agnes said.

* * *

In Weymouth, Jenner was alienating many in his congregation by his demand for more money; and Lenthall was preaching to a dwindling number of worshipers. As a consequence, Hull's services drew a few more people, but not enough to kindle his desire to reestablish a church there.

Riding with her father to Weymouth, Joanna was struck by the joyful manner in which he carried out his duties. The moment he mounted his horse, he became a man alive to his calling and to the spirit within him. He had made two trips to Salem, but they seemed to give him little satisfaction. Like Agnes, Joanna was reluctant to move to Salem, but for reasons much more personal. John Bursley attended the services in Weymouth, and he often spoke to her afterwards while she waited for her father. They had little chance to talk on his visits to Hingham.

Eager to learn more about him, she enlisted Tristram's help. They had gone to the Hobarts to get spices newly arrived from England. "What do people say about Master Bursley?" she asked her brother on the walk back.

"He has his own ship. That's all I know. Why do you ask?"

"I think he likes me," she whispered, though no one was about. "He never fails to ask about my health when he visits Father."

"You mean he wants to marry you?"

"Is that so hard to believe?"

"N-no," Tristram stammered, "but he's as old as." Her look made him swallow the rest of his statement.

"I want you to find out all you can about him," Joanna said. "But you mustn't let on that I want to know."

"What am I supposed to do? I can't just ask him if he likes you."

"You'll think of a way. And don't say a word to anyone else."

In carrying out her orders, Tristram hit upon a scheme that would promote his own interests. His love of ships and the sea, nurtured on the voyage to New England, was known at home. He need only get his father to ask Bursley to show him around the *Aurora* when next the ship was in port.

To his satisfaction, the visit to the ship was quickly arranged. He attended closely to Bursley's explanation as they inspected the master's cabin, the galley, and the crew's quarters; and he was filled with wonder and longing as he peered down into the hold and gazed up at the tall masts.

"Well, are you ready to sign aboard?" Bursley asked.

"They need me at home," Tristram said, recalling his mission. "And if Joanna gets married, I'll have even more chores to do."

"I didn't know Joanna was engaged." Bursley's casual tone failed to hide his heightened interest.

"She's not," Tristram said, pleased at the success of his ruse, "but girls her age get married."

"They do indeed," Bursley said. "Well now, would you like to climb into the rigging? I'll get one of the crew to show you the crow's nest."

Tristram readily agreed. Yet he wondered if Bursley was too old – or simply too dignified – for the climb. He could ask the young sailor assigned to the task for more information about the master. But the climb proved to be a challenge, his perch was often precarious, and the view aloft made him catch his breath. Not until he stood again on deck, exhilarated by his experience, did he think of asking any questions.

"If I should decide to become a seaman," he said, "how long would it take to learn everything I need to know?"

"You look to be quite a bright lad. One or two voyages ought to do."

"Where does the ship go?"

"Mostly, the master trades with Indians in Maine; but sometimes we sail down the coast to New York or Charleston."

"Is he a good master?" Tristram asked, getting back to the point of his mission. "Does he whip you if you do something wrong?"

The sailor laughed heartily. "I guess he might, if you did something really bad; but I never been witness to a flogging. Master Bursley is kinder than most. You'll have more to fear from the crew."

"W-what do you mean?" Tristram asked.

"Your initiation. How long that lasts is up to you." Despite his words the young sailor's smile was reassuring.

"I'll be ready when the time comes," Tristram said bravely. He was thinking that if Bursley married Joanna, he would have to protect him.

He thanked the seaman and Bursley, then ran home to report his findings to Joanna. "Master Bursley is a good man," he told her, "and I think he likes you."

* * *

Hull declined the offer from the church at Salem. Though he was mindful of Agnes' feelings, external events also influenced his decision. His brother William's widow in Colyton sent him word that his father had died at the age of eighty-four. He considered returning to England, but the cattle business required his full attention No doubt the news had reached George in Connecticut as well. Perhaps he was in a better position to help settle their father's estate in Crewkerne.

Closer to home, a delegation of church elders went to Weymouth to resolve a dispute between Jenner and his congregation over salary and other matters. An uneasy truce was established; and Jenner stayed on despite continued dissatisfaction with his ministry. Hull saw in this a sign that the authorities in Boston were guarding against his own return to the pulpit. The same would surely hold true in Salem. Better to devote his energies to being a successful businessman.

There was also the matter of Anne Hutchinson's baby. Following her banishment, she had delivered a mass of tissue that bore no resemblance to a human fetus. Winthrop described it as "thirty monstrous births, one for each of her thirty misshapen opinions;" and he cited her misfortune as proof that she had been rightfully banished from the colony. His verdict gained wide acceptance in Boston, but Hobart demurred.

"Her other children are normal in every respect," he pointed out to Hull. "I doubt this one was even a child."

Hull remained silent. He was himself prone to seek out signs and omens. Yet it troubled him that a woman's misfortune was being used to justify her punishment, as if evidence mustered against her by the General Court and the Church of Boston were insufficient. Winthrop's verdict on the baby bespoke a flaw in his own character. He regarded himself as an instrument for carrying out the will of the Almighty. Such hubris was not to be tolerated, and Hull was easily persuaded to forget Salem and set out on the road to Boston.

With Hobart's support he was easily elected as deputy from Hingham to the September session of the General Court. Anthony Eames, commander of the town militia, was reelected as the second deputy.

"The King is concerned with finances and civil unrest," Hobart said when he met with the two deputies to discuss the upcoming session. "He has little concern for the colonies, and Gorges is powerless to act on his own. Winthrop and the assistants are using old fears as a ploy to retain control and thwart the will of the deputies. I trust you'll both work to vest more power in the towns."

"If Winthrop has his way," Eames said, "his idea of a city on a hill will never be subject to popular vote."

"It's a noble dream," Hobart said, "but I fear he misreads human nature."

"I had a similar dream when I arrived," Hull said. "I wanted to establish an oasis of Anglican worship in this desert of Puritanism."

Hobart laughed. "And have you abandoned your dream?"

"I've set it aside for now," Hull said, "but I still hope that circumstances may warrant its resurrection."

* * *

At the September session of the court, held in the First Congregational Church in Boston, the deputies authorized Winthrop to send yet another letter to the Lords Commissioners excusing his failure to return the colony's patent. They skirted the issue of freemen's rights, except to banish John Underhill for maligning the court and publicly questioning its sentence. Underhill had been punished for claiming to receive the grace of God while smoking a pipe of tobacco, as well as for lewd conduct aboard a ship to England. For good measure, he was now accused of praying with a married woman behind locked doors. His case was referred to the church authorities. Winthrop was authorized to write a letter to George Burdett, a minister at Pascataquack in New Hampshire, about entertaining men like Wheelwright who were outcasts from the Bay Colony. The Governor also proclaimed a day of public thanksgiving for the arrival of ships and coming of the harvest. And the deputies conferred with church elders on the fashions and costliness of women's apparel, but no action was taken.

"Too many of their wives contribute to this particular disorder," Eames observed.

Hull raised no objection to a law that required excommunicated persons to make an effort to regain their church membership or be subject to fines, imprisonment, or banishment. He viewed the law as another step toward a theocracy; but having voiced his support earlier in the session for Ralph Mousall, an elected deputy from Charlestown, he declined to draw more attention to himself.

Mousall was accused of speaking publicly in support of John Wheelwright, a brother-in-law of Anne Hutchinson, who had been banished the previous year along with two other deputies who defended him. When it appeared that Mousall would be denied a seat on the court, Hull asked for permission to speak.

"As a newly elected deputy," he began, "I had resigned myself to sit quietly and absorb the wisdom of men more experienced than myself. Yet, in weighing the charges against Mr. Mousall, I feel obliged to voice my opinion. I do not defend Wheelwright or Mrs. Hutchinson, and I grant that banishment of people who pose a threat to the peace and welfare of the colony is justified. But to punish someone simply for voicing a contrary opinion is reminiscent of the restrictive authority I thought I had left behind me in England. I agree that heresy must be refuted; but the roots of this particular heresy have long since been exposed to the sunlight, and its leaves can be allowed to wither on the vine. I'm sure that we have more pressing business to attend."

His speech was greeted with silence until Winthrop rose to reply. "I thank the deputy from Hingham for reminding this court of the conditions prevailing in England that drove us to emigrate and to establish a colony with a new vision. But I must take issue with his concept of heresy. Vines, even when severed, can take root and form a new plant indistinguishable from their parent. This body is willing to consider all pertinent evidence in the case, but it has become abundantly clear that the public expression of private opinions on such matters can serve only to stir up the populace, resulting in civic unrest."

Hull started to rise, but Eames grasped his sleeve. "It's already been decided," he whispered. "Nothing you say will change their minds. Don't jeopardize your own seat."

Heeding his fellow deputy's advice, Hull made no reply. A vote was taken, and Mousall was denied his seat.

Hobart was waiting for them on their return to Hingham. In response to Hull's report, he adopted a more optimistic view of the matter. "At least Mousall wasn't banished. You accomplished that much."

"I fear my sole accomplishment was to incur Winthrop's enmity," Hull said. "I must admit that I felt rather useless in Boston."

"Satisfaction will surely follow upon more experience," Hobart said.

* * *

That winter Thomas Dimmock of Scituate, whom Hull knew from his dealings in cattle, proposed they petition the Plymouth General Court for a tract of land in that colony. Dimmock had emigrated to New England soon after Hull. His wife Ann was about Agnes' age, and he had a two-year-old daughter. A son had died recently at birth. He was in his late thirties, a short stocky man with a voice given more to bluster than command. Impressed by Dimmock's stoic acceptance of adversity, Hull lent a patient ear to his proposal.

"Ann and I need to make a fresh start," he concluded, "and you need more land for your cattle business."

Hull set down the pail of water he had filled at the town pump. "Where is this land located?" he asked.

"We won't know that until our petition is granted," Dimmock said.

"Would I have to move there?"

"Not at once. You could put a few cows on the land as a sign of occupancy, then move or not at your leisure."

"Why do you need me?" Hull asked.

"I have little status or influence in Plymouth. You're a merchant and a deputy. Your name will mean something to the court."

Hull stroked the beard he had grown since arriving in Hingham. "You can file your petition. But if the land they offer us is too remote or otherwise unsuitable, I warn you that I shall refuse to accept it."

The Plymouth Court agreed to rule on their petition at its spring meeting, and Hull thought no more of the matter. He had other business to attend. Agnes was due to give birth, and he was reelected deputy from Hingham to the March session of the General Court. Lethal, who was contending with Jenner for control of the Weymouth church, had been summoned to appear before the court to answer for statements pertaining to his religious beliefs. Hull recalled the bishop of Exeter, charged with being lenient on Puritans and forced to kneel before Archbishop Laud. Was Massachusetts so different?

Lethal's hearing was the first item on the docket. A church court had found him guilty of imbibing some of Anne Hutchinson's opinions, as of justification before faith. He was charged now with maintaining that all baptized persons should be admitted to the church without further trial. On hearing the charges and the evidence, Hull realized that Lethal's opinions corresponded closely with his own. But the sentiment of the court was clear. To defend Lethal would be tantamount to putting himself on trial. He sat tight-mouthed and with his eyes downcast as Lethal was forced to recant his heretical opinion, and as Winthrop issued a stern warning that the court would deal more harshly with any future errors in doctrine. Chastened in spirit and disillusioned as to his ability to effect any meaningful change, Hull endured the rest of the session in numb silence. He returned to Hingham convinced that he had failed the townspeople and his own calling, and that he had no future in the Massachusetts Colony.

That same month Agnes delivered her second child, a son named Benjamin. He was baptized by Peter Hobart. Hull would have liked to perform the ceremony himself, but decided it was better to cement his friendship with Hobart by honoring his jurisdiction.

He had given no further thought to land in the Plymouth Colony, and was surprised when Dimmock appeared at his door.

"The court granted our petition," he blurted before Hull could invite him to come in. "The land is in Mattakeese, about forty miles east of here. Much of it has been cleared, and there's plenty of marsh grass for your cattle. They agreed to transfer the title to us, provided we settle there by the end of the summer. I can move at once, and I've persuaded several families recently arrived in Scituate to go with me. We're sure to attract more settlers once we establish a town."

As Hull listened to this exuberant outpouring, his mind turned to how he would justify another move to Agnes. He needed her willing cooperation in this new endeavor. He had only one servant now. John Wood and Judith French had married when she became pregnant, and he had released them both from indenture shortly after the move to Hingham. He would have to rely on his children to help Agnes get settled.

"Have you nothing to say?" Dimmock asked.

Hull's eyes focused again on his visitor. "Forgive me, my thoughts were elsewhere. I know one or two families who may be willing to make such a move, but a town needs a church and a minister."

"I was relying on you to fill that role."

"I have no standing in Plymouth as a minister. To them I'm just a merchant and a deputy, and that is what I propose to remain."

They were still standing outside the cabin. Hull had decided that it was best to discuss this in private.

"There's a minister in Scituate named Lothrop, who was forced to leave England because of his religious beliefs," Dimmock said. "Now his congregation is beset with controversy over infant baptism. He may welcome a new home for himself and his followers."

"Then I trust you to enlist his support."

"How soon will you be able to move?"

"I'm not sure," Hull said. "I must speak to my wife first."

He had never been to Mattakeese, so he gleaned additional details from Bursley and others in Hingham. All were unanimous in praising the harbor and the fishing. But Agnes showed little enthusiasm when he told her what he had learned. Her attention remained focused on the child she was nursing. She looked up when he had finished his account. Benjamin emitted a small cry, but quieted as he regained contact with her breast.

"How will you benefit from such a move?" she asked.

"With more land at my disposal," Hull replied, "I can raise and sell more cattle. And I'll be free for good of Winthrop's influence."

"Does anyone live there, other than the Indians?"

"A few settlers, but not enough to establish a town. That will be up to Dimmock and myself and any others who join us."

"The place sounds so isolated. We'll be starting all over again."

"Mattakeese is readily accessible by sea," he assured her. "And if Bursley marries Joanna, we can rely on him to help us move. Perhaps the two of you can persuade him to go with us."

Agnes appeared somewhat mollified at the prospect. "That would certainly make it easier," she said.

* * *

On a Sunday in May, Hull rode to Weymouth. He insisted on going alone; for he wanted to rein in his emotions, and he feared the presence of his family might cause him to break down. A steady drizzle made travel on horseback treacherous; but the skies cleared as he arrived at Upham's house. Encouraged by this sign, he rose to address the remnant of followers gathered to hear him. He had left Hingham still undecided what he would say; but as his horse picked its way along the road that led over Great Hill, the thought struck him that this chance to begin anew in Mattakeese was a test of his faith. Dismounting, he knelt on the wet earth and acknowledged his readiness to do what appeared to be God's will.

In his sermon he likened his situation and his decision to that of Abraham. God was asking him to sacrifice something as dear to him as a firstborn son – his congregation and his calling as a minister.

"On this day four years ago," he said in closing, "we arrived in what was for us an alien land. By working together, we made that land our home. The town of Weymouth was born and has prospered. If man's success on this earth were measured solely in terms of material things, I should be satisfied. Yet in respect to what matters most, I account myself a failure. The present church in Weymouth is not the one I envisioned when I first came to New England. I hoped to change minds through understanding, tolerance, and compromise. I've learned from my experience as a minister and as a deputy to the General Court that the religious climate in this colony renders such an undertaking futile."

His voice broke, and he paused a moment before continuing. "I have decided to move with my family to a place called Mattakeese in the Plymouth Colony, where I hope to find or create conditions more congenial for someone of my convictions and temperament. Some of you have indicated an interest in accompanying me, and I am grateful for your continued confidence. I thank everyone here for your loyalty to me and to the Church. It saddens me to leave you, but I am heartened to hear that Mr. Newman, the minister chosen to replace Mr. Lethal and to heal the division in the Weymouth church, is imbued with a true sense of piety and reconciliation. I urge you to give him your full support. May God be with you, and may He smile upon us all in our future endeavors."

Nine

"Goals have a different look once you reach them."
(Barnstable, Plymouth Colony, 1639-1640)

Hull and Agnes, along with their household furnishings, reached Mattakeese harbor late in May, arriving on Burley's ship. The girls and younger boys accompanied them. Joseph and Tristram helped to drive the cattle that remained overland from Hingham. Hull had arranged with Standerwick in Somerset for a fresh shipment to the Plymouth Colony. Dimmock was already there, and the two groups set about erecting their palisado homes and planting crops. Reverend Lothrop and his congregation had not yet left Scituate, so the settlers pressed Hull to conduct services on a stone altar they erected for the purpose. He offered thanks for the extensive hay grounds or marshes, for the fine harbor that provided an abundance of clams and fish, for the pine trees that covered the gently rolling uplands, and for the meadows previously cleared by the Indians.

His new house was much larger than the one in Hingham. He thought thus to assure Agnes that this new home was to be permanent. The walls were made from wooden poles filled between with stones and clay. It had a roof of thatch, windows of oiled paper, and floors made of hand-sawed planks. The chimney was constructed from field stone up to the mantel. Above that was cobwork – a mixture of unburned clay with marsh grass as a binder. It was among the first houses to be finished, for the settlers also used it as their gathering place. Agnes took delight in arranging the furnishings, and Hull promised to have additional pieces sent over from England. At the end of the summer she happily announced that she was again pregnant.

In the autumn of 1639 the Mattakeese plantation became the town of Barnstable. Hull and Dimmock were elected deputies to the December session of the Plymouth General Court. The court was less concerned with matters of church doctrine, and more with keeping peace among the settlers, promoting their economic well being, and fostering good relations with the Indians and neighboring colonies. Hull was well satisfied with the choice he had made.

John Lothrop and his party, which comprised twenty-two families, reached Barnstable late in the fall. They received a warm welcome, and Hull opened his home to them for a day of thanksgiving. Following the service, he took Lothrop outside and pointed out his pasture, where a few cattle were grazing, while he rehearsed in his mind what he knew about this minister.

A Cambridge graduate, Lothrop had served for sixteen years as a minister of the Church of England before embracing the congregational principle that leadership authority is transmitted from God to a minister through the people rather than through a church hierarchy. Upon orders from Laud, then Bishop of London, he and several members of his flock were arrested and confined in Newgate prison. On the death of his wife he obtained his release by pleading that he had to care for his six children and by agreeing to go into foreign exile. With thirty-four families from Kent, he sailed for New England on the *Griffin*, arriving in Boston in the autumn of 1634.

Rather than settle there, he took his flock to Scituate in the Plymouth Colony, where he married his second wife. But a division in his church impelled him to seek a new home in Barnstable.

They gazed at the cattle for some time in silence. Hull stood half a head above Lothrop, and his body was hardened from working on his house. Lothrop appeared soft and rather plump in comparison. His face wore a kindly expression, but his grey eyes had a wary look. Having listened approvingly to his words of thanksgiving, Hull felt it incumbent upon himself to allay whatever fears Lothrop might have of a potential rivalry.

"I trust we can both follow our own pursuits as peacefully as those cattle. I did not come here to resume my ministry, and I shall not stand in your way as you establish your church. Meanwhile, my house is always available for services in bad weather."

"Dimmock led me to expect a church building would be ready when I arrived," Lothrop said.

"I didn't want to attract attention," Hull said. "I came to Mattakeese as a dealer in cattle. I don't intend to forego that occupation, though I confess that I'm still a minister at heart."

"I appreciate your candor,"Lothrop said. "My first concern is to build homes for my congregation before the winter sets in. A church will have to wait until the spring."

"Whatever talents I have are at your service. I request only that you make appropriate use of them."

Lothrop met his gaze without flinching. "I owe you that in return for your hospitality."

One of his first duties was to marry Joanna and John Bursley. The ceremony took place in the neighboring town of Sandwich.

"A wedding should be held indoors in a proper church," Agnes declared, and Hull readily concurred.

Bursley was often at sea, and Joanna stayed with her parents until her new house was built. Agnes was glad to have her help. In March Agnes gave birth to her first daughter. Lothrop baptized the child Naomi.

Hull had received the shipment of cattle from Standerwick. His business and family took up most of his time. Although he assured Agnes that he was content with his lot, his talks with Lothrop gave rise to some questions and misgivings.

For Hull the congregational system was the price he had paid for setting down in Wessaguscus. It was also the form of church governance that had cost him his post as a minister. Why had Lothrop set down in the Plymouth Colony, where most men wore the mantle of separatists? Was he opposed to the Puritan effort to reform the Church from within? And what impelled him to come to Barnstable?

From their talks Hull learned that the issue in Scituate, as in many churches, was the proper form of baptism. Lothrop held a moderate view. He accepted all forms of the sacrament – immersion, sprinkling, or laying on of hands – for infants or adults. But dissension arose in the congregation, and he seized on the promise of more land to take his band of followers elsewhere. Hull regarded the distinction as meaningless. For the most part he agreed with Lothrop, except on the central issue of the transmission of authority. Though he had willingly agreed to play a subsidiary role in the Barnstable church, it troubled him that the settlers who came with hin and Dimmock were in a minority. He told himself Lothrop had encountered adversities similar to his own, that he was an honorable man, that he could be trusted to honor their agreement. In his heart he was not so sure.

* * *

Bursley liked to described his marriage to Joanna as negotiated. Then, lest his listeners consider it a business arrangement, he would explain with a laugh, "Agnes gave me two choices if I wanted to marry Joanna. I could talk her father out of moving to Plymouth, or I could go with them. Most of my shipping was out of Weymouth, and I didn't want to move. But Agnes kept after me. She was worried that Joseph might stir up some trouble here with his preaching, as he did in Weymouth. When I spoke to him, he said he was only interested in his cattle business. I could see that he'd made up his mind to move, so I figured I'd better go along and keep an eye on him."

Bursley suspected from the start that the harmony between Hull and Lothrop would be subverted once the minister's party was no longer dependent on the earlier settlers for food and shelter. The first sign of a rupture surfaced in the spring, six months after Lothrop's arrival.

"It's started again, just like before," Joanna told him on his return from a rough voyage to Dover. "Mr. Lothrop has ordained John Mayo as a teaching elder."

Bursley opened his eyes and rolled over in the bed to face his wife. News of Mayo's appointment had reached him as soon as he came ashore. He knew Joanna had waited to raise the issue out of consideration for him. She did her best to make his homecoming a joyful occasion. He loved her for that. Time enough tomorrow to discuss whatever problems had arisen in his absence. Taking her in his arms, he assured her that all was well.

"Your father must have approved. He assisted in the ceremony."

"You don't understand. Mr. Lothrop has put his own followers in all the key positions in the church. Father is being cut off, just as he was in Weymouth. He doesn't say much about it, but it must hurt him that he has no official place in the church."

Church affairs were of no interest to Bursley, and family problems were still a novelty. "Your father founded this town," he said, stroking her hair. "He owns land and has his business here. He was elected deputy to the court in Plymouth. Without his aid Lothrop and his party would never have survived the winter. Surely they haven't forgotten that."

Joanna was not convinced. "He's being pushed aside. I'm afraid he'll look elsewhere for some way to exercise his ministry."

"He didn't come to Plymouth to be a minister," Bursley said.

"Father will always be a minister. You saw how pleased he was to hold services before Mr. Lothrop arrived."

"If he wanted to set up his own church, he could have asked the Plymouth authorities for permission."

"You know how he is," Joanna said. "He was ordained by the Church of England and needs no one's permission to preach."

"It wouldn't hurt him to bend a little."

"He's been bending ever since we came to New England. He has become a master of accommodation. Don't deny him his principles. That's all he has left."

"Let's not quarrel. I respect his principles and your concerns. I'm sure this can be worked out to everyone's satisfaction."

"Talk to him, John. He listens to you."

"I'll do what I can," Bursley promised.

* * *

Unknown to Joanna or Agnes, Hull had confronted Lothrop about the matter of Mayo's ordination. Lothrop made daily visits to the hill overlooking the harbor where the new church was being built, and Hull was on hand to greet him. They surveyed the progress, then stood gazing out at the sandy neck of land that sheltered the harbor on the north. A shallop carrying cargo and travelers from Plymouth or Boston rounded the point and headed for the town pier as they watched.

"I'm disappointed that you haven't made better use of my services," Hull said, his voice restrained but calm. "Mayo is a good man, but you must admit that I am much better qualified for the position."

"The congregation could have chosen you if they so desired," Lothrop said without looking at him. "I'm obliged to carry out their wishes."

"Surely they acted on your recommendation," Hull persisted.

"I thought you would consider the position demeaning, and I didn't want to cause dissension in the church."

Hull made no effort to conceal his displeasure. "You might at least have consulted me before offering me up as a sacrificial victim on the altar of church unity."

Lothrop turned to face him. "Church unity is not lightly dismissed. You've been in the same position yourself."

"I grant you that, but you have betrayed my trust."

"I'm sorry you feel that way," Lothrop said. "I had hoped you might assist me with Mayo's ordination."

Hull regarded it as a peace offering, a tacit recognition of his status as a minister. Lothrop's followers were in the majority. It was only to be expected that they would elect one of their own as reader. "That thought did enter my mind," he said, somewhat mollified, "but I feared you might take offense at such a request."

"So be it then," Lothrop said as they parted.

* * *

Bursley's house was not far from Hull's. In the evening the two men often walked to the docks, where Bursley obtained the latest shipping news, while Hull inquired about new arrivals. The advent of Lothrop and the establishment of a church were attracting commerce and newcomers to the area, potential customers for Hull's cattle.

"What do you think of Mayo as a teaching elder?" Bursley asked on one of these walks.

"He should do well," Hull said, quickening his pace.

"But you were ordained to teach," Bursley said, hurrying to catch up.

"If ever I want to preach again, I'm sure I can find a pulpit."

"Would you even consider that? You've attained every goal you set for yourself when you moved here."

"Goals have a different look once you reach them."

They had reached the docks, where several men were unloading cargo from one of the shallops that plied the waters along the New England coast. The *Aurora* lay at anchor in the harbor. When his inquiry about new arrivals received a negative response, Hull shook his head sadly.

"It's all due to Laud's restrictions on emigration. Without a steady influx of new settlers, I'm hard pressed to sell my cattle. But you can tell Joanna I have no intention of becoming an itinerant preacher."

Bursley laughed. "I'm sure she'll be relieved to hear it."

They spent another hour on the docks before retracing their steps.

"By the way, I need an apprentice seaman," Bursley said on the walk back. "I thought Tristram might be interested."

"He's a great help to us," Hull said, "but he'll welcome a chance to confirm his love for the sea."

"I'll speak to him tomorrow," Bursley said.

* * *

Hull was not reelected as a deputy to the June session of the General Court. He wasn't surprised. The same freemen who made Mayo a reader had now voted to replace him as a deputy. It was one more sign that his fortunes – in church, business, and community – were turning against him. To add to his trials, he was charged with trespass in a lawsuit brought by Nicholas Norton. He said he was trying to reclaim a cow that belonged to him, but the magistrate ruled in favor of Norton.

In this dark frame of mind, he approached Bursley at the end of the summer. The master was readying the *Aurora* for a voyage along the coast of Maine. "I need to get away and clear my mind," Hull told him.

Bursley was incredulous. "Why would you want to go to Maine?"

"I have good reason. Sir Ferdinando Gorges has obtained a royal charter for the province, and his young cousin Thomas is serving as the deputy governor. I met Thomas on one occasion while

I was recruiting followers in Batcombe. It may benefit me to assess the situation in Maine."

"Nothing changed when Gorges was named as Governor General of New England," Bursley said. "How will his royal charter for Maine make any difference?"

"That's what I hope to find out. If Thomas can establish a firm grasp on Maine, Sir Ferdinando may yet succeed in asserting his control over all the colonies in New England."

"The towns in Maine are quite independent," Bursley said. "Young Thomas may encounter some resistance. But I sail in a week. Where in Maine do you want to go?"

"Thomas resides in Agamenticus."

"I have cargo for Dover," Bursley said. "I can set you ashore in Agamenticus and pick you up on my return."

"That will serve my purpose," Hull said.

Bursley sailed for Maine in October with Hull as a passenger and Tristram as apprentice seaman. After dropping Hull at Agamenticus, he proceeded up the Piscataqua and Cochecho rivers to Dover, where he discharged his cargo and sought out shipments to other towns along the coast. On his return, he was greeted with yet another request.

* * *

Hull's reaction on viewing Agamenticus from the deck of the *Aurora* was disappointment. The settlement was tucked away inside the mouth of a river bearing the same name. Through the morning fog he saw several rude cabins among the trees that lined the river bank, a fishing boat moored in the river, another tied to a wharf, and some dugout canoes drawn up on the shore. The population, according to Bursley, was under a hundred. He pointed out to Hull the chapel on a hill and the tavern by the shore.

"Men have an easy downhill access to their weakness," Hull noted, "but must exert themselves to worship God, who is their strength."

Bursley laughed. "A good subject for one of your sermons."

Despite this observation, Hull's first stop after he disembarked was the tavern. Not because he had a great thirst, nor because it was so readily accessible. He went there to contact the person who could tell him what was happening in the community. The proprietor, a stocky florid-faced man named George Puddington, was happy to oblige.

Viewed from outside, the tavern appeared to be quite an ordinary dwelling. Only the interior distinguished it from the other cabins in the community. The great room was divided into two sections. The larger of these, located at the front of the building and including the fireplace, contained various handcrafted tables and benches. An array of pewter tankards lined a counter at the rear, and a keg of ale sat on blocks at one end. Puddington was alone in the tavern, but Hull could hear some activity behind the partition.

"I want to talk to Thomas Gorges," Hull said after he introduced himself. "Can you tell me where I might find him?"

"The governor?" Puddington said. "His manor house is a mile or so upstream at Point Christian, but you won't find him there. Last I heard, he was in Saco trying to get other towns to bide by his rules for the province."

"Has he had any success?" Hull asked.

"They don't see why we should make the rules. He's doing all he can to make Agamenticus the seat of government. People here in town respect him for that."

"I take it you're one of them."

"The governor does what he thinks is right and best for everyone. He made that preacher Burdett pay for doing my Mary in the straw. But you don't want to listen to my problems. Let me pour you an ale."

Hull accepted the offer. He kept no spirits in his home, but he was not averse to a draught when the occasion warranted. Puddington brought two tankards and joined him at one of the tables.

"I want to talk to anyone who's had dealings with the governor," Hull said.

"I've had dealings, all right. This Burdett showed up here a year ago, claiming to be a preacher. Well, Mary starts going to services up at the chapel. Next thing I know, he's preached her right into his bed."

"You say that Gorges made him pay for that?"

"Put him on trial in Saco. Burdett tried to talk his way out of it, but the governor fined him thirty pounds for adultery, plus five more for slandering my good name. When the preacher wouldn't pay up, the governor confiscated his property."

"And was your wife punished as well?" Hull asked, aware that in Massachusetts the woman in such cases often received an even harsher penalty than the man.

"After she gives birth, she has to wear a white sheet and stand in the church twice on a Sunday. I'm not excusing what she did; but that preacher seduced her, just like he did Ruth Gauch and who knows how many others. He says the Lord told him in a dream it was his mission to make love to the women in his congregation."

"Is Burdett still in town?" Hull asked.

"If he is, he wouldn't be likely to show his face here."

Hull left the tavern refreshed. Sir Ferdinando might be unable to govern his province in person, but his deputy appeared to be up to the task. And Agamenticus might need a minister to replace Burdett.

While waiting for the governor to return, Hull had ample time to look about the town. He spoke to fishermen who lived on Smith's Islands off the coast. They came regularly to sell their catch and have a drink at the tavern before returning home. They were simple, hard-working, and God-fearing men, like those in Northleigh and Batcombe, those who sailed with him from England. They spoke of their community on Hog Island, of the chapel where they prayed and sang hymns of praise, of their lack of a minister to preach the gospel and dispense the sacraments. He promised to have a look at the place. Not that he wanted to live on an island; but the prospect of a brief visit appealed to his hermitic nature. It would give him a chance to commune more closely with God. But first he must speak to Thomas Gorges and determine what plans Sir Ferdinando had for his province.

When the governor returned to his manor house, Hull hired a youth with a canoe to take him up river to Point Christian. Thomas Gorges took pride in showing off the house and grounds, and he claimed to remember his meeting with Hull in Batcombe. Thomas was twenty-two, slim, and clean-shaven. His steel gray eyes were like those of his uncle. Despite his youthful appearance, the mantle of authority appeared to suit him well.

The manor house had two stories and was shaped like a barn. It boasted glass windows throughout. A cobblestone fireplace ten feet wide and four feet deep dominated the great room. Thomas took special pride in a paneled study and a beer cellar lined with wood that extended under half the house. Despite these signs of elegance, the building appeared unfinished.

They walked in the garden. Many of the plants had turned brown from an early frost. Thomas pointed to a sundial he had installed. "It was made in Italy," he noted. "The place was badly run down when I arrived, but I've done my best to make the manor suitable for Sir Ferdinando should he decide to come to Agamenticus."

"Is he planning to live here?" Hull asked.

"He has so many plans, I find it difficult to assimilate them all. I'll be ready, no matter what he does. But what brings you to Agamenticus?"

"Sir Ferdinando once urged me to settle in Maine," Hull said, "but Massachusetts seemed to afford better prospects. I went to Wessaguscus and then to the Plymouth Colony. I find myself now a minister without a pulpit, casting about for some way to improve my situation. I understand you're trying to establish a new form of government in the province. Is that part of Sir Ferdinando's larger plan?"

Thomas smiled. "We'll be more comfortable if we talk in my study. I can offer you some brandy I brought with me from England."

Hull followed him into the house. While waiting for the servant to bring the brandy, he allowed his gaze to linger upon several shelves of books in leather bindings. No doubt Thomas had brought those with him as well. His own library was more modest, as befitted a minister; yet he would like to have access to such a collection.

"The borough government in Agamenticus is just an interim measure," Thomas said. "Sir Ferdinando has a loftier vision, the details of which are still a bit vague." He sipped his brandy, while weighing how much of that vision he should reveal. "A new form of government is easy to proclaim, but difficult to put in place. I'd like to paint a bright picture of Maine's future, but I see many obstacles ahead. Chief among them is the lack of men who are qualified to hold the reins of government. Vines and Godfrey are capable enough as agents, but they are easily swayed by the exigencies of the moment. If Sir Ferdinando wants Maine governed in accordance with his plans, he must come here himself."

"You appear to be doing a good job as his deputy," Hull said.

"My appointment is for three years. I'll stay longer if necessary, but I don't want to spend the rest of my life here. I miss the comforts and the stability of England."

Hull set down his glass. "Maine is known as a refuge for dissident ministers. What place has the Church of England in Sir Ferdinando's plans?"

"I gather you have a personal interest in the matter," Thomas said.

"To be honest, my purpose in coming here is to determine if I have a future in Agamenticus. I've been told that your last minister was fined for committing adultery."

"A minister is subject to the same punishment as any freeman, if he breaks the law. But I try not to get involved in matters of religion. The congregation chose Burdett. It's up to them to determine his fate."

"Is he still preaching in town?" Hull asked.

"I'm not sure. He threatened to take his case to an English court; but the charter forbids such appeals, so he has little likelihood of success. The church elders have already sent a call to John Ward of Newbury. He has yet to reply, but they seem confident that he will accept the post."

Hull took another sip of brandy, hoping thus to mask his chagrin at being too late upon the scene and his regret that Gorges' plans were not more advanced. "It may be just as well. I'm not yet ready to move to Maine."

"Now that I know your mind," Thomas said, "I'll keep you informed of any changes in church or political affairs."

"You can get word to me through John Bursley," Hull said. "I thank you for your good offices, and remember me to Sir Ferdinando when next you write to him."

On that note Hull took his leave of the governor. While waiting for the *Aurora* to return, he introduced himself to the church elders. In the absence of Burdett they invited him to preach. His reception was cordial but not enthusiastic. He was also drawn by the prospect of visiting the fishermen on Hog Island. They could get to know him, and he could learn about their concerns. Christ also preached to fishermen.

* * *

Hull leaned against the rail of the *Aurora* and gazed eastward. His face was radiant, as if the promised land were in view. "I feel that God wants me to go to Hog Island," he said.

"It's a desolate place," Bursley said. "A barren outcropping amidst a treacherous sea. Only fishermen live there."

"A good spot to meditate and plot the future course of my life."

"How long do you propose to stay?"

"No definite time. Just pick me up on your next voyage north."

"Did you speak to Thomas Gorges?" Bursley asked.

"He wasn't of much help," Hull replied. "He's doing his best to establish order in the province, but the situation remains unsettled."

Bursley was surprised to find a fair-sized village on Hog Island. Some of the fishermen had moved their families out there, and they had built a small chapel. Yet he couldn't understand why Hull would want to spend a month or more there.

"What shall I tell Agnes?" he asked in parting.

"Tell her I'm praying to God for help and guidance," Hull said.

Back in Barnstable Bursley described the island as a place remote from man and God. Joanna, now six months pregnant, was incredulous.

"How could you leave him alone in such a desolate place?" she asked. Bursley made no reply.

"When will he come back?" Agnes asked.

"I'll see to it that he gets home before Christmas," Bursley assured her. "What do you suppose he's looking for?"

"A congregation," Agnes said. "Joseph needs people to listen to him, but his audience shrinks every time we move. No one in Barnstable will follow him to Maine. I want him to be happy, but our home is here."

"You needn't worry," Bursley said. "Maine has little to offer him. And Hog Island even less."

Ten

"I shall preach where I like."
(Barnstable and Yarmouth, Plymouth Colony, 1641-1642)

"I found it appropriate somehow to preach to fishermen," Hull told Agnes on his return from Hog Island. "I felt an affinity for them, and they accepted me as part of the community. They hung on my words as if they were eager to become fishers of men. The experience was both humbling and exalting. I was as sure of my calling as when I arrived in Weymouth."

"What does that mean?" she asked. "Are you thinking of going to Maine as a minister?"

They sat at opposite ends of the long table in the great room of their house in Barnstable. A fire blazed in the hearth, while outside an early season snow fell lazily. The older girls were cleaning up after the evening meal. The younger children squatted near the fire coaching each other with their writing. They played the game each evening save Sunday.

"I have no desire to move to Maine at this time," Hull said. "I'm content to wait and see what plans Sir Ferdinando has for his province. But I have never ceased to be a minister."

"Such feelings have no place here," Agnes said. "Mr. Lothrop is the recognized pastor, and you have no authority to preach anywhere else in the colony."

"I have no intention of challenging Lothrop," Hull said, "but I'm free to preach wherever I'm invited. The congregational system has that benefit, and I shall take advantage of it."

"You should speak to him," Agnes persisted. "He keeps asking me why you went to Maine. My answers satisfy neither him nor me."

Hull rose abruptly from the table. "At the moment I have nothing more to say to Lothrop – nor to you."

The children seated by the hearth were quiet a moment, surprised by this uncharacteristic outburst. Then they resumed their game.

* * *

That winter John Lothrop noted in his journal: "Mr. Bursley's child dyed suddenly in the night & buryed at the lower side of the calves pasture." He much preferred to record a birth or marriage, but death too was the human portion. Yet the death of a child saddened him. Bursley seemed resigned to his fate, and outwardly Joanna was bearing up well. No doubt her father's counsel had eased her pain and her sense of loss. He hadn't spoken to Hull at length since his return from Maine; and he wondered if their hitherto cordial relationship had undergone a change.

The nature of that change was made clear by a note from Marmaduke Matthews, the minister in the neighboring town of Yarmouth. "Some few in my congregation appear to be dissatisfied with my ministry," he wrote, "and they have invited Joseph Hull to come and preach to them." After a lengthy and bitter characterization of the men involved, he concluded, "I am confident, with God's help, that these differences can be resolved, and that all involved can be brought to see the error of their ways. Meanwhile, I ask only that you discourage this Hull from accepting their invitation and thus exacerbating what is already a difficult situation."

Lothrop put off responding to this message. He agreed that any intervention from outside would only make matters worse in Yarmouth. Yet by supporting Matthews, he risked alienating the man who welcomed his party to Barnstable and provided them food and shelter. He knew Hull had faced dissension among his congregation in Weymouth. Perhaps he could be dissuaded on that basis from mounting the pulpit in Yarmouth. Yet Lothrop was reluctant to act until Hull broached the subject.

A week passed before Hull mentioned the invitation. They were walking home after the Sunday service, held in the newly built church. "I feel obliged to heed the call of people who need me," Hull concluded.

"I had a message from Matthews," Lothrop said. "I'm not privy to the difficulties that have arisen within his church, but I feel strongly that such problems are best resolved by the pastor and the elders. Calling in a minister from outside will cause more dissension and might splinter the congregation. You encountered that yourself in Weymouth."

Hull laughed bitterly. "What I learned in Weymouth, and what you must have learned in Scituate, is that people are not so easily persuaded to change their minds."

"Peace, Joseph. It's only natural that you should want a congregation of your own, but you're a valued member of our church and community. Why abandon that to stir up trouble in Yarmouth?"

"I'm not going there to stir up trouble," Hull said. "I shall assess the situation. If I can do no good, I shall give it up."

"It's not that simple," Lothrop said. "You relinquished your right to preach when you left Weymouth."

"Strange words from a man who was imprisoned for refusing to take an oath of conformity," Hull replied. "My rights, as you well know, derive from my ordination in the Church of England; and they cannot be revoked by the pronouncements of local courts or authorities."

Lothrop recalled his arrest in London for organizing clandestine church services and was silent. Facing the commission that put him on trial, he had declared, "I am a minister of the Gospel of Christ. The Lord has qualified me." He resented Hull's charge that he had changed his mind.

"What you propose to do is contrary to church rules and to the laws of the Plymouth Colony," Lothrop said.

"Under the congregational system the people in Yarmouth are free to choose their minister," Hull said. "In Weymouth that system was used against me. Now it may serve my purpose."

With that he turned and walked away. Lothrop watched him go. What more could he have done – threaten to expel Hull from the church? It hadn't come to that. Musing thus, he proceeded toward his own home. His wife greeted him at the door. She was cradling their infant son in her arms. Lothrop was filled with tenderness for Ann and for the child.

"I just tried to reason with Joseph," he said, "but he won't listen."

"Speak to Agnes. She'll have more influence," Ann said.

Lothrop nodded appreciatively. Taking the child in his arms, he followed her into the house.

The next day he saw Hull pass by on horseback, bound perhaps for Yarmouth. Whatever his destination, he would be gone for some time. Donning his coat, Lothrop climbed the hill to Hull's house. One of the girls ushered him into the great room. Agnes was busy cutting up squash.

"Don't let me interrupt you," he said. He had removed his hat and was turning it in his hands. Agnes motioned him to be seated.

"You're concerned about Joseph," she said.

Lothrop nodded. "I spoke to him yesterday, but I couldn't dissuade him from preaching in Yarmouth."

"Why shouldn't he? He has no opportunity to preach here."

"I understand how he must feel, and I do appreciate all he has done for me and our church. But I must respect the wishes of the congregation, else we too shall be plagued by dissension."

Agnes set down her knife and wiped her hands on her apron. "You have more followers. You can do as you like. What do you want with me?"

"I need to impress on him the consequences of preaching in Yarmouth. To put it bluntly, he risks expulsion from the church. I hope it won't come to that, but his actions put me in a position where I'm obliged to support a fellow minister. Perhaps you can speak to him. He has done so much good here in Barnstable. Why throw it all away."

"Yarmouth is only eight miles distant," Agnes said. "You speak as if we were moving away."

Lothrop paused. How far should he carry his threats? He admired Agnes, whose burden as a second wife was similar to Ann's.

Perhaps he could draw upon her friendship with his wife to enlist her support.

"Ann and I would hate to see you leave," he said, "but if Joseph is excommunicated, the ban would apply to the entire family – unless he goes to Yarmouth alone."

"He'll never do that," Agnes declared stoutly.

"Then persuade him to give up this mad idea."

"I'll speak to him, but I doubt that he'll listen."

"I ask no more than that," Lothrop said.

He could ask Ann to speak to her as well and reinforce the arguments he made. If Hull remained intransigent, the burden was on him.

* * *

Hull spoke openly about his interest in the Yarmouth church. When Agnes gave voice to her concern, he scoffed at the threat of expulsion. They were returning from the cemetery, where he went regularly of an evening to pray over the graves of the deceased. It was the one ministerial function he could still exercise without prior permission.

"He has to give token support to a colleague," Hull assured her. "I have more call upon his loyalty than Matthews does."

"But aren't you placing yourself in the same position as Mr. Jenner when he came to Weymouth?" Agnes asked.

"Not at all. The authorities in Boston sent Jenner to replace me. I'm answering a call from good men in the church, men whom Matthews alienated through his actions, men like Dr. Starr and Andrew Hallet."

"What has he done to lose their respect?" Agnes asked.

"Starr claims that he lacks tact and discretion; and that he tends to become vindictive if anyone presumes to challenge his authority."

"But Mr. Matthews is the authorized minister," Agnes said. "How can you replace him when you have no status in Plymouth?"

"My purpose is not necessarily to replace him. My presence will oblige him to address his faults, or else hasten his departure. I'm prepared to accept either outcome."

"That explanation won't satisfy Mr. Lothrop."

"I was a bit harsh at our last meeting," Hull said. "I'll talk to him again and make whatever peace I can."

"And I shall inform Ann of your intentions. She can plead your case better than you can."

Hull gave her a severe look. "I have no need to plead my case," he said. "I shall simply tell Lothrop what I plan to do."

"That's what I mean," Agnes said.

* * *

Yarmouth was founded before Barnstable, but had grown more slowly than its neighbor to the west, due in large part to the lack of a natural harbor. When Hull agreed to preach there, the town comprised some twenty-five families. Since use of the meetinghouse was proscribed by Matthews, he held his services at the home of Dr. Thomas Starr. Starr hailed from Kent in England. Not yet thirty years old, he had arrived in New England in 1637, and had served as the chief surgeon for a Massachusetts brigade in the Pequot war. But the slaughter of Indian women and children sickened him. He withdrew his support for Winthrop and the war, moved to Yarmouth, and devoted his skills to healing – both Indians and settlers. He had little respect for Matthews, who regarded Indians as less than human.

Aware of the schism in his church, Matthews paid another visit to Barnstable. "Your clear duty," he told Lothrop, "is to expel Hull from the church and to inform the Plymouth court of your action, so I can obtain a warrant for his arrest if he persists in preaching in Yarmouth."

Lothrop did not respond at once. They had gone outside to discuss the matter in private. He had no great liking for Matthews, regarding him as sound in his dogma but weak in his presentation. Now he sought a way to temper his actions toward Hull while honoring his colleague's demand.

"For the sake of his family, I shall try again to reason with Hull. If he remains obstinate, I'll take the action you request."

Matthews frowned. "He's not a man you can reason with," he said.

"That may be true," Lothrop said, "but I owe him that chance."

Matthews left less than satisfied. Lothrop, on his part, realized that if Hull were to leave, his own position as pastor would be secure. Not that Hull had questioned his authority, but the possibility, the threat, was ever present. He had entertained similar thoughts while Hull was in Maine. By supporting Matthews now, he antagonized Hull. If he took no action, he opened himself to criticism by church and civil authorities. He was still wrestling with this dilemma when he next encountered Hull at the town dock.

"Are you accomplishing what you hoped for in Yarmouth?" he asked.

Hull looked askance at him, as if any reply were fraught with peril. "I take it Matthews has paid you a visit," he said.

"He has indeed, but I have my own reasons for asking. I'm trying to decide what I should do next, now that you've chosen to ignore my advice."

"I suppose Matthews wants me expelled from the church."

"He mentioned it. In fact, he demanded it."

"What did you say?"

"I told him I wanted to speak to you first."

"Are you asking me to stop preaching in Yarmouth?"

"Listen to me, Joseph. We both have a calling that cannot, must not, be denied. I honor your desire to preach, and I understand your reasons for accepting this invitation. But in so doing you seek to divide an established church and to discredit a minster who, although he may have his faults, is nonetheless worthy, a minister who was installed by the proper authority. You place me in a most awkward position. I value your friendship; but I'm bound by the laws of the colony and by church rules to support Matthews."

Hull made no reply.

"Am I to gather from your silence that you are resolved to go on preaching in Yarmouth?" Lothrop asked.

"To do otherwise would betray my calling," Hull said.

"Then you leave me no choice," Lothrop said, bowing his head. "It saddens me to take this action, because I fear your family will also suffer."

"Do whatever you feel is right," Hull said as he walked away.

* * *

At the beginning of May, Lothrop wrote in his journal: "Mr. Hull excommunicated for his willful breaking of communion with us and joining himself a member with a company at Yarmouth to be their Pastor, contrary to the advice and counsel of the Church."

When he told Ann of this development, she sought on her own accord to rectify matters. She visited Agnes, who was nursing her newborn daughter Ruth, and proposed a plan of action.

"I know you don't want to leave Barnstable," she began, "and I'll hate to see you go."

"We seem to have little choice but to leave," Agnes said.

"If we put our heads together," Ann said, "maybe we can persuade our husbands to reconcile with each other."

"How do you propose to bring that about?" Agnes asked.

"If Joseph will agree to have Ruth baptized in Barnstable, I'm sure John will not refuse to perform the ceremony."

"But we've all been excommunicated."

"We must make them see it as a peace offering," Ann said. "It will at least open the door for reconciliation."

"I'll do my best," Agnes said, "but I doubt it will help matters."

"We must pray that it does," Ann said.

Their strategy was successful up to a point, and Ruth was baptized a week later. Yet the men failed to seize on the joyous event as an occasion to mend their differences. Lothrop did agree, at the urging of his wife, to delay promulgation of the church's censure. But his concession failed to alter Hull's resolve, and a fortnight later two wagons loaded with household goods moved down the hill past Lothrop's home. Agnes and the four younger children rode with Hull. The second wagon, driven by Bursley, bore three of the older girls. Ann dragged her husband outside to view the procession.

"Your threats have availed you nought!" Hull shouted when he spotted Lothrop. "I shall preach where I like. If I'm no longer welcome in the town I founded, I shall make a new home in Yarmouth." He drove on before Lothrop could frame a reply.

"They were good to us. I shall miss them," Ann said.

"Isn't there another girl?" Lothrop asked.

"Temperance will stay to help Joanna while her husband is at sea."

"And what about the oldest boy, Joseph?"

"He'll look after the cattle. They have no land in Yarmouth."

"I did all I could to shield Hull from his own folly," Lothrop said as he followed his wife back into the house.

"He meant you no harm," Ann said. "You mustn't punish his family any more. They'll suffer enough as it is."

"I'm content to wait and see what happens; but if Matthews pursues the issue, I'll have to inform the civil authorities of the church's edict."

* * *

Those who knew Marmaduke Matthews well described as a man of ardent temperament, eloquent, though not always logical or worldly wise. A native of Wales and a graduate of Oxford, he had arrived in New England in 1638, settling in Yarmouth where he built a meetinghouse that measured thirty by fifty feet. It had oiled paper windows and a thatched roof supported by posts fourteen feet long. From the entrance he looked out upon the cemetery to the north and upon his own house and lands off to the east. The view afforded him a sense of belonging and accomplishment, stiffening his resolution not to surrender to Hull. Since he had only token support from Lothrop, he must deal with this poacher himself.

After weighing the strength of the dissident faction within his church, Matthews took the offensive. Dr. Starr was fined for being "a scoffer and jeerer at religion." And William Chase, the carpenter who had built Starr's house, was censured for his language toward the minister and ordered to find sureties or else depart within six months. Dr. Starr and Andrew Hallet, the local schoolteacher, became sureties; so Chase was not forced to leave town; but he was relieved of his duties as constable.

Nor was Hull exempt from these retributive measures. His efforts to obtain land in Yarmouth were subject to endless delays; and he was forced to conduct his business, such as it was, from Barnstable. His son proved an able though not always reliable manager, and Hull found himself embroiled in several disputes over land and cattle.

By autumn the Yarmouth church was divided equally between the two rival ministers. They avoided each other, but the town was too small not to precipitate an occasional encounter. Hallet's general store was the scene of such a meeting. Hull had just learned that Samuel Hinckley was bringing suit against him over the sale of a lot in Barnstable. He derived little income from preaching in Yarmouth and had been obliged to sell some of his property to support his family. He was in no mood to placate his rival.

"You see that your efforts to be rid of me are of no avail," he said when he saw his rival.

"You have no right to preach here" Matthews countered, "and we don't need a minister of your persuasion. It's only out of consideration for your family that I refrain from presenting this matter to the court."

"I have a perfect right to preach wherever I'm needed," Hull shot back. "As for my persuasion, I'm here because your religious standards are so broad they can encompass almost any belief."

"My standards are my own," Matthews said. "Yours are dictated by Archbishop Laud."

They appeared ready to come to blows when old man Hallet stepped between them. "I'll thank you to take your quarrel outside," he said calmly. "You're upsetting the other customers."

Seeing no one else in the store, Hull stifled a laugh. But Matthews failed to see any humor in the situation. He stalked out, as if he expected his adversary to follow. Hull started to do so, but Hallet restrained him.

"Let it be," he cautioned. "You gain nothing by these arguments. You only add to the dissension that already exists."

"You're quite right. I had a like situation in Weymouth. Perhaps I should reassess my prospects for success here."

"You mustn't think that way," Hallet said. "Speak to my son and to Dr. Starr. I'm sure they have a more optimistic view."

Hull simply shrugged. Standing in the open doorway, he watched Matthews walk briskly in the direction of the meetinghouse.

* * *

Hull's house in Yarmouth was little more than a shed. The winter before his arrival it had been used to store grain and vegetables. He had no study, and privacy was a thing of the past. The family slept in a common chamber adjacent to the great room. He assured Agnes it was a temporary arrangement until his position in the town had been established.

"When I think of the house we left behind," Agnes said as she helped him on with his coat, "I can't help but wish we were back in Barnstable. Our life here isn't what we expected, and I see little sign of improvement."

Hull was on his way to talk to Dr. Starr. "I understand how you feel," he replied. "I'm equally disappointed in how this move has turned out. Those who invited me to preach in Yarmouth led me to believe they were in the majority, and that Matthews would soon leave town. I'm sure they honestly thought that would be the outcome."

"Everyone is now aligned either with you or with Mr. Matthews," she said. "What can change? What more can you accomplish?"

"You may be right. I rely on Starr to give me an honest answer as to whether anything can be done to alter the situation."

"You mean we could return to Barnstable?"

"It's not that simple," Hull said. "I'm an excommunicated person, though Lothrop seems oddly reluctant to publicize the fact. No doubt he's waiting to see how this turns out."

"You might make peace with him. He's a reasonable man."

"Lothrop would like to be rid of me for good. But let me talk to Starr and Hallet. If they take a dim view, I'll have to make other plans."

Agnes said no more, and Hull set out for the doctor's home. The path he trod was tree-lined and well back from the sea. Yarmouth had a shoreline but no harbor worthy of the name, a fact Bursley identified as a handicap for anyone who wanted to import cattle. But Hull's idea, once he established himself as a minister, was to turn the cattle business over to his eldest son and let him conduct it out of Barnstable.

He found Starr in his office in conversation with Andrew Hallet, the local schoolmaster. Hallet, whose father owned the general store, was some years older than Starr and shared his views. They listened attentively as Hull stated his concerns.

"We seem to be stymied in our efforts to oust Matthews," Hallet granted, "and the authorities won't approve a second church in Yarmouth. What more can we do?"

Starr ran his left hand along his face, starting below his right ear and ending with several thoughtful strokes of his neatly trimmed brown beard. "It seems that ministers exercise more control than doctors or teachers over how people think," he said. "I thought most of the freemen in town would be glad to see Matthews leave. But the fact that he hasn't presented his case to the court shows that he's still unsure of his ground. If we're patient and persevere, he may yet give in."

Hallet chuckled at that. The doctor would never admit he was wrong. "Matthews may have his faults, but he has the backing of the authorities. Not many freemen will oppose their leaders, be they civil or religious."

"They have families to consider," Hull said.

"I admit that we were premature in inviting you to preach here in Yarmouth," Starr said. "Since we haven't kept our end of the bargain, I won't blame you if you decide to go elsewhere."

Hull made a dismissive motion with his hand. "I too am at fault for thinking I could use the congregational system to my own advantage, even though I lacked the support of the authorities. Since we can neither unseat Matthews nor establish a second church, we had best give it up."

"I wish I could muster a contrary argument," Starr said. "Rachel and I both want you and your family to stay on, but I must own up to the fact that matters have not turned out as we hoped."

"I have no other place to go," Hull said. "Matthews must put up with me until God or fate choose to intervene."

* * *

In the autumn an emissary from Thomas Gorges brought word that Sir Ferdinando had formulated a plan for his province, that Hull might participate in Maine's glorious future, and that the deputy governor would be pleased to discuss the matter with him in person. He departed when Hull agreed, declining an invitation to spend the night.

"My dreams are at last linked with those of Gorges," Hull told his wife. "I must seize upon this opportunity."

They stood together outside their cabin as the messenger rode off in the direction of Barnstable, where Bursley's ship was waiting to take him back to Maine. The horse's hoofs threw up a wake of varicolored leaves, augmented by others that fell from the trees before settling on the road. A chill was in the air, a fire on the hearth; but Hull was oblivious to the cold.

"I know Sir Ferdinando is your patron," Agnes said, "but what is it about his latest plan that so excites you?"

"He has elevated Agamenticus to be the first city in New England and renamed it Gorgeana. I shall get all the details when I go to Maine."

"Are there enough people to make a city?"

"I'm sure Gorges has taken that into account."

"Winter is nearly upon us," Agnes said. "Go to Maine if you must, but find out what they have to offer before you decide to move again."

"I intend to survey the ground with great care," Hull assured her.

"How long will you be gone?"

"A fortnight perhaps, or it may take several months. It depends upon what part I am to have in Sir Ferdinando's grand scheme."

"Then you mustn't go alone," Agnes said decisively. "Elizabeth can go with you and keep house. That way you won't feel rushed to decide."

"I welcome her help and her company," Hull said. "She can give me a woman's perspective on conditions in Gorgeana."

"That thought had crossed my mind."

"But you and the children cannot spend the winter here," Hull said. "If I have to stay in Maine more than a month, you must return to the house in Barnstable. I'll speak to Bursley. He can help you move back."

"I shall do as you say," Agnes replied, "and I shall gladly accept whatever the future has in store for us, be it in Maine or here in the Plymouth Colony."

Taking his hand, she led him back into the warmth of the cabin.

* * *

When news reached Lothrop that the dissident faction in the Yarmouth church had failed to depose Matthews and that Hull had absconded to Maine, he considered the matter resolved. Having heard no more rumblings from his neighbor to the east, he was surprised to see Matthews on his doorstep early in March. He was trembling, either from the cold or from agitation. Ann made him sit by the hearth, where a fire was blazing.

"I've just had word that Hull is returning," he blurted before Lothrop could ask why he was there, "and that he plans to resume his ministry."

"What is there to resume?" Lothrop asked, drawing up a bench from the table. "He has no congregation in Yarmouth or anywhere else. And his family is back in Barnstable, though I have yet to see his wife in church."

Matthews ignored the question. "We must act now before he stirs up more trouble. I've petitioned the court to issue a warrant for his arrest, if he should attempt to preach in Yarmouth."

"So what would you have me do?"

"The court can't take any action without specific grounds. I informed them that he is an excommunicated person, but they have seen no order to that effect. I want you to notify them of your decision, so they can proceed."

"It was a hard winter for Agnes and the children," Ann interjected. "Arresting Joseph would be a cruel blow for them."

"I appreciate your concern, but Mr. Matthews and I can resolve this matter," Lothrop told her. Then, turning to Matthews, he said, "Forgive my wife's impetuosity. I often rely on her to point out the human consequences of my actions."

"Do you mean you refuse to notify the court?"

"Not at all," Lothrop said calmly, "but I want to speak to Agnes first, if only to confirm Hull's plans. We mustn't act too rashly."

Matthews had risen to his feet, his face flushed with anger. "Speak to her then," he said in obvious disgust. "I shall await further word from you." Snatching up his coat, he stormed out of the house, leaving the door open behind him.

"Matthews is making too much of this business," Lothrop said when Ann had shut the door. "The dissent in his church has made him a bitter man. I'll pay a visit to Agnes this afternoon, if she'll receive me. She seems to have cut herself off from everyone since returning from Yarmouth."

"Let me speak to Joanna first," Ann said. "She may have some knowledge of her father's plans."

"Neither she nor her husband are attending services," Lothrop said. "I suppose she blames me for her father's troubles. Yet it might be best to see what she knows before I take any action."

On her return from the Bursley house Ann reported, "Joanna claims to know nothing about her father's return, but she assured me that he has no intention of preaching again in Yarmouth."

"Then I shall harm no one by endorsing a warrant that forbids him to do what he has no intention of doing," Lothrop said.

* * *

Late in March the constable at Yarmouth received a court warrant for "the arrest of one Joseph Hull, if he attempt to practice his ministry, he being an excommunicant." Soon after that, Lothrop noted in his journal, "Our sister Hull renewed her covenant with us, renouncing her joining with them at Yarmouth, and confessing her evil in so doing with sorrow."

He closed the book, satisfied that his actions had effected at least one reconciliation. Would Hull follow his wife's example on his return from Maine? Such an event seemed rather unlikely, and after some reflection Lothrop had to admit that he would not be terribly upset if it didn't take place. Whatever happened, he would try to be charitable.

Eleven

"I stand before you like Job."
(Yarmouth to the Province of Maine, 1642-1643)

Beth was too full of strange new visions to sleep. Her life was moving in a new direction, and she was eager to experience whatever Maine had to offer. She knew already that she would like it there. She wondered if there were Indians in Maine, whether she could pick berries in the woods. She was eager to tell Tristram the news. He would be proud of her. He came to see her as soon as the *Aurora* arrived in port. The news had reached him that Hull would be sailing with them on their next voyage to Maine, but he was surprised by Beth's announcement that she would accompany him.

"I'm going to make sure we stay a long time," she declared as they walked along the deserted shore, pausing now and then to toss stones at the sea that covered the sandy flats frequented by fishermen at low tide.

Tristram laughed at her enthusiasm. "It's not so different from other places," he said. "But you may be in for a few surprises."

"Do you think Father will be happy there?"

"He'll be preaching to his own kind. That should make it easier."

"Agnes gave me a long list of questions about Maine," she said, heedless of his response. "I feel like a spy."

"I can help you answer them," Tristram said.

The voyage north was shorter than Beth expected. When she wasn't tending to her father, she was on deck watching Tristram as he went about his duties. He seemed fully grown, one of the men. She in turn was eager to accept the responsibilities of a woman, and she was proud that her father had chosen her to accompany him on this mission.

As the *Aurora* entered the Agamenticus river, Beth counted the houses on both banks. Gorgeana appeared to be a bit more populated than Yarmouth. In the harbor she saw dugout canoes, shallops, even a two-masted schooner. Master Bursley was telling her father about a man named Burdett.

"Did Mr. Burdett do something bad?" she asked them.

"Let's just say he was guilty of misconduct involving a woman," her father explained when Bursley was silent.

Beth thought he meant adultery, which was forbidden by one of the commandments; but she was afraid to ask. Her father changed the subject.

Once ashore, they found shelter in a small cabin near the chapel. The owner, a fisherman, was staying on Hog Island just off the coast. While Beth applied herself to making the cabin comfortable, her father met with the men in authority in Gorgeana and nearby villages. In the evening they would walk down to the wharf, where she watched the boats while her father spoke to the fishermen and the townspeople.

"Are we going to stay in Maine?" she would ask on the way home.

"It's still too soon to say," he would reply.

One day he was a bit more expansive. "I'm comfortable here. I feel I'm part of the community. In Massachusetts and in Plymouth, I had to worry about who my enemies were and what they were up to. Here I'm disposed to trust the men I meet, because we all have common goals."

Beth started to ask what those goals were, but a fisherman called out, "Good to see you, Mr. Hull. Would you like a cod for supper?" Her father produced his purse, but the man shook his head. "No charge."

"That's kind of you," her father said as he grasped the fish by its gills.

"Who was that man?" Beth asked as they climbed the hill to their cabin. She had insisted on carrying the heavy fish and was regretting it.

"I met him when I was preaching on Hog Island," he said.

When the cabin was in order, Beth set out to learn more about the new city of Gorgeana. In addition to a grist mill and a tidal-powered sawmill, it boasted a warehouse, a tavern, and a general store. An Indian path linked the houses strung along the river bank as far upstream as Point Christian. The governor's manor house was of special interest. She recalled the great houses in Devon and Somerset, but she had seen none like that in New England. She made her father promise to take her along when he visited Thomas Gorges.

"Sir Ferdinando had the manor built as his family seat in Maine," he said as they strode along the path, the river on their left. "That was seven years ago. It was in disrepair when Thomas Gorges arrived. He's working hard to restore the house to its original grandeur."

The manor house was by far the largest building Beth had seen in the colonies. The glass windows reflected the winter sun in a brilliant orange. Thomas Gorges agreed willingly to show her about. He was young and noble in bearing, and her attention on the tour was divided between her guide and what he pointed out – the cobblestone fireplace, paneled study, guest rooms, and beer cellar.

"It's not as grand as the homes in England," he told her, "but it should serve Sir Ferdinando's purpose."

His warm smile and optimism won her heart. She was glad that he was doing a fine job as deputy governor. That was her father's opinion, which she accepted without question. While the two men conferred in the paneled study, she explored the grounds of the manor. The outline of a formal English garden was clearly demarcated, but brown and sere now with the approach of winter. She resolved to come back in the spring when it was in full bloom.

"Thomas has accomplished a great deal in Gorgeana," her father said on the walk home. "I'm sure he'll do just as much for Maine."

"When will Sir Ferdinando arrive?" she asked.

"His coming may be little more than a dream," he replied.

* * *

Not long after his arrival Hull was invited to conduct a service at the chapel. A good crowd was on hand to hear him preach. Beth perched bird-like on her bench, eager to catch every word.

"I stand before you like Job," he announced. Beth smiled at that. His custom was to get the people's attention straight off with a bold remark that made them wonder what would come next. But this opening was new to her.

"When I came to New England seven years ago, I was convinced that I could erect a bastion of Anglicanism in the Massachusetts Colony. I was sure that many settlers, grown tired of Puritan rules, would flock to hear me preach. I was filled with pride in what I hoped to accomplish."

He paused, and Beth looked about her. Everyone appeared alert and expectant. Why would her father admit to a sin of pride? She didn't think of him as a proud man. What was he getting at?

"Much has occurred since then. A schism in my church forced me to leave Weymouth, and I took refuge in Hingham. But I could not preach there, and I was unable as a deputy to influence the actions of the General Court. I obtained a grant from the Plymouth court to settle in Barnstable; but another minister assumed control of the church there. Then my cattle business shriveled like a leaf in autumn. I responded to a call to preach in Yarmouth, and for that I was excommunicated. I come to you as a naked man, stripped of my ministry, my congregation, my hopes, and my pride. God has humbled His servant. But like Job, my heart and my soul cry out to bless the name of the Lord."

Beth wondered how her father would get out of this pit of humility he had dug for himself. Surely he didn't want to appear to the congregation as a man whom God had chastised. What kind of recommendation was that?

"You may rightly ask: why am I here in Gorgeana? I stand before you because I can see amidst the shambles of my ambition a spring of new hope that appears to be devoid of any pride. Before I left England, Sir Ferdinando Gorges told me of his dream for this province, but I was too enamored of my own purpose to mesh my dream with his. For seven years I have moved from place to place, learning by experience that I had erred in my judgment. I am now ready to devote myself to a much larger dream, a dream that is in the process of being realized by your deputy governor. I am grateful to Thomas Gorges for this opportunity to change my life and amend my past faults. My future and the future of Gorgeana lie in your hands and in God's. I am prepared to do His will."

Beth was moved by the sincerity of his words, and those about her seemed equally impressed. She waited for him at the rear of the chapel, eager to report her observations and ask him what would happen next.

* * *

Some days later Thomas Gorges paid a visit to their cabin. He smiled in recognition as she took his cloak and hung it on a peg. With him were two older men, whom he introduced as Edward Godfrey and Roger Garde. They took no heed of her as they surrendered their coats and hats. Her father motioned his guests to take seats near the fire, while he remained standing. Beth busied herself making tea, but she could hear and see all that transpired.

"People in Gorgeana are wary of a new minister," Gorges said. "You know about Mr. Burdett's troubles, and Mr. Ward was with us less than a year before he moved on. I have no authority to offer you the vacant post, but I do know that people were impressed by your remarks last Sunday."

"Especially by their brevity," Roger Garde said.

He was the shortest and most rotund of the three. As a rule, Beth liked short and jolly men; but something in Garde's manner put her off, perhaps the way he wiped his brow repeatedly in a not too clean handkerchief. She knew he was the mayor of Gorgeana, but that fact did not alter her opinion.

"No one here disputes your qualifications," Thomas Gorges continued. "We've come simply to confirm your availability, so we can present your name to the church elders. It's up to them to make the appointment."

"You needn't make your final decision now," Godfrey said. Beth noted that his voice was calm and reassuring, even soothing, "We can suggest a trial period. Let's say six months."

Beth gave a squeal of anticipation, then buried her face in her apron. When she looked up, her father had moved closer to the hearth. He took a deep breath, as was his custom whenever he had something important to say.

"I shan't equivocate. I seek a post that will allow me to fulfill my ministry as I was trained. I should be most unwise and ungrateful if I failed to grasp this opportunity. You may tell the elders that I am willing to stay on in Gorgeana, if the post is offered to me."

Beth was glad for her father, yet his words left her strangely cold. She suppressed a shiver. Maine was no longer a great adventure; it was to be her future home. Her father might be prepared for that, but she wasn't so sure.

"I'll have Bursley inform Agnes that we're staying in Maine for the winter," he said when the delegation was gone. "And I'll ask him to help her move back to Barnstable."

"When will we go home?" Beth asked.

"Nothing has been decided," Hull said. "I must see if they like me, and if I like them. But we should know where we stand by next spring."

* * *

The winter was a harsh one. Beth did all she could to make the cabin warm and tight against the wind and snow. She stuffed rags into the cracks around the windows, made a sand snake for the bottom of the door, and split wood for the fireplace – a never ending task. On Sunday she studied the faces of those about her in the chapel, then felt guilty for not paying closer attention to her father's sermon. But he was glad to get her reports on how the people were reacting to his preaching.

She also sought to get accurate answers to the questions Agnes had drawn up. What sort of goods did the stores in Gorgeana carry? A few ships from England made landfall in Maine before proceeding to Boston, and the general store had a good selection of household wares and materials.

Did they have enough food for the winter? Every family in town grew and stored vegetables, and the grist mill could grind twenty bushels of wheat with each tide. Thomas Gorges maintained a herd of cattle, and the staples of beef, pork, and fresh fish were supplemented by wild game – deer, moose, beaver, otter, and rabbit. They were in no danger of going hungry.

Was it safe to travel about? Not many Indians resided in that part of Maine. Her father said that diseases introduced by white settlers had severely depleted their numbers. The manor house at Point Christian sat on land vacated by the Wabanaki tribe. Thomas Gorges had tried without success to convert their Great Sagamore to Christianity. He advocated friendship with the Indians, but he discouraged excessive trade.

Did the people fear God and go to church? Attendance had grown since her father's arrival. As for fearing God, people in Gorgeana were much like anywhere else. The authorities were tolerant in matters of religion, hoping thus to attract more settlers.

Were the government officials easy to deal with? Her father seemed to get along with them. She liked Thomas Gorges and Edward Godfrey, but she wasn't so sure about Roger Garde.

Tristram carried her answers back to Agnes whenever the *Aurora* made port in Gorgeana, and he usually returned with more questions.

* * *

Before winter was out, the church elders offered to make Hull their permanent pastor, and he accepted the post. He sent word to Agnes of his decision, but it was early April before he and Beth boarded the *Aurora* for a return to Yarmouth. Bursley cautioned him that Agnes seemed less than enthusiastic about a move to Maine.

"The Plymouth court has issued a warrant for your arrest if you preach or set foot in Yarmouth," he continued. "I'm sure that Matthews is behind it, but Lothrop must have a hand in it as well."

They were alone on the quarterdeck of the *Aurora*. Beth had gone off to find Tristram and exchange news of the family. Hull was silent as he pondered the implications of Bursley's words.

"I suppose he told the court that I was excommunicated."

Bursley nodded. "Joanna is so angry she won't even speak to him, let alone go to church."

"Is Lothrop making things difficult for Agnes?" Hull asked.

"On the contrary," Bursley said. "She has reconciled herself with the church. I don't know if Lothrop persuaded her, or if she decided on her own accord. Anyway, she asked me to tell you."

"I'm sure there's more to it," Hull said.

When the *Aurora* docked in Barnstable, he proceeded directly to the home he had built there. Beth had to run to keep pace with him on the final hill. Word of their arrival had preceded them, and Agnes was waiting in the road with the children. Hull picked up and hugged each child in turn. They seemed uncertain what to do when he set them down, until Agnes urged Beth to shepherd them into the house. Left outside with his wife, Hull embraced and kissed her. After their lips parted, he continued to hold her tightly against his chest. In Gorgeana, alone and preoccupied with his future plans, he had little difficulty suppressing his carnal desires. Now, overcome by a wave of passion, he drew her out into the road that connected Barnstable and the town of Sandwich to the west.

"Where are you taking me?" Agnes asked, her voice subdued, as if she already knew the answer.

"Let's walk a bit," Hull said.

"What about the children?" she asked.

"Beth will entertain them with stories about Maine," he replied.

A light rain started to fall as they strolled hand in hand along the road. When they were out of sight of the house, he led her into a copse of pine trees. There on a damp bed of pine needles they satisfied their mutual hunger for each other.

"Bursley tells me you've rejoined the church in Barnstable," Hull said as they walked home. "You might have consulted me first."

"They were threatening to arrest you," Agnes said. "Mr. Lothrop said it would help us both if I returned to the church. I followed his advice."

"Joanna seems to have a different view of the matter," Hull said.

"Joanna has always been stubborn. I think she gets it from you."

"Lothrop has his own interest in mind," Hull said. "By forbidding me to preach, he hopes to be rid of me. Well, my plans accord with his desires. We're moving to Maine."

"You haven't asked me what I want," Agnes said softly.

Hull sat on a rock alongside the road."I know this is rather sudden," he said to placate her, "but you knew that I was prepared to resume my ministry if they offered me a post in Gorgeana."

Agnes had remained standing. "We've had to move four times already. Is there no end? It's very hard for me and the children."

Hull drew her toward him. She resisted at first, then sat beside him, her head bowed as if she were ashamed of her outburst. "What would you have me do?" he asked. "My duty as a minister is to go where I'm needed. The church in Gorgeana will grow along with the community. I can ill afford to let this opportunity slip by."

"Will Maine be any different?" Agnes said.

Hull put his arm about her shoulder. "I understand your feelings, but Maine is not the same as here or in Weymouth. Sir Ferdinando wants to create a model province loyal to Church and the Crown. If he succeeds, the King may expand his control to include all of New England."

"Beth says Gorgeana is just a fishing village," Agnes said. "How can a place like that fit into such a grand scheme?"

"Maine will be divided into eight counties," Hull said patiently. "Freeholders in each county will select deputies to assist the councillors and the deputy governor. The charter provides for a judge and officers of the court, a chancellor to determine property rights, a secretary, a treasurer, an admiral, and a marshal of militia. I shall be free at last of Puritans, whether they be reformers or separatists. Gorgeana may be small now; but it's destined to become the capital of New England – perhaps even the seat of a bishop."

"You make it sound a lot like Mr. Winthrop's city on a hill," Agnes said.

Her comment took him aback. "The plans of Sir Ferdinando are more likely to achieve fruition," he assured her. "Civil laws are the same in Maine as in England, whereas Winthrop adapts the laws to suit his own purpose."

"What if Sir Ferdinando should die?"

"Thomas Gorges is laying the groundwork so others can build on it."

"We'll be alone in this future capital of New England," Agnes said. "No one will go there with you, not even Joanna and John."

"When the new government takes root, people will flock to Maine from other colonies and from England as well. It's all coming together, Agnes. In Gorgeana I can do for the Church what Gorges is trying to do for the Crown. For once I'm in the place where God wants me."

"Don't misunderstand me, Joseph. I'm glad to see you so enthused about the future, and I shall not stand in the way of your dreams. But I need some time to prepare myself and the children for this move."

"The actual move can wait until summer. But you seem uneasy in your mind. Is there something else that troubles you?"

Agnes looked up at him. Her eyes were filled with tears, and her voice broke as she replied. "More than anything, I should like to return to England. Not right away. I know that is impossible. But at some future time. Let me have my dream."

Hull embraced her as she wept on his shoulder. They clung together for several minutes in silence. "I thank you for your honesty," he said at last. "I shall be equally honest. All in Maine is not quite as promising as I have pictured it. Sir Ferdinando may well die before his plans for Gorgeana can be carried out, and those plans may be overly ambitious. The new charter calls for forty municipal officers. Thomas has told him that such an order will require every man in the city to assume an office. So far he's received no answer."

"Still, it sounds like a noble plan," Agnes said.

"There are other factors as well," Hull pressed on. "The current strife in England threatens to distract the King's attention from the colonies. And Winthrop is eager to expand his jurisdiction. Massachusetts already controls a large part of New Hampshire, and future conflicts with Maine appear inevitable. I am bound to cast my lot with Sir Ferdinando; but events may intervene over which I have no control, and it may not turn out as I would like."

"I'm sorry I troubled you," Agnes said more calmly. "You must heed your calling. I am content to follow you to Gorgeana."

"Hear me out," Hull said. "I'm sorry that I didn't appreciate the depth of your desire to return to England. I can promise you this much. If my hopes for a future in Maine fail to materialize, we'll go back and start anew in England."

"I take comfort in that," Agnes said, "but I have another concern as well. Must you remain an excommunicated person? Surely the time has come to reconcile yourself with the church."

"I have no desire to make peace with Lothrop. My mind may embrace more charitable thoughts when I return in the summer. But I'm glad we had this talk. It bodes well for our future success and happiness."

"You might call it a good omen," Agnes said.

Twelve

"Where you lead, I shall follow."
(Gorgeana, Province of Maine, 1643)

On his return to Gorgeana, Hull spotted Thomas Gorges striding down the dock toward the *Aurora*. Before he could even wonder what the deputy governor might want that required such haste, Gorges was upon him. He was panting from his exertion.

"We must go to Boston at once," he said when he caught his breath. "How soon can you be ready to leave?"

Hull looked down at Beth, who was holding his hand. "I must get my daughter settled," he replied. "But why such urgency?"

"The future of Gorgeana is at stake. I'll explain as we walk. Let me take that satchel." He grasped the bag Beth carried and headed back the way he had come, without so much as a glance to see if they were following.

As they climbed the hill to Hull's cabin with Beth trailing a few steps behind, Gorges outlined his concerns. "As you may know, several years ago the Connecticut and New Haven colonies proposed a federation for mutual defense against the Dutch and the French. Delegates will meet soon in Boston to approve a charter for what Winthrop chooses to call the United Colonies of New England. Maine, of course, has not been invited to attend. No doubt Winthrop feels that his refusal to recognize Maine as an equal partner will make it easier for Massachusetts to expand northward."

"How did you learn of this meeting?" Hull was panting himself as he strove to match the pace of the younger man. Beth was falling farther behind; but she knew the way, and he wasn't concerned.

"Wheelwright sent me word of it from Wells. He had to leave New Hampshire when Exeter became part of Massachusetts. He was expressing his gratitude for finding a refuge in Maine."

"What do you hope to accomplish in Boston?"

Gorges paused to pick up a smooth and nicely rounded stone – one a boy might have found along the shore and dropped on his way home. "I must persuade Winthrop to reconsider his position," he said, fingering the stone in his free hand. "Many things have changed since our delegates were excluded from the first meeting of the federation – along with those from Providence Plantation and Rhode Island. In Winthrop's eyes their founders are outcasts and heretics who refuse to conform with the Puritan view of religion."

"We can hardly be described as outcasts or heretics," Hull said.

"Winthrop accuses us of harboring fugitives like John Wheelwright. Religious issues are certain to affect any decisions reached by the delegates. That's why I want you to come with me."

Hull glanced back over his shoulder. Beth was no longer in sight. "Who else is going?" he asked.

"Roger Garde can advise on political issues."

Hull had met Garde on several occasions. A woolen draper by trade, he came from Biddeford in Devon. Arriving in Maine in 1637, he served as recorder of the court before being elected mayor of Gorgeana. He struck Hull as a man of good character but volatile temperament.

"Why not wait until after the meeting?" Hull asked. "Then you'll see what you're dealing with."

"Afterwards may be too late," Gorges said, tossing the stone aside. "We must persuade Winthrop to accept Maine as a legitimate colony and an equal member of the federation."

"Why should he accept us now, when he rejected us before?"

"At that time the province had only a rudimentary government; whereas now we have a General Court, a chartered city as our capital, and a proprietor appointed by the Crown."

"But Winthrop regards Sir Ferdinando as the enemy," Hull said. "You can't change that."

"That's why I want you to come with me," Gorges said. "You know how Winthrop thinks, his strengths and his weaknesses. And having served as a deputy to the court, you must have contacts in Boston who can help us accomplish our goal."

Hull paused to catch his breath. "My relations with Winthrop are a bit strained," he said. "Yet he's the person we have to see. I consider him a fair and honest man, much given to disputation, but amenable to reason."

"Then we leave at once," Gorges exclaimed with evident satisfaction. "Can you be ready in the morning?"

"Beth will see to that," Hull said.

Setting down the satchel he was carrying, Gorges strode off. Hull waited for his daughter to catch up. Beth gave him a questioning look as she picked up the bag with both hands and followed him to their cabin.

* * *

Four years had elapsed since Hull was in Boston as a deputy from Hingham. Arriving from the north on horseback, he scarcely recognized the place. The town had expanded considerably, but its growth was still more haphazard than planned. Winthrop extended his hand to Thomas Gorges, but frowned when he saw Hull and Garde. He ushered them into his study and sent for additional chairs.

"What brings you to Boston?" he asked, his eyes fastened on Gorges. He seemed determined to ignore his other two visitors.

"I came to wish you success in forming a New England federation," Gorges replied. "England can only benefit from a union that ensures the safety and promotes the stability of all her colonies."

Despite his youth he spoke with confidence and appeared at ease. Roger Garde was obviously uncomfortable in these surroundings. The room was not overly warm, yet beads of perspiration were forming on his forehead, and he fidgeted with his hat. Hull sat calmly, content to observe the speakers and to assess the implications of their words. He wondered if Winthrop had noted the stress Gorges placed on *all her colonies.*

"That is the primary purpose of the United Colonies," Winthrop said, "but we have yet to agree on all the articles in our charter. I trust this will be accomplished at our next meeting."

"A meeting to which Maine is not invited," Gorges said. "Why are we left to stand alone? Maine is a buffer against the French to our north, just as Connecticut and New Haven are against the Dutch to their south. We are prepared to send delegates who can contribute to the deliberations and bring added strength to your union."

Winthrop's eyes shifted for a moment to Hull and Garde. He appeared to be asking himself whether these were the delegates he might expect. "That proposal was considered and rejected at our first meeting," he said calmly, as if he were sure of his ground. "We deemed it more important to maintain our unity of purpose, even if it meant sacrificing a measure of strength. Our goal is not just self-defense but the preservation of our common religion. Inclusion of outlaw settlements such as Providence and Rhode Island would only serve to introduce a disruptive element."

"Maine can hardly be called an outlaw settlement," Gorges said.

Hull seized on the opportunity to address what he considered the central question. "As for the preservation of our common religion, Maine is closer to you than the separatists in Plymouth."

Winthrop gave him a withering look before addressing himself again to Gorges. "Delegates from Maine represented a number of small enclaves, and there was much bickering among them. They were clearly not a united colony with common interests. For that reason we thought it best to exclude them from our deliberations."

"I'm here to speak about the future, not the past," Gorges said. "As you well know, we now have a stable government and a court system that conforms with English law. Inclusion of Maine in the federation is clearly of mutual advantage to all concerned."

"I'll present your proposal to the delegates," Winthrop said calmly, as if he anticipated this line of argument. "Unfortunately, they have already incorporated an article in the charter that precludes the admission of any new members to the federation. I cautioned against such a restriction, but to no avail. My goal now is the formation of the union. I will not jeopardize that."

Gorges looked at his clenched hands and was silent. He seemed to be searching for the right words. If the federation were limited to four colonies, Maine would be forever on the outside. Without strong support from Sir Ferdinando, the province would have to guard against French incursions from Canada and future encroachments by Massachusetts. Hull sensed that his own fate was also at stake in this talk.

Before Gorges could reply, Garde spoke up. "This federation serves your own purpose, which is to annex all of New Hampshire and Maine."

Gorges frowned. Winthrop merely smiled, confident that he had the upper hand and could afford to be gracious.

"I ask that you consider the points we have raised," Gorges said, a note of resignation in his voice, "and that you do what is right and just."

"I can only promise to speak to the delegates," Winthrop said. "Any decision is in their hands. I wish you continued success in governing your province, and please convey my best wishes to Sir Ferdinando."

Their meeting was clearly over, but no one made a motion to leave. Winthrop was the first to rise. The delegation filed out of the study and bade goodbye to the governor, who held the front door open for them. Once outside, each man appeared lost for a time in his own thoughts.

"Do you think any good will come of this?" Hull ventured to ask.

"I doubt it," Gorges said. "Winthrop has set his course, and only God can force him to change it. But we had to make the attempt."

* * *

In May of 1643 delegates from Massachusetts, Plymouth, New Haven, and Connecticut gathered in Boston and ratified the charter that created the United Colonies of New England. Rhode Island and

Providence Plantation were not represented. With regard to Maine, Winthrop wrote in his journal: "Those of Sir Ferdinando Gorge his province, beyond Pascataquack, were not received nor called into the confederation, because they ran a different course from us both in their ministry and civil administration; for they had lately made Acomenticus (a poor village) a corporation, and had made a taylor their mayor, and had entertained one Hull, an excommunicated person and very contentious, for their minister."

* * *

That summer Hull returned to Barnstable alone to put his affairs in order and to arrange for the removal of his family to Gorgeana. Young Joseph was suffering from an undefined illness and decided to accompany them. Hull sold what cattle he could in the shrinking market, turning the rest over to Bursley and Joanna, who declined to move. Tristram too was content with his life as a seaman.

Agnes was ready to depart, but she admitted she was sorry to leave Barnstable. "You mustn't think ill of me," she added, "but I became reconciled to a move by telling myself that Maine was a step closer to England." She was preparing the evening meal, and she didn't look at him as she spoke. "I want you to succeed in your ministry and to realize your dreams. Yet I can't help but feel that failure too would have its rewards."

"I appreciate your feelings," Hull said, though he didn't quite follow her reasoning. Gorgeana and Barnstable were equally close to England, and he refused to consider the possibility of failure. Rather than belabor the issue, he changed the subject.

"I have some news that should make the move a bit more palatable. John Heard has requested Elizabeth's hand in marriage.

He's a carpenter and a respected man in the community. I gave my consent. Beth is relying on you to help her prepare for the wedding."

"I'm happy for her," Agnes said, "but she's still so young. How did she meet this man when she was busy caring for you?"

Hull smiled in amusement, for it hadn't occurred to him to ask such a question. "I'm not sure. Perhaps Bursley had a hand in it."

"I couldn't have managed without Joanna in your absence," Agnes said. "Before we leave, you must speak to her. She's cut herself off from the church and from Mr. Lothrop since he issued that warrant for your arrest."

"The warrant is of no consequence. My future lies in Gorgeana."

"I told her as much, but she's still nursing her anger."

"I'll see what I can do," Hull promised.

He chose a time when Bursley was busy aboard the *Aurora*. Joanna prepared tea, then sat down across the table from him. Marriage and children had altered her looks and her demeanor. No longer a daughter to be chided or corrected, she was a mature woman, still respectful to her father yet capable of making her own decisions. She said as much when he broached the subject of her alienation from the church.

"I commend your loyalty," Hull said, "but that's all in the past. Agnes and I are concerned about you. We'll feel much better about leaving if you make your peace with Lothrop."

"How can I make peace with a man who repaid all the hospitality you offered him by ordering your arrest? I can't forgive him for that. Can you?"

Hull studied his daughter. She had given him an opening that he was not yet ready to take. He sipped his tea while he sought a way out of his dilemma. "I may have forgiven him already in my heart," he said at last. "Lothrop did what he thought was right. That's all anyone can do."

Joanna gave him a knowing look but remained silent.

"Be that as it may," he went on, "once I'm gone, you gain nothing from separation. Reconcile yourself with the church. Lothrop will gladly welcome you back, just as he did Agnes."

"I'll go to him," Joanna said, "if you promise to do the same."

Hull rose and paced the room. It was one thing to forgive Lothrop in his heart, quite another to admit he had erred by going to Yarmouth. Yet the arguments he had mustered against Joanna applied also to himself, and he owed it to his congregation in Gorgeana to come to them as a minister in good standing. He stopped pacing and faced his daughter. "I too must subdue my pride," he said. "Where you lead, I shall follow."

* * *

After Hull had left for Maine, Lothrop noted in his journal that Mistress Bursley rejoined the church and presented her second born child to be baptized. Then he added with evident satisfaction, "Mr. Hull in the acknowledging of his sin, of renewing his covenant, was received again into fellowship with us."

Thirteen

"Ambition in itself is hardly a cause for condemnation."
(Gorgeana, Province of Maine, 1643-1644)

Arriving in Gorgeana, Hull gave up his cabin and settled his family in a larger house acquired from a man who had decided to leave the province. In his absence Thomas Gorges had returned to England to fight in the civil war on the side of the Parliament. Lacking specific instructions from Sir Ferdinando, he named Richard Vines as the deputy governor. A physician and an agent for the Laconia Company, Vines had come to New England in 1630.

"A light has been extinguished," Hull said upon hearing the news. "The future of Maine is no longer so bright."

"Surely Mr. Vines is concerned about Maine's future," Agnes said with barely a pause in the task of putting things in their places.

"He lacks the prestige that Gorges enjoyed as a relative of Sir Ferdinando," Hull said. "Still, he's a man of broad experience and may rise to the task at hand. I wish him well."

"It's your concern," Agnes said. "I've enough to do getting settled here and preparing for Beth's wedding."

Taking the hint, Hull ended the discussion. Agnes did not wish to become embroiled in local politics, and she expected him to act in a like manner. Although he wasn't prepared to divorce himself entirely from the events of the day, he recognized the wisdom of her position. He assured her that his family and congregation had full claim on his efforts and allegiance.

The wedding took place late that summer in Gorgeana, with Hull officiating. The couple settled in Dover, an easy voyage by sea. Agnes looked forward to visiting Beth on occasion, when Bursley's business took him in that direction.

"I shall miss her," she confided to Hull after the ceremony.

He shifted his position in bed so that he cradled her with his body. "We mustn't think of ourselves," he said. "Let us be happy for her."

In the fall their joy gave way to grief over the death of Joanna's third child, christened John after its father. Bursley wept as he told them the news. The death of an infant was not uncommon; yet that of a namesake was doubly hard to bear – or so Hull reasoned as he sought to console his son-in-law.

Much was changing around him, not only in his family but in the community. He had a sense that he was no longer in control of his own life. To maintain his equilibrium, he devoted himself fully to his ministry and was gratified by a substantial growth in church attendance. He was doing his part. The rest depended on God's providence and the workings of fate.

* * *

As deputy governor Vines became embroiled in controversy with a man named George Cleeve. Hull knew little or nothing about Cleeve and had to rely on Edward Godfrey to shed light on these events. Godfrey had supported Hull's appointment as minister and was a frequent guest in his home. He was broad-shouldered with a warm smile that shone through a beard reaching from ear to ear. Like Vines and Cleeve, he had arrived in Maine in 1630 as an agent for Sir Ferdinando Gorges. As a party to the controversy from its beginning, he was able to give Hull a full account.

"When Cleeve came to Maine," he explained when the issue arose, "he was promised a tract of land at Cape Porpoise, or so he says; and he was angry when Sir Ferdinando had him evicted. Then about five years ago he returned to England and managed to convince Gorges that Vines and I had mismanaged the affairs of the province. I was called to London to answer the charge, and I secured a judgment in court against Cleeve. When Gorges learned of his duplicity, he reinstated Vines and myself as his agents. We thought that was the end of it, but last year Cleeve went back to England and persuaded Sir Alexander Rigby to buy up the old Plough patent issued by the Council for New England. That patent encompasses all the land between the Sagahadoc and Cape Porpoise."

"That's half of Maine!" Hull said.

"Then Rigby appointed Cleeve as his deputy to govern the newly created province that he calls Lygonia."

"Sir Ferdinando has a royal charter for the entire Province of Maine," Hull said. "Surely that outweighs a patent issued so long ago by a body now defunct."

"The Parliament decides these matters," Godfrey said, "and Rigby is an MP. A royal charter no longer carries the weight one might expect."

"Can't Gorges do something to stop him?" Hull asked.

Godfrey shook his head. "The Plough patent predates his charter and was never officially superseded. Sir Ferdinando was a member of the council that approved the patent."

Hull regarded this as information that was of little concern to him. Let Vines and Godfrey take care of the business of Gorgeana and the province. His duty was to God and to his congregation, and he made his position clear to town officials. But he did not hesitate to give voice to his opposition of further expansion northward by the Massachusetts Bay Colony.

He was surprised when Godfrey broached the subject of Cleeve again in the spring of 1644. They were returning from Hog Island, where Hull had performed a baptism while Godfrey sought to convince the fishermen that their allegiance was to Maine despite Rigby's claim that the island was part of Lygonia. The sea was calm, and they made slow progress toward the mainland.

"There's a storm brewing," the owner of the boat said, pointing to the dark clouds gathering in the southwest.

Godfrey let out the sail to better catch the light wind. "In more ways than one," he said as he fastened the line. Turning to Hull, he added in a lower voice, "We've had word that Cleeve is in Boston, trying to gain Winthrop's support for his claim to Lygonia. Vines wants me to present our case to Winthrop. I'd like you to come along."

"I promised Agnes I wouldn't meddle in public affairs," Hull said.

"She'll understand. You know Sir Ferdinando, and you represent the established church. Winthrop can't afford to offend either one."

Hull hesitated. The wind had freshened, as if in response to the boat owner's forecast, and he drew his hat down about his ears His reluctance to travel to Boston was not due to the nature of the mission. Godfrey's purpose was in line with his own hopes, as well as those of the province. What concerned him was a need to preserve his own role as a minister. For twenty years in England he had isolated himself from political controversies. Though he had served more recently as a deputy from Hingham and Barnstable, he attributed that temporary lapse to the loss of his congregation and his interlude in the world of commerce. Here in Gorgeana he was again at home in the ministry. To pose as an emissary for the Province of Maine would be presumptuous, a mockery.

"I'm sorry to disappoint you," he said, "but as a minister my duty is to my congregation and to my family. I have no business in Boston."

Godfrey was silent for a time. "Bursley's ship is in the harbor," he said at last. "Speak to him before you make a final decision."

Expecting an argument, Hull was surprised at this suggestion. "Bursley has nothing to do with it. He doesn't even live in Maine."

"He's aware of what's going on in the world. And you respect his opinion. You can give me your answer tomorrow."

"I shall speak to him in any event," Hull said. "The subject of Cleeve may come up, but I shan't introduce it."

"I shall call on you tomorrow afternoon," Godfrey said.

They made port ahead of the impending storm. Godfrey departed in some haste, claiming he had an appointment, while Hull lingered on the dock. Had Godfrey already spoken to Bursley? But no, the *Aurora* had arrived that morning, giving him no opportunity to plead his case in advance. Yet what Godfrey said was true enough. He did value Bursley's opinion, and it could do no harm to discuss the matter with him.

Instead of going straight home, Hull rowed out to the *Aurora*, which was moored in the river. He had glimpsed Bursley from the dock, and he felt they could talk more freely if Agnes were not present. Finding his son-in-law in his quarters, he proceeded directly to the subject at hand.

Bursley showed no surprise at the news. "I'm familiar with Cleeve and his activities," he said when Hull had finished, "but the future of Lygonia has less to do with Cleeve than with the outcome of the struggle between the King and Parliament."

"But Cleeve is in Boston now," Hull said, "and we can't ignore him. If Maine is split in half, Winthrop is sure to seize upon the opportunity to expand his control." He paused, surprised by the argumentative tone of his words. "That's the gist of what Godfrey said," he added as a disclaimer.

"Don't you agree with him?" Bursley asked.

"Of course I do. I'd like to help; but by going to Boston, I exceed my duty and authority as a minister. I may even jeopardize my prospects for advancement in the church." Hull bowed his head, ashamed at having disclosed his dormant hope of one day becoming a bishop.

Bursley had turned his back and was peering through the porthole. "That may be true," he said, "but Winthrop's decision whether or not to support Cleeve will be influenced largely by his religious convictions. That's probably why Godfrey wants you to go with him."

"The fact that Winthrop heeds the advice of the Council of Ministers doesn't mean he'll listen to me," Hull said.

"Who knows what questions may come up?" Bursley said. "Not only the future of Maine is at stake. Your future is tied to the preservation of what Gorges has built here."

Hull nodded in agreement. "I've often said that his dreams and mine are linked. That appears to be more true now than ever before."

"If we're finished with that matter," Bursley said, his face breaking into a grin, "I have good news for you. Tristram has acquired a half-share in a schooner. He's master of his own ship."

"Where did he get the money?" Hull asked.

"I put up some of it. A schooner is a good investment for a man who's young and ambitious. Besides, Tristram has a wife to support, and I've heard rumors of a child on the way."

Hull stared at him in surprise. "When did he get married?"

"I thought you knew," Bursley said, looking away. "Her name is Blanche. She's older than he is, and her reputation is a bit tarnished; but I'm sure they'll be all right."

"Does Agnes know?" Hull asked.

"I'm not sure. I leave that to you."

* * *

Hull questioned his wife as soon as he got home. Agnes looked up from the meat pies she was preparing for the evening meal. She seemed not at all surprised by the news.

"He spoke of Blanche the last time he was here," she said calmly.

"Did he say anything about her reputation?"

"Only that it was just gossip and slander, that her life had been full of difficulties, and that he was helping her to overcome her misfortunes. But he made no mention of a child."

"Why didn't you tell me?" Hull asked.

"He said Bursley was the only one who knew about the marriage. He was afraid you wouldn't approve of Blanche."

"I would need more reason than mere rumor and gossip not to approve."

"I assured him you would understand, and I thought he planned to tell you. He must have decided to wait."

The fact that Tristram had married without his knowledge made Hull wonder what wrong Blanche might have committed. A woman's reputation was not sullied without a reason, and it usually involved some sort of sexual or religious transgression. It struck him that he knew very little about his son's attitudes and beliefs, and he resolved to remedy that situation the next time Tristram was in port.

The talk turned to Hull's journey to Boston. "I'm reluctant to get involved," he told her, "but my future and that of Maine may well depend on whether we can persuade Winthrop not to lend his support to Cleeve."

"Will Mr. Winthrop receive you?"

Hull admitted he was apprehensive. "My presence may even hinder Godfrey's chances for success."

"He wouldn't have asked you to accompany him if he didn't think you could help," Agnes said.

Hull smiled gratefully at his wife. "I shall do what I can."

* * *

Winthrop had moved to a larger house. The smell of English leather that permeated his office struck Hull as a barrier designed to render him more distant. He recalled the odor of venison stew on his first visit – an odor that had made him welcome. Ten years had passed since that day, and Winthrop still clung to his vision of a city on a hill. Comparing the governor's mansion to his own modest dwelling, Hull had to admit that his dreams were fast fading. Bursley was right. Both his future and that of Maine were inextricably linked to events in England. Godfrey's mission was merely a delaying action. Yet it was nonetheless vital for all that.

Winthrop motioned them to be seated. "So you were sent by Vines," he said, peering down his nose at them. "Was he unable to come himself?"

"His situation is somewhat delicate," Godfrey said, "but he knows and approves of our purpose."

"And what is your purpose?"

"To caution you against placing too much trust in George Cleeve. He is driven by ambition and will resort to any measure to achieve his goal."

Winthrop stroked his beard. "Ambition in itself is hardly a cause for condemnation. People say that I too am ambitious. What specifically has Cleeve done to merit my distrust?"

"He slandered the reputation of an honorable man, a knight who has devoted his life and his fortune to the service of England – Sir Ferdinando Gorges." Godfrey's tone was matter of fact rather than accusing.

Winthrop raised his eyebrows at that. "I'm quite familiar with Sir Ferdinando's reputation. But how has Cleeve slandered him?"

"By misrepresenting his involvement in the Plough patent," Godfrey said, reciting the charge as if he were addressing a court, "and by circulating false reports of Gorges's death in order to bolster his own claims."

"I'm glad Sir Ferdinando is alive and well," Winthrop said. "Am I to understand that you've had some directions from him?"

When Godfrey hesitated, Hull spoke up. "His days are occupied in defending the land we all know and love. Our duty is to preserve the government he has set up in Maine until the strife in England is resolved."

Winthrop smiled at that. "Then you've had no word from England."

Godfrey had regained his composure. "Our directions are derived from the royal charter that encompasses all of the Lygonia tract. The claims made by Cleeve and by Sir Alexander Rigby have no validity."

"The English courts and the Parliament must rule on that," Winthrop said. "It's not for us to decide."

"But it benefits you nothing to recognize their claims now," Godfrey pressed on. "Wisdom would dictate that you wait for a ruling to be handed down on the issue."

"Cleeve bears a deed of assignment from Rigby. If I refuse to honor that commission, I appear to defy the Parliament." Winthrop's voice was soft yet decisive, as if he were familiar with this argument.

"You can honor it, while withholding active support until the courts in England have reached a decision."

Winthrop rose and went to the window. He appeared to be pondering Godfrey's proposal. "Will Vines do the same?" he asked, turning abruptly to face them. "Has he agreed to take no further action against Cleeve?"

"As deputy governor," Godfrey said, "Vines is bound to oppose Cleeve's effort to take control of the Lygonia tract, but he has promised to exercise restraint."

"Cleeve strikes me as a reasonable man," Winthrop said. "Ambitious for sure and perhaps a bit devious, but his concern is for Maine's future."

"Maine's future!" Godfrey scoffed. "His goal is to split the province in half!"

He appeared too upset to go on, so Hull took up the argument. "You do not serve your own interests by supporting Cleeve."

"My interests are not at issue," Winthrop said disdainfully. "I'll thank you to address the matter at hand."

"I seek only to point out that the interests of the Massachusetts Colony are better served by Sir Ferdinando's failure than by Cleeve's success," Hull said, adopting a conciliatory tone.

"Either outcome appears much the same," Winthrop said.

"On the contrary. If Cleeve and Rigby succeed in Lygonia, you must deal with a provincial government on your northern flank that has the backing of Parliament. On the other hand, if you delay their efforts to take control by simply withholding your support, you need only concern yourself with what fortune has in store for Gorges. Quite apart from the events in England, Sir Ferdinando is no longer a young man."

Winthrop looked puzzled. "You seem to argue against yourself."

"Not at all," Hull said. "Maine's future and our own are linked to that of Gorges. I have no choice. But it is clearly in your interest to wait and refuse to take sides."

"There is some wisdom in your argument," Winthrop granted. "I must recognize the validity of Cleeve's title, but I see no pressing need to assist him in carrying out his commission."

"That is all we ask," Godfrey said.

Hull was silent as they took their leave of the governor. "You seem less than pleased with our agreement," Godfrey said as they rode off.

"I fear it was just a ploy to be rid of us," Hull said. "Winthrop will take whatever action serves his interest."

"I trust him to keep his word," Godfrey said.

Fourteen

"His dreams and mine die with him."
(Gorgeana, Province of Maine, 1644-1647)

Godfrey kept Hull abreast of developments with regard to Lygonia. Cleeve had summoned a court at Casco to set up a government for the new province. Encouraged by Winthrop's promise of neutrality, Vines continued to question the validity of the patent, accusing Cleeve of counterfeiting the King's seal. Cleeve offered to let the magistrates in Boston rule upon the legitimacy of his claim; but Vines said he had no authority from Gorges to submit the title to arbitration. He arrested Cleeve's emissary and arraigned him before a court in Saco. Cleeve then sought to have Lygonia admitted to the New England Federation, but the commissioners denied his petition. To prevent open hostilities between the two rival provinces, a special court was convened in Boston. When neither side could persuade the jury of the merits of its case, the court advised both parties to live in peace until the authorities in England reached a decision.

Although Hull wanted to be kept informed, he made it known to Vines and Godfrey that he would no longer play an active role in public affairs, that he intended to devote himself to his family and his congregation.

* * *

When Tristram's ship entered the mouth of the river, Hopewell, Agnes' oldest son, broke the news to his parents. How he recognized the ship, never having seen it before, remained a mystery to them. As the morning passed with no sign of Tristram, Hull concluded that his son might want to speak to him alone. Tristram had always respected Agnes and obeyed her commands, but had never referred to her as mother. Anne had died when he was nine – old enough to remember.

Tristram spotted him from afar and came along the dock to greet him. He looked much the same, save for a fresh growth of beard; and he hugged his father with an eagerness that conveyed a newfound sense of self-assurance and equality. Marriage was a great step toward maturity, Hull reflected. He must take care in framing his queries about Blanche.

"Did you bring your bride with you?" he asked.

"Not this voyage," Tristram said. "She's not much of a sailor."

Hull studied the small coastal schooner tied to the dock. "And you're master of your own ship. I'm proud of you."

Tristram's face glowed in response to his father's praise. "I have to work just as hard as the crew, but it's a start."

"You look older with a beard." Hull had run out of neutral topics.

"That was my intent," Tristram said. "Would you care for a drink?"

"I could use a cup of cider."

Hull said no more until they were seated in a private corner of Puddington's tavern. His wife Mary, who seemed to be back in his good graces after her dalliance with Burdett, served them. Tristram drank his ale in silence, apparently uncertain how to begin.

"Bursley said something about a child," Hull offered.

"A son," Tristram said. "We kept it secret for Blanche's sake."

"Tell me about her," Hull said.

Tristram emptied his cup and pushed it aside. "You may remember her. Her parents owned the bakery in Northleigh. She was married there, but her husband died on the voyage across the Atlantic. She's a bit vague about what happened after that, and I don't press her with questions." He called for another ale, but simply stared at the tankard Mary set before him.

"How did you meet her?" Hull prodded.

"She was a servant for a family in Sandwich. Bursley had some dealings with them, and I spoke to her while he conducted his business. She told me she was expecting a baby. She was from Northleigh, so I offered to help. She said the only way anyone could help was to marry her." Tristram appeared lost again in contemplation.

"Who is the child's father?" Hull asked.

"It seems she was out in the woods, picking berries or something, and she got separated from the group. An Indian showed her the way back to the village – and a few other things as well, either then or later."

"You mean he raped her?" Hull asked.

"I don't think so. She's never said anything against him. She may have loved him – or thought she did. When she realized she was pregnant, her only choice was public disgrace or living with Indians. She was three months along when I met her. I was the first person she confided in."

191

"And you took pity on her." Hull lapsed into his ministerial mode. "A noble act, but a dubious basis for marriage."

"I admit that I felt sorry for her, but I married her because I love her. No one asked any questions before the boy was born. Now that he's older and looks more like an Indian, rumors are springing up about her character and her need to get married."

"Bursley said her reputation was tarnished even before that."

"Blanche doesn't say much about what happened when she first arrived in the colony."

"I can imagine her situation," Hull said. "An attractive young widow is all too readily branded as a woman of loose morals by those who feel their own marriage is threatened."

He paused to assess the effect of his words. By softening the cause of the gossip, he hoped to persuade his son to accept what was past and to deal rationally with what might lie ahead.

"I'm sure she'll tell me everything in good time," Tristram said.

"A sensible attitude, but you have a difficult decision to make. I don't like to suggest such a course; but it might be better for everyone if the boy were raised by Indians. I assume the father knows he has a son."

Tristram leaned far back in his chair. His shoulders relaxed, and a broad smile spread across his face. "Blanche spoke of that, but I was reluctant to agree. I was afraid she might want to maintain contact with her son – and with the father – so I offered to raise the boy as my own."

"And did she agree to that?" Hull asked.

"Not exactly. She's afraid the child will be a constant reminder of her past mistakes and an impediment to our love for each other. I had no answer for that, so we've made no decision."

"You have to think of the boy," Hull said. "If he is rejected by the community, he will grow up burdened by shame and guilt."

"But he can't just vanish," Tristram objected. "People are going to wonder what happened to him. What do we tell them?"

"It's best to say nothing. Let them assume the child died of natural causes. They'll forget it once you and Blanche have children of your own. But I must in good conscience ask that you have the boy baptized first. Where were you married?"

"I didn't want to get Mr. Lothrop involved, so we asked Marmaduke Matthews to marry us."

It was Hull's turn to smile. If Matthews had managed to put their past quarrels aside, he ought to act in like manner. "Then he should be willing to baptize your child. You needn't mention your future plans."

"And what do I tell the family?" Tristram asked.

"I leave that to you," Hull replied. "I won't say anything until you and Blanche have worked things out between you."

* * *

That winter the body of a man was found in the Agamenticus river. His head was severely bruised; and he had a deep gash in his side, as if somebody had driven a stake into him His sunken canoe was found nearby laden with clay. The body was identified as that of Richard Cornish, a local farmer. His wife Catherine and her lover, a man named Footman, were charged with murder. The corpse was observed to bleed profusely as each of them approached – a sure sign of their guilt. But Footman produced several witnesses to account for his whereabouts at the time of the murder. With the evidence provided by the bleeding corpse now in question, an additional charge of adultery was levied against Catherine; and several young men testified that they had enjoyed her favors.

Young Joseph was among those summoned. He admitted to his father that he had been intimate with the accused woman, but he hastened to add, "I wasn't alone. It was well known that she was available."

They were on their way home after a church service. The illness that plagued him in Barnstable had subsided, but he still felt as if it were lurking somewhere inside him, waiting to pounce. In the meantime he lived at home and did odd jobs in the community. Several weeks had passed since the discovery of the body, and the snow crunched under their feet as they walked.

"That's no excuse for adultery," Hull admonished him. "Still, it could help, when you testify, if you present yourself as only one of many victims who succumbed to Catherine's seductive charms. If you try to hide your guilt, you may become suspect as an accomplice to the murder."

Young Joseph grasped his hand. "Will you go with me to court?"

"Of course," Hull said, "but I'm powerless to help you."

"I just need to know you're there."

The trial was held in a courthouse erected as proof of Gorgeana's status as the seat of the province. Mayor Roger Garde presided as judge. Catherine Cornish had been in jail since the death of her husband. She was led in by a constable and thrust into a chair. Once seated, she adjusted the straight brown dress that reached to her ankles. Her smooth unblemished skin belied her age; but the aura of youth was diminished by her straw-colored hair. Uncombed and apparently unwashed, it gave her a wild and disheveled appearance.

Hull had thought of ministering to her in the jail, but he feared his intentions might be construed as an effort to protect his son. From his seat he noted her demeanor and actions. She glanced about coyly, smiling when she recognized a familiar face.

Young Joseph sat with lowered head and stared at his clenched hands, but Catherine failed to acknowledge his presence. When he was called on to testify, he followed his father's advice. His statements were accepted without question. Others also testified that they had enjoyed Catherine's favors, and it was noted that she had been admonished previously by the General Court in Boston for suspicion of incontinency. As for the murder, it was assumed that her husband had accused her of being a loose woman, at which she flew into a rage and killed him; or that she had found him burdensome and arranged with one of her admirers to do away with him.

Asked if she had anything to say in her defense, Catherine rose to her feet. Pointing her forefinger at the judge, she cried in a shrill voice that could be heard throughout the building and in the street outside, "It serves your own selfish purpose to be rid of me, Roger Garde!" She whirled about to confront the jury. "And yours as well, Edward Johnson! You're all hypocrites! You want to convict me to hide your own transgressions."

Johnson, a merchant well respected in the community, rose abruptly. Hull thought for a moment that his intent was to defend himself; but instead, he gathered up his coat and hat and left the room without glancing right or left. Garde fumbled with some papers until he could regain his composure.

"Have you finished?" he asked.

Having vented her anger, Catherine took her seat. Deliberations were swift. She was convicted and sentenced to be hanged.

Standing on the gallows, she steadfastly denied that she was guilty of murder. Johnson came forward and admitted publicly that he had committed adultery, but his belated confession had little effect on the large crowd that had gathered to watch Catherine die.

* * *

The winter snow was almost gone when Godfrey brought Hull the news that Archbishop Laud had been beheaded on Tower Hill.

Hull clutched the door frame to support himself. "Come in," he muttered in a voice that was barely audible. While Godfrey warmed himself at the fire, Hull sank down on a bench and buried his face in his hands.

"I knew he was in prison," Hull said, "but a year ago the Lords adjourned his trial without taking a vote."

"The Commons found him guilty of treason and of attempting to overthrow the Protestant religion," Godfrey said. "Then they forced the Lords to agree with their verdict."

"Couldn't the King do anything to save him?"

"I heard that the King issued a pardon, but Parliament ignored it."

"I disagreed with a good many of his ideas," Hull said, "but his death benefits no one. It will only strengthen the resolve of the Royalists, and it dashes all hope of a peaceful end to the conflict."

Godfrey turned his back to the fire. "I don't understand why he was executed. What did he do to deserve such a fate?"

"Laud tried to force the Scots to accept the *Book of Common Prayer*. When they resisted, the King had to reconvene Parliament in order to pay for his war against them. The Commons sought to impeach Laud for assuming tyrannical powers, fomenting rebellion, and subverting the true religion. He's been in prison for four years, but I never thought they would kill him."

"With Parliament in control, I fear for Maine's future," Godfrey said.

"As long as the King holds the reins, all is well," Hull said.

"You're too optimistic. He may still hold the reins, but the horses are half dead; and no one is at hand to provide a fresh team."

"We can only deal with our own situation," Hull said.

When Mayor Garde died unexpectedly during the summer, the city officials requested Hull to give the funeral sermon. Aware that Garde's death was widely considered proof of his complicity in the Cornish case, Hull felt obliged to address the issue.

"It pains me to admit it, but in our community a dead man is being placed on trial. In the minds of many here present Roger Garde stands, or rather lies before us, accused of a fault he vehemently denied while alive."

Surprise and discomfort were writ large on the faces of his audience, but he pressed on with his message. "Since he can no longer defend himself, I shall undertake that task. As evidence against him, we have the frantic claim of a woman charged with drowning her husband. I have also heard it said that, as a widower, the mayor was susceptible to carnal temptation. These same voices would have it that his death, following so closely upon the trial at which he presided, indicates that he was not wholly free of guilt. In Mayor Garde's favor let me point out once again that he was neither charged nor found guilty of any fault, nor did he confess to any. He remained single out of love and respect for his dead wife. Add to this a decade of public service to Gorgeana and to Maine as an agent, alderman, town clerk, recorder of the court, magistrate, and finally mayor. In my mind and heart, Roger Garde is innocent of any fault in this unfortunate matter. When you have weighed all the evidence, I trust that you will reach the same conclusion."

His message was well received. Rumors of the mayor's involvement with Catherine Cornish subsided, to be replaced by news from England that the Royalist cause had suffered further setbacks with Cromwell's victory over the King's army at Naseby. Forces loyal to the Parliament had also occupied Bristol. Gorges was a captive, though he was being treated with courtesy. In response to these events delegates throughout the province of Maine convened in Gorgeana and reconfirmed Richard Vines as deputy governor.

Meanwhile, Hull was engaged in private negotiations to purchase forty acres of marshland on the coast north of the city; and he inquired into the price of cattle. He realized it was probably a futile gesture, but he had to prepare for any eventuality. The farmer who sold him the land left at once for Massachusetts. Hull was surprised, but he gave the matter little thought.

* * *

Following the trial and execution of Catherine Cornish, young Joseph took to frequenting the tavern. This aggravated his chronic illness, and that autumn Hull presided at the funeral of his first-born child. In the weeks that followed, family members came to Gorgeana to express their sympathy and support. Hull derived some comfort from their visits, but the loss of his son weighed heavily on his spirit. He was often vexed by young Joseph's mismanagement of the cattle business in Barnstable and, more recently by his profligate actions in Gorgeana. Yet Joseph had helped to build the house in Weymouth, and he had facilitated the relocation to Hingham and Mattakeese and, more recently, to Maine. Kneeling alone in the tiny cemetery behind the chapel, Hull's thoughts drifted to the grave in Somerset where Anne was buried. He wondered if he would ever see England again.

His sorrow was alleviated by the steady growth of his family. Agnes gave birth to a boy, whom they named Samuel; and Elizabeth presented him with a grandson. He still awaited that bold stroke by Gorges that would create the diocese of Maine. But Ashton Court was wrapped in silence.

* * *

In 1646 Parliament replaced the commission that had sought to revoke the charter of the Massachusetts Bay Company with one more friendly to the Puritans. Vines promptly resigned and departed for Barbados. Henry Jocelyn was named deputy governor in his place. Jocelyn had come to Maine sixteen years earlier as an agent for Sir Ferdinando and the Laconia Company. He was much less belligerent than Vines. As magistrate on the provincial court, he had carried a message to Cleeve protesting his authority to govern that portion of Maine included in the Lygonia province. Their talks were friendly, though the results remained inconclusive.

No sooner had Jocelyn taken office, than Hull's longstanding friendship with Edward Godfrey was placed in jeopardy. The dispute arose over the marshland Hull had purchased. Godfrey claimed he had a lien on the land and had not authorized the farmer to sell it, while Hull maintained he had bought the land in good faith.

"I should not be penalized for the misdeeds of a man who has fled the province and is no longer available to make retribution," Hull told the judge hearing the case. "I submit that Mr. Godfrey should prosecute the real culprit in this case and seek to regain from him any losses he may have incurred."

"The matter at issue," Godfrey retorted, "is not my losses, but the right of the farmer to sell land he did not own. I seek no repayment from Mr. Hull. What I seek is the return of my land."

Their debate grew more heated until the judge intervened to say he had sufficient evidence and would consider the matter. His decision was in favor of Godfrey, and Hull was deprived of the land he had purchased as insurance against the future. As a result of these proceedings, Godfrey ceased to be a welcome guest in his house.

Jocelyn was reelected deputy governor in 1647. That summer Bursley brought news that Sir Ferdinando Gorges was dead. From the deck of the *Aurora* Hull stared at the slowly moving waters of the Agamenticus River – Sir Ferdinando's vanity had not extended beyond the city.

"Did he die in prison?" he asked.

"No," Bursley said. "He expired peacefully at Ashton Phillips."

"His dreams and mine die with him," Hull said as if in benediction.

"What will you do now?" Bursley asked.

"I've thought at times of returning to England," Hull said, "but what would I do there? I'm out of favor and out of fashion."

"I understand that Thomas Gorges is now a member of Parliament," Bursley said. "Perhaps he can help you."

"I find it strange that the relative of such an ardent Royalist should take the opposite side, but it's good to have an ally in the enemy's camp."

Hull was still mulling over his future plans when he received word of another death. The widow of his brother William had died in

Colyton, and he was heir to lands at North Farm and Goosemere. With the King in custody on the Isle of Wight, Hull concluded that the government and the church faced an uncertain future.

"I've decided to go to England and settle the estate," he told Agnes.

Her hands trembled at the news, and some of the water in the pot she was holding spilled onto the floor. "How long will that take?" she asked.

"I'm not sure. Six months. Perhaps as much as a year."

"Will we take the children with us?"

Hull smiled at this not so subtle reminder of the promise he had made to take her home. "The passage is costly, but we can take the young ones."

Agnes seemed satisfied with that; but as their arrangements for the trip progressed, she expressed some concern as to whether Naomi should go with them or stay behind.

"Temperance and Griselda can care for her," Hull said.

"They're both of marriageable age and have already agreed to look after the two older boys," Agnes said. "It's not right to burden them with an eight-year-old girl."

"Perhaps we can find someone else to take her in," Hull said.

"Whom do you have in mind?"

"I was thinking of Joanna or Elizabeth."

"They both have young children of their own to worry about. Besides, Joanna is all alone when Bursley is at sea, and Cochecho is on the edge of the wilderness."

"So what do you suggest?"

"We might take her with us," Agnes said.

They left it at that. In the days that followed, he sought for some solution that would be acceptable to Agnes. It wasn't so much the cost of an extra passage that led him to seek an alternative. In his mind this was to be a brief visit; and Agnes was pregnant. He didn't want to burden her with the care of more children than necessary. They would take Ruth and Samuel with them, but he was set on finding a temporary home for Naomi. One day he announced that he had business in Ipswich, a day's ride to the south.

"What business have you in Massachusetts?" Agnes asked.

"I'll tell you when I get back," Hull said.

His business was with Samuel Symonds, a magistrate in Ipswich who was somewhat older than Hull. Following the death of his father, he had disposed of his inheritance and emigrated with his family to New England. As a deputy to the General Court, he supported Hull in his futile defense of Ralph Mousall. They had remained in contact, meeting once when Hull was preaching in Salem, and again when Bursley's ship made port in Ipswich on the voyage to Maine.

Hull's business concerned Naomi, but he saw no purpose in telling Agnes until he determined that such an arrangement was feasible. He had delivered two steers to Symonds when he disposed of his cattle business in Barnstable. Payment had been deferred until Symonds had the means, or until Hull had a specific need. That time had now arrived.

Symonds readily agreed to take Naomi into his household, and the arrangements were soon concluded to Hull's satisfaction. Riding home, he framed his strategy for convincing Agnes that the girl would be safe and well cared for in Ipswich. He understood her desire to take Naomi with them; but the girl was rather frail, and the voyage was long and hard. He didn't know how long it would take to settle affairs in Colyton, or how much he might benefit from the transaction. Having Naomi with them would be a worry for him and an additional burden on Agnes. Armed with these arguments, he broached the subject as soon as he got home.

Agnes sat calmly at the table, her attention focused on a sock she was darning. Hull paced up and down in front of the hearth as he described the arrangements he had made in Ipswich.

"Symonds has a large house, as well as a daughter Naomi's age," he concluded. "I'm sure she'll be happy there."

"I know the voyage would be hard on her," Agnes said. "I'm just afraid she'll think we're abandoning her, even if it's only for a short time."

"If we have to extend our visit, or if we decide to stay in England, we can send for her," Hull said to clinch the issue.

Agnes stopped mending and looked up at him. "Is there a chance we might stay?" she asked, her voice at once hopeful.

"Much will depend on whether the King can regain control. I also want to assess the impact of Gorges' death on the future of Maine. We won't be able to judge that until we arrive. As it now stands, I fully expect to return to Maine after I complete my business in Colyton. That's why I want to travel as unencumbered as possible."

"I'm glad to be going home, if only for a visit," Agnes said. "I'll speak to Naomi and make her understand that we do love her and that this separation is only temporary."

A commotion outside the house drew them into the street. Men on horseback were riding westward out of the city Others were paddling their dugout canoes upstream.

"What's happening?" Hull called out.

"The manor house! It's on fire!"

When Hull arrived at Point Christian, the once proud mansion, designed as a residence for Sir Ferdinando Gorges, was in ruins. Godfrey approached him as he stood staring at the smoldering ashes.

"It's the end of an era," he stated solemnly.

"In more ways than one," Hull replied.

Fifteen

"We still have a King, even though he's in exile."
(Launceston, Cornwall, 1648-1656)

In the summer of 1648 Hull booked passage for England. Landing in Plymouth, he proceeded directly to Colyton where he settled Agnes and the children before tending to business. William had been dead for twenty years. Although his widow continued to occupy the house and property, there were claims against the estate and questions about certain provisions in the will. While Hull sought to straighten these matters out, England was engulfed in renewed conflict among rival political factions.

From his place of confinement on the Isle of Wight, King Charles had turned again to the Scots, promising to impose Presbyterianism in England in exchange for an army to fight against the forces of Parliament. This led to a Scottish invasion and to Royalist uprisings in the Midlands and in Wales. The fighting culminated in Cromwell's victory over the Scots at Preston. Angered by the King's unceasing efforts to prolong the fighting, the Army denounced him as a man of blood. But members of Parliament who supported the monarchy attempted once more to negotiate with him.

Colyton was not immune from this conflict. Cromwell's army had long since subdued active resistance in Devon, but royalist sentiment among the populace remained strong. With his future prospects in Maine dependent on the outcome of this struggle, Hull decided to delay his return to New England until the warring parties resolved their differences. Meanwhile, to support his family he sought a temporary post as minister. He tried to contact Bishop Hall, only to learn that the bishop had been evicted from his palace in Exeter and was himself a supplicant.

"It bodes ill for the future of England when a man of Hall's caliber is obliged to suffer such indignities," he told Agnes.

"Is there no one you can turn to?" she asked.

"I've written to Thomas Gorges and await his reply. But there is little likelihood that he will be able to help me. Such temporary appointments are beyond the purview of the authorities in London."

"Perhaps he can get you a permanent post."

Hull noted the eagerness in her voice. "I suppose he might, but I'm not ready for that. We must wait and see whether the Parliament reaches some compromise that will restore the King to power. In that event we can all return to Maine."

"Is that likely to happen?"

"It depends on whether the Army or the Parliament gains the upper hand. I hope Parliament prevails, but I'm prepared for the worst."

A week later Hull received word indirectly of a post in Launceston. He assumed Thomas Gorges was responsible but remained cautious. With Agnes about to give birth, he traveled to Cornwall alone and was pleased to find others like himself who respected Bishop Hall and sympathized with his plight. On his return he informed Agnes that he had been offered the post of vicar at St. Mary Magdalene. Christmas found the family settled in the rectory at

Launceston. And early in January Agnes bore a son, whom they named Reuben.

The church of St. Mary Magdalene boasted a square tower some three hundred years old. The main building dated from the sixteenth century and had three naves made of Cornish granite. A statue of the saint with her pot of ointment stood at one end of the church, and carvings on the exterior walls depicted various plants from which the ointment was made. Viewing these relics of Catholicism, Hull thought it odd that so much effort had been concentrated on commemorating a woman reputed to be a prostitute.

The walled city of Launceston was situated on the Tamar river. It had three gates, with Dunheved castle commanding the approaches from the east. The castle and the adjacent guildhall served as a seat for the regional assizes. The city reminded Hull of Exeter, and he commiserated once more with the plight of Bishop Hall. St. Mary Magdalene was nominally Anglican, but he knew that his words and actions would be subject to scrutiny and censure in light of the growing Puritan influence. He relied on his experience in New England to see him through.

January proved a momentous time for England as well. Angered by Parliament's willingness to negotiate further with the King, the Army marched on London. They proceeded to purge Parliament of Presbyterians and Royalists who wanted to retain the monarchy with reduced powers. The remaining seventy-five members were ordered to set up a High Court of Justice to try King Charles for treason. The trial opened on January 20, but the King declined to answer the charges against him and refused to recognize the authority of the court. The Commissioners labeled him a "tyrant, traitor, murderer, and public enemy" and found him guilty of high treason. On January 30 he was beheaded on a scaffold at Whitehall palace.

The execution of King Charles was condemned by every monarch in Europe, who saw it as a grave threat to the established order. The dignity he exhibited at the trial had won him much public sympathy; and to avoid any disorder, he was buried at Windsor rather than Westminster Abby.

Dismayed by these events, Hull unburdened himself to Agnes. "Laud is dead. Sir Ferdinando is dead. King Charles is dead. The Army controls the government. The future of England appears to be uncertain at best."

Agnes looked up from the rabbit stew she was preparing – a gift from a parishioner. "We're safe here in Launceston, aren't we?" she asked.

"For the time being," Hull assured her. "We can only wait until all this turmoil is resolved and we have a new king. Charles's son is the rightful heir; but he's presently in Scotland, and there is great animosity against the Presbyterians. Having deposed one king, the Army and what's left of the Parliament may decide not to install another in his place. That may well lead to a resumption of the fighting. We shall have to remain in England until our future path is more clearly visible."

Agnes wiped her hands in her apron and embraced him. "I'm glad to remain, but what of the children in Maine? Can we send for them?"

"Time enough to think about that when I know where my destiny lies – here in Cornwall or in New England."

"I worry about Naomi," Agnes said. "How long will Mr. Symonds be willing to keep her? Perhaps we can make other arrangements."

"If she is happy in Ipswich," Hull said, "I see no reason why she shouldn't stay on. I'll write to Bursley and ask him to look in on her. He can explain our situation to Symonds and work out a satisfactory agreement."

Several months passed before they received a reply from Bursley. He began by conveying greetings from Joanna and the children. "If you have not already heard of it," he went on, "allow me to inform you that John Winthrop is dead; but I see little advantage accruing to Maine from his demise. Parliament has confirmed Sir Alexander Rigby's title to Lygonia, which greatly strengthens Cleeve's position. When he heard about it, Henry Jocelyn resigned aa deputy governor. Godfrey has been elected in his place. For the moment the two rival provinces exist side by side in relative peace, while Massachusetts remains neutral. But no one can say how long that will last."

He went on to address the mission Hull had imposed in him. "I put in recently at Ipswich and am pleased to report that Naomi is in good spirits and seems content with her lot. Symonds is willing to keep her on as a companion for his daughter until you return to Maine. As for the boys, they are happy and well cared for in Gorgeana. They eagerly await your return home, as do Joanna and I and the rest of the family."

Agnes seemed reluctant to credit Bursley's glowing account, but she agreed to continue the arrangement with Symonds. "Promise me you'll send for Naomi if we stay in England," she said.

"You have my promise," Hull replied, "but you must remember that none of your children – save Reuben – were born in England."

"That will soon change," Agnes said, placing a hand on her stomach. Hull embraced her until she pushed him away. "If I don't finish this stew," she cautioned, "we won't eat tonight."

* * *

Following the execution of King Charles, civil strife broke out in Scotland and Ireland. Cromwell harshly suppressed an alliance of Royalist and Irish confederate forces. Meanwhile, Scots who were fearful of the newly declared Commonwealth, joined with Royalists in offering the Scottish crown to Prince Charles. In response to this new threat Cromwell invaded Scotland, captured Edinburgh, and advanced north toward Perth. In response, Charles moved his army south into England, where he hoped to gain popular support. Cromwell followed and defeated the Scots at Worcester. Fighting dragged on until 1652, when under a tender of union Scotland was granted thirty seats in a united Parliament, and Prince Charles sought refuge on the continent.

Launceston remained relatively peaceful throughout this period of renewed conflict. Under the Commonwealth, ministers who held posts once controlled by the royal court were replaced by clerics with Puritan leanings. Although his position was beyond the reach of Parliament, Hull felt much the same beleaguerment as when he arrived in New England.

Agnes was settled comfortably in the vicarage, built of granite that matched the church. Since her return to England, she had given birth to three boys – Reuben, Ephraim, and Isaac. A girl, Priscilla, born in 1652, lived less than three months. With a wife and five children at home and a reasonably secure position as minister, Hull was content to bide his time. The fact that Agnes was constantly pregnant ended any talk of returning to Maine. She saw it as a deliberate strategy on his part, but Hull denied the charge. Occasional letters from New England assured them that Hopewell and Benjamin were becoming more independent, and that Naomi was well cared for in Ipswich.

In the summer of 1653 the equanimity of their life in Launceston was shattered by the death of two-year-old Isaac. Agnes was disconsolate at the death of two children only a year apart. Hull assured her that he had no desire to add further to the family. She seemed relieved, but continued to grieve throughout the autumn and winter.

That fall eight women suspected of witchcraft were transported from the west of Cornwall to stand trial in Launceston. The trial was held in Dunheved castle within sight of the witches' tower where, according to legend, several witches had been burned to punish them for consorting with Satan. Hull placed no credence in such stories; but he did attend one session of the trial, when a rumor spread that the jurors appeared likely to find the women guilty and sentence them to be hanged. He sought permission to address the court, not so much in their defense, but in an effort to bring an element of reason into the proceedings. The women were quiet and withdrawn, and they displayed only a modest interest as he rose to speak.

"I do not deny that Satan exists," he began. "The Bible clearly attests on numerous occasions to his presence in the world. He manifests himself as a tempter or an unclean spirit. As such, he is to be resisted or driven out. But nowhere in the Bible is there any indication that he can be summoned or enticed to do the will of a human being, whether through potions or incantations or spells. Satan's aims are much grander than that. His goal is to overthrow God and to establish his own realm. To that end he is permitted to afflict mankind, to lure women and men along a path that leads to eternal damnation. But like God and His angels, Satan is a spirit, an evil spirit but a spirit nonetheless. God bids us to heed His voice, but we cannot command Him to speak. In like manner, we are admonished to resist the ploys of the devil; but he is not subject to our command."

Hull glanced about to gauge the effect of his words. The judge's features had wrinkled into a scowl. The jurors appeared to pay attention. The eight women exhibited no emotion. Hull pressed on with what was turning into a sermon. Well, so be it, he thought.

"You may reason that if Christians can pray to God to grant their wishes, a witch may logically pray to the devil for that same purpose. And if Christians pray for the speedy recovery of a relative or spouse, witches may beseech the devil to inflict pain and suffering on someone they have come to hate. But prayer, whether for good or evil, is by its nature a spiritual exercise. Its efficacy cannot be measured by human standards. If these women had simply prayed to the devil, they would not be here in this court. They are accused of performing specific acts toward a specific end. I maintain that their actions are spiritually neutral. They are comparable to those trappings of popery that the Church has rightfully proscribed. We don't chastise Catholics for using statues and beads and holy water. We simply pity them for the weakness of their faith. Neither should we punish these women for using potions, pins, and poppets, props that have no efficacy or value. We must resist the snares of Satan, but we must fight that battle in the realm of the spirit, not in this courtroom. Our laws are meant to govern how a man acts toward his neighbor, not how he deals with God or Satan. I thank you for hearing me out."

Hull left the castle without waiting for the verdict. He was satisfied that he had expressed what all rational men believed. He had done his bit to counteract the mass hysteria that often prevailed in such cases. Word reached him later that six of the women were released following the trial. The other two were confined for some weeks in prison, but no one was hanged or burned at the stake.

* * *

Hull kept an eye on political developments in London. With the rightful heir in exile, the Parliament split into factions. In December the Army intervened to name Oliver Cromwell the Lord Protector of England.

"What does it mean to be a Lord Protector?" Agnes asked.

Hull watched as she rehung some drapes she had taken down to clean. To assuage her grief, she sought to fill her days with household tasks of dubious necessity. On his part he found himself devoting more time than usual to his sermons and to the details of church administration.

"It means the Army is in full control of the government," he said. "Cromwell is a virtual dictator – like a king. Parliament has little power."

"How does that affect us?" she asked.

"Launceston is far from London," he said. "We should have no problems, as long as I confine my ministry to spiritual matters."

Agnes stepped down from her chair and stood back to view her handiwork. Satisfied that the drapes were evenly hung, she focused her attention on her husband.

"Does that mean we're staying in England?" she asked.

"We gain nothing by returning. The Province of Maine was annexed by Massachusetts a year ago, and Gorgeana is now the town of York."

"It's just as if Sir Ferdinando never existed," Agnes said.

"His son inherited the claim to the province, but he has shown little interest in pursuing his father's dream. With no guidance from England, Godfrey had to sign the articles of confederation."

"I'm glad to stay in Launceston," Agnes said, "but Naomi will think we've forgotten her. She's only thirteen. We can't abandon her to whatever fate a stranger may decree."

"Symonds may seem a stranger to you," Hull said, "but I know and respect him. Besides, Naomi is used to living in his household. If she wants to join us in Launceston, I can send for her as soon as things settle down. But if she wants to stay in Ipswich, I'll work something out with Symonds."

"A girl her age can hardly know what she wants," Agnes said.

"Still, forcing her to come to England benefits no one," Hull said. "I shall write to her and to Symonds. Once we know her feelings, we can better judge what course to pursue."

"I shall write to her as well," Agnes said. "I want her to know that we miss her, and that we want her here with us."

"Fair enough," Hull said.

"How do you like the drapes?" Agnes asked.

* * *

Naomi responded that she felt at home in Ipswich and had no great desire to go to England, but she would accede to the wishes of her parents. Symonds wrote that she was one of the family and that he was prepared to keep her in Ipswich, if that was what Hull desired.

"Perhaps we can visit her," Agnes said when she read the letters.

"An extended absence right now may jeopardize my position," Hull said. "Perhaps when the children are older and England has returned to a state of normalcy."

"We may have to wait a long time for that," Agnes said.

"We still have a king," Hull said, "even though he's in exile."

The family in New England continued to grow. Joanna had three daughters and a son. Tristram and Blanche had two children of their own and lived in Barnstable. Temperance had married John Bickford and lived in Oyster River. Elizabeth and John Heard were in Cochecho with their six children. Dorothy had married Oliver Kent and moved to Dover. Griselda was left alone in York to care for Hopewell and Benjamin. They were now seventeen and fourteen – old enough to look after themselves, as Hull pointed out. Agnes agreed, but her concern for Naomi was undiminished.

As Lord Protector, Cromwell sought to unite the country by pressing the war against Spain. He had a lesser interest in domestic and church affairs, and his influence was considerably weaker in Cornwall than elsewhere. Still, Anglican clergy who remained loyal to the King were prosecuted, and Hull was obliged to take care lest he give the authorities some cause to suspect him of harboring royalist sympathies.

He had little affection for the governing Protectorate, and he saw clearly that it would become ever more difficult for him to carry out his ministry. The conditions were similar to those that led him to emigrate to New England, yet strangely inverted. Then he had been chastised for not adhering to the doctrine and practice of the Church of England. Now he was in danger of being prosecuted for any overt leanings in that direction.

In this state of mind, he journeyed to Sennen at the western tip of Cornwall. Together with St. Levan, Sennen came under the Deanery of St. Buryan. The current Dean, one John Weeks, preferred London to the remote area called Land's End. He had served the Duke of Buckingham as domestic chaplain, and had supported royalist forces opposed to the Parliament. His position under the Protectorate was precarious at best. Hull learned these particulars from an associate in Exeter. He determined to explore the ground and stake a claim in case his situation in Launceston became untenable.

Agnes frowned when he told her. "I'm quite content here," she said. "I have no desire to move to the ends of the earth."

"Nor have I," Hull assured her. "But one misstep, and I may lose my post in Launceston. I need to prepare for any eventuality."

"Do what you must," Agnes said. "You know my feelings."

Hull stayed two weeks in Sennen. The church was only a mile from the westernmost point of England. The terrain was windswept and barren. The rugged coastline with its high cliffs and sheltered coves reminded him of Maine. The state of affairs in the parish was far less attractive. The Deanery of St. Buryan had not seen a resident Dean for more than three centuries, and the church records were in deplorable condition. Guided only by occasional itinerant ministers, the congregation had strayed from the straight path of Anglican doctrine and practice. Hull also visited the more impressive churches at St. Levan and St. Buryan, both within walking distance of Sennen, receiving a warm reception from everyone he met. He left with the feeling that he would be more than welcome if he should decide to return. But he saw too that his task there would not be an easy one.

Agnes listened to his report with some trepidation at first, and she appeared relieved as he detailed some of the drawbacks. "You need have no fear," he concluded. "Land's End holds little attraction for me. I shall seek instead to make my post in Launceston more secure."

"I'm glad to hear it," Agnes said.

His efforts were so successful that in the fall of 1655 Cromwell's council granted him an augmentation of fifty pounds for the education of twenty boys in Launceston. And in December, when Cromwell decreed that marriages no longer had to take place in a church, he performed the first civil marriage in Launceston. His responsibilities as a teacher restricted his ability to travel, and there was no more talk of a trip to New England. The four young ones occupied all of Agnes' time and energies. She seemed resigned to the continued separation from her three older children.

* * *

Hull never knew for sure how his appointment at St. Buryan came about. A year had elapsed since his visit to Sennen, and his tenure at St. Mary Magdalene appeared to be secure. Cromwell had abolished all deaneries and royal peculiars; but Hull had lost contact with Thomas Gorges, and he had no friends with political influence who could have recommended him .

"Someone I met there must have petitioned through church channels for my appointment," he told Agnes when he received the offer.

"But you said you had no intention of moving to Land's End," Agnes reminded him. "Have you changed your mind?" It was winter, and she was knitting a sweater for Samuel, who had outgrown his and was ready to pass it on to Reuben.

"It would be a permanent post and far removed from London."

"Far indeed!" Agnes said. "It's the end of the world!"

"Only of Cornwall. We'll be quite comfortable in St. Buryan, and we needn't move until spring."

Agnes was silent for a moment, as if she were reckoning the days. "Three months," she muttered. "I've had to pack more quickly in the past. At least this time I'm not pregnant."

Sixteen

"Any assistance I provide must be in secret."
(Launceston, Cornwall, 1656)

Preparations for the move to St. Buryan were scarcely under way when, late in January, George Fox and two companions were arrested and imprisoned at Launceston to await trial at the Lenten assize. Fox was well known for relishing disputation and for his ability to confound opponents. The city was awash in rumors about the new religion that required no intermediary between man and God. It was said that Fox had received divine inspiration for his teaching, that he met with Cromwell and gained a measure of tolerance but not approval for his Society of Friends, and that his arrest was on civil rather than religious grounds.

The prison was on Hull's rounds, but in response to his first inquiry he was told that Fox had no need of a priest and no desire to see one. He left it at that. To persist would draw attention to himself and might jeopardize his appointment at St. Buryan. But early in March rumors surfaced regarding the conditions under which Fox and his companions were being held and the treatment to which they were subjected.

"I want to help them," he told Agnes, "but any assistance I provide must be in secret."

"What do you propose to do?"

"First I must get the facts about how they are being treated. I can't act on rumor alone."

"I'll speak with some women in town," Agnes said. "They know what goes on in the prison."

"That would be most helpful," Hull said, surprised at her interest.

Agnes reported that the three men had refused to pay for their keep and that of their horses. "The jailor pockets their money but fails to provide the services. When they ceased paying him, he got angry and cast them in Doomsdale. The old woman I spoke to described it as a filthy hole where they keep condemned murderers."

"I've heard of the place, but I've never seen it," Hull said. "How long have they been there?"

"A week at least. The woman said she gave them a candle and a bit of straw to put on the ground. When they burned the straw to take away the stench, the jailor dumped excrement in the hole to put out the fire. I can't imagine such a thing."

Agnes soon brought further news. "The church warden's wife sent her daughter with some meat for the prisoners. The jailor had her arrested for breaking into the prison. Are people not allowed to bring in food?"

"They have to bribe the jailor first," Hull said.

Launceston prison was a stone structure on the castle grounds at Northgate. The jailor was a thin sallow-faced man well up in years. He had recently buried his second wife, amid talk that he drove her to an early grave. Hull put no stock in such rumors. His past dealings with the jailor had been less than amicable, so he stuck to the issue at hand.

"I've come to inquire about the three Friends who are awaiting trial," he said after a cursory greeting.

"You mean the Quakers," the jailor said. "They can't have visitors. Orders of the court."

Hull started to assert his rights as a minister, but thought better of it. He had not come to make Fox's acquaintance. He simply wanted to improve the conditions under which Fox was being held prisoner. To do that he had to deal with the jailor.

"Do you also have orders to withhold any food brought to them?" Hull asked. "If that is the case, I shall speak to the mayor."

"You mean that girl who was trying to smuggle food in without my knowing it. I'm bound to inspect all packages. I was only doing my duty."

"The church warden says the prisoners aren't getting the food he sends, food that he pays you handsomely to deliver. I can report that as well."

"No need for that. I was just trying to teach her a lesson."

"Then you'll drop your charges against her?"

"If she'll follow the rules from now on."

"I'll see to that," Hull agreed, "if you'll agree to deliver the food that's brought in for Fox and his companions."

"A poor man has to make a living somehow."

"How you make a living is your business – and God's."

"They'll get their food," the jailor said with a sigh of resignation – and obvious relief.

"Another thing," Hull said. "I would strongly advise you to let the prisoners clean out that hole where you're keeping them."

With that he departed, leaving the jailor with a surprised look on his sallow face. The next day Agnes reported that conditions for the prisoners had improved, at least temporarily.

* * *

"Will you attend the trial?" Agnes asked as she cleared the table after the evening meal.

It was the last week in March, and the rectory was littered with chests. All was in readiness for the pending move to St. Buryan.

"I must," Hull said. "But merely as an observer. Fox can speak for himself. I just want to see the man and hear his response to the charges against him."

"What is he accused of?" Agnes asked.

"Distributing papers that disturb the peace. Traveling in Cornwall without a pass. Refusal to take an oath of good behavior."

"You've been careful so long," Agnes said. "Why risk it all now just to satisfy your curiosity?"

"There's no risk in attending the trial."

"People who see you there will think you approve of his ideas. It would be better to let justice take its course."

"Justice can be rather fickle under the Lord Protector," Hull said. "They may not release Fox and his companions."

"How is that your concern?"

"England is too prone to imprison a man for his religious convictions. That's the unstated charge against Fox. Besides, three months in prison is punishment enough for whatever offense he may have committed."

"The man frightens me," Agnes said. "He makes himself out to be a prophet, and he claims God will preserve him from harm. They say the soldiers plotted to kill him on his way to prison, but he knew all about it and foiled their plans."

"You know a great deal about George Fox."

"Just what I hear in the market. The women are all afraid of him."

"The plot you refer to occurred in Bodmin," Hull said. "Nothing of that sort will happen in Launceston."

"At least, thanks to you, he's no longer in Doomsdale."

"I fear it's only a temporary respite," Hull said. "Public sentiment is against him, and what he says at the trial may inflame it even more."

* * *

The Lenten assize was held early in April in the hall of Dunheved castle, with the Lord Chief Justice of England, a Welshman named John Glynne, presiding. Also on the bench was Peter Ceely, mayor of St. Ives, where Fox and his companions were arrested.

From his place in the gallery Hull had an unobstructed view of the proceedings. Fox was brought in first, followed by his associates, Edward Pyot of Bristol and William Salt of London. Hull's attention was focused on George Fox. He studied him closely, searching for a physical characteristic that might distinguish him as a founder of a new religious movement, some feature that might set him apart from others; but he saw nothing very unusual about the man.

Fox was several inches short of six feet tall. His broad shoulders were accentuated by a plain straight outer garment of brown homespun that buttoned down the front and reached to his knees. His long dark hair fell naturally over his shoulders, partly concealing the white scarf he wore with a single tie about his neck. He was clean shaven, with a prominent nose and receding chin. His eyes were bright and alert; and he glanced about as he entered, as if eager to take in everything in the room. A sugar loaf hat with its high flat crown and wide brim lent a squashed appearance to his youthful face. He was no more than thirty – far too young to have gained such notoriety, Hull thought.

His companions were similarly dressed. They stood quietly while Justice Glynne took his seat. Then Fox proclaimed, "Peace be amongst you." His deep booming voice carried clearly to every corner of the room.

"Why do you not put off your hats?" Glynne asked. The three men made no move. "Put off your hats," he repeated. Still no response. "The court commands you to put off your hats."

At this point Fox spoke up. "Where did ever any magistrate, king, or judge, from Moses to Daniel, command any to put off their hats, when they came before him in his court? If the law of England doth command any such thing, show me that law."

"I do not carry my law books on my back," Glynne said.

"Tell me where it is printed in any statute book, that I may read it."

"Take him away," Glynne commanded.

The jailor led the three men off. Was the trial to end so soon and in this fashion? Hull was about to leave when the judge reentered the hall and called for the prisoners to be brought back.

"Where had they hats, from Moses to Daniel?" Glynne asked when they stood again before him. "Come, answer me. I have you fast now."

"Thou mayest read in the third of Daniel," Fox said, "that the three children were cast into the fiery furnace by Nabuchednezzar's command, with their coats, their hose, and their hats on."

"Take them away!" Glynne ordered again.

So ended the proceedings for the first day. Hull told Agnes about the impasse that evening over dinner.

"Why would they not remove their hats?" she asked. "Have they no respect for authority?"

"It's their custom. Neither will they bow, kneel, or swear an oath. They claim such forms of respect are reserved for God alone, and a judge has no right to demand them. There is some logic in their position."

"Will the judge give in to them?"

"He can't afford to do that," Hull said, "but he's not likely to argue scripture again. Fox appears to know his Bible."

At the next session of the assize, Justice Glynne adopted another course. Producing a printed sheet, he told the clerk to give it to Fox. "Are you the author of this seditious paper?" he demanded.

Fox looked at the paper without taking it. "Let it be read out in open court that I may hear it. If it is mine, I will own it and stand by it."

"Take it in your hand and look at it," Glynne said patiently. "Then tell me if it is yours."

Fox's hands remained at his side. "I desire that it be read, that all the country may hear it and judge whether there is any sedition in it or not. For if there is, I am willing to suffer for it."

After conferring with others on the bench, Glynne told the clerk to read the paper aloud. It was a long admonition against swearing an oath. Thus far, Hull reflected, Fox was clearly in control of the proceedings.

"I do own it to be my paper," Fox said when the clerk had finished, "and so might everyone here, unless they would deny the scripture. For is this not scripture language, the very words and commands of Christ and the Apostle, which all true Christians ought to obey?"

Hull saw nothing seditious in the wording of the paper. He waited for Glynne to reply; but the judge was apparently of like mind and let the subject drop, focusing again on the hats. He ordered the jailor to remove them. But when they were handed to their owners, all three of the men promptly put them on again.

"I desire to know for what cause we have lain in prison these nine weeks," Fox said before the judge could issue another order, "seeing that the court now objects to nothing but our hats. It is an honor God will lay in the dust, though you make so much ado about it. It is an honor which is of men, which men seek one of another, and is a mark of unbelievers."

"You forget that, as Lord Chief Justice of England, I represent the Lord Protector's person," Glynne said sternly.

Hull winced at this recourse to pomposity. The judge was clearly at a loss as to how to deal with this man. He looked at his associates on the bench, as if he were pleading for help.

Fox seized upon the opportunity afforded him. "We desire only that you do us justice for our wrongful imprisonment. Instead, you have brought indictments framed against us. They say that we came by force and arms, and in a hostile manner, into this court; when in truth we were taken up in our journey without cause by Mayor Ceely."

"May it please you, my lord," Ceely broke in, "this man went aside with me and told me how serviceable I might be for his design – that he could raise forty thousand men at an hour's warning, involve the nation in blood, and so bring in King Charles II. I would have aided him out of the country, but he would not go. I have a witness who will swear to it."

Hull regarded the charges as preposterous and was glad when the judge declined to examine Ceely's witness. Quick to press his advantage, Fox requested that the warrant committing him to prison be read in court, so all might hear the crimes of which he was accused. Glynne refused.

"It ought to be read, seeing it concerns my liberty and my life."

"It shall not be read," Glynne said.

But Fox was insistent. "It ought to be read, for if I have done anything worthy of death or of bonds, let all the country know it. Thou hast a copy of it," he said, turning to his companion Pyot. "Read it up."

"It shall not be read," the judge repeated. "Jailor, take him away. I'll see whether he or I shall be master."

The prisoners were led off. When they were brought back, Fox again requested that the warrant be read aloud. The justices were silent as Pyot read. "Peter Ceely, one of the justices of the peace of this county, to the keeper of His Highness's jail at Launceston, greeting."

Since copies of the warrant had been circulated before the trial, Hull was familiar with the charges. As the reading droned on, he silently congratulated Glynne for changing his mind. The request seemed in order and not unreasonable. Yet Hull also recognized that acceding to it was tantamount to an admission that Fox was indeed master in the court.

When the warrant had been read, Fox proceeded to question Mayor Ceely. "When and where did I take thee aside? Was not thy house full of rude people at our examination, so that I asked for a constable to keep the people civil? But if thou art my accuser, why sittest thou on the bench? It is not the place of accusers to sit with the judge. Thou oughtest to come down and stand by me, and look me in the face."

Hull considered it another point well taken. He expected Glynne to rule on the matter, but the judge remained silent. It began to dawn on Hull that Glynne's strategy was to let Fox talk until he said something to indict himself. If that was his plan, it had every chance of succeeding.

"Besides," Fox continued, "I would ask the judge and the justices whether Mayor Ceely is not also guilty of this treason, which he charges against me? He saith that he would have aided me out of the country, but I would not go. Do you not see plainly that Mayor Ceely is guilty of this plot and treason he talks of and hath made himself a party to it by desiring me to leave the country, demanding bail of me, and not charging me with this pretended treason till now, nor discovering it? But I abhor his words and am innocent of his devilish design."

"If it please you, my lord, to hear me," Ceely said when the judge made no reply, "this man gave me such a blow as I never had in my life."

"Mayor Ceely," Fox said, "art thou a justice of the peace, and tellest the judge in the face of the court and the country that I, a prisoner, struck thee? Prithee, where did I strike thee? And who is thy witness for that?"

"It was in the Castle Green," Ceely said, "and Captain Bradden was standing by when this man struck me."

"I desire his witness to be called," Fox said.

No one moved for a moment. Then Glynne nodded, and Bradden was brought into the court.

"Speak, Captain Bradden," "ox demanded. "Didst thou see me give Mayor Ceely such a blow as he saith?"

Bradden bowed his head and said nothing.

"Nay, speak up and let the court and the country hear, and let not bowing of the head serve the turn. If I have done so, then let the law be inflicted on me. I fear not sufferings, nor death itself, for I am an innocent man concerning all this charge."

When Bradden remained silent, Justice Glynne ordered the jailor to take the prisoners away. He fined them twenty marks each for not removing their hats and sentenced them to be kept in jail until they paid the fine.

* * *

Hull was stunned by the inconclusiveness of the trial and by the severity of the fine. Sixty marks was what he earned in a year. Fox would surely refuse to pay, even if he had the means. He would languish in jail for weeks or months. Was this English justice? Or was Glynne simply venting his vexation? Hull returned home feeling a certain sympathy for Fox and for the principles he had so vigorously defended.

"Fox was asking only for simple justice," he told Agnes as they retired for the night. He had been unusually quiet at the supper table.

The events of the trial occupied his mind – the vehemence of the defense, the lack of a meaningful prosecution, the unwarranted outcome. He thought of the three men in prison – perhaps back in Doomsdale. What had they done? What had been proved against them? They were there because of their beliefs and for no other reason.

"Can you do nothing else?" Agnes asked.

"Fox will surely place his case before the justices at the quarterly assizes in Bodmin," Hull said. "I could write to them stating my opinion of this last session in Launceston."

"Won't a letter draw attention to you?"

"It is my duty as a minister to declare this injustice. Besides, when the next assize meets, we'll be in St. Buryan."

Agnes did not question him further and was soon asleep. But Hull lay awake for some time, his mind too active for repose. What had made the deepest impression on him wasn't the trial and its outcome. It was the strength of character exhibited by George Fox. All Hull knew about the Society of Friends was that they wore simple garb, renounced violence, eschewed oaths, and sought spiritual guidance from an inner light. He found it hard to quarrel with the first three of these beliefs, but their claim that everyone, man or woman, was a minister to himself gave him pause. He saw in that assertion not only a threat to his profession, but a denial of divine revelation that was the root of Christianity. Yet these Friends didn't deny divine revelation. In fact, they remained ever open to it. They believed that God speaks, rather than God has spoken.

He had long respected a man's right to follow his own conscience in determining his relationship with God. It was this attitude that led him to tolerate the Puritan desire for reform. Lying in the dark, he told himself it was but a short step from that to acceptance of a direct communication with God. The saints had experienced visions of heaven, had seen and spoken to God. Was he prepared to exclude the common man from that communion? He saw Fox standing straight and determined before the judge, secure in his own beliefs, and felt obliged to ask himself if clergy were really needed. Did he perform a necessary function? Then he realized that however Fox might refer to himself, he too was essentially a minister, one who promulgates the word of God as it is revealed to him. Thus reconciled in spirit, he fell into a peaceful sleep.

In his letter to the justices at Bodmin, Hull was careful not to appear to support Fox. After pointing out some deficiencies in the proceedings at Launceston, he asked merely for a fair trial and a verdict based on the sum of the evidence presented. He learned later that Fox and his companions had been removed from Doomsdale on orders from the court at Bodmin. But they were not set free until September. News of their release from prison reached him at St. Buryan, where he was settling into his new life

Seventeen

"A wise man fastens upon truth wherever he finds it."
(St. Buryan, Cornwall, 1656-1659)

St. Buryan was about three miles inland, equidistant from Land's End and the south coast of Cornwall. In size and in character the village reminded Hull of St. Giles in Northleigh. However, the countryside was less wooded and became increasingly barren and rocky as one neared the ocean. He liked to walk along the cliffs on the south coast, and he would sit for hours at Land's End, watching the waves break against the rocks, peering out through the Atlantic fog, as if his gaze might penetrate all the way to Maine – now sadly a part of Massachusetts. He was content with his position, but his opinion of the Protectorate was unchanged. The Puritans, drunk with their power, had gone too far in restructuring the Church; and he was glad to be isolated and beyond their reach.

"I don't understand them," he told Agnes several months after their arrival in St. Buryan. She was clearing the table after the evening meal and did not pause in her work. "First they issue an edict stating that all who profess faith in God shall be protected in their religion. Then they appoint a commissioner for each county in

England to hear cases of ministers accused of plotting against the government. Anyone deemed scandalous, ignorant, or insufficient will be summarily ejected. What do they mean by insufficient? In God's eyes we are all insufficient."

"It doesn't matter what they mean," Agnes said. "You've done nothing like that, and you're certainly not plotting against anyone."

"I'm what they choose to call an ancient minister," Hull said, "one who returned from New England. But you're right. Here in St. Buryan I pose no threat to anyone."

He took care to reinforce that impression, concentrating his efforts on church matters and keeping his opinion of the government to himself. There was much to do in a parish so long deprived of spiritual guidance. He held regular services in each of the three churches covered by the deanery, and he instituted a program for building repair and for the maintenance of parish records. But most important, through his sermons and personal contacts with parishioners, he sought for ways to bring these stray sheep back into the fold.

News arrived sporadically from New England. Joanna, Temperance, Elizabeth, and Tristram were married with growing families. Tristram was master of a larger ship and was making regular voyages to the Caribbean. Dorothy was settled in Dover. Griselda was still unwed and living in York.

Agnes had even less word from the three children she left behind. Hopewell and Benjamin were doing well, though reports of their activities were sketchy and infrequent. Naomi's status in the home of Judge Symonds was now that of a semi-servant, insofar as she was expected to perform certain household duties in return for her keep. In her last letter she had adopted a brave voice, but Agnes thought she detected a hint that the girl was unhappy. She asked Bursley to check on her but had received no reply.

* * *

The parish of St. Buryan dated back to the tenth century and was dedicated by King Athelstan to Buriana, a holy woman from Ireland, in gratitude for his conquest of the Isles of Scilly off the coast of Cornwall. The church itself dated from the thirteenth century. Hull took pride in the fact that the stone tower was over ninety feet tall, as if the age and elevation of the building were linked in some way to his influence with the Almighty. The top of the tower resembled the battlements of a castle. From that vantage point he could see the entire coast around Land's End, as well as the church towers at St. Levan and Sennen. Looking over his domain, he felt that his position was safe and unassailable. With renewed confidence he set out to remedy the centuries of neglect that the parish had endured.

He held weekly services in all three of the churches. Sennen and St. Levan were an hour's walk from the rectory at St. Buryan. He enjoyed these walks, even in inclement weather. They cleared his mind and put an edge on his sermons. Each church had its own attraction for him. In St. Buryan he was at home, only a few steps from his family. Despite its barren surroundings, Sennen was but a short distance from Land's End, and on fine days he would stand on the rocks and gaze westward over the sea. He had failed to realize his dream in New England, and he wondered if the dream was still alive somewhere over the horizon.

But St. Levan was his favorite spot. It had a more sheltered and peaceful character. Situated on the south coast, it overlooked the fishing boats and cove of Porthuomo. The church was a century older than St. Buryan and steeped in tradition. It was said that the saint's name derived from Solomon, that he was the father of Saint Kybi, and that his body was interred in a small cemetery set into the cliff. There was also St. Levan's stone, a hemispheric rock the saint had split with his sword, predicting that when a mule laden with packs could pass through the cleft, the world would end. Hull put little stock in such legends; but young Samuel, who was going on eleven, seemed enthralled by the story and by the strange names of the local saints.

Saints were not all that occupied Samuel's mind. He listened to tales of a witch who had been executed in a nearby village for casting spells on her neighbors, and he examined an actual witch bottle used by a victim to retaliate against her tormentor. He knew that his father dismissed such stories or practices, but accounts of witchcraft involving swan feathers and poppets and fertilized eggs intrigued him.

He was also fascinated by the shipwrecks that occurred regularly along the south coast of Cornwall from Land's End eastward to Helford, Falmouth, and Penzance. These calamities were, for the most part, due to storms; and they spawned a breed of men known as wreckers who, upon hearing that a ship had gone on the rocks, put out in their small boats to salvage whatever cargo the ship contained. In St. Buryan it was just a job, like fishing or game keeping; but elsewhere along the south coast it was a profitable enterprise that attracted leading figures in the society. Sir John Killigrew, the vice admiral of Cornwall, had been charged with robbery, receiving stolen goods, and consorting with pirates. Wreckers were often tempted to cross the thin line between salvage and plunder, and Hull in his sermons stressed a respect for life and property. So he was not surprised by the story Samuel brought home late in the fall.

"I saw it all!" he cried as he burst into his father's study. He was panting for breath. "The wreckers spotted a sailor swimming ashore from the wreck. He looked almost dead as he staggered up out of the water. I thought they were going to help him, but instead they took his clothes and beat him until he ran off. It was terrible. I wanted to do something; but I was afraid to interfere. I ran all the way home."

"Sit down and catch your breath," Hull said. He placed his hands on his son's shoulders until the boy was calmer and breathing normally.

Samuel looked up at him. "What they did is wrong, isn't it?"

"Yes, it's wrong," Hull said, "and I do what I can to stop such things from happening. But men possessed by greed lose control of themselves and do things like you just saw. They may regret it later, but that doesn't excuse their actions."

"What will happen to the sailor?" Samuel asked with a sob.

"Someone will take him in and care for him," Hull said. "There are more good people than bad in the world. Always remember that."

"The men who go out to where the ship is wrecked, are they bad people? Are they stealing?" Samuel had ceased crying and seemed interested in acquiring more information. "One of them told me that anything washed away from a wreck belongs to whoever finds it."

"It's not that simple," Hull said. He wondered how much he ought to explain, how much the boy could grasp. "Their claim is based upon an ancient law of the sea that applies to wrecks with no survivors. King Charles ruled that watery items having no owner, whether on the surface or on the bottom, are the property of the crown; and he appointed the Lord Admiral to enforce his ruling. But Cromwell abolished that office, so the vice admirals for each county now keep the proceeds from shipwrecks."

"But this wreck had a survivor," Samuel said, "and the boatmen may have rescued others."

"I hope they did," Hull said. No point in burdening the boy with reports that wreckers were often more interested in plundering cargo than in saving lives. Such things had occurred elsewhere along the coast, but not in his parish – at least, not to his knowledge. Although Hull did not condone the plundering, he understood the temptation a shipwreck might provide for an impoverished population. But the stripping and beating of the sailor was a sign of lawlessness, and he determined to speak out against such criminal acts in his sermon on Sunday.

* * *

On their arrival in St. Buryan, Agnes had remarked that if they were any farther from London, they would no longer reside in England. Hull took it as a joke, for he was pleased to hold a post that seemed beyond the reach of Church and Crown. The rectory, long neglected, presented a challenge that Agnes struggled to overcome. Whenever they moved to a new place, he could rely on her to stifle any complaints until she had put their house in order. In St. Buryan that process occupied her for the better part of a year.

Ruth provided a willing hand in this endeavor. She was going on sixteen and eager to assist in the care of her three younger bothers. Her suntanned face and calloused hands bore evidence to the many hours she devoted to putting the grounds of the rectory in order, restoring the flower beds, and planting a vegetable garden. Agnes expressed some concern that the girl was working too hard and had no close friends.

Hull listened, but he saw no way to alter the situation. He attributed her behavior to a naturally awakening desire for a husband and family of her own. He was surprised when Agnes announced, "Ruth's problem is that she misses Naomi. They were inseparable as children in Gorgeana."

"They've been apart for eight years," Hull said. "Has Ruth expressed these feelings before?"

Agnes kept sorting patches for a quilt she was making. "She kept them to herself, but she's at an age when she needs a sister to confide in."

"She has you," Hull said.

Agnes smiled tolerantly at him. "It's not the same. Girls need to talk these things over with someone their own age."

Hull assumed these things were related to marriage and a husband. "Are you suggesting we send for Naomi?" he asked.

"It would help Ruth and put my mind at ease," Agnes said.

"Very well then," Hull said. "I'll contact Symonds and Bursley and ask them to arrange for her passage."

He expected Agnes to show some sign of joy. Instead, she looked down, and her hands clutched the patches of cloth in her lap. "Are you sure it's safe for a girl her age to travel alone? You know what conditions are like on those ships."

"Then I'll tell Bursley to deliver her himself," Hull said in evident exasperation. "I'm sure he has nothing better to do."

"Don't be angry with me. I was thinking that Benjamin or Hopewell might come with her. I'd like very much to see them again."

"They're all grown up and have their own lives," Hull said. "Still, there's no harm in asking. It will take some time to arrange all that."

"I know, but Ruth can look forward to seeing her sister again."

"I'll write to Bursley and carry the letter to Falmouth myself," Hull said. "If we're fortunate, a ship may be leaving for New England."

* * *

When Oliver Cromwell died in 1658, he was succeeded by his son Richard. The New Model Army, which had supported the Lord Protector, soon lost confidence in Richard. They removed him and reinstalled the rump Parliament that had executed the King. These two factions were quickly at odds with each other, and force was employed to dissolve the rump. With no Parliament and no leader capable of unifying the country, England was teetering on the brink of anarchy.

Amidst this uncertainty, Hull decided to put off his plan for Naomi until the government was more stable. "A cloud hangs over my future and that of England," he wrote to Bursley. "I pray for a return of the monarchy, but I'm not at all sure I would benefit from that outcome. My post in St. Buryan appears somewhat precarious. I've said nothing of this to Agnes, but she agrees with me that a visit to England is inadvisable at this time."

Amidst this turmoil and uncertainty, word spread that George Fox was again preaching in Cornwall. He was reported to be riling authorities in St. Ives on the north coast, some thirty miles distant. In the three years since his trial in Launceston, he had sought to discourage radicalism and to impose a more formal structure on the

Society of Friends in the hope that his movement would supplant both the Puritans and the Church of England as the leading religious group in the land. he adopted a diplomatic approach toward those in power, but the fervor of his preaching exhibited no hint of compromise.

Recalling Fox's confinement and his manner at the trial, Hull realized that his own feelings about the man and his teachings remained mixed. St. Buryan was too small to warrant Fox's notice. Still, he remained alert for any further accounts of the preacher's movements.

One Sunday, having conducted his service at St, Levan and greeted his parishioners, Hull went with Samuel to the small cemetery to meditate. Prolonged exposure in the New England colonies had made him fond of the sound of waves breaking on a rocky shore. And the notion of saints long deceased but ever ready to intercede on man's behalf intrigued him. Then he noticed a tall, broad-shouldered man with piercing eyes and a mane of dark hair standing at the gate. His worn clothing was wrinkled and dusty from travel. Recognizing Fox, he motioned to Samuel to leave them alone.

"Thou need not go," Fox said. "The Lord's business is equally suited for the ears of women and children."

Hull rose to his feet as Samuel ran off down the path to the shore. The two men faced each other silently across the slanted grave stones.

"And who has commissioned you to carry out the Lord's business?" Hull asked in the same even tone he might have used to ask the butcher if his lamb chops were fresh.

"My commission is from God," Fox replied. "I need no other."

"How does this business of yours affect me?"

"I come to speak of the ships that are wrecked on this coast."

"The shore is rocky, and the ocean is treacherous," Hull said.

"The nature of the land is God's gift, as are the vagaries of the sea. I find no fault in either, nor do I find the seamen in any manner negligent. But I deplore the activities of those people on land who, eager to profit from the misfortune of others and not satisfied with the goods that wash ashore, do tear the ship in pieces, not regarding to save men's lives, but fighting one another for the goods contained therein. If any man escapes with a little, they rob him of it and let him go begging up and down the country. Surely such ill-begotten goods will become a curse to those people. And surely their actions will be a curse unto thee, priest Hull."

"Who accuses me of condoning either the plundering of the wrecks or the actions of the men involved?" Hull asked.

"The deeds of thy parishioners speak of their own accord. Have people spent their money on thee for that which is no bread? I charge thee with failing to preach God's truth to those in thy care."

Hull remained silent a moment, not sure that Fox was done. His son's voice came up from the shore, as he mocked the shrieks of the gulls. Recalling Samuel's tale of the sailor stripped naked and sent off begging, he was tempted to repeat elements of his sermon deploring such wanton disregard for life and property. But Fox appeared to have no interest in words other than his own.

"If I am to be held responsible for the deeds of my parishioners," Hull said calmly, "I can offer no defense. What would you have me do?"

Fox seemed surprised at this acknowledgment of guilt, but quickly regained his composure. "I would have thee pray for enlightenment."

"My enlightenment will not bring about what my words have thus far failed to accomplish," Hull said. "I judge you to be a man of action as well as principle. What action on my part will stop the plundering?"

"If I were thee, I should stand in their path while invoking God's laws against thievery. I should command them to look within their hearts, where those laws are indelibly inscribed."

"Have you found that approach successful?" Hull asked.

Fox gave him a scornful look. "I have been sent to remind those in authority of their duties, not to perform those duties for them."

"I envy your detachment," Hull said. "You point out the problem, and leave me to wrestle with the solution."

"If that is thy final word," Fox said, "I shall shake off the dust of this place from my feet. So it is written."

"Nothing in life is final," Hull said. "That is my present thought."

Fox turned to go, but paused to look back. "Solutions come from within," he said. "Heed thy inner voice, and God will show thee the path."

Then he vanished as suddenly as he had appeared; and Samuel was calling out from across the cemetery. "Who was that man?"

"I think he was my conscience," Hull said.

Taking his son's hand, he led him up the hill, past the church and the apocalyptic stone, and onto the road toward St, Buryan and home.

"You often preach against the pillaging of wrecked ships," Agnes said when he told her of the encounter. "Why didn't you defend yourself?"

"Men like Fox are impatient for results," he replied. "They think nought of efforts. I trust God to take mine into account."

Agnes was not appeased. "He might at least have thanked you for what you did for him in Launceston," she said.

"In his own fashion, he did thank me," Hull said. "He came here on what was really a pastoral mission. Many of his ideas are quite sound. A wise man fastens upon truth wherever he finds it."

"Is he gone now for good?" Agnes asked.

"He stirs people up and charges those in authority with negligence, then moves on to the next town."

"And are you planning to go out with the children when next a ship goes on the rocks and block the way to the wreck?"

Hull laughed. "The sight of us would surely stop the wreckers in their tracks." His tone became serious. "There is too much of the prophet in Fox. Human nature is not so easily modified."

* * *

Before leaving the west of Cornwall, George Fox penned a letter to priests and magistrates which began with the admonition: "Take heed of greediness and covetousness, for that is idolatry; and the idolater must not enter into the Kingdom of God." In the ensuing pages, he mentioned only one man by name.

"Do not take people's goods from them by force out of their ships, seamen's or others', neither covet ye them; but rather endeavor to preserve their lives, and their goods for them; for that shows a spirit of compassion, and the spirit of a Christian. But if ye be greedy and covetous of other men's goods, not mattering what becomes of the men, would ye be served so yourselves? If ye should have a ship cast away in other places, and the people should come to tear the goods and ship in pieces, not regarding to save the men's lives, but be ready to fight one with another for your goods, do ye not believe such goods would become a curse to them? And may ye not as surely believe, such kind of actions will become a curse unto you? When the spoil of one ship's goods is idly spent, and consumed upon the lusts, in ale-houses, taverns, and otherwise, then ye gape for another. Is this 'to do as ye would be done by,' which is the law and the prophets? Therefore, priest Hull, are these thy fruits? What dost thou take people's labour and goods for? Hast thou taught them no better manners and conversation, who are so brutish and heathenish? Now all such things we judge in whomsoever."

"It won't affect my position in St. Buryan," Hull told Agnes when he saw the letter, "but neither will it do me any good. Even if the letter has no wide distribution, it is a matter of public record and may well influence some future decision regarding me and my family. I would rather it did not exist."

"Is there nothing you can do?" Agnes asked.

"Nothing that will do me any good," Hull said. "To respond or to protest my innocence will only draw more attention. Better to let it lie and hope that no one in London lays eyes on it."

Eighteen

"I feel as if I no longer have a home in England."
(St. Buryan and Southwark, 1660-1662)

When the wave of anxiety created by Fox's visit had subsided and the sea was again calm, the people in St. Buryan and neighboring parishes turned once more to the latest news emanating from London. Responding to the anarchy that had gripped England, General George Monck – appointed by Cromwell to govern Scotland – marched south with his army to restore order in the government. His negotiations with Charles, who was an exile in Holland, resulted in a statement of Charles' conditions for accepting the crown. In April 1660 the Parliament restored the monarchy and declared that Charles II had reigned as the lawful King ever since the execution of Charles I in 1649. He returned to England in May to the acclaim of the populace in London, and his coronation took place the following year.

"We have a King," Agnes commented when news of his accession reached St. Buryan. "Our future is secure."

"Now the recriminations will begin," Hull said. "Who knows what charges may be levied or for what causes men may be prosecuted?"

While in exile, Charles II had endorsed liberty of conscience in matters of religion; but once on the throne he quickly restored the Church of England to its former status and reinstated university officials removed under the Protectorate. Although Hull approved of these actions in principle, he was apprehensive as to how far such measures might be carried. Would the King revive the deaneries and reinstate Dr. Weeks in his post at St. Buryan? He kept his fears to himself, not wishing to alarm Agnes; and he was glad when a letter from Tristram focused their attention on other matters.

Since his return to England, Hull's only news of Tristram had come through Bursley; and it was with some trepidation that he read the letter. Tristram assured them that Blanche and the children were well, before launching into a lengthy account of a commission from the authorities in Boston. His orders were to transport a man condemned as a Quaker to a deserted island off the coast and leave him there in mid-winter to starve or freeze to death. Instead of carrying out this commission, he took the man to Sandwich and found refuge for him with the Indians.

"Won't the authorities punish him if they find out?" Agnes asked when Hull read her that portion of the letter.

"To leave a man to die in such a manner is akin to murder," Hull said. "What Tristram did was an act of charity. I applaud his decision."

On the last page of the letter, which Hull did not share with his wife, Tristram expressed his approval for many of the principles held by the Society of Friends, such as their rejection of violence as a solution to differences between men and nations. He ended by asking for his father's opinion on the subject.

Hull deduced from the nature and wording of this request that Tristram was on the verge of becoming a Friend himself. He was surprised that Fox's influence had already spread to the colonies. Recalling the trial at Launceston and the confrontation at St. Levan, he found it difficult to approve of a man so reluctant to compromise, even with regard to such a minor issue as removing his hat. In some ways he was akin to prophets of old in that his mission was to proclaim an ideal that men must strive to attain, even though they were certain to fall short. Yet Hull hesitated to regard Fox as a true prophet.

"I applaud many of the positions taken by these Friends," he wrote to his son, "and I shall not try to dissuade you from joining their ranks. I would, however, caution you against excessive zeal and a rigidity that can brook no compromise. Men's hearts are not changed by harangues or by restrictions. Conversion is a gradual process, not a single act or moment of enlightenment. I agree that a man must heed his inner voice or conscience; but I reject the notion that all men are equally qualified to testify to the truth. We discard tradition and ritual at our peril. As long as you consider any new course in the light of your conscience, I shall have no quarrel with your choice. May God aid you in reaching a decision."

* * *

In the autumn of 1660 a carriage drew up outside the rectory, and a tall dignified looking man got out. He looked about him, as if to get his bearings, and had some difficulty unlatching the gate. Hull watched him from the window of his study. He had never met Dr. Weeks, the deposed Dean of St. Buryan; but he knew instinctively the identity of his visitor and the nature of his business. He went quickly to open the door himself.

"I'm John Weeks," the man said, offering his hand.

"Joseph Hull. Please come in."

"I come here with mixed feelings," Weeks said when they were seated in the study. "I'm glad to find everything in good condition. But I take no pleasure in telling you that I have been reinvested as Dean of St. Buryan in what is once again a Royal Peculiar."

"I rather expected that," Hull said, "but I didn't think you would come here yourself."

"I admit this is my first visit to St. Buryan – indeed, to Cornwall," Weeks said with a laugh that seemed more forced than genuine. "I've spent most of my life in or near London."

"Are you visiting, or have you come to take possession?"

"My position is somewhat uncertain. I've been reinstated, but I'm currently out of favor at court. That may change, but it behooves me for the present to retire to a spot that is some distance from London."

"And that spot is St. Buryan," Hull said.

"It seemed a logical choice," Weeks said, "but I wasn't sure what I would find here. I must admit I am pleasantly surprised."

"I've done my best to put things in order," Hull said. He had the impression that if the rectory were now as he found it seven years ago, Weeks would already be on his way back to London.

"And I thank you for that," Weeks said. "I made inquiry in the town before coming here. The people appear well satisfied with your pastorate. Under normal circumstances, I would ask you to continue on as vicar. But things being as they are, I have no choice but to take possession of the deanery I have long neglected."

"Will you leave again, once you get an appointment in London? I ask not for my own sake, but for the people in St. Buryan. They deserve a pastor who is willing to reside in their midst and minster to their needs."

"I can understand your feelings," Weeks said. "I should have the same concerns, were I in your place. If I could answer your question, I should be better able to make some arrangement that might benefit both of us. As it is, I can only thank you for what you have accomplished here and offer to help you in any way I can. Do you have a place to go?"

"I had hoped I might stay on," Hull said, swallowing his pride, "if not as vicar, then as your assistant – at least until I can find another post."

"I should like nothing better," Weeks replied, "but certain factors mitigate against what you suggest. The Parliament is considering another act of uniformity, and your loyalty to the Church has been questioned."

"have done nothing disloyal," Hull objected.

"You were appointed to this post by a Puritan Parliament under the Protectorate. Authorities in the Church view that as cooperation or approval."

"So I'm to be branded a Puritan sympathizer."

"It is unfortunate, but I see no way open for you to stay in St. Buryan. Quite frankly, it would hurt my chances of obtaining a position at court."

Hull wanted to vent his anger against such obvious injustice and against the selfishness of this man sent to replace him. But he had his family to consider. "You asked if I had a place to go," he said. "If you know of a post anywhere in England, I shall be grateful for your help."

"I have a colleague in Surrey who might welcome an assistant. I can provide you with a letter of reference."

"That's just across the river from London," Hull said. "I may attract the notice of church officials."

"Those in authority tend to take a long view," Weeks said. "They often overlook what is right under their noses."

* * *

The letter of reference provided by Dr. Weeks led Hull to a post at St. Saviour in Southwark. The church was situated on the south bank of the Thames near the bridge to London. The vagaries of administration in the Anglican Church had rendered St. Saviour virtually autonomous with respect to selection of its ministers. The rector was sympathetic to Hull's plight and regretted that the only position available was as under-master in the grammar school. He was pleased to learn that Hull had experience as a teacher in Launceston. Established by letters patent in the fourth year of the reign of Queen Elizabeth, the free school served both the rich and poor youth of the parish. Given his straitened circumstances, Hull was glad to accept the post.

St. Saviour was by far the grandest church Hull had ever served. Dating from the thirteenth century, the long majestic nave with its gothic arches dwarfed that at Launceston or St. Buryan and rivaled the cathedral at Exeter. At the east end of the church was a Lady Chapel – leased out for a time as a bakery but restored under King Charles I. Beyond that was a smaller chapel that contained the canopied tomb of Bishop Andrewes, who had helped translate the

Bible. But Hull was most impressed by the immense square tower with its four pinnacles that overlooked the flat land on that side of the Thames. He had to climb almost three hundred stone steps to look out over the ramparts at London across the river. Samuel accompanied him on occasion and seemed as much taken with the scene as his father. Standing on top of this tower, Hull was struck by the irony of his position. He was as close to God as he was likely to get, yet his future as a minister was precarious and wreathed in uncertainty.

He kept these thoughts to himself. Agnes was finding it difficult to adjust to life in the city. Contributing to her discomfort was the character of the locale. Southwark and Lambeth had been incorporated into the city of London, but the two boroughs retained much of their traditional character as a refuge for thieves and vagabonds. The streets at night were unsafe to traverse. Aware of this danger, Hull kept his children at home after dark. Accustomed to run freely about the countryside, they chafed under this restriction. He told Agnes the situation was temporary, that he would look for a more suitable post; but he had little hope of finding one.

As Weeks had predicted, Parliament passed an act of uniformity that required strict adherence to the *Book of Common Prayer* and to the rituals of the Anglican Church. The wheel had come full circle, and Hull found himself in much the same position that had led him to emigrate to New England twenty-five years earlier. Through a contact in London, he learned that all ministers appointed under the Protectorate were suspect, and that his chances for reinstatement were slight. He was advised to stay put and not draw attention to himself.

"The times are conspiring against us," he told Agnes one night as they prepared for bed. "I feel as if I no longer have a home in England."

"Conditions may change for the better," she said. "The King could order an amnesty and forgive all that happened in the last dozen years."

"That seems rather unlikely," Hull said.

"You've done nothing wrong. Why can't you go to the bishop and clear yourself of any charges they may have against you?"

"My guilt is due solely to circumstance. I can't change that."

"What other choice have you?" Agnes asked.

"I see none at present," Hull said. "I can only hope for the best."

* * *

At fifteen, Samuel had inherited much of his father's curiosity about the world. From the tower of St. Saviour, he would point toward London and ask about the various landmarks in the city. He knew his way about Southwark better than his father, having explored all of the nearby streets and alleys thoroughly by day. He would ask about what the family had experienced in Weymouth, Hingham, Barnstable, Yarmouth, and Gorgeana. And he was eager for news about his siblings in Maine.

Ruth, who was twenty, expressed a particular interest in her sister Naomi. She asked why they were still separated; and she stored all Naomi's letters in a box under her bed, Agnes having relinquished them after an initial reading. Hull assured her that he wanted the family to be reunited, but the time and place for that joyous event were still indefinite. Ruth nodded as if she understood, but he knew she wasn't convinced it would actually occur.

One evening early in the spring as Hull was reading in his study, the door burst open, and Ruth stood there before him. Her clothing was disheveled, and she panted for breath. She grasped the door handle with both hands, as if for support. Her face registered fear and alarm, and she was on the verge of tears. Rising from his chair, Hull went to her side.

"What is it, Ruth?" he asked, placing his hand on her shoulder to calm her. "What has happened?"

"It's Samuel," she cried. "He's in trouble."

"Where? What kind of trouble?"

"We were walking home, and two men appeared from nowhere. One man grabbed me, but Samuel made him let go. He told me to run home. I didn't want to leave him, but he insisted. I looked back once. They had knocked him down and were beating him. I felt so helpless."

"Where did this happen?" Hull asked.

"Over toward the bridge. I'll show you."

Hull grabbed his coat and a walking stick and followed Ruth out of the house. A fog had rolled in off the Thames, and the air reeked of smoke from nearby dwellings. Samuel and Ruth had obtained permission to attend a party given by a church warden whose newly wed daughter planned to emigrate to the colonies. The warden lived only a few blocks from the church. The party was in the afternoon, and they promised not to stay too long.

As he hurried along the dimly lit cobblestone street, trying to keep up with his daughter, Hull wondered what he would do if the men were still there. He could use his walking stick if necessary, but as a weapon it seemed woefully inadequate. He pressed on behind Ruth, telling himself his son's assailants had likely fled.

That proved to be the case. Ruth had stopped ahead of him and was kneeling beside a body in the street. "Please, God, let him not be hurt," Hull prayed as he approached them.

Samuel looked up and winced as he essayed a smile. His face was bloody. His clothes were torn. He was having difficulty breathing.

Hull bent down over his son. "Are you able to walk?" he asked.

"I think so," Samuel gasped. "They stole my purse. There wasn't much in it. I guess that made them angry, so they kicked me. The next thing I remember was Ruth wiping my face."

"Come lean on me," Hull said. "I'll take you home."

"I can help too," Ruth said.

Together they got Samuel to his feet. He grasped his side. "My ribs hurt," he said, "but I think I can walk."

Flanked by his father and Ruth, he took a few steps, while favoring his right leg. "I must have twisted my ankle too."

"Put your arms on our shoulders," Hull said.

Samuel did as he was told, and they made their way slowly home. Agnes was at the door to meet them. She took charge of Samuel, cleansed the blood from his face, bound up his ribs and ankle, and put him to bed. When she was done, Hull stayed with his son, while she attended to Ruth, who was sitting in the parlor staring into space. They were still talking when he finally left Samuel asleep and prepared for bed.

"Is Ruth all right?" he asked when Agnes joined him.

"She's badly shaken. Samuel is a man and will soon recover. But Ruth says she never wants to go out again."

"Give her time. She'll get over it," Hull said.

"She's unhappy," Agnes said as she put on her nightdress. "Ruth knew several young men in St. Buryan, but she has no prospects here. Those ruffians grabbed her first. Who knows what they would have done if Samuel hadn't tried to defend her? Southwark isn't safe for women and children."

"I understand your concern," Hull said, "but what can I do?"

"Are there no positions away from the city."

"I can make some inquiries, but ministerial posts are scarce for those out of favor. It's as if my name were on some list being circulated by the church hierarchy."

Agnes was silent for a moment. "What took place tonight makes me wonder if Naomi is safe all by herself. Her last letter disturbed me."

"I don't know what you mean. She sounded quite cheerful."

"She made no mention of Judge Symonds or his family. I can't help but feel that she's in some kind of trouble."

"If that were the case, someone would have told us."

"Naomi was always a private child," Agnes said, "and she's been cut off from us for most of her life."

"I can't do anything about it until our future is secure," Hull said.

In the weeks that followed, he contacted several ministers whom he knew in England; but there were no posts available, and his inquiries were not well received. Even a classmate at Oxford, who held a position of importance in the Church, expressed reservations about his allegiance.

"You can well imagine how it must look to the authorities. You emigrated to escape censure by the Bishop of Bath and Wells, and who knows how many heretical ideas you absorbed in New England?

On your return you received two choice appointments under the Protectorate. You were ejected from your post at St. Buryan following the restoration of the monarchy. None of that can be considered a recommendation. My advice would be to return to the colonies."

In the fall he had a letter from Bursley. He had spoken to Naomi himself. She was still in the employ of Judge Symonds, but Bursley seemed deliberately vague about her circumstances, stating simply that she was a grown woman and anxious to live independently. She had said nothing to him about a reunion with her parents.

"He knows more than he's telling us," Agnes said after she read that portion of the letter. "Why didn't she write herself?"

"Read the rest of it," Hull said.

"The church in Oyster River needs a minister," Bursley wrote. "I mentioned your name, and the wardens were receptive. They are willing to wait upon your decision. Oyster River is near to Dover. As you know, Temperance, Elizabeth, and Dorothy are all married and live in the area; and Benjamin and Hopewell own land there."

"You never told me you asked Bursley to find a post," Agnes said when she had finished reading.

"I didn't. I simply kept him informed about what is happening in England. He took the rest upon himself – with some prompting, no doubt, from Joanna."

"It will be hard to return. I'm used to living in England."

"I know, but I'm tired of constantly making a new life for myself," Hull said. "I want to settle someplace where I can live in peace."

"I'd like that too," Agnes said. "It hasn't been easy for me either."

"You can check on Naomi and visit the other children; and Ruth's prospects for finding a husband will be much better in New England."

"At least Oyster River is an English name," Agnes said. "It's not nearly as ominous as Wessaguscus or Mattakeese."

Hull laughed at that. "I shall respond to Bursley at once."

He took her hand and drew her down on the bed, pulling the blankets over them. She snuggled up beside him. Raising himself on one elbow, he kissed her on the lips. To his delight, she responded to his ardor and reached out to embrace him.

Nineteen

"It is not our custom for women to preach."
(Oyster River Plantation, 1662-1663)

Save for a storm at sea, Hull's second voyage to New England in the summer of 1662 was without incident. With Agnes and four children he traveled by small boat up the Piscataqua River to Great Bay, then up the Oyster River to his destination. The settlement straddled the river and comprised roughly sixty families. Hull's house was situated on the south bank adjacent to the church. William Williams, his neighbor and a church warden, introduced him to the community.

Williams had also served on a committee of residents who, tired of crossing the river to attend services at Dover Neck, voted to call their own minister and to allocate twenty pounds annually for his support. Dorothy and Temperance, aware of their father's circumstances; assured their husbands that he would be willing to return to New England. Their husbands, Kent and Bickford, then persuaded the committee to offer him the post.

The congregation was smaller than Hull expected, but he took up his post eagerly His sermons, prepared with care and forcefully delivered, garnered for him a modest reputation in the region. In the new church, built in anticipation of his arrival, he preached and administered the sacraments in accordance with Anglican tradition and practice. Oyster River was now part of Massachusetts; but with the King and Church once again in control, he looked forward to carrying out his ministry in relative peace.

Agnes felt some initial dismay that Oyster River – like Wessaguscus and Mattakeese – was designated a plantation, but she took comfort in the prospect of being reunited with her three oldest children. Benjamin owned land off to the south, and Hopewell stayed with him when he was in the area. Hull had promised to send for Naomi as soon as they were settled. She was also delighted to see the grandchildren, many of them for the first time. Temperance lived half a mile distant, Dorothy a mile farther to the east, and Elizabeth close by in Cochecho. Joanna and Tristram were in Barnstable, but they would find their way to Oyster River in due time. Griselda was still unmarried and living in what was now York.

The younger boys adjusted readily to their new home. Samuel was fascinated by the tales of Indians and witches then current, and he passed them on to Reuben and Ephraim. Ruth held a bleak view of the place and her future there, yet she looked forward eagerly to the reunion with Naomi.

* * *

Shortly after Hull's arrival in Oyster River, a young woman came to his door. She was short in stature and fragile in appearance. Her dark hair framed a pale unblemished face, lending her a doll-like appearance. She wore a long brown garment suitable for travel and carried a satchel. She studied him without speaking, a questioning look in her pale green eyes.

He was trying to place her when Agnes cried out, "Naomi!" They embraced each other, and Naomi started to cry.

Hull hugged her in turn, but she was stiff and tense in his arms. "I'm sorry I didn't recognize you," he said as he led her into the house. "I was planning to go to Ipswich next week, but now you're here."

Naomi was still on the verge of tears. "I've waited fourteen years for you to come and take me home," she said.

"You're home now," Agnes said, easing her into a chair. "You must be hungry. I'll fix something while you speak to your father."

Hull had the impression that Agnes knew something he was about to find out. He faced his daughter, a grown woman now, across the table. He had convinced himself that their separation was unavoidable, but Naomi might view it in a different light. Her demeanor betrayed no anger, only regret and a thinly veiled accusation of neglect.

"I trust you were well cared for by Judge Symonds," he said.

"I'm never going back there," Naomi said vehemently.

"You don't have to go back," he assured her. "This is your home. Now tell me what happened in Ipswich."

Naomi seemed to relax a bit. "Have you seen Joseph?" she asked.

On his arrival Hull was surprised to find that Temperance had a five-year-old child named Joseph. He could recall no reference to the boy in letters he had received in England; but Temperance wrote infrequently, and he may have forgotten. Bickford seemed reluctant to talk 6about the child. His excuse that Temperance had simply neglected to mention it struck Hull as unconvincing.

"Is Joseph your son?" he asked.

"Yes," Naomi said.

"Who is the father?"

"He was a servant in the house. He came into my bed when I was sixteen. I suppose I half invited him. Mr. Symonds was furious when he found out I was pregnant. He sent the servant away. I'm sure he would have liked to be rid of me too, but he felt he had an obligation to you. I was wholly dependent on him, so I did as he said."

Hull rose and paced the room. He glanced at Agnes, but she seemed preoccupied with the preparation of the meal. Although his vexation was directed largely at Symonds, it extended to Naomi for her complicity in what had occurred, and to himself for his failure as a parent. Yet he admired her candor in admitting that she shared any guilt.

"Then Symonds arranged for Temperance to take the child."

Naomi nodded. "He paid her to take care of Joseph. He said it would avoid a scandal and protect my good name. I asked him to contact Dorothy, but he said Temperance had been married much longer and another baby in the house would attract less attention."

"Why didn't Temperance take you in as well? And why wasn't I notified?" Naomi cowered in her chair at this outburst, and Hull hastened to soften his tone. "I'm sorry," he said, resuming his seat. "I'm the one at fault. I should never have left you alone."

"Mr. Symonds said it was best not to worry you; that you were too far away to do anything. We all agreed to keep it secret, and I promised to serve him until you got back. I didn't know it would take five years."

She turned away, stifling a sob. Hull reached out and grasped her hand. "Did Symonds treat you well?" he asked.

"After that happened, I was more of a servant than one of the family."

"Does he know you're here?"

"Yes. He encouraged me to come."

"Did you need encouragement?" Hull asked.

"I was afraid you had forgotten about me."

Agnes wiped her hands on her apron and hugged her daughter once again. "We never forgot you," she said, "but something always came up to prevent us from sending for you."

"Our lives were at the mercy of events," Hull said. "But I know how you must have felt, and I regret the pain and distress I caused you."

"That's all in the past," Agnes said. "You and Joseph have a home here in Oyster River."

"Yes, of course," Hull said. "Symonds shouldn't be paying for the boy's keep. I'll find some way to reimburse him. But why did you say you would never go back? Did something else happen?"

Naomi nodded. "This past year two of his indentured servants refused to stay with him unless he paid them for their work. They claimed that under English law they should be free after seven years, but Mr. Symonds said his contract called for nine years of service. He had them arrested. I had to testify in court."

"About what?" Hull asked. "How were you involved?"

"About what they said to Mr. Symonds."

"And what was that?"

"They said they hadn't agreed to the contract, that they had served the customary term, and that they should be paid for their work. Everyone in the house wanted Mr. Symonds to let them stay on as hired men, but he wouldn't listen and had them thrown in jail."

"How did the magistrate rule?" Hull asked.

"He said the contract was legal and they had to stay two more years. Mr. Symonds was angry at me afterwards. He said that my testimony made him look like a tyrant."

A pause ensued as Hull absorbed her story. Naomi seemed unsure what to expect from a father she hardly knew. "You can stay here as long as you like," he said at last. "I shan't treat you as a servant nor as a sinner. You've suffered enough for your transgressions and from my neglect."

"How will you treat me?" she asked.

"As a daughter. Go now and eat what Agnes has prepared. Then you're coming with me. We have something to do."

"Where are we going?"

"To get Joseph and bring him home."

From the pleased look on her face, he knew he had said the right thing. He watched her eat – quickly and deliberately, as she had while a child. At the end of the meal Ruth returned with the three boys in tow, and another tearful reunion ensued.

They went that same afternoon to retrieve Joseph. Temperance was cool toward Naomi and seemed reluctant to surrender the boy to her care. Hull had to assure her that the child would have a home with him and Agnes. The boy hung back at first, but gradually warmed to the fact that this was his mother and his grandfather.

As Hull was preparing to leave, Bickford took him aside and spoke of repayment. "Symonds helped us care for the boy, but it wasn't enough to cover what he's cost us these past five years."

The implication was clear. He had abandoned Naomi and was therefore responsible for the consequences of his neglect. "Is Temperance of like mind?" Hull asked.

"My wife and I speak as one," Bickford said. "We only ask you to do what is right and just."

"I'm disappointed that Temperance expects payment for what has been an act of charity toward her own sister," Hull said.

"Her half sister," Bickford corrected him. "Was it an act of charity to leave Naomi alone among strangers?".

"I admit my fault," Hull said, "and I shall do what I can to make amends; but my concern now is to provide a home for Naomi and her son." On that note they parted, but Hull's relationship with Temperance and her husband remained strained.

Naomi and Ruth lightened the housework, giving Agnes time for an occasional visit to Dover. Samuel was eager to help his father and often rode with him on trips to nearby towns. Reuben and Ephraim, now thirteen and twelve, were glad to take charge of Joseph. For Hull the boy was a constant reminder of his failure to provide for his daughter. He was prepared to make restitution for his neglect, but Naomi's future was subject to her own decision. He would offer advice if she asked for it – or even if she didn't.

* * *

The woods were ablaze with yellow and red as Hull strode toward the church that autumn morning. His pace had not slackened, despite his age. On entering the church, he gave passing notice to two young women seated on a rear bench. The service proceeded in the usual manner until he mounted the pulpit to deliver his sermon. He had no sooner introduced his topic than one of the women stood up. She was plainly dressed, as if for traveling. Her features, despite her youth, were rather coarse; and her complexion was marred by red blotches. The other woman, who was similarl7y attired but more attractive, remained seated.

"My name is Mary Tompkins," the standing woman announced in a shrill voice. "My companion is Alice Ambrose. We are members of the Society of Friends, and we desire to give testimony before this gathering."

"It is not our custom for women to preach," Hull said, making an effort to be polite. "Please take your seat, and allow me to continue."

"Do thou bid me be silent in a house of public worship?" Mary asked. The question was addressed to him, but her eyes scanned the faces of those who turned to see the cause of the disturbance. "Would thou deny me the right to declare before God and this assembly what is in my heart? Do thou fear those who testify to the truth within them?"

She sounded as if she had learned her catechism at the feet of the master. To control his mounting anger, Hull called upon his respect for George Fox and his teachings. But he also knew from experience that any reply would add fuel to the debate. Their purpose was clearly to disrupt the service. He refused to surrender his pulpit.

"I respect your right to address God in your own manner," he said, "and you are free to lecture any who will listen to you later in the day. But if you persist in disturbing our worship, I shall have you removed."

Alice was now on her feet. "We desire to be heard!" she cried in a loud voice. "Our mission on this earth is to hear and heed God's voice, and to speak His truth as it is made known to us. Is that not thy calling as a minister of the gospel? It is our duty as well."

Hull glanced at Williams and another warden who were stationed by the door. Taking this as a signal, they seized the women by the arms. Alice offered no resistance as Williams led her out of the church. Mary, however, began to struggle; and Hull descended from the pulpit to aid in her removal. The other warden, a man named Davy Daniel, had her about the waist but couldn't budge her. Hull caught her flailing arms and held them tightly, as together they half dragged and half carried her outside.

Back in the pulpit, he realized that his prepared sermon had lost much of its relevance. "I ask you to forgive these women for interrupting our service," he said to gloss over the incident. "We are indeed called to testify to the truth that is within us, but there is a time and a place for such private testimony. Sunday morning is my designated time to speak what is on my mind and in my heart. You come to receive whatever guidance I can give you by my words and through the sacrament. If Mary Tompkins has something to say, let her wait until this service is over. Then you can decide for yourselves whether to listen to her."

As Hull left the church, he noted a small gathering around the two women. Mary loomed above the crowd. He couldn't make out what she stood on, but her words rang loud and clear through the crisp autumn air.

"Priest Hull pinched me!" she cried, exhibiting her bare arm. "You can see the spot where he pinched me."

Hull went rapidly to where Agnes stood waiting for him. Taking her gently by the arm, he led her away from the scene.

"Is there any truth in what that woman said?" Agnes asked.

"None at all. Daniel and I may have been a bit rough in removing her from church, but I never pinched her or touched her inappropriately."

"People are listening to her," Agnes said.

"That is their right," Hull replied.

Walking by the river that evening, he met his neighbor Williams, the warden who had ejected Alice Ambrose. Agnes was friendly with his wife, and Ruth or Naomi often minded his children. Williams lacked any formal education, but his common sense approach to the vicissitudes of life commanded Hull's respect.

"Those women held a meeting this afternoon on the green," he told Hull. "Mary Tompkins repeated her claim that you pinched her, and she accused Davy Daniel of striking her so hard in the stomach it forced her to fall backwards. She even offered to show her bruises to the doctor, but he couldn't be found."

"Daniel never struck her," Hull said. "I was right there and would have seen it. And I certainly didn't pinch her. "

"I can't say that I'd blame you if you had," Williams said. "I'm not accustomed to such close contact with a woman other than my wife."

"That statement does you no credit, William."

Williams bowed his head. "Forgive my human frailty."

"Is that why you attended the meeting – to contact Alice again?"

Williams laughed. "I confess she made an impression on me, and her demeanor struck me as rather admirable. I was offended by Mary's antics; but Alice was perfectly calm and submissive as I led her from the church, like she was drawing upon some hidden strength."

"What else did they say at this meeting?"

"Something about listening to our inner voice. That made some sense to me. But not very many people listened to them."

"Do you know where they came from?"

"They said they were last in Dover, talking to some people at the inn. The priest arrived and started to argue with them; but he got frustrated and threatened to have them arrested. So they crossed the river and came here."

"I know the priest. His name is Rayner."

"They broke the law today by interrupting your sermon," Williams went on. "Say the word and I'll have the constable run them out of town." Hull sensed from his tone that the warden's heart was not in his offer.

"Let them be," he said. "They'll leave soon of their own accord."

The women departed the next day, but stories about his treatment of them persisted and were embellished for weeks afterward. Agnes and Ruth were vocal in support of his innocence, but he thought he detected a gulf between himself and some women in the parish. Naomi said nothing about the incident, and he vowed to renew his efforts to regain her trust.

* * *

The bond that had sprung up between Naomi and Ruth following upon their joyful reunion soon showed signs of weakening. They often went their separate ways, and Hull noticed that they no longer carried on lengthy and intimate conversations just out of earshot. He broached the subject to Agnes one evening in bed, not to complain or to criticize his daughter, but merely to verify his observations.

"I've noticed it too," Agnes said.

"I suppose it's only natural," he added when she did not continue. "They were separated fourteen years, and they're starting to discover how far their paths have diverged."

Agnes rolled over to face him. Her nightdress was tied at the neck, an indication that she was not in the mood for sexual relations. They had agreed on this sign early in their marriage to spare each other embarrassment and injured feelings. But tonight Hull's sole concern was to get her opinion on the subject under discussion.

"Naomi has known at least one man, and she has a child," Agnes said. "Ruth is still virgin. That gulf is hard to bridge. Naomi really ought to find a man who will marry her."

Hull thought about that for a moment. None of Agnes' children was married, and she probably regarded marriage as a ready solution for Naomi's problems He wasn't so sure.

"She spends a lot of time with Williams' wife and their children," he said. "I don't object to her visiting them; but I have to wonder what it is she finds next door that she can't find here at home."

"In the Symonds household she was either a guest or a servant," Agnes said. "She's not used to being part of a family group and may find it constricting. Besides, Williams' oldest daughter is married. I imagine Naomi talks to her. And Joseph has children his own age to play with."

"Why can't she talk to Temperance?"

"Temperance still blames her for deserting her son, or for giving birth to him. I'm sure she blames us too for abandoning Naomi."

"What about Dorothy then?"

"She's eight years older and lives on the other side of town. Besides, Naomi may prefer to talk to someone outside the family."

"I didn't realize there was such a gulf between us. She makes me feel inadequate as a father and a minister. I help others to overcome their emotional and spiritual problems, but I cannot help my own daughter."

"Don't rush her. She'll talk to us when she's ready," Agnes said.

"I hope you're right," Hull said.

* * *

Before Christmas, Hull went to Dover with Agnes and Samuel to buy some personal items that were unavailable locally. While Agnes lost herself in the shops, Hull went to the church to get Rayner's opinion of the two women, Mary and Alice, and of the Society of Friends.

Samuel set off to explore the town. He was still mindful of the beating he had sustained in Southwark, and he appreciated the security of a peaceful and law-abiding community. There were occasional rumors of Indian unrest, but a boy of sixteen could roam the streets of Dover with no fear of harm from the residents. Many people he met had heard of his father, and everyone seemed to know Bursley. Whether loitering on the waterfront or strolling on the village green, Samuel felt safe and at home.

On his way back to rejoin his parents, he noticed a group of people gathered outside the meetinghouse. Pushing his way through the crowd, he came upon three women stripped to the waist. Their hands were bound with a rope that was fastened to the tail of an oxcart. They had their backs to him and were crouched down hugging their knees. Suddenly aware of the cold, he tightened the scarf about his neck. A few paces off a man with a whip stood motionless, as if waiting for a signal.

"What's going on?" he asked a man standing beside him.

"They're Quakers, and they're being run out of town."

"What have they done?"

"They broke the law."

"But why does that man have a whip?".

"It's their punishment. Run along now. It's nothing for you to see."

One of the three turned her head, and Samuel recognized her as the woman who was put out of the church in Oyster River. He fled the scene, determined to find his parents and report what was happening. His father would know what to do.

* * *

Hull found Rayner at home. The minister, a short pudgy man with a round and florid face, was glad to recount his experiences with the two women. He had been summoned to the inn by several of his parishioners. The women, along with two men who lived in Dover, were attempting to persuade their listeners of the truth of their beliefs.

"I asked them politely why they were in Dover," Rayner went on. "They were all silent at first. Then that Tompkins woman asked me what I had against them. I said they had no respect for magistrates or ministers or church doctrine. She wanted to know what doctrine I was referring to, so I cited the Trinity as an example."

"And what was her response?" Hull asked.

"She said she acknowledged the Father, the Word, and the Spirit, who, as she put it, 'bear record in heaven.' But she denied they are persons or constitute a trinity. I tried to prove it to her, but she was too set in her ways to heed my words. One of the men who was with them said the Bible was falsely translated, that 'person' really meant 'substance.' I saw that they had closed their minds to reasonable argument, so I decided to leave them in their ignorance. They accused me of abandoning my flock, and I regret to say that some of my parishioners were tempted by these heretics to alter their allegiance."

"Was that the end of it?" Hull asked.

"They fled before I could have them prosecuted," Rayner said. "I thought I had seen the last of them, but two days ago the same two women and a third arrived in Dover. This time I was ready for them and had them arrested. Here is a copy of the warrant issued by the magistrate."

Grasping a sheet of paper that lay on his desk, he held it out. Hull took it with some apprehension. He was familiar with the laws regarding heretics in the Massachusetts Bay Colony, but Dover was far removed from Boston. Surely here the laws were not so strictly enforced.

The warrant was addressed to the constables at "Dover, Hampton, Salisbury, Newbury, Rowley, Ipswich, Wenham, Linn, Boston, Roxbury, Dedham, and until these vagabond Quakers are out of this jurisdiction." Hull read further.

"You and every one of you are required in the King's Majesty's name to take these vagabond Quakers, Anna Coleman, Mary Tompkins, and Alice Ambrose, and make them fast to the cart's tail, and drawing the cart through your several towns, to whip them upon their naked backs, not exceeding ten stripes apiece on each of them in each town; and so convey them from Constable to Constable till they are out of this jurisdiction, as you will answer it at your peril; and this shall be your warrant. Per me, Richard Walderne, at Dover, dated Dec. 22, 1662."

Hull gave the paper back. "Did you know their punishment would be so harsh?" he asked.

"It's the law. They were evicted from Dover once before. They should have considered the penalty before they came back."

"And where are they now?" Hull asked.

"I imagine they are in the custody of the constable," Rayner said with a finality that brooked no further argument.

* * *

As Hull was leaving the minister's house, he saw Samuel running in his direction. Breathlessly, his son blurted out what was taking place at the meetinghouse. "Can't we help them?" he pleaded.

"They broke the law," Hull said. "But come with me. Perhaps we can do something to mitigate their suffering."

Arriving at the scene, Hull recognized Mary Tompkins and Alice Ambrose. All three women were squatting down out of modesty and to shield themselves from the cold. In response to Hull's question, the constable said that they were waiting for the mayor to start the march. Hull went up to the women. Removing his coat, he used it to cover Mary's shoulders. Taking his cue, Samuel put his coat around Alice. An onlooker did the same for Anna Coleman, a small bent woman. She smiled gratefully at him.

The constable approached Mary and put his hand out to seize the coat. "The law requires them to be stripped to the waist," he declared.

"But not until their punishment begins," Hull said. "Forcing them to stand here in the cold is needless cruelty."

The constable met Hull's unflinching gaze. "I don't like this any more than you do," he said as he drew back his hand. With that he walked off and resumed his place at the head of the procession.

The women barely had time to warm themselves before the mayor arrived and the constable gave the signal to proceed. The coats were cast aside, the cart set in motion, and the first lashes applied. Hull sensed that the man wielding the whip was exercising some restraint – either out of pity, or so not to offend the onlookers. Even so, each woman winced and cried out as the whip fell on her bare back. Hull watched the procession move off toward Hampton, the next town on their route out of the jurisdiction.

Samuel had shut his eyes as the first lashes were applied. "I don't understand," he said on the way back to where Agnes was waiting. "They preached in Oyster River, and you didn't have them beaten and run out of town. You just let them go on their way."

Hull faced his son. "Some people claim these women are preaching heresy, and they passed laws to protect us from such false doctrine. I believe that truth alone can overcome error. Laws are of little avail."

"Do you think those women are heretics?" Samuel asked.

"There is some truth in what they say – and perhaps some error. But heresy or not, they don't deserve to be treated in such fashion."

Samuel seemed to be satisfied with this explanation. Hull placed a paternal hand on his shoulder as they went back to rejoin

Agnes. He gave her a brief account of the event, omitting the more painful details. But lying beside her in bed that night, he stated his concern in greater detail.

"I'm not sure where the truth resides," he said. "Archbishop Laud claimed to know the truth; and he had a dissenter's ears cut off. Puritans came to New England to practice their version of the truth, and they beat or banished anyone who disagreed with them. The Friends seek the truth by heeding their inner voice, but they lack tolerance for those they regard as false ministers. It seems that when a society decides to eradicate dissent, truth becomes indistinguishable from mere opinion."

Agnes grunted in agreement, then rolled over and was soon asleep.

In the days that followed, Hull was alert for any news regarding the fate of the three women. It was reliably reported that on the road to Hampton the constable had offered to let the women ride part of the way on horseback. They refused, demanding that he either carry out his orders to the letter or release them. The constable who took custody of them in Hampton was lenient in administering the ten lashes prescribed by the court. When they reached Salisbury, the next town on their march, the constable there decided on his own initiative to release them. The women were said to have taken refuge with a Major Shapleigh in Kittery.

Though he was pleased that humanitarian instincts had prevailed, Hull knew that others professing to be Friends would soon come to preach in the area. Persecution merely inspired them to greater effort. What was this faith that, like Christianity before it, bore such indignity willingly and emerged stronger than before? Hull still decried their tactics, but he had to admire their tenacity and dedication. And he saw clearly that he would have to deal with them in the future.

Twenty

"A man must save his own soul."
(Oyster River Plantation, 1663)

Snow blanketed the earth when Tristram arrived in Oyster River. His ship was docked at Dover, and he had left his first mate to oversee the discharge and taking on of cargo. After eating the meal Agnes prepared, he expressed a desire to see his sisters, Temperance and Dorothy. Hull offered to accompany him. A month had passed since the beating and expulsion of the three women. He wasn't sure how closely Tristram had allied himself with the Society of Friends, but he hoped his son might help him to frame a response toward these missionaries of a new religion.

"I congratulate you on your success as a ship master," Hull said as they walked. "Bursley taught you well."

"We still help each other when we can," Tristram said, "but I don't see him very often."

"Why not? You live in the same town."

"One of us is always at sea." Tristram paused, as though he were reluctant to continue. "Blanche and Joanna don't get along very well."

Hull had listened to varying assessments of Blanche's character since his return. Temperance considered her as little better than a harlot. Elizabeth was more circumspect, and Dorothy claimed to have no direct knowledge of the matter. Hopewell and Benjamin declined to offer an opinion. He hadn't broached the subject to Naomi or Ruth, since they had met Blanche only once as young children.

Hull was inclined to reserve judgment regarding Blanche. On her only visit to Gorgeana shortly after she married Tristram, she had made a favorable impression on him. Agnes was quick to point out that she was on her good behavior. Though Hull tended to dismiss recent rumors of infidelity, he respected Joanna's judgment. Tristram's words troubled him.

"As long as you're happy together," he said, "what others say or think is of little consequence."

"I regret being away from home so much." Tristram said no more.

Hull decided not to press the issue. "I hear you've become a Friend," he said. "What led you to take that step?"

They had reached a promontory where the river broadened out to Little Bay. Tristram's eyes followed a shallop as it plied its way upstream. He seemed uncertain how to reply. "I have yet to join their society," he said at last, "but I'm favorably inclined toward them."

Hull leaned against a fallen tree. "Have you heard of my encounter with Mary Tompkins and Alice Ambrose?" he asked.

"There was some talk of them on the docks at Dover, but your name wasn't mentioned."

"The whole incident was unfortunate." Hull went on to describe his confrontation with the two women. "I have no quarrel with their mission," he concluded, "but they ought to respect my right to preach without interruption."

"I met Mary Tompkins once in Salem," Tristram said. "She has a volatile temperament and is possessed by missionary zeal. For the most part, Friends are content to live at peace with their neighbors."

"It isn't enough to say she was overzealous," Hull persisted. "I've heard of others just like her."

"People like Mary are misguided," Tristram said. "George Fox is also wrong, if he condones or encourages such behavior."

Hull related his encounters with Fox in Launceston and St. Buryan. "Fox was forthright but respectful," he concluded. "He never resorted to violence, preferring to debate and confound his opponents. I can't say the issues between us were resolved. I told him what I thought, and he did the same. We parted without animosity. But it's no use trying to talk to people like Mary Tompkins."

"You shouldn't be too hard on Mary. Women aren't accustomed to stand up and give testimony."

"Let her give testimony in her own church, not in mine. I've had enough interference with my ministry."

Tristram hoisted himself onto the tree trunk beside his father. His eyes glinted in the light off the snow, and he appeared to be enjoying their discussion. "What you say is true, but it doesn't justify the persecution they undergo. Do you know the laws against Quakers?"

"I imagine they're much the same here as in England."

"At first they were arrested and sent back to England. When they kept coming, the General Court declared them heretics and ruled that anyone convicted of preaching Quakerism shall have an ear cut off. It they do it again, they lose the other ear. For a third offense their tongue is bored with a hot iron."

"Is that law still in effect?" Hull asked.

Tristram ignored the question. "Now, according to a law passed last year, wandering Quakers who have no permanent dwelling nor occupation shall be punished in the manner you witnessed in Dover. If convicted again, they're branded on the left shoulder with an "R" – for reprobate, I suppose. For a third offense they are banished under pain of death. You used to say that no one should have to suffer because of their religion? I haven't forgotten what you taught us."

"But what should I do with someone like Mary Tompkins? Would you have me debate her in my own church?"

"At least you didn't have her arrested and run out of town."

"There have been too many banishments," Hull said. "We need a peaceful solution."

Dorothy was pleased to see her brother again, but their visit with Temperance was a bit strained. Agnes had made provisions for Tristram to stay the night. He was glad to spend time with the three younger boys, whom he had never seen. That evening he had a lengthy talk with Naomi. Hull never knew what was said, but she seemed more at peace as a result.

* * *

Shortly after Tristram's visit, Hull learned from Naomi that Mary Tompkins and Alice Ambrose were again in Oyster River and lodged in the home of William Williams. He wondered why they were spending their days indoors instead of preaching on the green or harassing him in church. Naomi could provide no answer, so he went next door to satisfy his curiosity.

Williams seemed flustered when he asked to see the women. "I just want to speak to them," Hull assured him. "I don't intend to report them to the authorities. But I am curious as to why you're sheltering them."

"To tell the truth," Williams said, "they've convinced me to join their society and become a Friend."

"I trust you've given the matter careful consideration," Hull said.

"I've thought about it ever since they were last in Oyster River. Now that I've spoken to them, I've made up my mind."

"Why are they here?" Hull asked.

"They can better answer that," Williams said.

Hull followed him to a storeroom at the rear of the house, where the women sat at a table reading a pamphlet. They appeared to recognize him, but gave no indication of surprise or interest. Hull stood just inside the doorway with Williams close behind him.

"I come here not as a minister, but as a neighbor who is concerned for your safety and welfare," he said. "Since you are not speaking openly, I take it you are fleeing from the authorities. Tell me what happened. Perhaps I can be of some assistance."

"And why would thou want to help us?" Mary Tompkins asked.

"My warden is about to join your ranks, and my son is quite sympathetic to your cause. As for myself, I've seen enough persecution to know that it serves only to strengthen the resolve of those persecuted."

"We returned to Dover three days ago," Alice Ambrose said when Mary was silent. "We stayed with a family of like mind and troubled no one. When the constable found out we were in town, he came by night with his brother and dragged us out through the snow to a boat they had moored on the river. I tried to get out of their boat and was made to swim alongside in the icy water. I would surely have perished, but the Lord sent a sudden violent storm that forced them to put ashore. We took shelter in a cabin without any heat. My wet clothing was frozen like boards about my body. In the morning they turned us out of doors into the snow and the cold. We came here and were taken in by this kind man, whom thou dost know, and to whom the Lord has revealed the truth of our message."

"Now that thou know our history," Mary said, "what neighborly assistance can thou provide?"

"Be not so bitter, Mary. I mean thee no harm." Hull stopped, surprised that he had spontaneously adopted their form of address. "Your sufferings speak to my heart and my conscience. I have no desire to interfere with your mission."

"All very well, but how can thou help us?" Mary asked.

"My son, of whom I just spoke, is master of a ship and is preparing even now to depart from Dover. If you can make your way downstream to Little Bay, he can pick you up on his way out to sea. I don't know his next port, but he'll put you ashore wherever you like. He's already done as much for others of your faith."

Mary studied him closely, as if she were seeking a sign that would allow her to disbelieve what he had just said. Finding none, her features took on a brighter cast. "The Lord has moved thee to come to our aid, and I thank thee for harkening to His voice."

"I've been listening to His voice for many years," Hull said. "On this occasion His words and His will are perfectly clear. Go in peace, and may God protect you and keep you well."

Back home, Hull sent a messenger to learn the date of Tristram's departure and to alert him to the women's plight. Passing the information along to Williams was a simple matter. A few days later he was pleased to learn that the women were safely on their way to Jittery, presumably to recuperate at the home of Major Shapleigh.

* * *

Toward the end of May, Bursley arrived in Oyster River, bringing news of Joanna and the family in Barnstable. But Hull could tell from the restless way he paced the room that he had something more on his mind, something that had to be discussed in private. After they had eaten, Hull led the way outdoors. They sat on a bench he had constructed in the shade of a great oak tree. From there he had an unobstructed view of the church.

Bursley seemed unsure how to begin, so Hull proceeded to describe his encounters with Mary and Alice. "Several Friends have been in the area since then," he concluded, "but I've had no further problems with them. They're still being persecuted in Dover. One woman was placed in the stocks and spent four days in prison for questioning the minister. And a man was whipped through three towns for accusing the magistrate of oppression and laying snares for the innocent."

"Such persecution is prevalent throughout the colonies, with the exception of Rhode Island," Bursley said. "While you were in England, several Quakers were put to death in Boston; and the courts ordered Quaker children to be sold into slavery in order to pay for pew rents owed by their parents."

"All this forces me to reconsider my position as a minister. Do I want to live and preach in a colony that enacts such laws and carries out such punitive measures?"

"Quakers aren't the only ones who suffer," Bursley said. "Accusations of witchcraft are on the rise, especially in the

Connecticut Colony; but cases have been tried in Massachusetts as well. An elderly woman from Hampton was convicted of being a witch and is now in prison in Boston. But what can anyone do?"

"I have no good answer," Hull said. "When those in authority are afraid, the people suffer."

"If you're unhappy in Oyster River," Bursley said, "I have a solution. Your old congregation in York is in need of a minister. I'm sure they would welcome you back."

"York is but twenty miles distant and no different from Oyster River. I fail to see how such a move resolves the problem"

"Hear me out," Bursley said. "Two years ago the fishermen and their families on the islands petitioned the General Court for a separate township, citing their isolation and the uncertain weather that makes travel to the mainland difficult. The court has established the town of Appledore, which includes Hog Island and all the others."

"What has that to do with a post in York?"

"They can't afford a minister on the islands, but you might easily arrange to serve them in conjunction with your duties at York. The two posts combined will make a good living. You know Hog Island well and can decide how much of your time you need to spend there."

Picking up a fallen branch, Hull traced a crude map of York and the islands in the earth at his feet. He studied it for some time in silence before tossing the stick aside and turning his attention to Bursley.

"Your suggestion merits consideration. My needs are simple; and as you say, I know the territory. But we're just getting settled in Oyster River. I doubt that Agnes will take to the idea."

"There's one way to find out," Bursley said.

* * *

Several days passed before Hull broached the subject to his wife. "I have made no decision," he said, "but it's an opportunity worth exploring. I can provide guidance for people who know me and accept me as I am. I'll have no need to pretend."

"Your mind seems to be made up," Agnes said. "It seems to be your destiny to move from place to place. I've grown accustomed to it."

They were seated by the hearth after the evening meal. "I don't want to decide this alone," Hull said.

"You provide guidance to the people in Oyster River. They all know you. If you leave now, they'll think those women drove you out."

"There may be some truth in that," Hull said, staring into the embers. "When I first came to New England, I was eager to do battle for the souls of men and ready to face all adversaries. That struggle has brought me much wandering and heartache. It seems that a minister is not commissioned to save souls, but only to encourage and guide those who are reaching out for salvation. A man must save his own soul."

"People are saying that you helped those women escape, and that you're on the verge of becoming a Friend yourself."

"People can say and think what they like. I dealt charitably with Mary and Alice, but more will follow. I haven't the heart or the will to confront a new wave of zealots. We were content when we lived in Gorgeana; and I found peace on the islands, though my vision was too clouded to see it. The men on Hog Island are uncomplicated. All a fisherman wants from God is a good catch. He goes where the fish are biting. I could take a lesson and do likewise. But you haven't told me how you feel about the move."

"Griselda is in York," Agnes said, "and I know what to expect; but I tell you straight out that I have no desire to live on Hog Island."

"I need spend only two days a week on the island. The fishermen have even built a chapel. They may well be my true congregation."

"Then I agree," Agnes said. "We shall move to York."

Hull made the appropriate inquiries, and he promised to remain in York as minister for as long as the congregation wanted him. He moved there with his family in the late spring. Naomi opted to remain in Oyster River. He arranged for her to board with Williams, though he was aware in so doing that he had surrendered her to the opposition. But there were worse fates than becoming a Friend.

Twenty-one

"The Province of Maine has been reborn."
(York and Hog Island, 1663-1665)

Hull looked forward to a measure of serenity amidst the familiar surroundings of York. He suffered from no serious disability; but he was sixty-eight, and his body was attuned to that fact. His walks were not as long as they used to be, his pace not as swift. But his mind was active, and he applied himself diligently to preparing his sermons and ministering to his congregation.

He had promised Agnes in advance of the move that he would take no active role in the political life of the town, and for the most part he remained true to his promise. Yet he was aware of the political unrest swirling about him.

After the restoration of the monarchy, the heirs of Rigby and of Gorges – a grandson also named Ferdinando – had renewed their respective claims to the provinces of Maine and Lygonia. Though Rigby's heirs found no favor in court, the King seemed favorably disposed toward rewarding Sir Ferdinando's lifelong devotion to the Crown. A legislative committee appointed by the Parliament upheld the rights of Gorges' heirs and declared that Massachusetts had usurped its authority over the province.

But officials in Boston were also presenting their case. Heartened by a gracious response from Charles II, the General Court proclaimed him King and sent two ministers to England. In the summer of 1663 they obtained a letter from the King confirming the charter of the Massachusetts Bay Colony. But they also brought back to Boston a copy of the Act of Uniformity, which compelled Puritans to accept the doctrines of the Church of England or leave the church.

In Maine, meanwhile, many towns had refused to send delegates to the General Court. Both sides were waiting to see when and how the decision reached by the legislative committee would be implemented. Such was the situation when Hull assumed his duties as minister in York. And so it remained until the summer of 1664, when Charles II signed an official letter expressing his pleasure

It was addressed: "To our trusty and well-beloved subjects and inhabitants in the Province of Maine, and all whom it may concern. We greet you well." After acknowledging the legitimacy of Sir Ferdinando's initial claim, the King cited the substantial resources expended by Gorges in establishing the province and praised him for his steadfast loyalty to the Crown. He went on to restate the decision of the legislative commission and to accuse Massachusetts of unjustly depriving the rightful proprietor of the issues and profits of his property and of blocking commissioners who sought restitution. The King's letter concluded: "We have therefore taken the whole matter into our princely consideration, and have thought fit to signify our pleasure in behalf of Ferdinando Gorges, the present proprietor, and do require you to make restitution of the Province to him or his commissioners, and deliver to him peaceable possession thereof, or otherwise without delay show us reasons to the contrary."

"The Province of Maine has been reborn!" Hull exclaimed when he saw the letter. He hurried home to share the news with his family.

"I feel fulfilled," he told Agnes. "Our trials have not been for nought. We need only wait for the King's decree to be carried out."

She regarded him steadily across the dinner table. Ruth looked up at him but continued to eat. Samuel, caught with a fork full of beans, set them back on his plate. His face beamed with a joy equal to that of his father. The two youngest, Reuben and Ephraim, displayed little interest. Griselda, a regular guest at the family table, stopped eating but made no comment. She lived alone near the church. Hull had offered to take her in, but she said she was accustomed to solitude.

"Will Massachusetts relinquish its hold on the province?" Agnes asked.

"The authorities will have to obey the King's command," Hull said, refusing to countenance her negative attitude. "Maine is a reality."

"Don't misunderstand me, Joseph. I'm glad that the King has decided to act, but such changes take time."

"I'm content to wait," Hull said as he resumed eating.

"I know little about politics," Griselda said, "but I've lived in York for twenty years, and I listen to the local gossip. After we became part of Massachusetts, many Puritan families moved here. They control the government and will undoubtedly support the officials in Boston."

"They won't have a choice," Hull said. "The King has spoken, and that's the end of it."

Samuel broke the silence that ensued. "Will you take me to Hog Island with you sometime?"

"Of course," Hull said. "It's good to meet different types of people. You might do worse than become a fisherman."

"I don't see what you find so attractive on that island," Agnes said. "Those fishermen are a rude lot, if you ask me. I've spoken to their wives. They all yearn for a less precarious existence."

"They are certainly simple uneducated men; but they work hard, provide for their families, and go to church. I'm sure God has reserved a special place in heaven for fishermen."

"Do you go fishing when you're out there?" Samuel asked.

Hull smiled. "I have other duties, but I've landed a few big ones."

"I wish you'd do your fishing closer to home," Agnes said.

"I must go where they're biting," Hull said.

* * *

Hull was still riding a wave of elation when Bursley put in at York later that summer. "The King has spoken!" he said gleefully as he helped Bursley climb up on the dock. "Maine is again an independent province."

"I've heard about it," Bursley replied. "The mood in Boston is far from joyful. I would describe it rather as cautious."

Hull's brow furrowed. "Cautious? The matter is settled."

Bursley smiled. "Then let us repair to the tavern and celebrate."

He hefted his satchel and followed Hull to the waterfront tavern where Puddington and his wife Mary still served the local populace. There Hull expanded on the King's letter, which he had almost memorized. Bursley downed a tankard of ale as he listened.

"You can imagine how happy I was when I read that letter. All the efforts made by Sir Ferdinando and myself have been justified."

"It's certainly good news," Bursley said, "but Massachusetts has been given an opportunity to present reasons as to why the King should change his mind. That will surely lead to further delays."

"This is no time to take a dark view," Hull said. "Let us rather savor our victory." He raised his tankard high and toasted a bright future for the Province of Maine. Bursley lifted his tankard to eye level, then set it down.

That winter and into the spring it became evident that the King's letter was not of itself sufficient to effect a change of government in the province. The General Court in Boston decided that the people in Maine still needed assistance and protection, and that the government they had freely chosen should not be hastily vacated. The court directed civil officials in York to perform their duties as usual and named a resident magistrate to hold court sessions in the town.

Hull was aware of these developments, but he seldom spoke of them at home. He remained confident that Maine would soon become an independent province. He left it to other men to work out the details. His task was to minister to the faithful in York and on the islands. But he knew also that the Puritan element wielded considerable influence, not only in the town but in his own congregation. He didn't mention that either, lest he worry Agnes.

He was spending more time on Hog Island. What had begun as two days a week expanded to three days in the spring of 1665. With the advent of summer he was often away from home four days out of seven.

Although the family was not in need, Agnes was dismayed at what seemed to her an abdication of his responsibility. When Bursley stopped by on his way to Dover, she enlisted his help. "I'm worried about Joseph," she told him. "I can't believe those fisherman require so much of his time."

"Have you discussed it with him?" Bursley asked.

"He says he finds peace on the island. All well and good, but he has responsibilities in York too."

"I'll speak to him," Bursley agreed.

The following day, while his ship was discharging cargo, he paid a boatman to take him to Hog Island. He had visited the place on a number of occasions, but was unaccustomed to approaching it by small boat. The craggy cliffs on the south shore appeared taller and more forbidding, the trees more stunted and windswept. Much of the wood had been used to build ships or feed fireplaces during the harsh winters. The sailboat put into a cove on the western shore, the only safe anchorage on the island. A number of fishing boats were moored in the harbor.

"Why aren't they at sea?" he asked the boatman.

"There's a wedding going on in the chapel," was the reply.

The houses clustered near the harbor appeared vacant as Bursley made his way to the small chapel the fishermen had built. Several ministers had preached on the island, but none lasted more than one winter. Hull spoke often of an affinity with these fishermen, but Bursley wondered if the feeling was mutual.

The doors of the chapel were open, and he recognized Hull's voice as he approached. Sliding into a seat at the back, he listened. Hull's manner of delivery was still forceful, but his movements were slower. He looked tired, and his words lacked their former spark.

"It is written that a husband shall cling to his wife, and that the two shall become as one flesh. In most instances the woman is the first to die, and the man is obliged for the children's sake to take a second wife – or even a third. But the conditions on Hog Island are somewhat different. It is often the husband who is lost at sea, and the wife who must find another man to provide for her. I don't mean to sound a solemn note on so joyous an occasion. I merely advise wives to cling to their husbands in equal measure, for they know not what trials life has in store for them. So I say to this young couple: love and embrace each other always, and be grateful for whatever future God may provide."

Rather a strange sentiment on such an occasion, Bursley thought as he waited for Hull outside the chapel. Yet others had nodded in agreement. It was for them simply a fact of life.

"What brings you out here?" Hull asked.

"Agnes is concerned about you," Bursley said as they walked down the hill to the harbor. "She says your parishioners in York are wondering why you spend so much time on this island. Are fishermen such great sinners?"

Hull laughed heartily. "On the contrary. This is the most satisfying and peaceful ministry I've had in my entire life."

"Are you avoiding the royal commissioners?" Bursley persisted.

"That's part of it," Hull said. "I wish them success in carrying out the King's orders, but as a deposed minister I remain suspect in their eyes."

"They're here to restore the province to Sir Ferdinando's heirs, not to check on you."

"I know, but I don't want to risk attracting their attention."

"You might have told that to Agnes."

"She would surely worry if she thought I had to hide from them."

Bursley leaned against a wagon that stood alongside the road. "Can I tell her that once they leave, you'll spend more time at home?"

"Tell her what you like," Hull said. He kicked at a stone, but it traveled only a foot or two before settling in the dust. "There's something else. Some members of my congregation in York are seeking to replace me. It's the Puritan set. If they gain the ascendency, I shall need a place to preach and a source of income. I receive twenty pounds annually for my services on Hog Island. We can make do with that if need be."

"You must tell Agnes something to allay her concern about you."

"Once the commissioners finish their work, many Puritans will leave, and we can celebrate the rebirth of Maine. That will alleviate my problems."

"It may take them longer than you think," Bursley said. "The authorities in Boston won't relinquish their control without a struggle, and they have a good deal of local support."

Hull regarded him scornfully. "You sound like Griselda. Believe me, in six months we'll be free of Massachusetts, and any influence the Puritans have gained here will evaporate."

Bursley realized it was useless to argue the point. Hull was obviously happy in his assurance that a bright new day had dawned for himself and the province. There was nothing to be gained by casting doubt upon his rosy future. "I hope you're right," he said.

* * *

The King's commissioners had designated York as the seat of the provincial government they sought to establish, and they spent a good deal of time there that summer. Hull continued to preach on Hog Island. To appease Agnes for his lengthy absences, he suggested that she accompany him to the island. She appeared to be pacified by his invitation, although she didn't admit it to him.

Hull got reports on what the commissioners were doing. After appointing justices of the peace in each of the major towns, they constituted these justices as a court and ordered residents of the province to obey this established authority. But the commissioners also forbade the agents for Massachusetts and for Gorges to disturb the residents of Maine until the King made known his pleasure.

"Are they saying that the case is still open?" Agnes asked when she heard the ruling.

"They're just being impartial," Hull replied.

All that summer and into the fall he remained steadfast in his belief that the matter was resolved and that the King, having already expressed his pleasure, would not change his mind and rule in favor of Massachusetts. Faced with pessimistic assessments that they would have to wait months or perhaps years for a final ruling, he declared simply, "I'm content to wait, knowing that Maine is free."

Despite some initial resistance, Agnes did accompany him to Hog island in fine weather, leaving Griselda to care for the children. She was with him early in October when he collapsed during a service in the chapel. Two men carried him outside and set him on the ground with his head and shoulders against an oak tree. Another man fetched some water, and Agnes used a handkerchief to bathe his forehead.

"I'll get a fisherman to take you to York," she told him when he was breathing normally. "The doctor there has a degree from Edinburgh. He'll know what's wrong and what to do."

"I'm not up to a boat trip right now," Hull said, his voice weak but steady. "If I'm to die, let it be here on the island where I've found a measure of peace. I've done my best to provide for you and the children in this life. I trust that God will do the same when I'm gone."

"He will, Joseph," Agnes said. "He will."

Hull recovered fully from this episode – or so he assured Agnes. During the weeks that followed, he continued to serve the fishermen on the island. They were a boisterous lot who celebrated their successes and bemoaned their failures at the local tavern. Hull accepted this as a human failing; even as he preached against excesses. No one on the island questioned his authority, nor was he called upon to justify or defend what he preached. God alone could approve or disapprove of his words and actions. For once, the reality corresponded with his dream.

* * *

Hull died on the 19th of November 1665 on Hog Island. Samuel was with him at the end and brought word back to Agnes and the family. His funeral service at the church in York was well attended, and the mayor paid fitting tribute to his dedication and his accomplishments in both the political and spiritual realm.

Disagreement arose within the family as to where he should be buried. Most of the children were of the opinion that his body should be interred in York. But Bursley and Samuel supported Agnes in her desire to carry out Hull's wishes, and his body was returned to the island for burial

Agnes was named the administrator of his estate. With Bursley's help she filed an inventory totaling 52 pounds, 5 shillings, 5 pence – including 10 pounds for books and 20 pounds owed to him for his ministry on Hog Island.

"I'll go out there and collect what they owe him," Bursley offered.

"No," Agnes said. "Joseph would not have insisted on payment, and I can make do without it."

"Then I'll tell them to use the money for a suitable memorial."

"I think Joseph might like that," Agnes said.

NEW ENGLAND WAKES

A Novel of Tristram Hull and
the First Quakers

One

"The devil is plying his trade here in Boston."
(Massachusetts Colony, July 1656)

"The devil is plying his trade here in Boston."

Tristram Hull caught the words as he entered the tavern at the Red Lyon Inn, an ordinary located near the docks in the north end of town. The speaker was John Norton, a middle-aged man in clerical garb. Tristram had seen him before at the inn but knew little about him, only that he was a minister and an outspoken supporter of Governor Endicott.

"I thought we put the devil to rest when we hanged Ann Hibbins on the Common a month ago," a rum merchant said. His neatly trimmed red beard and tailor-made clothes attested to his status in the community. As the master of two merchant ships Tristram had business with him on occasion.

"A fine show it was, that hanging," a swarthy laborer from the docks said. "Annie shed nary a tear when they put the noose around her neck."

Nicholas Upsall, proprietor of the Red Lyon, spotted Tristram and motioned to him to join the group at the long table. He walked with a slight limp, which he attributed to age. A full apron served as his badge of office. Without being asked, he drew a tankard of ale for Tristram, then sat down beside him at the table.

"Ann Hibbins struck me a woman of wisdom and discretion," he said. "Her husband William, God rest his soul, was a deputy and assistant to the governor. I can't believe that she practiced witchcraft or consorted with the devil."

"I knew her husband," the rum merchant said. "As a magistrate he voted to condemn Goodie Jones for witchcraft. It's ironic that his widow should be hanged for the same offense."

"You'd think as deputy governor, Bellingham could have saved her," Upsall said. "She was his sister, after all."

"He tried," the merchant said, "but Endicott persuaded the General Court to overrule the magistrates and find her guilty. I'm sure his death sentence made for bad blood between them."

"Annie sued me once," the laborer said. "Claimed I charged her too much for some work I did. She was excommunicated for treating workers the way she did. I can't say I shed any tears when she was strung up."

"Maybe she deserved to be excommunicated," Upsall said. "but not to be hanged as a witch. Her only fault was that she had more wit than those who accused her."

"A woman shouldn't put herself forward as she did," Norton said. "But it's not Ann Hibbins I have in mind when I speak of the devil. I mean the two Quaker women who arrived on the *Swallow*. I thought we were safe at this far remove from that heretical sect. Now that their emissaries have arrived on our shores, we must impress on them that they are no more welcome here than in England, where many of their number have been whipped and branded for preaching their poisonous doctrines. Bellingham wisely put them in jail."

"They broke no law by coming to Boston," Upsall said. "What have they done to warrant being imprisoned?"

"It's not what they've done," Norton said. "It's what they plan to do that should concern us all. They brought with them a hundred pamphlets filled with their blasphemies. Bellingham had every last one of them burned."

"They made a lovely fire," the laborer said. "The executioner tossed them into the flames one at a time, like he was giving each pamphlet one last chance to repent."

Tristram nudged Upsall. "They say Bellingham did all this. Where is Governor Endicott?"

"He's in Salem for at least a fortnight," Upsall said. "Bellingham is acting as governor."

"I confess my ignorance of Quaker doctrine," the rum merchant said. "I've heard that they refuse to swear an oath or remove their hats in court."

"Those are minor matters," Norton said. "They claim that men and women can communicate directly with God through their own inner spirit."

"I can see why they're in jail," Tristram muttered.

Norton gave him a scornful look. "That's where they belong. At my behest all of the jail windows have been boarded, lest good God-fearing people be infected by contact with them."

Upsall turned to a young man in seaman's garb who had remained silent throughout this exchange. "You serve aboard the *Swallow* and had some contact with the women. What's your opinion of them?"

"I steered clear of them," the sailor said. "I couldn't stomach all that jabber about inner voices. Otherwise, they seemed decent enough."

"Decent in manner perhaps," Norton said, "but deluded in the belief that this inner voice, of which you speak, is the voice of God. The devil is behind such blasphemy."

"We're back to the devil!" Upsall said. "I have some work to do."

He rose and motioned to Tristram to follow him. They left the group at the table to their talk of devils and witches.

* * *

Tristram had frequented the tavern at the Red Lyon Inn since he acquired his first ship, a coastal schooner called *The Catch*; and he regarded Upsall as a second parent. His own father had returned to England some eight years ago and been caught up in the turmoil of the civil war. As an ordained Anglican minister he was keeping a low profile at a safe distance from the Lord Protector in London. Upsall spoke little about himself, but Tristram had gleaned a few facts about his past. He came to New England with the Winthrop company and for a number of years operated an inn in Dorchester, where he sheltered Roger Williams briefly after he was banished from Massachusetts. Now with his wife Dorothy he managed the Red Lyon in Boston. Built of red brick and wood, the inn had three stories and boasted twenty-four windows. A two-story addition housed the tavern. Unlike the Blew Anchor and State's Arms, which catered to magistrates and deputies to the General Court, patrons of the Red Lyon were chiefly workers, tradesmen, and sailors.

Upsall led the way through a public room, where Dorothy was setting up for the evening meal. They entered a small parlor used by ladies for their talk after dinner. If an itinerant fiddler performed in the public room, they could crack the door and enjoy the music. Now the parlor was deserted.

"You were wise to stay out of that talk in the tavern," Upsall said as they took their seats. "I'm concerned about the two Quaker women. Given Norton's influence, I fear they are being ill treated."

"I know very little about Norton," Tristram said. "Who is he?"

"He came to Boston three years ago from Ipswich. Endicott often calls on him to defend orthodox positions before the General Court."

"Why does he hate Quakers so much?"

"I think he's afraid of what they stand for. The idea that God speaks directly to everyone who is willing to listen must be anathema to a minister."

"How long will they be in jail?"

"That's hard to say. Bellingham has accused them of being a threat to the peace, but he needs some legal grounds to banish them from the colony."

"Maybe he's waiting for Endicott to get back from Salem."

"I think he wants to take action himself. He hasn't forgiven Endicott for hanging Ann Hibbins, and he'd like to be governor again. This is his chance to win favor with the magistrates and deputies to the court."

"How are you involved in all this?" Tristram asked.

"I just want to make sure they have enough to eat. But I'd also like to know why they came to Boston. They must have known what to expect."

"And how do you propose to find that out?"

"I've arranged to visit them at the prison tonight. I want you to come with me."

Tristram half expected the answer. "I thought no one was allowed to speak to them."

"The turnkey is a friend of mine."

"Why do you need me? You could go by yourself."

"I hear the younger one, Mary Fisher, can be quite abrasive. She might he more willing to talk to a man her own age. You can eat at the inn before we go, and I'll put you up for the night when we get back."

"I never refuse a good meal," Tristram said, "but I prefer my cabin aboard ship to a room in your garret."

"An upstairs chamber is free," Upsall said, "and Dorothy will make sure the bedding is fresh. Will you come with me?"

"I'll admit that I'm curious. Do they really talk with God?"

"I believe they listen and wait for God to speak to them," Upsall said. "But apart from their religious beliefs, I admire their dedication and courage."

"What good does dedication and courage do them if they're not allowed to preach?"

"That's what I want to find out. I need to know why Bellingham and Norton are so fearful of them. I suspect they're still clinging to Winthrop's dream of fashioning a church and a government that will serve as a model for the world. But his dream died with him. Many of those who are newly arrived in New England have other goals and different dreams."

"One thing hasn't changed," Tristram said. "The authorities are still eager to banish anyone who holds different religious beliefs."

"I'm waking to a conviction that what a man believes is his own concern," Upsall said, "something between him and God. A number of men feel as I do. These Quakers may find ready ears for their message."

"If every man has to establish his own connection with God, the result will be chaos," Tristram said. "We need ministers to guide us along the path to salvation. I'm my father's son in that respect."

"I met your father once when he was a deputy from Hingham. He stopped by my ordinary in Dorchester on his way to Boston. He struck me as a tolerant man with a thirst for justice. I'm sure he'd be concerned about the fate of these women, even if he couldn't agree with what they preach. I take it he's still in England."

"He has a post at Launceston in Cornwall. In his last letter he spoke of attending the trial of the Quaker George Fox, who is in prison there. He was quite impressed by the man, so you're right. He would be concerned."

"Then you'll go with me tonight?" Upsall asked.

"I look forward to one of Dorothy's fine meals."

* * *

Leaving the inn, Tristram crossed a courtyard framed on two sides by the barn and the brewing house. He paused to drink at the pump before relieving himself in the necessary next to the pigsty, then proceeded briskly down Richmond Street to the wharf where his second ship, the *Hopewell*, was undergoing minor repairs in preparation for a voyage to the West Indies.

As he walked, he questioned the wisdom of involving himself with the Quakers. He was no Puritan, though he was obliged as a freeman to join the church in Yarmouth and listen to the minister's cautionary sermons. His father had taught him to look to heaven rather than hell, to fear God rather than the devil. Was that what Quakers meant by an inner voice?

He had reached the waterfront. Even with the sails on her foremast and mainmast lashed to the yardarms and those on her mizzenmast furled, the *Hopewell* presented an imposing sight. He was part owner of the barque and looked forward to the day when she would belong entirely to him. Another voyage or two to the West Indies should enable him to reach that goal.

In the master's cabin he rummaged through the papers on his table until he found the letter from his father. It was headed, "St. Mary Magdalene, Launceston, Cornwall, 12 April 1656." He passed over family news about a pending move to St. Buryan, focusing his attention on the last paragraph.

"I recently attended the trial of George Fox who, as you may have heard, is a principal founder of that sect commonly known as Quakers. He has been in prison in Launceston since January. As a minister of the Gospel, I find some of their teachings naive and primitive. But their beliefs were not a major issue at his trial. Charged with distributing papers that disturb the peace and refusing to swear an oath, he was found guilty and returned to prison. I was impressed by his simple dress, his carriage, his knowledge of Scripture, and his manner in addressing the court. He managed somehow to assume the role of magistrate and place everyone else on trial. I know not whether he has divine inspiration, as he claims; but I feel certain that we shall hear more of these Quakers in the future. Your loving Father, Rev. Joseph Hull."

Why would his father express admiration for a man who saw no need for ministers? Had he begun to waver in his loyalty to the Church of England? More likely, his favorable opinion of George

Fox was inspired by the same spirit of tolerance that brought about his frequent moves after he came to New England.

Tristram was eleven at the time, and the voyage across the Atlantic had instilled in him a love for the sea and ships that remained strong after two decades. He was happiest at sea, where he could commune directly with God and nature. He had at least that much in common with the Quakers. Odd that this letter from his father should coincide with their arrival in New England, an omen perhaps of things to come. His father was ever alert for such portents. Tristram was more attuned to signs of upcoming calms and tempests; whether at sea or in his marriage.

Strange also that the two Quakers were women. Could religious conviction inspire a woman to become a missionary? Why would George Fox entrust such a vital task to women? Tristram laughed as he tried to picture his wife as a missionary. With five children in the house Blanche had no time for preaching. Yet she had managed to find time for John Gorham, the most recent instance of her misbehavior.

Tristram had accepted or overlooked previous rumors of her misdeeds while he was at sea, but this affair with Gorham was too public to be ignored. It was termed an assault, yet the magistrate who fined them both seemed to have some doubts. Tristram had first learned about Gorham some weeks earlier, but repairs to the *Hopewell* and preparations for his next voyage took him to Boston before he could resolve the issue. He wanted to settle the matter before he sailed to the West Indies. If the facts pointed to Blanche's complicity, he was still undecided whether to punish or forgive her. Though he was inclined by nature toward leniency, the time might have come to take a firmer stand. He did not consider himself a model of virtue, but his lapses were few and distant. And he had to think of the children.

Upsall was generally aware of his problems at home, but Tristram had not mentioned this latest instance involving Gorham. He might raise the issue after they returned from their visit to the Quakers. He realized that his interest in them was piqued not so much by the new religion as by the fact that they were women in trouble. That was what had drawn him to Blanche thirteen years earlier. What he learned at the prison might cast some light on his own circumstances.

Two

"Do thy devil's work. Thou art no man of God."
(Massachusetts Colony, July 1656)

Upsall led the way through the dark and narrow streets of Boston to the jail located in Prison Lane. The ground floor was built of stone with walls reputed to be three feet thick. The jailer, a hairy muscular man past middle age, admitted them to the building. A large room across the front served as a common room for his family and a reception area for visitors. Their sleeping quarters were in the upper story built of wood. The room was simply furnished with a table and benches near the fireplace. A work bench and sideboard stood against the far wall. The jailer's wife, a stout woman the same age as her husband, was darning socks by the light of a tallow candle. She seemed oblivious to the strong animal odor it gave off. She gave them a cursory glance as they entered, then resumed her labors.

The jailer unlocked a door at the rear of the room, then stood aside to let them enter a hallway that extended the full width of the building. He followed, bearing another candle. A single window at one end of the hall was boarded up on the inside. The massive wooden door at the other end was barred and locked. Several cells opened off the hall. The jailer handed the candle to Upsall and unlocked one of the doors.

311

"You can stay until the candle needs snuffing," he said.

"Are the other cells occupied?" Upsall asked.

"Nobody here but these women."

"We won't be long," Upsall said as he entered the cell.

He had described the women in general terms on their walk, so Tristram could identify the older one as Ann Austin. According to Upsall, she was married with children in England. A wisp of grey hair protruded from her bonnet. A dress of homespun reached to her ankles. Her defiant look softened a bit as Upsall politely introduced himself and Tristram.

The younger woman, Mary Fisher, was somewhat shorter than her companion. She was similarly attired, her auburn hair exposed and tied in a bun. She regarded them warily, as if reserving judgment until they stated the reason for their visit.

The women sat on a crude platform that was built into the far wall. It was no wider than a seaman's cot and held their straw bedding. A small table and a chair stood in a corner of the cell by the door. Upsall set the candle on this table. Its odor failed to overcome the smell of urine from a chamber pot visible under the platform. Dampness crept up through the plank floor, adding to the oppressive atmosphere. A sudden draft caused the candle to flicker.

"Why are thou here?" Ann asked.

"Is it not our Christian duty to visit those in prison?" Upsall asked.

"Thou might have brought us some food. I fear that our jailer has orders to starve us."

"I didn't know. I'll see to it that you're properly fed."

"Thou must have some other reason for thy visit," Mary said.

Upsall laughed. "You're quite right. I'm curious as to why you left the comforts of England, when you must have known how you would be received here in Boston."

"Comforts indeed!" Mary said. "We're quite familiar with English prisons as well."

"We were moved by the spirit to spread the word of God in these American colonies," Ann said.

"I had not thought that God made His purpose so clear."

"If thou heed the prompting of thy inner voice, God's purpose will be made known to thee. But thou must be patient and persist."

"Your inner voice seems to have led you to this prison cell."

"It is right that we carry out God's will in this manner."

While Upsall spoke to the women, Tristram focused his attention on Mary Fisher. Something about her appealed to him, her eager and open expression, the manner in which she deferred to her older companion, the suggestion of a well-proportioned body under her plain clothing.

"The authorities who cast you in prison are equally convinced that they are doing God's will," Upsall said.

Ann was quick to respond. "They heed the dictates of a creed that was handed down to them from past generations, a creed they proclaim so loudly that their inner voice can obtain no hearing. If they would remain silent, God's true purpose would be revealed to them. I bid thee, carry that message back to those who sent thee."

"We are here on our own accord," Upsall said.

"Do you harbor no anger or resentment against men who treat you as if you were criminals?" Tristram asked.

Mary spoke up, as if designated to respond to one her own age. "It is not in our nature to harbor resentment or to assign blame. Their actions arise from the darkness that pervades their spirit. Our task is to make them see the light within them. Men may put us in prison, but our message will not be confined by walls of stone."

Her words grated on him. His father too had devoted his life to spreading God's word. She was not the only message bearer. "Perhaps they are guided by a different light," he said.

"One can only act in accordance with the light one sees and the voice one hears." Mary's tone was softer, almost conciliatory. "The men who put us here acted out of fear and ignorance. Our lot now is to suffer persecution for the sake of justice. So it is written in the book thou and others like thee profess to be thy guide."

"It's a hard saying. In my heart I'm not sure I can subscribe to it."

"Just be quiet and let thy heart's voice be heard."

"How does one attain this quiet?" Upsall asked.

Mary deferred to her companion for a response.

"At our meetings we sit quietly and listen," Ann said. "Those who hear the voice within them may be moved to testify to its message. We are sent to establish a meeting in Boston, where the need is exceeding great."

"You've been in prison since you arrived. How can you presume to know what Boston needs?"

"We can only follow where the spirit leads us."

"You will find it difficult to carry out such a mission," Upsall said. "The authorities in Massachusetts will tolerate no religious opinions that differ from their own."

"In England minds have been changed in an instant, and many are guided by a new light. But to heed our message, people must first hear it."

"They may hear, but they will not listen."

"There are men like thee who are willing to listen."

Upsall appeared stunned by her statement.

Before he could reply, the door of the cell flew open, and the jailer entered. "Bellingham and that minister are outside," he said. "If they find you here, I'll lose my post. You must hide."

Taking up the candle, he ushered them into the adjoining cell and locked the door behind them. It was almost identical to the one they had just left. Tristram groped his way to the platform and sat down. Upsall remained standing in the dark. Neither spoke as footsteps sounded in the hall outside the door. A voice from the women's cell reached their ears.

"I smell tallow. Are you providing your prisoners with candles?"

"Who is that?" Tristram whispered.

"It's Bellingham." Upsall's voice came out of the darkness.

"What you smell is my candle," the jailer said.

"So you say."

"These are the women you asked about," the jailer said.

"I trust you are being well treated," Bellingham said.

"We don't complain." Ann's voice seemed unruffled. "How long dost thou intend to keep us here?"

"Until the court determines a suitable penalty for your offense."

"I see no offense," Ann said. "What crime have we committed?"

"Your presence is crime enough. We have no room for heretics."

Tristram recognized Norton's voice.

"Is it heresy to follow the light that guides us?" Ann asked.

"I'm not here to argue such matters," Bellingham said. "Why have you come to Boston? What do you propose to do here?"

"We can propose nothing while in prison," Mary said.

Ann cut her short. "Our inner spirit led us to this place. We intend no harm. Our only wish is to speak openly about our beliefs so people may judge them on their merits."

"What you wish is a license to spread a heretical doctrine that is contrary to the word of God as expressed in the Bible," Norton said.

"Our beliefs arise from the same book," Ann said.

"If thou art a true Christian, order the jailer to return the Bible that was taken from us," Mary said.

Norton ignored the comment. "Do you hold that prior generations have wrongly interpreted the Bible?" he asked.

"What is written in the Bible was inspired by the spirit," Ann said. "That same spirit still speaks to our hearts and minds. We need only listen to ensure that our words and actions are in accord with God's purpose."

"Enough of this blasphemy! Your words are not from God. They are inspired by Satan. In all likelihood you bear his mark on your body."

"We bear no mark produced by this devil of thy fancy," Ann said.

"I shall determine that for myself," Norton said.

"I hope you know what you're doing," Bellingham said. "I told you that I have little faith in the devil or his marks."

"This case is quite different from that of your sister," Norton said. "The devil has numerous guises. These women are either witches or false prophets. In either case the devil is at work in them. I smell his presence."

"What assails thy nostrils is stale urine," Mary said.

Her comment drew no response.

"Any examination of these women is and must remain unofficial," Bellingham said, "unless of course you find what you seek."

"Women in outward appearance," Norton said, "but their words and their mission identify them as minions of the devil. Once I find his mark, they will cause no further trouble to you or anyone else in Boston."

Some light crept through a crack in the planks that separated the two cells. During this exchange Tristram had made his way to this wall.

"Sit down," Upsall whispered. "You don't want to watch."

"We came here to see how they're treated," Tristram said.

Pressing one eye to the crack, he took in the scene in the next cell. Norton hovered over the two women, who were seated on the platform. Bellingham stood with his back half turned. The jailer leaned against the door, the tallow candle on the table at his side.

"The marks that thou seek mean nothing," Ann said.

"That is yet to be determined," Norton said. "Now if you will be remove your clothes, I shall proceed with the examination."

"Thy request is unwarranted. We must refuse."

"Then the turnkey will remove them for you."

The jailer straightened up. "If you please, sir, my wife is near at hand. It would be more proper if she carried out your orders."

"You're quite right," Bellingham said. "Summon your wife."

"I only thought to have as few witnesses as possible," Norton said.

No one moved as they awaited the arrival of the jailer's wife. The four remaining figures viewed by candlelight formed a tableaux similar to a painting Tristram had seen as a boy on a visit to Bristol with his father. That was before his mother died, before his father remarried and brought the family to New England.

Once inside the cell the jailer's wife placed her hands on her hips and sniffed the air. "Your duty is to empty their chamber pot," she said. "I can't be doing everything myself."

"I was busy," the jailer muttered. "I must have forgot."

"Never mind that," Norton said. "If you will assist these women in removing their clothes, we can get on with the examination."

"What is it you're looking for?" the jailer's wife asked.

"The devil has a variety of telltale signs: bite marks, black spots, warts, scars, extra teats, birthmarks of an odd shape."

"If I find the like, I'll let you know. Now step out in the hall, so I can get to work."

"I must remain here," Norton said.

"It seems only proper that we wait outside," Bellingham said.

"I insist on staying," Norton said. "I know the devil's signature, and I know where to look."

"Have it your way. I'll be out in the hall."

"You must stay too," Norton said. "We'll need a second witness in court. My testimony may not suffice, and this wife is easily intimidated."

"Say you indeed! We'll see about that."

"No offense," Norton said. "I meant that you're not accustomed to a court setting and the questioning."

"I shall stay," Bellingham said, "but I refuse to watch."

The jailer had made no move to leave his post by the doorway.

"We won't be needing your help," his wife said.

Muttering to himself, he stepped out and shut the door behind him, reluctantly it seemed to Tristram. Norton moved the table closer to the platform and positioned the candle so it shed maximum light. Bellingham had turned his back on the proceedings.

"Let's get on with it. Off with your clothes," the jailer's wife said.

The two women remained seated.

"Either you take them off yourself, or my husband will help me to undress you. Take your choice."

Mary rose from the bed. She stared at Norton until he averted his gaze. Tristram watched as she removed her outer garment and unfastened her bodice. She stepped out of her petticoat and undid the pockets. Clad in her shift, she sat down, kicked off her mules, and pulled off the stockings that came to her thigh. Finally, dropping her shift, she stood naked in the light of the single candle.

Tristram pressed his eye closer to the crack. Her body was as he had imagined it, firm breasts, a slender waist, and narrow hips. Blanche was broad, flaccid and somewhat pudgy, a consequence of child bearing. He didn't fault her for that. The comparison was unworthy.

"All right now, where do I start?" the jailer's wife asked.

"I prefer to examine her myself," Norton said.

"That hardly seems proper for a gentleman and a minister."

Norton gave her a scornful look. "My only interest in this woman is to ferret out the devil's work and recognize his mark. Hold the candle close, so I can see what I'm doing."

Turning to Mary, he said, "Let down you hair. I need to examine your head."

Mary did as she was told. Norton ran his fingers over her scalp, parting her hair carefully as he proceeded.

"Hurry it up," Bellingham said. "The candle won't last very long."

"The jailer can fetch another if need be," Norton said. "The devil is wont to conceal his mark in the hair or in body cavities, where it's not readily visible. My examination must be thorough, or it's of no use."

He had finished poring through Mary's hair and was scrutinizing her face and neck. He had her raise her arms so he could inspect the hair in her armpits. Then he turned to the jailer's wife.

"If you'll lift her breasts, I need to look under them."

"I'm perfectly capable of lifting my own breasts," Mary said.

Tristram's forehead ached, but he kept an eye pressed to the crack as Norton worked his way down Mary's body. She held herself rigid, staring straight ahead.

"Please have your husband heat some water and fetch his shaving equipment," Norton said, turning to the jailer's wife.

She was standing to one side with a watchful eye on the minister. "And why would you need that?" she asked.

"I need to examine her private parts."

Mary looked Norton full in the face. "I will not submit to such an indecency." She sat on the platform, her legs pressed tightly together.

"Either you let this good woman shave you so I can see clearly, or I'll have the jailer restrain you while I examine you as I did your head." Norton's tone was imperious.

The jailer's wife had stepped forward. "You'll do no such thing," she said. "Nor will I shave her." Turning to Mary, she spoke more softly. "Lie on your back and let me part the hair so he can look."

Mary appeared to weigh her options. Then she lay back, shut her eyes. "Do thy devil's work. Thou art no man of God."

Norton bent over her, his hands clenched behind his back His legs trembled as he concluded his examination. When he was done, he stood back. Mary got up and quickly donned her clothes. Norton's expression showed that he had failed to find the mark he sought.

Tristram withdrew his eye from the crack in the wall. He rubbed his forehead to relieve the pain.

"Is she good looking?" Upsall asked.

"You could have a look for yourself," Tristram said.

"I don't care to look upon a woman who is beyond my grasp."

Tristram resumed his position. Mary had finished dressing. Norton appeared to have calmed himself.

"You're next," he said, turning to Ann Austin.

As Ann proceeded to disrobe, her age became ever more apparent. Tristram turned away out of propriety.

"What's going on?" Upsall whispered.

"He's examining Ann for marks of the devil."

"God help them both if he finds anything," Upsall said.

When Tristram looked again, Ann was getting dressed. Norton stood with his head lowered, staring at the floor. His shoulders sagged.

"Well, did you find anything?" Bellingham asked.

"The older woman has a black spot on her back, but it bled when I pricked it with a pin. The other one hasn't a blemish."

"Then I must find some other way to rid the colony of this plague."

"The devil may still possess their mind and tongue," Norton said. "Give them time, and they'll convict themselves by their utterance."

"Let us go," Bellingham said. "You've done all you can."

Norton glanced at the women, who had turned their backs on him. The jailer's wife glared at him, as if to say, "I hope you're satisfied." He drew himself up and followed Bellingham out.

When they had left the building, the jailer unlocked the cell where Upsall and Tristram took refuge.

"Are you done with the women?" he asked.

"I doubt that they're in any mood to speak to us now," Upsall said. "But tell me, why aren't they being fed properly? Are you starving them to line your own pockets."

"I have my orders," the jailer said.

"I thought as much. I'll give you three shillings a week, if you'll promise that the food I send in will get to them."

"I risk losing my post."

"I'll make it five shillings. Is it a bargain?"

The jailer considered a moment. "You have my promise," he said

"And give them back their Bible," Upsall said as he was leaving. "It's of no use to you."

* * *

Neither man had much to say on the walk back to the inn. Upsall appeared occupied with his own thoughts, while Tristram grappled with the impression Mary Fisher had made on him. Viewing her nude body was only one factor. Her self-assured manner and her quick responses, coupled with her deference to a senior, struck him as attractive qualities. But most of all he admired her dedication, her conviction that she was in the right place and doing the right thing, her confidence in the ultimate success of her mission. He realized that Ann Austin was responsible in part for these impressions, but he chose to give Mary the benefit. He felt certain that she possessed all of these qualities, whether outspoken or pent up within her. She was like the master of a ship who sets out on a voyage, aware of the dangers and difficulties that lie ahead, but confident in her ability to meet and overcome them. She seemed a good deal like himself.

Blanche had always been dependent on him. She had proved time and again that she was unable to manage on her own. This business with Gorham was but the latest example of her weakness and poor judgment. She was a servant before he married her, and a servant she remained, too willing to accede to the demands of others. He had given her a home and a refuge, but she seemed incapable or unwilling to guard the gates in his absence. His time at sea contributed to the problem; but he had to provide for his family and knew no other trade. It was up to Blanche to adjust to the circumstances of their marriage.

They entered the inn by the tavern door. Upsall drew two tankards of hard cider and joined Tristram at a table. The tavern was empty except for two of the militiamen. A pair of bayberry candles provided the light. Their fragrant aroma was a welcome antidote to the oppressive tallow at the jail. Upsall said they added a certain quality to the inn.

"I'd call our mission a success," Tristram said. "We accomplished all that we set out to do."

"Wait!" Upsall cautioned. "We're not alone."

They sipped their cider until the militiamen rose and climbed the stairs to their garret room.

"Now we can talk," Upsall said. "We could be fined for visiting the women. I don't care about that; but I don't want anyone to know I intend to keep them from starving."

"The conditions in their cell would kill me," Tristram said. "I need fresh air. I don't see how they endure it."

"For them food is more important. In some ways they're fortunate. If Endicott were here, he'd treat them even worse."

"I can't imagine anything more humiliating than that examination. Why would Bellingham agree to it?"

"He wants to banish them, but we have no law that says they can't be here. Norton probably suggested a charge of witchcraft or heresy as a quick way to get rid of them."

"But if he found that mark, they'd be hanged as witches."

"I doubt that Norton believes in witchcraft, but he does believe the ideas being spread by these Quakers are inspired by the devil. He's willing to use any tools at hand. Bellingham would be wise to set them free. They would soon provide him with sufficient cause for banishment. Norton was right about that."

"I feel sorry for them. They came this far only to be cast in prison. They don't deserve such treatment."

"There's little I can do, except to make sure they don't starve."

"Now that you've talked with them, what do you make of their ideas?" Tristram asked.

Upsall downed the rest of his cider before replying. "Their notion of an inner voice is not so different from the conversion experience that our ministers require for admission to the church."

"I never had a conversion experience," Tristram said. "My father was a minister, and I was admitted to the church by default."

"I was an original settler and automatically a church member," Upsall said. "That was the rule before the ministers settled on a conversion requirement. But I was excommunicated five years ago for withdrawing communion from the fellowship of the church, as they put it. I can't see that I'm any the worse for it."

"My father was excommunicated by the church in Barnstable, but he was reconciled before he went to Maine."

"What was his offense?"

"He was accused him of preaching in Yarmouth without approval. I don't know what he had to do to get reinstated."

"Then your father and I have something in common. I haven't felt or acted any differently since I was excommunicated. I suppose I've had what the Quakers call a personal relationship with God. I'd like to learn more about them and what they believe."

"They can't very well instruct you while they're in jail."

"No, but they brought pamphlets with them."

"I thought Bellingham had them all burned," Tristram said.

"Such measures are seldom very thorough," Upsall said. "I think you know Simon Kempthorn, master of the *Swallow*. You might ask him whether any pamphlets escaped the fire."

"Why don't you ask him? He must come by the inn on occasion."

"If I show any interest in the Quakers, I draw attention to myself. I can't afford to do that."

"I can look him up in the morning. Wasn't it enough to put the women in prison? Why did Bellingham have to burn their pamphlets?"

"Burning the book is easier than silencing the ideas it contains."

"Are the women still in danger of death?"

"No one has yet been hanged for heresy."

"I keep thinking about that examination," Tristram said. "How could they endure being probed like that by a man."

"Examined by one man and observed by another," Upsall said.

Tristram laughed. "I won't deny that I found Mary attractive, but I have a wife and children at home."

"How are things with Blanche?"

"I fear she is once again in trouble."

Upsall knew about Blanche's past indiscretions, but Tristram had always spoken of them after the issue was resolved. Despite his decision to seek advice from Upsall, he hesitated to speak about his current problem.

"A man was fined for assaulting her at night," he continued, "and Blanche was fined for not crying out. I wish I could believe that's all there was to it."

"Once lost, trust is hard to regain," Upsall said when Tristram was silent. "But unless you have evidence that she's at fault, make your peace with her. Treat her as you have in the past, with patience and forgiveness."

The advice warranted no further elaboration. Tristram picked up his tankard of cider, saw that it was empty, and set it down again.

Upsall broke the silence. "When do you sail for the West Indies?"

"Not until mid-August."

"Doesn't it trouble you that the plantation owners use slave labor to produce the sugar and molasses you bring back?"

"I deal with the product," Tristram said. "How it's made is on their conscience."

"I'm not sure I can agree with that," Upsall said.

Three

"I didn't want to alarm the children."
(Plymouth Colony, Spring 1656)

The assault on Blanche had preyed on Tristram's mind for some weeks before he broached the subject to Upsall. But business and family concerns took him away from home before he could inquire more fully into the matter. And a longstanding caution in matters concerning his wife made him reluctant to act rashly in a manner he might later regret.

His first word of trouble came not from Blanche but from his sister Joanna. She was on the dock when *The Catch* made port in Yarmouth. It was a warm spring day, and she had cast aside her winter garments in favor of lighter attire. Her trim figure and vitality belied her thirty-six years and the fact that she had four children. She was the oldest of his siblings and the first to marry. Her husband, John Bursley, was master of a merchant ship, and like Tristram was often at sea.

Tristram was surprised to see Joanna waving to him. The timing of his return from a voyage was never definite. Perhaps she had come over from Barnstable to spend the day with Blanche and happened to spot his ship. Or was her presence there a sign of trouble?

"I'm glad you're home," she said as he stepped onto the dock.

"Are the children and Blanche all right?" he asked.

"The children are fine," Joanna said as she freed herself from his embrace, "but Blanche had a rather serious problem while you were gone."

Tristram sighed. "What has she done now?"

After thirteen years of marriage he was not yet inured to his wife's periodic waywardness, leading to charges of unseemly conduct or behavior unbecoming a woman. He had managed in the past to pacify those Blanche offended. Peace at home was restored only when she was once again pregnant. She was currently nursing their fifth child, a daughter born during the winter.

"Blanche and John Gorham were summoned to appear before the magistrate," Joanna said. "Gorham was charged with assaulting her at night. He pleaded guilty and was fined forty shilling, but Blanche was fined fifty shilling for not crying out. I saw your ship and thought you might want to know about it before you went home."

She paused to let Tristram absorb the news. Gorham owned a grist mill and a tannery in Barnstable. He was married with five children. Tristram couldn't imagine why he would assault Blanche. Unless she had invited it.

"Did it happen at home? Were the children involved?"

"I'm not sure. Blanche keeps changing her story. My husband went to the hearing with her. He knows more than I do, but he's at sea now."

"I'll get at the truth," Tristram said.

"Don't be too harsh on her," Joanna said. "Gorham pleaded guilty. I'm sure he's the one to blame."

"I wish I could be sure. I've had this kind of problem with Blanche before, as you well know."

"Remember that you had some problems yourself before you were married," Joanna said.

Tristram laughed. "Sisters never forget anything."

"Nor do wives. Give Blanche a chance to explain. She should have her story straight by now."

"A straight story isn't always the truth."

Joanna ignored his comment. "And stay away from Gorham. You don't want to end up before a magistrate yourself."

"I'll hear what Blanche has to say, but I may have to talk to Gorham. He was there and should know the facts."

"I've said my piece. Now I have to get back to Barnstable. You can call on me if you need advice."

"Seems like you've pretty well exhausted your supply."

"Good-bye, Tristram. Give my regards to Blanche."

Joanna strode off with a swift sure pace. Tristram watched her until she was out of sight. Her youthful vigor contrasted with Blanche's matronly appearance and manner. What did Gorham see in her that was so attractive? Or was Blanche attracted to him? Mulling these questions over in his mind, he set off for home.

* * *

On returning from a voyage it was his custom, after he greeted the children, to retire with Blanche to the chamber where they slept. He hoped none of the children were involved in this affair. But Blanche's appearance before the magistrate was public knowledge, and Mary must be aware of it. The others were too young to know anything was wrong. Sarah was six, Joseph four, John two, and Hannah four months.

Blanche greeted him as usual; but her embrace seemed less ardent, and her smile struck him as tentative. The children were as demonstrative as ever in their welcome.

"Tend to the young ones," he told Mary. "Your mother and I have something to talk about."

The girl appeared uneasy as she ushered the three youngsters who could walk outside. Left alone in the house with the baby, neither he nor Blanche made a move toward the chamber. She straightened her apron, which had no need of it; then stood stolidly near the hearth.

He planned to ask first about her health and that of the children, but now he blurted out, "What's this I hear about you and John Gorham?"

Blanche seemed to expect the question and launched at once into an explanation. Listening to her, he recalled previous instances when she sounded equally convincing. But perhaps this time she was telling the truth. He would try to keep an open mind.

"Before you went away, I ordered a leather satchel at the tannery. When I stopped by to ask about it. Gorham apologized for the delay and said he would get at it right away. The next day he came to the door after dark. He had the satchel in his hand. He wanted to come in, he said, so I could hold it up to a candle and have a good look at it. I said I could look at it with no help from him, and asked him to wait outside. When I went back, he grabbed me. He said the only payment he wanted was a kiss. I could tell from his manner that he wanted more than that. I tried to push him away. We struggled and fell to the floor. Then something must have frightened him, because he let me go and ran off into the night."

"Joanna said you had to appear in court and were fined for failing to cry out when he assaulted you."

"I didn't want to alarm the children."

"How did the magistrate get involved?"

Blanche appeared to be confused by the question. "It came out at the hearing that a man serving on the grand jury happened to pass by and see us. I have no idea what he thought was happening, but he felt it was his duty to report it to the constable. The whole affair was unfortunate, but it was no matter for the court."

She spoke without emotion, displaying no sign of contriteness or regret, as if the incident had happened to someone else and was of slight importance. Tristram found her account too smooth and well rehearsed. Blanche had been involved much too often in such difficulties.

"Why would Gorham come to the house? He must have thought you would welcome him."

Blanche bristled at his question. "I certainly did not invite him to assault me, if that's what you mean to imply."

"I'm just trying to understand why the magistrate ruled the way he did," Tristram said. "I want the truth."

"I told the magistrate what happened, like I told you; but he chose to believe Gorham's story instead."

"What story? Joanna said Gorham pleaded guilty."

"I've told you what happened. Believe it or not, as you like."

Tristram knew it was futile to question her further. In the past he had yielded to Blanche's ultimatums to maintain peace in the family. But the magnitude of her fine troubled him. Why was she fined at all if Gorham admitted to the assault? His prior experience stood in the way of acceptance and forgiveness.

"I'd like to believe you," he said, "but I feel that you're not being completely honest. We can talk again when we're calmer."

"If that's what you want," Blanche said.

* * *

Tristram was reluctant to confront Gorham until he had done what he could to verify Blanche's account. Bursley would know what occurred at the hearing and why the magistrate fined both parties to the assault, but he was at sea. A ready source of information was the local ordinary owned by Edward Sturgis, though much of what one heard there was rumor or gossip.

Sturgis had kept the inn more than a decade. Tristram considered him a friend, and had on occasion delivered liquor to him without having it inventoried. Sturgis was well over forty, but from his youthful look and cheerful manner they could have been brothers. He had a wife and three or four children. Tristram was unsure of the number.

The inn was not nearly as spacious as the Red Lyon in Boston. It had two stories, with two rooms on each floor. The tavern was at ground level with a chamber for guests above. The family occupied the other two rooms. As Tristram arrived, two men came from the tavern, tankards in hand, and sat on a bench outside the entrance. Sturgis greeted him as he entered and poured him an ale.

"Are you home for a spell now?" he asked.

"Maybe a week or so. Then I want to check on my half sister in Ipswich and visit relatives in York and Oyster River. I haven't seen Naomi for some time."

"Is she the one your father placed with Judge Symonds before he went to England?" Sturgis asked.

"That's right."

"How old is she now?"

"Sixteen, or thereabouts."

"You're lucky she has someone to keep an eye on her. My oldest is about that age, and I worry about her getting in trouble."

"Speaking of trouble," Tristram said, "do you know anything about what happened between Gorham and Blanche while I was away."

Sturgis glanced about him before he replied. "All I know is what I heard here in the tavern. There was a lot of talk about it at the time."

"Someone reported it to the constable? Do you know who it was?"

"It was Crow. He claimed it was his duty to report it."

"John Crow?"

"The other one, Yelverton."

"What was he doing around my house at that hour of night?"

"He claims he happened to be passing by, but some say he was hired by Sam Mayo's wife to spy on Blanche. Seems she has a grudge against her because of that business a few years back."

That business was a complaint lodged against Blanche by John Willis of Duxbury for striking his stepdaughter and interfering with her service as a domestic in Mayo's family. Blanche had defaulted by failing to attend the hearing and was issued a warning to desist.

"That has no bearing on the case," Tristram said. "The magistrate must have based his decision on hard evidence. What did Crow see that he felt bound to report?"

"He said he saw Blanche and Gorham embracing each other at the door of your house. Then something startled Gorham, and he ran off. Crow claims that Gorham admitted to the assault to hide what was really going on between them."

"You mean they were seeing each other?"

"I'm sure that's what he meant. He never said how he came to know about it. I've heard comments about how they look at each other, but I know of nothing to indicate they were having an affair."

"You're friendly with Gorham. What did he have to say?"

"He claims it was all a misunderstanding. He and Desire have six children and a seventh on the way. Why would he chase after Blanche?"

"In that kind of chase," Tristram said, "it's hard at times to tell the hunter from the one being hunted. What you say seems to jibe pretty well with Blanche's story, but I want to get all the facts before I face Gorham."

"Are you planning to have it out with him?" Sturgis asked.

"It may come to that," Tristram said.

* * *

In the days following his return home neither Tristram nor Blanche spoke any further of the assault. They slept together but made no move to reach out to each other. During the day an uneasy truce prevailed. He was grateful that the children were too young to notice. All but Mary.

"Is something wrong between you and Mother?" she asked one day when they were outside the house.

"Nothing we can't work out between us," he said.

"Is it about her having to see the magistrate?"

Tristram wondered how much she knew about what had transpired that night. He refused to ask her. She was too young to be dragged into his domestic problems.

"You needn't worry," he said. "Everything will be all right. Your mother and I understand each other very well."

Mary seemed to be satisfied by his reassurance.

He needed to speak to Bursley, but he wasn't expected back for a fortnight. Ample time for a visit to Naomi and his siblings in Maine. A few days at sea might help to clear his mind.

* * *

Instead of taking Naomi with him to England, Tristram's father had placed her with Samuel Symonds in Ipswich, a man who served with him on the General Court. She was eight at the time. He intended to return within a year, but the Civil War and the ascendency of Cromwell as Lord Protector had obliged him to remain in England.

Symonds had a daughter about the same age, and Naomi appeared to adjust well to her new home. She spoke at length of her childish affairs; but as the years went by, she seemed to lose interest in her family. She was now sixteen. Tristram's visits to Ipswich were infrequent, due largely to the duration of his voyages along the coast and to the West Indies.

Symonds had a large house overlooking the harbor. His household included a number of servants. His clothes and his erect carriage lent him a dignified air that befitted a man of his status in the community.

He greeted Tristram at the door and ushered him into the parlor. "We need to talk before you see Naomi," he said by way of explanation.

"Is something wrong?" Tristram asked. "Is she ill?"

"You might call it that. She's expecting a baby."

"Who is the father?"

"One of my servants. I've dismissed the man, but we must decide what to do with the child when it's born. I thought one of your sisters in Maine might care for it until Naomi is able to assume that responsibility. I'm willing to contribute something toward the child's support."

"And what do you get in return?" Tristram asked.

He sensed that Symonds had some sort of business arrangement all worked out. He could understand that. He was in business himself.

"I would expect Naomi to perform some service in my household to compensate me for any expenses I might incur in raising her child."

"Isn't she already a servant in your house?"

"We've always treated her as if she were one of the family, but the baby changes all that."

"What if she wants to keep the baby with her?"

Symonds frowned. "I want what is best for Naomi. I'd like to spare her the disgrace and shame of bringing up a bastard child in a town where she's well known."

"And you avoid any scandal in your own household."

"That too. Will you speak to your sisters?"

"I plan to see Temperance and Dorothy in Oyster River. I can ask if one of them would be willing to take the baby."

"I've drawn up an agreement. It's wise in such matters to specify the obligations of all parties involved. We can sign it while you're here. That way your sister will know what she's agreeing to."

"I'd like to speak to Naomi before we sign anything."

"Of course. She and my daughter Ruth are in the garden. They've become inseparable. Of course that will have to change, now that Naomi is no longer a child."

Tristram restrained a surge of anger. Directed to the garden, he found Naomi sitting on a bench alone. Had she already been ostracized?

His contact with his half sister over the years had been limited. He was a veritable stranger to Naomi. She was an infant when Bursley took him on as an apprentice seaman. Since then he was much at sea, and his family occupied the rest of his time. He wondered if she would even agree to discuss her situation with him.

"I'm glad you're here," Naomi said as she rose to embrace him. "I thought the whole family had forgotten about me."

They sat side by side on the bench. She was taller, her face more freckled, than he recalled from past visits. The hair peeking out from her bonnet was as dark as ever, and the loose garments she wore showed no evidence that she was losing her slim figure. But her overall appearance and attitude were indeed more mature. She was, as Symonds indicated, no longer a child.

"I understand you're expecting a baby," he said

Naomi glanced at her stomach. "I think it's beginning to show."

"Symonds said one of his servants is the father. Did the man force himself on you?"

"It wasn't his fault," she said. "I suppose I half invited him."

"No matter now whose fault it was. We have to decide what to do about it."

Tristram went on to explain the plan as Symonds had presented it.

"I told him I wanted to talk to you first," he concluded. "If Dorothy or Temperance agree to take the baby, are you content to give it up?"

"Do I have any choice?" Naomi asked. "What else can I do?"

He didn't blame her for being bitter. It would have been far better for Naomi if their father had taken her with him to England.

"Symonds wants you to become a servant to compensate him for supporting the child."

"I'm quite accustomed to that."

"He claims you and Ruth are close friends and that you're treated as one of the family."

"He can claim what he likes. The truth is, I've been nothing but a servant ever since Father sent word that he was staying in England."

"I suspected that you weren't very happy here," Tristram said.

"It's not so bad. Judge Symonds is strict, but he treats me fairly."

"Then you'll do as he suggests?"

"I'd like Dorothy to have the baby, but I've no say in that either."

"Maybe they'll offer to take you in along with the baby."

"They could have done that years ago, if they wanted me."

Tristram sensed that she was accusing him as well. He had but one child at the time. He might have offered to care for Naomi until his father returned. The truth of the matter was that neither he nor any of his sisters was asked to take her in. He didn't blame his father for that. He had gone to England to settle the estate of his brother William's widow, planning to return within a year. It made sense to put Naomi in a home with children her own age. When, for some reason Tristram could not wholly fathom, he was unable to return, it made equally good sense to leave her in Ipswich, where she was presumed to be happy.

Still, he might offer now to take Naomi and her child into his own home. The problem was, there was no room for them. Placing a bastard child and its mother with a wayward wife would only compound his own problems and do neither of them any good. He might speak to Joanna, but he thought it best to approach Temperance and Dorothy first. They might well agree to take the baby. He wouldn't suggest that they take in Naomi as well. That would be asking too much.

"I'm on my way to Oyster River now," he said. "Symonds has drawn up a contract to make it all legal. He wants us to sign it, but I won't sign anything unless you agree."

"Do you advise me to do as he says?"

"As you say, we have little choice."

"I don't want Father to know about the baby," Naomi said. "Not now anyway."

"I trust we can keep it a secret."

The next day when he set sail, Tristram had the contract in hand. It stated the terms of Naomi's service and specified how much Symonds would contribute for the child's support. The judge insisted that Tristram sign too as a witness that Naomi was not acting under duress.

Thus armed, Tristram traversed the Piscataqua River to Great Bay, then up the Oyster River to his destination. In addition to two sisters, two half brothers, Benjamin and Hopewell, lived in Oyster River plantation. Another sister, Elizabeth, lived farther upstream in Cochecho, bordering on Indian territory. Naomi hadn't mentioned her brothers in the course of their talk, so Tristram decided to present his case only to Dorothy and Temperance.

He approached Temperance first. In his estimation she was more likely to refuse. That would put pressure on Dorothy to take in the child, which was the outcome Naomi preferred. The reaction of Temperance to his proposal was initially as he expected, but her attitude changed when he produced the contract. After consulting with John Bickford, her husband, she agreed to give the child a home until Naomi was old enough and had the means to provide that care. They made no offer to take in Naomi as well, and Tristram did not broach the subject.

Following a visit to his other relatives in the area and a brief stop in York to see his unmarried sister Griselda, Tristram returned to Ipswich, where he delivered the signed contract to Symonds. He promised Naomi he would come by more often in the future, but added that he was often at sea on long voyages. She said she understood. With mixed feelings as to what he had accomplished, he left her with Symonds. But before returning home to Yarmouth, he stopped in Boston to check on the *Hopewell*, which was undergoing repairs for a voyage to the West Indies later in the summer.

Four

"Why did the magistrate blame you more than Gorham?"
(Plymouth Colony, Summer 1656)

All this was fresh in Tristram's mind as he retired to his room at the Red Lyon after visiting the Quakers in prison. He was determined to settle matters at home before he sailed for the West Indies. After he talked to Bursley about what took place in court, he would decide whether or not to confront Gorham. He might also speak to the magistrate. He wanted to learn all he could before raising the subject again at home.

Blanche had entered his life when he was eighteen, an apprentice to Bursley. She was a servant indentured to a family in Sandwich and was pregnant by an Indian she encountered in the forest. Having broken family ties by going off to sea, he was moved to marry this free spirit and release her from shame and servitude. He liked her flashing eyes and her unruly blonde hair, her thirst for life and experience. Heeding his father's advice, he persuaded her to relinquish the child to its Indian father. Yet at times like this he wondered whether she had yielded to the brave's strength, as she said, or whether she had willingly coupled with him. Her silence in the face of Gorham's assault seemed to signify a degree of acquiescence.

But before he left Boston, he had a promise to keep.

The next day he rowed out to the *Swallow*, a ship similar in size and rigging to the *Hopewell*. Kempthorn received him cordially but with obvious caution. He was about thirty years old. His broad shoulders and swarthy features commanded attention, though he appeared too heavy for his short stature. He seemed skeptical at first of Tristram's interest in stray pamphlets, but agreed to search the area where the Quakers slept.

"I didn't want to take them aboard," he said, "but I had no choice. It was either that or risk losing my connection on Barbados. Do you know Thomas Rous?"

Tristram shook his head. "Who is he?"

"He has one of the largest sugar plantations on the island. Both he and his son John have become Quakers. He practically ordered me to take the women to New England. They've been nothing but trouble ever since I agreed to give them passage."

"What kind of trouble?" Tristram asked.

"They had half of my crew listening to their inner voice instead of tending to business and sailing the ship. One of them even tried to make a Quaker out of me, but I would have none of it."

Tristram wondered if it was Mary Fisher, but dared not ask lest he let on that he had seen and spoken to the women.

"When I reported that I had two Quakers aboard," Kempthorn said, "Bellingham had me confine them to the ship until he decided what to do with them. I didn't want to tell him who paid for their passage to Boston, but he pried it out of me. When I mentioned Rous's name, Bellingham had them put in jail. I was glad to be shed of them."

"I've heard talk that he wants to send them back to Barbados."

"He can do what he likes with them, as long as I'm not involved. I don't need any more aggravation. I'm getting married in September. What are you going to do with these pamphlets you're looking for?"

"Give them to a friend. That's all I'm willing to say."

"It's none of my business. I doubt that we'll turn up anything. The man who searched the ship seized all he could find."

They had entered the fo'c'sle. In the dim light Tristram discerned bunks and bedding and sea bags belonging to the crew of the *Swallow*. He was inclined to agree that their search would be fruitless. Then he asked himself where he might hide a pamphlet, if he were in a similar position. The obvious answer was in the bedding of one of the crew.

"Is this where they slept?" he asked.

"Somewhere around here. I didn't check on them very often."

Tristram rummaged through all the bedding in the vicinity, his fingers alert for any unusual object that might be hidden there. He was beginning to despair of finding anything, when the young seaman he had encountered at the Red Lyon appeared on the scene.

"What is it you're looking for?" he asked.

"Any pamphlets the women brought with them," Tristram said.

"They were all carted off to be burned."

"Every last one of them?"

"All they could find. A couple of men who listened to their talk were given pamphlets, but they couldn't make any sense of the words."

"Where are those pamphlets now?"

"Unless they heaved them over the side, they're likely tucked away in their seabag. Shall I see what I can find?" he asked Kempthorn.

Kempthorn nodded, and the seaman ran his hands through several of the bags. He grinned broadly as he held up two pamphlets.

"May I take them with me?" Tristram asked.

Kempthorn seemed uncertain how to respond.

The seaman spoke up. "They'll be glad to get rid of them. I can vouch for that."

"You can tell them there's a free meal waiting for them at the Red Lyon," Tristram said. "And for you as well."

"I'll do that," the seaman said, handing over the pamphlets.

Tristram stuffed them inside his shirt. After thanking Kempthorn for his cooperation, he rowed back to shore.

That afternoon he delivered the pamphlets to Upsall. "The price was three free meals," he said.

* * *

Satisfied that all was in order on the *Hopewell*, Tristram left the mate in charge of repairs and returned home to spend time with Blanche and the children. Neither of them made mention of Gorham. Three days later, hearing that Bursley's ship was in port, he paid a visit to his sister.

Joanna had several loaves in the chimney oven, and the aroma of baking bread permeated the hall. "John will be back soon," she said. "You look as if you have weighty matters to discuss."

"You're right as usual," Tristram said. "I still haven't resolved this business about Blanche and Gorham."

"Didn't Blanche tell you what happened?"

"I don't think she told me the whole truth. When I asked why she was fined ten shillings more than Gorham, she shrugged it off as a whim of the magistrate. There has to be more to it."

"Gorham was the one fined for assault," Joanna said. "It seems to me your quarrel is with him, not with Blanche."

"I suppose so, but she has a certain reputation in the town. Sturgis says there's still some talk about it."

"If you think Blanche is to blame, tell her so. But you may not like what she has to say."

"What do you mean by that?" Tristram asked.

"You and John are two of a kind. You're off at sea for weeks and months at a time, and you feel that your wives should be content to keep house and care for the children. I don't condone Blanche's behavior, but I can understand why she might listen to someone who offers her some affection in your absence."

"So you think she's partly responsible."

"All I said was that I could understand it if she were."

"Have you ever been tempted in that way yourself?"

"Only a brother would ask a question like that."

"Or a husband," Tristram said.

"I won't say it hasn't happened," Joanna said, "but I've never given in to such a temptation. Now are you satisfied?"

"You've just confirmed what I already know about you."

The sound of a man's voice raised in song reached their ears.

"I hear John coming. I'll leave you two to talk in private."

That was how Joanna dealt with life's vicissitudes. Having voiced her opinion, she left the decision to others. Tristram wondered where she had acquired that trait. As a minister their father was undisputed head of the household. Their mother had died when they were children, and their stepmother Agnes was rarely more than an obedient helpmate.

Bursley greeted him warmly. His weatherbeaten looks attested to his age, but his movements were those of a much younger man.

"What brings you here?" he asked. "Did you come to say goodbye to Joanna before you leave again for the Indies?"

"I came to thank you for supporting Blanche in her trouble with Gorham," Tristram said. "But I'd like to know what happened when she appeared before the magistrate."

Bursley frowned. "Joanna said you two had worked all that out."

"We've talked about it, but I still have some questions."

"Let's take a walk. That's a subject for the open air."

Bursley led the way outside. A short distance from the house he leaned against a tree and ran a hand over his beard.

"Blanche asked me to go with her," he said. "I could see that she was upset. It was all fairly straightforward. She claimed Gorham assaulted her, and he didn't deny it."

"Why did the magistrate fine Blanche? He must have felt that she invited it, that it wasn't actually an assault."

"Is that what you think?" Bursley asked.

"It's not the first time I've had reason to suspect her, as you well know. She says her reason for not crying out was that she didn't want to alarm the children."

"That sounds like a valid reason."

"I was hoping that you might know something that would help me get at the truth."

"You seem to have decided where the truth lies."

"Do you think Gorham would assault a woman in her own home?"

"He might, if he thought she encouraged him. Maybe he went too far before realizing he was mistaken."

"Sturgis said that Yelverton Crow witnessed the assault and filed the complaint."

"That was rather curious," Bursley said. "Blanche was the one who charged Gorham with assault. Crow never granted that what he saw was a struggle. He kept harping on the fact that Blanche didn't cry out for help."

"Maybe that's what influenced the magistrate to fine her too."

"Suppose Blanche admits she was unfaithful. Will you leave her?"

"I can't do that. We have five children. They need a mother."

"Then your best course is to accept her story of what happened."

"Joanna said pretty much the same thing."

"Gorham may have chosen to pay the fine for assault rather than create a scandal."

"Do you think I should speak to him?" Tristram asked.

"That's up to you," Bursley said. "Just take care, or you're apt to find yourself facing the magistrate."

* * *

Gorham eyed Tristram warily as he entered the grist mill. He was over forty, clean shaven, with rugged good looks. The noise made by the grinding stone and the creaking of the vanes as they turned in the wind made it impossible to talk. He motioned Tristram to wait for him outside. Several minutes passed before he appeared, and Tristram wondered if he might be rehearsing his defense.

"I've wanted to talk to you," he said before Tristram could speak. "I owe you an apology. I don't know what your wife told you, but it was all a misunderstanding."

"What do you mean by a misunderstanding?" Tristram asked. He hadn't expected an immediate peace offering.

"I went to your house that evening to deliver a leather bag your wife ordered. It wasn't ready when I promised it to her, and I wanted to make amends. I followed her inside when she went to fetch payment. I thought she invited me to come in, but she turned to block my way and lost her balance. I tried to catch her and cushion her fall. We were both on the floor, when I saw your oldest girl. She was staring at us from the loft, and she had a puzzled look on her face. I expected Blanche to say it was all right, but she shoved me out of the house and shut the door behind me. The next thing I knew, I was charged with assaulting her."

Like Blanche's story, Gorham's explanation struck Tristram as too well considered to be fully credible. Mary's role in the incident was a new piece of information. Why had Blanche omitted such an important detail?

"Were you aware that someone outside saw you?"

"That came out at the hearing. Crow thought he saw an assault and reported it to Rock, the constable."

"Did you give the magistrate your account of what happened?"

"I didn't get the chance. Blanche had already told her story, and I didn't want to contradict her. I could see that she was scared and upset, so I decided to plead guilty and pay the fine. It was the easiest way out."

It sounded all too plausible. "I'm still not convinced it was only a misunderstanding," Tristram said.

Gorham's face reddened, but he controlled his anger. "Ask your wife. She'll tell you it's the truth."

"I've spoken to her. She never mentioned losing her balance. She claims you tried to kiss her."

"That's what she told the magistrate. I doubt that he believed her."

"Are you saying she lied?"

Tristram straightened and clenched his fists. He stood half a head taller than Gorham, but otherwise they were well matched.

Gorham took a step back and raised both hands, the palms open. "I was just fined for assaulting your wife," he said. "I'm not looking to be charged with anything else. I was wrong to go to your house after dark; and I apologize for the trouble I've caused you."

"Will you promise to stay away from Blanche in the future?"

"I don't know what you're implying, but you have my promise."

"Then for the time being I accept your apology."

On that note they parted. Though pleased that their talk had been amicable, Tristram was vaguely dissatisfied with the results. If they only made contact when Blanche was falling, why would she charge him with assault? Why claim that he tried to kiss her? Even if Gorham's apology seemed rehearsed, it might prove helpful in drawing the whole story out of Blanche. He thought of questioning Mary as well, but dismissed the idea. Her version of what she had seen might be based more on fantasy than on fact. He would talk again to Blanche and try not to appear belligerent.

* * *

The following day they set out on an evening walk along the trail that led to Barnstable. When Blanche paused to rest, Tristram sat beside her on a fallen tree trunk.

"There's something I need to know," he said, taking her hand. She tried to withdraw it, but he tightened his grasp.

"If it's John Gorham you want to talk about," she said, "that's over and done with."

"I'm just trying to understand what happened that night."

"I told you everything. He wanted to kiss me. I tried to push him away. Then something scared him, and he ran off."

"You didn't mention that Mary saw you."

"Who told you that?"

"I spoke to Gorham. He claims it was a misunderstanding."

"What else did he have to say?"

"That's not important. What was it that Mary saw?"

"Have you spoken to her as well?"

"I haven't, and I won't. That's why I'm asking you."

"Mary saw us there on the floor. I tried to explain to her that I was in no danger; but she was too upset to understand. She kept insisting that I go to the constable. I didn't know what ideas she had in her head or what she thought she saw; so I told her I would, just to calm her down. I didn't intend to do it. Then that nosey scoundrel Crow insisted he saw us hugging each other. I was scared and felt the only way out was to say I was being assaulted. It was the truth."

"But why did the magistrate blame you more than Gorham?"

"You'll have to ask him about that. He kept harping on my failure to cry out. I finally asked him whether he would want his children to see something like that. It shut him up, but he still fined me."

"Gorham says you tried to stop him from following you inside; that you lost your balance and he tried to catch you before you fell. He says there was no struggle."

"He can say what he wants," Blanche said, her eyes flashing. "I've told you what happened. You can believe whomever you like."

"I want to believe you, Blanche; but the magistrate must have had some reason for fining you more than he did Gorham."

"Maybe he thought we were lovers. Is that what you think too?"

"I'm not sure what to think. Just tell me that Gorham had no reason to think you'd be pleased to see him."

"I don't know what he may have thought. I didn't ask him to come to the house, and I didn't invite him in. If he says otherwise, he lies."

With that Blanche withdrew her hand, got to her feet, and walked rapidly back the way they had come.

Tristram watched her until she was no longer in sight. It was not the outcome he hoped for. Nothing was settled. She had neither admitted nor denied that she and Gorham were attracted to each other. She did say that it was over and done with. But what did she mean: the business with the magistrate, the affair with Gorham, or both? Had the fine led her to put an end to whatever was going on between them?

Tristram had little confidence in that assessment, nor any notion of what to do next. Should he forgive her and put it out of his mind? Should he remain on the alert for future transgressions? And what of Mary? What had she witnessed, and how had it affected her?

He forced himself to think of his upcoming voyage to the West Indies. Two months at sea might enable him to view the situation with greater clarity. It had worked in the past. Yet the fact that Blanche would be alone gave him pause. It would be a trial period for both of them.

Five

Back in Boston Tristram busied himself with final preparations for his voyage to the West Indies. The *Hopewell*'s cargo consisted of flour, fish, meat, and staves used to construct barrels for the molasses he would carry on his return voyage. He didn't need Upsall to remind him that this trade depended on slave labor. He had never transported slaves himself. Thus he salved his conscience while still reaping the profit.

Several days before he was due to sail, he stopped by the Red Lyon to inquire about the Quaker women. The weather had turned humid, usual for mid-August. His clothing was damp from intermittent showers. Upsall was not there. Dorothy said he would be back soon, so he sat down at the long table to wait.

"I need to talk to you," a voice behind him said.

He turned to see Kempthorn at a side table. He stood up, and they shook hands; a little too warmly, Tristram thought. Was he in trouble over those pamphlets? He hoped Kempthorn had not implicated him in that business. He had no time for a court appearance.

"When do you sail for the West Indies?" Kempthorn asked.

"Within the week," Tristram said.

"Will you make port in Barbados?"

"Most of my business is on St. Kitts and Nevis, but I put in at Bridgetown on occasion. Why do you ask?"

"I have a problem with those Quakers. Since I had the misfortune of bringing them to Boston, Bellingham has ordered me to take them back where they came from."

Tristram made the connection at once. "You want me to take the women back to Barbados."

"That's the idea," Kempthorn said.

"Why can't you take them yourself?"

"I think I told you, I'm getting married next month to Mary Long. Her father owns the Three Cranes in Charlestown. I'm not planning to make another voyage right away."

"Why not take your bride to Barbados? Her maiden voyage." Tristram intended the comment as humor, but it fell flat.

"Bellingham wants the Quakers out of Boston this month. I can't get a cargo that fast, and I don't want to postpone my wedding."

"Does Bellingham know you're getting married?"

"That's of no concern to him. He wants to be rid of those women. I don't expect you to do it for nothing. I can give you a letter of introduction to Thomas Rous, the planter I told you about. He lives in the parish of St. Philip and has one of the largest plantations on the island. I'm sure he'll have a full cargo for you on your return voyage."

Tristram's first inclination was to turn down the proposal. It was one thing to gaze briefly on Mary Fisher's naked body, quite another to have daily contact with her on a lengthy voyage. But his contacts on St. Kitts and Nevis were not as lucrative as he wished. Barbados had become the most prosperous island in the West Indies. It would be to his advantage to have a connection there.

"The last time we talked, you said the women were nothing but trouble," he asked. "Now you want me to take them aboard."

"I won't lie to you. A day out of Bridgetown I was sorry I agreed to give them passage. They're hard to deal with, especially the younger one. She wanted everyone to listen to their inner voice. I soon set the crew straight about whose voice they had to heed, if they expected to get paid at the end of the voyage."

Tristram was thoughtful. Taking the women to Barbados posed no great inconvenience for him. Despite what Kempthorn had said, he did not view them as troublesome. Their preaching did not concern him. He could not picture himself as a Quaker. But the prospect of getting to know Mary Fisher better was attractive. Who could tell what might result from having her aboard the *Hopewell*?

Reining in his imagination, he made what he considered a rational decision. He would treat the two women with respect and courtesy, neither seeking nor avoiding contact with them. Where that might lead was up to them. He told himself he had no ulterior motives regarding Mary Fisher, and he almost believed it.

"Having two women aboard will be a burden," he said, so as not to appear overly eager, "but I think I can manage it."

"I see Bellingham tomorrow morning," Kempthorn said. "If we go together, we should be able to convince him that you're in a much better position than I am to carry out his wishes. The way the order is written, I must either transport them or cause them to be transported. It would take a month to ready the *Swallow* for another voyage. If we inform him that you can remove the women within a week, he can't very well refuse."

"I'll meet you in the morning," Tristram said.

"And I'll draw up that letter of introduction to Rous," Kempthorn said. "You won't regret it."

With that he rose and left the tavern.

* * *

"I hear you've been talking to Kempthorn."

Tristram turned to greet Upsall. "Bellingham has ordered him to take the two Quakers back to Barbados on the *Swallow*. But he's getting married next month and wants me to take them. The wording of the order gives him a way out. I'm leaving next week, and he says Bellingham will be glad to get rid of them."

"He's right about that. Did you agree to do it?"

"For a price. I get a new contact in Barbados."

"And you get to see Mary Fisher again."

Tristram smiled. "That thought did occur to me. Have you spoken to the women recently?"

"I saw them a week ago. I wanted to make sure they were getting the food I send in. Conditions in the prison are no better; but they aren't starving, and they have their Bible back."

"Have they passed a law banishing Quakers?"

"There's no law, but the court ruled that the two women pose a threat to the community. That's how Bellingham can send them back to Barbados. But you'll need his approval for your deal with Kempthorn, unless you propose to transfer the women after you put to sea."

"Kempthorn has a meeting with him tomorrow morning. Do you think Bellingham will refuse?"

"The timing is in your favor, and the fact that Kempthorn is getting married should help. Bellingham had to overcome some obstacles to his own marriage. It was quite a scandal at the time."

"What sort of obstacles?" Tristram asked.

"Bellingham was fifty, widowed, and the governor. She was twenty and engaged to a friend of his. He avoided the banns by performing the ceremony himself. The magistrates agreed to hear the case, but he refused to be questioned. As governor he was chief magistrate, so the case died."

"Kempthorn warned me that the women might be troublesome. I didn't let on that I'd met them."

"They'll be disappointed and unhappy," Upsall said. "They came here on a mission and failed to carry it out."

"Maybe their mission wasn't a complete failure," Tristram said.

"What do you mean?"

"Have you read those pamphlets I gave you?" Tristram asked.

Upsall nodded. "I told the women about them. They were pleased that some of their literature escaped the fire."

"Did they try to convert you?"

"They seek to convince anyone who will listen to them. Not that they see anyone except the jailer, and he turns a deaf ear. I asked them a few questions, and they had a ready answer. I can see why their beliefs are anathema to those in authority. But we've had enough whipping, hanging, and banishment, whether it's for heresy or witchcraft. A man should be free to follow whatever truth his mind and conscience reveals to him. On the day of judgment we'll answer to God, not to Endicott or Bellingham."

"That sounds like the inner voice the Quakers listen to."

"There's some truth in what they preach," Upsall said. "I can see why Bellingham wants to banish them. Their ideas threaten the peace of the community and the livelihood of ministers of the gospel."

"I'll be glad when I'm at sea again," Tristram said. "I need to clear my head. Not so much of the Quakers, but of personal matters."

"Have you made peace with Blanche?"

"It's more of a truce. I have several different accounts of what took place, and I don't know which one to believe. I'm counting on this voyage to calm my mind. Perhaps my inner voice will reveal the truth."

"I can give you one of my pamphlets," Upsall said.

Tristram laughed. "I'm sure the women will be glad to assist me."

* * *

Richard Bellingham ran his hands lovingly over the desk in the governor's office as he awaited the arrival of Simon Kempthorn. Were he now the governor, as he had been twice and was determined to be again, the Quakers would be on their way back to Barbados by now. No need for a court ruling or that fruitless and distasteful examination for signs of the devil. Now word had arrived informing him that Endicott would remain in Salem for a fortnight. He had some freedom to act on his own initiative. Let the governor make what he would of it when he returned.

.The ruling lay on the desk before him. Bellingham read the final words again. The magistrates had found the two women "not only to be transgressors of the former laws, but to hold very dangerous, heretical, and blasphemous opinions; and they do also acknowledge that they came here purposely to propagate their said errors and heresies, bringing with them and spreading here sundry books, wherein are contained most corrupt, heretical, and blasphemous doctrines contrary to the truth of the gospel here professed amongst us."

Several ministers had requested that the women be examined yet again. In their eyes it was a short step from heresy to witchcraft. But the death of his sister remained fresh in his mind. He had no stomach for any more hangings. It was enough to send these Quakers back where they came from. All he needed now was Kempthorn's agreement.

When the clerk announced his arrival, Bellingham was surprised to see that he was not alone.

"Grant me the liberty, your honor, of introducing Tristram Hull," Kempthorn said. "He is master of the *Hopewell,* and is now readying for a voyage to the West Indies."

Bellingham studied the man who stood before him. He had never dealt with Hull, but he recalled his father, an excommunicated minister whom Winthrop had labeled contentious. It was a term that men had often applied to him, one that he was proud to own. He turned his attention to Kempthorn. From his downcast eyes and obsequious manner, Bellingham gathered that a plea of hardship was in the offing.

"I trust you've come to inform me that you will take the Quakers back to Barbados at once," he said.

"I've read the order, your honor; and it states that I can either take them or arrange for them to be taken. I'm getting married in a few weeks and a voyage to Barbados would disrupt my plans. Master Hull here has agreed to carry out your order."

"You may be right about the wording of the order, but I'll need a much better reason to approve any change to the expressed wishes of the magistrates. Your marriage plans are of no concern to me."

Kempthorn appeared unflustered by the rejection.

"Master Hull is ready to sail tomorrow," he said. "Even if I put off my marriage, I would need at least three weeks to prepare for a voyage. I feel confident that your honor will take my situation into account and approve the change I propose."

Bellingham accepted the deference as his due, but he was angered by the subtle reference to the measures he had taken to facilitate his own marriage. Kempthorn had brought the Quakers to Boston, and he must pay the price to remove them. Then he realized that in three weeks Endicott would be back from Salem. It would be out of his hands. Ridding himself at once of the Quakers was definitely to his advantage. But he could keep this annoying sea merchant on the hook a while longer.

"You should have considered all that before you provided passage for these Quakers," he said.

"I acted in good faith, your honor. I was wholly ignorant of their purpose in coming to Boston until I was well under way and it was too late to turn back. I would remind your honor that I reported them to the proper authorities as soon as I made port."

"You're not to blame for their actions, but I hold you responsible for their presence in Boston and for their removal. You will post bond for one hundred pounds to ensure that they do return to Barbados. You'll get it back when I see a written statement to that effect signed by the governor of the island."

Kempthorn appeared taken aback by this demand. "Posting such a bond will pose a great hardship for me," he said.

Bellingham was not finished. "The magistrates also ruled that the Quakers shall return to Barbados on the ship that brought them to Boston. I'm reluctant to accept bond from a party who will not carry out the action agreed upon. Perhaps Master Hull is prepared to post the bond."

Hull's face had darkened, and he made a motion to rise.

Kempthorn put out a hand to restrain him. His shoulders sagged. He started to speak, but appeared to think better of it and was silent.

"May I suggest a course of action that is in accord with the ruling?" Hull asked. "I trust it may be agreeable to all parties concerned."

Bellingham regarded him sternly. Was the son to prove himself as contentious as the father? "What would you suggest?" he asked.

"Kempthorn can post the bond and take custody of the women. He can then transfer them in private to my custody. I'll guarantee their arrival in Barbados and get a written statement from the governor. Kempthorn can retrieve his bond on my return."

"And what do I tell the magistrates when they see the *Swallow* at anchor in Boston harbor?" Bellingham asked.

"I can assure your honor, they'll see nary a trace of the *Swallow*," Kempthorn said.

Bellingham stroked his chin thoughtfully. As long as Kempthorn posted the bond, what ship the Quakers were on was of no consequence. The assurance that they would be gone before Endicott returned overrode any doubts he might have as to Hull's trustworthiness.

"I need know nothing about a transfer of custody," he said. "You can work that out between you."

"I thank your honor for this consideration," Kempthorn said. Hull had no further comment.

"You can post your bond with the clerk before you take custody of the women," Bellingham said as they rose to leave.

When they were gone, he heaved a sigh of satisfaction. He would be rid of those troublesome Quakers, and another marriage would take place as scheduled. A fair day's work.

* * *

"I thought for a while that Bellingham was going to turn down our proposal," Kempthorn said as they walked toward the harbor. "What made you think of transferring custody?"

"He felt bound by the court ruling," Tristram said. "I realized that any arrangement we made about the Quakers would have to be carried out in private. We needn't have gone to him at all."

"I'm glad we did. If something goes wrong, he can't say he didn't know about it."

"Nothing will go wrong. You get married as planned, and I get a contact in Barbados." Tristram made no mention of another contact, that with Mary Fisher.

"I thank you for that," Kempthorn said. "But you saw to it that I have to post the bond."

"You needn't worry," Tristram said. "You'll get it back."

On their way to the wharf they worked out the details of a plan to transfer custody of the women. They parted, leaving Tristram to ponder what provisions he might make for the women aboard the *Hopewell*.

There was an extra bunk in his cabin. He pictured Mary Fisher asleep in that bunk; but such an arrangement lacked propriety, and word of it would get back to Blanche. To quarter them in the forecastle with the crew would only invite trouble. He might create space below on the cargo deck; but they would be isolated and subject to possible molestation, and there was no time for such extensive renovations. He settled upon a cabin in steerage. He could share his quarters with the mate who was displaced, giving up his own privacy to ensure theirs. It was a small sacrifice.

Whether or not he established a bond with Mary Fisher, the voyage to the West Indies should prove interesting. It was sure to be different. He was not accustomed to having women aboard. He usually left on amicable terms with his wife. And his contact on Barbados might prove fruitless. He had dealt throughout his life at sea with the uncertainties of nature, but he prided himself on maintaining order in his personal affairs. He felt he was about to enter upon foreign territory unprepared.

Six

"Some areas of our lives are always open to doubt."
(Aboard the *Hopewell* at Sea, Summer 1656)

Kempthorn posted the bond and took custody of the women at the prison. The transfer to the *Hopewell* was accomplished without incident. As soon as they were aboard, Tristram hoisted sail and set his course for Barbados. The voyage would take from two to three weeks, depending on the weather. The length of his stay depended partly on how long it took to dispose of his cargo. Yet another uncertainty.

If he expected gratitude for providing the women with passage, he was disappointed. They were not confined to their quarters, but they kept to themselves and had little to say to him.

When pressed to speak, Mary was decidedly abrupt. "We return to Barbados against our will. It's of no consequence who takes us, be it thou or Master Kempthorn."

Ann was somewhat kinder. "We thank thee for the privacy of our quarters. On the voyage north we had to guard each other at night for fear of being molested in our sleep."

"You'll have no problems like that," he assured her.

To make sure of it, he ordered his crew, mates as well as seamen, to respect their privacy. Anyone he found disregarding the order would be dismissed upon arrival in Barbados. He also granted the women access during the day to the command deck.

"I don't want you to feel like prisoners," he told them, "and you'll be out of the way as the crew carries out their duties."

It also made them more accessible. He had a number of questions he wanted to ask them. He told himself it was just curiosity, but he knew in his heart that he had other motives. They thanked him for his offer, but seemed hesitant to take advantage of it.

Tristram had ample time to reflect on his problems with Blanche, but he saw no resolution nor any way to proceed. Quaker teachings might provide some guidance regarding marital relations. If he could gain the confidence of Ann Austin, a married woman, he might gain some new insight into his problems at home. It could also pave the way for further contact with Mary Fisher.

For several days the women kept to themselves, speaking to others only when it was essential. They seemed loath to mount the ladder to the command deck. Realizing that any meaningful communication was up to him, Tristram approached Ann Austin as she walked on the main deck.

"I trust the meals are satisfactory," he said, falling in beside her.

"I thank thee. They are quite adequate."

"I understand you have a family in England."

"I have five grown children in London."

"I have five as well. My oldest is nearly eleven."

"How old is the youngest?"

"Only six months."

"Then thy wife must care for them while thou art away. It must be a lonely life, married to the master of a ship."

Tristram saw an opening, but he was suddenly reluctant to take it.

"She manages quite well," he said. "I do my best to make up for it when I'm home. But you're right. It's hard for her, yet I see no way to ease her burden. I must provide for my family, and this is the only trade I know."

"And a profitable one, if I err not," Ann said.

"We live in modest comfort."

"What is thy business in Barbados, if I may make bold to ask?"

"My cargo consists of flour, meat, and barrel staves. On the return voyage I carry a load of molasses."

"Art thou aware of the role that slaves play in harvesting the sugar cane and converting it into molasses?"

Tristram smiled. This was why Ann agreed to talk to him. "Is your religion opposed to slavery?" he asked.

"Not officially; but many Friends, including myself, regard it as a crime to enslave one's fellow man."

"I have no direct dealings with slaves."

"Yet thou do profit from the work of their hands."

"That is true," Tristram said, "but the crime, if there is one, lies with someone else."

He decided it was futile to seek advice from this missionary. Based on her comment about his wife, he felt certain that Ann's sympathy would be with Blanche. She might not condone her behavior, but she would lay his problems with Blanche on his own doorstep. There was some truth in that, but it didn't help in plotting his future course.

* * *

Mary Fisher was the first to venture upon the command deck. The seas had turned choppy, and she used both hands to steady herself as she gazed westward toward an unseen shore. Tristram joined her at the rail.

"You're alone," he said. "Is Ann all right?"

"She's a bit unsettled in her stomach," Mary said. "I thank thee for inquiring about her."

From where he stood Tristram had a good view of her slim figure and well-scrubbed features. Blanche's face had filled out like the rest of her body. Not that he found her any the less attractive for that; but Mary had a fresh and youthful look, one that emerged even by candlelight. He dismissed the thought, but not until he had conjured up a mental picture of her naked body.

"May I ask why you came to Boston, when you might have led a much easier life as a missionary in England?"

Mary gave him a skeptical look, as if she sought to detect his true intentions. "Why is that of interest to thee?"

"Fate has thrown us together," he said, meeting her gaze. "We should get to know something about each other."

She looked again out to sea before responding to his question.

"Only the wealthy can choose what sort of life they will lead. I was an orphan. As a young girl I was employed as a housemaid by a family in the north of England. I had resigned myself to my lot in life. Then I heard George Fox preach, not in a church but on the village green. I was thrilled by his words and saw another course for my life. Under his guidance I was moved to take a different path, a path that led me to New England. Thou knowest the rest of my story."

Tristram had not expected such a full account. For a moment he was at a loss for words. Then he realized that she was waiting for him to respond in kind. He hesitated to confide in her that fully. He had hoped for such a talk, but he was uncertain where it might lead.

"I grew up in Devon," he said. "My father is an Anglican minister. He brought the family to Massachusetts when I was eleven. He settled in Weymouth, but was obliged to relocate to Hingham, then to the Plymouth Colony and to Maine before he returned to England."

"What choices has life made for thee?"

Tristram knew what she meant. She wanted to know about him, not his father. Recalling Kempthorn's words, he felt she had begun her efforts to convert him. In revealing his past, he must proceed with caution.

"When I was fifteen, I was apprenticed as a seaman to my sister's husband, John Bursley. He helped me to buy my first ship and stood up for me when I married. He's become like a second father to me."

"And thy real father is now in England?" Mary asked.

"He has a post at Launceston in Cornwall."

"We had word before we left England that George Fox was in jail in Launceston. They say he assaulted an official."

"Strangely enough, my father mentioned him in his last letter. He attended the trial. Fox was found guilty and returned to prison."

"I thank thee for this news, sad though it may be."

"My father was impressed by his words and demeanor," Tristram said. "Perhaps they became acquainted."

He tried to imagine such a meeting and stifled the laugh that welled up in his throat. He hastened to apologize. "Prison is no cause for mirth, as you well know."

"Our teacher once said we have not truly lived unless we spend at least one night in prison. I gather that experience is foreign to thee."

"What benefit can one derive from being in prison?"

"One confronts the true face of humanity. The innkeeper who sent us food revealed his true character. As did the jailer and the minister who examined us for marks of the devil."

"Those in authority in Boston are afraid of new ideas."

"What about thee? Art thou fearful as well?"

Tristram detected a twinkle in her eyes. Did Mary view him as a likely prospect for conversion? If that was her purpose, it might prove a favorable wind for further talks. He took great care in framing his reply.

"If the ideas answer my questions or help to solve my problems, I'm willing to examine them for their merit."

"And do our ideas have merit?"

"I know very little about your ideas."

His reply was impulsive, yet it served his purpose. He was curious about Quaker beliefs, and it seemed a good way to maintain contact with Mary. But before she could reply, Ann Austin mounted the ladder to the command deck and joined them at the rail.

"What is the gist of thy talk?" she asked.

"Master Hull is interested in what we believe as Friends," Mary said. "I was about to inform him of our willingness to instruct him."

"You may call me Tristram, if you like."

Ann gave him an icy look. "Master Hull will do nicely for now."

* * *

The next day Mary kept her distance, resting in her cabin or taking air on the main deck. Ann had doubtless advised her to exercise caution. Tristram could think of nothing he had done to offend Ann. It was clear that he would have to win her confidence in order to foster contact with Mary. But talking to Ann was not easy. She seemed loath to discuss her situation or her future plans. Her digestive system rejected the pottage served up by the cook, and she was often indisposed in her cabin.

"I can ask the cook to provide something more palatable," he said, "though your choice of food is somewhat limited."

"It's not the food," she said, "I'm always like this aboard ship."

"I understand. Let me know if you have need of anything."

He was glad he had not confided in Ann about his troubles with Blanche. He felt he had formed a certain bond with Mary. Alerting Ann to his marital problems would raise a warning flag and might have a chilling effect on Mary's attitude toward him.

Ann's weak digestive system did provide him with opportunities to speak to Mary in private. He spotted her seated on a hatch and invited her to join him on the command deck. She readily accepted. Moderately high waves caused the ship to roll, but she traversed the deck and climbed the ladder with confidence.

"You seem to have acquired your sea legs," Tristram said.

"This is my third voyage. I've crossed the Atlantic to Barbados and sailed north to New England."

"Is your companion feeling any better."

"I thank thee for asking. Ann was improved when I left her."

They stood once again at the rail, looking to starboard toward the land that lay beyond the horizon. The sun was shining, and a steady breeze filled the sails of the *Hopewell*.

"We were talking of prisons," Tristram said. "I trust you and Ann suffered no indignity at the hands of the authorities in Boston."

"We were spared the whip, but the minister examined us for marks of the devil. He would do better to examine his own conscience."

Tristram felt his face redden. He looked away, lest she notice. "At least you got your Bible back," he said.

"The innkeeper saw to that," Mary said. "I suspect we can thank him also for the return of our beds."

It was a custom for jailers to confiscate the bedding of inmates as part of their wages. Upsall had probably paid to get it back.

"I'm sorry if you were treated badly."

"We experienced worse in England."

Groping for something else to say, Tristram recalled her interest in his own past. "It must be frustrating to travel so far only to be turned away by the people you came to help. I remember how my father felt when his congregation in Weymouth voted to replace him. For a time he doubted his ability as a minister and raised cattle instead."

"Thou speak always of thy father," Mary said. "Art thou free of all doubts and vexations in thy own life?"

He thought of his vexations with Blanche, but he wasn't ready to share his problems with a woman his own age who had never married. "I was eleven when I crossed the Atlantic. I knew then that I wanted to go to sea, and I've never regretted my decision."

"Thou art indeed fortunate," Mary said. "I trust thou likewise have no regrets about the other big decision in thy life. Ann says most men have doubts about their marriage."

"How did you know I was married?"

"There is a married look about thee." Mary paused a moment. "I also heard one of the crew refer to thy wife and children."

Tristram laughed. "I wedded at nineteen. I won't deny that I have on occasion doubted my decision, but I remain happily married."

Mary appeared to be staring at the wake of the ship. "We all have doubts at times," she said. "Shortly after I began to preach, I was arrested and spent more than a year in prison, where I was stripped and beaten. I wasn't sure I had chosen the right path. But with the aid of my teacher I persisted and was called to spread our message in New England."

"What of the way you were treated in Boston? Surely that gave you some cause for doubt."

"I now have the strength and resolve to accept such setbacks. But I do envy thee. A master of a ship has no cause or time for doubt."

"Some areas of our lives are always open to doubt," Tristram said. "But I shan't burden you with my personal concerns."

Mary did not insist, and they left it at that.

* * *

They spoke more often after this exchange. Tristram was glad to have penetrated her wall of reserve, but Mary remained cautious. He had a vaguely defined goal of greater intimacy and was eager to hear more about her life and her beliefs. But what if he succeeded? Did he intend to use her to gain a measure of revenge on Blanche? His mind was not at all clear on that point. Whatever came of this would depend largely upon Mary.

"What will you do when you get to Barbados?" he asked at one of their meetings. "Will you try to return to New England?"

"I have a mind to go to Newport," Mary said, "but Ann is opposed to that idea."

"I had no idea you wanted to go to Newport. I thank you for not asking me to take you there on this voyage."

"I'm aware of thy commitment to Master Kempthorn. Would the decision have been so difficult?" she added with an impish grin.

Tristram fancied she might be flirting with him. He was not adept at that game, but he ventured a try. "If you're truly serious about going to Newport, I might take you there on my return voyage."

He pictured Mary alone on his ship. Left to fend for herself, she might be more inclined toward friendship, wherever that might lead them. She was studying him with what he took to be new respect and wonder.

"Would thou really consent to take us to Newport?" she asked.

"If that is your wish." He noted that she had inserted Ann into the question. "My agreement with Kempthorn and Bellingham is to leave you in Barbados. Nothing prevents me from bringing you back, as long as it's not to Boston."

"Ann and I have made no final decision about our future. Our true path will be revealed to us when we get to Barbados. But I do thank thee for thy kind offer. It's more than I expected from one of thy kind."

Tristram suppressed a surge of anger. "What are my kind? I'm no Puritan like the majority of people in Boston. I have no desire to punish others for their beliefs, even if I don't agree with them."

"Dost thou deny that what we speak is the truth?"

"I know not enough of what you speak, either to deny or accept it."

"Would thou like to know more?"

"I'm perfectly willing to listen to you."

"Not to me," Mary said. "Thou must listen to thy own inner voice."

Tristram felt he had taken a major step toward gaining her trust and confidence. Where it might lead depended on Mary, and she had a mind of her own.

Seven

"Thy aim is not to comfort, but to convince him."
(Aboard the *Hopewell* at Sea, Summer 1656)

Mary confided in Ann about her latest talk with Tristram. Though she was aware of his interest in her, she assured herself that what she felt was simply relief to be treated with respect, even deference. She recalled the beatings she had endured at the hands of the students when she sought to preach at Cambridge. There were many in England who had heeded her message, but her success was tempered by constant danger to her person. Apart from the brief respite on Barbados, she had been subject to abuse, persecution, and imprisonment ever since she began to follow the dictates of her inner voice. She was no stranger to doubt.

When moved by the spirit to go to the American colonies, she had dared to hope for a warmer reception. Her experience in Boston proved it was not to be. People were much the same on either side of the ocean. The men who left England to escape from persecution had become persecutors in their own right. Thanks to Master Hull, who remained attentive to their needs and comfort, this voyage was relatively free of anxiety and stress. It gave her a chance to reflect upon her past life and her future plans.

"He seems ever willing to converse," she told Ann as they lay in their bunks. "I do believe at times that he is flirting with me."

"Thou must have done something to encourage him," Ann said.

"I've done nothing more than speak to him in a civil manner."

"What are thy feelings toward him?"

"He has treated us very decently. He has even offered to take us to Newport on his return voyage, if that is our wish."

"What was thy response to that?"

"I told him we were awaiting further guidance."

"I would remind thee that our mission is to convince people of the truth of our message, not to invite men to flirt with us."

"I've given him no cause," Mary said indignantly. "Any kindness he has bestowed on us has been of his own volition."

"We might turn his kindness to our advantage, as we did with the innkeeper Upsall."

"He is the only seed we planted in Boston that promises to take root," Mary said. "At least our trip was not totally useless."

"Master Hull may prove to be another such seed," Ann said.

"He has expressed an interest in our beliefs," Mary said. "I shall do my best to water that interest."

"Thou art not alone in this endeavor. By acting together, we shall have more chance of success."

"With due respect, I feel certain he will be more receptive to our message if I speak to him alone."

"Be careful, Mary. Thou art treading on perilous ground. I fear thy interest in Master Hull may exceed the bounds of thy calling."

"He has a wife and children. I assure thee that my sole aim is to open his eyes to the light within him."

"He is also young and far from home," Ann said.

"I promise to give him no false impression of my purpose."

Ann said no more. Her regular breathing and an occasional snort told Mary she was asleep. Did Ann see something to which she was blind? Was she attracted to Master Hull? Since becoming a missionary, she had experienced no feelings of that sort. But no man beyond the society had treated her in so kindly a fashion. She was mulling these questions over in her mind when sleep overcame her.

* * *

Midway in the voyage to Barbados the *Hopewell* encountered foul weather, and Tristram was too busy to advance what he jokingly termed his courtship of Mary Fisher. He knew that her interest in him was in all likelihood part of her mission. Yet his hopes were rekindled when the sea calmed and she mounted the ladder to the command deck uninvited.

"I trust you and your companion weathered the storm without too much discomfort," he said.

"Yesterday was bad for both of us," Mary said. "I feel much better this morning, but Ann is still indisposed."

"Our moods seem to mimic the weather," he said, "calm one day and stormy the next."

"Nature is quite mindless," she said. "Humans differ in that we can strive to fashion the events in our lives. We can remain calm in the face of adversity or rale against our fate."

"Is that my first lesson?"

Mary laughed. "A wise man once said we should devote our time and energy to changing what can be changed and accept that which is not subject to our intervention. Human nature is subject to change. Soft words may inspire a calm response."

"Surely you have recent evidence of the opposite. Your purpose in coming to Boston was peaceful, and your words were a threat to no one; yet the response was anything but calm. You spent five weeks in prison, and you might well have been hanged as a witch."

Tristram realized he had just admitted to more knowledge than he ought to have. He assured himself Mary was unaware that he had observed the examination in the prison cell.

She seemed not to notice his momentary confusion. "In the face of intolerance we must stand our ground and be willing to suffer persecution for the sake of our mission."

"I find it difficult to exercise such restraint."

"As long as we harbor resentment in our hearts, we cannot forgive. It is by forgiving that we overcome those who would do us harm."

She sounded like a preacher. "Do you feel no anger toward those who imprisoned you?" he asked.

"They acted in accordance with beliefs imposed on them by higher authority. Our mission is to convince them to heed the voice which resides within their own hearts."

"How can you convince them? You're going back to Barbados."

"More will follow us. Our message will be heard."

"Women are more forgiving by nature. Men find it hard to pardon those who have done them wrong."

"Dost thou speak from thy experience?" Mary asked.

Tristram laughed. He was indeed thinking of Blanche. He might find it in his heart to forgive his wife, but he still harbored anger against Gorham. He chided himself for walking away without questioning the man's account. Mary was awaiting his reply.

"I have reason to believe my wife is unfaithful."

It was out before he had time to reconsider. He regretted not so much the statement, as the audience he had chosen. What did Mary know of marriage? But having broached the subject, he saw no way to retract his words. He gave her a brief account of the assault and the court action. He knew he was seeking her sympathy, her assurance that he was in the right and that Blanche bore most of the blame for what had occurred.

"I'm not married," Mary said when he finished, "but I'm told that in most cases infidelity is equally the fault of both parties. Accept some of the blame thyself, and it will be easier to forgive thy wife."

"I'm often at sea and away from home, but I can't change that."

"Even if thou are blameless, it remains thy duty to forgive."

"Forgiveness can be seen as a sign of weakness," Tristram said. He felt uncomfortable at this turn in the conversation.

"It takes strength to oppose the general custom. But men as well as women are persuaded by their inner voice."

"I do appreciate your advice," Tristram said, anxious now to bring their talk to a close. "Your words have been useful."

"We have made a fair start," Mary said.

A fair start indeed, he thought; but he wasn't sure what had been started, nor where it would lead.

* * *

On entering their cabin, Mary could read the questions in the look Ann gave her before she asked them.

"How went thy talk? Has the seed been watered?"

"He's has a problem with his wife," Mary said. "I think I was able to bring him some comfort."

"Thy aim is not to comfort but to convince him," Ann said sternly.

"I merely sought to impress on him our common need to forgive and be forgiven. He seemed to take heed."

"I must warn thee not to involve thyself in his personal life. Our duty is merely to answer his questions. Let him apply what we say to his own problems."

"He's a decent man and seeking the truth," Mary said. "I assure thee, I have no feelings for him."

"Does he attend a church?" Ann asked.

"We didn't discuss that. His father is an Anglican minister."

"Then our task is doubly difficult."

"As long as he's willing to listen, I see no harm in talking to him," Mary said. "It is our mission to nourish the seed we plant that it may take root and bear fruit at some future time."

"That is true, but take care lest he have thee singing hymns and quoting the *Book of Common Prayer*."

"If he starts to sing," Mary said, "I shall terminate our lessons."

Ann laughed. "It is good to retain a sense of humor about our task. I have faith in thee to proceed with wisdom and caution."

Mary determined to continue their talks. She had a duty to answer Master Hull's questions. His objections were a test of her worthiness as a missionary. She would use his doubts to strengthen her faith in her own beliefs. Thus fortified, she was alert for opportunities to speak to him. In fact, it seemed to her that he sought her out.

She spent hours at the rail studying the wake of the ship. It had a mesmerizing effect on her. She was startled when he appeared at her side.

"This pleasant weather is unusual," he said. "It's the season for storms in these latitudes."

"One storm was quite enough for me," Mary said.

"I've thought about what you said when last we spoke." His smile was unforced, and he appeared at ease.

Mary too experienced less restraint than in their prior talks. She felt more inclined to be attentive, willing to learn as well as teach. She was not accustomed to such feelings and found them rather pleasant.

"Hast thou determined to forgive thy wife?" she asked.

"I hope we can forgive each other."

"For what fault must thou be forgiven?"

"No one is without fault."

"That is thy inner voice speaking to thee."

"What is this inner voice that guides you?"

"It is the spirit, a divine light that resides and shines in each of us. It is always there, ready to guide us if we will only listen."

"The spirit that moved you to come to Boston seemed unaware of how you would be treated."

"The spirit is good and true. We learned much about the forces that oppose the spread of our message in the New England colonies. That will prove useful in planning for the future."

"Then you've decided to return to New England."

"We've made no decision. The spirit within us must guide our next move." He appeared put off by her reply. She waited for his next question.

"Many people rely on the Bible as their spiritual guide. They look to ministers to interpret what God has revealed. Would you forego that help and guidance?"

Mary realized that they had arrived at the crux of the matter. She chose her words carefully. "The Bible has served us well as a basis for what we believe today, but its words are centuries old. I cannot believe that God spoke once and then was silent. Revelation is ongoing. How can one worship a God who has nothing more to say?"

"I was brought up to believe that God speaks to us through those ministers who are devoted to His service, and also in response to prayer."

"Prayer requires no response," Mary said. "Its true purpose is to make us receptive to the promptings of the spirit. As for ministers, they preach many different messages. How are we to know which one is right? And they proclaim the same message to multitudes of people who differ in many ways. When our inner spirit speaks, the message is only for us."

She knew she was on dangerous ground. If she hoped to convince him, she must tread lightly on the topic of ministers. But her background and experience governed her speech. She could not say otherwise, even if her words alienated the man she wanted to impress. For she admitted now what previously she had only sensed, that she wanted not only to convince Master Hull of the truth of her message, but to persuade him of her merit as a woman. She wanted him to see her as a person, not as an advocate of some new doctrine. She wanted him to like her as she liked him.

He appeared to ponder her words before replying. "I'm willing to grant that God can speak to us in a variety of ways. One of them may well be through an inner voice. But we must heed his message no matter how it is transmitted to us. The words I heard from my father in my youth are just as true and helpful as anything my inner voice can tell me today."

"Then thy father is different from the ministers I've encountered. The words they spout are placed in their mouths by someone in authority over them, a bishop perhaps. The only spiritual authority we recognize is that of Jesus Christ."

"You yourself are a minister of sorts," he said.

"I am a messenger, but thou need not accept what I say. Listen to and heed thy own inner voice."

"If everyone were to follow the dictates of his own inner voice, I fear we should have nothing but chaos."

"There is but one true voice," Mary said. "We should not be afraid to trust in it when it speaks to us in the stillness of our hearts."

"I'm willing to listen, but I doubt I shall hear anything."

"If that is thy attitude, then thou will surely hear nothing."

She sensed their talk was at an end. She pressed his hand as a sign of encouragement, then watched as he mounted to the command deck. Ann had come on deck, and she hastened to join her.

"Hast thou succeeded in convincing thy pupil?" Ann asked.

"He is well trained by his father to respect the clergy," Mary said, "but he is willing to get acquainted with his inner voice."

"Did I see thee press his hand in parting?"

"It was a spontaneous gesture. It meant nothing."

"Not to thee perhaps, but he may give it a different meaning."

"I answer his questions. His interest is in our beliefs, not in me."

"Take care, Mary. Questions can prove to be flattery in disguise."

"Thou hast no cause for such a comment."

"If his interest is solely in what we believe, why has he ceased to question me? In his eyes I no longer exist. He sees only thee." Ann's look was triumphant.

Mary had no answer. They spoke again of what they would do when they reached Barbados. Friends were tolerated by the governing authority on the island, but they had met with opposition from plantation owners and from clergymen of all faiths. Should they cast their lot with the nascent community of Friends on Barbados, return to New England, or strike out on a new path? They resolved to be patient, to wait and listen.

When she was alone, Mary allowed herself to speculate upon the prospect of continuing the relationship with Master Hull. She had done her best to convince him. They had reached not so much an impasse as a truce. Any further discussion was up to him. She must tell that to Ann. It would put her mind at ease. In her own mind she was reluctant to leave it at that. She wondered if their paths might cross after they reached Barbados.

* * *

Tristram held up the hand Mary had pressed in parting. What did it mean? Was it a calculated move on her part or just a gesture of good will? His efforts to get closer to her had placed them on a more friendly footing. She was no longer on guard against him, no longer avoided his company. Yet he saw no prospect for contact with her in Barbados. He had business with the planter whose name Kempthorn had provided. Mary was sure to have plans that did not involve him. His one hope was that the spirit would direct her to go to Newport.

Meanwhile, he would listen to his inner voice as he had promised , but he doubted that God had anything to say to him.

Eight

"I can always provide a bed and a woman for your comfort."
(Barbados, September 1656)

On arriving in Bridgetown, Tristram's first business was to obtain an official affidavit attesting to the safe arrival of the women in Barbados, a document Kempthorn could present to recover the bond he had posted. He requested an audience with Daniel Searle, the governor, but in light of Bellingham's attitude toward Quakers he was uncertain how he would be received. Mary had indicated that the authorities were tolerant of the first Quakers to arrive, but that may well have changed in the months she was away. The ministers were sure to oppose such a policy. He had no idea how much influence they had upon the government.

He took the women with him to Government House, leaving them in an anteroom when he was ushered into the governor's office. Searle rose to greet him as he entered. He was young, tall, and slender. He had a well tended mustache and wore a white suit, the customary garb of British colonial officials serving in a tropical clime. Tristram stated his business and produced the affidavit that Kempthorn had prepared.

Searle studied it for a moment. "Where are the women now?"

"They're waiting outside," Tristram said.

The governor rose and went out to the anteroom. He was gone for several minutes. Tristram couldn't make out what was said, but he thought he heard Searle address Mary by name.

"I trust my signature is sufficient for your purpose," he said as he reentered his office, "or would you prefer a witness?"

"Your signature and seal are enough," Tristram said, laying claim to more knowledge than he possessed.

Searle signed the document. Folding it neatly, he applied a patch of hot red wax, pressed upon it the official seal of his government, and gave it to Tristram.

"Will there be anything else?" he asked.

"I'm a little surprised at the lack of animosity toward Quakers in Barbados," Tristram made bold to say. "In Boston these women spent five weeks in prison before they were banished from the colony."

Searle smiled. "I'm aware of Governor Endicott's attitude, but his actions are not my concern. I do my best to distance myself from religious controversies. Quakers are much like the clergy. They all insist on telling us what we must do to be saved. As long as they cause no disturbance, I see no reason to treat them differently from anyone else."

"I must say that I find such an attitude refreshing," Tristram said.

"What is your business on our island?" Searle asked.

"I'm master of the *Hopewell* at anchor in the harbor. My first order of business is to dispose of my cargo of flour and barrel staves. I also bear a letter of introduction to a planter named Thomas Rous."

"I know him well. He is a man of some influence and has recently aligned himself with the Quakers. He now refuses to furnish horses or men for the troop of militia on the island. I suspect his son John is behind these activities. The son appears more zealous than the father. If they persist, I'll be forced to take action against them. I say this not to discourage you, but to apprise you of the situation as it exists."

"I shall remain on guard in my dealings with him," Tristram said.

This was why Kempthorn had been so willing to introduce him to Rous, even though it meant a loss of trade for himself. It was Rous who pressed him to transport the two women to Boston, and his dealings with the Quakers had brought him nothing but trouble. Hence his eagerness to sever all ties with them, wherever they might be.

"One of my goals as governor is to promote trade," Searle said. "If I can assist you in any way, feel free to contact me."

Tristram thanked him and took his leave. Outside the building he bade good-bye to Mary and Ann. He watched as they merged with the crowd in the market area. They seemed to know where they were going. He wondered if he had seen the last of them, or would they meet by chance in the coming days? He hoped so.

* * *

Thomas Rous had a plantation in St. Philip parish, located in the southeast section of the island and more than an hour by carriage from the harbor at Bridgetown. According to the driver, the plantation was one of the largest on Barbados, covering some four hundred acres and tended by nearly three hundred field hands and servants.

"You mean slaves, don't you?" Tristram asked.

The driver, a black man, shook his head vehemently. "I not say that word in my carriage. Not good for business."

Tristram turned his attention to the land through which they were passing. The gently rolling hills reminded him of those around Yarmouth, except here the country was more open with fewer trees. The planters had taken advantage of this in establishing their crops. He had an occasional view of a house in the distance, but none bordering on the rough dirt road they traveled. The driver turned down a lane between fields of sugar cane and drew up before a house that was several times as large as any building in Yarmouth or neighboring towns. It stood on a rise and commanded an expansive view of the surrounding fields.

Thomas Rous was seated on a shaded veranda from which one had a distant view of the ocean. Tristram had seen sugar plantations on Nevis and St. Kitts, but none this large. When he introduced himself and stated the purpose of his visit, Rous insisted that he spend the night. He paid off the driver, having assured Tristram that he would get him safely back to Bridgetown. Tristram readily agreed. He could conduct business at his leisure, and he looked forward to a good meal in an elegant setting, a welcome change after weeks at sea.

Rous was in his late forties, his face deeply tanned save for a well trimmed mustache. He insisted that Tristram rest before dinner. Business could wait until they had eaten. His wife and his son John joined them at table along with several younger children. Looking at the china and crystal set before him, Tristram thought of the simple meals he enjoyed at home. The dinner included pork and veal, fresh vegetables, and an abundance of fruits such as pomegranates, guavas, and papayas, all served with a wine that suited the dish. Black servants moved about silently throughout the meal. He was certainly not in Yarmouth.

After dinner Rous led the way to his study. He offered his guest a snifter of brandy and broke out a box of cigars. Tristram had transported tobacco grown in Virginia, but he had not taken to smoking it. At Rous's urging he agreed to give it a try. After a thinly disguised cough, he settled into a pretense of enjoying the cigar. By the end of the evening with some assistance from the well-aged brandy he no longer had to pretend.

"I've been on Barbados twenty years," Rous said. "When I arrived, tobacco was a major crop on the island. But Virginia tobacco drove down prices on the London market, and I turned to cotton. More equipment was needed to remove the seeds and gin and card the fiber, but with the labor of indentured servants I managed to eke out a reasonable profit."

"But now you're growing sugar cane," Tristram said. He was not overly interested in an economic history of the island.

"Cane has been our salvation. At first we had to compete with the Portuguese planters in Brazil. When the Dutch seized their province, the planters revolted and torched the mills and fields of cane. Some of them relocated to Barbados and taught us their methods. Now we have a good share of the market. I'll have John show you around the plantation in the morning, if you like."

"I accept with pleasure," Tristram said.

Their talk turned to the business at hand. When Tristram presented his letter of introduction, Rous expanded on the nature of his relationship with Kempthorn.

"Simon is a business man. He was intent on buying at the lowest possible price. I don't blame him for that, but he would often take only a part of what I produce. Said he had other contacts, or there was no space left on his ship. If you'll agree to pay a fair price and take all I produce, we can do business."

"I'll take as much as my ship will hold," Tristram said, "but so far I've been unable to sell the flour, meat, and barrel staves I have aboard."

"I can help you to dispose of your cargo," Rous said.

"Then I see no reason why we can't come to an agreement."

They smoked and drank for a time in silence. Tristram had never experienced wealth. While his body voiced its approval, his mind sought to make peace with how it was acquired. He saw nothing terribly wrong with slavery. The blacks who served dinner were smiling and appeared to be content with their lot. He knew little about the conditions under which the field hands lived and labored. He decided to reserve judgment until he had toured the plantation and to enjoy all his host had to offer.

"I've heard reports of your other business," Rous said. "Barbados is a small island, and word spreads fast. I speak of the two Quaker women who returned. I gather they were not welcome in New England."

Tristram gave a brief account of the banishment of the women and his involvement with them. "I was surprised to find that Governor Searle is so tolerant of Quakers," he concluded.

"Searle was appointed governor by Cromwell, but he also owns a plantation. In consequence he must balance his own interests and those of Barbados against the rulings of our self-designated Lord Protector. I must say that he's been quite successful."

"I had to see him regarding the two women," Tristram said. "He told me that you too are a Quaker,"

Rous laughed. "I'm more than halfway to becoming one. I never had much use for ministers. The notion that God can speak to me directly if He has a mind to has a certain appeal. But I must say that most of my decisions are based on my economic interests."

"Then it was in your interest to persuade Kempthorn to transport Ann Austin and Mary Fisher to Boston."

"Is that what he told you? In that instance my motives were purely altruistic. The women were determined to go to New England. I used my influence to get them there. Any member of the society would have done as much. Of course I was also doing Searle a favor. They had caused him a lot of trouble, and he wanted to be rid of them."

"What sort of trouble?" Tristram asked.

"Searle found their tactics harsh and disruptive. On a Sunday they shouted down a minister in the midst of his sermon, demanding that he let them testify to the inner light that was in them. He had them escorted, as he put it, to the outer light."

"Are all Quakers like that?"

"Most of them have adapted to the customs of the island," Rous said. "They keep to themselves and educate their own children. Several have even acquired a plantation and purchased slaves in the market."

"The Quakers I spoke to are opposed to slavery," Tristram said.

"Some of them have tried to convince slaves of their truth. A few even advocate granting slaves their freedom. They don't get very far."

Tristram noted that Rous spoke mostly of them, rather than us. He was apparently a Quaker only when it suited him. Or to put it in his terms, he was halfway along the road to becoming one.

"Governor Searle said that you failed to provide horses or men for the militia. Is that also based on religious principles?"

Rous's smile was transformed to a frown. "He can think that, if he likes. Actually, it's for economic reasons. The militia captures slaves who flee to the hills in the north and returns them to their owners. I don't see it as a big problem. It costs less to buy another slave."

"How many Quakers are on Barbados?" Tristram asked.

"More arrive on each ship from England. They keep coming here because Searle seems not to care, as long as they behave themselves. Let's talk about something more pleasant. How do you like Barbados?"

"I've hardly had time to form an impression of the island."

Rous raised his glass. "I'll see to that before you leave."

"What do you mean?" Tristram asked.

"Only that I'll arrange for John to show you the plantation in the morning. That should give you a better idea of the people you're dealing with. I'd take you around myself, but I have to prepare for a meeting in Bridgetown."

"I look forward to it," Tristram said. "Now if you'll excuse me, I'd like to turn in. I want to be fresh in the morning."

He noted a smile on Rous's face as he took leave of his host.

* * *

Tristram was awakened by a movement in the bed that was not his own. Turning on his side, he saw a black girl lying beside him. Moonlight through the window painted the curves of her naked body. He too wore no clothes due to the heat. His body prompted him what to do, but his mind gave him no justification for doing it. He told himself it was a custom of the island, a sign of hospitality. But that excuse did not suffice.

He thought of Mary Fisher. Alone in his cabin, would he have tried to make love to her? It was just a fantasy in which he had indulged, secure in the conviction that Mary had no such inclination. He had fed his fancy in similar fashion in the past, while remaining for the most part faithful to Blanche. The difference now was that he was reasonably certain that she had been unfaithful to him.

The girl at his side was no doubt a slave, a gift from Rous intended to seal their business agreement. By rejecting her he might well damage his prospects for future trade. He denied that a desire for revenge against his wife influenced his decision to take the girl in his arms.

She offered no resistance and made little response as he penetrated her. No matter. If anything, it lessened his feelings of guilt. When he was done, he pushed her away and was soon asleep. When he awoke the next morning, she was gone. It was better that way. The act had involved no love. It hardly qualified as adultery. He had merely yielded to a natural bodily need.

"I trust you enjoyed the night with us," Rous said over breakfast with a sly wink. His wife and his son John were also at the table, but the younger children were still in their rooms.

"I was quite comfortable," Tristram said, "and I thank you for your hospitality."

"John has agreed to show you around the plantation. I want you to feel confident about our agreement. It always helps to know something about your business partner."

"I'm not lacking in confidence, but I want to see your plantation."

As he ate, Tristram studied the young man designated to be his guide. John Rous was in his early twenties. He was half a head taller than Tristram and sported a small beard not quite as brown as his hair. Though clearly alert during the talk, he uttered few words in his father's presence. Tristram wondered whether his silence indicated deference or a variance of opinion.

When they had eaten, John led the way to a row of buildings a fair distance and downwind from the main house. In the first shed two teams of oxen were harnessed to a shaft that turned massive wooden rollers.

"This is our sugar mill," John said before he could ask. "The first step is to extract the juice from the sugar cane. The cane has to be pressed right after it's cut or the juice starts to sour."

"You must keep quite a large herd of livestock," Tristram said.

"We have about fifty oxen. We used horses at first, but we found that they couldn't work as long and were more subject to injury."

John moved on to a structure with a thatched roof but open at the sides, where s dozen or more black slaves were stirring and skimming the contents of several large copper kettles suspended over a wood fire. Their upper bodies were bare and covered with sweat. Several of them sang in rhythm with their task in a language foreign to Tristram.

"The juice that was extracted by the rollers has to be boiled and refined so crystals can form," John said. "The trick is to ladle it from one copper to the next at just the right moment for maximum yield and purity. These men are called boilers, and they're proud of their skill."

"Are they rewarded for their skill?" Tristram asked.

John gave him a look verging on suspicion. "I suppose they have the satisfaction of knowing that their task is one of the most important on the plantation."

Tristram got the message, but he determined to probe more deeply into the living and working conditions of the slaves. John was moving on toward the next station, and he hurried to catch up.

"The syrup from the last copper goes into this pan. When it has cooled enough, it's packed into hogsheads and taken to the warehouse."

He led the way to a long shed, thatch covered but enclosed on the sides. Inside were dozens of large barrels suspended on beams above what appeared to be a catchment basin.

"After the molasses has drained off," John said, "the raw sugar or muscovado is ready to be shipped."

"But you ship the molasses as well," Tristram said.

"We sell what we can. The residue is fed to the livestock, or else it's distilled into rum. Not very good rum, but it keeps the slaves happy."

"How many slaves do you own?" Tristram asked.

"We need about two hundred to cultivate and harvest the cane and process the sugar. Another thirty maintain the grounds or work as servants in the main house. Without the slaves we couldn't make a profit."

"There are few slaves in New England," Tristram said, "but we do have a number of indentured servants."

"My father had indentured servants at first. They no sooner learned the trade than their time was up. Slaves are more stable. There's some loss due to sickness or death; but we can get replacements in the market."

Tristram noted that he spoke in the plural, as if he were merely a participant in a business controlled by his father. "How do you feel about slavery?" he asked.

John looked at him intently. "Why do you ask?"

"According to Mary Fisher, Quakers are divided on the subject."

John glanced about, as if to make sure that he was not overheard. "Personally, I hate the idea of slavery; but I know our prosperity depends on it. So I carry on and keep my mouth shut around my father. I'm trapped in a system I can't change without destroying my own way of life."

"There must be some escape," Tristram said.

"Not on Barbados. I'd like to go to New England like Mary Fisher, but my father depends on me to oversee labor on his plantation."

"Do you know Mary Fisher?"

"I met her before she left, and we'll probably meet again now that she's back. She's filled with zeal and dedicated to the cause. It's a wonder she didn't convince you to join the society."

"I can't say she didn't try. But why does your society send women as missionaries to places where they suffer all kinds of indignities?"

"We go where our inner voice directs," John said, "women as well as men. It's easier for someone like Mary. She has no ties on Barbados or at home in England. I have a comfortable life here, and it's hard to break away. All I can do is warn the inhabitants of the island of the dangers that lie ahead."

"What sort of dangers?" Tristram asked.

"Slaves are human beings. They want their freedom as much as we do. A few have fled to the hills in the north. Planters want the governor to order the militia to round them up and return them to their owners, but so far he's been reluctant to act unless they cause trouble. For my part I've persuaded my father not to support the militia. It's a small gesture, but I'm proud of it."

"He claims he did it for economic reasons," Tristram said.

"That's his guiding principle," John said. "But he did it. That's the important thing."

Did John approve of how his father conducted business? Did he take slave women into his bed? Surely for an unmarried man it must be a constant temptation. Tristram thought it best not to ask. He had begun to regret his own weakness. No need to tell the world about it.

"I want to see the field hands at work and how they live," he said.

"I'll gladly show you the fields," John said. "The slave quarters are best viewed from a distance."

When Tristram made no reply, John had a stable hand harness two horses. They circled the plantation, while he explained the growth and the harvesting of sugar cane. Tristram had never seen cane fields up close. He was surprised that the cane was twice as tall as the men and women who used machetes to cut it. The slaves wore a minium of clothing, little more than colorful rags.

John was explaining the division of labor in the fields. "Cutting requires the most skill. The cane has to be cut close to the earth, because sugar is more concentrated at the base. Trimming the stalks quickly and efficiently is an art in itself. The cutters take real pride in their work."

"It looks like they sweat a lot," Tristram said.

"They drink water flavored with sugar and lemon when they're in the fields, and they get a portion of rum at the end of the day."

They gave a wide berth to the slave village, located in a gully on land that was unsuitable for planting cane. Viewed from a distance, the shacks appeared to be constructed of nothing but sticks. Tristram reined his horse about, intending to ride closer; but John called him away.

"The place stinks," he said. "They're not very sanitary. I'm trying to improve their living conditions, but my father is concerned about the cost. Why are you so interested in slaves?"

"I don't see many where I'm from. Are they all from Africa?"

"Most of them come from the west of Africa. We buy them at the slave market in Bridgetown. "

"How much does a slave cost in the market?"

"A good strong male Negro can bring fifteen to twenty pounds on the market. Women cost less than that, though some of them are equally good workers. My father handles all that. Watching a slave auction makes me sick. He just laughs and says I'll get over it. I don't want to get over it. I want to get far away from it."

"If you decide to go north, stay away from the Massachusetts and Plymouth colonies," Tristram said. "Rhode Island and New Amsterdam are more tolerant of different religious opinions."

"I'll keep that in mind," John said. "Perhaps we'll meet one day in your part of the world."

"I hope we do," Tristram said.

* * *

Rous insisted that Tristram stay for the noon meal, after which he provided a carriage to convey him back to Bridgetown.

"You're welcome to spend a night or two here whenever you're in port," he said as Tristram took his leave. "I can always provide a bed and a woman for your comfort. It's safer than in Bridgetown."

"Do you avail yourself of such comfort?" Tristram asked.

"On occasion," Rous said. "A little variety promotes happiness in a marriage. Don't you agree?"

Tristram evaded the question. "How does your wife feel about it?" he asked.

"She's learned to accept it. It's part of who I am. As long as I don't neglect her, she doesn't complain. I'm not promiscuous. I take a slave to bed only if she suits me."

"And when one no longer suits you, another is available."

"They're my property. If you're opposed to slavery, you're in the wrong business."

"I don't give it much thought," Tristram said. "As you say, our mutual livelihood depends on it. And it has other advantages."

Rous laughed. "I'm glad we understand each other."

Nine

"I'm going to buy one of those women."
(Barbados, September 1656)

Tristram found a ready market for his cargo in Bridgetown. He had no further contact with the governor, and he wasn't sure whether Searle's influence was a factor. His agreement with Rous made a trip to St. Kitts unnecessary, and he was able to sail for home sooner than anticipated. He declined to spend another night at the plantation. It would cloud his efforts to resolve his problems with Blanche.

There was also the prospect of having Mary Fisher aboard on the voyage north. He had heard nothing of her since their arrival in Barbados. Perhaps that was all for the best. She would only distract him, and he needed to think clearly about the business at hand.

He met her by chance on a street in Bridgetown. She stopped when she saw him, and he sensed she wanted to talk. Her dress was of a lighter fabric but equally plain. She was alone.

"I sail at the end of next week," Tristram said after they exchanged greetings. "Will you return to New England or remain in Barbados?"

"I shall do neither," Mary said. "I am called by the spirit within me to return to England and wait for my future path to be revealed."

Tristram was surprised to experience a sense of relief. Not that he regretted his offer to take her to Newport, but he stood to gain nothing by having Mary aboard. Any hope he entertained of a closer relationship had been dashed by her behavior and her preaching. He told himself it might be different if Ann Austin were absent, but he didn't believe it. Mary was dedicated to her missionary work. She had neither time nor inclination for romantic entanglements. He tried to hide his feelings, but she saw through his feeble attempt.

"It is better for both of us that I do not return. I accomplished my mission in Boston. Others will follow and continue the work. Meanwhile, men like Upsall, and perhaps thou, can prepare the ground for them."

Tristram recoiled inwardly. Did she think she had converted him? "I have a better understanding of your beliefs, and I thank you for that," he said, "but I'm not ready to join your society."

"A father's example is not easy to set aside," Mary said. "Fortunately or not, I have no such barrier in my life."

Tristram waited for some further explanation, but she was silent. He decided to change the subject.

"I've come in close contact with slavery on Barbados, and I'm trying to sort out my feelings about the practice. I deplore the conditions in which slaves live and work, but my livelihood depends on it. Ann told me that your society is not officially opposed to slavery."

Mary appeared to relax, as if she were glad to be on safer ground. "Many of our teachers consider slavery and the slave trade to be a great evil," she said, "but in Barbados slavery is ingrained in the culture and the economy of the island. We try to discourage the planters from using slave labor, but that struggle will not be soon or easily won. "

Tristram described his tour of the sugar plantation and his distant view of the slave quarters. He thought it best not to mention the black girl Rous had ordered to sleep with him.

"It's a pity thou failed to look inside the stick houses. Slaves have little or no furniture, and their diet consists of root plants and corn meal mush, with an occasional dish of vegetables or salted fish. Was it a large plantation?"

"About four hundred acres," Tristram said.

"I've been studying the matter," Mary said. "With four hundred acres under cultivation the owner earns about fifteen thousand pounds. He spends roughly five hundred pounds a year to maintain his slaves. We're making some progress in getting the planters to provide slaves with better food and housing. Some of them admit we're right on moral grounds, but they all claim that economic conditions make it impractical for them to change the manner in which they do business. I believe they are driven by greed, but thou must judge that for thyself."

"How can you reconcile your moral principles with a practice you consider to be a great evil?" Tristram asked.

"Wisdom requires us to be realistic. We change what we can and trust that the rest will follow in due course."

"What was it you hoped to change in Boston?"

Mary laughed. "A few noble minds. That must suffice for now."

Did she really believe he was destined to become a Quaker? Well let her think so. There was no harm in that.

"Hast thou ever witnessed a slave auction?" Mary asked.

"I have not, nor do I intend to."

"We mustn't blind ourselves to the wrongs that surround us, even if it we are powerless to right them. Thou hast seen but half the picture of what it means to be a slave. There's an auction in progress on the green. If thou hast a mind to attend, I can accompany thee."

Tristram allowed himself to be persuaded. Though he had given up any romantic thoughts about Mary, he was still attracted to her and glad to spend time in her company. As long as she was willing to play the role of teacher, he was content to remain a student.

She took him past one of the wharfs on their way to the auction. "I want thee to get the true smell of slavery," she said.

Tristram had noticed the slave ship when it made port a few days earlier. It was larger than the *Hopewell* and carried a maximum cargo of human freight. He had encountered the stench of slave ships before, but never this close. The scent of excrement, sweat, and death made him gag.

"Are you casting off?" he asked a seaman, who was checking the lines that held the ship alongside the wharf.

"We've got orders to anchor in the harbor as soon as the auction is over. They don't want us stinking up the town. Can't say I blame them."

"Are there any slaves aboard?"

"Just the sick ones. They'll be ready for market in a day or two."

"How do you stand the smell?"

The seaman shrugged. "You never get used to it," he said. "Once they're all ashore, we flush out the hold. Outbound we can breathe the fresh sea air."

Mary pulled him away. "Half of them die of starvation or disease on the voyage here from Africa. The slave traders regard it as the price of doing business."

The market was a fair distance from the wharf, where the stench of slavery could not penetrate the nostrils of the plantation owners who had come into town for the auction. They gathered around a wooden platform set up at one end of the village green. A row of wagons along the edge of the green waited to transport the human cargo back to the plantations. The auction was already in progress when Tristram and Mary arrived. The men mounted the platform clad in little more than a loin cloth. Their arms and legs glistened in the sunlight.

"Why are they sweating?" he asked. "It's not that hot, and they're not doing any work."

"Before slaves are brought to market," Mary said, "they're sprayed with hoses to wash off the smell from the voyage. Then their bodies are smeared with grease to make them shine and cover up any blemishes."

Planters were invited to inspect the merchandise before bidding commenced. They seemed interested primarily in muscles and teeth. Men were made to open their mouths, like horses on the block. Tristram paid close attention to their eyes. Those who looked down seemed to command a better price than those who glanced around out of curiosity or defiance. the price for male slaves ranged from eight to fifteen pounds. Those who stirred no interest among the buyers were taken to a pen separate from those who were awaiting sale.

"What happens to them, if they aren't sold?" Tristram asked.

"When the auction is over," Mary said, "the gates of the pen are opened, and the planters are free to take anyone they want."

When all the men were sold, the women had their turn. The buyers who ringed the platform appeared to relax. Tristram noted a new gleam in their eyes. The male slaves had been strictly business. The females, some of them at least, were for pleasure.

"The attractive ones become house servants," Mary said, "maids or cooks or whatever else their owner requires. The others work in the fields cutting cane alongside the men."

"How is it they're all so neatly dressed?" Tristram asked. "They surely didn't wear those clothes during the voyage."

"The trader has them wear cheap dresses, so they'll look better and command a higher price. It doesn't always work, because the buyers get to inspect them first."

An inspection was in progress as she spoke. The auctioneer touted the woman on the block as a healthy young virgin. Several planters were engaged in checking her head and feeling her breasts. One of them had put his hand up under her dress. He shook his head and left the platform.

"How do they put up with it?" Tristram asked.

"They have no choice," Mary said. "I doubt that they understand what's happening to them."

Tristram recalled the girl who had shared his bed at the plantation. Was that to be the fate of these women? Such a custom would never pass muster in New England.

One after another the women mounted the platform to be fondled and probed and sold to the highest bidder. Tristram felt sorry for them and increasingly angry at the planters. He regretted his own weakness at the plantation. He should have sent the girl away without touching her. Why had the fidelity and morality instilled by his father abandoned him?

"I'm ready to go," Mary said. "This business depresses me."

"I'm going to buy one of those women," Tristram said. "I want to take her back to New England and set her free."

He moved toward the platform before Mary could reply. She cried out after him, but he couldn't make out her words. The auctioneer was motioning for him to come up and inspect the black girl who stood with downcast eyes on the block. Tristram shook his head. He wasn't buying her body; he was buying her freedom. The bidding commenced. He waited until it approached its peak and slowed before signaling to the auctioneer.

"Ten pounds!" he called out, aware that this was two pounds more than the previous bid.

A momentary silence ensued as the planters turned to stare at him. He took no notice of them. He was equally blind to the appearance of the girl offered for sale. His mind absorbed only her frightened and helpless look, her yellow dress, and the chant of the auctioneer. He had made it his duty as a Christian to save one person from a life of servitude.

"Sold for ten pounds!"

All eyes were on him as he mounted the platform. He paid the ten pounds and took possession of the girl. As he led her back to where Mary waited, he read the knowing looks of the plantation owners. He didn't care what they thought. He subscribed to a different code of conduct.

Once free of the crowd, he stopped to look at the girl. He judged her to be in her teens. Her face bore the marks of a past sickness or of ill treatment, and she walked with a slight limp. He would have liked her to smile at him out of gratitude; but she simply stared at the ground, her arms folded across her breasts. He turned his attention to Mary. To his surprise her look expressed both anger and sorrow. He had expected her approval.

"What have thou done?" she cried. "Thy rash action bodes no good for this poor girl."

"I propose to set her free," he said. "Is that not a good?"

"Free to do what? What is there for her in New England? The girl speaks no English. She's nothing but a slave in thy care."

Her admonitions caused him to consider that he might have acted rashly. Yet his intentions were noble, and he was prepared to do whatever was needed to carry them out. He looked again at the girl he had bought. Her expression was one of fear and bewilderment.

"You may be right," he said, "but I intend to do what is right and best for the girl when I get home."

"If thou art truly interested in doing what is best for her, sell her to a planter, so she can stay in Barbados with her kin. In New England she'll have no one but thee."

"I intend to help her make a life for herself. I shall take her into my own home for a time. My wife will be glad to have some help."

He was making it up as he went. It was beginning to dawn on him what he had undertaken, the commitment he had made, the effort required to make this slave a free woman.

Mary gave him no time to consider. "Thy own home indeed!" she said scornfully. "And doubtless for thy own purpose, which is no different from that of these planters. Thy wife will recognize thy intentions as soon as she sees the girl."

"You have no cause to accuse me in such fashion," Tristram said. But even as he spoke, he wondered if his indignance was partly pretense.

"I took care not to provoke thee. This poor girl is defenseless. Thou can do with her what thou will."

Though chastened by the vehemence of Mary's outburst, Tristram was not ready to accept her verdict. "Her defense lies in her ignorance of the language," he said.

"If thou are determined to take the girl to New England, thou might at least explain to her what is in thy mind. She has no knowledge of what lies ahead of her."

"How can I explain anything to her?"

"I would urge thee to find an interpreter."

"I'll do more than that. I'll give her a choice. She can either come with me, or she can stay in Barbados with her own people. I shall abide by her decision. She is already free in my eyes."

"I leave her in thy care," Mary said. "I hope thy wisdom is equal to thy compassion." With that she turned and strode off.

Tristram watched her go. When he looked again at the slave girl, he was surprised to see Rous standing next to her. He hadn't noticed the planter during the auction, but his eyes had been fastened on the platform. Rous's knowing smile put Tristram at once on the defensive.

"I know what you think, but I bought the girl for quite a different reason. I'm going to give her a better life in New England than she could expect here in Barbados. Eventually she'll be a free woman."

"That's very noble of you," Rous said, "but eventually is far off. In the meantime you're free to do with her what you like, or what your wife will tolerate."

"I can assure you that I have no such intentions. She will be a paid servant in my home until she can live on her own in the community."

"You're a lot like my son John, impetuous and quick to act before you think. I suppose it comes with being young, though I don't recall such a phase in my own life."

Tristram relaxed. "I'll admit that I acted on impulse."

"Whether or not your motives were selfless," Rous said, "your act indicates that you're a man of like mind, a man I can trust. I wish you and your slave girl happiness and good fortune."

Tristram started to muster a further argument in his defense, then paused to reconsider. Rous had made up his mind about him and the girl. Nothing he said now was apt to change his opinion. The best course was to cement their agreement by letting Rous think what he would.

"I'm glad I passed the test," he said. But he vowed in his heart to prove that Rous was wrong.

* * *

Tristram's search for an interpreter took him first to the slave ship. He reasoned that someone on the ship must have communicated with the slaves during the long voyage from Africa. The girl followed a few paces behind him. Her pace slowed as they approached the ship, and the look on her face was akin to terror. Realizing that she must think his intent was to put her back aboard, Tristram sought to reassure her through gestures and signs that all was well. She seemed to understand something of what he was trying to tell her, yet she refused to set foot on the gangplank. He had no choice but to leave her on the wharf, while keeping her in view as he spoke to a seaman who was working on deck.

"We don't try to talk to them," he said in response to Tristram's question. "We feed them while they're alive and throw them overboard if they die."

"Someone has to give them orders," Tristram persisted.

"The mate's ashore, but he won't be much help. You could ask at the slave market. They must speak to them before they auction them off."

Out of the corner of his eye Tristram was aware of a black man in uniform striding toward the spot near the gangplank where the girl waited. He shouted something as he approached, but his words were meaningless to Tristram. The girl's look of terror was rekindled as the man seized her by the arm and attempted to draw her away.

"Let her be," Tristram called down to him. "She belongs to me. I just bought her at the auction."

The man in uniform came to attention and saluted. "I'm sorry, sir. I think maybe she run away."

"I thank you for doing your duty," Tristram said.

The man saluted again, did an about face, and strode off the way he had come.

Tristram turned back to the seaman. "Run away!" he said. "Where would she go?"

The seaman shrugged. "No telling what these blacks have in their heads. We get them straight out of the jungle."

"They're human beings," Tristram said, "just like you and me."

"If you say so. But they sure don't look like us, and their talk is so much animal babble."

Tristram left him to his work and rejoined the girl on the wharf. His chief concern was to set her mind at ease. He felt sure that a return to the slave market would only add to her anxiety. The Quaker community in Bridgetown might be willing to help him. Some of them were opposed to slavery and wanted to convert slaves to their beliefs. But to do that they would need an interpreter.

In response to his inquiries, he was directed to a ramshackle two-story building on the edge of town. The room on the second floor was furnished more like a parlor than an office. A stout middle-aged woman gave him a dubious look as he entered, but her attitude changed when he mentioned Mary Fisher. He stated his reason for coming and asked about an interpreter.

The woman frowned. "Did Mary agree with thy plan?"

"It was Mary who suggested an interpreter. I promised her I would get the girl's consent before I took her to New England. I understand that you have some contact with slaves, so I thought you might help me."

"Help thee to get the girl's consent?"

"That's why I'm here," Tristram said.

"I know a few words in one of their languages. I can try to make myself understood."

The girl stood near the door with her hands clasped in front of her. She seemed apprehensive but no longer afraid. The woman motioned her to sit down and drew up a chair beside her. They spoke in a language that meant nothing to Tristram. The woman's speech was broken and labored, but the slave girl appeared to understand.

Her responses were fluent, and she repeated them as often as necessary.

"She says her name is Tamika. The planters choose names for their slaves. I would advise thee to do the same. It will make it easier for her to live and gain acceptance in your community."

"Tell her I'll call her Tami," Tristram said.

The girl smiled as the woman sought to convey his message.

"She says Tami is a form of endearment, a name that a man would use for his wife."

Tristram felt his face redden. "Tell her I have a wife, but I'm still going to call her Tami."

The two women were occupied for some time, using both gestures and words to communicate with each other.

"Tami wants to know what will happen to her. I tried to explain what she can expect if she stays in Barbados, but I don't know what to say about New England. What sort of life will she have there?"

"Tell her she'll work in my house. She'll help my wife and tend to our five children. When she's ready, she can live in the community and do whatever she wants. She'll be a free woman."

"Will the community accept her?"

Mary had asked the same question. "I'm confident that in time the townspeople will grow accustomed to seeing her about and accept her as one of them."

"And what of thy wife?"

"She'll be pleased to have some help."

"I speak not of help. Art thou quite certain thy wife will welcome a young black woman into her house?"

Tristram essayed a laugh. Mary had brought that up as well. "I can assure you that I have only Tami's best interest in mind. I want to give her a chance to make her way toward becoming a free woman."

Turning again to the girl, the Quaker woman resumed their broken dialogue. Tami appeared to relax as they spoke. Once she glanced at him and smiled. Tristram assumed she had begun to grasp the implications of what he offered her.

"She wants to know what will happen to her if she refuses to go with thee to this place she never heard of and can't understand."

"I'll have to leave her with a planter named Rous," Tristram said, "unless your society is prepared to take her in."

"That may be our mission in the future, but at present we're not prepared for such an undertaking."

The two women conversed again. At last Tami said something in a tone Tristram took to be decisive.

"She agrees to go to New England," the woman said. "Of course, she has no idea where or what New England is. I tried to explain, but I doubt that she understood. May I ask, how will thou talk to her?"

"I can try to teach her some English on the voyage."

"Two members of our society are planning to go to New England. One of them is a teacher. She knows far more of the native language than I do. She might be willing to instruct Tami in exchange for their passage."

The proposal would surely be of benefit to Tami. Yet Tristram had looked forward to teaching Tami himself. It would build her confidence in him and convince her that he had her welfare in mind. Whether it proved to be difficult or easy, it presented a challenge for him. Yet if he declined to provide passage for the two Quakers, it would raise questions about his own intentions toward the girl. He decided to compromise.

"I just fulfilled the terms of a bond to return two members of your society to Barbados. It is hardly in my interest to bring anyone back with me. Perhaps on my next voyage. But I'm willing to pay this teacher you mention to instruct Tami while I'm in Bridgetown."

Recalling his offer to take Mary Fisher back with him to Rhode Island, Tristram wondered if word of his refusal would get back to her. He trusted her to understand that she was a special case and that his offer did not extend to the entire Quaker community.

The woman regarded him closely. "I understand thy position. I'll speak to the teacher today. She can contact thee; that is, if she's willing."

"Tell her she can find us aboard the *Hopewell*," Tristram said.

He thanked her and left. Tami followed him willingly. She seemed more comfortable now in his presence. Back on the *Hopewell* he installed her in the same quarters the Quaker women had used on the voyage south. She smiled at him in gratitude. She was no doubt unaccustomed to private accommodations.

The next day the teacher sent word that she was willing to take Tami on as a pupil. Tristram escorted the girl to the address given in the message. The teacher was an older woman, short and stocky, her face pockmarked by some childhood or tropical disease. After conversing for a time with Tami, she laid down the terms for her tutelage. Her words and her manner made it clear that they were not negotiable.

"The girl will stay here with me. Otherwise I cannot possibly teach her enough English so she can communicate with thee. As for the price of my services, we can work that out when she departs. If that is acceptable to thee, I am prepared to begin her instruction at once."

"I readily agree," Tristram said. "It's more than I hoped for."

Leaving Tami in the custody of the teacher would also relieve him of the responsibility to care for and protect her during the remainder of his stay in Bridgetown.

"I'm grateful for your time and effort," he added.

"Thank Mary Fisher for putting in a good word on thy behalf."

The teacher smiled at him, as if she were enjoying his confusion.

"Send me word when thou are ready to sail," she went on, "and I'll deliver Tami to the *Hopewell,* is it?"

Tristram nodded, and they shook hands. Saying good-bye to Tami, he experienced a pang of regret. He felt that he was abandoning her. She smiled at him, as if to say she understood.

In the days that followed, he concluded his business with Rous and supervised the loading of the sugar and molasses that comprised his cargo. The task kept him fully occupied, and he was doubly grateful to be free of the burden of looking out for Tami. He would have liked to seek out Mary Fisher and thank her for interceding with the teacher on his behalf, but the loading of cargo and preparations for departure kept him fully occupied.

A day prior to sailing Tristram sent a message to the teacher. Early the next morning he spotted three women approaching the *Hopewell.* He was expecting Tami and the teacher, but he was surprised and pleased to see Mary in their company. As Tristram descended the gangplank to greet them, Tami left the other women behind and stationed herself alongside him on the wharf. She was clad in a bright green dress that was better fitted to her slender body.

"She's been a good student, quick and eager to learn," the teacher said. "I've taught her all I could, with a little help from Mary here. I leave it to thee to complete the task."

"I'm deeply grateful to you," Tristram said. "Feel free to name a price for her instruction."

"I have no need of thy money. Thy promise to provide passage for us on thy next voyage is sufficient payment."

The teacher hugged Tami. "I wish thee well in thy new home."

"I thank thee," Tami said.

Tristram laughed. "I didn't expect you to make a Quaker of her."

"I can speak in no other fashion," the teacher said.

"Then I forgive thee," Tristram said.

They shook hands in parting. He thought he detected a tear on her pockmarked cheek as she turned and strode off briskly along the wharf.

Mary remained behind. She had said nothing during the exchange of custody. Now she handed over a cloth satchel she was carrying.

"I've assembled a few items Tami will find useful in her new life," she said. "I've also come to apologize for my abrupt departure after the auction. Truth to tell, I was quite angry at thee at the time. But I've come to know Tami a little better these past few days. She is quite excited about going to a land where there is no slavery, and I'm convinced that she has made a wise decision. So I too wish thee well in this undertaking."

"I'm glad to have your approval," Tristram said. "Have you made a decision regarding your own future?"

"I've made arrangements to return to England. I'm certain that my future awaits me there, though that future has yet to be revealed to me."

"Whatever it is, I wish you better success than you had in Boston."

"Boston was not a failure," Mary said. "I have evidence of that at this very moment."

Tristram thought it best not to argue the point. He was glad of this opportunity to say good-bye to her, and he wanted to part on good terms. If she chose to think he had absorbed some of her beliefs, he saw no harm in letting her believe it. It could be that she was right.

Ten

"She's a free woman, and she belongs to me."
(Aboard the *Hopewell*, Autumn 1656)

Not long out of Bridgetown Tristram realized that having Tami aboard would be more of a problem than he expected. By their demeanor and the fact that they were a pair, the Quaker women had established and maintained a certain barrier between themselves and the crew. But Tami was timid and alone, a stranger in a foreign land. She had a private cabin, but no way to fasten the door; and initially she was left to fend for herself on the main deck.

The second day at sea, having framed a tentative plan for teaching Tami more English, Tristram went in search of the girl. He needed first to gauge how much she had learned from the teacher in Bridgetown. She was not in her cabin, but he saw nothing unusual in that. She spent much of her time on deck staring at the wake created by the ship as it cut through the waves. He attributed her desire for fresh sea air to memories of her long confinement in the hold on her last voyage from Africa.

Stepping out on deck, he directed his gaze along the leeward side of the ship. Tami was nowhere in sight. As he made his way forward, one of the crew gestured toward the fo'c'sle. Tristram thrust open the door and entered the crew's quarters. As his eyes adjusted to the dim light, he made out the figure of the cook bending over one of the bunks. A second figure was stretched out on the bunk. It was Tami. She was clothed and appeared to be waiting submissively for whatever was to happen to her.

"Let her go!" he called to the cook.

The man looked at him in surprise. "She's a black slave," he said. "I spotted her all alone on deck, so I figured she was fair game for anyone who had a hankering after her."

"Well, she's neither fair game nor a slave. Now get out of here."

Tristram helped Tami to her feet and led her to her cabin. Leaving her there to rest, he summoned the entire crew and addressed them from the command deck.

"I want every one of you to understand this," he said. "The woman is a passenger on this ship. I hold myself responsible for her safety while she's aboard. You will keep your distance from her, and you will respect her privacy. She's a free woman in my eyes, and you will treat her as such. Anyone who molests her in any way will forfeit his wages for the voyage. Is that perfectly clear?"

The crew murmured their assent; but he could sense that they still had doubts about Tami's status or about his motives. He vowed to be on guard in dealing with the girl, lest idle rumors become part of the cargo he carried back to Yarmouth. With this in mind he conducted her first lesson in English in plain view on the command deck. But the uncertain weather and a lack of comfort made that location impractical as a classroom.

Henceforth, for an hour each morning and afternoon he met with Tami in his cabin. Since he doubted his ability as a teacher, he enlisted the aid of a mate who had once taught school; the same mate who was forced to give up his quarters to the Quaker women and now to Tami. He hoped thus to further her education, allay any talk among the crew, and maintain proper decorum in their relationship.

Tami always wore the green dress. Tristram took this as a sign that she regarded her lessons as an event worthy of more formal attire, though he was also aware that her wardrobe was limited. Her willingness to learn the language filled him with joy, and he looked forward to these sessions as much as she did. The teacher in Bridgetown had given her a Quaker pamphlet as a learning tool; but many of the concepts it contained were foreign to her experience. She no longer used thee and thou in addressing him, and he had no desire to reinforce whatever religious ideas she was exposed to in Barbados. He brought out a Bible his father had given him; and they read simple stories from the Old and New Testament, using them to round out her instruction.

He also granted Tami access to the command deck. Between the lessons he drew from her not so much an account as an impression of her experiences prior to her arrival in Barbados. He gathered she was from a place or a tribe in Africa called Ibo, and that she was abducted, sold to a slave trader, and placed on a big ship. She seemed eager to tell him about conditions aboard the slave ship. To make it easier for her to explain what she meant, he showed her the cargo deck and the hold. There he coaxed from her a broken account of what the trip across the Atlantic was like.

From her own words and those he put in her mouth, he learned that she was forced to lie on a shelf, where she was wedged among dozens of other men and women. As more and more slaves were herded aboard, she could no longer lie flat on her back but had to turn on her side. Thus she remained throughout the voyage, except for a brief time each day on deck to eat and get some fresh air. The men were shackled to the shelf, but she was spared that added discomfort. The hatches were covered with canvas in rough weather to prevent water from flooding the decks below. This cut off any air circulation to the hold. The stench of vomit and excrement was pervasive and caused many slaves to become ill. With each roll of the ship Tami prayed she might die, or that the ship might sink. She survived, but many about her did not. After a storm the living were brought on deck, while the dead were cast over the side. Later in the voyage she had room once again to lie on her back.

Tristram felt certain that her eagerness to tell her story was due in part to the contrast between her close quarters on the slave ship and the freedom of movement she enjoyed on the *Hopewell*. He took her facial expression and the tone of her voice as an indication that she had begun to realize she was no longer a slave. He wondered if she had been molested aboard the slave ship, but some questions were better left unasked.

Anticipating rough seas, Tristram steered a course that took him along the coast to Jamestown in the Virginia Colony. There he planned to obtain fresh food and honor a commitment to one of the tobacco growers. There was little space left on the cargo deck, but with a bit of reshuffling he might be able to placate the grower and maintain their connection.

The ship was still some distance from Jamestown when he spotted the mate coming out of Tami's cabin. He appeared flustered when he saw Tristram and passed by without saying a word. Tristram realized he was in a quandary of his own making. By maintaining a respectful distance from Tami himself and impressing on the crew that she was a free woman, he invited them to get better acquainted with her. She may well have invited the mate into her cabin. He was after all one of her teachers. To question her would convey the message that despite his fine words he still regarded her as his property. His only recourse was to confront the mate. It dawned on him that he was jealous.

Following Tami's next lesson the mate volunteered an explanation of what had happened. "With this turn in the weather, I needed a scarf I'd left in her cabin. Tami started talking to me. She wanted to practice what she just learned, and I must have lost track of the time. When I passed you on my way out, I realized how it might look to you; but I was too confused to say anything. I apologize for any concern I may have caused you."

It sounded like a reasonable explanation. "I did wonder what you were doing in her cabin," Tristram said. "Maybe I'm overly protective of Tami, but I can't help feeling responsible for her welfare."

"You have good cause to be protective. Some of the crew grasp at any opportunity to speak to her."

"What about the cook?"

"He's kept his distance, but I can tell from the way he looks at her that he would welcome a chance to be alone with her."

"I thank you for the warning," Tristram said. "Keep your eyes open for signs of trouble, so I can head it off."

"I'll do that," the mate said. "Truth to tell, I've begun to feel quite protective toward Tami myself."

* * *

Although Tami's cabin was private, it was accessible to anyone. Tristram thought of installing a bar on the door so Tami could lock herself in while she slept. But such a measure would only frighten the girl. When persistent vomiting and diarrhea kept her confined to her cabin, Tristram saw a solution to the problem.

"I'll have a doctor look at her when we arrive in Jamestown," he told the mate. "Meanwhile, I'll care for her in my cabin. You can have your quarters back."

"I understand your concern," the mate said. The expression on his face was inscrutable.

Tristram had experience caring for his children when they were ill. Now he took full charge of Tami's recovery. He supervised what she ate, cleaned up after her, and saw to it that she was comfortable. Tami ventured an occasional wan smile in response to his ministrations. He took it as a sign that she appreciated his concern.

When the *Hopewell* made port in Jamestown, Tami was no longer vomiting, but she remained weak. Tristram hired a carriage and set off with her to find the only doctor in the settlement. On arriving at his house, they were told that the doctor would be back shortly. While they waited, Tristram sought to tell Tami what she might expect when she saw the doctor. In the midst of his explanation she fell asleep, her head nestled on his shoulder.

That was how the doctor found them on his arrival. He was short and stocky and had white hair, though he did not appear to be much over fifty. He seemed surprised to find a black girl in his office. Tristram told him who they were and why they had come, then detailed the course of Tami's illness and the measures he had taken to effect her recovery.

The doctor nodded approvingly during his account. He proceeded to question Tami about her symptoms, with Tristram acting as interpreter. Satisfied that he had all the facts in the case, he turned to Tristram.

"What she has is a fairly common malady," he said. "I'll prepare some medicine she can take right now, along with a tonic that will help her regain her strength. I'd like to see what effect the medicine has before she leaves, if that is possible. It will take two or three hours. Perhaps you have something you'd like to do in the meantime."

"I do have business to tend to," Tristram said. "I'll come back for her when I'm finished."

He explained to Tami that he was leaving her in good hands and would soon return. He trusted that she understood. She gave him what he took to be a brave smile as he left.

His business took longer than expected. When he returned to the office, Tami was gone.

"I tried to tell her you were delayed," the doctor said. "She insisted that she could find her way back to your ship."

"Was she feeling any stronger?" Tristram asked.

"I think so. She responded well to the medicine I gave her. Would you believe that she helped me prepare it. She seemed to be familiar with the herbs I was using. She even rejected some and suggested others. What she said made good sense, so I let her dictate her own cure."

"Did you notice which way she went when she left here?"

"She was headed toward the docks. I made sure of that."

Tristram paid the doctor his fee and left in the carriage. The town had a main street along the river bank and several side streets. He had the driver stop so he could ask anyone they met about a black girl in a green dress. Tami had insisted on looking her best for the doctor.

426

A man who was walking near the docks said he had seen a woman in a green dress. "A young fellow was helping her into a carriage. She was a bit unsteady, like she was weak or pregnant or something."

"Can you describe the carriage or the horse?"

"The carriage was closed and rusty red in color. It had some sort of emblem painted on the door. The horse was light, almost white."

"Did you notice which way they went?"

"The last I saw of them, they were headed west out of town."

Tristram got back in his carriage. If Tami had been taken to one of the many tobacco plantations that surrounded Jamestown, he might never see her again. He was debating what to do next when the driver spoke up.

"There's an ordinary out that way. The young fellow may have stopped for a drink."

"Let's go then!" Tristram cried.

He climbed up next to the driver and urged him to whip his horse into a fast trot. As they approached the ordinary, he spotted a carriage and a white horse. The horse was tethered to a rail in front of the inn. Tristram got down and ran toward the door of the tavern. In passing the carriage, he noticed the emblem on the side.

Several men were seated at tables in the smoke-filled tavern. They stopped talking and drinking as Tristram entered. There was no sign of Tami. A burly man sporting a rusty brown beard, whom he took to be the innkeeper, called out to him.

"What can I do for you, mate?"

"Did a man and a black girl wearing a green dress come in here a short while ago?"

"Can't say that I've seen anyone fitting that description."

"There's no need to cover for him," an older men seated at one of the tables said. "You'll find them upstairs."

Tristram mounted the stairs two at a time. At the top he faced two closed doors. In the first room a clean-shaven young man in his twenties, his shirt open at the neck, was kneeling over Tami and trying to raise her dress. He ventured a smile as Tristram burst into the room.

"You can have a go at her as soon as I'm done," he said.

Tristram took him by the belt and yanked him away. As he lay sprawled on the floor, Tristram put a foot on his chest. The man looked up at him in surprise.

"What's the matter with you? She's nothing but a slave girl, most likely run off from one of the plantations."

"She's a free woman, and she belongs to me," Tristram said, aware as he spoke of the contradiction "What's more, she's sick and just saw a doctor. I'm taking her back to my ship."

"She ought to have said she was sick."

"Would that have made any difference?"

The young man relaxed. "Probably not," he said, forcing a grin.

Tami had managed to get to her feet. Tristram took her hand and led her to the door. The young man said nothing further.

The men in the tavern looked up again as Tristram passed through with Tami on his arm, but they made no comment. He helped her into his carriage and got in beside her. The driver had turned his horse around, and he headed toward the docks without any instruction.

Back on the *Hopewell* Tristram sought to calm Tami and make her comfortable. The tonic the doctor prescribed for her had disappeared in the confusion. Tristram promised to have it replaced before he sailed. Tami ventured a wan smile in response.

"Thank you, Master Tristram," she said.

* * *

Having concluded his business and stored the tobacco aboard the *Hopewell*, Tristram prepared to leave Jamestown behind. He had obtained another bottle of tonic for Tami. She felt much stronger and was eager to resume her English lessons. The mate still served as a teacher. But Tami continued to share his cabin, while the mate remained in his own quarters. The crew heard only that she was still recovering from her sickness.

The third day out they encountered rough weather. When it came time for Tami's lesson, the mate was fully occupied on deck. Tristram wanted to cancel the lesson, but her look of disappointment made him feel like a father who has failed to fulfill a promise to his child. Alone with her in his cabin he motioned to her to sit at his table, while he stretched out on his bunk. She listened intently as he read about the wedding feast at Cana. His procedure was to read a story and explain it to her, then have her read it again with him. He wanted to build on the foundation laid by the teacher in Barbados, who insisted that Tami learn to read and speak English.

The table where she sat was but a few steps from his bunk. When she was puzzled by a word or phrase, he held up the Bible for her to see. An occasional smile told him that she was following the story, though he wasn't sure what it meant to her.

When the lesson was over, he closed the Bible and gave it to her. As she was replacing it on the shelf, a wave caused the *Hopewell* to lurch heavily. Tami lost her balance and fell on the bunk. The foreign scent of her body was not unpleasant. She felt warm and soft as she lay on top of him. She had gained some weight since he bought her at the auction, but she was still frail from her weeks on the slave ship.

They remained motionless in that position. Tami seemed to be awaiting a signal from him to rise. He sensed that she was offering herself to him, either out of gratitude or because she felt it was expected of her. He recalled the slave girl at the plantation. But Tami was different. She would be part of his household. If he made love to her now, would she not expect as much when he got home?

Unconsciously he had begun to caress her back, an action that was natural for him when Blanche was in his arms. His hands told him that Tami had little if anything on under the green dress.

"Make me yours," she whispered in his ear.

Tristram hesitated a moment, awaiting orders from his body, then complied with her request.

* * *

For the rest of the voyage north Tami remained in his quarters. He told the crew it was for her protection, that he was simply reinforcing his order that she was off limits to them. He was sure they had reached their own conclusion about what was going on, but he no longer cared what they thought. He had no wish to end his sessions with Tami. Time enough to break it off when they were no longer at sea. Somehow he would make her understand that it could not continue after he got home. Perhaps there was a story in the Bible to illustrate that point.

The sea had calmed, and a favoring wind drove the *Hopewell* along at good speed. He arrived in Boston a day earlier that expected.

It was not exactly home, but he decided to break the news to Tami at once. It would give her time to adjust, and he could test his own resolve.

"You know I have a wife and children at home," he told her.

"I know," Tami said.

"My religion says a man should love his wife and no one else. That means we can no longer lie in bed together. It's better for both of us if we stop now. We need time to change the way we think about each other."

"I not understand," Tami said. "You not like me any more?"

Tristram frowned. This was going to be harder than he thought. He had no idea what meaning she attached to concepts like religion, marriage, and fidelity. Perhaps where she came from a man could keep several wives and sleep with whomever he pleased.

"I do like you, but my wife will be angry if I make love to you."

Tami was silent. She appeared bewildered.

Tristram had a sudden inspiration. "Did you belong to one man in Africa?" he asked.

"I not old enough for that. Then men come and take me away."

"Let's say you did belong to one man. Would he still make love to other women?"

"Man make love to any woman he like."

Tristram saw only one approach open to him. "Do you know what it means to be a slave?" he asked.

Tami appeared to wince. "You say I not slave any more."

Tristram paused. He hated to go down that road, but he saw no alternative. "After I bought you, I said you would be a free woman when you're ready. You're not ready yet to be free. You're still my slave. Do you understand?"

"I do what you say," Tami said, looking away.

"That's right, and I say we cannot make love any more."

The expression on her face told Tristram he was being too harsh

"It's not because I don't like you," he added. "It's because I have a wife and children at home."

"I do what you say," Tami repeated.

Tristram could tell she was about to cry.

Eleven

"Only to warn you against the course you are pursuing."
(Massachusetts Colony, Autumn 1656)

Tristram's first business in Boston was to ensure that Kempthorn recovered his bond. Since the *Swallow* was not in the harbor, he sent word of his arrival to Kempthorn in Charlestown.

"Are you happily married?" Tristram asked when they met.

"I am," Kempthorn said, "and I have you to thank."

Tristram showed him the paper Governor Searle had signed.

"That should satisfy them," Kempthorn said.

The clerk in the governor's office scrutinized the paper with great care. Having assured himself that all was in order, he secured the hundred pounds that Kempthorn had posted to guarantee the safe arrival of the two Quaker women in Barbados. He seemed reluctant to relinquish the money. Kempthorn finally had to snatch it out of his hands.

Free of this responsibility, Tristram attended to the disposition of his cargo. Realizing that he needed someone he could trust to watch over Tami while he was ashore, he enlisted the aid of the mate who had helped to teach her English. Tristram felt he was sincere in his desire to protect Tami, and she showed no sign of fear in his presence. If he had an opinion about where she slept, he kept it to himself.

Several days went by before Tristram had a chance to visit the Red Lyon Inn. He took Tami with him. He had it in mind to introduce her to life in New England; but he had also begun to question the wisdom of his undertaking, and he wanted Upsall's advice on how best to introduce the girl to Blanche. If Upsall met Tami face to face, he would have a better idea of what they were dealing with. Tristram did his best to prepare her for what was to come, but he wasn't sure himself what that was.

Upsall was clearly surprised when he saw Tami. They sat in the tavern with three tankards of cider before them, while Tristram launched into an explanation of how and why he had acquired the girl.

"I may have done something foolish while I was in Barbados," he said. "Mary Fisher persuaded me to attend a slave auction. This girl was on the auction block, and the growers were leering and fondling her. I was moved to save her from a lifetime of slavery, where she would be forced to accommodate the plantation owner and anyone else he ordered her to sleep with. So I bought her, and here she is."

Upsall put down his tankard so hard some of the cider spilled out. "What sort of life will she have in Yarmouth?" he asked.

"She'll be a servant in my home until she makes a place for herself in the community. Then she'll be a free woman."

"Free to do what?"

"Whatever she has a mind to do. I'll give her something for her service. She can set herself up in a business of some sort."

"How does your wife feel about all this?"

"I haven't been home yet," Tristram said. "But having a servant in the house should make things easier for her."

"Blanche may not see it that way."

Tristram contemplated the pool of cider Upsall had made. Tami appeared stoic and withdrawn. She had not touched her cider. He doubted that she understood what they were saying.

"You mean she'll think I had another reason for buying the girl."

"Was there another reason?" Upsall asked.

"At the time my motives were entirely unselfish, but on the voyage north in a weak moment I took her to bed with me."

"Then you should be prepared for problems at home."

"I've tried to make it clear to Tami that from now on she's nothing more than a servant."

"Such resolutions are easily made, and just as easily broken."

"Well, I own her now. I'll just have to make the best of it."

"If you want my advice, I'd get her out of your house as soon as possible. Farm her out as a servant to a friend or a relative. You'll still be able to keep an eye on her, but you won't be tempted to sleep with her."

"I can't do that," Tristram said. "She'll think I'm casting her out. I'm all she has to hang on to right now."

"That's part of your problem," Upsall said. "Blanche is sure to be suspicious. Wouldn't you be, if you were in her position?"

"I suppose I would," Tristram admitted.

"You good master. I good slave," Tami said.

Upsall seemed surprised. Then he laughed. Tristram joined in; but he wondered if she was making a simple statement, or whether she knew enough of the language to be setting a condition.

The conversation turned to the two Quaker women.

"I trust they're safe in Barbados," Upsall said.

"They are indeed," Tristram said, "and Simon Kempthorn is now a happily married man."

"Did the young one convince you of the truth of their message?"

"No, but we talked a lot on the voyage south. I have a better opinion of the Quakers and what they're trying to do."

"A second group arrived from England shortly after you sailed," Upsall said. "Eight of them this time."

"Are they in jail too?" Tristram asked.

"Where else would they be? They're charged so far with intending to disrupt the peace, but Endicott has requested the Commissioners of the United Colonies to establish some general rules for dealing with Quakers and other heretics who come here from foreign countries. He wants a law that prohibits them from landing in Massachusetts."

"I thought there was a law," Tristram said.

"That court ruling only applied to the two women."

"Have the Commissioners acted on his request?"

"They proposed that all Quakers, Ranters, and other heretics who enter the colonies or spring up among us be secured and removed beyond our borders. I think that's the way they put it. Now it's up to the General Court to pass such a law."

"Do you think they will?"

"There's some opposition to it," Upsall said, "but Endicott has a lot of influence. He'll get it passed."

"Why doesn't he just send them back where they came from like Bellingham did?"

"He tried that on their arrival. A man named William Brend acted as their spokesman at the initial hearing. He has some training in the law. I wasn't there, but I heard he had quite a heated exchange with Norton."

"The minister who examined the two women?"

"The same. It seems Norton asked him if he agreed that Scripture is the sole rule of faith. He cited St. Peter, something about the sure word of prophecy, the light that shines in a dark place, and the day star that rises in our hearts. But Brend got him to admit the sure word refers to the word of God as manifested within the heart and soul, and that this eternal word is a sufficient rule and guide. Then he asked Norton how the conscience that guides his actions differs from the inner voice that Quakers heed."

"What did Norton say to that?"

"As George Fox might say, he was confounded. Endicott realized that any charges of heresy might be turned against him. Maybe he recalled the trial of Ann Hutchinson. Whatever his reason, he decided the best solution to his problem was a law preventing Quakers from landing in Boston."

"But if Norton was confounded, as you say, why are Brend and the others still in prison?"

"Instead of answering him, Endicott warned Brend not to break our ecclesiastical laws, lest he stretch by a halter. Then the magistrates ordered the Quakers to be confined until measures can be taken to determine their fate. There's talk that they should be whipped or branded, but for now the jailer just has to make sure they speak to no one and have no paper and ink at their disposal."

."Are you smuggling food to them in jail?" Tristram asked.

"The fewer people who know what I'm doing, the better," Upsall said. "I've been in contact with them, and I'm doing what I can to make sure they're well treated."

"Then it's my turn to ask the same question. Have they convinced you? Are you now a Quaker?"

Upsall was silent for a moment. He glanced at Tami, as if to assess her ability to keep a secret. Turning to Tristram, he said, "I trust you not to repeat what I say. I have indeed been convinced of the truth these Friends proclaim. I have yet to tell anyone. I'm not afraid to admit it, but it would hamper my efforts to assist them."

"It's sure to come out," Tristram said. "Have you considered the consequences?"

"I think of little else," Upsall said. "I've discussed it with Dorothy. I'm prepared to take a stand when the time comes, but that day has yet to arrive. It may be sooner than we think."

* * *

Tristram was alone on his next visit to Upsall at the Red Lyon. They were hardly settled at a table when they heard a drumbeat, followed by sounds of a commotion in the street outside the inn. Upsall rose and went to the door. Dorothy and Tristram stood at his elbow. A crowd had gathered about the town crier, who stood on his box at the intersection of North and Richmond streets. He held a scroll above eye level, as if the phrases he was about to utter originated somewhere on high.

"Whereas, there is a cursed sect of heretics lately risen up in the world, which are commonly called Quakers, who take upon them to be immediately sent of God, and infallibly assisted by the Spirit of God to speak and write their blasphemous opinions, despising government, and the order of God in the churches and common wealth, speaking evil of dignities, reproaching and reviling magistrates and ministers, seeking to turn the people from the faith, and gain proselytes to their pernicious ways."

"It's the usual rhetoric they use to describe Quakers." Upsall said when the crier paused to catch his breath. "I've heard it ever since this last group arrived. I suppose there's an element of truth in it, but most of it is groundless assertion."

"Listen!" Dorothy said. "He's reading again."

"By authority of this Court be it ordered and enacted, that what master or commander of any ship, bark, pinnace, ketch, or any other vessel that shall henceforth bring into any harbor, creek or cove, within this jurisdiction, any Quaker or Quakers, or any other blasphemous heretics as aforesaid, shall pay or cause to be paid the fine of one hundred pounds to the Treasurer of the country,"

"He said henceforth," Tristram noted. "Kempthorn can relax."

"That what Quakers soever shall arrive in this country from any foreign parts," the crier went on, "or come into this jurisdiction from any parts adjacent, shall be forthwith committed to the house of correction, and, at their entrance to be severely whipped, and by the master thereof to be kept constantly to work, and none suffered to converse or speak with them during the time of their imprisonment."

Upsall's look had darkened. "To whip Quakers for their beliefs is contrary to the principles on which the colony was founded. The deputies seem to have forgotten why they left England."

The crier was reading again. The next article exacted a fine of five pounds from anyone who should knowingly bring into the jurisdiction any Quaker book or writing, or conceal such book or writing in his house.

"Now they're talking about you," Tristram said.

"And you as well," Upsall said. "You gave me the pamphlet."

The crier read on. "If any person within this colony shall take upon them to defend the heretical opinions of the said Quakers, or any of their books or papers as aforesaid, if legally proved, shall be fined for first time forty shillings; if they shall persist in the same, and shall so again defend it, the second time four pounds; if still, notwithstanding, they shall again so defend it, and maintain the said Quakers heretical opinions, they shall be committed to the house of correction till there be convenient passage to send them out of the land, being sentenced in the Court of Assistants to banishment."

"You were wise not to announce that you're a Quaker," Tristram said. "As long as no one knows about it, you're safe."

"I refuse to be banished for my opinions," Upsall said.

The crier had not finished. "Lastly, be it hereby enacted, that what person or persons soever shall revile the office or persons of magistrates or ministers, as is usual with the Quakers, such person or persons shall be severely whipped, or pay the sum of five pounds."

He rewound the scroll and prepared to move on to the next corner. Upsall left the shelter of the tavern and stepped out into the street.

Dorothy sought to restrain him. "You're too wrought up to think clearly. Go back inside and calm yourself. Tomorrow you can decide what to do about this law."

Upsall brushed her hand aside. "There is but one way to deal with a law like this."

With that he strode to the same spot where the crier had stood. The crowd had begun to disperse, but many of them turned back as he began to speak. The crier too had stopped to listen. Upsall's voice carried for a long distance; even to the ears of Endicott, as some were later to state.

"People of Boston, hear what I have to say! I am not a magistrate or a minister. You know me simply as a citizen and an innkeeper. But my conscience compels me to declare that it is wrong to whip and banish and cast people in prison merely for setting foot on the soil of Massachusetts. The assistants and the deputies should be reminded why we left England and emigrated to these shores. As a Christian I am bound to oppose a law that forbids me to comfort those who are afflicted or in prison. This new proclamation is not in accord with the laws of any church or state with which I wish to be associated. I view it is a sad forerunner of the heavy judgment that is due to fall upon this country."

"What would you have us do with these Quakers?" someone cried.

"I speak only of what I would not do," Upsall said. "I would not whip them, starve them, or deny them the solace of visitors. But I've said enough. I for one shall act in accordance with the teachings of Scripture. I ask you to do the same."

He made his way back to the tavern. Dorothy hugged him as he entered. "That was well spoke," she said. "I'm proud of you."

"Your pride may well bear a heavy price," Upsall said. "My little speech will not go unnoticed."

His prediction was borne our the next day. Tristram was at the inn as a constable read the pronouncement. He had come out of admiration for his friend's stance and out of curiosity as to what would happen next.

"Nicholas Upsall, you are hereby summoned to appear before the Court of Magistrates the morning of Thursday, the sixteenth of

October, to account for your words spoken in a public place, namely a street near the Red Lyon Inn. Failure to appear will result in a fine or imprisonment."

"I'm sorry to be the bearer of this message," the constable added on his own accord. "I feel sure that you'll be cleared of these charges."

"I wish I were sure of that," Upsall said when he was gone.

"You're a respected citizen of Boston," Tristram said, "one of the first freemen in the colony. It's your right to speak out against a law that is contrary to our beliefs and our tradition."

"I fear my statement will be construed as evidence that I'm either a Quaker or a sympathizer. In the present climate, that is no small offense."

"I shall go with you to court."

"If you do," Upsall said, "you'll be branded with the same stamp. But you might slip into the gallery and bear witness to what takes place."

"You can depend on my presence," Tristram said.

* * *

Upsall appeared in court on the date ordered. Governor Endicott presided over the hearing. Bellingham was also present. Tristram joined a small group of supporters and curious onlookers in the gallery.

The clerk rose and read the charges. "Nicholas Upsall, you are charged with reproaching the honored magistrates, for speaking in public against a law passed by the General Court against the sect of Quakers, and for sympathizing in word and in deed with the said sect of Quakers. What say you to these charges?"

Upsall responded in a voice as strong as that he employed outside his inn. "I spoke out against a ruling that is contrary to English law in that it punishes people for no recognized crime. It is my right and my duty as a freeman to protest such a miscarriage."

"Your speech is like that of the cursed sect of Quakers," Endicott said. "I fear that you have imbibed from the same cup that nourishes their heretical opinions."

"The Scriptures are my nourishment," Upsall said. "They instruct me to feed the hungry, to visit those in prison, to comfort the afflicted and persecuted. This law forbids me to act out of Christian charity."

"That is a matter best addressed by the clergy. Mr. Norton, what is your opinion of the claims just voiced by the defendant?"

Norton was not seated on the bench with the magistrates. Tristram recalled Upsall's claim that the minister often advised Endicott on matters of religion. He pictured Norton as he examined Mary Fisher for some sign of the devil's mark. He regarded the minister as a zealot bent on weeding out and punishing heretical opinions, whether expressed or simply held.

"The Sermon on the Mount does state that the merciful are blessed and shall themselves obtain mercy," Norton said. "But that same sermon also states that those who hunger and thirst after justice shall be satisfied. This colony was and remains founded on a thirst for justice, a hunger that cannot stomach heresies intended to delude and corrupt the populace. By their efforts to express and publish such heresies, this sect of Quakers has offended against justice. It is our duty as Christians to prevent them from spreading their pernicious lies, lies that are clearly intended to lead astray those whose faith would otherwise remain strong."

"I thank you for your assessment," Endicott said.

Bellingham asked to speak and was recognized. "We often hear that justice should be tempered by mercy, but the obverse is equally true. I am of the opinion that mercy unconstrained by justice is a feeble thing."

"A point well taken," Endicott said. "Unbridled mercy leads only to weakness. Our strength and future as a colony is based on the justice of our laws and our mission. Does anyone else wish to express an opinion?"

A magistrate who voted against the law was recognized. "I agree that these Quakers must be restrained, and I have no objection to sending them back where they came from. But by subjecting them to such physical punishments simply because they are Quakers, we risk alienating decent citizens who oppose such harsh treatment for no apparent offense."

"You gave voice to a similar argument before the law was passed," Bellingham said without being recognized. "I would remind you again that it is our duty to make laws that promote the general welfare. With this in mind we must do all within our power to prevent the introduction and spread of these pernicious beliefs in our colony."

The dissenter remained standing. "Nicholas Upsall has endorsed a view expressed in this chamber and prevalent in the community. He's said nothing to indicate that he subscribes to such beliefs himself."

"He has spoken out publicly against the law and has urged others to disobey it," Endicott said. "He is also guilty of supporting the Quakers who are now in prison."

"We have heard no evidence to that effect."

"You shall have your evidence. Summon the turnkey."

Up in the gallery Tristram felt his head shrink down between his shoulders. Was he about to be drawn into this hearing? But the jailer said only that Upsall was providing the Quakers now in prison with food and writing materials. He made no mention of Mary Fisher and Ann Austin.

"Is there any doubt but that the defendant, Nicholas Upsall, has been grievously corrupted by these Quakers?" Endicott asked when the jailer had finished testifying. "Granted that Scripture urges us to feed the hungry; but nowhere is it written that we are to assist heretics to spread their false doctrine by providing them with pen and paper. His actions are a clear demonstration that he is a Quaker sympathizer."

Tristram waited for someone else to speak in Upsall's defense, but the magistrates appeared cowed by the governor's words.

Endicott turned to face Upsall. "Have you anything to say before this court votes to determine your fate?"

Upsall drew himself up. He looked at each magistrate before he spoke. "Only that in a spirit of tenderness and love I feel bound to warn you against the course you are pursuing."

"Your warning is duly noted," Endicott said. "Let us proceed."

The vote was not unanimous, but most of the magistrates endorsed Endicott's verdict. A satisfied look spread over his face as it became clear that he would have his way. Tristram took it as a indication of smugness. Endicott rose to pronounce sentence. Upsall remained on his feet.

"For reproaching the honored magistrates and speaking against a law made and published against the sect known as Quakers, the defendant, Nicholas Upsall, is sentenced to serve four days in prison and fined twenty pounds. For providing aid and comfort to the said Quakers, he is hereby banished from the colony. Failure to depart this jurisdiction within thirty days will result in further fines and imprisonment."

Upsall displayed no emotion as the bailiff escorted him from the chamber. He had obviously expected the judgment.

* * *

Endicott wasted no time in applying the new law to the Quakers in prison. He ordered the master of the *Speedwell* to return them to England at his own expense and to post bond of a hundred pounds as a guarantee. The master refused, saying he had violated no English law in bringing her free-born inhabitants to this part of her dominions. After four days in jail he complied with the order. Some eleven weeks after their arrival the eight Quakers left Boston aboard the *Speedwell*.

From the deck of the *Hopewell* Tristram observed their departure. It took him a week in all to dispose of his cargo. His business in Boston completed, he took passage with Tami on a shallop bound for Yarmouth.

Twelve

"You can bet he had his way with her."
(Plymouth Colony, Autumn 1656)

Blanche did not expect Tristram to return home from Barbados for another week. She had resolved in his absence to avoid contact with John Gorham, but her good intentions had been overcome on one occasion by his persistence. She was not in love with him; but he was ready at hand, whereas Tristram was off at sea. She blamed him for leaving her so long and so often alone. He knew she was vulnerable, in need of constant love and affection. Now that he was home, she could be strong again.

"I have a surprise for you," Tristram said as he disengaged himself from her embrace. "Look outside."

Blanche did as she was bid. A few steps behind him stood a young woman, more of a girl, short, slight of build, and very black. She clutched a cloth bag to her chest as if for warmth. The flimsy green dress she wore provided scant protection against the autumn chill. Blanche's first thought was to offer her a coat. Then a more pressing question occurred to her.

"Who is she? What is she doing here?"

"I brought her back from Barbados," Tristram said. "She can help you to care for the children and manage the household ."

He stood silently, as if awaiting her approval.

"Is she a slave?" Blanche asked.

"I bought her at the slave market in Bridgetown," he said. "I intend to set her free as soon as she can manage it. In the meantime she can work as our servant. Her name is Tami. Tami, this is my wife Blanche."

Tami ventured a smile as she bowed.

"Does she speak English?" Blanche asked.

"She had some lessons before we left Barbados, and I taught her as much as I could on the way home. She's quick to learn, but you'll have to be patient in explaining things to her."

"The poor girl's cold. Tell her to come in and get warm."

Tristram motioned to Tami to follow him inside the house. There he hugged each of his children. They had hung back, deterred no doubt by the sight of this strange black woman.

"Say hello to Tami," he told them. "She's going to stay with us for awhile and help your mother. She speaks a little English, but you can help to teach her a lot more. Will you do that for me?"

"I'll teach her all I know." Mary's eyes and her smile bore witness to her eagerness to begin the task.

The young ones seemed unsure of what it all meant. They smiled uncertainly as Tami knelt and greeted each of them in turn, repeating their names as Tristram introduced them. Blanche was pleased to see that Tami accepted them so readily. She could use help with the housework and the children. Tristram was right about that. But her gratitude gave way quickly to curiosity. Why did he purchase Tami? What beside English did he teach her on the voyage north? He had a few things to explain.

Blanche waited until they were in bed that evening to broach the subject. Tami had retired early, pleased to be sleeping in the loft with the young ones. Tristram had displayed unusual ardor in their lovemaking. She took it as a sign that he had forgiven her for that business with Gorham. Her own infidelity was problem enough. She wasn't prepared to cope with his rejection. But she still wanted an answer to the questions that flooded her mind as she lay beside him.

"Whatever possessed you to buy that slave girl?" she asked.

"I felt sorry for her. I had just visited a sugar plantation and saw how the slaves live and how they're treated."

"But what were you doing in a slave market?"

"I agreed to take two Quakers to Barbados on the *Hopewell,* so Simon Kempthorn could get married. In return he put me in touch with a planter named Rous. Rous's son John showed me around the plantation."

"You haven't answered my question," Blanche said.

"One of the Quakers dragged me to a slave auction. I was prepared to see men being auctioned off, but I hated the way that planters examined the women before they placed their bids. You'd think they were buying a horse they could hardly wait to ride. Tami looked so bewildered by what was happening that I felt I had to help her. It was impulsive and foolhardy, but I'm glad I did it."

It crossed Blanche's mind that if planters viewed female slaves as sexual objects, Tristram might have entertained a similar thought. But she was in no position to levy accusations. His compassion for an unfortunate girl was praiseworthy, and Tami would be a help to her. She would reserve judgment as to his motives.

"I'm glad too," she said.

* * *

Tristram lay in the dark, sated from making love to his wife. He was surprised by the urgency he had displayed. Was it true passion or guilt about Tami? They had coupled every night on the voyage north. Despite his explanations and assurances, she still thought of herself as his slave. She was available to him. To confess all that to Blanche would serve no purpose. She had been less than honest about her relations with Gorham. He was under no obligation to be completely open with her.

Yet he asked himself if he was any different from the planters he had described to Blanche. He liked to think that Tami had come to him of her own volition, but was she really free to choose? As his slave she had simply anticipated his needs and done his bidding. He wasn't at all sure that being in his home had changed her thinking in that respect.

The next day with Blanche present he explained to Tami his plan to grant her freedom. She would remain as a paid servant in his house until she was able and willing to live on her own. It was up to her to decide when she was ready. Tami listened dutifully, but asked no questions. He doubted her ability to grasp the full significance of what he said, but he felt confident that an exposure to freedom would bring with it an appreciation of his offer. Meanwhile, he would treat her as is she were already free.

Having established the guidelines governing Tami's service, he repaired to the local ordinary. He told himself he wanted to get the latest news from Sturgis; but his mind and his ears were alert for any talk about Blanche and Gorham. A refusal to ask questions sometimes produced a good deal in the way of answers.

Sturgis was intrigued by his account of the slave auction and his decision to buy Tami. He leaned forward, his elbows on the table, his gaze fixed on Tristram. His expression bespoke simple curiosity rather than any lasciviousness. But his look changed to one of puzzlement and concern as Tristram sought to explain Tami's status in his household.

"If I were you, I wouldn't try to pass Tami off as a free woman," he said when Tristram finished his account. "People around here should have no trouble in viewing her as your servant, but they're not ready to accept a black woman who claims to be free."

"Tami won't claim anything for a long time," Tristram said. "At the moment her freedom resides solely in my own mind."

"Then I wish you luck with your noble experiment."

"I don't see it as noble, nor as an experiment. You'd have done the same thing under the circumstances."

"I doubt that," Sturgis said, "but I'm eager to have a look at her."

"You want me to bring her here?"

Sturgis paused to reflect. "That might not be advisable."

"I promise that you'll get to meet her. Now I want to know what happened while I was away."

Sturgis recounted several quarrels over cattle ownership and land boundaries, along with two cases of drunkenness in his establishment, one of them involving a fight with the constable.

"Gorham's wife gave birth to their fourth son," he went on. "They named him Jabez."

"Have you heard any more talk about him and Blanche?"

"There's always talk. Give people something to chew on, and they can't leave it alone. They're like a cat with a mouse. But no one can point to anything specific."

"Maybe they're being more careful since they were both fined."

"I doubt there was ever anything between them," Sturgis said. "He admitted that he assaulted her. I think he lost his head that one time and did something he regretted. We've all been guilty of that. Why don't you talk to the magistrate? At least he can tell you why he fined them both."

"I may well do that," Tristram said.

* * *

The magistrate had a long grey beard and was as old as Tristram's father. He had held the post for many years and was regarded as a fair and reasonable man. He exhibited no surprise on finding Tristram at his door. His welcoming smile appeared to be paternal, if not actually benevolent.

"I've been expecting you," he said. "You want to know why I fined your wife fifty shilling."

Tristram nodded. This might be easier than he expected.

"Let's walk a bit," the magistrate said. "I tend to talk more freely out in the open."

They were a good distance from the house before he spoke again. "I had no need of evidence in arriving at my decision. Blanche claimed that Gorham assaulted her, and he didn't deny it. The verdict was clear."

"I was told that Yelverton Crow reported the incident," Tristram said, "and that he placed another interpretation on what he saw."

"Crow was in no position to determine what took place that night, though I was persuaded that he had some grounds for his suspicions. But lacking any hard evidence to the contrary, I had to accept the testimony of the two participants."

"If Gorham admitted that he was guilty, why was Blanche's fine heavier than his?"

"In levying fines I took into account the circumstances involved, the characters of both parties, and the consequences of my action. On one hand I had Gorham's standing in the community; on the other Blanche's reputation for, shall we say, indiscretion. I have no doubt but that Gorham admitted to the charge of assault to protect his family and Blanche as well. He wanted to avoid a more serious charge."

"You mean adultery?" Tristram asked.

"I gathered from the circumstances surrounding the alleged assault and from Blanche's manner that she was not wholly innocent. I fined them both as a warning and to teach them a lesson. I'll say no more. As far as I'm concerned, the case is closed."

"I wish I could say that," Tristram muttered.

He thanked the magistrate and left, his need for information only partly satisfied. He remained ignorant of what had actually occurred that night. He was left to weigh Gorham's account against the story Blanche had told him. He had nothing to gain by confronting Gorham again. All he could do was remain alert for any further signs of indiscretion.

* * *

"Are you mad at Mother?" Mary asked.

Tristram was taken aback by his daughter's question. He thought his actions and manner since his return from Barbados indicated exactly the contrary. Despite his resolution not to involve Mary in his troubles, he was curious as to what had put such an idea in her head. She had opened the door, yet he remained hesitant to enter. He would simply peek inside.

"What makes you ask that?"

Mary looked down in confusion. "I don't know," she stammered. "Mother was acting kind of strange while you were gone."

"What do you mean by strange?"

"Like she's hiding something she doesn't want me to know about."

Tristram gathered from her manner that Mary was more disturbed by Blanche's actions than by his behavior toward her.

"She's still upset about her appearance before the magistrate," he said to allay her concern. "We agreed not to worry you about something you wouldn't understand. Maybe that's the secret you think she's hiding."

Mary seemed to consider his explanation. "I think it was something else," she said. "Sometimes she went out for no reason. I asked her where she went, but she said I was too young to understand. Everyone thinks I'm not old enough to know about things like that. I'm eleven now."

Tristram frowned. "How often did she go out?"

"Two or three times."

"Was she any different when she got back?"

"I'm not sure what you mean." Mary appeared frightened. "She looked happy. That's all."

He knew he had gone far enough, but he was powerless to shut the door Mary had opened. He wanted to know more. He had to know all that she could tell him.

"Has it happened again since I got home?" he asked.

"No, but things aren't like they were before. You don't kiss Mother any more when you come home."

"It's complicated," Tristram said. "I'm not sure I understand it all myself. But your mother and I aren't mad at each other. We're just trying to work things out about the trouble she had with John Gorham. That's how grownups deal with problems that come up in their lives. I'm glad you and the other children were asleep that night."

Mary's gaze drifted to the ladder that led to the loft. She seemed to weigh something in her mind. "I wasn't asleep all the time. I saw them by the door. They were close together. I think they were kissing each other."

Tristram paused to consider where this talk was leading. What else could Mary tell him? He wanted to know all about that night, but he was reluctant to get his information from this source. In the end his curiosity prevailed.

"What else did you see?" he asked.

"Then they were lying on the floor for a long time."

Mary burst into tears. Tristram took her in his arms to console her.

"Were they making love?" she asked between sobs.

"It may have looked that way, but that's not what they were doing."

What else could he say? Mary seemed to be reassured. He held her hand until she had calmed. When he released her, his curiosity drove him to ask one more question. He hoped to her it would seem innocuous.

"Have you seen John Gorham since that night?"

"I saw him once in the store. He said hello and went on his way."

Tristram decided to let it go at that. To probe any further into what Mary saw or thought she saw would only bring on more tears.

* * *

Standing outside the meeting house on a Sunday morning, Blanche debated whether she should wait for Tristram or start for home. He had lingered after the service to talk to a fellow merchant. Tami was at home in charge of the children. With a servant in the house she had no excuse for her absence from church. The minister suggested once that Mary was old enough to care for her siblings, but Blanche felt uneasy standing in the house of God. She hadn't seen Gorham since Tristram's return from the West Indies. She wished her husband were more often at home, yet something within her looked forward to his departure. It was hardly a proper attitude for worshiping God.

Blanche gave little thought to whether Tristram was faithful to her. She assumed that he might avail himself of an opportunity on land, if one presented itself. But most of the time he was at sea. He never spoke of such matters, and she did not wish to be informed. She was in no position to hold him accountable for his actions. They were on his own conscience.

As she waited, still indecisive, she became aware of two members of his crew who were carrying on a conversation not far from where she stood. At first she paid no attention to them. Only when their talk became more heated did she attend to what they were saying.

"You're just mad because he kept a close watch on the girl, and you couldn't get close to her."

"A close watch is right! At the end of the voyage she was sleeping in his cabin."

"She was sick and recovering."

"You can bet he had his way with her when she got better. I hear she's a servant in his home. That should be real handy."

One of the men put a finger to his lips and drew the other away. Blanche pretended she had heard nothing. She recognized the accuser as the cook. The other man was one of the mates. She was certain they were referring to Tami. What they said struck too close to home to be ignored. The girl slept in her house and cared for her children. Tristram might still be having his way with her. Remaining faithful to him while he was home enabled her to place part of the blame on him for her lapses while he was away. Those were the boundaries she had set in her own mind, and she expected him to adhere to the same rules.

She decided to wait for Tristram to conclude his business. Gorham came out of the church, accompanied by his wife and children. Desire was her name, but it was more suitable for him, Blanche thought. It was during Desire's last pregnancy that Gorham had taken a fancy to her. He glanced in her direction, but passed on without a greeting. He knew the rules.

Tristram rejoined her, and they set off for home. Blanche waited until they were well away from the meeting house before giving voice to her concern. "I just heard two of your crew talking about you. From what they said, I gather that you had Tami in your cabin."

Blanche wasn't sure whether the look he gave her was puzzled or questioning. He appeared to be asking himself what she was getting at, or how much she knew.

"The mate was there too," he said. "We were teaching her English. My cabin was a convenient place "

"They said she slept in your cabin for part of the voyage."

He had a ready answer for that as well.

"I had to protect her from the crew. A few of them felt Tami was aboard for their enjoyment."

"One of the men said she was sick and you wanted to care for her."

"That's why I took her into my cabin, but I had good reason to fear for her safety if I left her alone."

"The other one claimed you had your way with her, as he put it."

His laugh was rather forced, Blanche thought.

"The cook was the biggest offender. Was it he you overheard?"

"He was one of them. I didn't recognize the other. They seemed to know that Tami is now our servant."

"That's the reason I brought her home," Tristram said. "I made no secret of it to the crew. I think it's working out quite well. The children all like her, and she likes them. Have you any doubts about her?"

"My doubts are about you," Blanche said.

"Tami is our servant, nothing else. I'll be as happy as she is when she becomes a free woman."

Blanche noted that he had neither admitted not denied having his way with Tami while she was in his cabin. Yet he seemed sincere in his assurance that the girl was nothing but a servant in their house.

She should be satisfied with that. She had no evidence to the contrary.

"I'm sorry," she said. "I couldn't help but be suspicious."

Tristram felt that he had emerged relatively unscathed from this latest encounter. He could let it go or take the offensive. He had suspicions of his own that were just as warranted as those Blanche had raised.

"It's all due to your own behavior," he said. "I hear that you and Gorham saw each other while I was away."

He spoke without thinking and regretted his outburst at once. He had determined not to involve Mary in their problems.

Blanche's face reddened. "Who told you that?"

"There's been talk at the tavern and elsewhere."

"That's nothing but talk. Why would I see a man who admitted that he assaulted me? "

"The magistrate didn't believe your story at the hearing, and I find it hard to believe you now."

"Well, I find it hard to believe that you never laid hands on Tami in your cabin," Blanche shot back.

Realizing that his own footing was none too sure, Tristram decided to compromise. "Maybe we should both try to forget what did or didn't happen in the past and think of the future."

"What do you mean by that?"

"No matter what took place in my cabin on the voyage north, you have my word that I won't lay a hand on Tami as long as she's a servant in our house."

Blanche realized that he admitted no wrongdoing, yet his assurance regarding Tami provided her with some comfort. Seeing Gorham involved some risk. With Tami around a meeting would be even harder to conceal. She wasn't even sure that she wanted to see Gorham again. Tristram was proposing a solution whereby they renewed their pledge of fidelity. Any lingering suspicions would remain unexpressed. She could get along with that if he could.

"And I promise that whatever happened that night, I'll avoid any contact with John Gorham in the future."

But there was another issue to be addressed.

"The real problem," Blanche continued, "is that you're off at sea for months at a time, and I'm here alone. If you were home more often, it would make things much easier for both of us."

"I've decided not to make any more trips to the West Indies," he said. "For years I've felt that as long as I deal only with the products of slave labor, how those products are made need not concern me. On my last voyage I saw what slavery really is, and I hated what I saw. That's why I had to save Tami from that life."

"Where will you go instead?"

"I can arrange to trade with other colonies up and down the coast. I'll still be away from home, but for much shorter periods."

"That will be a big help," Blanche said, and she meant it.

Thirteen

"I've grown accustomed to doubt."
(Plymouth Colony, Winter 1656-57)

When Tristram stopped again at the Red Lyon Inn, the thirty days granted Upsall to leave the colony had elapsed. Tristram wanted to find out where his friend had gone. Upsall's wife Dorothy was in the tavern, engaged in a heated conversation with the local constable. Standing by the entrance, Tristram had no difficulty making out their words.

"I tell you he's gone," Dorothy said. "I don't know where he is."

"I'd like to believe you," the constable said, "but the governor has good reason to think he's in Boston. I have orders to search the premises."

Dorothy appeared flustered. "Have either of you seen my husband this past week?" she asked, turning to two men seated at a table.

"Not I," one said.

"Nor I either," the other agreed.

The constable brushed this aside. "I think he's hiding somewhere here at the inn. Please stand aside so I can carry out my orders."

Dorothy had spotted Tristram by the door, but she didn't venture to speak to him until the constable had completed his search of the tavern and moved on to other parts of the inn.

"I need to talk to you once he's gone," she whispered.

Tristram sat at the long table, ordered a hard cider, and pretended to ignore her. Some time passed before the constable reentered the tavern. His face bore a look of disappointment.

"He doesn't seem to be here," he said to no one in particular.

"If I were in his place," a man at the table said, "I'd hide in a place where you'd never think to look for me."

"And where would that be?" the constable asked.

"I don't know. Maybe in the Boston jail."

They both laughed at the absurdity of it.

"If any of you see him or know where he is," the constable said, "it's your duty to report it to the authorities."

"We'll do that," the men said in unison.

As soon as the constable was gone, Dorothy beckoned to Tristram to come to the parlor. "This is the second time in a week they've searched the inn," she said.

"Why do they keep coming back?" Tristram asked.

"It's that minister, Norton. He barged in here last night after hours. Nicholas just had time to hide, but I think Norton caught a glimpse of him. We decided it wasn't safe for him to stay here any longer."

"Where is he now?"

Dorothy gave a mirthless laugh. "Would you believe it? He's at the jail. I don't know if that man was joking, or if he knows something."

"I don't think the constable took him seriously," Tristram said.

"We can't be too careful. I have to get word to Nicholas that the authorities are looking for him."

"And you want me to carry the message."

"You have to help him escape."

"Why is he still in Boston?"

"He had no place to go. He felt certain that Endicott would pardon him on the basis of his past service to the community."

"I'm not sure I can help," Tristram said, "but I'll go to the prison."

"Will they let you in to see him?" Dorothy asked.

"I was there not long ago. I think the jailer will remember me."

"Tell Nicholas I send him my love," Dorothy said.

"I'll be sure to do that," Tristram said.

*　*　*

He waited until it was dark before making his way to the prison. It was a moonless night, and the streets of Boston were deserted. The jailer greeted him as if he were expected. Carrying a tallow candle, he led the way to the same cell the Quaker women had occupied. Upsall rose from the platform as they entered. The jailer set the candle down and left.

"I hoped you would come," Upsall said.

"You're in danger," Tristram said. "They searched the inn again today. Endicott got word that you haven't left Boston. Dorothy said you had no place to go. But you can't stay here."

"That's what I want to talk to you about."

Tristram glanced about the cell. Everything was much the same as before, except for a canvas bag ready at hand on the platform. Upsall was apparently prepared for flight.

"We have to get you out of here," he said. "Then we can talk about where to go and what to do next. If you're ready to leave, I can take you aboard *The Catch* ."

"That sounds like a step in the right direction," Upsall said.

The voice of the jailer, raised unnaturally, reached them from some spot outside the cell. "It's not customary. Visitors aren't allowed at this time of night."

"I'm not visiting," was the reply. "I have orders to search the jail."

"Whose orders?"

"Governor Endicott himself."

"Well, you'd see better in the daytime," the jailer said. "Where do you want to start?"

"Right here where you live. I'll check the cells afterwards."

Upsall had doused the candle. "What do we do now?" he asked.

"Leave it to me," Tristram said.

He tried to sound confident, but had no idea what he would do. By the time the constable had searched the front rooms, Tristram had formed a plan of action. As the cell door was opened, he lurched into the hallway, nearly knocking the jailer down.

"I'm not drunk," he shouted, his voice slurred. "I'm going home, and you can't stop me."

The jailer stepped back in surprise, but he was quick to recover. "The only place you're going is back in your cell."

They grappled in the hallway. Tristram was much younger and stronger than the jailer. He made it appear that he was getting the upper hand, while taking care not to break free.

"Give me a hand here!" the jailer cried.

The constable joined in the struggle. Together they forced Tristram back into the cell and locked the door on him.

"He's a strong one," the constable said. "Who is he?"

"A sailor off one of the ships in the harbor. He was brought in for fighting in the street after he was thrown out of a tavern. My orders are to let him sleep it off and release him in the morning."

"I need to search his cell," the constable said.

"As you wish, but you needn't count on me to help you restrain him. He nearly broke my arm just now."

A moment of silence ensued. Sensing some indecision on the other side of the door, Tristram cried, "I hear you breathing! Let me out of this cursed hell hole! I'm going home."

It was enough.

"Very well," the constable said. "Let's check the next cell."

Tristram and Upsall waited in the dark. The jailer alerted them when the constable was gone. Upsall picked up his canvas bag and headed for the door. Tristram was close behind. He noted that Upsall slipped the jailer a coin on his way out.

"My ship is this way," Tristram said as they reached the street.

"I have to see Dorothy before I go," Upsall said. "I want to tell her I'm safe and in good hands."

Tristram wanted to dissuade him from a return to the inn, but Upsall was already headed in that direction. Realizing that argument was useless, he resigned himself to this new danger. He was not familiar with Boston streets at night, and Upsall took a route that bewildered him. They met one man, perhaps a night watchman, en route to the inn. Upsall made no attempt to avoid him. He simply hurried past as if he had important business, leaving Tristram to sweat out a valiant attempt to match his equanimity.

Upsall slipped into the Red Lyon by a back door, while Tristram waited in the brewery. He understood Upsall's feelings, but he doubted that he would risk as much to bid farewell to Blanche. Perhaps he would feel differently in thirty years, when he was Upsall's age. He was still pondering the question of marital relationships when Upsall returned.

Their path now led toward the harbor. Tristram was more familiar with this route, but he had to run to keep up. Upsall's pace slowed as they reached the wharf.

"Is that your ship?" he asked, pointing to *The Catch*.

Tristram nodded. Once aboard he gave orders to a crew member to summon him if anyone approached, then led the way to his cabin.

"You're safe here for now," he told Upsall. "We'll be ready to sail by mid-morning."

"Shouldn't we leave before daybreak?" Upsall asked.

"I need to get the rest of my crew aboard, and a coastal schooner leaving port isn't likely to attract attention. Besides, Endicott has banished you from the colony. Why would he want to stop you from leaving?"

Upsall's shoulders sagged, and he uttered a deep sigh. He looked older than his sixty years and was glad to rest on the single bunk in the cabin. Tristram sat on the edge.

"Why are you still here?" he asked. "Why didn't you leave before your thirty days were up?"

"My wife and my livelihood are in Boston," Upsall said. "I have nothing anywhere else. Dorothy wants me to stay with her brother in Dorchester; but they'd be sure to find me, and he'd be in trouble too. Where would you suggest I go?"

"I have relatives in Maine. I can ask one of them to take you in."

"That's still part of Massachusetts," Upsall said.

"There's Rhode Island or New Haven or even New Amsterdam."

"I want to be close to home, so I'll know when it's safe to return."

"Endicott isn't likely to have a change of heart any time soon."

"I suppose you're right,"

"What will happen to the Red Lyon now that you're gone?"

Upsall waved his arm in a gesture of dismissal, as if the subject were of little importance. "Dorothy can manage the inn until I get back."

"That leaves Plymouth," Tristram said, "but Governor Bradford is hand in glove with Endicott when it comes to Quakers. Still, someplace else in the colony might be safe enough. I know someone in Sandwich who thinks for himself."

"Who is he?"

"His name is William Allen. We came over from England on the same ship. I'm sure he'll be willing to help you."

"Then Sandwich it is!" Upsall said.

A moment later he was asleep.

* * *

The next morning with Tristram at the helm *The Catch* put to sea. Once the schooner was well under way, he sent word to Upsall that it was safe to come on deck.

"I feel like a free man," Upsall said, taking a deep breath of the sea air. "Speaking of freedom, how are you managing with that slave girl you bought in Barbados? Has your wife accepted her?"

"Tami has made herself a part of the household. The children love her, and Blanche seems glad to have some help."

"And how do matters stand between you and Blanche? Have you resolved that business about the assault?"

"We've reached an agreement. I promised not to touch Tami while she's a servant in my house, and Blanche promised that she wouldn't see Gorham again."

"But you still don't know what happened between her and Gorham. You're in constant doubt as to how she'll behave while you're off at sea."

"I've grown accustomed to doubt," Tristram said.

"If I were you," Upsall said, "I'd take some action. Do something to put it all behind you."

"What would you have me do? If I charge Blanche with adultery or threaten to put her away, who will care for the children? If on the other hand I simply shut my eyes to her faults, do I not give her free rein to continue? You may regard me as indecisive, but my indecision keeps our marriage on an even keel. I prefer the doubt and uncertainty, the occasional flare-ups, the tears that accompany forgiveness and reconciliation, to any resolution I can fashion in my mind."

"I understand your position. Forgive me for my insensitivity."

"Besides, I'd be playing the hypocrite to censure Blanche for a transgression of which I too am guilty. I've begun to think that my decision to make love to Tami was really a means to preserve my own marriage. By assuming an equal guilt myself, I relinquished my right to judge Blanche."

"I suppose you might look at it that way," Upsall said.

Both men were content for a time to let the sea and the motion of the ship sway their thoughts. Upsall finally broke the silence.

"You say that Tami is like one of the family. Has she also made a place for herself in the community?"

"People in Yarmouth seem a little suspicious of her," Tristram said.

"Because she's a slave?"

"What bothers people is that I don't treat her like a slave. Tami may be a paid servant longer than I expected."

"You mean you pay her in addition to feeding her and giving her shelter?" Upsall appeared incredulous.

"That was our agreement when I brought her here."

"I suspect Mary Fisher had a hand in that."

"Mary warned me that Tami would be out of place in Yarmouth. Maybe she was right."

"You need to give people time to get used to her."

"Tami knows a lot about herbs. When we saw a doctor in Virginia, she practically concocted her own medicine. The word has spread that she possesses healing powers."

"That may help her, but you can't change the color of her skin."

"I'm still determined to make her a free woman."

"It won't be easy," Upsall said.

* * *

They reached Sandwich that same afternoon, but it was growing dark when Tristram knocked on the door of William Allen. Allen greeted him warmly and ushered both men into the hall of his home. After hearing Upsall's story, he and his wife Priscilla agreed to shelter him. Allen seemed to be interested in his connection with the Quakers.

"Who are they?" he asked. "What have they done to be persecuted in such a manner?"

"They landed in Boston and brought some pamphlets with them," Upsall said. "It's not what they've done. It's what they believe. Endicott regards their religious ideas as heretical."

"Are you one of them?" Priscilla asked. "Is that why you were banished?"

"I was accused of feeding Quakers in prison. I wanted to stay in Boston and tend to my business at the inn, but I had to speak out against a law that punishes Quakers for setting foot in Massachusetts."

Tristram recalled his talks with Mary Fisher. "Endicott may banish them as a threat to peace and order, but they intend to keep coming despite laws and persecution."

"I'm glad to hear it," Upsall said.

Tristram wasn't surprised by this admission, but he wondered how Allen would interpret it.

"Many of the new immigrants aren't Puritans and have come here for reasons other than religion," Upsall said. "Most of them are attracted by the prospect of free land. Change has arrived on our shores. Endicott may be able to postpone it, but he can't stop it."

"We've just rid ourselves of the minister we had in Sandwich," Allen said. "His preaching was no longer relevant to our needs. I'm eager to hear what these Quakers have to offer. You're welcome to stay with us as long as you wish, but try not to draw attention to yourself. The authorities already have their eye on us."

"The authorities don't know where I am," Upsall said, "but you have my promise."

Tristram went away satisfied that he had found a safe refuge for his friend. He had fulfilled his duty. Now he had business and problems of his own to attend.

* * *

Tami continued to fit herself into the household. The children were eager to teach her English. Mary was particularly fond of her.

"It's like having an older sister," she confided to her father.

Blanche still had some reservations, but she and Tami shared the household chores amicably. She appreciated the girl's uncanny ability to come up with a remedy when the children took sick.

Tristram had peace at home, and for that he was grateful. But the community was another matter. People were willing to tolerate a slave girl in their midst as long as she was respectful and subservient. They balked when Tami attended church and sat with Tristram in his pew.

Mr. Miller, the minister, spoke to him in private after the service. "Understand, I don't object to a black slave attending services, but several people have approached me and voiced their displeasure at her presence. I take that to mean she was too obtrusive. To preserve harmony in the congregation, it might be better for the time being if she stayed at home until people are more accustomed to seeing her about."

Tristram smiled at the contradiction in the minister's advice. Yet if his goal was to make Tami a free woman, he could not let the matter drop.

"You're putting her in the same category with the Indians. Tami is neither a savage nor a slave. She's a servant in my home, and I expect the people of Yarmouth to treat her as such."

"God has ample room in his heart for heathens," Mr. Miller said, "but their conversion is best accomplished in private. I'm perfectly willing to undertake Tami's instruction in the Christian faith, if that is your aim. I have her welfare in mind, but attending services will only confuse her and offend others. Whatever you intend for her, I'm sure you don't want that."

"My father too is a minister," Tristram said. "He taught me enough about the Christian faith to enable me to instruct Tami myself."

Mr. Miller seemed relieved. "That is your choice," he said.

* * *

Tristram saw Upsall again a week before Christmas. Winter had gripped the land. He was chilled on the ride to Sandwich. After tending to his horse, he was glad to warm himself at Allen's hearth and sip the cider Priscilla set before him.

"The authorities have found me out," Upsall said when they were settled. He sounded almost cheerful.

"How did that happen?" Tristram asked.

"Someone must have told Governor Bradford that he had a heretic in his midst. Shortly after I arrived, I was summoned before the Court of Assistants. They informed me that I wasn't welcome in Plymouth because I had openly opposed the law regarding Quakers and was a threat to good order. When I asked if Plymouth had such a law, I was told that the court considered itself bound by a decision of the Commissioners of the United Colonies regarding Quakers."

"But you weren't banished for being a Quaker," Tristram said.

"I told them that. They said the authorities in Boston had branded me as a sympathizer. I reminded them that the law made no mention of sympathizers. That stopped them for a moment. But after conferring they decided that giving aid was the same thing, and I would have to leave the colony. I said it was winter, and I had no other place to go. They agreed to let me stay until the first of March, if I behave myself."

"Did they want to know who brought you here?" Tristram asked.

"I think they knew the answer. You needn't worry. I gave them my promise. My sole desire is to get back to my wife and the Red Lyon."

"You made me a promise too," Allen said without rancor. "Whether or not you're a Quaker, you've talked about nothing else since you got here, both to me and my friends as well."

"I don't consider myself a Quaker. I'm preparing myself and those around me for the next wave of missionaries that Tristram has assured me is on the way."

"Like John the Baptist," Priscilla said.

Upsall laughed. "Many people are receptive to the idea that God will converse with us if we remain quiet and listen to the spirit within us."

"Take care the authorities don't hear that kind of talk," Tristram said. "It's not easy to return home, once you've been banished."

"I've told him that, but he won't listen," Allen said. "Though I must admit that Priscilla and I are among those who are receptive to his ideas. We gather on a Sunday morning and wait for the spirit to speak to us, but so far no one has heard his inner voice."

"It's not a regular Quaker meeting, and we're careful whom we invite," Upsall said. "We discuss some of their beliefs, as outlined in that pamphlet you obtained for me. You're welcome to join us."

Upsall was looking directly at him. Was he already included in their number? Caution told him the time had come to distance himself from this circle of potential Quakers.

"I'll think about it," he said. "Where do you intend to go when you leave the colony in March?"

"I haven't given it much thought. For now I feel certain that I'm in the right place. I may defy the court and stay in Sandwich."

"Then you're breaking the promise you made. You're not behaving yourself, and I can see trouble ahead."

"If there's trouble," Upsall said, "it won't be of our making."

* * *

The invitation preyed on Tristram during the weeks that followed. Though he had no great desire to attend their meeting, he cared and had a stake in what happened to his friend. If Upsall remained in the colony, Tristram saw that his part in the saga was not over. The court knew how he got there. Based on what had happened to Kempthorn in Boston, he could even predict the outcome. He broached the subject to Blanche toward the end of January.

"Sandwich is a long hard ride in mid-winter," she said. "What do you hope to get out of it?"

"I've known Upsall for many years," Tristram said. "I owe it to him as a friend to caution him against the course he's pursuing. He's on the verge of becoming a Quaker himself."

"Seems to me that's his decision," Blanche said.

"I don't want to change the way he thinks, but I can at least point out the consequences to himself and his family, if he defies the authorities and remains in the colony. It's not too late for him to change direction."

"Aren't you taking a risk by attending the meeting?"

"I have to save Upsall from himself."

"Go, if you must," Blanche said, "but don't come back a Quaker."

The following weekend Tristram had some business in Sandwich. He stopped by Allen's house on the way home. It had snowed during the night. Allen tethered his horse in the barn, where it would be warm and out of sight. On entering the house, Tristram saw five people assembled in the hall. In addition to Allen and Priscilla the gathering included Upsall, Richard Kirby and Elizabeth Newland. It was soon evident that Upsall was in charge of the meeting.

"Before we seek to free our minds from distraction and heed the prompting of the spirit," he said, "does anyone wish to speak?"

"My daughter Sarah and Jane Launder have been ordered to appear in court," Kirby said. "They interrupted our minister in the midst of his sermon. Sarah claims the spirit moved her to protest his meaningless and erroneous preaching. They're charged with disturbing the peace."

"I was wondering why they weren't here," Allen said.

"They feared it might draw undue attention to our meeting."

"What did they object to in the minister's sermon?" Upsall asked.

"He was saying that God has spoken, that the Bible is a sufficient guide on how to conduct our lives. Sarah cried out that God still speaks and reveals Himself to those who are quiet and willing to listen."

"Were you there?" Upsall asked.

"I'm ashamed to say that I remained in my seat while Sarah and Jane were removed from the church."

"Women are courageous when it comes to proclaiming the truth," Elizabeth Newland said.

Recalling the courage exhibited by Mary Fisher and Ann Austin, Tristram was tempted to agree with her; but a picture of his father presented itself. Surely a minister had a right to preach in his own church, whatever his message might be.

"Theirs is not the only truth," he said. "I suspect they made more enemies than friends by their actions."

Upsall broke the silence that ensued following this pronouncement. "The spirit bestows courage at will," he said. "It has nothing to do with gender. Everyone has a right to heed his own conscience."

"You too may be suspect for what your daughter did," Allen said.

"You're right," Kirby said. "Perhaps I shouldn't have come."

"We're breaking no law," Upsall said. "We simply discuss matters of common interest."

"But we try to establish contact with the same spirit that moved the two young women to protest," Allen said. "The authorities in Plymouth may use that to brand us all as Quakers."

"I don't know enough to be a Quaker," Upsall said. "If the court objects to my activities, I'm ready to pay the price. Now let us be silent and allow the spirit within us to enlighten our thoughts and guide our actions."

Tristram's thoughts were in turmoil. To quiet them he recalled his efforts under the tutelage of Mary Fisher to get in touch with his inner voice. It was more difficult than it sounded. But now, surrounded by others of like mind, he sensed a solidarity that was lacking in his previous attempts. His father's sermons had often evoked in him a similar feeling. But he was no longer a child or pupil heeding the directions of a parent or teacher. He was a man seeking the right path to what lay ahead. He had attained a measure of inner peace when the silence was shattered by a heavy knock on the door, followed by a demand to, "Open up!"

"It's the constable," Kirby said. "I recognize his voice."

"You're not part of this," Allen said, addressing Tristram. "Leave now, and no one will know you were here." He pointed to a window at the rear of the house.

Tristram shook his head. "I choose to stay. I have as much right to be here as anyone else."

Allen opened the door and greeted the constable by name. "What can I do for you?" he asked.

"I have a summons for you and Nicholas Upsall and any others here present to appear before the Court of Assistants at their next session." He handed Allen the paper.

"What are the charges?" Upsall asked.

"Holding unauthorized meetings on the Lord's Day and some other words I don't understand."

The constable's eyes fastened upon Tristram. "You aren't a freeman in Sandwich," he said. "Who are you, and what are you doing here?"

"My name is Tristram Hull, and I'm from Yarmouth; but I'd be pleased and honored to appear in court with my friends."

"In that case I'm pleased to add your name to the list."

* * *

The Court of Assistants met in the town of Plymouth the first week in February. In addition to the small group at Allen's house, Jane Launder and Sarah Kirby were responding to their summons. Tristram rode along with those who had been ordered to appear. John Newland, Elizabeth's husband, and William Launder, Jane's father, also joined the procession.

The assistants met in the same chamber used by deputies to the General Court. A smattering of curious onlookers were at the back of the room. The eight defendants sat in front facing the seven assistants.

"We have a slight advantage in numbers," Tristram thought, "but I fear the weight of the law is on their side."

The two young women were ordered to rise as the clerk read the complaint against them. "Sarah Kirby and Jane Launders, you are charged with disturbing the public worship of God on the Lord's day at Sandwich by opposing and abusing the speaker standing among them."

"What say you in your defense?" the chief assistant asked.

"We did oppose the minister as stated," Sarah said, "but I know of no abuse to his person. We were moved by the spirit to object to untruths that issued from his mouth."

The chief assistant cut her off. "The court can neither sanction nor take exception to the words a minister utters in his sermon."

"We have no other defense for our actions," Sarah said.

The assistants consulted among themselves before delivering their verdict. "Since you admit to the charges as stated, you are sentenced to be whipped in the public square. But recognizing that William Launder, here present, has petitioned this court for mercy on behalf of his wife and his children, the sentence imposed on Jane Launder is hereby suspended, and she is warned to offend no more. The clerk will read the next complaint."

Launder embraced his daughter, and they left the room together. Sarah smiled at her father as she was led away by an officer of the court. Kirby started to rise but was ordered to resume his seat.

"Nicholas Upsall, Richard Kirby, Elizabeth Newland, William Allen, Priscilla Allen, and Tristram Hull, you are charged with frequently meeting at the house of William Allen in Sandwich on the Lord's day and at other times, at which meetings you do inveigh against the ministers and magistrates to the dishonor of God and contempt of the government."

"Who will speak for the accused?" the chief assistant asked.

Allen took a step forward.

"What say you to these charges?"

"It is true that we have met in my home on occasion to discuss the issues of the day and the state of our own spiritual welfare. I am not aware that such gatherings are contrary to any law of this colony. I deny that we have shown contempt toward any minister or magistrate. To act in such a manner is to dishonor the God in whom we all believe."

"The constable can testify that you met on the Lord's Day," the chief assistant said, "and that you were wont to sit quietly for periods of time, much like that accursed sect of heretics known as Quakers. Do you deny these charges?"

"I've had my say. I have nothing more to add."

The assistants conferred briefly among themselves. Then the six remaining defendants were ordered to rise while sentence was passed.

"Richard Kirby and Elizabeth Newland, you are hereby fined five pounds each for your participation in the aforesaid meetings. William and Priscilla Allen, you are fined ten pounds jointly for hosting the meetings. Nicholas Upsall, your license to stay in the Plymouth Colony until spring was contingent upon your good behavior. By organizing and setting the tone for these meetings, you have broken the terms of that license. You are hereby ordered to depart this colony by the first of March. Failure to comply with this order will subject you to further punishment as decided by this court. Tristram Hull, since it appears that you were not a regular attendee at the aforesaid meetings, no fine is levied on you. However, this court is aware that you were instrumental in transporting Nicholas Upsall to the Plymouth Colony. You are hereby ordered to remove him from this colony by March first. Failure to do so will render you subject to a fine of fifty pounds."

Tristram stepped forward. "Upsall has already been banished from his true home in Boston. Where should I take him now?"

"Where you take him is not our concern," the chief assistant said. "Leave him on an island to perish from the cold, if you will."

"Your words and attitude do dishonor to the God in whom you profess to believe," Upsall said from where he stood.

The chief assistant ignored him. "This court is adjourned."

Following his appearance in court, Tristram left at once for home. He had no desire to witness Sarah's punishment. The others remained to support Kirby and his daughter. He had no idea where to take Upsall when the time came. He would leave that decision to him. Of one thing he was certain. He refused to leave him on an island to perish.

Fourteen

"Why are you protecting a witch?"
(Plymouth Colony, Winter 1657)

Tristram shut the door of his house against a cold March wind. He was back from Boston, where he had readied the *Hopewell* for a voyage to New Amsterdam. The ship lay now at anchor in Yarmouth harbor, and his crew were enjoying some time with their families while he waited for the man he was ordered to remove from the colony.

"Have you heard from Upsall?" he asked.

"No word as yet," Blanche said. "Take you coat off and listen. We have a problem with Tami."

He glanced toward the table, where Tami and the children were engrossed in their own conversation. Blanche had taken to talking about the girl as if she were absent or could not understand.

"What has she done?" he asked, his voice just above a whisper.

Blanche took the hint. She waited until he hung his coat on a peg and was warming himself by the hearth.

"It's partly my fault. You know how we rely on Tami to prepare potions for the children when they're sick. She has a way with herbs and whatever else she puts in them. Well, about a week ago Charity Bicknell came to the door. I was surprised to see her, because she

482

tends to ignore me when we meet in town. But there she was at the door, saying that her daughter was sick with a fever and begging me for some of the medicine we give to our children. How she knew about that, I have no idea."

"Did you give her the medicine?"

"She was desperate and pleading for help. How could I refuse? She took it and left with hardly a work of thanks. I heard later that the girl had died in her sleep. I felt sorry for the child, and that was it. But now I hear that Charity is blaming her daughter's death on the potion I gave her. She's telling everyone that Tami put a curse on the girl."

"That's ridiculous," Tristram said. "Tami had no way of knowing you would share the medicine with anyone."

"You'd think people would realize that. Yesterday when I was in Hallet's, two men came in. As soon as they saw me, they started talking about Tami. They called her a witch. When I spoke up for her, they were rude and insulting."

"What did Hallet do?" Tristram asked.

"He had to threaten to send for a constable. As they left they kept shouting about what ought to be done to a witch like Tami. You have to get her out of the house. It isn't safe for her to stay here."

"I see no need for that. It will all pass over in another week."

"What if it doesn't? I can't protect Tami while you're away, and I'm afraid for the children."

"I can't just cast her adrift."

"You must do something before you go."

"While I'm waiting for Upsall, I'll try to find out who's spreading this talk about witches. Have you said anything to Tami?"

"Not yet," Blanche said. "I didn't want to scare her."

"She must realize something is wrong," Tristram said. "I'll speak to her first. Then I'll try to set matters straight in the village."

When he had warmed himself and eaten, he took Tami aside. "Some people say that your medicine for the fever killed a young girl."

"I not give medicine to girl." A puzzled look had replaced Tami's customary smile.

"Her mother begged Blanche to give her the medicine. Now she's blaming you for the girl's death. I'm sure she would have died anyway."

"Everyone is angry at me?"

"Not everyone. I can explain what happened, but it will take some time to convince people that it wasn't your fault."

"You make things all right," Tami said.

"I'll do my best," Tristram said.

The next day he sought to gauge the public sentiment toward Tami. Not that he doubted Blanche's view of the situation, but women tended to see things as worse than they really were. All that was required to rectify matters was a reasonable explanation. But it soon became apparent to him that the accusations against Tami had struck a responsive chord. Rumors were rampant about her familiarity with the devil and black magic. He also sensed a certain resentment against himself for injecting a black slave into the community and treating her as an equal. One tradesman went so far as to offer him a remedy for the spell Tami had cast upon him and his family.

The first of March, the date set by the court for Upsall's departure, had come and gone. In a message to Tristram he had declared his intention to stay in Sandwich. Having served as a constable himself, Tristram knew what would happen in that event. When the authorities learned that Upsall had defied their order, a constable would be assigned to deliver him into the custody of a fellow constable from Yarmouth. He in turn would ensure that Upsall left the colony in the company of Tristram Hull, as ordered by the court.

Upsall's decision to stay put presented a problem. Tristram had business to tend. He couldn't stand by indefinitely waiting for his friend to be arrested. The *Hopewell* was ready to sail. He wasn't sure that Upsall would consent to go to New Amsterdam. Tristram viewed it as a sanctuary for refugees in search of religious freedom. The founders of the Plymouth Colony had found refuge in Holland before emigrating to New England. They seemed to have forgotten that Upsall's position was once their own.

A week into March the constable came to Tristram's door with Upsall in tow. Having been assured that Upsall would leave the colony in three days or less, the constable departed with a warning that he would be on the dock to witness their departure.

Seated by the fire that evening, Tristram and Upsall addressed the future. Blanche and Tami were nearby teaching the older children how to sew. They seemed oblivious to what the men were saying.

"I hoped the authorities would forget about me," Upsall said, "but I refused to hide. I had work to do."

"What sort of work?" Tristram asked.

"Our little circle of prospective Quakers has grown since your last visit. I had to prepare the ground, so Allen can carry on the work until the next missionaries arrive."

"He may have a long wait. Quakers have been forbidden to land in Plymouth as well as Massachusetts."

"That won't stop them," Upsall said. "Where are you taking me?"

"To New Amsterdam. The Dutch authorities are fairly tolerant in religious matters. I'm sure you'll be welcome there."

"My family and livelihood are in Boston, and I have a stake now in Sandwich. If I go to New Amsterdam, I'll never return to New England."

"Where then?" Tristram's tone betrayed his exasperation.

"Perhaps Rhode Island. It's closer to home."

"Do you know anyone there?"

"While the second group of Quakers were in prison, I helped them exchange letters with a man named Samuel Gorton. He offered to provide them with a refuge in Rhode Island. But the master of the *Speedwell* was under a strict bond to take them back to England, so the plan bore no fruit. In his letter Gorton stated that many people in the Rhode Island Colony would be receptive to the Quaker message."

"Is Gorton in Newport?" Tristram asked.

"He's in a place called Warwick, but I'd rather go to Newport. It's a much larger town and a major seaport. When the next group of Quakers arrives, they're very likely to choose Newport as a base for their work."

"Newport poses no problem for me. It's right on my way. I can set you ashore and continue on to New Amsterdam."

"I ask for nothing more," Upsall said. "When do we leave?"

"I'll muster my crew tomorrow," Tristram said. "We can sail the next day. I'll send word to the constable."

"What do you propose to do about Tami?" Blanche asked.

Upsall turned to look at her. "Is there a problem with the girl?"

Tristram explained the situation. "The people in town have calmed down a bit," he went on, addressing Blanche. "I'm sure Tami will be quite safe while I'm away. Just keep her close to home."

It was as close to a lie as he had ever come, but he was convinced that what he heard in town was just talk. Tami was in no real danger.

"When it comes to witchcraft, it's hard to tell what people think," Upsall said. "For your wife's peace of mind it might be better to get Tami out of the house. Is there someone she can stay with while you're away?"

"We could ask Joanna to take her in," Blanche said.

"Before I do that," Tristram said, "let me see how matters stand. I have to go to Hallet's in the morning, and I'll take Tami with me. I won't send her away just because a few ignorant people think she's in league with the devil."

"I not know any devil," Tami said.

"You have to consider the effect this is having on her," Upsall said.

"That's why I'm taking Tami with me to Hallet's. If people talk of witchcraft, I want to gauge Tami's reaction to it."

"You may also be gauging their reaction to Tami," Upsall said.

"Try not to antagonize anyone," Blanche said.

"I promise, as long as they don't antagonize me."

* * *

Seated side by side on the wagon, Tristram and Tami set out for the general store. Her face bore no sign of fear, but she sat a little closer to him than usual. On reaching Hallet's, he sent her in with a list of items he had drawn up, promising to follow along as soon as he tethered the horse. In that way he could better judge the general attitude toward her. If there was a problem, he was ready at hand to intervene.

He had just finished hitching his horse to the rail when Tami came back. She looked distraught and was on the verge of tears.

"Man not give me what I want. Call me witch. What is witch?"

"Someone who talks to the devil. You're not a witch."

Tristram took the list she clutched in her hand and helped her up on the wagon. "You wait here," he said. "I'll be right back."

"I not want to stay alone," she said.

"I'll be inside. If you're afraid of anything, call and I'll come out."

"I do what you say, Master Tristram."

Her method of address always brought a smile to his face. Tami smiled bravely in return. On entering Hallet's, he looked about. A man at the back left quietly as he approached the counter. Old man Hallet was dead, and his son Andrew had taken over the store. Normally he was quite garrulous. Today he tended strictly to business.

"I'm aware of all this talk about devils and witches," Tristram said when he had the items he wanted. "You know very well that none of it is true. From now on I expect you to treat Tami like one of my children."

"When you're in business," Hallet said, "what you know doesn't always determine what you say and do. I saw you outside and decided not to wait on Tami. I didn't want to antagonize my other customers and lose their trade."

"Where else would they go? You're the only store in Yarmouth."

"It's a matter of good will. People should come here because they want to, not because they have to."

"I trust that applies to me as well."

"Of course. I'm sorry I treated your servant badly, but I feared for her safety. I wanted to get her out of the store before she got hurt."

"I'll bring her back in, so you can apologize to her."

Hallet's face bore a pained expression, but he did not reply.

Tristram stepped outside. A group of men had gathered around the wagon. Tami sat rigidly, her hands clasped to her breast, looking up at the sky. She might have been praying.

"Devil's spawn!" one man shouted at her.

"Leave her alone!" Tristram cried. "She's done you no harm."

The group parted to let him stow his purchases in the wagon. He looked up at Tami, who still stared heavenward. To take her back into the store would only prolong this unpleasantness. Climbing up beside her, he applied a whip to his horse. Unaccustomed to such treatment, the animal bolted ahead, scattering the men in its path.

"Stay away from our children!" one of them called after her.

When the town was behind them, Tristram reined in the horse and turned to Tami. She was trembling. He put an arm about her shoulders.

"You're safe," he said. "They can't hurt you now."

She clung to him with both hands. Her body shook violently, and her tears wet his neck. She seemed unwilling to let go.

"It will be all right," he said, stroking her hair. "You can stay with Joanna until I get back. I'll take you there tomorrow."

"What they do to witch?" she asked.

"Don't worry. There are no witches here or anywhere else."

He wasn't sure his words were reassuring, but Tami stopped crying and seemed more relaxed. They drove home in silence. She leaned against him on the seat. He did not push her away.

* * *

"I'm glad Tami will be out of the house," Blanche said, "and Joanna can use an extra pair of hands with the children."

Tristram had concluded his account of the incident at Hallet's. Tami was outside with the children, and Upsall had gone for a walk.

"It's not only Tami's safety that concerns me," Blanche went on. "Mary has taken a liking for her. Tami is teaching her how to recognize wild herbs and make potions. I'm afraid some of this talk about witches will rub off on her if Tami stays with us."

"I didn't realize she and Mary were that close," Tristram said.

"You're not at home to see these things."

"By the time I return, all this talk will have died down, and you'll have Tami back."

"You'll have her back as well," Blanche said. "I've noticed how her eyes follow your every movement. She idolizes you."

Tristram wasn't sure how to respond. It wasn't quite an accusation. Blanche stated it simply as a fact.

"I'm her guardian," he said. "I proved it today at Hallet's. It's only natural that she should be grateful."

"But you enjoy having a slave girl in the house, someone who has to obey your commands. A grateful slave is even better."

"Tami will one day be a free woman."

"That's what you say, but she still regards you as her master."

"I can't help that," Tristram said. "It's not what I intended when I brought Tami home, and it's not what I want. When I get back, I'll see what I can do to change her attitude toward me."

"See that you do," Blanche said.

The next morning as Tristram was planning how to deliver Tami to Joanna, she descended the ladder from the loft. She was fully dressed and had her satchel in hand.

"I not go to Joanna," she said. "I go with you to Newport."

Her voice conveyed a note of assertion that Tristram found wholly foreign to her. She spoke not as his servant or slave, but as his equal. His first thought was that Blanche was behind this decision, but a glance in her direction told him that she was equally surprised by Tami's announcement. Upsall also looked up with interest.

"You won't be staying with Joanna forever," Tristram said. It had struck him that she must have a wrong idea about his reason for sending her away. "As soon as I get back, you can come home again."

Tami's expression didn't change. "People here not like me. I make much trouble for you. It is better I go to Newport."

"But you don't know anyone in Newport."

"I know Master Upsall," Tami said.

Upsall smiled at her claim. "You seem to have a free woman on your hands much sooner than you expected," he said.

"She doesn't know what she's doing," Tristram said. "She's not yet ready to live on her own, not in a place that's totally strange to her."

"What she says is true," Upsall said. "The people here have turned against her. She'll never be truly free in Yarmouth."

"You must admit that she's become a problem for us," Blanche chimed in. "Maybe Newport is the place for her."

Faced with opposition on all sides, Tristram was silent.

Upsall was the next to speak. "We might take Tami with us and see what there is for her in Newport. If she decides to stay, I could look out for her until she gets settled."

"What do you propose to do in Newport?" Tristram asked.

"I have no clear idea. Maybe I can open an inn. It depends on how long I'm there."

"Then it is all right I go with you," Tami said.

"You said from the start this was what you wanted," Blanche said. "The time has come to let Tami go."

Tristram wondered again if Blanche had a hand in this. Her ready acquiescence struck him as overly eager, almost rehearsed.

"She's been a big help to you," he said.

"I managed by myself for twelve years before she came. I can get along without her."

"I feel that I'm abandoning her," Tristram said. "She's not ready. It's best for her if I take her to Joanna."

"Apparently Tami doesn't agree with you," Upsall said. "You said you would know when the time came to set her free, because Tami would tell you. It seems to me she's telling you."

"But what will she do in Newport?" Tristram asked.

"We won't know that until we get there," Upsall said. "I just hope her reputation doesn't go with her. She'll have a hard enough time fitting in without being suspected of witchcraft."

"Is Tami going away for good?" Mary asked. She had come down from the loft and stood now next to her friend.

"We haven't decided yet," Tristram said. "There's some talk in the village that she's a witch. She may get hurt if she stays here."

"Tami's not a witch," Mary said.

"We know that; but some people think she is. So far I haven't been able to change their minds."

"Will they hang her like they do in Boston?"

"We don't hang people here, but they'll make life miserable for her." Tristram realized that he was now arguing against himself.

"Can we visit her if she goes to Newport?" Mary asked.

"That will depend on a lot of things."

"As long as I know I'll see her again, she can go," Mary said.

Tristram laughed. "I'm glad I have your permission. There's a lot to do before we sail in the morning. I'll decide about Tami tonight. In the meantime she can stay here."

"It seems to me you've already decided," Upsall said.

* * *

Throughout the day, while Tristram made final preparations for the voyage, his thoughts reverted to Tami's declaration of freedom. He could not stifle a sense of loss at the thought of her departure, the loss of one who looked up to him and did his bidding. With Blanche and the children Tami had shown signs of independence, but his word was always her law. Her decision to go to Newport came as a shock. Instead of congratulating himself on having achieved his goal, he blamed Tami for making her choice without consulting him. He wanted to be the architect of her future happiness, to have a part in bringing it about.

She was not yet ready to live alone in the community, be it in Yarmouth or Newport. Her speech might be adequate, but she was not equipped to deal with public sentiment toward slaves and blacks. The incident at Hallet's store bore that out. He shuddered to think what might have happened, had he not been there to protect her. He told himself he had only her welfare in mind in resisting her impulse to flee, and by the end of the day he almost believed it.

Returning home at dusk, he found several men stationed in front of his house. They stood silently as he approached.

"Why are you here?" he asked.

"We've come for the black girl," one of them said.

"She's done nothing to hurt you or anyone else. Now go home and get some sleep." He entered the house without waiting for a response.

Upsall met him at the door. "They started to gather about an hour ago," he said. "They've done nothing as yet. They seem to be waiting for others to join them."

"I'll never surrender Tami to them," Tristram said.

"Nor should you, but Yarmouth is no longer a safe place for her. In light of what's outside, Newport may be the only solution."

Tristram glanced at Tami, who was seated at the table. The satchel was nearby. She seemed calm, but he read the apprehension in her eyes.

"I guess you're right, but first I need to persuade that crowd outside to go home."

"First we have to get Tami out of the house," Upsall said. "It's for her own safety. They'll leave once they realize she's not here."

"I'll take her to the *Hopewell*," Tristram said. "You can talk to the crowd after I'm gone."

Upsall shook his head. "If they see you're not here, they'll know where you went."

"I can take her." Mary's eyes sparkled at the prospect. "I know the way so no one will see us."

"You'll do no such thing," Blanche said. "It's too dangerous."

Tristram had witnessed this aspect of Mary's character before, but this was no childish adventure. Before he had a chance to second Blanche's objection, Upsall was outlining a plan for Tami's escape.

"You and I and Blanche will confront the men out front," he said. "They won't be suspicious if they see all three of us. We can keep them occupied while Mary and Tami slip out the back way. You can go to the ship after the crowd disperses."

"We'll hide near the dock until you get there," Mary said.

Tristram saw no alternative, and Blanche grudgingly agreed to the plan. Tristram took down the musket from his days in the militia .

"Give the gun to Blanche," Upsall said. "It's less threatening."

When Tami and Mary were ready, he motioned for Tristram and Blanche to step outside. He was right behind them. The crowd of men now numbered more than a dozen. Several of them held torches. Seeing three people at the door, one with a musket, they retreated a few paces.

"We want the witch!" one of them shouted.

"She's not here," Tristram said. "Go home to your wives, and may the light of reason dawn on you with tomorrow's sun."

He laughed quietly at his own rhetoric. He was sounding like his father. But the crowd was not mollified.

"Where is she? Out in the woods consorting with a black devil?"

"Or brewing up another magic potion?"

"She's beyond your reach," Tristram said.

"Why are you protecting a witch?"

"She's not a witch. I use her potions for my own children. The Bicknell girl would have died with or without the medicine."

"You're not a doctor!"

"We'll find out where she's hiding!"

"Then we'll decide whether she's a witch or not!"

"If you don't believe me, one man can search the house. Then go home and leave us in peace."

A man stepped forward. Blanche handed the musket to Upsall and followed the man into the house. The crowd was silent as they awaited the results of the search. Several minutes passed before the man reappeared.

"There's nobody in there except the children," he said.

"All of them?" someone asked.

"I guess so. I didn't count them."

With their prey seemingly out of reach, the crowd lost interest. When the last man was gone, Tristram slipped out at the back. When he reached the dock, Mary stepped out of the shadows. Tami was clinging to her hand and obviously frightened.

"I can take it from here," he said. "You're a brave girl."

"Take care of Tami," Mary said as she hugged him.

"I promise. Go on home, and don't let anyone see you."

The two women embraced. Then Mary ran off into the darkness. Tristram waited until she was out of sight, then rowed out to the *Hopewell*.

The familiar surroundings of the cabin appeared to have a soothing effect on Tami. It was here they had made love on the voyage north from Barbados. More than four months had passed since then. He had managed to control the passion she aroused in him, and Tami seemed to have done the same. But the thought of it now rekindled his desire to hold her in his arms. There was no risk, no one to disturb them. The crew were spending a last night ashore with their families. To go home and leave Tami there alone was out of the question. Upsall and Blanche could handle the crowd if they returned.

A resumption of their lovemaking would place him in an awkward position. How could he adopt a righteous stance with Blanche, if he was guilty of like behavior? If he became suddenly tolerant, she was sure to suspect something was amiss. By yielding to his desire, he was doomed forever to playing the hypocrite.

To calm himself and gain time, he made up the extra bunk where Tami was to sleep. She watched his every movement. Her eyes told him that her thoughts were in a similar vein. He had promised Blanche that he wouldn't touch Tami as long as she was a servant in their home. But that restriction no longer applied. Tami had declared herself to be independent. She was now a free woman.

Having arranged the bedding to his satisfaction, he turned abruptly, aware that some change had occurred while he was thus occupied. Tami's coat and dress lay in a heap on the floor. She was in his bunk, the covers drawn up to her neck. She smiled at him. Was this her parting gift, her way of thanking him for all he had done for her? If he made love to her now, would she expect as much whenever he made port in Newport? Was that indeed his intention? While pondering these questions, he removed his clothes and got under the covers beside her.

Fifteen

"Safety is no longer my primary concern."
(Rhode Island Colony, 1657)

Upsall came aboard early the next morning. The crowd had not returned. The constable watched from the dock as the *Hopewell* set sail. A cold northwest wind was blowing as the ship rounded the tip of Cape Cod and caught the swells of the Atlantic. Tristram stood at the helm on the navigation deck. Tami was resting below. Out of propriety and to forestall any further expressions of gratitude, he had installed her in his own cabin for the overnight voyage to Newport, while he bunked with Upsall in steerage.

He had no regrets about their lovemaking, yet he told himself it must not continue. Tami had made her decision. Ready or not, she was on the verge of becoming an independent woman. She would have more than enough obstacles in her path when she got to Newport, without the added burden of breaking free from him. Yet, much as he admired her courage and resolution, he found it difficult to accept her new status. She was his child, though more than that, and he was reluctant to surrender all responsibility for her future welfare.

Upsall had suggested Newport as their destination, but he seemed now unsure of the reception that awaited them in the Rhode

Island Colony. "I have no fear for myself," he said as he huddled against the cold wind, "but I worry about Tami. They might not accept a black woman in Newport without a white master. What will we do if they turn her away?"

"I could take her to New Amsterdam," Tristram said.

"Maybe Gorton would take her in at Warwick," Upsall said.

"We won't know until we get to Newport," Tristram said.

The ship lurched, and Upsall lost his balance, catching himself up against the rail. "I'm going below," he said. "Maybe Tami is up and about. If I'm to watch over her in Newport, we need to get better acquainted."

It crossed Tristram's mind that Tami might one day be moved to show her gratitude to Upsall as well, even though he was over sixty. She had no reason as yet to be grateful, but Tristram relinquished the helm soon after and went below to join them.

The voyage was cold and rough but otherwise uneventful. They arrived in Newport the next day and prepared to go ashore.

"I think we should leave Tami on the ship," Upsall said. "She'll only make matters more difficult for us. Let's settle one problem with the local authorities before we present them with another one."

"It's all of a piece," Tristram said. "Either they accept both of you, or we go somewhere else."

"I apologize. I was thinking only of myself."

Upon landing at Long Wharf, they spotted a fisherman unloading his catch and asked him where they might find the governor.

"You mean Roger Williams? We don't see much of him. Most of the time he's up in Providence. The man you want is John Clarke, but he's in England trying to get us a charter. You might talk to Nicholas Easton or John Coggeshall. Maybe they can help you."

"Which one of them owns the most land?" Upsall asked.

"That would be Easton."

"Where can we find him?"

"He has a house in town, but his main holdings are over the hill and past the beach. You might do better to wait for him in the square. He's bound to show up there sooner or later."

Upsall said he was up to the hike, and they set off in the direction indicated. Tami drew curious looks from the people they met. They made their way along the curved strip of beach and out onto a point of land that lay beyond. The house ahead of them was not as pretentious as those in Barbados, yet Tristram deemed it more elegant than any in Yarmouth.

Easton's greeting was warm and hospitable. "What business brings you to Newport?" he asked when they were seated in his study.

He too was in his sixties, yet alert and vigorous. A tanner by trade, he had a certain air of the clergyman about him. He reminded Tristram of his father.

Upsall detailed the course of events that had led to his banishment from Boston and Sandwich. "I've heard that people in Newport are more tolerant of different religious opinions," he concluded. "I come here in the hope of finding a temporary place of refuge."

"I too was banished from Boston nearly twenty years ago," Easton said. "I have heard of these Friends of whom you speak. I and others like me would welcome an opportunity to learn more about them. I'm not in a position of authority at present, but I daresay I have some influence. I see no impediment to your setting down here in Newport."

"Is there also a place here for this woman?" Tristram asked.

Easton appeared to notice Tami for the first time. "I'm not sure I know what you mean. Is she not your slave?"

"She was once," Tristram said. "I've granted her liberty. She's free to pursue whatever future course in life she may choose."

He stopped at that. To mention the charges of witchcraft levied against Tami would only make it more difficult for her to gain entry and acceptance in Newport. Easton appeared to reflect. When he spoke, it was in a flat tone, as if he were giving voice to his thoughts.

"After we joined with Providence Plantation and became a single colony, we passed a law to prevent slavery from taking root in any of our four towns. Roger Williams, who is now the governor, favors the law; but merchants in Newport feel it hampers their trade. So we have a law on the books that is not enforced."

"Then there are slaves in Newport," Upsall said.

"A few. This woman would be readily accepted as such. I have no experience with a slave who has been freed from servitude."

"Then your law doesn't prevent a free black woman from seeking refuge here," Tristram said.

"Has she been banished as well?" Easton asked.

Tristram decided that Tami's cause was best served by telling the truth. "She was wrongly accused of practicing witchcraft in Yarmouth."

Tami was seated with her hands in her lap during this exchange. "I not a witch," she said now, her dark eyes flashing.

"I thank God that witchcraft has gained no hold in Rhode Island," Easton said, "but I'm not sure that Newport is prepared to accept a black woman who claims to be free."

"If that presents a problem," Upsall said, "I can appoint myself as her guardian until she establishes a place for herself in the community."

Easton reflected again. "If she lives with you, people will regard her as your slave," he said.

"They can think whatever they wish," Upsall said. "It will become evident in time that she is free to do what she wants."

"Such a gradual introduction to the community might forestall any problems," Easton said. "You can try it and see how it works out. I won't stand in your way."

"You mean to say that she'll be a curiosity," Tristram said.

"She'll certainly be a first," Easton said.

Tristram stayed in Newport several days, long enough for Upsall to make fruitful contact with a local innkeeper recommended by Easton, and long enough for Tami to find work at the inn as a maid. In taking his leave, he promised to maintain contact with both of them and to make port in Newport when possible. Whatever other motives he had, they remained unexpressed even to himself.

* * *

Autumn was well advanced before Tristram kept his promise and landed again in Newport. He went at once to the inn. Tami was delighted to see him and eager to tell him about her accomplishments. In addition to her work as a maid she was helping out in the kitchen. She no longer lived with Upsall, but rented a room in the town.

"I have time now," she said proudly. "I show you where I live."

Her room was a short distance from the inn. It was larger than he expected. A lean-to added at the rear of the local blacksmith shop, it had been the smithy's home prior to his marriage. The arrangement and order of the simple furnishings reminded Tristram of his home in Yarmouth.

"I make fire in shop every morning, so smithy sleeps longer with new wife," she said.

"What else do you do?"

He realized that the question could be taken two ways, but Tami seemed oblivious to any ambiguity.

"I make medicine. Some day I have shop and sell much medicine to people. Then I am free woman like you promise."

He wanted to say that she was already free, but felt she would not understand the distinction between working at the inn and being a servant in his home.

"You tell Mary and children I sorry I not see them," she went on.

"They miss you too," Tristram said.

That was true in part. Mary spoke often of Tami and what she had learned from her. For the younger ones she was a fading memory. Blanche seldom mentioned her. Tristram was more at home now, limiting his trade to colonies north of Virginia; and his relations with Blanche had improved as a result. To his knowledge she no longer had any contact with Gorham.

He had given as his chief reason for visiting Newport a desire to see what Upsall was doing. Blanche need not know that he had checked first on Tami and been to her room. If she inquired about

Tami on his return, he would say simply that she still worked at the inn.

As he took tea in the home she had fashioned, he was pleased yet somewhat chagrined that Tami seemed to be doing quite well on her own. No doubt Upsall was to thank for her rapid adjustment and her newfound independence. Tristram had anticipated this day ever since he bought her at auction, yet he was saddened by its arrival. In her talk and her attitude it was evident that she no longer saw him as a master.

She stood in front of him, her arms akimbo. She had removed her coat and was clad in a work dress and apron. He wondered what else she had in her wardrobe. How did she spend her time when she was not at the inn or brewing medicine or making fires? Was there a man in her life?

"I must go back to inn soon," she said as if in reply to his question, "but have time to get in bed, if you like."

Taken aback by her words, Tristram groped for a response. Was this what she expected of him? Was this why he had come? The thought had crossed his mind and been dismissed. Although he still felt a certain responsibility for her welfare, he was resigned to becoming a figure in her past. Her brazen offer indicated that in her eyes he was more than that.

"That's not why I came," he said, taking her hand. "I wasn't sure what I would find, what I would accomplish by coming here. Now I know what I have to do. I came to set you free."

Tami looked puzzled. "I not understand. I am free woman now."

"In all respects but one. You still feel that you owe me a debt, and you think that getting into bed with me is the price you have to pay."

"You not want to get in bed?"

"I may want to, but I'm not going to. You owe me nothing. Do you understand what I'm saying? You owe nothing to anyone. That's what it means to be free."

Tami appeared to consider his words with care. "It sound like you say good-bye, like I not see you again," she said in a voice that was barely more than a whisper.

"Of course you will. I can visit you whenever I'm in Newport. I still care about what happens to you, and I'm willing to help you in any way I can. But we won't get in bed together."

"I do as you say, Master Tristram."

She smiled as she withdrew her hand. Satisfied that they had reached an understanding, Tristram took leave of her. Back aboard the *Hopewell* he wondered at his ability to withstand this latest temptation. He had acted with her best interest at heart, but he was aware that he had also liberated himself.

* * *

Upsall had left the inn and was working at a tavern near the docks. Tristram delivered a letter from Dorothy, then waited as he read it. Upsall was smiling as he refolded the letter and stuffed it in his pocket.

"Dorothy appears to be managing quite well in my absence," he said. "Do you see her often?"

"I stop by the inn when I'm in Boston."

"Tell her I miss her. I'll give you a letter to take back."

"I'll see that she gets it," Tristram said.

Upsall had little to say about Tami, merely acknowledging that she had made a place for herself at the inn. He knew about her plan to open a shop and sell medicine.

"When the time comes I'll do what I can to help her get started," he said, "provided I'm still here."

"Where else would you go?" Tristram asked.

"I'm not sure. Another group of Friends has just arrived in Newport on the *Woodhouse*. I believe you know one of them, a man from Barbados named John Rous."

"I met him on my last voyage to the island. Both he and his father had become Quakers. I'm not surprised to find him here."

"He's staying with Easton and seems to have convinced him to join the society."

"Easton seemed receptive when we spoke to him in the spring."

"He has an open mind on the subject of religion, but open minds can entertain strange ideas. According to Rous, he maintained at one time that both the devil and God dwell within us and are waging a perpetual struggle for our soul, and that grace is the signature of the Antichrist. I don't see how a man can live with a notion like that."

"How do you know so much about Easton?"

"Rous invited him to attend an informational meeting."

"It sounds like the next wave of missionaries we talked about."

"You might call it that. Their plan is to set up a base of operations in Newport. They won't be persecuted here, and they'll have a place of refuge if they're banished from neighboring colonies. Roger Williams was opposed to them, but he's no longer president of the colony. Benedict Arnold took office back in May. He resides in Newport and has a more liberal view."

"How can I get in touch with Rous?" Tristram asked.

"We're holding a meeting tomorrow evening. I'm sure Rous will be there. You're welcome to attend and see what's going on."

"I could lay over for another day," Tristram said.

"The meeting is at my house," Upsall said. "Have you changed your opinion of the Quakers? As I remember it, you objected to their insistence that everyone can hear and heed God's voice in his own heart, that we have no need for ministers."

"I remain my father's son in that respect," Tristram said. "But I also question the wisdom of some of their tactics. I understand it is common practice in England for Quakers to interrupt a minister during his sermon and to shout him down. That strikes me as very like the intolerance of such men as Norton and Bellingham. Quakers may speak directly with God, but other men prefer to listen to a minister. As I said at Allen's house, theirs is not the only truth. There are many paths to salvation."

"You make a valid point," Upsall said. "I'll bring it up at one of our meetings. I suspect that such actions are the result of the persecution Quakers have suffered at the hands of the authorities and the established clergy. Once we are free to practice what we believe and to proclaim our message in peace, there should be no need for the tactics you decry."

"And when will that day arrive?" Tristram asked.

Upsall laughed. "So far God has been reticent about that."

* * *

Tristram arrived at the meeting at the time designated. In addition to Upsall and John Rous, Christopher Holder, John Copeland, Humphrey Norton, and Robert Fowler, the master of the *Woodhouse*, were in attendance. Tristram spoke to Rous before the meeting started. He had to be reminded of their encounter on Barbados.

"I'm sorry I didn't recognize thee at once," he said. "My life has undergone a good many changes during this past year. I'm no longer the same person who showed thee about my father's plantation."

"You were already a Friend when we met," Tristram said.

"I was dabbling with the idea in Barbados," Rous said. "It was a fashionable way to rebel against authority. Now I'm committed to the cause and eager to spread the good news."

"Did Mary Fisher have a hand in convincing you?"

"She was an inspiration for me until she returned to England. She assured us that we would be welcome here in Newport. I thank thee for putting me in contact with her."

Tristram recalled only that he had mentioned her name in his talk with Rous, but he let it pass. "Do you know where she is now?" he asked.

"Only that she's in England and waiting for a calling."

Tristram wondered what it meant to have a calling. Had his father been called to become a minister. Had he been called as a youth to go to sea? Was it as simple as that to know what God wanted?

"Were you called to come to New England?" he asked.

"I seized an opportunity to join a group of Friends bound for New Amsterdam and Newport," Rous said. "I suppose I saw it as a calling."

"Now that you're here, what do you plan to do?"

"My immediate task is to spread the seed in Newport, then await God's direction regarding the future."

"And the others in your group, do they have plans as well?"

"That will all come out at the meeting," Rous said.

As host for the evening Upsall convened the meeting, which lasted nearly two hours. No one appeared to be in charge, nor was there a ready agenda. People spoke as the spirit moved them. Tristram had experienced something like it at Allen's home in Sandwich, but this group of Quakers seemed to be remarkably comfortable with silence. Long periods of time went by without a word being spoken. Still, by the end of the session, they had made a number of decisions. Tristram assumed they were based upon the prompting of their inner voice.

Holder and Copeland determined to leave in a fortnight for the island of Martha's Vineyard. Their intention was to use the island as a gateway to Sandwich in the Plymouth colony. Upsall had doubtless touted it as fertile ground for their missionary work. Fowler offered to transport them in the *Woodhouse*. Norton and Rous had plans to travel directly to the seat of government in Plymouth when their task in Newport was finished.

No one mentioned Boston, so Tristram was surprised when Upsall drew him aside after the meeting adjourned and gave voice to his intention to return home.

"I have to see Dorothy and the Red Lyon again," he said.

"It's not safe for you in Boston," Tristram said. "They'll arrest you on sight and put you in jail."

"I know people there, and I know my way around the town. If they imprison me, at least I'll be close to my family."

"Endicott is pressing the court to pass a new law that mandates even more severe punishments for any Quakers who return to Boston after they've been banished. He'd cut off their right ear and bore a hole in their tongue with a hot iron. He won't be satisfied until he can hang them."

"Safety is no longer my primary concern. I'm too old to spend the rest of my life in exile."

"When do you plan to return?" Tristram asked.

"When the spirit tells me the time is right," Upsall said.

Sixteen

"I want to be a Quaker."
(The New England Colonies, 1666)

During the winter of 1665-66 Tristram received word that his father had died on Hog Island in the Isles of Shoals. Reverend Joseph Hull had returned to New England three years earlier, having been evicted from his post in Cornwall following the restoration of the monarchy in England. Tristram had seen him on several occasions after his return, first in Oyster River and then in York. He seemed to be in reasonably good health when they last met, and news of his death came as a shock.

That winter was unusually harsh, and it was March before Tristram could set a course for Maine. He wanted to pay his respects to his father, to console his stepmother Agnes, and to look in on Naomi, his half-sister. He offered to take Blanche with him, but she declined.

"I met your father only once, before he went to England," she said. "Besides, you'll want to see the rest of the family. I'd only be in the way."

Tristram had to agree with her. Over the years of their marriage Blanche had little opportunity and less inclination to establish any sort of a bond with his sisters, Elizabeth in Cocheco, Temperance and Dorothy in Oyster River, and Griselda in York. Joanna was the only one in the family with whom Blanche was at all friendly. Tristram did not fault her for that. He saw his sisters in Maine only on rare occasions; and none of them, with the exception of Elizabeth, approved of his marriage. His father and Agnes had remained impartial.

Late in March Tristram sailed on *The Catch* for York in the newly restored Province of Maine. Agnes was the executor of his father's estate. She appeared to have matters well in hand and had been out to Hog Island.

"I'm indisposed at the moment to make another visit to his grave," she said, "but you might offer to take Naomi with you. She's visiting with Griselda at the moment. I have no idea how that came about."

"Is Naomi well?" Tristram asked.

"I worry about her. Her two brothers are talking about a move to Piscataway, and she doesn't get on well with her stepsisters. Your Father and I were hurt by her refusal to come with us when we left Oyster River. Now she's cooped up in the house of a Quaker named Williams. I've heard that she's involved with a married man. It's too bad, because she has a home in York whenever she likes. You can tell her that when you see her."

"How does she feel about Father?"

"You'll have to ask her," Agnes said. "But I'm sure a visit to his grave will do her good."

Tristram had planned to see Naomi in Oyster River on his return, but the prospect of taking her along to Hog Island appealed to him. On a visit to Ipswich he had found her decidedly bitter about her situation and her future prospects. Then Judge Symonds cast her out for testifying against him in a case that involved two of his indentured servants. She took refuge with her parents, newly returned from England, and reclaimed custody of her child. When Tristram last saw her in Oyster River, she appeared outwardly cheerful; but he sensed she was floundering in her effort to make a place for herself in the community. That was roughly two years ago.

* * *

Hog Island was almost deserted at that time of year. Many of the fishermen who made a living there chose to spend the winter months on the mainland. An elderly man who loved the island led Tristram and Naomi up the hill beyond the church to the grave. A simple well-joined wooden cross marked the site. Attached to the cross arm was a grapevine wreath, now withered and dried. The islanders owed his father twenty pounds when he died, a debt Agnes forgave provided they use the money for a suitable memorial. She had asked Tristram to determine what the islanders had done to commemorate their pastor. Was this the extent of their tribute?

He stood there for some time, Naomi at his side, while swirling snow stung his cheeks and a biting wind chilled him to the bone. His happiest memories of his father dated from childhood, the ten years at Northleigh in Devon prior to the death of his mother in childbirth. His father had married again before emigrating to New England. But as a minister of the Church of England he failed to fit in with Puritans in Massachusetts or separatists in Plymouth. He had finally found a safe haven in the Province of Maine.

Tristram liked to say that he had jumped the family ship by signing on as an apprentice to Bursley and going off to sea. Once he had his own vessel, he did his best to maintain contact with his father and his sisters in Maine, but his visits were brief and infrequent. Looking down now at the grave, he told himself that Naomi was not the only one orphaned when their father returned to England. For more than a decade men like Bursley and Upsall had assumed that role in his life. He didn't blame his father for his long absence. A minister had to carry out what he took to be the will of God.

Naomi's head barely came to his shoulder. Even bundled up against the weather, she appeared rather frail. Bending down, she broke off a twig from the wreath and put it in the pocket of her coat. She stumbled in rising, and Tristram helped her regain her feet. She smiled at him in gratitude.

They had spoken little as yet about their common father. "I can tell you better how I feel about him after I see his grave," she said on the brief voyage to Hog Island.

It was late in the day and snowing heavily when they left the grave site. Tristram opted to lay over on Hog Island and return to York the next day. It would give him a chance to speak at length to Naomi. He tried to frame some questions that might induce her to reveal her true feelings.

"Now that you've seen his grave, are you reconciled with Father?" he asked when they were secure in his cabin.

Naomi gave him a suspicious look. When he said nothing more, content to await her reply, she appeared to relax. Several minutes passed before she spoke.

"He did what he thought was best. He didn't expect to be gone so long. I was bitter for a time, and I still can't help but blame him and the rest of the family for leaving me alone in Ipswich all that time."

"I didn't realize you were so unhappy there," Tristram said.

"Don't get me wrong. I wasn't mistreated. I just felt cast off and abandoned. Nights were the worst. I'd lie awake wondering what I had done to deserve such a fate."

"I imagine it was hard for you to give up your son?"

"Judge Symonds said he was protecting my reputation; but I never understood why I had to stay in Ipswich, why I couldn't go with Joseph."

"It's partly my fault," Tristram said. "I was glad to get Temperance to care for the boy. I didn't think to include you."

"You're not to blame," Naomi said, venturing a grin. "She and her husband took him in only for the money the judge agreed to pay for his upkeep. Now they're claiming that it wasn't enough to cover their expenses. Temperance would never have accepted me too."

They shared a hearty laugh at his sister's expense. Tristram sensed they had just come a little closer together.

"Besides," Naomi went on, "Judge Symonds wanted to keep me as a servant. I was useful to him. He gave no thought to what I wanted. After Joseph was born, I was nothing but a maid in his household."

"Well, you're a much better judge of his character."

"Judging the judge," Naomi said, laughing again.

While she was in a good mood, Tristram decided to bring up a more serious question. "The last time I saw you, you seemed happy to be reunited with your parents and your son in Oyster River. Why did you stay behind when they moved to York?"

Naomi stared at him, as though seeking to read his motives.

"You needn't answer unless you want to," Tristram said. "I was just wondering if Williams has made a Quaker out of you."

"Not yet, but he says it would help me make a new life for myself."

"You can have a new life in York. Agnes has a home for you there."

"I thought Mother had a hand in this," Naomi said. "I'll tell you why I stayed in Oyster River. I met a man I like. I'd marry him, if he asked me. He's a carpenter and works mostly on boats."

"Is he in a position to marry you?"

"You must know that he has a wife somewhere, or you wouldn't ask a question like that. Who told you?"

"I forget who told me," Tristram said. "I'm not going to advise you what to do. You probably had plenty of that from Father before he died."

"I think he gave up on me. You can tell Mother I'm grateful for her offer, but I can work things out by myself."

"Maybe I can meet this man when I'm in Oyster River."

"I'll try to arrange it," Naomi said. "And thanks for your interest. It's more than I get from the rest of the family."

* * *

Nicholas Upsall died in August of 1666. Tristram kept track of him on visits to Dorothy at the Red Lyon Inn. Upsall had returned to Boston three years after Tristram took him to Newport. He was promptly confined in the Boston jail, where he was watched over and aided by his friend, the turnkey. When the authorities saw that he was influential and was drawing people to him, they isolated him in the Castle in Boston Harbor. After two petitions by Dorothy for his release, abetted by a royal edict ordering an end to the persecution of Quakers, Upsall was removed to the house of her brother, John

516

Capen, in Dorchester, but forbidden to return to Boston. There, despite a court injunction not to "corrupt any with his pernicious opinions" or teach the "diabolical doctrines and horrid tenets of the cursed sect of Quakers," he remained active in Quaker affairs.

Other Quakers had fared even worse. Holder and Copeland had their right ear cut off when they returned to Plymouth after being banished. In 1658 the General Court of Massachusetts ordered the banishment of all Quakers, visiting or resident, upon pain of death if they returned. While still in prison, Upsall arranged to fence in a pit where the bodies of William Robinson and Marmaduke Stevenson were thrown after they were hanged for defying that order. Two more Quakers were hanged before the edict from Charles II in the fall of 1661 ended that practice. But a new law requiring that Quakers, both men and women, "be stripped naked from the middle upward, and tied to a cart's tail and whipped through the town," remained in effect long after that date.

Tristram learned of these laws and penalties from Dorothy on his visits to the Red Lyon. Through contact with her husband she kept herself current on all matters concerning Quakers. Although he steadfastly declined to become a Quaker himself, Tristram remained sympathetic to their cause and their beliefs. On several occasions he was fined by the court in Plymouth for rendering them assistance. And he recalled with satisfaction a visit to Oyster River, when at his father's behest he transported two Quaker women to a safe house in Kittery. They had been whipped and nearly drowned for preaching in the neighboring town of Dover. He viewed their rescue as a tribute to his friendship with Mary Fisher.

Dorothy broke the news of Upsall's death. "It grieves me that I wasn't by his side. But my brother was there and assured me that he died peacefully. I had to fight for permission to return his body to Boston, so he could be buried on Copp's Hill."

"If you have time," Tristram said, "I should like to see his grave."

"I can make the time. He had a number of acquaintances toward the end. The Quakers seemed to regard him as a hero or patriarch."

"I regret that I didn't see him more often in recent years. I would have liked to take him on a voyage to Newport; but that was impossible, given the conditions of his confinement."

"You proved yourself a true friend when he most needed one."

"You were a long time without him. It must have been hard."

"I saw him quite often while he was in Dorchester, but keeping the inn these past ten years without his help has been hard. I did it for his sake. Now that he's gone, I'm ready to give it up."

"I trust he left you well provided for," Tristram said.

"His estate was valued at more than five hundred pounds."

"I admire him for remaining a Quaker to the end."

Dorothy laughed. "Even beyond that. In his will he left them all his books and papers, his feather bed and bedstead, his pillows, sheets, and a rug, along with some other provisions."

"Were you tempted to become a Quaker yourself?"

"I listened to Nicholas, but I could never understand why he was so taken with their ideas. It brought him nothing but grief in his old age."

"He saw them as victims of injustice," Tristram said.

"He was right to speak out in their defense, but he needn't have become one of them. He's lucky they didn't cut off his ear or put a hot iron to his tongue."

"Or hang him on Boston Common, like those other unfortunate souls," Tristram said. "Thank God, the King put an end to that."

"You've had a good deal of contact with Quakers," Dorothy said. "Have you joined their society?"

"I always felt that if I became a Quaker, I would be disloyal to my father and betray all that he taught me. He died last year, so now I can make up my own mind."

"You haven't answered my question."

"My daughter Mary married a Quaker and seems content to worship God in their fashion. As for me, I'm not yet a Quaker; but one never knows what may lie ahead in the fogs of the future."

"I wish Nicholas had felt that way," Dorothy said. "He might have saved us both a lot of heartache."

Since Upsall had served as a guardian and benefactor to Tami while he was in Newport, Tristram felt obliged to give her a personal account of his death. Soon after his visit to Dorothy, he determined to include Newport as a port of call on a voyage down the coast. He had paid several visits to Tami since he left her in Upsall's care a decade ago. She continued to live alone. Though he gave no thought to renewing their relationship, he liked to think she might be tempted. But the example he had set on his visit to her room at the blacksmith shop and his parting words seemed to have made a lasting impression on her. Tami remained free in every sense.

He expected some opposition from Blanche. Their relations had stabilized over the years, but they remained watchful of each other. Since the incident with Gorham, she had done nothing to attract public attention. Tristram in turn had abandoned all commerce with the West Indies, and he rejected an opportunity for a trade route between Boston and London. Short voyages along the coast from

Maine to New York were sufficiently lucrative and enabled him to spend more time with his family. And the coastal trade was untainted by the sweat and blood of slavery.

In response to his announcement that he planned to visit Tami in Newport, Blanche surprised him by saying, "Take the boys with you."

"They haven't seen Tami since she left us," he said. "I doubt they even remember her."

"John has been after you to take him along on one of your voyages. This is your chance to keep the promise you made him."

Tristram regarded his wife closely. Was this a resurgence of her old mistrust? Or was she attributing motives to him that applied more properly to herself? She had no cause for concern, yet he admitted that he would have preferred to see Tami alone. It added a not unpleasant tension to a visit to recall what once had been and to wonder if it might be again.

"I suppose I could take them along," he said.

Tristram picked up yet another passenger on a visit to his married daughter in Sandwich. When he chanced to mention that he was going to Newport, Mary said she had fond memories of Tami and would like to see her again. He was left to wonder if she too might have some hidden reason for her request.

* * *

So it happened that on a bright day in late autumn Tami found four people in front of her house. She recognized Tristram at once, though he had been an infrequent visitor of late. After greeting him, she turned her attention to the others in the group. The young woman was smiling at her. The two boys hung back, unsure where they were or why they had come.

"Is it Mary?" she asked.

Mary simply nodded.

"You grow since last time I see you. I hear you married now and have a baby."

"Two babies," Mary said. "It's good to see thee again."

Tami turned her attention to the boys, who were using their big sister as a shield. "And this is Joseph and John."

"They've grown a bit too," Tristram said.

Tami approached each boy in turn. They stiffened as she hugged them. She invited them all to come inside.

"I have some sad news," Tristram said when they were settled. He and Mary sat across the table from her, while Joseph and John stretched out on the floor near the hearth. "Nicholas Upsall is dead."

His statement garnered Tami's full attention. "Where did he die?"

"In Dorchester. He lived with his wife's brother, because he was forbidden to return to Boston."

"I glad he not die in prison. I never meet his wife."

"Her name is Dorothy."

"He take good care of me when I come to Newport. Then he go back to Boston, and I not see him again."

"I saw him shortly before he died. Prison had left its mark on him, but he was still strong in his Quaker beliefs."

"I go one time with him to Quaker meeting. I feel at home there. Not so much at other church in Newport."

"Do you go to meetings now?" Tristram asked.

"Sometimes I go, but it is not the same."

"Do you still earn a living with your sewing?"

Tami pointed to a basket near the hearth. "I make medicine too, but not kill anyone in Newport."

She smiled at Tristram as she spoke, and he laughed in return.

"Sarah and Hannah are big girls now?" she asked, turning to Mary.

"Sarah is quite a young lady," Mary said. "I expect she will marry one of these days. Hannah is only ten, but she acts much older than that."

"They not remember me." Tami stated it as a fact.

"I'm afraid not," Mary said. "But I remember. That's why I came."

"I have some business in town," Tristram said. "You and Tami can talk while I'm gone. I'll come back for you when I finish."

The two boys rose from the hearth, as if to follow their father; but a motion from Mary changed their minds, and they stayed where they were.

"I have herb garden behind house," Tami said when Tristram was gone, addressing the boys. "How much you know about herbs?"

"I know a lot about plants of all kinds," Joseph said.

"You and John see how many you can name. Mary and I talk. We come out when we're done. Maybe make a test."

Joseph was eager to accept the challenge. Drawing John behind him, he went out to the garden.

"Your face tell me you want to talk something serious," Tami said when she was alone with Mary.

"It's about my mother," Mary said. She paused, as if unsure how to proceed. "She hasn't always been a good wife to my father.

She was unfaithful to him at least once that I know about, but I suspect there were other times."

"I remember talk when I am in Yarmouth," Tami said.

"I want to forgive my mother in my heart, but I get angry when I think of the heartache she's caused my father. She claims he's as guilty as she is. That makes me more angry. But if it were true, if I knew my father was also unfaithful, perhaps I could accept my mother as she is."

"You want know if your father make love to me," Tami said.

"I have no right to ask, and I don't blame thee for not answering," Mary said, her face flushed with embarrassment. "But it's important to me, and I promise not to tell anyone."

Tami rose to put a log on the fire. It gave her time to think. She was inclined not to answer the unspoken question, but she liked Mary and wanted to help her reconcile with her mother. But how was she to reply? Should she defend Tristram and deny any improper involvement? After all he had done for her, she owed him that much loyalty. Mary would be satisfied with a lie.

She paused while stirring the embers to induce a flame. She was thinking like a servant, like the slave girl he bought at auction. Through her own efforts in Newport she had become a free woman. Free to make her own decisions. Free to follow her instincts as a woman. Returning to the table, she sat next to Mary and took her hand.

"I want you listen and understand what I say. Mister Tristram save me from life as slave. He make me free woman. I want to thank him, but have only myself to give him. He understand and accept my gift. Mister Tristram is a good man."

"When was the last time he accepted thy gift?" Mary asked.

"On night when he save me from men who call me witch, night you take me to boat. Sometimes when he visit me here in Newport, I want to say thank-you again, but he love your mother."

Mary used the back of her hand to wipe a tear from her eye. "I understand," she said, "and I thank thee for being honest with me."

"You have good mother. You listen to heart and be good daughter."

"I'll do my best. I feel better now that we've talked."

"You and other children always welcome here in my house," Tami said. "Your father too." She tried to make it sound like an afterthought, and Mary seemed to take it as such.

"I gather thou art comfortable and happy in Newport," Mary said.

"I have good life here as free woman," Tami said.

"I'm glad for thee. That's what Father wanted."

Tami was glad that Mary did not pursue the question of happiness. She had blamed Tristram at first for leaving her alone in a strange place. It was Nicholas who helped her establish herself as a seamstress and healer of the sick. He urged her to marry one of her own kind, as he put it. But all the black men in Newport were slaves. To marry one of them was to risk a return to servitude. It wasn't worth the price.

What she told Mary was the truth. Tristram had made no further effort to renew their relationship. On several occasions she had spotted his ship in the harbor and wondered why he neglected to visit her. She would have liked to believe that he didn't trust himself to be alone with her, that he had brought the children along today, not so they could meet her but as security. She knew it wasn't true. He had never really loved her. Not like he loved his children and his wife. His gift to her was freedom, and for that she was forever grateful.

She had noted earlier the cautious manner in which Tristram made certain movements, and she recalled a previous visit when she gave him medicine for a pain in his chest. Not wishing to alarm Mary and the boys, she inquired in private about his health after he returned from his business in town. He thanked her for her concern and assured her that he was fine.

It struck her when they were gone that he hadn't mentioned his wife. Mary was the only one who spoke of her mother. Did he wish to spare her feelings? Blanche had never confided in her, but Tami felt they had a good deal in common when it came to men. She was glad Mary hadn't asked about her relations with Nicholas.

* * *

"Why was Nicholas Upsall in prison?" Joseph asked.

His mission in Newport accomplished, Tristram was at the helm of the *Hopewell* steering an eastward course toward home. John stood within easy earshot. Mary had gone below to rest.

Tristram regarded his son with surprise. Joseph was old enough to have some knowledge of the way of the world, old enough to deal with the truth. John would have to make what he could of their conversation.

"Upsall had to leave Boston for protesting a law that barred Quakers from entering the colony. Then he was banished from Sandwich for holding meetings like a Quaker service. He went to Newport and became a Quaker himself. When he returned to Boston, he was arrested and put in jail."

"Why did he go back?" Joseph asked.

"He missed his wife, but also because Quakers seem moved by the spirit within them to go where they aren't wanted."

This was getting pretty deep. He had no desire to burden Joseph with his own questions about religion; but neither could he brush aside his son's interest or curiosity. He decided to compromise by providing some details about the last years of Upsall's life. That seemed safe enough.

"He was in prison for three years in Boston. I saw him after he was released. He remained active in Quaker affairs, but he couldn't go home. He spent the rest of his life in Dorchester."

"Was he your friend?" John asked.

Tristram looked at his younger son. He hadn't seemed to be paying much attention to the conversation.

"Father rescued him and took him to Newport," Joseph said, as though proud of his knowledge.

"Where did you hear about that?" Tristram asked in some surprise. Joseph was six at the time, and the topic seldom came up at home.

Joseph's pride gave way to a sheepish look. "We went to a Quaker meeting while you were away at sea. The people there told us about it, after they found out who we were."

Tristram was silent, unsure what to say next

"Is there something wrong with being a Quaker?" John asked. His eyes were as bright as ever, but his brow was wrinkled in puzzlement.

"It depends on where you live," Tristram said, surprised again by the course their talk was taking. He had intended for some time to speak frankly to his sons about the vicissitudes of life, what they could expect as they grew older, what decisions they might have to make, what pitfalls they should avoid. That time seemed to be at hand.

"Not any more," he said. "For a time the authorities in Boston felt they had to punish anyone who worshiped in a different way. Quakers were banished from the colony. Some were imprisoned, whipped, and branded. Four of them, including a woman, were hanged on the Commons."

"They hanged a woman!" John seemed aghast at the thought.

Tristram wondered if the boys were still too young for this kind of talk. But he had gone too far to stop. "The first Quakers to arrive in Boston were women. They were imprisoned for five weeks before being banished."

"Did you know them?" John asked.

"Yes. They were just like us, seeking guidance on how to live a good life, looking for answers to questions that have no final answer in this life."

Tristram realized that he was rambling on now for his own benefit. The faces of the boys expressed their bewilderment. He reminded himself that his older son was only fourteen. He wasn't much older than that when he was apprenticed to Bursley as a seaman. All the father figures in his life, his own father, Bursley, and now Upsall, were dead. For a moment he felt like an orphan left alone to make his way in life. He shook himself back to the present moment.

"That's how things were in Boston. Then about five years ago King Charles ordered an end to the persecution. Now in most places Quakers can hold meetings without fear of being punished. Like the one you attended without my permission."

The boys looked at each other as if they were unsure whether this was a reprimand or simply a statement of fact.

"Did you rescue any other Quakers?" John asked. He seemed to have taken over the role of interrogator.

"Your grandfather, the minister, asked me once to smuggle some Quakers out of Oyster River," Tristram said, disarmed by the question. "I suppose you might call that a rescue."

"Did grandfather like Quakers?"

"He respected them, and he was opposed to the persecution they had to endure because of their beliefs."

"Are you a Quaker?"

Tristram laughed. He had asked himself that question on occasion in recent years. He had yet to answer it to his own satisfaction. Yet he had to frame a reply that would satisfy his son without transplanting the doubt and resistance that lingered in his own mind.

"Quakers have a simple unfettered approach to religion and to God that I find attractive," he said. "But many of them have been disruptive in their efforts to convince others that God still speaks directly to man through the spirit. I refuse to deny the need for ministers. I suppose I got that from your grandfather."

He wondered how much of this they understood. Religion was not as important a factor in their lives as it had been in his. They were free to assess Quaker beliefs on their merit and without bias.

"Did you like the Quaker meeting you went to?" he asked.

The boys exchanged looks, as if uncertain how to respond. Joseph finally undertook to answer the question.

"The people just sat on benches and waited for the spirit to speak to them. I listened as hard as I could, but I never did hear any voice inside me. Maybe the spirit only speaks to certain people."

"I haven't heard it either," Tristram said.

"Is Mother a Quaker?" Joseph asked.

"What makes you think that?"

"Some Sundays we don't go to services. Mother says we can talk to God wherever we are. Is the spirit speaking to her?"

Tristram doubted that Blanche was in touch with her inner spirit, at least not the one Quakers had in mind. But who was he to judge?

"Quakers say the spirit speaks to everyone," he said. "Some people don't hear it because they don't pay attention. You have to be real quiet and listen real hard."

Both Joseph and John appeared to be satisfied with that response. Tristram felt it advisable to change the subject.

"Now that you've been to sea and visited another colony, have you any better idea about what you want to do when you grow up?"

"I want to have a farm and grow things," Joseph said, "and I'm going to take part in town affairs, just like you do."

Tristram was currently a selectman in Barnstable. He had served on several juries and acted as agent for the town in the purchase of land from the Indians. Though he would have liked his older son to take over the trade he had established among the colonies, he voiced no objection to his choice of an occupation. There was still John, who had always shown an interest in ships and the sea.

"And what about you?" he asked the younger boy. "Do you want to be master of a merchant ship like your father?"

John nodded vigorously. His brow furrowed, and he appeared lost in thought. Then he looked up at Tristram and smiled.

"I want to be a Quaker," he said.

NEW ENGLAND RISING

A Novel of Conflict and Resistance
in the Colonies

One

"You might kill your own brother."
(Plymouth Colony, Late Autumn 1675)

John Hull, twenty-one years of age and a mariner by trade, opened the door of his modest cottage in Barnstable to a man he recognized as the local constable. "What brings you here so early in the morning?" he asked.

"The authorities in Plymouth have ordered the town to provide twelve men for a campaign against King Philip and his cutthroat band of Indians. I trust we can rely on you to defend the colony."

John was more attuned to life at sea than to events on land, and the summons took him by surprise.

"How long will the campaign last?" he asked.

"A month or two. No one knows for sure."

"When do I have to report?"

"Friday morning at the training field. Bring your flintlock and powder and enough provisions for three days."

"Where will we be going?"

John smiled at his use of the plural. The constable was old and bent, well suited for the role of messenger; but he would never pass muster as a militiaman.

"You'll find that out when you report."

"Who's in charge of the local militia?"

"Captain John Gorham."

John frowned. "I'll be there," he said.

The constable repeated the time and place of the muster, then strode off toward town at a pace that belied his age.

John watched until he was out of sight. His mind was a jumble of thoughts. His legs were better attuned to maneuvering the deck of a schooner than to trekking over fields and through forests. As mate on a merchant ship sailing out of Boston, his concerns were with cargo, weather, and dreams of one day being master of his own vessel. He knew little about the trouble that had started that summer when Philip's warriors burned the settlement at Kickemuit. More attacks had occurred since then. He wasn't sure how many.

He shut the door of the rude one-room cottage that was his abode on land. His quarters aboard the ship were less spacious, but more congenial to one of his temperament. When ashore he felt separate from the world around him. No one relied on his knowledge and skill. He was less of a man.

"Who was that?" his sister Mary asked.

Her question recalled John to the present. She sat by the hearth, where a blazing fire dispelled the chill in the autumn air. She was eight years his senior, slight in stature, with brown hair. She had married a Quaker named Joseph Holway. They had five children and lived in the neighboring town of Sandwich. But whenever she was in Barnstable visiting their mother, she checked on whether he was at home or off at sea.

"A messenger," John said. "I've been summoned to serve in the militia. I have three days to get ready."

"What of thy obligations on the ship?"

"It's undergoing repairs in Boston. We sail for England in March."

"Will thou be back in time?"

"He said a month or two. If the campaign lasts much longer than that, I'll pack up and come home."

"How do thou feel about going off to fight Indians?" Mary asked.

"We've always had good relations with the local Mashpee tribe," John said. "Father negotiated with them for a number of land purchases. I've no quarrel with the Indians, but I have a duty to defend the colony."

"Our peaceful nature comes from Father. He never joined the Society, but he went to jail for supporting Friends who were being persecuted by the authorities in Plymouth."

"That may be, but I owe a good deal of it to your example," John said.

Mary smiled in acknowledgment. "I see no need for this conflict. Governor Winslow could have tried harder to keep the peace or at least limited the fighting to just one tribe."

"How do you know so much about it?"

"We're friendly with Robert Harper. I've told you about him. When they hanged William Leddra for being a Quaker, he caught the body as it was cut down from the gallows and arranged for a decent burial. He's active in the Society and keeps abreast of what goes on in the colony."

"Something else troubles me," John said. "John Gorham has been placed in charge of the local militia."

"The man who assaulted Mother?"

John nodded. "I hardly know the man, but the thought of serving under him in this campaign makes me uncomfortable."

"Better thou than thy brother," Mary said. "Joseph speaks nothing but ill of Gorham."

"Having Mother in the same house is a constant reminder. I want to talk to Joseph before I report."

"Will thou mention Gorham?"

"His name is sure to come up," John said. "But your point is well taken. I'm the right person for this task."

Later that day after Mary had departed, he reflected on her comment about Gorham. The assault had occurred some twenty years earlier. He was two years old at the time. It had always struck him as odd that his mother was ordered to pay a heavier fine for failing to cry out when assaulted than Gorham paid for pleading guilty to the assault. He came in time to realize that there must have been a liaison between them, but the subject was never mentioned among members of the family. He wondered how much Mary knew about it.

* * *

Blanche Hull greeted her younger son with a warm embrace. She saw him only for brief periods between his voyages to England, and his visits were a welcome surprise. At fifty she had gray hair and walked with a slight limp, the result of a hip injury.

"John! I'm glad to see you. Mary said you were home."

"Just while the ship is undergoing repairs," John said.

"Come in. Joseph will be back soon, but Mary is still here."

"I need to talk to Joseph."

"Is something wrong?" Blanche asked.

"No. I just want to settle something in my mind."

"Shall I make some hot cider while you wait?"

"I'd like that," John said.

Mary emerged from a back room. "I'll make the cider while thou talk with John," she said.

Blanche considered inviting him into her bed chamber, where they could speak in private. That addition to the house was bequeathed to her by her husband in his will. She was grateful to Tristram for providing her with a degree of separation. Joseph had inherited the rest of the house and the land surrounding it.

John sat down at the long table. Blanche took a place opposite him She hated the onset of winter. Tristram had died in December. He was her first love, the man who saved her from disgrace and gave her five children. The three girls were happily married. Neither John nor Joseph seemed so inclined, but they were still in their twenties. She didn't blame them for waiting. Tristram was eighteen when he married her, but that was under different circumstances.

"How long will you be home?" she asked.

"We sail for England in March," John said.

"Be sure to stop by occasionally for a meal."

"I'll be glad to. How are you and Joseph getting on?"

The question caught Blanche off guard. She assumed he must discuss such matters with his brother, but he had never raised the issue so openly.

"Why do you ask?"

"I was wondering what you'll do if Joseph gets married."

"What gave you that idea? Do you know something I don't?"

Mary set the pan of cider on a rack by the hearth to warm. "I know of no woman in his life," she said, "but it's bound to happen one day."

"When that day comes," Blanche said, "I'll just have to make peace with his wife. I have nowhere else to go. Besides, I have a right to stay in this house for as long as I live."

"I'm sure Joseph has no intention of putting thee out," Mary said.

"Enough of this. I'll deal with that when the time comes."

When Joseph returned, Blanche set about preparing a meal while the men conversed at the table; but she attended closely to what they said. Mary moved about as her interest in their talk dictated.

"I've been summoned to serve in the militia," John said after the brothers had greeted each other.

"I thought ship officers were exempt," Joseph said.

John laughed. "Only the master of the ship is exempt. What I want to know is, why are we still fighting Indians? I thought we defeated King Philip's tribe and forced him to flee."

"That's true. But Metacom, or King Philip as we call him, has joined up with the Nipmucks and tribes in Connecticut. They burned homes at Springfield, and sixty men were ambushed and massacred at Bloody Brook."

"It's a shame," John said, bowing his head. "We've always been on good terms with the Indians hereabouts."

"That's all over. All Indians are now under a cloud of suspicion."

"Why doesn't Governor Winslow seek aid from the King?" John asked. "A company of British regulars could end this uprising. Calling on militia to respond to each attack just drags things out."

"Winslow and Governor Leverett in Massachusetts fear that asking for help from England will compromise their authority."

"I question that," John said. "The talk in London is that King Charles has drained the royal treasury in his war with the Dutch. And he's busy securing his throne against a rising tide of Catholic influence. He has little time or interest in the American colonies."

"Winslow is largely responsible for this trouble with the Indians," Mary broke in. "His demands that they turn in their weapons and give up title to their lands stoked resentment and suspicion on both sides."

"You can't blame Winslow for what's going on," Joseph said. "He and Leverett are simply defending the colonies."

"I blame him for the way friendly Indians are being treated."

"What do you mean?" John asked.

Mary was eager to explain. "A peaceful community of praying Indians, people we persuaded to become Christians have been isolated on Deer Island in Boston harbor, where they may die from cold and starvation. When John Eliot defended them, he was threatened with death. I don't justify what some tribes have done, but this suspicion of all Indians will only prolong the war."

"It can hardly be called a war," Joseph said.

"Call it what thou will," Mary said. "It's been going on for six months and seems to be spreading."

"That's because all Indians are savages at heart."

"Many tribes are still loyal to the colony."

"They want protection from their enemies, and it's in their interest to trade with us. Now their true nature has been revealed. We have no choice but to drive them back."

"John has reservations about that," Mary said.

"I'm willing to serve," John said, "but I'll make a poor soldier. I can't see myself killing anyone."

"You might get someone to take your place," Joseph said.

John ignored the suggestion. "That's not all that concerns me. Gorham is in command of the militia."

Blanche stopped stirring the pot of stew.

Joseph broke the silence that ensued. "He's an experienced officer."

"It's just that serving under him will be awkward," John said.

Blanche stood straight, the spoon in her hand. "If you're referring to what happened years ago," she said, "I have better things to think about."

"We can discuss Gorham later," Joseph said. "I'm hungry, and that stew smells wonderful."

"There's something else you should know," Blanche said.

Her face was flushed as she faced them. She paused, aware that all eyes were fixed on her. Did she want to reveal what she had kept secret so long? What did she hope to gain? Joseph had made up his mind about Indians, but there was hope for John. He was the one called to serve.

"When I was young, I served a family in Sandwich," she said, looking at John. "They sent me out into the woods to pick wild berries. One day I chanced upon an Indian. He forced himself on me, and I got pregnant."

She paused to measure the effect of her words. Her sons stared at her, their mouths open. Mary calmly ladled stew into pewter bowls and set them on the table. She appeared to know what was coming. Had Tristram said something to her before he died?

"The family threatened to cast me out, and I was frightened. I hardly knew your father. He would visit them on occasion, and he always spoke kindly to me. I decided to tell him my plight, not expecting him to do anything. I had to tell someone. He offered to marry me, likely out of pity more than love; but he spared me the shame of bearing a bastard son."

Blanche paused again. No one spoke.

"Tristram convinced me to give up my baby. He arranged for someone in the Mashpee tribe to take him in. I never saw him again."

"Why are you telling us this?" John asked.

"You're going to fight Indians. I want you to know that you might kill your own brother."

"Little chance of that," Joseph said. "The Mashpee tribe is loyal."

"You just said all Indians are under suspicion."

Joseph had no immediate response.

"Do you know anything else about our brother?" John asked.

"Your grandfather, the minister, insisted that the baby be baptized before we gave him up. We called him Christopher. I don't know what name the Indians gave him."

"That's all very well," Joseph said, "but if I meet an Indian in battle, I won't stop to ask his name or religion before I shoot."

"I'm glad you told us," John broke in before Blanche could reply.

"We should try to find him," Mary said.

"Now that you know," Blanche said, "do what you will."

"We can decide that after I get back," John said.

"It's quiet this time of year," Joseph said. "I can go in your place. You and Mary can look for our lost brother while I'm away."

"Thanks for the offer, but it's best that I report on Friday," John said.

* * *

The first flakes of snow were falling as the brothers climbed the hill behind the house. Now that the trees were bare, John could see the slate grey waters of the bay. Beyond the northern horizon workers at a shipyard in Boston were repairing the mizzenmast of his ship damaged in a November gale. It struck him that if he were injured in this campaign, he might be unable to sail for England in March. He banished the thought as unworthy of a mariner. If it was his destiny to be injured, it would be at sea.

"So you're concerned about serving with Gorham," Joseph said.

"I'm not sure how to deal with him," John said. "Do I pretend to know nothing about what happened between him and Mother?"

"It's Gorham's problem. Let him worry about it."

"But what do I say if he brings it up?"

"That depends on how you feel about it."

"I want to forget what he did to Mother."

"I wish I could," Joseph said, "but you can only forget what's past."

"What do you mean?"

"Mother is still seeing him on occasion."

"Are you sure of that?"

"I live with her," Joseph said. "I can tell when they've been together, and I hate it. Gorham has a wife and children. Whichever one of them keeps it going, it's not right."

"What does Mary say about that?"

"If she knows, she doesn't talk about it."

"I'll just try to avoid Gorham," John said.

"He's likely to do the same," Joseph said.

They walked back toward the house. Joseph's arms swung in cadence with his stride. John's hands were clenched behind his back.

"What do you think of our Indian brother?" Joseph asked.

"We should try to find him, but I don't want Mary to get involved."

"I was joking about that."

"I'm afraid she took you seriously."

"We have to think about how the Indian will feel," Joseph said. "He probably knows nothing about his birth. Telling him he has a white mother won't improve his standing in the tribe. It's best to leave it alone."

"You could be right. I'll think about it."

"You do that," Joseph said. "My mind is made up."

* * *

John walked his sister to the barn, where her horse was tethered. "Be careful on the ride home," he cautioned her.

"Thou needn't worry," she said. "The Indians hereabout are friendly."

"Did you know we had an Indian brother?" John asked.

"A half-brother," Mary said. "When all this trouble with the Indians started, Mother said she had something to tell me if I swore to keep it to myself. I told her I couldn't swear to anything. She said it wasn't important and could wait. But when she mentioned the Indian and getting pregnant, I remembered something Father said about Mother having a child before they were married."

"From what she told us, it seems that the Indian raped her."

"Most likely she feared for her life and felt she had to submit."

"Maybe that's what stopped her from crying out when Gorham assaulted her," John said. "We should ask her."

"Some questions are best left unasked," Mary said.

"You never told me what you saw that night."

"No, and I see no good reason to tell thee now."

"I ought to know what happened in case Gorham brings it up."

Mary unhitched her horse, leaving John to wonder whether she was deliberating or ignoring him. Saddle in hand, she turned toward him.

"I think Gorham pleaded guilty of assault to spare her and himself."

"You mean they committed adultery?"

"I was only ten at the time. I no longer have a clear picture, but I remember thinking it didn't look like he was assaulting her."

John realized that he had to satisfied with that explanation. "At least Gorham was the only one," he said.

"I'm not so sure. She wasn't a widow very long."

"You mean Hedge was already on the scene before Father died?"

Mary ignored the question. "I don't blame her for marrying again. She had four children to provide for."

"Did Hedge really leave her only twelve pence in his will?"

Mary laughed. "It makes for a good story. Hedge claimed that Mother abandoned him, but she had good cause for leaving. He refused to accept her children in his home. He already had a raft of children by his first wife. Mother didn't stay long enough to remember how many."

"Did Father know she was unfaithful?" John asked.

"He never said anything, but he must have suspected."

"I suppose he put up with it for our sake."

"He was guilty as well," Mary said. "With Tami, the slave girl he brought back from Barbados to care for us when we were young. I got that from Mother."

"I hardly remember Tami from that time," John said. "I met her years later when Father took Joseph and me with him to Newport."

Mary proceeded to saddle her horse, while John looked on in silence.

"Joseph thinks Mother is still meeting Gorham," he said.

"I'm too far away to know about that," Mary said. "I doubt he cares very much what she does."

"You're wrong. He told me he hates it. Do you think he'd do Gorham some harm, if he had a chance?"

"Joseph is inclined to act on impulse. He might well seize upon an opportunity to get revenge."

"Maybe that's why he offered to take my place."

"He was being kind. He knows thou are already a Quaker at heart. I'll convince thee yet to join our Society. And Joseph as well."

"I'm afraid he's a hopeless case," John said.

"Don't be too sure. I have a plan in mind."

Mary failed to elaborate, and John did not press the issue. "Are you serious about trying to find our Indian brother?" he asked.

"I am indeed. We'll search for him when thou return."

"What if we find him? He was brought up as an Indian. He may resent being told he's something else."

"I just want to know whether or not he's alive. We can decide what to do afterwards."

Mary swung herself into the saddle. Seated astride the horse, she smiled down at him as if the matter were settled.

"I know a couple of Indians," John said. "I can ask them if they know anything, but I doubt that I'll learn very much."

"Someone in the tribe may remember what happened," Mary said. "Indians have long memories."

"I'll see what I can find out," John said.

He chose to ignore her desire to participate in the search.

* * *

On Friday morning John made his way to the training field, a flat plot of land on the edge of town set aside for drilling militia. The weather had turned milder, but he wore a heavy coat in anticipation of cold days ahead. In addition to a flintlock and powder, he carried a pack with provisions slung over his shoulder. Arriving at the field, he looked about to see who else had been recruited for the campaign. Then he spotted his brother.

Joseph sat with his back against a tree. His weapon and equipment were piled beside him. He appeared to be dozing, but he opened his eyes as John approached. "Hello, brother," he said. "I've been expecting you."

"What are you doing here?" John asked.

"I'm taking your place. You said you'd make a poor soldier. They need men who are ready and willing to fight."

"I had some doubts, but I'm here and ready to serve."

"You can go home. I'm better suited for this task."

"You might have told me what you planned to do," John said.

"I didn't want an argument."

"I hope you're not doing this to settle your grudge against Gorham."

"Where did you get that idea?"

"If you hate it that he still sees Mother, you must hate him too."

"I wouldn't call it hate. I'm just bitter against both of them. But I'm here to fight Indians. How I feel about Gorham has nothing to do with it."

"Would you revenge yourself on him, if you had a chance?"

"I hadn't thought about it. I suppose I might."

"Then I won't let you do this."

"It's too late. I'm already on the rolls. You can look for our Indian brother while I'm away."

John made no attempt to hide his relief. On his way to the training field he had tried in vain to picture himself in the act of killing an Indian. Joseph's tone was not accusing, and he much preferred the challenge of finding a lost brother, or half-brother.

"You said that was a bad idea."

"That's how I feel, but it will take your mind off Gorham."

"Do you know where you'll be going?" John asked.

"All I know so far is that we're joining up with other militia from the colony in Taunton," Joseph said.

"Are you sure you want to do this?"

"I wouldn't be here if I weren't sure. Go home, John. Look in on Mother while I'm away. She'll be worried about me."

Joseph rose, gathered up his equipment, and strode off to where the militiamen were gathering about Gorham. John watched him go, then turned and retraced his steps toward home.

Two

"Take heart, men! They're almost out of powder!"
(Narragansett Country, December 1675-76)

The second of December was designated a day of prayer in the United Colonies. The next day twelve militiamen from Barnstable set out, along with two Indians who had volunteered as scouts. At Taunton they rendezvoused with other groups of Plymouth militia, then moved on to the Seekonk River to join forces with militia from the Massachusetts Colony.

Joseph was surprised to learn that the entire force was under the command of Governor Josiah Winslow. A son of the first governor of the Plymouth Colony, his attitude toward Indians was well known and markedly different from that of his father. Whereas Edmund Winslow had sought the cooperation and loyalty of the native populace, a policy carried on by his successors Bradford and Prence. Josiah distrusted all Indians, even those who were loyal to the colony and those who had embraced the Christian religion.

Joseph didn't question Winslow's decision to ship several hundred noncombatant Indians to Spain to be sold as slaves, even though they had been assured of amnesty. The tender feelings expressed by his sister Mary were only laudable in times of peace. The size of the force gathered at the Seekonk River convinced him

548

that he was about to engage in a genuine war. The fewer Indians he had to face, the better.

His reflections were cut short by a summons from General Winslow to muster for instructions. The general was on horseback as he addressed the body of men from Plymouth Colony.

"We have but two companies of militia from Plymouth, but we are not alone in this endeavor. We shall fight alongside four hundred brave men from Massachusetts and three hundred from Connecticut. A thousand militia will take part in this grand effort to defeat our common enemy. My aides in this campaign are Samuel Moseley and Benjamin Church. Both of them are thoroughly familiar with Indians and their ways. We know that Metacom has been busy enlisting the support of other Indian tribes in attacks on settlements throughout the United Colonies. Many colonists have lost their homes or their lives in these attacks. It has become abundantly clear that his goal is to foment a general uprising against us."

Winslow paused, wheeling his horse about before resuming. Joseph was in the forefront of men listening to his words. He nodded approvingly. So far he was in agreement with all the general said.

"The greatest threat now facing the United Colonies is the likelihood that the Narragansett nation will join in this general uprising of Indians. In that event we shall be hard-pressed to defend ourselves and may well be driven back to the boats that brought us to these shores. Our mission is to forestall that possibility. If anyone thinks the Narragansetts have shown no hostility toward us, I can assure you that is not the case. They are providing a refuge for Indian women and children, and many of their warriors are fighting alongside the Nipmucks and other hostile tribes."

He paused again as if to let his words sink in. "We have reliable information that hundreds of their warriors are gathered in a rude fort in the Narragansett country, which lies between the colonies of Rhode Island and Connecticut. We'll proceed to Smith's garrison in Wickford and join forces with the militia from Connecticut. If we take the Indians by surprise, we can accomplish our purpose with little loss of life. I expect every man to fight bravely, and I trust we shall all return to homes that are forever secure from Indian attack."

The men near Joseph murmured their assent, and several cheered as Winslow concluded his remarks. Joseph did neither. A surprise attack by a thousand militia was clearly impossible. His weather sense told him more snow was on the way, and he envisioned a long arduous march. They would be cold and tired, while the Indians would be fresh and warm behind the walls of their fortress, however rude.

* * *

It was snowing steadily as the militia from the Massachusetts and Plymouth colonies reached Providence. Roger Williams came out to confer with Winslow. Huddled against the driving snow, he appeared smaller in stature than the mythic figure Joseph had pictured since childhood. Word spread that Winslow had rejected a request by Williams to await the outcome of further negotiations with the Narragansetts, insisting that his militia press on to their destination at Smith's Garrison.

On the way to Wickford the militiaman ahead of Joseph tripped on something buried in the snow. Joseph helped the man to his feet. He was in pain, having sprained an ankle; and he leaned heavily on Joseph for support.

They had taken no more than a dozen steps, when orders came from above to "Leave him and move on!"

Joseph looked up at the older uniformed man on horseback. Gorham gave no sign of recognition.

"If we leave him here, he'll freeze to death," Joseph said.

"He can make his way back to Providence."

"I can go along and make sure he's all right. I'll catch up with the company at Smith's Garrison."

"Let him get there on his own," Gorham said.

"I'll be all right," the injured man said. "I just need to rest my ankle."

"It's a long way back to Providence," Joseph said.

"That's his concern," Gorham said, prodding his steed. "Move on."

Joseph did as he was ordered. Glancing back, he saw the injured man seated with his leg drawn up. He was rubbing the ankle with his bare hand. His flintlock rested against the shoulder bag he had placed beside him. He waved to Joseph, then resumed rubbing. Gorham rode ahead, his horse barely visible in the driving snow. Joseph uttered a curse, then plodded on.

When the militia reached Smith's Garrison, word awaited them that Bull's Garrison a dozen miles to the south, where they were to join up with militia from Connecticut, had been attacked and burned. When Winslow's forces reached the burned-out garrison, they received more bad news. The supply ships that were supposed to meet them had not arrived. Short of provisions and deprived of shelter, Winslow ordered an attack on the Narragansett fort the next morning.

Joseph got little sleep that night. His bed was the frozen ground, his blanket a fresh layer of snow. At five in the morning the combined force of nearly a thousand militiamen set out. An Indian named Peter offered to guide them to the Indian fortress hidden in the depths of a great swamp. Winslow assured his men that the frozen earth would provide easy access, but there was considerable grumbling in the ranks.

"I don't call wallowing in snow up to my knees easy."

"By the time we get there, we'll be too tired to fight."

"All I want is a good meal and a warm bed."

"I hope Winslow knows what he's doing."

The Plymouth company under Gorham kept to high ground, where the snow was less deep. But this prolonged the march, and it was early afternoon before they reached the swamp. Dense undergrowth slowed further progress. Some Indians were sighted, but they vanished without an exchange of shots.

"So much for a surprise attack," a man near Joseph muttered.

Ordered to press on into the swamp, Joseph bulled his way through the underbrush. He assured himself that the scales were weighted in their favor. The militia from Plymouth and Massachusetts had been augmented by three companies from Connecticut and a hundred Pequot warriors, natural foes of the Narragansetts. Indians defending the fort lacked sufficient powder to ward off a sustained assault by such a large force. At least that was the message that came down from Winslow. Joseph had no reason to doubt it.

The Massachusetts militia led the way, followed by the men from Plymouth. Joseph's first view of the fortress brought him to a halt. He stood for a moment in awe of what the Indians had constructed, what Winslow had set out to capture. The campaign seemed at that instant almost foolhardy.

A palisade wall of tree trunks some twenty feet high surrounded the fort, which was located on an island in the midst of the swamp. At each corner was a tower made of tree limbs, from which defenders could fire upon anyone attempting to scale the walls. In front of the fort was a moat and a thick hedge of clay and brush. Massive tree trunks laid across the frozen moat provided access to the entrance gate. A frontal assault on the fort might succeed, but at what cost in lives?

Winslow had apparently reached the same conclusion. He ordered the Massachusetts militia to fan out in an arch, while the men from Plymouth stationed themselves at the rear of the fort to cut off the avenue of escape.

From his position at the rear the fort appeared to Joseph somewhat less formidable. The palisade and hedge barrier extended to the back, but he could make out a section of the wall where the logs were horizontal and only shoulder high. Several men at a time might mount this barrier and enter the fort. Did this gap serve a purpose, he wondered, or was the fort unfinished?

Winslow had moved to the rear and was consulting with two men, whom Joseph took to be Church and Mosely. No doubt they were pondering the same question. They parted company and moved out of his view.

Their decision was soon apparent. Two companies of Massachusetts militia took up positions and attempted to storm the gap at the rear of the fort. Both captains leading the charge fell as they scaled the barrier. Several men made it over the logs, but a withering volley from the towers that flanked the rear wall forced the militia to fall back.

A second assault on the gap proved no more successful. Crouched behind a tree, Joseph fired at cracks in the nearest tower. When all appeared hopeless, a group of militia from Plymouth managed to capture one of these structures, which allowed them to fire directly into the fort. Encouraged by this success, Winslow called upon the Connecticut militia to launch an attack on the gap. They succeeded in removing part of the log barrier, and a fair number penetrated the fort.

A cry went up. "Church is calling for volunteers! It's now or never!"

Without giving the matter any thought, Joseph joined a group of men gathered around Benjamin Church. He knew Church only by reputation, as a leader who had escaped the Indian ambush at Stony Brook without a single casualty, a man who had dissuaded two chieftains from aligning themselves with King Philip, a man who knew what he was doing.

A number of Indians had left the fort and were firing at militia from among the trees. On Church's command the small group of volunteers took up positions behind these Indians. His orders were passed along the line.

"Wait 'til they stand, and you'll have a brave shot."

Joseph fired with the rest. A number of Indians fell. The others fled in confusion, many of them back into the fort. Church ordered his men to follow. To Joseph's surprise, the entrance gate at the front was now open. Once inside the fort the band of men ran unopposed through a maze of tents and other primitive structures. No women or children were in evidence.

The fleeing Indians took refuge in a blockhouse that faced the gap in the rear wall of the fort. Crouched behind a tent, Joseph realized why the first two assaults had failed. Men trying to scale the log barrier were an easy target. The space between the blockhouse and the gap was littered with bodies of the dead and injured. But most of the logs had now been removed. Militia entering the fort by that route were greeted only with sporadic volleys from the blockhouse.

"Take heart, men! They're almost out of powder!" Church cried out.

While awaiting further orders, Joseph took stock of his surroundings. The area behind the blockhouse and extending to the front wall of the fort was a veritable sea of tents and rude huts. Some militia were fighting Indians among these dwellings. He turned his attention to the blockhouse. From his vantage it appeared to be vulnerable. Built of limbs like the corner towers of the fort, it was elevated on wooden poles to provide good visibility for the defenders. But the poles were slender and spaced too far apart. He judged the structure to be rather unstable and was not surprised at Church's next order.

"Get under the blockhouse and put your shoulders to it! We can bring it down!"

As Joseph stood up to carry out the order, he saw Church clutch his groin and fall. He and several others rushed to his side.

"I'm all right," Church said. "Bring down that damn blockhouse."

Two men dragged Church out of the line of fire. Joseph joined the group of men under the blockhouse. The firing was now sporadic, and some Indians were shooting arrows. Church's men put their full weight against the poles supporting the structure. Joseph heard a loud crack as the poles split and the blockhouse crashed to the ground.

He joined in the cheer that went up, but his satisfaction was short-lived. A man next to him fell with an arrow in his back. Turning quickly, Joseph saw that several Indians had emerged from the toppled blockhouse. One of them with bow raised appeared to be taking dead aim at him. Before he could react, he was pushed violently aside, lost his balance, and fell to the ground. Looking up, he saw one of the scouts who had volunteered to serve with the Barnstable militia. He was clutching an arrow that had lodged in his chest. Joseph raised his musket and fired at the Indian. His aim was true.

Joseph removed the arrow. The scout's eyes were glazed, and he had ceased breathing. Aware that he was in an exposed position, Joseph took cover. Church's band had regrouped and was firing at Indians as they emerged from the blockhouse. He made his way to where Church lay propped against the rear wall of the fort. His uniform was soaked with blood, but he was still giving orders.

"Get word to Winslow that the fort is ours. Tell him not to burn it. We need the food and shelter."

Joseph ran to the gap in the rear wall. He found Winslow and Mosely just outside the fort. In a tone intended to convey its urgency, he delivered Church's message.

"Church is wrong!" Mosely said. "Many Indians are still in the fort. They're hiding in the tents. We have to burn everything."

"Give the order!" Winslow commanded.

Joseph ran back to tell Church. He had it in his head that the wounded man might still manage to countermand Winslow's order.

He found Church barely conscious from loss of blood and unable to speak above a whisper.

The tents and other structures inside the fort were put to the torch. Militiamen fired at all who emerged, mostly women and children. Sickened by the slaughter, Joseph dropped his musket and sank to the ground. He wanted to weep, but no tears were forthcoming. He barely heard the cry that went up around him

"They're torching the walls! We have to get out of here!"

The palisade walls and the towers that flanked them were ablaze as he made his way out of the fort. Indians of all ages were slain as they fled into the swamp. Two men had carried Church to safety. As Joseph sought to rejoin his company, he spotted Gorham on foot and favoring his right leg.

"Are you hurt?" he asked.

"I took an arrow in my thigh during the battle," Gorham said.

"What happened to your horse?"

"I think an Indian stole it."

"Do you need help?"

Gorham laughed bitterly. "We all need help. God willing, we'll get it. Go on ahead. I'll be all right."

Winslow had given orders not to pursue the fleeing Indians. Cold and exhausted, Joseph and those around him had but one thought, to return to the safety and warmth of Smith's Garrison. It was already dusk, and a fourteen-mile march lay ahead of them. Once out of the swamp they found the snow in many places knee deep. With Winslow and a scout leading the way, they proceeded in single file, each man following in the tracks of the man ahead.

"I hope we're going in the right direction," Joseph remarked to the man behind him.

"Just keep your eye on the man ahead," was the reply.

Joseph gave no thought to pausing for rest. He knew that he had to keep moving in order to survive. Seeing that stragglers were being left to fend for themselves, he fell back in line to see how Gorham was holding up. He spotted him hobbling along, one hand on his injured thigh.

"I had a fall," Gorham said. "I think the wound is bleeding again."

"Let me have a look at it."

Gorham extended his leg. Someone had slit the pants and applied a bandage, the material held in place by a leather thong. A block of wood under the thong served to maintain pressure. The bandage had slipped, and blood was oozing from the wound. Joseph repositioned the bandage and fastened it in place, adding some strips from his own shirt.

"Who put on the bandage?" he asked.

"One of our Indian scouts."

"Can you keep going?"

"I'll make it, if I can stay on my feet."

"I'll keep an eye on you in case you need help."

"I should be up front leading our company," Gorham said, "not back here being nursed."

"We do what we can," Joseph said.

He fashioned a walking stick from a low-hanging limb and gave it to Gorham, then fell in behind the injured man. The thought struck him that, if Gorham were to die, it would be just punishment for how he treated Blanche. But any desire for revenge abated as he encouraged Gorham to keep moving forward. It was more important that they survive.

Gorham was managing better with the aid of the stick. With every hour and mile Joseph became more concerned about his own ability to keep plodding ahead in the cold and the darkness. The snow reflected some light from the sky, enabling him to keep those ahead of him in view. He lost track of the time. His one concern was to keep moving. He gave no thought to rest. He realized that once seated in the snow, he would be unable or unwilling to get up. It would be all too easy to fall asleep, never to wake again. He had no idea how close they were to their goal. The march seemed interminable. Perhaps they were lost, doomed to wander in the snow until they dropped from exhaustion.

Gorham was limping badly, and Joseph lent him an arm for support. Not fully conscious of his decision, he felt a need to aid Gorham to reach Smith's Garrison. Keeping watch on the wounded man's progress helped to take his mind off his own fatigue and aching limbs.

"Keep going! It's not much farther!" he urged, if Gorham faltered.

After what seemed an eternity, a cry went up along the line. Joseph made out the shape of buildings ahead. They had reached Smith's Garrison. He was ravenously hungry, but above all else he wanted to sleep. He could eat later.

* * *

On waking, Joseph scrounged up a few crusts of bread and some venison stew. Provisions at the garrison were in short supply. Only one ship had made it through the ice that clogged the northern part of the bay. Word spread that hundreds of Indians had died in the swamp fight and many others were prisoners. He saw no sign of prisoners. No one know where they were, but only the Plymouth militia had found refuge at Smith's Garrison.

Their first duty was to bury the dead. How their bodies had been transported to Wickford was a mystery to Joseph. Forty graves were dug just outside the garrison. The earth beneath the snow was soft enough to allow for proper burial. A brief ceremony accompanied the interment. The Indian who saved Joseph's life, a scout known only as Thomas, had been left behind in the fort. Joseph said a silent prayer for him as the dead were laid to rest.

The living were eager to go home, but Winslow was not yet satisfied that he had rendered the Narragansetts powerless to take part in the larger conflict. When he got word that a band of warriors who had survived the swamp fight were trekking north, presumably to join up with the Nipmucks in Massachusetts, he ordered his militia to pursue the fleeing Indians. The order was met with grudging consent or outright hostility.

"I've had enough," one man told Joseph. "Some of us are leaving for home tonight. You can join us, if you like."

"You mean you're going to desert?" Joseph asked.

"We did what we set out to do. We've buried too many men. We're cold and hungry. Winslow can't expect anything more from us."

"I want to go home as much as you do," Joseph said, "but I trust Winslow has a good reason for his decision."

"Reason or no reason, he's asking too much," the man said.

"Leave, if you like," Joseph said. "As for me, I'll go home when Winslow says our job is done."

The pursuit of the fleeing band of Indians proved futile. They were not eager to fight and easily evaded the militia. The weather continued cold and harsh. Short of supplies and unfamiliar with the terrain, the Plymouth militia were rewarded with nothing more than exhaustion, hunger, and low spirits. When Winslow ordered withdrawal, Joseph heaved a sigh of relief.

But their ordeal was not over. The long march back to their point of muster still lay ahead. Tired and hungry, they foraged what food they could from settlements along the way.

Upon arriving in Taunton, Winthrop disbanded the two companies of militia. Joseph joined a group of men on the road to Barnstable. Gorham's wound had been treated. He was again on horseback; but they had little contact along the way. Joseph got home late in January. He had been gone for nearly eight weeks.

Three

"His name Ataquin."
(Plymouth Colony, Winter 1675/6)

January arrived, and Mary had no further word from John about their half-brother. Had he lost interest in trying to locate him? If they were to mount a search before John sailed again for England and before Joseph returned from serving in the militia, she would have to take the initiative. During a break in the weather she paid a visit to her mother in Barnstable. She was greeted by John, who said he was fulfilling his promise to look after Blanche in his brother's absence.

"Have thou had any word from Joseph?" she asked.

"These campaigns can involve more than one battle," John said.

"Are thou not concerned about our brother?"

"Joseph can take care of himself."

Mary felt that he was seeking to reassure her, rather than believing it himself. She watched as he put another log on the fire in the hearth.

"Where's Mother?' she asked.

"She's resting in her chamber," John said.

"Then we can talk in private. Have thou learned anything about our half-brother?"

John stirred the embers until the flames shot up. "I had very little success," he said without looking at her.

Mary was silent, waiting for him to continue.

"I spoke with several Indians I know. None of them remembered a white child being raised by the Mashpee tribe."

"How old were the Indians thou spoke to?"

"My age, or a little older."

"We need to find someone who can recall what happened more than thirty years ago."

"Who might that be?"

"Every tribe has a wise man whose role is to remember past events and pass them on to the next generation. Sort of a tribal historian."

"Where do we find this wise man, if he exists?" John asked.

"It shouldn't be too hard. We can ask the chief."

"That won't be so easy. The Mashpee tribe only summers in this area. They're now in their winter home"

"Perhaps one of the Indians thou know can tell us where he is."

"I doubt that the chief will tell us anything. Joseph is right. The Indian we're looking for has no idea his mother was white. He may not want to know. Being a half-breed is no mark of honor."

"We needn't tell him. I just want to know where and who he is."

"I can ask a few more people," John said.

"Do it today. We can look for him before I return home."

"Doing this together is too dangerous and may complicate things."

"Indians respect women," Mary said. "They'll be more apt to answer our questions if I'm with thee."

John smiled. "You seem to have it all worked out," he said.

* * *

John's inquiries revealed that, although the Mashpee tribe had moved to its winter home, there was an Indian who stayed behind because he was too old to accompany them. The man John spoke to wasn't sure whether this old man was still alive.

"Where can I find him?" John asked.

"What you want with old man?" the Indian replied.

John wasn't given to lying, but he recognized the need for caution. "I have a question to ask him," he said. "It's a private matter."

The Indian proceeded to trace lines on the ground, explaining as he drew. John was familiar with the area south of Barnstable. As a boy he accompanied his father Tristram on a mission to purchase land from the Mashpee tribe, and he had traded knives or kettles with the Indians. The spot indicated was new to him. He asked a few more questions, then committed the crude map to memory.

Mary was eager to set out on their quest. "If this old man has the answers we want," she said, "we won't need to find the chief."

"You may be right," John said.

They set out on horseback early the next morning, warmly dressed and with provisions for three days. The territory to the south was wooded but relatively flat, and they made good progress. Upon sighting the ocean, they turned westward as directed. Within a mile of their goal they encountered an Indian on foot who was younger than they were. When John explained their mission, he agreed to lead them to the tribe's summer encampment.

A number of wetus in varying stages of disrepair formed a rough circle. Their outer coverings of reed mats had blown loose in the wind or disintegrated under the weight of the snow, exposing the framework of bent cedar poles. John noted open spaces where more wetus had stood. He recalled hearing that they could be disassembled and transported to another location.

Two of these mound-like dwellings were covered with overlapping strips of bark and appeared to be habitable. Their guide led them to the larger one and stood aside, beckoning them to enter. They had to bend low to get through the entrance. Straightening up, John saw an old Indian with a deeply wrinkled face. He sat cross-legged on a straw mat by the fire pit. His eyes were closed, and he appeared lost in meditation.

John started to speak, but Mary motioned for him to wait. Looking about, he saw that the interior walls of the wetu were lined with bullrush mats to preserve heat from the fire. A slightly raised platform along one side was covered with animal furs. He assumed this was where the Indian slept.

The old man had opened his eyes. He did not seem surprised at their presence. He motioned to them to sit by the fire pit and warm themselves. When they were seated, John produced a kettle made of iron and offered it to the Indian. The man turned it over in his hands, examining it from every angle. He nodded approvingly and set the kettle down at his feet.

"Why you come here?" he asked.

John glanced at his sister. Mary was ready with an answer.

"Many years ago my mother gave birth to a boy whose father was a Mashpee warrior. The child was raised as an Indian, and Mother never saw him again. We've come to learn about our brother, his name and whether he's still alive."

The old man appeared to ponder the request. "How many summers has your brother?" he asked at last.

"Thirty or more," Mary said.

"What name of your father?"

"Tristram Hull."

The Indian was silent. John wasn't sure if he was seeking to recall the past or deciding how to frame his reply. He glanced again at his sister. Mary appeared to be waiting calmly, unconcerned by the delay. He admired her attitude and was glad he had agreed to bring her along.

"I not free to speak about brother," the Indian said at last. "Must get word from chief."

"Where do we find the chief?" John asked

Mary gave him a reproving look. The old man just stared at him.

"If it is in thy heart to ask the chief to permit thee to speak," she said. "we shall await his answer."

The old man's features softened as he turned his attention back to Mary. "I send messenger to chief," he said.

"My brother and I thank thee," Mary said, rising to leave.

"He might at least have offered us food and shelter," John said when they were outside.

"Well he didn't, so we must make the best of it."

"Why won't he tell us where the chief is and have done with it?"

"He remembers our brother," Mary said. "He just needs permission to tell us what he knows."

"I'm sorry I interrupted you. It seemed like a reasonable question."

"It sounded like an order. No wonder the old man took offense."

"From now on I promise to keep my mouth shut."

"We need to find shelter," Mary said. "Perhaps the Indian who guided us to this place can help."

They found him in the other wetu that looked habitable. He appeared to be busy gathering equipment for his journey.

"I take message to chief," he said when he saw them. "You sleep here until I come back."

Mary thanked him. After he left, they ate some of the provisions they had brought along and settled in for the night. She felt one of the fur hides covering the spot where the Indian slept.

"These should keep us warm," she said, "but there's hardly room here for the two of us."

"You take the bed," John said. "I've slept on the ground before."

The next day Mary insisted on waiting until they were called. When the summons came, the old man motioned them to sit, then addressed Mary.

"I have memory of white man who come to us with baby. He brave man now in our tribe."

"Can you tell us his name and where he is?" Mary asked.

"Chief say it better I speak no more."

Mary was visibly disappointed. John started to speak but restrained himself. They thanked the old man and took leave of him.

"At least we know he's alive," Mary said as they prepared to return home. "That's something."

"We can do better than that," John said. "The messenger may know the name of the Indian he was sent to ask about."

"What makes you think he'll tell us?"

"Perhaps he can be persuaded."

John found him waiting to reclaim his dwelling. His body tensed as John approached. He appeared ready for whatever this white man might do.

John produced a hunting knife from his pack and offered it handle first to the Indian. "Take it," he said. "It's yours."

The man looked at it skeptically. "What you want?" he asked.

John laughed. "You're right. I do want something. You were sent to the chief to ask about an Indian in your tribe. I want to know his name."

"Old man say tell no one."

"This is between you and me. The old man will never know."

The Indian regarded the knife, then reached out and grasped it by the handle. His face brightened as he hefted the knife and made several swipes in the air. Then he held out the knife to John.

"I not want trouble with old man and chief," he said.

"I understand," John said amiably. "You can keep the knife."

The Indian was silent as he stared at the knife in his hand.

"His name Ataquin," he said as John turned to walk away.

* * *

John was with Blanche when his brother returned home. Joseph had a haggard look and appeared exhausted as he warmed himself at the hearth.

"Next time you can fight your own war," he declared.

"You said you were eager to fight Indians," John said.

"Indians yes, but the sight of women and children being slaughtered made me sick to my stomach."

"You mean you had to kill women and children?" Blanche asked.

"I watched. There was nothing I could do to stop it. When Winslow gave the order to burn the fort, the militia shot anyone trying to escape."

His voice broke, and he turned his head away.

"What kind of fort was it?" John asked after a moment of silence.

Joseph described in some detail the Indian fortress and the struggle required to capture it. There were tears in his eyes as he finished his narration. John waited for him to compose himself. Blanche had a sober look.

"The Narragansett tribe was neutral in this conflict," Joseph said. "They may have provided a haven for women and children of other tribes, but they didn't support Metacom openly. Now they're at war against us. No one knows how this will end."

"Will there be another call for militia?" John asked.

"There may be a call, but I for one don't intend to answer."

Joseph left the hearth and sat at the long table. His tone became more cheerful as he changed the subject.

"When do you sail for England?" he asked.

"Early in March. I hope the fighting will be over when I get back."

"I wouldn't count on it," Joseph said.

John decided to wait until his brother was more his customary self before he discussed the subject of their Indian half-brother. They were enjoying a tankard of ale at the local tavern.

"How did you get on with Gorham?" he asked.

"I resolved a good many things during the campaign," Joseph said.

He went on to describe the march back to Smith's Garrison. "Men who were injured and couldn't keep up froze to death. Gorham had a leg wound. I could have left him to die, but I didn't. I felt sorry for him. When you mentioned his name just now, I felt no anger or resentment. I've forgiven him for what happened to Mother. He wasn't solely to blame."

Joseph drained his tankard of ale and ordered another. "Now it's your turn," he said. "Did you locate our Indian brother?"

"We spoke with an old Indian," John said. "He remembered Father leaving a baby with the Mashpee tribe, but he would only say that the boy is now a man and one of the tribe. I did find out his Indian name. Does the name Ataquin mean anything to you?"

"I don't know many Indians," Joseph said. He lapsed into silence. His eyes appeared to be focused on some distant object. The tankard of ale rested on the table forgotten. John waited patiently for his brother to return.

"This campaign changed my attitude toward them. During the battle for the fort an Indian saved my life. He took an arrow that was meant for me. If it weren't for that Indian, I'd be dead."

"Who was he?" John asked.

"A scout who volunteered to go with us."

"He must have been from the Mashpee tribe," John said. "Do you know his name?"

"I had no chance to ask him," Joseph said.

A fit of laughter wracked his body as he repeated his last words. It gradually subsided, and he bowed his head and wept.

"I never spoke to him, and he died to save my life. Maybe that's why I couldn't leave Gorham to freeze to death."

"Is Gorham all right?" John asked.

"A surgeon said his wound is healing, but the long march home in the snow took a lot out of him. He wasn't quite himself the last time I saw him."

"We might visit him and see how he's doing," John said.

"You can go,"Joseph said. "I'm done with Gorham."

* * *

As Mary warmed herself at his hearth, John was struck by her serious demeanor. "I take it this is more than just a friendly visit," he said.

"Joseph told me about the Indian who saved his life," Mary said. "It made me think of Ataquin. It would be ironic if our newfound brother gave up his life to save Joseph."

"I had the same thought," John said.

"We have to make sure he's still alive," Mary said.

"How can we do that? All we know abut him is that he volunteered to accompany the militia as a scout."

"That may be enough."

"I don't understand."

"I want to visit Gorham, and I want thee to go with me."

"What can he tell us? He doesn't know what happened to Joseph."

"He was a captain in the militia. He may know the scout's name."

"He'll only know the name some white man gave him."

"That's a start. Let me warm up a bit before we go."

571

"It's too late in the day. You can rest here tonight, and we'll set out first thing in the morning."

Mary agreed. She had arrived on horseback. John had no horse, but he had a shed to shelter her steed. The next day after a trip to the local livery stable they set out for Gorham's house.

His wife Penelope appeared somewhat puzzled as she greeted them, but she ushered them without question to the chamber where Gorham lay propped up in bed.

"He has a fever," she said. "It's from his exposure on that march. He nearly froze to death."

Gorham's face was flushed, and he was breathing heavily. He seemed uncertain who they were. Mary calmly stated their relationship to Joseph.

"He asked about thy condition," she said.

"I owe my life to your brother," Gorham said. "Thank him for me."

"I will, but we're here for another reason too. We hope thou can tell us the name of an Indian who served as a scout for thy company of militia."

"What do you care about Indians or their names?" Gorham asked.

John winced at the question. Would Mary admit their mother had given birth to an illegitimate child, that their half-brother was a Mashpee Indian? Such matters should be kept within the family circle.

But she had a ready answer. "Joseph spoke of a scout who fought hard and was killed in the battle. If thou can identify him, we'll get word to the Mashpee chief about his bravery."

Gorham looked askance at Mary as if he doubted her explanation. "You say this Indian was a scout?" he asked.

"That's as much as Joseph could tell us about him," Mary said.

"We had two scouts. One of them helped to guide us to the garrison in Wickford after the battle. The other one, the one we called Thomas, must be the one who died."

"Do you know his Indian name?" Mary asked. "The chief may not recognize him as Thomas."

"I may have heard it. I don't remember," Gorham said. "These Indians have names you can't even pronounce."

Mary appeared unsure what to say next.

"Was it Ataquin?" John asked.

Gorham turned his head. "That sounds like it. I can't be sure."

His expression posed a question without framing the words.

"An Indian I know spoke about a warrior named Ataquin who served as a scout with the militia," John said. "His name just came to me as we were speaking."

Gorham appeared to accept his explanation. "Now that I think about it, I'm quite sure that was his name."

Mary was visibly shaken by his words, but Gorham was looking at John and appeared not to notice. "We thank thee for this information," she said, "and we hope thou will soon recover from this illness."

Gorham was seized by a fit of coughing. Penelope sprang to his side with a basin and a napkin. He brought up a large amount of green phlegm, and she went to dispose of it.

"I fear that may not be the case," Gorham said when she was out of hearing. "Now that you're here, I want to apologize for the trouble I caused your mother and your family. None of it was her fault."

"We accept thy apology, and we thank thee," Mary said.

John would have liked to continue the conversation, but he saw that the subject was making her uncomfortable. Gorham was coughing again as they left the house. Penelope shut the door behind them

"Do you believe what Gorham said about Mother?" John asked.

"He's near death," Mary said. "He told us the truth as he sees it."

"I think he decided that was why we were there, and he thought it was what we wanted to hear."

When Mary did not respond, he changed the subject.

"How will Joseph react when he learns that the Indian who saved his life was his brother?"

"We made that connection in our minds before we came," Mary said. "Joseph may have done the same. I'm more concerned about how Mother will take the news. She just learned that he was alive."

"She doesn't know we spoke to Gorham," John said.

"Perhaps we shouldn't tell her," Mary said.

Four

"It served no purpose and left me sick at heart."
(Plymouth Colony, Spring 1676)

Joseph was first to get word of Gorham's death. He passed the news on to Mary on her next visit. John was at sea on his way to England.

"When we spoke to him, he told us the affair with Mother was all his fault," Mary said. "John thinks he took the blame for our benefit."

"It no longer matters," Joseph said. "I made my peace with Gorham during the war."

"How is Mother taking it?"

"If she shed any tears, it was in her room."

"At least she has only one death to contend with," Mary said. "Unless thou told her about our half-brother."

"I've told her nothing, nor do I intend to. Are you here to see Mother, or have you some other purpose in mind?"

"Thou are right on both counts. We have a neighbor named Robert Harper. He's about Father's age. In some respects their lives have been much the same. I think thou should meet him."

"I gather from what you say that he's a Quaker."

"He is," Mary said. "He's been in prison for his beliefs."

"What business do I have with him?"

"Thou have much in common. He's opposed to this conflict, and he deplores the way some Indians are being treated."

"How I feel about Indians is personal, and I have no desire to join your Society."

"It will do thee no harm to talk to him," Mary said. "I can ask him to stop by when he's in Barnstable, if thou agree to receive him."

"If it will make you happy," Joseph said.

* * *

Robert Harper looked older than fifty. His forehead and cheeks were furrowed; not so much by weather, Joseph suspected, as by care. He moved with a degree of caution, but his eyes sparkled. His manner was gracious as he greeted Blanche. She bade the men to take a seat while she prepared a light repast, an offer Harper was glad to accept.

"I understand that thou took part in the recent campaign against the Narragansetts," he said as they faced each other across the long table. "I'd like to hear about thy experiences, if thou care to share them."

"What I experienced is personal," Joseph said.

"I respect thy feelings, but I've heard that hundreds of Indian women and children were killed in that battle. I hoped thou might confirm or deny those reports."

"I chose to serve in the militia. I must live with what I saw and did."

"This war affects us all, Indians as well," Harper said.

"Did Mary tell you our Indian half-brother died saving my life?"

"I know nothing of that," Harper said. He appeared pensive, as if he were restructuring his thoughts. "I also saw a man die, a man I regarded as my brother. It was some years ago, but I still think of him."

Joseph regarded his visitor with new respect. "You want to know what I did," he said. "I helped to capture an Indian fort in a swamp."

He went on to describe in some detail the attack on the fortress and the march back to the garrison in Wickford. "I volunteered to fight Indians," he concluded, "not to slaughter women and children."

"Who gave the order for the slaughter?" Harper asked.

"Winslow ordered us to burn the fort. I suppose the militia killed any Indian they saw in retaliation for our losses. Many of our men were ashamed afterwards of what they had done."

"Were thou also ashamed?"

"When I saw mothers and their babes killed as they fled the burning fort, I wept. I felt separate from what was happening around me. It served no purpose and left me sick at heart. I want no more of it."

Joseph brushed the tears from his eyes.

Harper waited for him to regain his composure. "Winslow's efforts to render the Narragansetts powerless had the opposite effect. Those Indians who survived have joined forces with the Nipmucks, and tribes that were neutral have rallied to Metacom's cause. Settlements in the Rhode Island and Massachusetts colonies have been burned, and hundreds of colonists are dead. Even Providence did not escape."

"I haven't kept up with the reports," Joseph said. "I just want to be left in peace, far apart from battles and killings."

"That is becoming ever more difficult," Harper said. "The Pequots and Mohegans are still Metacom's enemies; but if all the tribes were to unite, it would spell disaster for the colonies."

"When will it all end?"

"No one knows. Metacom no longer controls events. Even if he were to die, the fighting would go on."

Blanche set out cheese, some freshly baked bread, and two tankards of cider. Both men were quiet for a time as they ate.

"There's another aspect of this struggle that troubles me." Harper paused, as if he were asking for Joseph's permission to continue.

"What is that?"

"Many Indian captives are being sent to Bermuda or Spain and sold as slaves. Even women and children seeking refuge and protection have been enslaved. John Eliot has issued a warning that such practices will alienate tribes who are still loyal to us, but those in power appear to be consumed by a hatred for Indians. And slavery is profitable. I doubt that Winslow could put a stop to it, even if he had a mind to."

"I admit that I felt some hatred when I volunteered," Joseph said, "but the campaign against the Narragansetts has changed my attitude."

"Mary seems to think thou will join our Society one day."

Joseph laughed. "She would like that. I think she has her mind set on convincing me and my brother John to become Quakers."

"What are her chances of success?" Harper asked.

"My grandfather was ordained as an Anglican minister. My father was sympathetic toward Quakers, but he could never agree that ministers are of no use. A family tradition is hard to overcome."

"What is thy opinion of ministers?"

"I attend services sometimes, when I'm not busy on the farm; but I fall asleep during the sermon. I feel that I've heard it all before."

"Thou are already listening to thy inner voice," Harper said. "On thy next visit to Sandwich come with Mary to our meeting. Thy spirit may be telling thee something of great interest."

"I'll think about it," Joseph said.

* * *

In June Joseph was summoned to serve again in the militia.

"I served for two months this past winter," he told the constable.

"You took your brother's place. This summons is for you."

"I've had my fill of killing Indians. I must decline to serve."

"Will you hire someone to take your place?"

"I cannot ask someone else to do what I would not do myself. I'll accept whatever fine or punishment the authorities mete out."

"Is that your final decision?"

"It is," Joseph said.

As the constable walked away, it struck Joseph that the stand he had taken would likely change the course of his life. Had he acted on impulse, or was he truly committed to his position? He needed to talk to someone. John was in England, and Blanche would only smile and offer no comment. He decided to speak to Mary, aware that she would interpret his decision as a sign that he was ready to become a Quaker. Perhaps it would be wise to take her suggestion and talk to Harper as well.

* * *

Mary was pleased to see Joseph at her door. Before she could decide how to carry out the next phase of her plan, he made it easy for her.

"I need to speak with Harper."

"We're readying to go to meeting," Mary said. "I'm sure Harper will be there. Thou are welcome to join us."

Holway had come up beside her. He was a good husband and father, but retiring by nature. Mary wished the two men were closer friends. She was glad Joseph had taken to Harper. That was more important at the moment.

Holway claimed the two-mile walk to meeting fostered a receptive mood for heeding one's inner voice. He used his carriage only when Mary was pregnant. They had six children ranging in age from four to fourteen; but only the older ones accompanied them.

Harper was outside the meeting house when they arrived. As Mary had anticipated, his eldest daughter was with him. She allowed Harper to make the introduction, but she noted the spark of interest in Joseph's eyes as he shook hands with Experience.

They entered the meeting house together. Harper drew Joseph to the left of the partition where the men were seated, while Mary and Experience joined the women on the right. Once they were seated, Mary had no view of her brother. The unprogrammed meeting lasted two hours. Three men and a woman were moved by the spirit to speak. Mary found it difficult to attend to her inner voice. Her mind was busy devising ways to prolong the contact with Harper and his daughter without making her intentions too obvious.

Joseph again saved her the trouble. As they left the meeting house, he drew Harper aside. "I'd like a few words with you at some time," he said.

"If Mary is agreeable, thou are welcome to join us for the midday meal," Harper said. "My wife Prudence will be pleased to meet thee."

"I have no objection," Mary said, perhaps a little too eagerly.

"Then it's settled. My home is a mile in the opposite direction."

"That is no obstacle," Joseph said.

With a nod to his sister, he set off with Harper. Experience followed behind with her mother. Taking her husband's hand, Mary headed for home.

* * *

"We can talk as we go," Harper said.

Joseph glanced back at Experience and Prudence.

"Thou can speak freely," Harper said. "My wife and daughter are all too well acquainted with the ways of the world."

"When we last spoke," Joseph said, "I told you my attitude toward Indians had changed and that I wanted no more of this ongoing conflict with Metacom. I've just refused to respond to a summons to serve again in the militia. I don't regret my decision, but it raises some questions in my mind. I know Quakers are opposed to violence on principle, but what is one to do in the present circumstances? How can a man refuse to defend his family and his home against Indian attacks?"

"Thou raise a thorny question," Harper said. "George Fox and other leaders in our Society don't advocate violence, but neither do they proscribe it. Every man must follow the dictates of his inner spirit in that regard. I too am of a mind that the killings thou described were wrong, and that violence must be avoided whenever possible. But we all have a natural inbred desire to defend ourselves and those we love."

"Then how can we refuse to fight in defense of those settlers who are in danger of losing their property and their lives?"

"Thou must decide that for thyself. I too have reservations about the origin and the purpose of this war against Indians. In thy position, having witnessed such needless slaughter, I would probably adopt the same course. But in some situations I might well do otherwise."

"At times I feel like a traitor for refusing to serve in the militia."

"Thou are no traitor so long as thou allow thyself to be guided by the spirit that resides within thee."

"Maybe I ought to consider becoming a Quaker," Joseph said.

Harper laughed. "Thou might do worse."

* * *

"I've told Prudence all about thy farm," Harper said during the meal. "It's a large responsibility for a young man."

"I've managed the farm ever since I was eighteen," Joseph said. "I inherited it from my father."

"I understand that thou also care for thy mother," Prudence said. "She must be a burden for thee?"

Joseph laughed. "Not really. Blanche makes her own decisions, but she tends to all the household tasks. I need only concern myself with work on the farm."

"Still, it must be awkward at times to have her so close by," Prudence persisted. "Mothers like to control their children, no matter how old they are."

Experience spoke up. "I don't feel that I'm being controlled."

"That's because thou take after thy father," Prudence said.

"Blanche has her own room," Joseph said. "Father provided for that in his will."

"Thy father was a wise man," Harper said, suppressing a chuckle.

The conversation at table continued in that vein. Joseph spoke of his brother John and his three sisters.

"We're well acquainted with Mary and her family," Prudence said. "She's a wonderful wife and mother."

"And the Holways are loyal member of our Society," Harper added.

When they had finished eating, Joseph accepted an invitation from Experience to view her father's land. After crossing a grassy meadow where cattle were grazing, they climbed a low hill and sat on a fallen tree trunk at the edge of a wood. He sensed that she came there often. Unsure of what to say, he waited for her to speak.

"Thou are fortunate to have a sister like Mary," she said. "She's older than I am, but we're good friends. I seek her advice on countless matters."

"It's good to have someone to turn to for advice," Joseph said. "I'm grateful to your father for our conversation after the meeting."

"I admit that I listened with interest to thy talk with Father. I too am opposed to violence, but I have no personal reason for my feelings. They arise largely from Father's experiences as a Friend and a defender of our beliefs."

"I'm afraid I have ample reason," Joseph said.

"If thou can bear to speak of it, I should be pleased to listen."

Joseph found himself giving her a full account of his service in the militia. Despite the fact that she was younger and a woman to boot, he spoke without reserve of the battle for the Indian fort, the sacrifice made by his Indian half-brother, and the march back to Smith's Garrison.

"I saw too many brave men die, let alone the women and children," he concluded. "I want no more."

"I can understand how thou feel," Experience said. "Father has been persecuted and cast in prison for his beliefs. I've suffered none of that myself, but I'm aware of the hatred and injustice that prevails here in the colonies."

"I know something of your father's reputation. But what you say adds to my respect for him."

Experience made no reply. Joseph realized that he liked this girl, her serious yet unassuming manner, her politeness and strength of character. Equally pleasing to his eye was her trim figure and unblemished complexion. As he wondered how to resume their talk, she came to his aid.

"I should be pleased to know thy impression of the meeting we all attended this morning."

"I remember going to a Quaker meeting when I was young. I must admit that I was bored."

"Were thou bored today as well?"

"Not at all, but I attribute that to the company I was in."

"That is one purpose of the meeting. We derive peace and pleasure from sitting quietly in community with our friends and neighbors, while we open ourselves to the promptings of our inner spirit."

"I'm afraid I felt no such promptings today," Joseph said.

Experience laughed merrily. "They are an exception rather than the rule, but it's quite wonderful when they occur."

"Did you experience such promptings this morning?"

"I did indeed, but I could not testify to them in public."

"You mean that your spirit also gives you private advice."

"Much of what I gather from our meetings is personal. That is the nature of our relationship with the spirit within us."

"You're even more persuasive than your father."

Joseph averted his gaze, pretending not to notice a blush on her face.

"We should get back," she said. "I thank thee for speaking openly of what is on thy mind. I trust my replies were of some benefit to thee."

"They were indeed," Joseph said. "I came to speak to your father, but my visit has been doubly fruitful."

Five

"Tell Joseph to marry that girl."
(Plymouth Colony, Summer 1676)

When Blanche became ill, the local apothecary referred to her malady as consumption. Despite his efforts on her behalf, her condition deteriorated. John was back from England and helping to care for his mother. Mary was quick to arrive. To Joseph's surprise and delight, she was accompanied by Experience Harper.

"She often ministers to the sick," Mary explained.

Joseph did not question her credentials. Following their initial talk, he thought often of Experience, and he had made another trip to Sandwich.

"I gather thou did not come all this distance just to see me," Harper commented on that occasion. "I believe Experience is out in the barn."

Joseph was silent, but he felt his face redden.

He found her cleaning out the stalls. She greeted him warmly, then suggested a walk to their spot on the hill. They spoke at some length of their backgrounds and present circumstances. Joseph outlined his plans for the farm, while Experience allowed that marriage and a family were in her dreams for the future. On the way back to the house he ventured to take her hand. Shielded from view by the barn, they kissed and resolved to see each other more often. But summer was a busy time for Joseph, and his promise was more easily made than kept.

He hadn't notified Experience of Blanche's illness. Mary had obviously passed the word along. The fact that she had come of her own volition bode well for their future. She and Mary stayed with Blanche all that night. Toward morning they summoned the men to her bedside as she took her last breath.

Citing her absence from worship, the local minister declined to hold a church service for Blanche; but he agreed to pray at her grave. Mary and Experience offered to stay on after the burial, and Joseph was glad to accept. He needed to talk to someone about his relationship with his mother.

"Mostly I felt sorry for her," he told his sister, "but there were days when I hated her. I couldn't help blaming her for Father's death."

Mary had suggested a visit to Blanche's grave. They stood looking at the freshly dug earth, Joseph on one side, the two women on the other.

"How was she in any way responsible?" Mary asked.

"The medicine you found at his bedside," Joseph said, "the potion he got from the slave girl Tami on our visit to Newport. The bottle was nearly full. Father was sick for several weeks. It ought to have been almost empty."

"Why would Mother neglect to give him the medicine?"

"So she could marry Hedge. You must have been suspicious too, or you wouldn't have told me about the medicine."

"I'm sorry I mentioned it," Mary said. "I was angry at Hedge. We had to appoint guardians for my sisters when he refused to accept them into his house. He should have told Mother of his intention before he married her. But there's a simple explanation for the medicine. Father probably bought more than one bottle."

"Whatever she did is buried along with her," Joseph said.

"I believe thou are wrong about thy mother," Experience said.

Joseph stared at her in surprise. This was a family matter? What did she know about it?

"Mary and I heard her last words."

"What were they?" he asked.

"She said to tell thy father she loved him."

"She must have been delirious," Joseph said.

"I think she wanted to set our minds at ease," Mary said, "to make things right before she died."

"It makes no difference," Joseph said. "She was unfaithful to Father while he was alive. I suppose she was grateful to him for marrying her; but despite what she said, I don't believe she ever loved him."

"She didn't blame him for her indiscretions," Mary said. "She held herself responsible for the lapses in her life."

"You mean she couldn't help but act that way?"

"Not everyone can be strong and righteous," Experience said.

Rather than argue with her as well as Mary, Joseph was content to let the matter rest.

Later in the day, when he and Mary were alone, she confided in him that Blanche had made another request before her death.

"And what was that?" he asked, feigning indifference.

"She said, 'Tell Joseph to marry that girl.'"

"She only met Experience once."

"Mothers may make mistakes in their own lives, but they seem to know what's best for their children."

"Does that mean you agree with her?"

"I know the Harpers well. Experience would make thee a good wife."

"It's a little soon to speak of marriage." Joseph felt no anger at his sister, nor was he inclined to dismiss her recommendation. "I suppose I'd have to become a Quaker," he added after a pause.

"It might help if thou did," Mary said.

After this exchange with his sister, seeing Experience about the house evoked thoughts of marriage; and he fastened upon an innocuous incident as an indication that she might be receptive. He had just finished his morning ablutions and was wearing only pants and shoes when Experience emerged from Blanche's room, where she and Mary slept.

"Good morning," he said cheerfully. "Did you sleep well?"

Experience stopped in the doorway. "Please put on thy shirt," she said, her face reddening.

Joseph complied, but he drew his own conclusions from her request.

* * *

Holway had transported Mary and Experience to Barnstable in his carriage, but he left it to Joseph to get them back to Sandwich. Joseph opted to take Mary home first, giving him an opportunity to be alone for a time with Experience.

He told her about his father's association with the first Quaker women to arrive in New England, how he took Mary Fisher and Ann Austin back to Barbados on his ship after they were banished from

Boston, how he rescued Nicholas Upsall from persecution by the Plymouth authorities. It occurred to him as he spoke that he was in effect stating his own credentials for becoming a Quaker. He found talking to her pleasant and surprisingly easy.

Experience listened with interest. "When I was three years old," she said, "Father was banished from Boston for arranging a decent burial for William Leddra after he was hanged. That's what they did to Friends at that time. Now they fine or imprison us for refusing to swear an oath of loyalty."

Joseph nodded in agreement. "I suspect those fines are a steady source of income for the colony."

"I was only eight when my mother died. Father married again a year later. I've grown to accept Prudence, but I can't say that I love her."

When Joseph made no response, she apologized.

"I'm sorry to go on like this about myself when thou just buried thy mother. What will thou do now? Will it change thy life in any way?"

"I'll go on managing the farm," Joseph said. "It will feel strange to be alone in the house, but I suppose that will pass."

When Experience was silent, he fastened the reins and turned to her in hope of another kiss. She was willing, but she pushed him away when he placed his hand on her covered breast.

"I appreciate thy feelings, Joseph," she said, "but for the sake of our future happiness, I think we should wait until we are husband and wife. If thy mind is not set on marriage, please say so now."

Taken aback and a bit bewildered by her words, he managed to say, "For my part I'm not averse to the prospect of marriage."

"I'm glad we understand each other," Experience said.

Joseph unfastened the reins and continued along the dusty way to her home. She kissed his cheek in parting, then ran into the house. Driving back to Barnstable, he experienced an exhilarating sense of freedom. He felt ready and eager to embrace whatever the future might hold in store for him.

* * *

From his vantage point on the main deck John watched the slow procession of Indian men and women as they mounted the gangway. Their hands and legs were shackled, but their eyes flashed as they looked about before entering the hold of the ship. They were ignorant of their destination and what awaited them there. What did it mean for a person to be deprived of freedom and endure life as a slave in a foreign land? He was aware of the practice, but he had associated it primarily with men and women brought from Africa to labor on plantations in Virginia or the West Indies.

His eyes fastened upon a young woman clad in a leather garment that reached to her thighs. She stood frozen in place at the foot of the gangplank, seemingly reluctant to board the ship. One of the guards prodded her legs with a stick. She stumbled and fell back against the man behind her.

The woman reminded John of the girl Tami, whom his father bought at a slave auction in Barbados. She had cared for him as an child until his father set her free. He recalled visiting Newport at the age of twelve and trying to identify the herbs in her garden. He wondered if the handful of blacks in Barnstable who worked as farmhands or house servants were free and paid for their labor.

As the Indian woman crossed the deck of the ship, she paused for a moment to gaze back. He sensed that she was bidding farewell to her native land. She looked at him, not in anger but with sadness and resignation, then descended into the hold. He was in no position to alter what was taking place; yet he felt compelled to take some action, be it only in protest.

The ship's master was tall and slender, a life at sea writ large on his weathered face. He looked up in surprise as John entered his cabin.

"Is there a problem with those savages?"

John was silent. He was well satisfied with his post. The master had treated him fairly and had recently promoted him. Was he being overly impetuous? Would he come to regret his action?

"The problem resides with me," he said at last. "My mind and heart tell me it's wrong to condemn these Indians to a life of slavery. Many of them have done nothing to warrant such punishment."

"Who knows what they've done? Whatever it is, it's of no concern to me. I don't choose my cargo. I'm paid to transport these Indians to Bermuda, and that's what I intend to do. I advise you to set your feelings aside and tend to the task at hand."

John experienced another moment of doubt. Perhaps the master was right. This was simply business. There was no place for personal feelings. Yet he couldn't ignore the look the woman gave him. He thought of his brother's account of the battle in the swamp and the needless slaughter of women and children. Surely this woman had waged no war, committed no crime.

"I cannot serve on this voyage to Bermuda," he said. "My conscience won't allow me to be a party to the enslavement of innocent people."

"You're a man born to the sea," the master said. "Take my advice and sleep on it. We can talk again in the morning."

"That will serve no purpose. My mind is set."

"You leave me no other choice but to relieve you of duty. Unless you change your attitude, you'll find it hard to get another post."

"I'm willing to take that chance," John said.

* * *

"I thought you were at sea," Joseph said when he saw his brother.

"The ship was transporting Indians to Bermuda to be sold as slaves," John said. "I refused to sail on a slave ship and was relieved of my post."

"I didn't know you felt that strongly about slavery."

"It's wrong to profit off human lives."

"The authorities don't know what to do with Indians they capture," Joseph said. "They can't release them, because they fear another uprising."

"Do you view slavery as the answer?" John asked.

"I'm simply stating facts," Joseph said. "I think a major uprising is unlikely. King Philip is was betrayed by one of his own warriors. His head is on display in Plymouth. People are flocking to see it, but I'll not be one of their number. Those tribes still fighting will have to sue for peace."

"I hope you're right," John said.

"What will you do now?" Joseph asked.

"I'll seek another berth, perhaps on a ship with a Quaker master. Then I can go to sea with a clear conscience. Of course, the best solution is to get a ship of my own."

"Are you able to do that?"

"I've saved a little, but not nearly enough."

"I wish I could help, but my profits go back into the farm. Perhaps Holway can assist you."

"He and Mary have five children," John said. "Don't worry. I'll find a berth. Meanwhile, I thought I might help out here on the farm."

"I can use an extra hand for the harvest. Working together, maybe we can put aside enough to buy you a share in a ship."

"And enough for you to get married."

Joseph laughed. "I've been to Sandwich a few times, but I doubt that Experience will marry me unless I become a Quaker."

"Have you been to their meetings?"

"A few, but I have yet to hear from my inner voice. All I can think about in the silence is what I'll say to her afterwards."

"That sounds pretty serious," John said.

"While we're both working on the farm, you can use Mother's old room," Joseph said, seeking to change the subject.

"That room is better suited for a married couple," John said.

* * *

The evils of slavery were a frequent topic in the Harper household. Joseph was of like mind, but he had come to see Experience and was not prepared for her father's proposal.

"The authorities in Plymouth have more than a dozen Indians penned up waiting to be transported to Spain and sold as slaves. The ship is in the harbor. I have a plan to free them, but I'll need thy help."

"You've been in trouble before," Joseph said. "I have a clean slate. I prefer to keep it that way."

"We're in no danger of going to jail," Harper assured him.

"Where are these Indians from, and what have they done?"

"Some were promised protection if they surrendered. None of them deserve this. Their only crime is being an Indian."

"Why are they being shipped to Spain?" Joseph asked.

"Slaves bring a better price in Spain. My plan is to free them without alerting anyone, so they can escape with no risk of being recaptured."

"And how do you propose to do that?"

"We'll wait until they're all aboard the ship. The night before the ship sails, I'll bribe the guards to let us smuggle them ashore."

"What about the master and crew?"

"Most of them will be ashore in the arms of their loved ones."

"It sounds risky," Joseph said. "A lot could go wrong."

"Nothing we can't deal with. Are thou with me?"

Joseph was inclined to refuse. Why endanger his body and reputation just to free a few Indians? Then he considered what Experience would think of him if he refused to help her father. By agreeing, he was sure to gain favor with her. The plan seemed reasonable with a fair chance of success.

"Have you done this sort of thing before?" he asked.

"There's a first time for everything," Harper said.

* * *

Early the next morning Joseph and Harper set out for Plymouth on horseback. On their arrival they saw a three-masted barque tied to the dock. Harper appeared to be studying the terrain.

"Thou can wait here," he said. "I have to do this alone."

"What is it you plan to do?" Joseph asked.

"I need to find out when they sail and who will be on guard."

"I'll try to act inconspicuous while you're gone."

"Don't act," Harper said. "Just be thyself."

He strode confidently along the dock and boarded the ship. Joseph leaned on a piling. Despite his efforts to appear casual, he felt out of place. No one seemed to notice, nor did anyone ask why he was there. But he was greatly relieved when Harper returned.

"We're in luck," Harper said. "The ship sails tomorrow, and the night guards are in a tavern nearby. Let's go and buy them a drink."

"Is that what you mean by a bribe?" Joseph asked.

"It will loosen them up, make them more receptive."

They found the men seated on a bench in the tavern. Joseph listened with admiration as Harper struck up a conversation, plied them with rum, and ingratiated himself by pretending to know all about Spain. He expounded on the beauty of Spanish women and emphasized that they had to have money in their purse when they went ashore. Having aroused their interest, he spoke of his desire to free the Indians.

"Most of them weren't involved in the fighting. The only thing they did wrong was accept our promise to protect them if they surrendered. But instead of the safety they expected, they get to spend the rest of their lives as slaves in a land they know nothing about. Put yourself in their place, and try to imagine how they must feel."

The two men exchanged glances as he spoke, but made no comment.

"We'd like the money," one of them said, "but if the Indians escape, we have no reason to go to Spain."

Harper was ready for the question. "It may delay the voyage a week or so, but the ship owner can easily find a like cargo in Boston."

The men nodded in agreement, and arrangements were soon made. The Indians were to be transferred to the ship that very evening. Harper laid out his plan for the rescue. They all shook hands in parting.

"Let's go before they change their minds," he whispered to Joseph.

Toward nightfall they watched from a distance as the Indians were herded along the dock and up the gangplank onto the ship. Joseph counted fourteen, including two women.

"Is there a market for Indian women in Spain?" he asked.

"I suppose so, but the first market is on the voyage," Harper said.

They passed the evening in the tavern, where some of the crew were drinking more than eating. Harper waited until they were drunk, then led the way to the waterfront, where he had arranged for the use of two boats.

"I trust thou know how to row," he said.

"I can manage," Joseph said, "but why do we need boats?"

"Would thou have us parade the Indians along the dock and down the main street of town?"

Joseph was silent. Harper appeared to know what he was doing.

"We'll wait until everyone is asleep except the guards," Harper said. "Thou can rest in the boat, if it suits thee."

"I couldn't sleep, if I tried," Joseph said.

Shortly after midnight they rowed across the harbor and approached the ship from the water side. One of the guards lowered a line, and Harper clambered aboard. Joseph waited in his boat. There was no moon. He could make out only part of the dock and a vague outline of the town. He struggled to keep the two boats alongside the ship. Harper was taking a long time. Joseph feared that something had gone wrong with their plan.

Harper's head appeared at the rail above him, and a woman lowered herself into one of the boats. Joseph counted the Indians as they slid down the line. Was there room enough for everyone? He told himself that Harper must have taken that into account in his planning.

Both boats were soon full. Harper was the last to descend. Taking up the oars, Joseph rowed quietly away from the ship. The Indians in the other boat followed his lead. They had gone several hundred yards when a clamor erupted on the deck of the ship. Torches were held over the side. Harper told Joseph to row as fast as he could, heedless of the noise. Cries from the ship drowned out the sound of their passage, and they were soon safely lost in the darkness Seeing that Joseph was tiring from the added load, Harper took the oars. From then on all the men took turns rowing.

"Won't the guards be punished for aiding the escape?" Joseph asked.

"I bound and gagged them," Harper said, "but loosely enough so they could free themselves and sound the alarm."

"Where are we going now?"

"We'll let the Indians decide that."

As though following Harper's direction, the Indians in the other boat took the lead. They beached their boat on a wooded promontory some miles south of the village. Following a brief exchange, which Joseph interpreted as words of gratitude, all but one disappeared into the woods. The remaining Indian said he was an outcast from his tribe, and Harper allowed him to stay.

"What will you do with him?" Joseph asked.

"I have no idea. Right now we have to get away from here."

It was still dark when they beached the two boats near the spot where their horses were tethered. At dawn they were well on their way to Sandwich.

Prudence had a meal ready for them. The Indian seemed doubtful at first, then opted to taste the food on his plate. He was soon wolfing it down, oblivious to all else. Joseph too had a hearty appetite. It struck him as he ate that Experience was especially solicitous.

Harper drew Joseph aside after they had eaten. "The authorities will soon be at my door asking what I know about this escape. Have thou a place for this Indian on thy farm?"

"Why would they question you?"

"I have a certain reputation."

"I ought to discuss this first with my brother," Joseph said.

He was reluctant to get involved in this part of Harper's enterprise, but the warm smile Experience had bestowed on him at table was persuasive.

"I suppose I could take him off your hands," he said. "But I have a request to make in return."

"What might that be?" Harper asked.

Joseph took a deep breath. "With your permission I'd like to propose marriage to your daughter Experience."

"I think she's expecting it," Harper said.

Six

"I have a duty to protect him as a brother."
(Plymouth Colony, 1676-81)

Sponsored by Harper and coached by Experience and Mary, Joseph was soon accepted by the community of Friends in Sandwich. He was married that autumn. His satisfaction was heightened in the spring when Experience announced she was pregnant. She gave birth to a boy. They named him Tristram after his paternal grandfather.

Save for scattered incidents in the northern provinces, the war with the Indians appeared to be winding down. Joseph improved the buildings on the farm and added to his holdings of cattle. Experience managed the household and tended to the needs of her son. They named their next child Joseph.

Harper came regularly to see his grandsons, also passing on news about the family and the colony. "I just spent two days in jail for refusing to take the oath of fidelity or pay the fine," he said after he had bounced Tristram on his knee and held young Joseph in his arms. "I'm tired of this annual ritual. The authorities know that swearing is contrary to our beliefs. It's just a source of income for them."

"Two days is a fairly light sentence," Experience said.

"Someone else paid the fine. Have they knocked on thy door?"

"I took the oath before I joined the Society," Joseph said. "I suppose I should repudiate it."

"Better leave well enough alone," Harper said.

"Is there a place where Friends are left in peace?" Experience asked.

"I was getting to that," Harper said. "I'm going to buy a piece of land in Kings Towne in the Narragansett country. I'm told we can worship there without restriction or fear of imprisonment."

"It sounds too good to be true," Experience said.

"It may be worthy of thy consideration as well," Harper said.

"The Narragansett country holds bitter memories for me," Joseph said, "and I can't give up the farm. But I wish thee and Prudence well."

"I hope we shall still see thee on occasion," Experience said.

"The grandchildren are a strong incentive," Harper said.

* * *

Harper moved later that year, but getting settled in his new home was harder than he expected. He sent word apologizing for his failure to keep his promise and expressing the hope that they might visit him.

"The children are too young for such a journey," Experience declared to her husband, "but I'm eager to know more about the Narragansett country. I urge thee to go there and find out how well Father is doing."

"I too am curious as to what he finds attractive in such a remote place," Joseph said.

"Have thou any thought of moving there?" Experience asked.

Joseph laughed. "Fear not. I'm perfectly content where I am."

He made the trip to Kings Towne on horseback. At times on the way something reminded him of his long march as a militiaman. He tried not to dwell on the outcome of that campaign, but he felt duty bound to stop off in Wickford and render homage at the graves of his fallen comrades.

Harper was eager to show him around the property he had acquired. He introduced Joseph to the fledgling community of Friends and urged him to consider a move to Narragansett.

"I'm impressed with Kings Towne," Joseph said, "but I was born and raised in Barnstable. Experience is content there, and I have no reason to sell the farm. If we were to move, it would likely be to West Falmouth. A man named Gifford has established a colony of Friends there. So far they've been free to meet without interference or penalty. I may well buy land there simply as an investment for our future and that of the children."

"West Falmouth is still part of the Plymouth Colony," Harper said, "but thou are wise to plan ahead. My concern is with present conditions. I shall say no more, if thou will promise to bring Experience and the children with thee on thy next visit to Kings Towne."

"I'm sure she would like that," Joseph said.

* * *

Following the birth of his third child, a daughter whom they named Mary, Joseph had yet another visit from the constable.

"By order of the court," the man recited, "all bond servants are to be released from their contracts, so they can pursue their own livelihoods. You are directed to give up all papers related to their terms of service."

Joseph had been alerted to this new regulation at a monthly meeting of Friends. Authorities in Plymouth had acted without benefit of law to cancel articles of apprenticeship and release bond servants. But their ruling applied only to those whose masters were Friends. He had just tended to a sick calf; and he looked forward to a hearty meal, followed by a good night's rest. He was in no mood to accede to this unjust ruling.

"I trust that all landowners are subject to this order," he said.

The constable looked away. "At present it applies only to Quakers," he said in a tone much less imperious.

"I shall gladly comply when everyone is bound by the same rule," Joseph said. "Besides, I have no bond servants." He regretted his words at once, but it was too late to retract them.

The constable looked toward the barn, where the Indian was hitching up a work horse. "What about that man?" he asked.

"He's working here of his own free will."

"I'll just ask him a few questions."

The constable stepped toward the barn, but Joseph blocked his path. "Not until this ruling applies to everyone in the colony."

"I shall have to report this to the magistrate."

"Do what thou must," Joseph said. "Thou have my reply."

The constable turned and stalked off. Joseph entered the house and sat with his head bowed.

"Is something wrong?" Experience asked.

"The constable wanted to question the Indian. When I refused, he said he had to inform the magistrate."

"Does he know the Indian is a fugitive?"

"I doubt that he could make him out as an Indian. But I aroused his suspicion. I'm sure he'll be back."

"We might send the Indian away for a time," Experience said.

"I need him on the farm, and it will look suspicious if he's gone."

"What do thou propose to do?" Experience asked.

"I'll have to think about it," Joseph said.

A week later a neighbor reported that the constable had asked him about the man working on Joseph's farm. "I said he was an Indian. You've spoken quite openly about it, so I had no reason to lie to him. When he wanted to know how you came to have an Indian working on your farm, I said he'd have to ask you about that."

"Did he say anything about an order from the magistrate?"

"Not that I remember, but I could tell he was up to no good."

Joseph broached the subject to Experience that evening. "It's just a matter of time before they seize him as an escaped slave."

"There must be some way to save him," she said.

"The fall harvest is in. We might go away somewhere for the winter. Come spring it should be safe to return."

"Where would we go?"

"I told thee about a community of Friends in West Falmouth. I could get a neighbor to look after the farm while we're away."

"We might visit my father," Experience said. "He speaks well of the Narragansett country. We could see for ourselves."

"It's just a temporary problem. Besides, this is our home; and the farm is the work of my hands. I can't leave all that behind."

"Then release the Indian. Let him find another place of refuge."

"Don't forget that I owe my life to an Indian." Joseph's stern look bespoke his disappointment at her suggestion. "Thanks to thy father, I was able to repay part of that debt by rescuing this Indian from a life of slavery and offering him shelter. I have a duty to protect him as a brother."

"I'm sorry," Experience said. "I didn't realize thou harbored such strong feelings. I rely on thee to do what thou think best."

* * *

A neighbor with grown sons agreed to care for their livestock while they were away. Joseph promised to sell him the property if by chance he decided to remain in West Falmouth. By the first snowfall the whole family was settled temporarily on a small farm abandoned by its owner.

William Gifford welcomed them. A slender muscular man in his late twenties, he was married and had four children.

"My father bought this land nearly a decade ago," he told Joseph. "Our little community is self-sufficient. We preserve our independence by remaining apart from the rest of the town. We raise or grow everything we need. What we can't produce, we learn to do without. So far the authorities have left us in peace."

"I'm not prepared to cut myself off from the outside world."

Gifford smiled. "Thou are free to do what best suits thee, as long as thou adhere to the principles of honesty, equality, simplicity, and frugality that guide our community."

"I have no quarrel with thy principles," Joseph said. "But I could use some help getting settled. Can thou recommend someone?"

"Thou might be of some service to me personally," Gifford said. "My younger brother Christopher recently returned home. He left after being fined for speaking contemptuously against dispensers of the word of God."

"I see that as no great fault."

"His fault lies in calling attention to himself and to our community. But he's a strong lad and a good worker."

"I'm willing to talk to him."

"I'll send him to thee on the morrow."

Gifford was as good as his word. Christopher had broad shoulders and dark wavy hair, and he was as fluid in his motions as a dancer. He took easily to the tasks laid out for him and was quick to develop a friendship with the Indian. Joseph was pleased to call on him as needed during the winter.

With the arrival of spring Joseph made a brief visit to his neighbor in Barnstable and was assured that all was well on the farm. He also learned that the constable had made several inquiries in his absence.

"I told him you wouldn't be back until spring," the neighbor said.

Joseph managed to control his anger. "Thou ought not to have said anything. Now he'll be waiting when I return."

"I'm sorry. If it's any help to you, my sons will gladly care for your property this summer, or as long as you're away."

Joseph suspected his neighbor may have had a method and motive for his disclosure to the constable. He also realized that he gained nothing by severing their relationship. He had toyed with the idea of developing the farm in West Falmouth. Experience seemed content there and seldom mentioned their former home. He made arrangements for his neighbor to manage the farm until further notice. By leaving the date of his return indefinite, he hoped to avoid further inquiries by the Plymouth authorities.

Experience voiced no objection to his decision. Christopher agreed to work four days a week, citing other responsibilities. When questioned, he said those responsibilities did not include a wife and family. With his help and that of the Indian Joseph set about the spring planting. He made needed repairs to the barn and moved some cattle from his farm in Barnstable.

"It looks as if thou plan to stay for a spell," Gifford commented when he saw all this activity.

"The place needed some fixing up," Joseph said.

* * *

The summer was marked by hard work but otherwise peaceful. On a bright afternoon in September a stranger arrived at the farm on horseback. The man identified himself as a constable from Sandwich.

"What do thou want with me?" Joseph asked, feigning bewilderment.

"It's been reported that you're sheltering a fugitive Indian."

"I have only laborers in my employ," Joseph said.

"As I rode up, I saw a man by the barn. He looked like an Indian."

"Thou are mistaken. He's a local youth I hired to work in the fields."

"Then you won't mind if I ask him a few questions."

The constable took a step toward the barn, but Joseph blocked his path. "Say thou that I lie?"

"I'm just doing my duty," the man said.

As he tried to push past, Joseph seized his arm. The struggle ended with Joseph on the ground and the constable straddling his chest. Christopher had come up from the barn. When he tried to separate them, the constable struck him in the face, bloodying his nose. He retaliated with a blow to the man's eye. Joseph had regained his feet. Confronted now by two men, the constable took a step back and brushed himself off.

"You'll be seeing me again," he said as he mounted his horse.

Experience had emerged from the house during the struggle. Seeing that Joseph had no visible injuries, she turned to Christopher, whose nose was bleeding profusely.

"Come inside and let me tend to that," she ordered.

Sweating from the struggle, Christopher followed her into the house. She gave him a clean cloth to use as a compress. Then she filled a pan with water and bathed his face and neck

"I think my shoulder is bruised as well," he said.

"Take off your shirt, and I'll have a look," Experience said.

Moistening another cloth, she gently cleansed the wound. Christopher submitted to her ministrations. When her covered breast brushed against his cheek, he looked up at her, his face flushed with embarrassment.

Experience smiled, as if she hadn't noticed. Yet she was keenly aware of the smooth unblemished skin on his well-tanned back and chest. Joseph came in, and she banished such unworthy thoughts. That night she dreamt that a stranger who resembled Christopher held her in his arms and kissed her. The following day she sensed that he was looking at her in a different way. But by the end of the week she had put the incident and her attendant feelings out of mind.

Her intention as she left the house was to check for eggs. The entrance to the chicken coop was through the barn, a benefit for her and the chickens. She was surprised to find Christopher seated on a bale of hay.

"I thought thou were out in the fields with Joseph," she said.

"I came in to get a flask of water from the well."

"Is the bruise on thy shoulder still painful?"

"It hasn't bothered me. I've almost forgotten about it."

"I can have a look at it while I'm here."

The words were out before she could reflect on their import. He gave her a curious look as he removed his shirt. She was at once aware of the same feelings that had gripped her as she dressed his wound. The bruise had almost healed, but she couldn't resist pressing lightly on the skin around the edges.

"Does that hurt?" she asked to mask her impulse.

"It feels good," he said, turning toward her.

Experience found herself in his arms, and he was kissing her as in her dream. She tried to pull away, but he held her tight as he drew her down to the floor of the barn and ran his hand up her leg.

"This isn't right," she said, making only a feeble effort to stop him.

She shut her eyes as he hoisted her skirt, then waited for what she knew was coming next.

* * *

Both Joseph and Christopher were summoned to appear before the magistrate. Joseph pleaded guilty to assault, but he denied that the Indian was either an apprentice or a fugitive.

"I regard him simply as a laborer," he said.

"How did this laborer come to be in your employ?"

"He was a free man and came willingly."

The magistrate agreed that the ruling by Plymouth authorities was discriminatory in that it applied only to Quakers, and he declined to enforce it. He was also quick to render his verdict on Christopher.

"Your brother William has contributed a great deal to this community, but that doesn't lead me to excuse you for resisting an officer of the court. Since your account seems to indicate that the constable initiated the struggle, I'm inclined to let you off with a warning. I trust you have learned a lesson from this incident and will act accordingly in the future."

Both men gave assurances that they would henceforth respect the law and those who enforce it. Seated quietly in the chamber, Experience placed a meaning on the magistrate's words that she hoped was private.

Joseph remained troubled by what had occurred. "It's not just the Indian who concerns me," he told his wife. "The Plymouth authorities know of our community. They're enforcing regulations and levying fines that we came here to escape. When they hear of this incident, they may not accept the magistrate's opinion."

'Would thou return to Barnstable?" Experience asked.

"I thought I might explore the opportunities in Kings Towne."

"Will thou go there alone?"

"It's the wisest course. I don't want to burden thee with another move until I've examined the ground. I'll leave right after the harvest."

Experience had a moment of panic. She was resolved that there would be no repetition of what had occurred in the barn. But Christopher might have other ideas, and she feared the affair might come to light. Could she rely on Joseph to understand and forgive her weakness? He had never forgiven his mother for her indiscretions. She had no wish to put him to that test.

"Thou seem to forget that my father is already in Kings Towne," she said. "We can visit and be close to family. If thou make up thy mind to move, I want to contribute to that decision. I won't be left behind to fend for myself and wonder what's going on."

Joseph knew Experience to be strong-willed, but he did not expect such vehemence. She was right. Harper had gone before them, had in effect prepared the ground for their move. He wrote in glowing terms of his life in Kings Towne. No laws directed exclusively at Friends. No fines for refusing to take an oath of loyalty. A life of peace and hard work free of interference by the authorities. Joseph could understand her eagerness to be reunited with her family, or at least visit them. There was no more to it than that.

"We can all stay with thy parents," he said. "It will give us time to make a wise decision. We'll take the Indian with us."

* * *

The move took place late in the fall. Since further discussion had led to the possibility that they might well settle in Kings Towne, Joseph loaded two wagons with their belongings. Upon their arrival he noted the excitement and joy with which his wife greeted her family. His quest for information about the area evolved quickly into a search for a suitable home.

Backed by Harper, he was able to purchase a parcel of cleared land near the shore. With the help of the Indian and local labor he built a two-story house that was comfortable but not ostentatious. The following spring his family was able to occupy their new home. Soon after that Experience gave birth to her fourth child and proudly presented the baby to her parents.

"We've decided to call him Reuben."

"What made thee decide on that name?" Harper asked.

"I think it came to me in a dream," she said.

Joseph laughed. "Experience suggested it. I agreed because the name is in my family. I have an uncle somewhere named Reuben."

Joseph was soon a vital part of the community. He helped to form a local meeting of Friends, and he made his home available for that purpose. In addition to farming he established himself as a cooper and undertook to breed horses suited for riding. Experience gave birth to their fifth child. Joseph insisted on naming him John, following a visit from his brother.

He had sold the family farm in Barnstable to his neighbor shortly after the move to Kings Towne, using the proceeds for his business ventures and to help John acquire a half share in a ship he could call his own. But he still had certain holdings and interests in Falmouth. He undertook that journey in the winter and contacted his friend Gifford.

With greetings out of the way Gifford became suddenly more serious. "Christopher is in trouble again. Perhaps thou can talk to him."

"What sort of trouble?" Joseph asked.

"He struck a local constable on the head with a walking stick. He acts rather strangely, absenting himself from meetings and disappearing for days with no explanation. He's contemptuous of ministers and civil authorities. He won't listen to me; but thou were once a good influence on him, and he respects thee."

"Where is he now?"

"He owns a piece of land in Sakanesset," Gifford said. "Thou may find him there."

"I have some business out that way."

"If thou can persuade him to attend our meetings, we can give him the support he needs to get back on the right path."

"I'll do what I can to help," Joseph promised.

His business was with a landowner named Hatch, who had once expressed an interest in buying cattle. He wanted to bring pressure on the current occupant of his farm to pay him for livestock he had left behind when he moved to Kings Towne. His business completed, he was surprised to find Christopher in the barn where he had left his horse.

"How do thou come to be here?" he asked.

"I might ask the same," Christopher said. "I do odd jobs for Hatch on occasion. It puts a few shillings in my pocket and keeps me independent."

"Thy brother said thou are in trouble with the authorities."

Christopher laughed. "I regard it as persecution."

"He said thou struck the constable and bloodied his head. What led thee to do such a thing?"

"The man has had it in for me since we were charged with assault. The magistrate didn't do me any favor by letting me off without a fine."

"Have thou thought of moving away and starting life anew?"

"The authorities would like that," Christopher said. "I won't be driven from the land I inherited from my father."

Joseph was suddenly aware of a man at the entrance to the barn. He recognized the constable who had questioned him about the Indian, the man he was once accused of assaulting.

"Christopher Gifford," the man recited, "I have orders to conduct you to jail for failing to appear at your hearing set for Wednesday last."

"How did you know where to find me?" Christopher asked.

"I followed your friend. I figured he might know where you were."

Christopher glared at Joseph. "So I have you to thank for this."

"I had no idea thou were here," Joseph said.

"Will you come along peacefully?" the constable asked.

Acting on impulse, Joseph stationed himself in front of Christopher. "To take him into custody," he said, "thou must contend with both of us."

"I don't want a fight," the constable said, "but you'll both be charged with resisting authority, and you won't get away with it this time." With that he turned and walked away.

"Why did you take my part?" Christopher asked when he was gone.

"I promised thy brother that I would do my best to persuade thee to attend meetings. They're always willing to help members in good standing."

"If I were in good standing, I wouldn't need their help."

"They're ready to welcome thee back, but thou must take the first step. I ask only that thou attend the next meeting."

"I owe you something," Christopher said. "I promise to consider it, and I thank you for your support today."

He was as good as his word. Before returning home, Joseph was glad to see Christopher at a meeting. Both men were summoned to appear again before the magistrate. Joseph pleaded guilty to resisting authority. He was fined five pounds, but payment was waived when his friend Gifford pleaded on his behalf. Christopher's more substantial fine was also reduced when he agreed to pay twenty shillings to the constable for his head wound.

Seven

"There is no Narragansett River."
(The Narragansett Country, 1682)

"I regret that when thou decided to move thy family to Kings Towne, I made no mention of the ongoing border dispute with Connecticut," Harper said. "At the time I didn't regard it as a major problem. I realized that our neighbor to the west would continue its efforts to absorb the Narragansett country, but I didn't think the dispute would lead to violence."

"I'm aware of the problem," Joseph said, "but I know little about the background of the controversy."

"Then allow me to enlighten thee," Harper said. "When the King's Province, the Narragansett country as we know it, was created nearly twenty years ago, the border with Connecticut was set at the Pawcatuck River some miles to the west of here. But when the Indian wars ended, Connecticut laid claim to the entire province by right of conquest."

"That's a false claim," Joseph said. "Most of the militia who fought against the Indians were from Massachusetts and Plymouth. I was there."

Harper nodded in agreement. "They also cited a contract with the Indians that extended their territory to the Narragansett River."

"There is no Narragansett River," Joseph said.

"They claim the river referred to in the contract is Narragansett Bay, so all of the Narragansett country is rightfully part of Connecticut."

"Have there been any efforts to settle the dispute?"

"Rhode Island offered to compromise, but Connecticut seems set on expansion. In that respect they're just like Massachusetts."

"How did Rhode Island get involved?"

"Magistrates from Rhode Island exercise authority as justices of the peace in the King's Province. Our traditional ties are in that direction, but now Connecticut is sending settlers across the Pawcatuck River to reinforce its claim. Two men from Westerly were abducted and are being held for ransom because they spoke out in favor of Rhode Island."

"I take it thou have not been silent about the issue," Joseph said.

"My feelings are well known. Prudence is worried about my safety. I tell her we're a good many miles from the Pawcatuck river, but fear and unrest are spreading throughout the province."

"Can't the King settle the issue for once and all?"

"We have but a faint voice in Court. I fear that we shall have little say in the final decision."

"I'll reassure Experience, if she shows concern," Joseph said.

"Thou are in no immediate danger" Harper said, "but I advise thee to take care to whom thou express thy opinions."

* * *

Residents of the Narragansett country maintained good relations with Rhode Island. But that colony was a pariah in the eyes of its neighbors, even though it had a royal charter and Newport had become a major port. Joseph was not given to worry; but he heeded Harper's warning as he developed his land and promoted his business ventures, obtaining permits to sell horses in all of the neighboring colonies.

Experience received word one morning that Harper had failed to return from a trip to Westerly. She roused Joseph and broke the news. "That's right on the Connecticut border. Prudence is sure he's been abducted."

"I wonder what he did to warrant being abducted," Joseph said.

"Are thou implying that he's to blame?"

"Not at all; but if I knew what he did or said, I might better judge whether his captors are taking him to New Haven or to Hartford. Did anyone witness his abduction?"

"The message says that he didn't return home and that Prudence fears the worst. That's all I know."

"It's not much to go on, but I'll do what I can to find him."

Saddling his horse, Joseph set out for Harper's farm some miles to the southwest. Prudence could tell him nothing more. As he continued along the road to Westerly, a young boy blocked his path.

"Are you chasing the men I saw last night?" he asked.

"What men did thou see?" Joseph asked.

"Four men on horseback. One of them had his hands tied. They passed right by my house. I was out looking at the stars because I couldn't get to sleep. I knew something was wrong, so I followed them."

"Which way did they go?"

"There's a fork just down the road. They went to the left."

Joseph thanked the boy. If the men took the road toward Westerly, their initial destination was likely New London. Riding steadily, he arrived there late that afternoon. He tethered his horse near a building he took to be the courthouse. A group of men were gathered outside. Their talk was about a court hearing to be held the next morning.

"One of those farmers from Narragansett who love Rhode Island, and a Quaker to boot. It should be quite a show."

Joseph sought to devise a plan in line with what Harper had told him about the purpose and course of such abductions. He could easily pay a fine imposed by the court, but Harper might not recognize the court's authority. Though Joseph felt less strongly about such matters, he respected Harper's position. He had to find another way.

A crowd had gathered at the courthouse when Joseph returned the next morning. He was in time to see Harper escorted into the building. He joined those who followed along and took a seat at the rear of the chamber. Harper refused to stand as the magistrate entered. A sheriff and his deputy pulled him to his feet, while a clerk recited the charges against him.

"Inciting the officials and populace of the eastern part of Connecticut known as the Narragansett country to reject and oppose the jurisdiction of Connecticut over that territory."

"What have you to say in your defense?" the magistrate asked.

"I was abducted and brought here against my will," Harper said. "This court has no jurisdiction over my activities."

"I shall make note of your statement. Do you swear to speak only that which you know to be true?"

"I cannot and will not take an oath to that effect."

"I gather from your refusal that you are a Quaker?"

"I belong to the Society of Friends."

"Since you refuse to defend yourself, it is useless to proceed with this hearing," the magistrate said. "I order you to pay a fine of five pounds, plus five more pounds for disrespect of this court."

"I must refuse to pay the fine, even if I had the means at hand."

"Then I must sentence you to be confined until you find the means."

When the magistrate had departed, the sheriff and a deputy took Harper by the arms and dragged him from the chamber.

Outside the building Joseph watched as they conducted the prisoner to the jail. This development fit in with the plan he was forming in his mind. At the local livery stable he arranged for the use of another horse. Toward dusk he returned and tethered the two horses outside the jail.

Bursting into the building, he announced in an authoritative voice, "As ordered by the Governor of Connecticut and the New London court, I come to conduct Robert Harper to prison in New Haven."

The jailer appeared dubious. "Nobody told me about that."

"He refused to pay his fine and is being held for ransom. I have orders to take him off your hands."

"I don't know you. Have you got something in writing?"

The jailer seemed willing to accept the reason for the transfer, but he was being cautious. Joseph produced an official looking paper from his bag. The jailer studied it from every angle, as if to make sure it was genuine. Joseph remained calm. He was on firm ground, having inquired beforehand as to whether or not the man could read.

"It's late in the day and a long ride to New Haven," the jailer said. "Why not wait until tomorrow?"

"I have word that a rescue party is on its way here. It's to your own advantage that I take him off your hands now."

"Are you sure you can handle him by yourself?"

"I have horses outside. If you'll fasten his hands, I can manage."

"Wait here while I fetch him," the jailer said.

When he had disappeared into a back room, Joseph put the paper he had presented back in his bag.

Harper feigned anger when he saw Joseph. "Where are thou taking me now?" he demanded.

"You're being held for ransom in New Haven," the jailer said.

"By whose authority?"

"I have my orders."

The jailer tied Harper's hands and fashioned a leash, which he handed to Joseph. "He's all yours. I'm glad to be rid of him."

Harper tried to pull away, but Joseph held tight to the leash. Outside he helped Harper to mount his horse. The jailer watched from the doorway as they rode off in the direction of New Haven.

On the outskirts of town Joseph freed Harper's hands. "Wait here while I return thy horse to the livery stable," he said.

"We'll need two horses for the ride home," Harper said.

"I have my scruples too," Joseph said. "They can accuse me of lying, but I'm not a horse thief."

"The jailer said thou had an order to release me into thy custody," Harper said. "How did thou manage that?"

"I showed him my permit to sell horses in Connecticut," Joseph said. "It bears the seal of the colony. I figured that would be enough to convince a man who can't read."

* * *

In the following months Joseph expanded his business and assumed a prominent role in the community. He and Experience hosted meetings of Friends and remained in close contact with her parents. The incidence of abductions declined, due in part to reports that the King had ordered the formation of a commission to settle the border dispute. Harper made it a point to keep abreast of the issue.

"The commission is meeting at Smith's castle in Wickford," he told Joseph one day in the spring.

"Who is representing the Narragansett country?" Joseph asked.

Harper uttered a bitter laugh. "No one. They're all from Plymouth, Massachusetts, and Connecticut."

"What about Rhode Island? Have they no voice?"

"Rhode Island is a thorn in their side," Harper said. "It was never part of the federation."

"Then the outcome has already been decided."

"That's a fair assessment of the situation," Harper said. "We could go to Wickford and present our case," he added after a pause.

"You mean we should take it upon ourselves to represent the King's Province?" Joseph asked.

"If we don't, no one will speak up for us."

"I doubt that the commission would recognize us."

"We'll find out when we get there," Harper said.

Smith's castle was a long two-story saltbox structure with a central chimney and numerous windows for use in repelling attacks.

The building was new to Joseph, having replaced the garrison burned by Indians in the uprising that followed the swamp fight; but the nearby plot of ground with forty graves was all too familiar. He had helped to dig some of them. The wooden markers placed there nearly ten years ago had deteriorated but were still legible. Joseph paused there for a moment before entering the building.

A clerk was posted at the door of the room where the commission was holding its hearings. He asked for their credentials.

"We represent the King's Province, the territory under discussion." Harper tried to make it sound official.

The clerk was unimpressed. "The King's Province is not a party to these hearings," he said. "I have orders to bar any unauthorized persons."

"Surely we can be allowed to witness the proceedings."

"Take a seat away from the door, and I'll submit your request to Lieutenant Governor Cranfield."

"Thank you. We appreciate that."

"Who is Cranfield?" Joseph asked when they were seated.

"He's from New Hampshire, but he's hardly impartial."

"What if they won't let us in?"

"Don't say anything. Let's see what happens."

The clerk wrote a note, but he left his post to find someone to deliver it. Harper was quick to seize upon the opportunity. Pulling Joseph along with him, he entered the large room where the hearings were in progress. No one took notice of them as they found seats at the back.

Joseph recognized the man holding the floor as an official from the Plymouth Colony. He listened intently to what he was saying.

"As for the claim made by agents from Connecticut that the territory in question belongs to that colony by right of conquest, I would remind the commission that the campaign against the Narragansett Indians was waged largely by militia from Massachusetts and Plymouth under the command of Governor Josiah Winslow. The Connecticut militia had but a supporting and somewhat questionable role in our glorious victory at the great swamp."

Joseph was on his feet. Ignoring Harper's tug on his sleeve, he spoke in a loud and clear voice. All heads turned, and all eyes were focused on him

"My name is Joseph Hull. My home is in the Narragansett country, and I speak as someone who fought at the great swamp."

Cranfield wrapped with his gavel for order. "You, sir, are neither an agent nor a delegate authorized to speak before this commission. Please sit down. The gentleman from Plymouth has the floor."

Joseph refused to be silenced. "The Narragansetts had been peaceful up to that time. Their territory was invaded with dire consequences for both sides. I invite members of this commission to visit the graves of forty brave men who died in that swamp. They lie within easy walking distance."

"I repeat that you are out of order," Cranfield said. "If you persist in this tirade, I shall have you removed."

Harper was now on his feet. "In order to reach a fair decision about the border, all the affected parties should be heard. Since the King's Province is not represented here, this commission can only recommend a solution to the dispute. It's up to King James to decide.

Until then the province should remain as originally established, with Rhode Island maintaining civil jurisdiction."

Cranfield again wielded his gavel. "This is not a public hearing," he shouted. "Your comments and opinions are out of place. The bailiff will remove these men from the chamber."

Three men converged on Joseph and Harper; but before they could carry out their orders, the sound of musket fire outside the building caused everyone in the room to glance about in wonder.

Cranfield was the first to recover his voice. "Can someone tell me what is going on out there?"

The clerk entered from the hall. "Mounted militia from Rhode Island have surrounded the building," he announced. "The officer in charge requests to address the commission."

"It sounds more like a demand," Cranfield said. "Since we appear to have no choice, you may show him in."

A man clad in what passed for a uniform entered the room and strode to the front where the commission was seated.

"What is the reason for this interruption?" Cranfield asked.

The man produced a paper and read aloud. "By unanimous vote of the legislature, the Colony of Rhode Island and Providence Plantations refuses to recognize the authority of this commission to adjudicate the matter under consideration. The commission is therefore prohibited from keeping court within our jurisdiction. Failure to comply with this order will result in arrest and forcible eviction from the colony."

Without waiting for a response, the man turned on his heel and left the room. The silence following his departure was punctuated by the sound of a trumpet outside the building. All eyes turned to Cranfield.

"Under pressure I hereby adjourn this session of the commission. We shall resume our deliberations next week in Boston."

* * *

"The commission decided that jurisdiction over the King's Province belongs by right to Connecticut," Harper announced two weeks later.

Joseph looked up from a horse he was grooming. "We expected as much," he said. "But thou appear to be pleased. Is there something more?"

"Rhode Island has appealed to the King, citing the partiality of the commission and a lack of representation by all parties involved. The decision will have to be confirmed in London."

"Have we any hope that King James will rule in our favor?"

"I think not, but the process will take months, even years. Meanwhile, everything in the Narragansett country remains the same."

"So we continue to live in uncertainty," Joseph said.

"That's better than living in Connecticut," Harper said.

Eight

"To win her hand, thou must become a Friend."
(London, Autumn 1683)

When Joseph sold the family farm in Barnstable and settled in Kings Towne, a portion of the proceeds went to help his brother buy a half share in a ship. While crossing the North Atlantic, intent on establishing connections with merchants in London, John had ample time to reflect upon the course of his life and his newly acquired status. His contacts with women outside the family had thus far been confined to occasional and meaningless encounters in various ports of call. With nothing to offer a woman, he had given little thought to marriage or raising a family. Now as proud master of the brig *Ataquin* he began to give serious thought to following Joseph's example.

Mary had been prodding him to marry another of Harper's daughters. Experience's younger sister. She was seventeen, an eligible age; but John wanted someone a little older. A merchant in London might have an eligible daughter. Mary would have less reason to criticize his choice, if he brought back an English bride. He made what he felt were discreet inquiries among the handful of merchants with whom he was acquainted One of them agreed to put John in touch with an eligible young woman; but when the match

626

proved mutually unacceptable, the merchant declined to do business with him. He had few enough contacts in London and couldn't afford to alienate them by rejecting the women they thrust at him. But he had yet to fasten upon an alternative strategy.

On a bright sunny day in autumn he set forth on foot to visit the cathedral in Southwark where, according to family legend, his grandfather the minister had held a post shortly before he returned to New England. John crossed London bridge with supreme confidence, but he was soon lost in the maze of streets on the south bank of the Thames. As he looked about in bewilderment, he spotted a young woman carrying a wicker basket. From her purposeful stride he gathered that she was familiar with that part of the city.

"Excuse me," he called out. "Could you direct me to Saint Saviour?"

The woman paused to scrutinize him. Having decided apparently that he was sincere in his request, she gave him directions to the cathedral.

"I'd take thee there myself, but I'm going to visit my father in prison."

"Who is your father, and what has he done?" John asked.

The woman gave him a searching look before she replied. "Captain Edmund Tiddeman. The charge against him is unlawful meeting and riot. But in all likelihood thou have never heard of him."

"I presume he's innocent of the charges," John said.

The woman regarded him with apparent interest. "Pray tell me, what is it that leads thee to that presumption?"

John looked down in confusion. He wasn't prepared to defend what he intended as gallantry. To regain lost ground, he fastened upon her speech, which indicated she was a Quaker.

"I meant only that in thy eyes he must appear to be innocent."

"So thou think he may actually be guilty as charged." The woman's eyes sparkled as she spoke.

"I know not what to think," John said. "I meant no offense. If you'll permit me, I should like to go with thee to visit your father. I can see the cathedral another day."

"Thou seem uncertain as to whether to present thyself as a Friend."

"That aptly describes my situation. My brother and two sisters in New England belong to your Society. I am much at sea and have no opportunity to attend any kind of church service."

"How long will thou be in London?"

"I've yet to set a date for my return voyage," John said.

His answer was somewhat misleading in that he expected to sail in a week or two. He was first to break the awkward silence that ensued.

"I'm quite serious about my offer. I should like very much to go with you to visit your father."

"Perhaps we should first introduce ourselves. I'm Alice Tiddeman. My father served honorably in His Majesty's Navy. He's retired now and has shipping interests in Dover. And who may thou be?"

"I'm John Hull, master of the brig *Ataquin* at anchor in the Thames. My home is Barnstable in the Plymouth Colony. My father supported many Friends in New England while he lived. He died when I was twelve."

"I'm sorry," Alice said. "Thou are welcome to accompany me to the Counter in Tooley Street, where my father currently resides."

John altered course and fell in step beside her. He offered to carry the basket, and she seemed glad to relinquish it.

"Where I live Friends are fined or imprisoned for refusing to swear an oath of loyalty. I'm glad the King has ended such persecution in England."

"Thou are mistaken," Alice said. "More than a thousand Friends are currently in prison throughout the country."

"How long will thy father remain in jail?"

"At the Bridge-House sessions Justice Spiers sentenced him to six weeks in the Counter. I visit him every day so he has enough to eat."

John drank in her words and the music of her voice. He felt without thinking that he could gladly listen to more of that music.

"What is this Counter to which you refer?" he asked.

"The building just ahead. It's more properly the Borough Compter, but it has a small prison where people charged with misdemeanors can serve out their sentences. It was rebuilt after the great fire."

"What does that coat of arms on the facade represent?"

"The borough of Southwark," Alice said.

Upon reaching the building they were ushered into a holding area, while the jailer went off to fetch her father.

"The cells are at ground level," Alice said while they waited. "The floor above has a courtroom. Father will be pleased to speak to another man."

Edmund Tiddeman's stance was as erect as any young naval officer, and he moved with an ease that belied his age.

629

"This is John Hull, a mariner," Alice said. "He comes from a family of Friends in New England. I met him on my way to the Counter."

Though he was clearly surprised to see his daughter in the company of a stranger, Tiddeman's face brightened as they shook hands.

"I apologize for my present circumstances," he said. "I hope thou can stop by our house once I'm free to entertain thee in proper fashion. I don't normally approve of Alice speaking to strangers, but in this case she seems to have acted wisely."

"I approached her," John said. "I wanted directions to Saint Saviour."

Tiddeman's look became of a sudden wary. "What business have thou at the cathedral?" he asked.

John related what he knew about his grandfather the minister, his studies at Oxford, his ministry in Devon, his failed attempt to establish an Anglican parish in the Massachusetts Colony, his posts in Cornwall and London during the Protectorate. He spoke as well of his father Tristram, his association with the first women missionaries to arrive in New England, his rescue of a man they had convinced to become a Friend, his opposition to slavery. Tiddeman and Alice listened intently to his account

"I admire a man like thy father who carries out a mission at great risk to himself," Tiddeman said. "Many Friends have done the same. Some have given their lives for the cause."

"Four Friends were hanged in Boston," John said. "My sister-in-law's father was banished for arranging a burial for one of them." He hoped his effort to ingratiate himself with father and daughter was not too obvious.

"How is it thou are not a Friend thyself?" Tiddeman asked.

"After Father died, I lived for a time with my sister Mary who had married a Friend. But I stopped going to meetings when I went to sea."

"Thou bear a worthy pedigree. Thou should attend one of our meetings at Horsleydown after I get out of this place."

"I should like that," John said.

"I hate to see thee confined here," Alice said. "Will thou grant me permission to plead with Justice Spiers to shorten thy stay?"

"Thou have no basis for such a plea," Tiddeman said. "The Justice will only turn a deaf ear."

"I can say thou are old and in ill health."

Tiddeman laughed. "Others here are older than I am. As for being ill, there is no evidence of that."

"I might still try," Alice said.

"I would not have thee go to Spiers alone. I'll say no more."

"I shall be pleased to accompany her," John said.

Tiddeman regarded him sternly. "I don't presume to tell thee what thou should do, but I repeat that such a visit will be fruitless."

Alice produced bread and cheese from the basket she had brought. The talk while her father ate was about John's ship and his business dealings in London. Tiddeman brushed aside questions about his own naval career.

"That will keep for another time. Alice has heard it all before."

John did not insist. He felt he had made a good impression, and he had prospects for future meetings. He was content with that.

* * *

631

Justice William Spiers was seated at his desk when John and Alice were ushered into his study. He looked up but did not rise to greet them. Leaning back in his chair, he folded his arms across a copious paunch.

"What is it you want of me?" he asked.

Alice had rehearsed her petition. "I come to plead for the early release of my father, Captain Edmund Tiddeman, who is presently confined at the Counter in Tooley Street. I beseech thee to consider his advanced age and the effect of an extended term in jail on his fragile health."

"Ah, yes!" Spiers said. "He was one of that crew arrested for unlawful assembly at Horsleydown. Do you claim that he's innocent of the charge?"

"He was simply listening to his inner spirit in a peaceful manner when he was taken into custody. He did nothing to justify such a harsh sentence."

John winced at her assertion. To question the Justice's decision in the case was not calculated to effect Tiddeman's release. Yet he had to admire her directness and honesty.

Spiers was smiling. "You're not the first to question my judgment," he said calmly. "Nor, I suspect, will you be the last. We're not in court, so I'll allow for your loyalty and love for your father. However, Captain Tiddeman is as guilty of the charges as everyone else. I see no reason why I should treat him differently from other prisoners serving time in the Borough Compter."

John respected Spiers' decision. Yet he felt compelled to speak up in support of Alice's petition, if only to prove to her that he was on her side. "Allow me to say that Captain Tiddeman has rendered honorable service as an officer in His Majesty's Navy."

"And who are you, sir?" Spiers was no longer smiling.

"John Hull from the Plymouth Colony in New England, and master of the merchant vessel *Ataquin*."

"What is your relation to Captain Tiddeman?"

"None at all. I'm simply a friend of the family." That was stretching things a bit, but Alice's look was appreciative.

"Were you present at this unlawful assembly?"

"I know nothing of that. I speak out of respect for Captain Tiddeman."

"How long have you known the Captain?"

"I met him for the first time this morning."

Spiers fingered his monocle as he looked from John to Alice. "Your honesty is refreshing," he said. "I shall reduce Captain Tiddeman's sentence by one week, provided he behaves himself until the time for his release."

"We thank thee for thy consideration," Alice said.

Spiers regarded her sternly. "Don't misunderstand me. I have scant sympathy for Quakers. Now go before I change my mind about your father."

Taking Alice by the arm, John led her from the room. On the street he took leave of her, pleading some business in the city.

"When shall I see thee again?" she asked.

"May I call when I'm again in London and thy father is at home?"

"I should like that," Alice said. "And I thank thee for thy help."

* * *

"Thou can hardly expect a woman from a city like London to adjust easily to life in New England," Experience said. "She's sure to be miserable and homesick."

John had just related the details of his meeting with Alice Tiddeman and her father, this following an extensive tour of his brother's properties in the Narragansett country. He had thought a good deal about Alice during his voyage across the Atlantic. He was attracted to her; but he had to wonder if she would agree to marry a man from the colonies, a man who for the present could promise her only a hard life and an uncertain future. He had yet to establish a firm and reliable trade with merchants in London. He might be ready for marriage, but he had very little to offer a woman. He needed advice, and the best source was his older brother and his sister.

"Experience is right," Joseph said. "Thou should marry a farm girl."

"I have no business on farms," John said, "and I see no reason to start over when I've found a woman I like and who seems to like me."

Experience smiled. "Is she the only child at home?" she asked.

"I'm not sure. I have yet to visit her home."

"Daughters have a strong bond with their fathers. If he's old and in need of her help, she may not want to break that bond."

"You left your father when you married Joseph," John said.

"That was different. He had remarried, and he had other children. He wasn't alone, and he wasn't that old."

"Speaking of Harper," Joseph said, "he has a daughter who may well be receptive to an offer of marriage."

John stifled a frown. "Mary has already made me aware of that. I have nothing against your sister," he added, turning again to Experience, "but I want someone older."

"My half-sister," Experience said. "How old is Alice?"

"I believe she's about my age."

"If thou are set on an English bride," Joseph said, "be sure that she's aware of all the adjustments that lie ahead of her in the colonies."

"I plan to talk to Mary as well before I return to England," John said. "I want to see what she has to say."

"She'll give thee much the same advice," Experience said.

* * *

When John visited his sister, he was still mulling over the cautionary advice he had received from Joseph and Experience. Should he abandon his efforts to find a wife abroad and seek one closer to home? He was inclined to reject that idea. Alice had made too deep and lasting an impression on him. Yet his brother's words were well intentioned, and they had a certain validity.

Mary embraced him at the door. "Come in and warm thyself. I'm alone with the children. Joseph is at his shop."

Mary's husband had a blacksmith shop in Sandwich. John liked him, but they had little in common. What he wanted to discuss was personal in nature. He followed her into the house and stood with his back to the hearth.

"You're the one I want to talk to," he said. "I met a young woman in London. Her name is Alice Tiddeman, and she's a Friend like you."

"And thou are favorably inclined to make her thy wife."

"I'm not sure. Can I expect her to give up the comforts of London for a life in Barnstable? I spoke to Joseph and Experience. They feel she would be unhappy and homesick in New England. They think I'd be wiser to marry one of Harper's daughters."

"Why are thou opposed to that idea?" Mary asked.

"I want someone closer to my own age. Besides, how do I win the hand of a girl in Kings Towne. I have no business there?"

Mary appeared to be studying him. He toyed with his cap, wondering what she would say next.

"Is a lack of comfort the sole reason she might not wish to leave England?" she asked.

"No. She lives with and cares for her father. He's getting old, but he's in reasonably good health. I only met him once, and very briefly at that."

"How often have thou met Alice?"

John laughed. "Only once, but I have an invitation to call when I return to England."

"Thou must have made a good impression on both of them."

"Her father was in prison at the time. I went with her to the Justice who sentenced him and helped to get his sentence reduced."

"Why is he in prison?"

"He's charged with unlawful assembly and riot. According to Alice, hundreds of Friends are imprisoned throughout England on similar charges."

Mary appeared to be mulling over this new bit of information.

"Can I expect her to give up all she has in London and make a new home in New England?" he asked. "Is there any chance she'll agree?"

"How does she feel about it?"

"We haven't discussed it."

"I take it she's spent her whole life in London."

"As far as I know, she has."

"Is her mother living?"

"I don't know. As I said, I haven't been to her house."

" How did thou come to meet her?"

John laughed. "Would you believe I met her on the street?"

He went on to recount how he had offered to go with Alice to the prison and to the meeting with Justice Spiers. Mary ventured a smile as he eagerly narrated the details of that first meeting.

"Thou accomplished a lot at one meeting," she said. "I'm surprised thou didn't ask her to marry thee on the spot."

"In my heart I was ready to propose to her, but I wasn't sure how to present myself and my future prospects in the best possible light."

"First off, to win her hand, thou must become a Friend."

"I've already told her I'm so inclined."

"It may also help thee to show a willingness to reside in England for a time after the wedding."

"You mean I should make my home in London?"

'Thou can simply spend thy time there between voyages. Don't ask her straight off to leave home. Once her father has the pleasure of holding a grandchild, she may be more willing to come to New England."

"I haven't thought that far ahead," John said.

"Thou can offer her yet another incentive, a home where she's free to worship without fear of persecution."

"She won't find that in the Plymouth Colony."

"I was thinking of Rhode Island. There's nothing to hold thee here. Thou are master of thy own ship and can sail from whatever port thou will."

"I should hate to leave you behind."

"Thou can still visit us on occasion," Mary said.

"Then it's settled," John said. "As soon as I get back to London, I'll become a Friend and ask Alice to marry me."

Nine

"Do not presume to inform me of the law."
(London, Spring 1684)

Edmund Tiddeman's home in the Horsleydown section of Southwark was substantial yet unassuming. Before presenting himself at the door, John made some inquiries among his merchant contacts. He learned that the Captain had resigned his commission in the Royal Navy shortly after he became a Friend, that he was a widower who lived in modest circumstances, and that he had two daughters, one of whom was unmarried. John concluded that a willingness to reside for a time in England might serve him well in his courtship of Alice.

Tiddeman was no longer in prison, and he welcomed John to his home. Alice too greeted him warmly, then left to go shopping for their dinner. Seated in the book-lined study, John prepared himself for a barrage of questions about his background and circumstances. But Alice's father was bent on describing the harsh winter in London.

"I never saw anything quite like it. We had our first snow early in November. Toward the end of December it turned bitter cold. For seven weeks in January and February we could walk across the Thames on foot. Water mills were frozen, ships were ice-locked, horses couldn't pull the coal carts up the icy streets from the river, and trees were split by the long frost. Even salt water in the channel froze more than two leagues off shore."

John heard him out, responding with comments about the winter in New England. His patience and courtesy were rewarded when Tiddeman, having exhausted his description of what he termed the long frost, turned the conversation to more personal matters.

"If thou are still interested in our Society, thou are more than welcome to attend a meeting during thy stay in London."

"I am indeed," John said. "When is the next meeting?"

Tiddeman appeared pleased. "Sunday morning next. Come to the house at nine. We can all go together."

"I'll make it a point to be on time."

"After dinner I'll ask Alice to instruct thee in our practices, so thou will know what to expect."

"She'll have an eager pupil," John said.

Having established what John took to be the primary qualification for a suitor, Tiddeman proceeded to inquire into his background. This was more in line with what he expected, and he replied honestly to questions about his family and financial condition. Tiddeman's expression, rather grave at the outset, gradually softened during their talk. John gathered that his answers were satisfactory.

Alice had returned during this interrogation and was busy preparing the meal. She was quiet while they ate. Prodded by Tiddeman, John described his life at sea and his home in Barnstable. After the meal they retired to the parlor. Tiddeman excused himself, saying he had business to tend in his study. Alone with Alice, John waited to gauge what course she would set for their relationship.

"If thou attend our meeting on Sunday," she said, "thou should know that thy primary purpose is to heed the prompting of thy spirit. That is best done by freeing thy mind of external thoughts and distractions. Some people may be inspired to testify aloud, but thou need only be quiet and listen to thy inner voice."

"I went to meetings when I was young," John said. "The women made a lot of me because my father Tristram aided two women missionaries, the first Friends to arrive in Boston."

"Our meetings are much the same. We seek a direct relationship with God without the intervention of a minister. Some people may testify to the persecutions to which we're subjected, but most of that is done at a special meeting for sufferings."

"My father never became a Friend, but he was a peaceful man and opposed to slavery. I think I inherited some of those traits."

Alice gave him a look that he interpreted as new interest.

"Many Friends feel the same way, but the Society has no clearly defined policy on such matters. If thou desire to join us, thou would benefit from instruction by a teacher."

"I should be pleased to have thee as my teacher," John said.

Alice laughed. "I'm not qualified to teach, but I can go with thee."

"I would like that."

"How long will thou remain in London?"

"Long enough to become a Friend."

His response won approval from both Alice and her father. On his next visit Alice told him her father had arranged for lessons to start at once.

"How many lessons will there be?" he asked.

"As many as necessary," Alice said.

In the weeks that followed, she accompanied him to the home of the teacher and took part in the lessons. He attended the weekly meeting of Friends at Horsleydown. These contacts convinced him that he wanted her as his wife, and he resolved not to return home until he had a commitment.

"I'm still not in touch with my inner voice," he confided after the third meeting. "Will that bar me from becoming a Friend?"

"Thou must be patient," she said. "It will come in time."

Later that summer he asked permission from Tiddeman to take Alice aboard the *Ataquin*. "I want her to get an impression of my life at sea."

Her father readily agreed. John described for her the workings of the vessel. They toured all the decks and compartments, ending in the master's cabin on the main deck aft.

"It's much smaller than I expected," she said, "but it's quite cozy. Is there a place for passengers?"

"I don't have many passengers. There's some room in steerage and an extra bunk in my cabin."

His inference appeared lost upon Alice. "I've never taken an ocean voyage," she said. "I fear I should be seasick."

"That is quite likely, but it usually takes only a day or two to recover."

John waited for further questions or comments. When none were forthcoming, he asked, "Have thou any desire to make such a voyage?"

"Perhaps one day," Alice said. "For now I'm content to stay at home and care for Father. He would be quite lost without me."

John regarded that as an overstatement. Tiddeman appeared to be in reasonably good health. "When thou are ready," he said, "I shall be pleased to accommodate thee." He laughed to mitigate the effect of his boldness.

"In steerage or in thy cabin?" she asked in the spirit of their exchange.

"Whichever suits thy pleasure."

"I should be getting home," Alice said, suddenly more serious. "Father will be worried about me. I thank thee for the tour."

"He has no cause for worry. Thou are in safe hands," John said.

* * *

John became a regular guest in the Tiddeman house and at weekly meetings. He had developed an easy friendship with Alice and was even more certain that he wanted her as his wife, but Alice gave no sign that she was ready to get married. She spoke often of her duty to care for her father. John was prepared to cope with that obstacle. He was simply waiting for the right circumstance and impetus to broach the question.

On their arrival at the meeting house one Sunday they found the doors barred and locked. Members of the Society had gathered outside the building and were debating among themselves what to do. They finally opted to hold the meeting in the street as a protest against this unwarranted action by the local authorities. Several dissenters left, warning of reprisals; but the meeting went on with nearly thirty men and women in attendance. Some sat on the steps of the meeting house. Others stood in the street.

As an elder in the Society, Tiddeman took it upon himself to address the meeting. "Let us seek to understand this action which the authorities have taken, that we may forgive them in our hearts. May our understanding and forgiveness open their eyes and minds to tolerance and respect for our beliefs and our right for peaceful assembly."

John felt no inclination toward forgiveness. He stood with Alice at the fringe of the crowd in the street. Everyone around him seemed intent on listening to their inner voice, but no one was moved to testify. He remained more conscious of his surroundings than he was of what his spirit had to say to him. He found the noise of passing carriages and shouts from lorry drivers to clear the way not at all conducive to meditation. Alice seemed oblivious to the clamor in the street.

Recalling the warning of the dissenters, he scrutinized each carriage as it went by. He was the first to note the approach of a horse-drawn patrol wagon with two constables, one seated beside the driver, the other hanging onto a side rail. No one spoke up to alert the meeting. John too was silent, but he took Alice by the hand. She smiled at him but gave no indication that she was aware of the impending danger.

The patrol wagon stopped in the middle of the road, blocking traffic in both directions. One constable, club at the ready, dismounted and made his way through the gathering to the door of the meeting house.

"This gathering is unauthorized and unlawful," he called in a loud voice. "All men are under arrest and will come along in the wagon. Women may go home and tend to their proper business."

"Come away!" Alice said. "Thou have no part in this."

John started to follow her, but the second constable had stationed himself on the outskirts of the gathering. He seized John by the arm and drew him roughly toward the wagon. John was inclined to pull free, but noted that the other men offered no resistance. If that was required of him to become a Friend, he determined to pass the test. He caught Alice's eye as he got into the wagon. Her look of concern seemed to harbor a hint of admiration.

The patrol wagon was packed with men. No one spoke as it swayed and bounced on its way to what Alice had once termed the Counter. Though it was familiar ground for John, he had never been inside a cell. Slightly more spacious than the patrol wagon, it was equally overcrowded. The men took turns sitting on a built-in platform that served as a bed.

That afternoon all those arrested were marshaled upstairs for a hearing before Justice Spiers. One of the constables read the charge. "Unlawful assembly in a public street and blocking traffic, resulting in a riot."

"Have you any response to the charge?" Spiers asked.

"Traffic was not blocked until the patrol wagon arrived," Tiddeman said, "and any riot that occurred was not of our making."

"Then you admit to the charge of unlawful assembly."

"We held our meeting in the street because the doors of the meeting house were barred against us, an action that was in itself unlawful."

"Do not presume to inform me of the law," Spiers said.

He proceeded with the sentencing. Tiddeman, as spokesman and a repeat offender, was remanded to Newgate. The other men were sentenced to serve six or eight weeks in the Borough Compter. When it came John's turn, Spiers scrutinized him closely.

"I know you," he said. "You're the master of a merchant ship from New England. You and a young woman came before me to plead for the man I just sent to Newgate."

"I am that person, your Honor," John said. He felt it expedient to show respect and forego the informal address preferred by Friends.

"Then I advise you to return to your ship and steer shy of any further involvement with these Quakers. If you wish to seek that young woman's hand in marriage, choose some place other than their meetings."

'I have yet to express such an intention," John said.

"I understand," Spiers said. "Go now, before I change my mind."

John left the building, but he did not return to the *Ataquin*. He went instead to the Tiddeman home to inform Alice of the sentence imposed on her father and to offer his support.

She seemed surprised to see him. "How is it thou are not in the Counter with the others?" she asked.

"Justice Spiers remembered me. I think he regards me as an outsider. Perhaps we can help thy father by paying another visit to the Justice."

"Now that Father is confined in Newgate," Alice said, "Spiers would only declare the matter is out of his hands."

"Are visitors allowed at Newgate?"

"I'm not sure, but I intend to find out."

"I should be pleased to go with thee," John said.

"And I should be glad of thy company," Alice replied.

* * *

The weather had turned hot. John would have preferred to be at sea with a fresh breeze in his face. Then he thought of Tiddeman in prison and of Alice alone at home. His proper place at the moment was in London.

He saw Alice at the meetings, which were being held in Tiddeman's home until the Friends could regain access to the meeting house. He also continued his lessons with the elder, who was preparing him for membership in the Society. And he accompanied Alice on visits to her father in Newgate. When they asked how long he would be there, they were told that the length of his sentence was indefinite.

The prison was located on the other side of the Thames, a good thirty minute walk from the Tiddeman home. Alice visited her father almost daily in the afternoon. John had moored the *Ataquin* in the pool of London. He called for Alice at home or met her at the south end of London Bridge, then walked with her to the prison. He would take the basket she carried. Prisoners had to supply much of their own food. Her face hardened as the stench emanating from the prison told them their destination was nigh.

"I don't know how he suffers it," she said. "All about him men are sick or dying from the pestilence. He'll be fortunate to come out alive."

John could find no words to console her. To his mind Newgate was aptly described by native Londoners as a hell hole. They met her father in a dimly lit visitor area, a privilege for which Tiddeman had to pay. At the end of their visit John's clothing reeked of sweat, vomit, and excrement. The odor lingered on the walk back to Horsleydown. He left Alice at the door of her house. She did not consider it proper to invite him in.

When John was accepted as a member of the Society, Tiddeman congratulated him. His situation was unchanged, but he had contracted one of the many diseases rampant in the prison.

"We must get him out of there," Alice said. "He'll die if we don't."

"I'll see what I can do," John said to comfort her.

"What can thou possibly do?"

"I'm not sure, but I have a plan that may work."

His crew was anxious to get to sea, and merchants in London were pressing him to set a date for his return voyage to New England. He couldn't wait indefinitely for Tiddeman's release, and he was determined to help Alice. With this in mind he went alone to the prison.

"Where is Alice? Is she all right?" Tiddeman asked.

"She's well and safe at home," John said. "I'm here for a personal reason. With thy permission I'd like to ask Alice to marry me."

"I've been expecting it. Thou have my permission, of course. It's Alice thou must convince. She thinks I'll be lost without her to care for me. The truth is that I'm quite capable of managing by myself. Thou can tell her I said that. I'll tell her myself, if she gives thee an argument."

"I'll do that. And I thank thee."

"I may also benefit from thy proposal. Prisoners are often released in order to attend the wedding of a son or a daughter. Thou might use that as an argument in thy proposal."

"I've heard talk of that," John said. "Is there something I can do to bring it about?"

"Thy task is to convince Alice to marry thee," Tiddeman said. "I can tend to the rest."

John left the prison feeling confident. All he needed now was the right occasion for his proposal. Since he no longer went for instructions, his time with Alice was limited to Sunday meetings and visits to Newgate. The latter option offered a better chance for success. If she agreed, they could break the news at once to her father.

* * *

London Bridge was lined on both sides with shops. John was midway across before he fastened upon a clear plan of action. He would wait until he had a clear view of the Thames. Not that he planned to jump if Alice rejected him, but he felt more comfortable within sight of water, more at home. Alice should have no doubt that she was wedding a mariner.

He nearly despaired of finding an open space on the bridge and was framing an alternate plan. Then near the north bank he caught a glimpse of the river. Taking Alice's hand, he led her to the rail. For several minutes they looked at the water as it flowed slowly toward the English Channel. There was too much refuse and waste from the slaughter houses to entice him to jump in under any circumstances.

Gathering courage, he turned to her. "I have thy father's permission to ask thee to be my wife."

Alice continued to gaze down at the river. "Thou must realize that my father is seriously ill," she said at last. "He will need someone at home to care for him when he is released from prison. I would be most ungrateful for all he has given me, if I were to abandon him now and go off to New England."

John was prepared for her objection. "Thou need have no concern on that score. I shall make London my port between voyages. Thou can stay at home and care for thy father while I'm at sea."

649

"I'm pleased that thou would do that much for me," Alice said. "What else are thou prepared to do?"

John sensed from her coy smile that she had made her decision and was playing him as one plays a fish that has taken the bait.

"I became a Friend in the hope of marrying thee."

"That strikes me as a poor reason for changing thy belief."

"I was already so inclined. Thou did but provide a motive."

"I'm glad of that. I suspected as much."

John played his last card. "If thou agree, thy father may be released from prison to attend the wedding."

"Even if his release is unconditional," Alice said, "he'll soon be charged with some other offense."

"I have nothing more to offer thee," John said, "only my love and a comfortable living in the place of thy choice."

"That is quite enough," Alice said. "I gladly accept thy offer."

Ten

"I take this my dear friend Alice Tiddeman to be my wife."
(London, Autumn 1684)

Late in October John and Alice entered the meeting house and sat quietly with her father and the elder who had provided instruction, facing family, friends, and other members of the Horsleydown meeting. All the requirements had been met. They had written permission from Tiddeman to wed. The fact that John's parents were dead had facilitated matters in that respect. They had presented their proposal to the community at a monthly meeting and gained their approval for the marriage.

John left it to Alice to determine the proper time for them to rise and say their vows. She assured him she would know the right moment. He presumed she would listen to her inner voice. He sat erect on the hard bench and looked straight ahead, but he cast an occasional nervous glance sideways at Alice. She appeared perfectly calm.

Tiddeman had been released from Newgate to attend the wedding. John was looking at him when he felt Alice take his hand. They stood up together. He had memorized the vows they were to exchange. She pressed his hand as a signal for him to begin.

"Friends and people, I desire thee to take notice that in the fear of the Lord and in the presence of this assembly, I take this my dear friend Alice Tiddeman to be my wife, promising to be to her a faithful and loving husband until death shall separate us."

John relaxed and waited for Alice to speak.

"Friends, in the fear of the Lord and before thee in this Assembly, I take this friend, John Hull, to be my husband, solemnly promising through the Lord to be to him a faithful and loving wife until death shall separate us."

She sat down and pulled him down beside her. All was quiet until Tiddeman rose and addressed the assembly.

"I welcome my friend John to my family and to this assembly. I entrust my daughter Alice to his care, with the assurance that he will be kind to her and give her offspring. May they have a long and happy life together, and may the Lord keep him safe while at sea."

No one else was moved to speak, but all present signed the record as witnesses when the meeting was over. Among them were Alice's sister Mary and a middle-aged woman named Prudence. Alice said she was a cousin on her mother's side with whom she had occasional contact.

"I gather that your husband is a mariner," Prudence said after she congratulated the newlyweds.

"He is indeed," Alice said, an element of pride in her voice. "He's master of his own ship and makes regular voyages to New England."

"My son speaks constantly of going to sea. May I send him to your husband for advice, or perhaps for training on his ship."

John did not wait for Alice to reply. "By all means," he said. "What is the boy's name?"

"Charles," the woman said. "Charles Wager."

* * *

To John's surprise, Tiddeman accompanied them back to the house and settled himself in the study. He had assumed that Alice's father would have to return to prison right after the ceremony.

"When I was released, no one mentioned a time or a date for my return," Tiddeman said in response to his question. "I propose to remain at home until someone comes to take me back."

He had survived in Newgate due to his willingness to pay for better accommodations and for additional food and water. But he was a victim of disease and of the lice that infested the prison. The day after the wedding he kept to his bed, saying he felt out of sorts. A doctor was summoned and diagnosed his malady as gaol fever. For a month Alice was fully occupied in nursing him back to health. When he recovered, his face was drawn and his body wasted.

Meanwhile, John pacified the London merchants by arranging to sail for New England in December. Some of his crew had taken berths on other ships, but he soon enlisted a full complement.

"I'd be happy to have thee aboard," he told Alice. His tone indicated that he did not expect her to agree.

"My father needs me at home," she said.

"I understand," John said, "but I had to ask. Thou are welcome to sail with me at any time."

"I never doubted it," Alice said.

* * *

Shortly before John was due to sail, the newlyweds had a visit from Prudence Wager. She lived in another district of London, so contact was infrequent. When John appeared puzzled, she hastened to introduce herself.

"I'm Alice's cousin, and this is her nephew. I spoke to you about him on the day of your wedding."

John regarded the blonde-haired, wide-eyed youth who stood on his doorstep. His clothing was neat and clean, but worn and not the best fit. The sleeves were a trifle short, the pants too high on his legs. He was an inch taller than John, slim and muscular. His bright smile conveyed a sense of anticipation and confidence.

"Yes, of course," John said.

Alice saved him from further confusion. "Prudence! And Charles! It's good to see thee again. Come in. I'll make tea while thou speak to John. I assume that is the purpose of thy visit."

"It is indeed," Prudence said, "but I should like some tea."

She waited until Alice had left before continuing. "I don't know how much Alice has told you about my circumstances."

"I know very little about thee or thy son," John said.

"I can understand that. My husband died shortly after Charles was born. I've done my best to bring him up and give him a good education. It hasn't been easy. My father did not approve of my marriage. He gave us barely enough support to keep us alive. I tell you this in confidence."

To spare her further embarrassment, John turned to the boy. "If I remember rightly, it is thy wish to pursue a life at sea."

"I like ships," Charles said. "I like to visit the docks on the Thames; but I have yet to sail on the channel, let alone the ocean."

"That is the purpose of our visit," Prudence said. "Please forgive me if I speak bluntly. Would you accept Charles as an apprentice, so he can learn the trade of a seaman? It would be a great service to him and to me as well."

John stroked his new grown beard. Taking on an apprentice involved time and no small expense. Normally he could expect compensation, but Prudence was in no position to pay him. What she proposed was of some benefit to him. He would have an extra hand aboard, one who worked for only his keep. He studied the youth before him. Charles sat straight and calmly in his chair. He appeared not at all apprehensive, as if his uncle's approval was assured.

"I'll take thy son on my ship," he said, "but thou must understand that he will be under my control. His life will henceforth be tied to my voyages across the Atlantic. Of course, he is free to visit thee when the *Ataquin* is in port. Are thou wiling to give thy son into my care under these conditions?"

"I am," Prudence said. "I expected no less."

"And what about the boy? Is he also in agreement?"

"He can speak for himself."

"I agree wholeheartedly," Charles said with a bright smile, "and I thank you for this chance. I promise you won't regret your decision."

"As you can see, we don't belong to the Society of Friends," Prudence said. "Charles feels duty bound to honor his father's memory in that respect."

"Not all of my crew share my beliefs," John said. "I should be sore pressed to put to sea if I made that a requirement."

"Then it's settled. I can hire a solicitor to draw up the agreement."

"That won't be necessary. This is all in the family. Charles is free to leave whenever a life at sea no longer suits him."

"I see little chance of that," Charles said.

Alice returned with tea, crumpets, and a saucer of lemon curd. "I trust thy business has been concluded," she said as she poured.

"I've agreed to take Charles on as my apprentice," John said. "From now on he'll be like a son to us."

Alice smiled, but she made no further comment.

* * *

After a rough voyage across the ocean John made port in Boston, where he conducted a large portion of his business. While there he found time for a visit to Sandwich. He was eager to tell his sister about his marriage.

Mary was overjoyed at the news. "So thou are now a Friend."

"I'm a member of the Horsleydown meeting in London," he said, an element of pride in his voice.

"When can we expect to see thy bride?"

"Her father is ill. She can't leave him alone. I admire her devotion."

"So thy home will be in London."

"For the time being. I know not what the future may hold."

"Then I have something to look forward to," Mary said.

"Have thou heard from Joseph?" John asked.

"I've had no word from him since thou were last here."

"I want to expand my trade route to include Newport. Perhaps I can visit him before I return to London."

"I miss talking to Experience," Mary said. "Please give my love to her and Joseph and the four children. I suspect another may be on the way."

"I thought thou had no word from them."

"Nor have I. Reuben is nearly two. She's due for another child."
John laughed. "So that's how it is. I'll have to remember that."

"Is Alice expecting?"

"I won't know that until I return to London."

"While thou are in Newport, thou might look in on Tami, our old nursemaid," Mary said. "I've had no word about her in years."

"If she's still there, I promise to look her up," John said.

* * *

John had long considered adding Newport to his trade route, and he resolved to contact some merchants there before he returned to London.

He had been in Newport before; so he knew how to get to Kings Towne. Accompanied by Wager, he rowed across the east bay to the island of Conanicut. Crossing the Atlantic, the youth had demonstrated an affinity for all things bearing on seamanship. Any doubt John may have had about his decision to take on an apprentice had long since been put to rest. Wager did not seek or expect special treatment, but John sensed his disappointment at not being invited to go with him to Sandwich.

To compensate for this failure, John took the boy along on his visit to Joseph, saying he wanted someone to man the oars. A narrow path a mile long crossed the island. There he hired a boatman to ferry them over the west bay to the Narragansett country.

Joseph was pleased to see him. As Mary had anticipated, Experience was indeed pregnant. She set about preparing a meal, while the brothers exchanged news and views. Wager entertained the two older boys, Tristram eight and Joseph six. They paid rapt attention to his stories of life at sea.

Joseph spoke of his involvement in the Society of Friends. "We're using my home until a meeting house can be built. I'm preparing to serve as a teacher. Our community continues to grow, and we hold our meetings without interference."

"Hundreds of Friends are in prison in England for unlawful assembly, refusing to pay tithes, or take an oath," John said. "For all I know, Alice's father may again be one of them"

He went on to expound on the joys of married life.

"When will thou bring thy bride to New England?" Joseph asked.

"I can't say. Alice has undertaken to care for her father as long as he needs her. I agreed to that when we married."

"Is he seriously ill?" Experience asked.

"He was suffering the effects of prison fever when I left. Until he's fully recovered, my home port will be London."

"When thou come back, thou should settle in Kings Towne," Joseph said. "Friends in Plymouth are still fined for their refusal to take an oath of loyalty. Alice will be much happier here than in Barnstable, and we can work together for our own good and that of the Society."

John laughed. "The brothers Hull. If I do leave Barnstable, I'll likely settle and conduct my trade out of Newport."

"Thou will at least be close to us," Experience said.

"I hope Alice will be happy here?" John said. "She's lived in London all her life. It will be a change for her."

"Women are more adaptable than thou give us credit for," Experience said as she stirred the pot of rabbit stew.

"I'll bear that in mind," John said.

* * *

Several merchants in the Rhode Island Colony expressed an interest in establishing a regular trade with London, and John resolved to make Newport a regular port of call. His last task was to keep his promise to Mary. He vaguely recalled Tami's modest dwelling and her herb garden, and he was gratified that the reality corresponded with his mental picture. But the woman who appeared at the door was a stranger to him. Twenty years had aged Tami beyond his recognition.

"Master John!" she cried. "Is it really you?"

She invited him in, brewed a pot of herbal tea, and prodded him for news about the family. She seemed pleased to hear that he was married. When he had a chance to ask some questions of his own, he learned that Tami was well established as a medicine lady in the community.

"People pay me what they can," she said. "It's enough for my needs. As you can see, I live very simply."

"Thy home is quite comfortable," John said.

Tami smiled. "All that's missing is a man."

John sought to imagine his father's relationship with this dark old woman. He gave it up, concentrating instead on learning more about her. By the end of his visit he had come to appreciate her fierce independence and her love of nature.

"You look quite healthy," Tami said as he prepared to leave. "But if you ever feel sick, come and see me."

John allowed that he suffered occasionally from a pain in his left hip. He departed with a bottle of lineament, having promised to convey her love to his siblings.

* * *

In London the situation was much the same. Tiddeman had recovered from the gaol fever, but he remained in poor health. He had offered to share his home with the young couple. John welcomed the arrangement. He was assured that Alice would be safe while he was at sea, and she could continue to care for her father.

"I've spent no more time in Newgate," Tiddeman said in response to John's question, "but Friends are still subject to arrest and persecution."

But John's first thought on his arrival was the realization that Alice was carrying their first child. He made no effort to hide his tears of joy.

"If it's a boy, we'll call him Tiddeman," he said.

"And if it's a girl?"

"Both of us have a sister named Mary," John said.

"Then Mary it shall be," Alice said.

She spoke to him in private about her father. "I do what I can to safeguard his health, but I'm afraid another stay in prison would kill him."

"We might persuade him not to attend meetings," John said.

"He says he has a duty to testify until Friends are free to gather without fear of reprisal. I fear that day is still distant. He plans to attend a meeting for sufferings on Friday."

"I've never been to a meeting like that," John said.

"They take place four times a month. A fourth of the members attend each meeting, and each one has a chance to testify to any ill treatment or persecution. Everything is recorded in a book, so it won't be forgotten."

"Will thou attend the meeting?"

"Only men are allowed to testify. Besides, in my condition I don't go out unless I have to."

"I understand," John said. "Thou must tire easily."

"It isn't that. People I know will accuse me of living in sin, people who aren't Friends. I don't believe in sin, but it still bothers me."

"Why would they say a thing like that?"

"The civil authorities don't recognize the vows we exchanged as a legal marriage contract."

John made no response, and they let the matter drop.

* * *

On Friday John and Tiddeman set out for the meeting house. The street door was once again barred, and they entered through a panel at the rear of the building. The windows had been shuttered on the inside to avoid attracting attention. Seated on a bench beside Tiddeman, John leaned forward to listen to the litany of fines and imprisonments borne by members of the Horsleydown meeting. One by one they testified to their encounters with justices, recorders, constables, and juries.

Some members spoke of fines levied for absence from public worship, failure to pay tithes, or refusal to swear an oath. Others had been arrested for unlawful assembly and riot. The fact that a constable was summoned was enough to constitute a riot. Most of those cases involved an informer, usually a woman. If a group had been arrested or imprisoned, a spokesman recited the list of punishments.

Having undergone that experience, John was familiar with the court procedures. In some cases the decision of a jury was at variance with the facts. One man was fined twenty pounds for attending a meeting, even though witnesses testified that he was absent. Another was fined when the name on the warrant was not his. Men who refused to pay fines were sentenced to prison and had their goods and property seized to satisfy the judgment against them. Fines and seizures ranged from ten to thirty pounds. Prison terms varied from a week in the local compter to several months in Newgate.

One case in particular commanded John's attention. For failure to pay a fine of ten pounds the man's home was occupied for nearly a week, while a constable oversaw removal of his household possessions valued at three times the amount of the fine. On the third day as the family was roasting a shoulder of mutton, porters seized the spit and dripping pan, the dishes and knives, the chairs and table. The family borrowed a platter to set the meat on and sat on the floor while they ate.

"Why are people being fined for holding a meeting in their own home?" John asked on the walk home.

"If five or more persons are present, other than family members, it's considered unlawful assembly," Tiddeman said.

"What happens to the money garnered from the sale of household goods that are confiscated?"

"It goes in the general treasury. Any balance is supposed to be returned to the owner, but it often ends up in the constable's pocket.""I understand that King James is a Catholic," John said "Are things likely to improve under his reign?"

"He needs the support of the Anglican Church," Tiddeman said. "His religion has thus far been a private matter. I don't expect any immediate relief from our sufferings."

* * *

John was in Horsleydown for the birth of their daughter Mary. Alice remained in bed for two weeks following the delivery, and a nursemaid was brought in to help care for the baby. Tiddeman was delighted with his new granddaughter, and John never tired of cradling his first offspring in his arms. In the evening the men retired to the study to discuss the situation at court.

"During the summer King James squashed rebellions by the Duke of Monmouth in England and the Duke of Argyll in Scotland," Tiddeman said. "But the opposition seems to have reawakened his distrust of his subjects."

"What do thou mean by distrust?" John asked.

"Before King Charles died, the Parliament tried three times to pass a law that would exclude James from succession to the throne because of his religion. They didn't succeed, but that sentiment still persists. In response he has increased the size of the army and placed the new regiments in command of Catholic officers from abroad who are loyal to him. Needless to say, both the Parliament and Church authorities are upset by his actions."

"Will it end in another civil war?" John asked.

"I hope not," Tiddeman said. "I don't want another Lord Protector."

* * *

John continued to neglect his trade, and merchants in London had to press him to make voyages to New England. Late that summer he prepared to sail again for Boston and Newport.

"I know thy father is not in the best of health," he told Alice, "but one day I should like thee to come with me to New England. I want thee to see it, and I look forward to the day when we can make it our home."

"I hear reports that in the colonies Friends are also fined and cast in prison" she said. "Would thou have me abandon the comforts of London to no advantage?"

"That is still true in Plymouth and Massachusetts, but we need not settle in Barnstable. In the Narragansett country, where my brother lives, Friends can worship without interference. And in Rhode Island even the governor is a member of our Society."

"But isn't New England still pretty much a wilderness?" Alice asked.

"Newport is a busy seaport. Not like London, of course; but I feel we could be happy there."

"Once Father no longer needs me here in London, I shall gladly follow thee to the Indies, if that is thy wish."

"As long as he stays out of prison, he should continue to get better."

"I'll do my best to keep him out of trouble. But thou know very well that he'll pursue whatever course he sets his mind to."

John smiled in acknowledgment. "I trust thee to be his compass."

"That is more easily said than done," Alice said.

* * *

Another year passed, and John continued to make London his home port between voyages. Talking with Tiddeman, he gathered that the political climate in England was undergoing a change. Alice's father seemed more relaxed, and he spoke less of prison or sufferings.

While preparing to sail for New England, John once again broached the subject to Alice. He had made the offer before in private, but this time Tiddeman was with them at table. John had not alerted him in advance, but he hoped for his support.

"Thy cabin is ready," he said, "if thou choose to accompany me."

"I can't leave Father alone," Alice said. "Perhaps on thy next trip."

Tiddeman broke the awkward silence that ensued. "Thou have placed my needs above thy own for nearly two years. I'm grateful for thy devotion; but my health is much improved, and King James issued a declaration of indulgence this past spring. The time has come for thee to make a life for thyself with thy husband."

John was privy to the politics of the day; but he pled ignorance, hoping thus to help his cause. "I thought that applied only to Catholics."

"He suspended the penal codes, so Catholics can worship without being arrested for nonconformance with Church of England regulations. But Friends now enjoy the same benefits. I'm grateful for that."

"That may be true," Alice said, "but most of the Anglican bishops are opposed to the declaration, and King James is at odds with the Parliament. Thou must admit that the situation is unsettled."

"That is always the case," Tiddeman said. "The time has come for thee to heed thy husband's wishes rather than my needs."

"What if thou take ill? What will thou do?"

"I'm quite able to care for myself. I can hire a nurse if necessary."

"But thou will be alone in the house."

"Thy sister Mary can look in on me from time to time, and I can call upon members of the Society."

"It distresses me to be separated from thee."

"Thy place is with thy husband," Tiddeman said. "It will pleasure me to know that thou and thy daughter are aboard his ship when hr sails."

"If that is thy true sentiment," Alice said, "I shall gladly abide by thy wishes and those of my husband."

John was silent, but in his heart he was well pleased.

Eleven

With his wife at his side on the navigation deck, John brought the *Ataquin* safely through the narrow entrance to Narragansett Bay. Alice had endured repeated bouts of seasickness on the long voyage across the North Atlantic. Upon viewing the islands of Aquidneck on the starboard side and Conanicut to port, she shed tears of joy. She stood with arms outstretched, as if she were eager to touch dry land.

"If I had to choose between those two islands," she said, "I'm drawn to the one on the left. It has more charm."

John laughed. "I'll make note of that, but thou have yet to see either place. No need to make a hasty decision."

The *Ataquin* had sustained damage to the sails and mizzenmast in the rough crossing. John relaxed as he made anchor in Newport harbor. His eyes took in the sprawling settlement of wooden houses that stretched up the hill away from the waterfront. Only one of a handful of makeshift piers and wharfs bore any resemblance to those along the Thames in England.

"Newport has a competent shipyard," John said. "They can make needed repairs to the ship while we establish our new home."

"I confess that I'm a little apprehensive," Alice said. "I'm a stranger here and know nothing about the people and customs."

"My brother and his wife will make thee welcome. Thou will soon feel at home and among family".

"I'm eager to meet Joseph and Experience. Do they live nearby?"

"The Narragansett country is west of here, just beyond the island that struck thy fancy."

"Then we may settle halfway between," Alice said.

* * *

"Welcome to the Dominion of New England and to what is now the town of Rochester," Joseph said.

John had just introduced his wife and their year-old daughter Mary. He had no comment. His immediate concern was to make his newly acquired family acquainted with that of his brother. The political situation in New England could wait. Experience meanwhile had trotted out her own children. Tristram, was nine, Joseph seven, Mary five, Reuben three, and John one.

John felt a renewed kinship with his brother. They had both married Friends and were raising families. They were soon to be neighbors, or within easy reach of each other. The children could grow up knowing their cousins. All was as it should be.

Joseph raised the subject again as he was showing off his holdings. He seemed particularly proud of his stable of horses.

"Being a dominion has one advantage," he said. "I can sell horses to the other colonies without restriction."

"I had word of a dominion before I left England," John said. "Are all of the colonies included?"

"First it was Massachusetts, Plymouth, New Hampshire, Maine, and the Narragansett country. Now they've added Connecticut and Rhode Island."

"What brought all this about?"

Joseph leaned against the rail fence of an enclosure where his horses ran free. "Last year an order came down setting up a provisional commission under Joseph Dudley from Massachusetts. But his charter didn't arrive until this past spring, and his efforts to change things met with resistance. The magistrates he appointed refused to serve, he has limited sources of revenue, and his order to make churches available for Anglican services was ignored. All he's accomplished here is to rename the town, and no one pays much attention to that."

"Is Dudley still in control?"

"Edmund Andros is now the royal governor."

"Wasn't he governor of the New York Colony?"

"The same man."

"Can he accomplish more than Dudley?"

"He'll have more authority and military backing. It remains to be seen what he does with it."

"Alice's father says that the King wants more uniformity in how the colonies are governed. The dominion is a step toward that end."

"Is that thy opinion as well?"

From the tone of his brother's question John sensed some opposition. "I'm not sure. It seems to makes good sense."

"I'm inclined to fear the worst from a royal governor," Joseph said.

"Tell me more about thy plans for this land," John said.

"I still ply my trade as a cooper. I have plenty of trees on the property. As the land is cleared, I can breed more horses. That trade is quite lucrative, at least for the moment. There will always be a demand for barrels."

"Who does the work? Thy children are too young for such labor."

Joseph laughed. "Some time ago I helped to rescue an Indian who was in danger of being sold into slavery. He's now my foreman. He recruits all the workers I need from the local tribe."

"So thou have a steady source of cheap labor."

"I pay them a fair wage. I feel that I owe them that for all the women and children who died at our hands in the swamp fight."

When the brothers returned to the house, they found their wives engaged in a different topic of conversation.

"I was asking Alice where thou plan to settle," Experience said.

"We have yet to decide," John said.

"There's good land available here in Kings Towne," Joseph said.

"I'll be sailing out of Newport. Living on this side of the bay would make it hard to conduct business Alice has taken a fancy to Conanicut. We'll decide after we have a look at the island."

"Wherever it is, we'll be able to visit each other," Experience said.

"I should like that," Alice said.

* * *

Some nine miles long and a mile in width, Conanicut boasted grassy meadows and broad marshes. The Narragansett Indians had made the island their summer home. The island was purchased by authorities in Newport and used as pasture for sheep and cattle. Then two prominent residents, William Coddington and Benedict Arnold, acquired the island and sold off lots. A town was established in 1678 and named Jamestown. This much John learned from contacts in Newport before he set out with Alice to view the island.

A descendant of Arnold met them on the pier at the east end of North Ferry Road. "Are you planning to settle in Jamestown?" he asked.

"We're looking for some suitable land," John said.

"There's a nice piece at the north end of the island, if three hundred and fifty acres suits your purpose. It includes some swamp land, but the high ground near the west shore would be ideal for a house."

"That should make it easy to visit Joseph and his family," Alice said.

"Let's have a look at it before we make any decisions," John said.

The land proved to be as the agent described it, and they soon agreed on a price. With the aid of the crew from the *Ataquin* and recruits from the town, a stately house with two levels and a central chimney was ready to be occupied by the following spring. John's apprentice Wager took a personal interest in the design and construction of the house. As one of the larger homes on the island, the structure was referred to in some quarters as the Hull mansion. The major settlement on the island was several miles to the south on land owned by Coddington, but John was satisfied to have ready access to the north ferry.

* * *

Joseph had just confirmed that the horses were properly bedded down when he saw a group of his Indian workers waiting outside the barn. He prided himself on how he treated laborers on his property. But he sensed from their uneasy manner that this group was a delegation of some sort.

"Have thou something to say?" he asked an Indian who had stepped forward and appeared to be their spokesman.

"Man say he own land. Tell us to move away."

"What man?"

"Man from company."

"The Atherton Company?"

The Indian nodded.

Joseph called to mind what he knew and what Harper had told him about the Atherton Company. None of it was good. The company was formed prior to the trouble with Metacom. From its foundation the proprietors had preyed upon unsuspecting Indian sachems, plying them with strong spirits so they would sign deeds transferring ownership of their lands to the company. Supported by authorities in the United Colonies, the Atherton Company at one time laid claim to all land in the Narragansett country not specifically deeded to English settlers. But the Rhode Island Colony had challenged their claim and appealed to the Crown for a definitive ruling. The King and Lords of Trade had yet to reach a decision. As far as Joseph knew, that was where the matter stood.

"Tell the people in thy village not to worry," he said. "I'll look into it and see what I can do."

The Indians expressed their gratitude and dispersed, leaving Joseph to ponder his next move. He had given little thought of late to the Atherton Company. With the establishment of a dominion the matter may have taken a turn of which he was not aware. He could rely on Harper to have the latest information on the subject.

Harper greeted him warmly. "I'm pleased to see thee, Joseph. I trust Experience and the children are well"

"Quite well, thank you."

"I can tell from thy demeanor that something is troubling thee."

"The Indians who work for me have been ordered to vacate their village. I'm not sure who gave the order." Joseph went on to describe the concerns of the delegation that had approached him.

"Thou can blame Dudley for that," Harper said. "In an effort to assert authority, he sent a commission to settle various affairs in the Narragansett country. Half of the commission were proprietors of the Atherton Company. They obtained a ruling that squatters on land claimed by the company must deal with a committee from the company or leave."

"Indians can hardly be called squatters," Joseph said.

"Most Indians move about with the seasons. Those who work for thee stay in one place. That's why they're being dispossessed."

"Who's in charge of this committee, and where can I find him?"

"I'm not sure," Harper said. "Thou might contact Richard Wharton. He's a proprietor of the company, and he was on Dudley's commission."

"How is it thou are so well-informed on the subject?"

"Thou are not the first to approach me with similar problems."

"What else can thou tell me about Wharton?"

"I've never met the man. He lives in Boston and has extensive land interests in New Hampshire as well as Narragansett. That's all I know."

"I thank thee for thy help," Joseph said.

"No need for thanks. Will thou stay for dinner?"

"Another time. I have to talk to Wharton."

After several inquiries Joseph finally caught up with him. It was late in the day, and Wharton had just left the home of one of his targets. The squatter stood shaking his fist as Wharton walked toward his horse.

Though this was hardly an ideal time or place, Joseph was determined to put the matter to rest. "Richard Wharton," he called without dismounting.

Wharton appeared startled. "That's right. And who might you be?"

"Joseph Hull, a land owner in this Narragansett country."

"If you have a valid title to your property, I have no business with you," Wharton said dismissively.

"It's not my property that concerns me," Joseph said. "I employ a number of Indians in my business."

"And what is your business?"

"I'm a cooper, and I sell horses. The Indians who work for me have been ordered by someone from the Atherton Company to vacate land they have occupied as long as anyone can remember."

"I had no part in that," Wharton said. "It was probably Hutchinson who made the decision based on the facts of the case."

"But thou are in a position to do something about it," Joseph said.

"What would you have me do?"

"Let them remain on land that is rightfully theirs."

"That, sir, is your opinion. They do occupy the land, but they have no legal title to it. They don't own it. We do."

"Indians know nothing of ownership. Land was granted to them for their use, not as a possession."

"That is their misfortune. It's up to us to educate them."

"Then thou refuse to remedy the situation?" Joseph asked.

"I won't intervene in Hutchinson's decision," Wharton said. "Speak to him, if you have a mind to; but I doubt that he'll do what you want. Now if you'll excuse me, I must be on my way."

With that he mounted his horse and rode off.

Based on Wharton's response, Joseph saw the futility of talking to Hutchinson. It was clearly up to him to resolve the problem. The next day he summoned the man who had served as spokesman for the Indian delegation. He explained in simple terms the role of the Atherton Company and the contested legality of its claim to Indian lands.

"What you say is, we must go," the Indian said.

"Just until the case is decided," Joseph said. "In the meantime thou can tell the people in thy village that they are free to make their home in the wooded portion of my lands."

"I tell them, and my people thank you."

The man walked off toward a group of Indian workers near the barn. Their excitement was evident as he told them the news. Some workers spotted Joseph and raised their arms in a show of appreciation. He waved in response, then entered the house to tell Experience what he had done.

"That was kind of thee," she said.

"I had no choice," he said. "I hope I don't regret my decision."

* * *

One day while his house was still under construction, John spotted Wager in the company of a tall muscular black man. A look of apprehension or fear was evident in the man's eyes.

"This is Ben," Wager said. "I found him hiding on the waterfront in Newport. He said he escaped from a ship in the harbor, where he was being held as a slave. I agreed to hide him until the ship left."

"Where did thou hide him?" John asked.

"I recalled that you spoke once of a black woman in Newport who could cure a variety of illnesses."

"You mean Tami," John said.

Wager nodded. "When I mentioned your name, she agreed to take Ben into her house until the ship sailed. Now he needs work and a place to stay. You'll need help on the farm. He's big and strong and eager to work."

"He's a fugitive. What if his owners come to reclaim their property?"

"He's willing to take that chance."

"What makes thee think I'll agree to shelter him?"

"Your brother said that you refused to serve on a ship that was taking Indians to Spain to be sold as slaves."

"Indians are different," John said.

"I fail to see the difference," Wager said.

"Blacks are property. An Indian is a free man."

"Both are being displaced and forced to serve a foreign master. The black woman Tami said your father was opposed to slavery."

John paused a moment to reflect. Wager was presumptuous in his conclusion, and he was clearly overstepping his bounds as an apprentice. Yet he had shown initiative, a willingness to make decisions and stand up for them. Leadership qualities should be nurtured and encouraged, not stifled.

"Does Ben speak any English?" he asked.

"He worked on a plantation in Virginia. His master called him a troublemaker and sold him. All he wants is to be a free man."

"It will cause less comment in town if he remains a slave for now."

"Then you'll take him in?"

"He can help with the planting, and I'll need someone to look after things while I'm at sea. Alice has enough to do, and she may be expecting."

* * *

Ben proved quite knowledgeable about what was required to operate a farm, and John soon had sufficient confidence in him to undertake another voyage. When the spring planting was done, he sailed for England

On his arrival in London he looked in on Alice's father, as was his custom. Tiddeman expressed a keen interest in the progress of the Dominion of New England under a royal governor.

"I hear Andros is meeting with a good deal of opposition," he said. "What has he done to stir up so much resistance?"

John had been too occupied in the construction of his house to attend to what was happening in Boston. But his brother had kept him abreast of developments following the arrival of Andros. He had little doubt but that Joseph was a contributor to the opposition cited by Tiddeman.

"For one thing he's has abolished the governing assembly in each colony," John said. "A council he appointed makes the laws, which he must approve. Meetings are held in Boston, and delegates must travel at their own expense; so only those from Massachusetts and Plymouth attend. The other colonies have little voice in what happens."

"How are thou and thy family affected?"

"My brother Joseph is opposed to the tax on livestock. As for me, I don't like a tax on imported alcohol; but taxes are needed in order to govern."

"What of the rigid enforcement of the Navigation Acts?" Tiddeman asked. "Thou must feel the effects of that?"

"It has reduced the quantity of foreign goods shipped to ports in New England, but my trade is chiefly with merchants in London."

Tiddeman sighed. "I commend thee for thy tolerance in these troubled times. For myself, I know not what position to take on the King's continuing efforts to make England more Catholic."

"He had thy approval when he issued his declaration of indulgence," John said. "What has he done to change thy mind?"

"We do benefit from some of his rulings, but he's overreaching. He received the papal nuncio at court, and now he's purging office holders and replacing them with his Catholic favorites. We don't want a return to Rome."

"Will we have another civil war?" John asked.

"I sincerely hope not, but the King has lost whatever Church support he had earlier in his reign."

"I'm glad to be so far distant from court," John said.

"The King is my problem," Tiddeman said. "Yours is with Andros."

Twelve

"I fear we have some dark days ahead."
(Rhode Island Colony, Autumn 1687)

When John returned home in the fall, he was eager for news on what had occurred in his absence. His brother proved to be well-informed.

"Resistance to the dominion and to Andros has spread throughout the colonies," Joseph said.

"Has he imposed additional taxes?" John asked.

"It's more than that. He's issued an order that limits town meetings to once a year for the election of officials. Meetings for any other purpose or at any other time are forbidden. The order violates the Magna Carta, which guarantees that taxation must be approved by representatives of the people."

"Aren't the people represented on the governing council in Boston?"

"Nearly all of the council members are large landowners. Many have connections to the Atherton Company, including the one from Narragansett country. Small farmers and merchants have no voice."

"What else has he done?" John asked.

"It's a long list. Ministers in Boston were ordered to make their churches available for Anglican worship. When one of them resisted, Andros demanded the keys to the building, so services could be held there."

"Things like that have little or no effect here," John said.

Joseph gave his brother a stern look. "If thou seek something closer to home, Andros has ordered all land titles issued under previous charters to be recertified. The new titles contain a quit claim provision to raise money."

"Have thou obeyed that order?"

"I have not, nor do I intend to. It's a lengthy process, and the outcome is uncertain. Most local landowners have chosen to ignore the law rather than risk losing title to their lands."

"Are there no restrictions on his power?" John asked.

"All of the colonies have had their charters revoked. Officials in Connecticut hid their charter in an oak tree. Andros seized their official seal, so the government can't function. His only weakness is a need for money. He has appointed a commission to review the tax laws in each colony and recommend a uniform code for the dominion. But the final decision is up to Andros, and he's sure to favor the big landowners."

"How can thou say that resistance is spreading?"

"Resistance by individuals. We can disobey or ignore the laws. That's all we have left."

"There may be some hope. In England the Church and the Parliament are opposed to the King's policies favoring Catholics. Alice's father feels that a popular revolt is in the offing."

"And then what?" Joseph asked.

"We can only wait and see," John said.

* * *

John had business with Walter Clarke, the former and now deposed governor of Rhode Island. They were conferring in the paneled study of his home in Newport when they were interrupted by his brother-in-law. His face was flushed, and he was breathing hard.

"I've just come from the ferry in Portsmouth," he said. "Andros is on his way here to demand the surrender of our charter."

"Well, he won't get it," Clarke said. "My uncle got that charter from Charles II at great expense to himself. I'm not about to give it up."

"What do you propose to do?"

John rose as if to leave, but Clarke motioned him to stay. "We must hide it," he said.

His brother-in-law uttered a mirthless laugh. "Do you have any particular oak tree in mind?"

"Andros has been governor nearly a year," John said. "I'm surprised that he hasn't already seized our charter."

"He ordered us to give it up," Clarke said, "but we always had a ready excuse, some reason for delay. This is the first time he's come here himself."

"We have to get it out of the house," his brother-in-law said. "This is the first place he'll look. Give it to me."

"Where do you propose to hide it?" Clarke asked.

"I have no idea, but time is short."

John's mind was racing. He wasn't opposed to the Dominion of New England and was willing to abide by its regulations, though he was troubled by reports that Andros was using the office of royal governor for personal gain. Then he thought of his recent talk with

Joseph, of the growing influence of large landowners, of the unresolved claim by the Connecticut Colony to the Narragansett country. What if Rhode Island were to lose its charter, while Connecticut retained that document? What would that mean for Joseph and for himself?

"I'll hide the charter aboard the *Ataquin*," he said. "Andros can't search every ship in the harbor."

The two men stared at him in surprise. Clarke was the first to speak. "That sounds reasonable. Unless you have a better idea," he added, turning to his brother-in-law.

"Not at the moment."

Clarke unlocked a cabinet behind his desk, took out the scroll, and gave it to John, who tucked it inside his coat. As he left the house, he noticed a man who seemed to be trying hard to ignore him. It struck him that Andros might well have anticipated their attempt to hide the charter and dispatched someone to ride ahead and spy on Clarke. If so, he too might now be a suspect. On his way to the harbor he glanced back frequently to see if anyone was following him.

Back aboard the *Ataquin* he explained the situation to Wager. "I want thee to conceal the charter somewhere on the ship. Thou needn't tell me the exact location. If I'm questioned by Andros, I can honestly say I have no idea where it is."

Wager's face bore a strained expression. "The charter of every colony has been revoked," he said. "I thought the royal governor had your support."

John regarded him in surprise. It wasn't a refusal, but Wager clearly had reservations about his request. "I respect the governor's authority," he said, "but I can also understand the desire of people in

Rhode Island to retain their hard-won charter, even if it is of no value at present. I'm a colonist as well as a British subject. I see no disloyalty in what I'm doing."

Wager appeared to consider this argument. The muscles in his face relaxed, and he ventured a smile. "I don't question your loyalty. But you will grant that the charter has some value as a symbol of the independence that the colonists once enjoyed."

"I'll grant you that," John said.

"Be that as it may," Wager said, "the man you saw outside Clarke's house has likely identified you. When they can't find the charter there, the next place they'll look is here on the ship."

"Have thou a better plan?"

"You might hide it somewhere on your property in Jamestown."

"I won't have them upsetting Alice," John said. "I shall remain aboard the *Ataquin*. If I was followed, they'll find me here and not at home. I trust thee to carry out my wishes."

"Is that a request or an order?" Wager asked.

"I ask this of thee as thy uncle and a member of the family."

"Give me the charter," Wager said. "I'll find a safe place for it."

John handed over the scroll. He spent the night in his quarters. At dawn he was awakened by a demand to come aboard. A boat had pulled up alongside the *Ataquin*. John recognized one of the men.

"Thou are welcome to come aboard," he said. "How can I help thee?"

"You were seen yesterday leaving the home of Walter Clarke," the man in charge said. "An important document is missing. We have orders to search your ship."

"I have no document, but thou are free to conduct thy search."

The men clambered aboard and fanned out to search the fo'c'sle and the cargo hold. The man in charge inspected John's cabin as well as those in steerage. Frustrated, he summoned his men and bade John an angry farewell.

Later that day Clarke sent word that Andros was on his way back to Boston. John looked about for Wager, but he was not aboard. One of the crew said he had spent the previous night ashore. John resigned himself to wait.

Toward evening Wager returned and gave John the scroll that had been entrusted to him. After examining the charter to make sure it was intact, John extended his thanks.

"How did thou manage to preserve it?" he asked.

"I decided that the safest thing I could do was keep the charter in my possession and hide myself." Wager said.

"And where was thy hiding place?"

"You'll recall that on one occasion I concealed Ben for several days with the medicine woman Tami. I said she could do you a service by putting me up for a night. I felt that Andros' men would never think to look there."

John laughed heartily. "I must thank Tami. And I promise to repay thee one day for thy service."

"You owe me nothing," Wager said. "Remember, we're family."

The next morning John went ashore and returned the charter. Clarke thanked him profusely for his loyalty to the colony.

"How did Andros react when he couldn't find it?" John asked.

Clarke produced an object from a drawer in his desk. "I shall keep this as a measure of his anger."

John recognized the object as the official seal of the colony, or rather as part of that seal.

"The seal was on my desk," Clarke said. "Andros smashed it on the floor. He said the whole colony would suffer a like fate unless we submit to his rule and recognize his authority."

"What did he mean by that?" John asked.

"I'm not sure," Clarke said. "The important thing is that we still have our charter. It's a sign that one day our rights will be restored."

* * *

John had offered once before to take Alice to England to see her father, but she declined. He did not argue the point. He was proud of his family and his home on Conanicut and pleased that Alice had taken so well to life in New England. He had Experience to thank for that. The women had frequent contact with each other. Joseph's boys were eager to row their mother across the bay and visit with their cousin Mary. Experience was not loath to take the oars herself, if circumstances dictated.

With the arrival of spring, as John was preparing the *Ataquin* for the next voyage, he repeated the offer, expecting the same response. He was surprised when Alice appeared to consider it before she replied.

"Mary is going on three; and as far as I know, I'm not expecting. If I'm ever to see Father again, this seems to be an appropriate time."

They arrived in London toward the middle of May. Tiddeman was overjoyed to see Alice again, and he never tired of entertaining his young granddaughter. John spent his days tending to business in the city, but in the evening he could be found in Horsleydown. After the meal he retired to the study with Tiddeman to discuss local events or the situation in New England.

"My brother has a disdain for Andros and an antipathy toward the Dominion of New England," he said one evening in response to a question by Tiddeman.

He went on to detail some of the complaints raised by Joseph. "As for me," he concluded, "I'm content to obey the laws enacted by legitimate authority, even though I may not like some of them."

Tiddeman heard him out before responding. "Thy brother seems to object chiefly to the restrictions on legislative assemblies."

He feels that he no longer has a voice in government," John said. "He also claims that Andros is abusing his authority."

"I still feel that the King and the Lords of Trade are acting in the best interest of the colonies," Tiddeman said. "Thy brother must realize the difficulties involved in governing so many separate colonies, each with its own distinct charter. Under a royal governor the same laws apply to all."

"Joseph's concern is that Andros makes the laws. Colonists have no say in the matter."

"All laws proposed in the colonies must be approved by the King," Tiddeman said. "It's true that without a duly elected assembly, colonists no longer enjoy the same rights that we in England take for granted. But in time they will come to recognize that they also derive benefits from this form of government."

"I'm not so sure about that," John said. "But for the most part we are loyal subjects, and I trust we shall remain so."

He was still in London when the Queen gave birth to a son and heir to the throne. News of the royal birth shattered Tiddeman's equanimity. He did not hesitate to vent what was troubling him.

"I fear we have some dark days ahead," he said.

"Why is that?" John asked.

"The fact that the King now has a son and an heir apparent to the throne will stir up fears of a Catholic dynasty. I've heard rumors that some members of Parliament have already written to ask William of Orange if he would be willing to come to England and assume the throne."

"The King has managed thus far to remain on reasonably good terms with the Parliament and the Church," John said. "Why would a son and heir alter that relationship?"

"King James seems to be moving ever closer to Rome. He welcomed a papal nuncio to the court, and he gave Magdalen College over for use by Catholics. Now he's prosecuting the Archbishop of Canterbury and six other clerics for seditious libel because they petitioned him to withdraw his declaration of indulgence."

"Why would anyone in England want a foreign ruler?" John asked.

"William is wed to the King's older daughter Mary. She was next in line to the throne until the King had a son, and she was raised a Protestant."

"Might King James actually be deposed?"

"Only if both parties in Parliament and the bishops agree to it."

Alice had been listening to their conversation. "Speaking of babies," she said, "I'm quite certain that I'm expecting another child."

"Some good news at last," Tiddeman said.

"I'll cut my business dealings short," John said. "We can sail for home in a fortnight."

"I had hoped for a longer visit," Tiddeman said. "Are thou sure that is the wisest course? If thou wish, I can arrange for thee to have the baby here in London."

"It will be best if Alice delivers at home," John said.

"I agree with John," Alice said. "My place is in Jamestown. But I see no need to hasten our departure. I can wait another month before we leave."

"Then we sail in a month," John said.

* * *

Alice gave birth to a daughter Catherine as the first snow of winter was falling. John experienced a sense of relief. Alice had suffered through a rough voyage from England, and he feared the baby might be affected. But the midwife assured him that, as far as she could tell, Catherine was healthy and without defect. Nonetheless, he put off another voyage to London until the spring. Experience promised to look in on Alice regularly, and he trusted Ben to look after the farm. He set sail toward the middle of April.

Most of his trade was out of Newport, but he had maintained some lucrative connections in Boston. He arrived there to find the populace in revolt. All over town people were demanding the arrest of Andros.

John was not surprised by this turn of events. Rumors of a major upheaval in England had circulated throughout the winter. It was said that William of Orange had landed in England, many officers in the army had deserted, and the King had fled to France. The latest news was that James had been accused of abdicating the throne, and Parliament had offered the crown to William of Orange and his wife Mary.

This report had stirred the colonists in New England to revolt. When John and Wager stepped ashore in Boston, they were swept up in a mass of people on their way to the Town House. Wager had been promoted to mate following the episode with the Rhode Island charter.

Simon Bradstreet, the ex-governor, and other officials were standing on the balcony of the Town House, while a town crier read a declaration of grievances. From his position in the rear of the crowd John caught only an occasional phrase in the rather lengthy document.

"Horrid Popish plot. Our charter was condemned. Without any liberty for an assembly. Malicious and unreasonable. A people dutiful and loyal to our King. Andros arrived as our Governor. To make laws and raise taxes as he pleased. A crew of abject persons fetched from New York. Extraordinary and intolerable fees. Illegalities done by these horse-leeches."

John's mind drifted away from the speaker to his own contacts with dominion authorities. Save for his efforts to preserve the Rhode Island charter, he had no direct dealings with Andros and his company of horse leeches. Which was not to say that he was unaffected by the regulations and changes imposed by the royal governor. The crier was getting to those, and John moved closer.

"People in New England were all slaves. Treated with multiplied contradictions to Magna Carta. Unaccountably fined and imprisoned. No man was owner to a foot of land in all the colony. The raising of taxes without an assembly. Packed and picked juries have been very common things among us. Caused the lands to be measured out for his creatures to take possession. Again briard in the perplexities of another Indian war. Our poor friends and brethren now under Popish commanders. We did nothing against these proceedings but only cry to our God. We therefore seize upon the person of those few ill men which have been the author of our miseries. Firmly believing that we have endeavored nothing but what mere duty to God and our country calls for at our hands, we commit our enterprise unto the blessing of Him and advise all our neighbors to join with us in prayers and all just actions for the defense of the land."

Shouts of approval punctuated the reading of this declaration. As the crier finished, a clamor gained strength among the crowd.

"On to Fort Mary!"

John and Wager were caught up and swept along in a general movement toward the place where Andros had his residence. They arrived as several colonial militiamen mounted the steps of the building. A British soldier was at every window. An officer appeared at the door and spoke to the militiamen. The import of his words was relayed back through the crowd.

"Governor Andros wants no bloodshed. He's willing to negotiate with proper representatives of the colony."

Faced by armed soldiers and what seemed a reasonable demand, the crowd gradually dispersed. John and Wager returned to the *Ataquin,* where the crew was loading cargo for the voyage.

John decided to extend his stay in Boston. He wanted to report on the outcome of these events when he got to London. He was well positioned to witness the next chapter. A British warship, the *HMS Rose,* was moored in the harbor. Early the next morning a longboat put off from the *Rose* and headed toward the wharf where the *Ataquin* was docked.

A group of men in nondescript clothing had arrived at the end of the wharf. In their midst was a man whom John identified as Andros. He saw it as an obvious attempt by the governor to escape. A group of colonial militia stationed on the wharf moved toward the band around Andros. A warning shot from the longboat brought the militia and the men with Andros to a halt. They stood facing each other until Andros took matters into his own hands.

"Hold your fire!" he called to the men in the longboat.

He gave another order to those surrounding him. John couldn't hear what was said, but they all turned and left the wharf at an unhurried pace. The militiamen stood their ground and watched them go. The longboat reversed course and headed back toward the *Rose*.

"He said he wanted no bloodshed, but what will he do now?"

John turned at the sound of Wager's voice. "He'll have to negotiate with Bradstreet."

"It might be better for everyone if he escaped," Wager said.

"You may be right," John said.

Later that day word spread that Andros had agreed to a meeting with the council headed by Bradstreet. John and Wager were part of the crowd that gathered to watch the governor as he emerged from his headquarters at Fort Mary. Andros entered a waiting carriage and was escorted under guard to the Town House. People lining the streets or peering from windows hurled jeers and insults at the carriage. A progressively larger crowd formed behind it as it moved along.

John was eager to learn the outcome of negotiations. The crowd at the Town House grew ever more restless as time passed with no word from inside. A cheer went up as Bradstreet appeared on the balcony. He waited for quiet before addressing the crowd.

"We have informed Governor Andros that we are determined to have the government of this colony in our own hands. He rejected our demands and has been placed under arrest. With his arrest we are once again our own masters. I urge you to return to your homes and not to vent your grievances against the governor or his associates. Rest assured that we shall deal with him justly and in accordance with his station."

Another cheer greeted his announcement. Several militiamen came from the building. They had a firm grip on Andros, who was clad in a purple surcoat that came to his knees. He glared defiantly at the crowd.

Shouts of "String him up!" and "Hang the traitor!" erupted as people recognized the royal governor.

The militiamen shouldered their way through the crowd and pushed Andros into a waiting carriage. Most of the crowd fell in behind the carriage as it moved off. John and Wager lingered outside the Town House.

A young British soldier who had accompanied Andros to the meeting emerged from the building. Several colonists moved to seize him. Thrusting aside those who stood in his path, Wager freed the frightened youth and pushed him back inside.

"Your quarrel is with Andros," he shouted in the silence created by

his action. "This boy has done you no harm. He was just doing his duty. Take your protests to the prison, where Governor Andros can hear them."

"Who are you to tell us what to do?" one man shouted.

"We're all British subjects," Wager said. "We owe our loyalty now to the new King and Queen. Be patient and wait for the changes that are sure to come."

What was left of the crowd appeared satisfied with his words. They began to disperse, most of them in the direction the carriage had taken. John and Wager followed along. On arriving at the prison, they spotted the carriage off to one side. The area around it had been cleared, and a squad of militia restrained the crowd. John took a position to the right of the prison entrance. He was just in time to see two men clad in green garments that passed for uniforms escort Andros from the carriage to the door of the prison. One of them carried a musket as a badge of authority. A third man, whom John took to be the jailer, stood waiting at the entrance.

Andros offered no resistance. He held his head up and looked straight ahead, ignoring those in the crowd who cheered as he entered the prison. No sooner was he out of sight than they began to question each other.

"What does it mean?"

"Is he gone for good?"

"Can we really govern ourselves again?"

John turned to Wager. "Change is indeed in the air. Whether it's for better or worse remains to be seen."

"We may learn more when we get to London," Wager said.

With that they returned to the *Ataquin.* The next day news spread on the docks that Andros had been transferred to Fort Mary, which was now under colonist control. Satisfied that the revolt had achieved its purpose, John set sail for England.

Thirteen

"I take no satisfaction in the outcome of this encounter."
(Dominion of New England, Spring 1689)

With the accession of William and Mary to the throne and the flight of King James, relations between Protestant England and Catholic France became even more strained. King Louis had offered earlier to help James retain his crown; but fearing an adverse reaction in England, James declined the offer. But once in exile, he summoned support for an effort to take back the throne that was rightfully his by birth.

John learned all this from Tiddeman upon his arrival in London. It served to explain what had occurred toward the end of his voyage across the Atlantic. Wary of French reaction to the deposition of a Catholic monarch, he hugged the south coast of England. But off Weymouth in the English Channel the lookout reported an armed ship under full sail bearing down on the *Ataquin* from the southeast.

"What flag does she fly?" John asked.

"She flies no flag," was the reply.

"She looks like a Frenchman, probably a privateer," Wager said, tightening his grip on the wheel. "Shall I change course for Weymouth?"

"We can't outrun her," John said, "and by the time we come about, she'll be upon us. We must determine her intent."

As if in response the approaching ship fired a shot across the bow of the *Ataquin*. John spotted several dozen men on her deck, ready to board.

"If we put in closer to shore, she may veer off," Wager said.

"It's worth a try," John said, "but there's no fort close by. I'm afraid we must resolve this on our own."

"Several of the crew have pistols. We might fight them off."

"Thou know well how I feel on that score," John said. "I'm loath to lose the ship and cargo, but our lives are of far greater value."

"I value my life as well. Yet it seems cowardly to surrender without some show of resistance."

Wager looked away, embarrassed by his criticism of the ship's master and his own uncle. "I'm sorry," he said. "It's your decision."

"I'm going below," John said. "Thou can take command."

In his cabin he paced back and forth, his hands clenched behind his back. He expected to hear cannon fire as the enemy ship drew near, but all was quiet. The *Ataquin* remained on course with no reduction in speed. Had Wager opted to surrender? Unable to restrain his curiosity, John stepped out on the main deck.

The privateer was closing fast. A man with a horn was calling on him to surrender. Wager held the wheel steady and made no reply. The privateer veered off to starboard, putting her in position to fire a broadside as the *Ataquin* changed course to avoid collision. But John saw the maneuver as an advantage to himself.

"If thou put the helm a little more to starboard," he called to Wager, "thou might run her down!"

Wager nodded and did as directed. The privateer fired an ineffective volley from her cannon before the *Ataquin* struck her amidships. The force of the collision threw John to the deck. Regaining his feet, he mounted the navigation deck to assess the damage.

The privateer had been virtually cut in half. Many of her crew were in the water, and those who remained aboard soon followed as the ship sank slowly beneath the waves.

"Put her about!" John ordered. "We must rescue as many as we can."

Wager obeyed at once, but the seas were heavy under a stiff wind. By the time the *Ataquin* reversed course and returned to the site of the collision, not one of the privateer's crew was to be seen. John stood for some time at the rail, scanning the sea for survivors. Giving it up at last, he turned to face his mate.

"That was a brilliant maneuver," Wager said.

"Thou were already on course to do as I suggested," John said. "But many men have died. I take no satisfaction in the outcome of this encounter."

Upon reaching port in London, he reported the sinking to the proper authorities. The news was cause for relief and rejoicing, for the privateer had been preying on British commerce for some time.

"I shall forward your report to the Admiralty Office," the official told John. "I'm sure you'll be hearing from them."

* * *

"I'm glad everything went well for Alice," Tiddeman said when John informed him about the birth of Catherine. "I was concerned that the long voyage might affect the delivery."

After a brief exchange about Tiddeman's health, which he claimed to be quite tolerable, their conversation turned to the state of affairs in New England. John told him about the Boston uprising and the arrest of Andros.

"When I left Boston," he concluded, "Andros was being held at Fort Mary, his headquarters. Bradstreet has promised to treat him in accordance with his station, but some people want him to be tried and imprisoned."

"I knew the colonies were dissatisfied with Andros," Tiddeman said, "but this uprising, as thou describe it, goes much deeper than that."

"I agree," John said. "It was a revolt against the policies of the King and the Parliament."

"It's easy to blame the man sent to carry out a policy," Tiddeman said. "It's much harder to persuade those who made the policy to change it."

"What do you suppose will happen to Andros?" John asked.

"He did what he was sent to do. If the colonial authorities in Boston feel he abused his power, they have recourse to the courts in England."

"Will the policy change, now that we have a new king?"

"William is too busy consolidating his power to have much concern for the colonies. England has welcomed him, but there's opposition in Scotland and Ireland."

"Where is King James?"

"He's said to be raising an army in France to regain the throne," Tiddeman said, "and he's likely to have the support of King Louis. Catholic monarchs tend to support each other. Louis is currently at war with the Dutch. With William of Orange on the throne, England is likely to be drawn into that conflict."

"That may explain my encounter with a French privateer," John said.

He went on to give an account of his battle in the English Channel. Tiddeman listened attentively.

"Thou will hear from the Admiralty," he said when John had finished. "They may decide to give thee a medal."

"I want no medals," John said. "My concern is what effect this will have on colonies in New England. Will our charters be restored? Will we be able to govern ourselves?"

"A friend of mine at Court says that may have become more likely. Have thou heard of a man named Richard Wharton?"

"My brother Joseph spoke of him. His company claims title to much of the Indian lands in the Narragansett country."

"I think that claim was voided," Tiddeman said. "Wharton has been in England trying to persuade the Lords of Trade to recommend appointment of another royal governor. Increase Mather is also here advocating a policy of self-government for the colonies."

"All I know about Mather is that he's a minister," John said.

"The two sides had equal support; but now Wharton is dead, and the balance is likely to shift toward Mather's position."

"Joseph will be glad to hear that."

"What are thy feelings?" Tiddeman asked.

"I can carry on my trade under a charter or a royal governor. I'd like the Navigation Acts to be less strictly enforced; but that seems unlikely if England gets involved in another war."

"As long as Louis is on the throne in France, I see no prospect for a lasting peace in Europe," Tiddeman said.

"Has King William restricted the way Friends worship?" John asked.

"The toleration act is still in place, but Parliament will surely try to revoke or modify it. I don't know what position William will take. The Dutch are quite tolerant when it comes to religion. We can only hope for the best."

* * *

When word of the sinking of the privateer reached the Admiralty Office, John was summoned to appear before them.

"We wish to commend you on the heroism and seamanship displayed by yourself and your crew," an Admiralty spokesman said. "Your decisive action in ridding the nation of this scourge was in the best tradition of the British Navy. It speaks well of your character and your loyalty as a British subject. I am pleased on behalf of this office to offer you a commission in the Navy with the rank of captain. What say you to our offer?"

John pictured himself pacing his cabin while Wager was on deck in command of the *Ataquin*. The Admiralty had apparently received no word of that. He paused a moment to think. He knew what he would say, but he had to take care how he framed his reply.

"I appreciate thy confidence in my seamanship," he said, "but I cannot accept praise or reward for an action that is not without regret. I did what I felt to be necessary; but many men died as a result, and their deaths weigh heavily on my spirit."

"We understand, but you will accept a commission."

"I must decline. If thou wish to reward someone, I can recommend my mate, Charles Wager. He was at the helm of the *Ataquin* and carried out what was merely a suggestion on my part. It was his seamanship and bravery, not mine, that led to the sinking of the privateer."

The spokesman consulted a moment with others on the bench. "The Admiralty extends its thanks for your service to the Crown," he said, "and we shall consider your recommendation."

John left the Admiralty Office wondering if he had acted in his own best interest. A commission in the Navy was a guarantee of lifelong security, and Alice might welcome the opportunity to return to London. He assured himself that she would resist such a temptation. Yet he would have liked to discuss the matter with her before making his decision.

When he reported the exchange to her father, he was heartened by Tiddeman's response. "I would love to have Alice nearby and be able to visit my grandchildren, but thou need have no doubts or regrets. Our personal comfort is less important than the principles that govern our lives. Thou have made the right choice."

"I shall tell Alice my decision met with thy approval," John said.

"I'm sure she feels as I do," Tiddeman said.

Before returning to New England, John got word from the Admiralty that his recommendation had been considered, and they were pleased to offer his mate a midshipman's berth in the Royal Navy.

"I'm sorry to leave your service," Wager said, "but this is my chance to fulfill a dream I've had ever since childhood. I'm grateful for all that you taught me. I shall remember you and your family for the rest of my life."

"I respect thy choice, and I wish thee success," John said.

* * *

Back in Boston after an uneventful crossing of the Atlantic, John was eager to find out what had transpired in his absence, what changes had come about since the April uprising. He learned that Massachusetts had reverted to its old form of government. While awaiting restoration of the charter, the authorities were proceeding as if it were already in place. A general sense of relief and good will prevailed after three years under the dominion. When he inquired into the fate of Andros, he was told that the former royal governor was imprisoned on Castle Island in Boston harbor. John recalled the promise Bradstreet had made to Andros upon his arrest. He dismissed the thought. It was none of his business.

As fate would have it, the welfare of Andros soon became his business. The *Ataquin* was tied to a wharf while her cargo was unloaded. Awakened by loud voices, John went on deck to investigate the cause of the disturbance. In the darkness he could make out nothing on land or at sea.

"What's going on?" he asked a crew member.

"Three men in a boat to seaward. They want to come aboard."

John peered over the side, but could make out little more than what he had been told.

"Who are thou, and what is it thou wish?" he called out.

"Governor Andros requests permission to come aboard."

Taken aback, John was at a loss how to respond. He realized he was dealing with an attempt to escape. He was being asked, or ordered, to assist. Did he want to get involved with these men? Did he have a choice? Why had they chosen him to aid in their escape? He had never spoken to or dealt with Andros. The closest he had come was when he helped to preserve the Rhode Island charter. That was hardly a recommendation.

But the pressing decision was whether or not to allow Andros to board the *Ataquin*. He wasn't committing himself to anything by acceding to the governor's request. He could decide what to do after he heard him out.

"Permission granted to board on the wharf side."

"The governor prefers to board here. Throw us a line."

A line was dropped, and two of the men clambered aboard. The third man stayed in the boat and rowed off into the darkness. Andros was the first to board. John thought he recognized the other man, but he failed to establish any connection. After ordering one of his crew to shelter the man, he led the way to his cabin. Stepping aside, he motioned Andros to enter. Once inside he lit a lantern and addressed the governor, who had yet to speak.

"I take it thou have escaped from Castle Island, but why have thou come to me for assistance?"

"You were recommended," Andros said.

"May I ask by whom?"

"That's neither here nor there. I must get away from Boston, the farther the better."

"Where is it thou wish to go?"

"My preference would be England."

"I just arrived from London. The ship is in no condition for another voyage across the Atlantic."

"I feared as much. Then let it be New York. I have connections there and can rely on them to get me away from this hotbed of rebellion."

John had no desire to go to New York, but neither was he prepared to refuse the governor's request for help. He needed more information.

"When I left Boston in April, thou were being held at Fort Mary. How did thou came to be imprisoned on Castle Island?"

"You must ask Bradstreet about that. But put no faith in what he tells you. He's not a man of his word, as I discovered to my sorrow."

"Were thou ill treated in the prison?"

"What rankled most was the indignity of my confinement."

"How did thou manage to escape?"

John was stalling for time, while he sought a reasonable alternative to New York. Andros' stern look proclaimed his impatience.

"My men plied the guards with liquor," he said. "But all that is past. I'm here to discuss the future."

"I must unload some cargo," John said. "It will arouse suspicion if I leave port now for no apparent reason."

"How long will that take?" Andros asked.

"Two or three days."

"Tell your men to work longer hours. I'll make it worth your while when we get to New York."

"My next port is in Rhode Island, Newport." John was still seeking a satisfactory and diplomatic way out of this predicament.

"Newport is out of the question," Andros declared. "The people there are very uncooperative."

"They abided by all the laws issued under the dominion."

"That may be true, but I prefer not to test the loyalty of men like Walter Clarke. If you are a true subject of the Crown, as I was led to believe, you will take me directly to New York."

"Walter Clarke need have no knowledge of thy presence," John said. He was formulating his plan as he spoke. "There will likely be a ship in the harbor that is bound for London. I can arrange to have thee transferred before it sails. Thou will be on thy way to England as thou desire."

Andros said nothing. From the expression on his face John sensed he was suspicious of the proposal. But his look gradually changed to one more akin to gratitude, and he ventured a smile.

"I was well advised to place my trust in you," he said. "You shall be rewarded, if it is in my power to do so."

"I seek no reward," John said. "I'll have one of my crew prepare a cabin for thee. Thou must stay out of sight until we sail."

"You may rely on that," Andros said.

John smiled with satisfaction. He had gained time to consider his position before deciding upon a final course of action. His proposal was made in good faith, but he might change his mind when he got to Newport.

* * *

Two days later the *Ataquin* sailed from Boston with Andros onboard. He kept to his cabin, emerging only for an occasional turn about the deck. His aide, as he termed the man who accompanied him, fetched his meals and dined privately with the governor.

John was pleased with this isolation, although he had not ordered or suggested it. The less his crew saw of Andros, the better for everyone. The aide was more visible, and John soon identified him as the soldier whom Wager had protected from the crowd when Andros was arrested. Neither of them referred to that incident, but the aide seemed to express his gratitude by his willingness to talk.

John ventured to ask about the conditions on Castle Island, where Andros had been imprisoned. He felt that information might bear upon his decision.

"I wasn't there with him," the aide said, "but I made regular visits to the island. I never saw his cell. We met in a room near the entrance. I brought in food when the Governor said they were starving him."

"Did he suffer any physical punishment?"

"He wasn't beaten, if that's what you mean. When he got sick, he was told no doctor was available; and he would have to cure himself. I brought him medicine for a stomach ailment. That was his biggest problem."

Another time John asked the aide how Andros managed the escape.

"I smuggled rum in, knowing the guards would find and confiscate it. My associate, the other man in the boat, slipped by them undetected and hid. When they were drunk, he unlocked the gate, and we took the Governor away in the boat. You know the rest."

John started to ask why he had selected the *Ataquin* rather than some other ship, but thought better of it. He was satisfied that he knew the answer. On yet another occasion he raised the subject of what Andros expected or hoped for when he got back to England. The aide had a ready answer.

"He figures he'll be a free man. The Governor was doing the job he was sent here to do, and those who arrested him realized that. They didn't know what to do with him, so they decided to put him in jail until they made up their minds. He was there almost four months."

"Why didn't they send him back to England?" John asked.

"The Governor says they were set on punishing him, but they couldn't decide how to do it."

John had all the information he needed. He recalled that Tiddeman had said much the same thing about Andros. The governor's faults were grievous enough to warrant his being brought to trial, but he had made an effort to establish the Dominion of New England on a firm footing. Let the Boston authorities air whatever grievances they might have in an English court. His course was clear. He would keep his promise to Andros.

* * *

On his arrival in Newport, John moored the *Ataquin* in the harbor rather than tying up at a wharf. He needed time to inquire what ships were due to sail for England and to persuade the master to provide passage for Andros and his aide.

His efforts were finally successful. As he was returning to his ship to break the news to Andros, he noticed a boat alongside the *Ataquin*. On deck two men were holding Andros. A rope ladder had been lowered into the boat, and they appeared to be directing him to climb down. Another man in the boat stood ready to receive him.

"What are thou doing?" John called out when he was within range.

"We've seized Governor Andros," was the reply. "We're sending him back to Boston."

John recognized the speaker as Peleg Sanders, a deputy whom he had encountered in his dealings with Walter Clarke. He was about to ask how they knew Andros was aboard when Sanders spoke up again.

"My orders are to thank you for your cooperation in his capture."

John remained silent. Better to say nothing until he knew all that had occurred in his absence. He watched the boat carrying Andros and his aide draw away and head toward the long wharf.

Onboard the *Ataquin* John demanded an explanation. "Who told the authorities Andros was on this ship?"

"One of the crew must have done it," his mate said.

"Find out who it was. I want to talk to him."

With that he retired to his cabin to reflect on the situation. He was not exactly upset by the turn events had taken. He had considered doing the same thing himself. Now fate had intervened and made the decision for him.

"Come in," he called in response to a knock.

A rigger named Carr entered with cap in hand. He appeared nervous as he stood just inside the door. "You wanted to see me?"

"Did thou fetch the constable to arrest Andros?" John asked.

"I can explain," Carr said.

"Please do."

"When I found out who was aboard, I figured you were going to turn him in as soon as we got to Newport. When it didn't happen, I decided you must be under pressure to say nothing. So I did my duty as a citizen and told the authorities. Was I wrong?"

John was silent, while Carr fidgeted with his cap. The explanation was perfectly logical. He couldn't fault the man for the conclusion he had reached, and he was thankful at heart that his crew regarded him as someone whose loyalty was to the colony. He had nothing to gain by telling them he had other plans for Andros.

"No, thou did well," he said. "I commend thee for thy decision. Thou may return to thy duties."

When Carr was gone, he speculated on the fate of Andros. Would the authorities in Boston punish him for trying to escape, or would they finally return him to England to face trial? They were shed of him as governor. What more did they want?

Fourteen

"If I still be slave, maybe I have man and children."
(Rhode Island Colony, Winter 1690/91)

That winter two-year-old Catherine came down with a fever.

"The tonic we got from that man who calls himself a doctor did her no good," Alice told her husband. "What else can we do?"

"I know of a black woman in Newport named Tami who deals in homemade remedies," John said. "People say her potions are quite effective."

"The woman who sheltered Ben before we took him in?"

"The same woman. My father bought her as a slave. Then he set her free and helped her to settle in Newport. I went with him to visit her when I was twelve, shortly before he died. I still remember her herb garden and the bottles of medicine."

"We must go to her at once," Alice said.

"Thou should go," John said. "Thou can describe the child's illness much better than I can."

"I can't leave Catherine and the baby alone."

Alice had given birth to their first son during the summer. They named him Tiddeman after his grandfather.

"I'll watch them while thou are gone."

"How do I find this Tami?"

"Ben can go with thee. He knows where she lives."

Alice gathered her bag and set off with Ben set for the ferry. The sail across the east bay to Newport took about an hour. Ben admitted that he knew the house, but he was unsure how to get there. Alice asked the first man they saw for directions.

"You mean that crazy medicine woman. Her place is on the far side of the basin behind the long wharf. But I'd advise you to stay clear of her. People say she's a witch."

Alice thanked him and set off with Ben in the direction indicated. The man's words made her pause outside Tami's home. The grounds were well kept, but the cottage was in need of repair. She stared at it as if she were trying to determine the character of its owner from its outward appearance.

Ben interrupted her reflections. "Shall I knock?"

"If thou would," Alice said.

Ben rapped sharply on the door, then stepped aside. The woman who opened looked younger than Alice had pictured her from John's description. Her clothing was well worn but clean. Her dark piercing eyes regarded them questioningly.

"My daughter has a fever," Alice said. "The medicine we gave her is of no use. I was told thou might have something to help her."

"Come in," the woman said in a strong voice.

Alice entered the house. She assumed without checking that Ben was right behind her. The great room was simply furnished but comfortable. A fire blazed in the hearth, and she smelled freshly baked bread. Reassured, she took the chair that was offered her.

"How old is the girl?" the woman asked.

"She was two in December."

"How long is she sick?"

"This is the third day."

"Does she cough or throw up?"

"No, it's just a fever. I brought the medicine she was taking."

"Let me see."

Alice took the bottle from her bag and handed it over. The woman removed the cork and sniffed the contents. Her grunt meant nothing to Alice.

"You wait here," the woman said.

She went into a back room and returned a few minutes later with an amber bottle. The hand-written label read "For Fever."

"You give child one spoon of medicine with food morning, noon, and night. She much better tomorrow."

"How much do I owe thee?" Alice asked.

"Who send you to me?"

"I'm Alice Hull. I believe thou know my husband John."

Tami seemed to regard her with new interest. "How many children you have?" she asked.

"Two girls and a boy."

"John's brother and sisters, are they well?"

"His brother Joseph live in Kings Towne," Alice said. "His sisters are in the Plymouth Colony. They're all quite well."

"I know them when they very young."

"John remembers meeting thee just before his father died."

Tami took a moment to reply. Her expression was strained, as if she were in pain. "I not sorry when he die."

"Why do thou say that?" Alice asked in surprise.

"He bring me to Newport, then forget me. I have nobody here."

"Are thou not grateful that he made thee a free woman?"

"If I still be slave, maybe I have man and children. They call me crazy old woman, but they still come for medicine when they sick. Sometimes I want poison them."

"Why are thou telling me this?" Alice asked.

"I want you tell John."

"We go now," Ben said.

Startled by his voice, Alice turned to see him standing by the door.

Tami appeared to regard him for the first time. "I know you," she said. "You hide here until English gentleman find place for you."

Ben looked away. He seemed embarrassed by her statement. "I have good home now," he said.

Tami's expression softened. "John is good man. He not to blame that I crazy old woman."

"Let me pay thee, and we'll be on our way," Alice said.

"I not want money."

"Let her have her way," Ben said softly.

"We thank thee for thy help," Alice said.

"I sorry what I say about John's father," Tami said.

Ben steered Alice toward the door. Once outside he set the pace to the ferry landing. They were well away from the house before either one spoke.

"That man who gave us directions was right," Alice said. "She is a bit crazy. I'm afraid to use the medicine she gave me."

"She make medicine before she know your name," Ben said.

Returning home on the ferry, he appeared lost in thought. Alice made no comment on his silence. She had enough to think about. She gave Catherine the medicine as soon as she got home.

At supper that evening John listened carefully to her account of the meeting with Tami. "My father did all he could for her," he said. "He took her to Newport and gave her a chance to start a new life. When I saw her, she appeared to be doing quite well. But I'm sorry for neglecting her."

"It's not thy fault that she became a lonely and bitter woman," Alice said. "She admitted as much."

"We're both in her debt," John said. "Catherine is much better since thou gave her the medicine."

"I thought Ben acted a bit strange when Tami recognized him," Alice said. "It made me wonder if there was something between them."

"That's his affair," John said. "It's best we keep out of it."

* * *

When John arrived in London the following spring, he was eager to break the news of Tidddeman's birth to Alice's father.

"I've been hoping for a son," John said.

"Every man wants his family name to be carried on," Tiddeman said, his face beaming. "Are Alice and the other children well? We've had a good deal of illness in London. I was sick for some weeks myself."

John assured him that all was well in Jamestown. Their talk turned to the state of affairs in England and the colonies.

"When James and his army landed in Ireland bent on regaining the throne," Tiddeman said, "he was accepted there as the rightful king. But he was defeated, and Ireland has acknowledged William as their sovereign."

"Where is James now?" John asked.

"He fled back to the continent."

"Then we're still at war with France."

Tiddeman nodded. "War is the proven way for a new king to confirm his rule. I'm surprised it hasn't spread to the colonies."

"There is some trouble with the French colonies in Canada," John said. "We've had enough turmoil. A period of peace would be welcome."

"That has been the wish of mankind since the dawn of creation. All I and thou can do is strive to maintain peace in our own families."

"I'm doing my best," John said. "We're fortunate that my brother Joseph and his wife live nearby."

"Now that his crown is secure," Tiddeman said, "William may attend more to governance of the colonies."

"Will he appoint another royal governor?"

Tiddeman shrugged. "I doubt the sentiment in Parliament has changed in that regard. Speaking of Andros, he was tried in England and acquitted of the charges levied against him by the people in Boston. He's now governor of the Virginia Colony."

"Then the uprising in Boston served no purpose."

"I wouldn't say that. I think the King got the message."

Tiddeman's opinion was borne out soon after John returned home. The Rhode Island charter was reaffirmed; and to settle the border dispute with Connecticut, the Narragansett country was incorporated into the Rhode Island Colony. John Easton was elected governor after the death of William Bull. Regular town meetings were permitted, land titles were restored, and residents of Kings Towne were glad to shed the name of Rochester.

Plymouth had never been granted a charter. Along with Massachusetts and the territory of Maine, it was incorporated into a newly created Province of Massachusetts Bay with Sir William Phips as governor. But Phips had not yet arrived in Boston, and the colony continued to govern itself.

Taxes imposed by Andros remained in effect. The war with France dashed John's hope that trade restrictions under the navigation acts might be relaxed. Indian tribes allied with French forces in Canada were burning settlements along the border, and militia were called up to repel the attacks.

* * *

Joseph had a broad market for his horses, barrel staves, and farm produce, and Indians continued to toil in his fields and in his workshop. The Atherton Company claims having been revoked by an English court, the local tribe was again resident on its native land. He took pride in the fact that, unlike some of his neighbors, he declined to own slaves. Despite a decades old law prohibiting the importation of slaves in the Rhode Island Colony, the market for free labor remained active and was a lucrative source of income for some shipowners.

He was glad that John was not involved in the slave trade. He had mixed feelings about Ben, but that was his brother's business. When he found Ben at his door one night toward the end of the harvest season, he took him to be a messenger.

"Is something wrong?" he asked.

"Nothing wrong, Master Joseph. Ben run away."

Joseph frowned. "Come in, and we'll talk about it."

Ben removed his cap before entering. He remained standing near the door until Joseph beckoned him to take a seat.

"What did John do that caused thee to run away?" Joseph asked.

"Master John treat Ben fine."

"Then what brings thee to my door at this hour?"

"Man on next farm say he be free after seven years. I want be free man too."

"Does my brother know how thou feel?"

"Master John say it better for me if I be his property."

"What do thou want me to do?"

"Indian who work for you get money Ben work harder than Indian. Save money to get married and have children."

Joseph turned to Experience, who was listening to this exchange. "I can't put him to work on my farm. What would John say?"

"Speak to thy brother," she said. "Thou can work things out. We'll send Tristram over in the morning to let him know Ben is here. Right now I'll fix a place for Ben to sleep."

"You going tell Master John?" Ben asked.

"I'll tell him just what thou told me. I'm sure he'll listen."

"I do as you say, Master Joseph."

When John got the message, he traveled at once to Kings Towne to reclaim his property. He had been searching for Ben in Newport and was surprised that he had sought a haven with Joseph.

"Where is he?" he asked when his brother opened the door.

"He's in the barn," Joseph said. "We need to talk."

"What is there to talk about. He ran off. I've come to take him home."

"Have thou no interest in why he left?"

"I gather thou are about to tell me," John said angrily.

"Peace, brother. I know thou treat Ben well. He admits it. But I think thou should be aware of his feelings."

"Ben has always been grateful to me."

"True, but he sees nothing different in his future. He wants to be paid for his labor so he can marry and have children. He needs a dream."

"I don't treat him like a slave. It's just better for everyone in town if they see him as one. Would thou have me set him free?"

"I ask nothing of thee. I speak only of how Ben feels. He just wants to be like an indentured servant, no better or worse."

"And if I decline, will thou refuse to give Ben back?"

Joseph laughed. "Of course not. Ben is thy property."

John was silent for a time. "I promise to consider his wishes," he said at last, "provided he comes back with me today."

"I'm sure he'll agree to that," Joseph said.

Fifteen

"From this day forward the Negro Ben is a free man."
(Rhode Island Colony, 1693-1695)

John's hope that King William's war with France would not spread to the colonies in New England was dashed by the appearance of French privateers off the coast of Rhode Island. Still troubled by the fate of those drowned in the English Channel, he refused to arm the *Ataquin* with cannon required for self-defense. As he sought an alternative that would permit him to undertake a voyage across the Atlantic, he had a visit from Thomas Paine.

Paine had recently built a home on the east shore of the island. He had a reputation for piracy and was reputed to have some association with the notorious Captain William Kidd. John had no business dealings with him and regarded him simply as a fellow shipowner. He took Paine at his word that he was no longer on the grand account and wished to be regarded as a respectable member of the community.

Paine declined John's invitation to come inside. "This matter is better discussed in the open air," he said.

"We can walk over to the shore," John said.

They had gone some distance before Paine stated the reason for his visit. "You must be aware that some French privateers are lurking off the coast. They pose an immediate threat to people on Block Island."

"I've been putting off my next voyage to England due to the threat," John said. "How many ships are there?"

"Three or four. Each captain is bent on serving his own interest, but they do support each other in a battle. That's why I'm here."

"I don't understand," John said.

"I've heard stories that you sank a Frenchman in the English Channel. I need some help in fighting these privateers."

"My ship is unarmed, and my crew are ill equipped for battle."

"That is easily remedied," Paine said. "Governor Easton has granted me the authority to take whatever measures I think appropriate in defense of the colony. I'm prepared to do battle with these Frenchmen, but two ships stand a better chance of success than one ship alone."

John was silent. He sat on a rock and stared out across the west bay. Paine waited patiently for a response.

"As thou well know," John said at last, "I belong to the community of Friends and am opposed to conflict. I regard the incident thou refer to as a sad day in my life. I had relinquished command of my ship, but I feel responsible for the outcome and the loss of life. The death of scores of men who drowned weighs heavily on my spirit."

"Does that mean you refuse to do battle with these privateers?"

"I cannot deny that I have a duty as a freeman to defend the colony. Thou can make use of my ship for thy purpose, if thou will; but I must decline to serve as commander. I cannot speak for members of my crew."

"Without you the ship may be a liability rather than an asset."

"I'm sorry. I can do no more."

"Very well, I accept your offer," Paine said. "I bid you good day."

With that he turned abruptly and strode off.

John continued to stare out across the bay. In his mind he pictured the privateer going down with all aboard, while he looked on powerless to save the drowning men. If Paine regarded him as a coward, so be it. He could not risk a repetition of that scene.

A week later word spread on Conanicut and along the waterfront in Newport of Paine's victory over the fleet of privateers off Block Island. John got an account of the battle from one of his crew who had volunteered to serve with Paine.

"We had two ships against five of those privateers Paine told us not to worry. He said we had the advantage because he knew the waters off the coast like the back of his hand. When we got to Block Island, he put a dozen armed men ashore to keep the French from landing on the island. Then he maneuvered his two ships into shallow water, so he wouldn't be surrounded by the Frenchmen and could fight them one at a time on equal terms. The battle lasted all one afternoon before the French called it quits and sailed off to the west. They must have lost a hundred or more men in the fight. One man on Paine's ship died when he was hit by a cannonball. When it was all over, he told us to go home; while he went after the ships that fled."

John had been scanning the deck of the *Ataquin* during the crewman's account. "I see little or no damage to the ship," he said.

"We were close in to shore," the crewman said. "Paine did most of the fighting. It seemed like he was protecting us."

* * *

720

The message from Tami said only that she wished to see him.

"I'm planning to be in Newport one day next week," John said. "I'll look in on her, if I have time."

"We owe her more than that," Alice said.

"Thou mean the medicine she prescribed for Catherine?"

"Not only that. Have thou ever thanked her for helping to preserve the Rhode Island charter?"

Alice's demand for quicker action surprised him. He couldn't recall when he told her about that incident.

"I didn't want to draw attention to her at the time," he said. "I'm sure she's forgotten about it by now."

"Women have long memories," Alice said. "Someone ought to recognize her contribution to the independence of the colony."

"I can get Governor Easton to draft a note of appreciation."

"I'm sure she would prefer a few pounds."

John laughed. "Thou are probably right."

"While there thou might also persuade her to forgive thy father for abandoning her."

"That's a tall order, but I'll see what I can do."

In Newport the next day he traversed the narrow cobblestone streets to the cottage where Tami grew her herbs and purveyed her tonics. The door opened a crack to his knock. The face that peered out at him was that of a girl, whom he judged to be no more than eighteen. She regarded him with apprehension, as if she were about to slam the door in his face.

"Tell thy mistress that John Hull is here in response to her message."

"Miss Tami in garden," the girl said. The frightened look on her dark face had faded. "Come in and take seat. I tell her you here."

John did as he was bid. The room was free of any sign of Tami's trade. He saw no evidence of tonics, salves, or powders. Not a bottle was in sight. But the girl's reference to a garden confirmed that he had not mistaken the address. He rose as Tami entered. The black girl was no longer in sight.

"I hope wife and children are well," Tami said.

"Everyone is well," John said. "I got thy message. But I've also come to thank thee belatedly for helping my apprentice, Charles Wager, to preserve the charter of our colony. Governor Easton has granted thee five pounds for thy service to the colony. I'm sorry it took so long."

John handed her a small bag of coins. Obtaining recognition for Tami from the governor might take weeks. He had yet to decide whether he would seek reimbursement. Tami set the bag on the mantel above the hearth without opening it or counting the contents.

"You say thank you to governor for me," she said. "I glad you and Alice are together and all are happy."

John paused a moment to consider her choice of words. Was this a veiled reference to what Alice had described as abandonment by his father Tristram? He found it hard to understand why Tami bore a grudge against a man who had rescued her from a life of slavery and made her a free woman.

"Thou seem to be prospering," he said in an effort to steer the talk in a different direction. "I see thou have taken on a woman as thy assistant."

"She not assistant. She slave girl. She run away from master in Salem. People call her witch and bride of Satan. I hide her and tell her not to answer door. She never go out. She afraid master look for her."

"How did she get here from Salem?" John asked.

"You hear story from ger. Nakumba, you come out now."

The young girl entered the room, her eyes downcast. "I sorry I open door. I think someone maybe sick and need medicine."

"It all right this time," Tami said. "Nakumba, this is John Hull. He good man. Has big farm in Jamestown. You say how you come to Newport."

The girl ventured a glance at John. "Why he want to know?"

John laughed to reassure her. "Did the family in Salem call thee Nakumba?" he asked.

"They call me Dolly. I not like that name. I not toy for children."

Tami spoke up. "My real name Tamika. His father call me Tami."

From her tone of voice John couldn't tell whether the comment was a criticism or simply an acknowledgment.

"I'd like to hear thy story," he told the girl. "But please sit down."

"It better I stand." Nakunba paused as if to collect her thoughts, then continued. "They hang many women in Salem for being witch. Girl in family where I work ask me go with her to woods. I cannot say no. She meet other girls, dance around fire, make strange sounds. I watch. Then men come and tell master they want arrest woman who cast spell on children. They call me witch and say I must see judge. I run away. Hide on ship. Good man on ship give me food and water, not say where I hide. I very sick on ship. Man bring me here. I safe now."

The girl's eyes were fixed on the floor during her account. She looked at John as if to gauge his reaction. He was too taken aback to speak.

"Now you know story," Tami said, breaking the silence. "Long time ago people call me witch. You too young to remember."

"My sister Mary says that's why Father brought thee to Newport."

"Tristram good man. I sorry what I say to your wife."

John accepted her apology without comment. He hadn't expected the reconciliation to be so easy. "What will become of this girl?" John asked.

"She need place to start new life. I think maybe on your farm."

The thought had crossed John's mind, but he wasn't sure how Alice would feel about it. "Why don't thou keep her as thy assistant?" he asked.

"I have no money for feed two people," Tami said.

It struck him that she made no mention of Ben. Was that all Wager's doing, or was it her idea to bring Ben to his attention?

"I already have one slave," he said. "I'm not sure I need another."

"She not slave any more. She now free woman."

"She escaped, but that doesn't mean she's free. She has good cause to fear that her master will be looking for her."

"Why he want to bring her back?" Tami asked. "Judge say she a witch and hang her."

John saw a certain logic in her argument. "So thou want me to take the girl in and pay her for her labor."

"I think that good for her," Tami said.

"If she is now a free woman," John said, looking at Nakumba, "she must speak for herself. Is that what thou desire?"

"That my wish," the girl said softly.

"In that case Nakumba should see where she'll live and what her duties will be before she decides. And Alice must also agree."

Tami turned to the girl. "You go with Master John and meet wife. She nice woman. Find out what she want you to do."

Nakumba nodded, but she appeared tense and uncertain.

"Is it all right if I call thee Cumby?" John asked.

"Cumby a nice name," the girl said.

* * *

On the ferry Cumby sat with her head turned toward the water. John suspected she was hiding the fear that was evident on her face ever since they left the sanctuary of Tami's cottage. He had tried to reassure her to no avail. Now as he sat beside her, his expression defied anyone to ask about his companion. But the only other passenger was a man from the village, who seemed little inclined to talk.

Ben was waiting with a farm wagon at the ferry landing. John simply introduced Cumby without explaining her presence. Ben regarded her with interest. The girl appeared to relax on the wagon. Her face brightened as they drew up to John's house; and she ventured a smile when she spotted Alice, who had come out to greet her husband.

"Alice, this is Cumby," John said. "If thou agree, I'd like to keep her to help thee with the children and the housework."

Alice eyed the girl with some suspicion. Cumby wore a green shawl over her plain brown dress. She gripped a satchel that contained all her worldly belongings. Any trace of a smile had vanished.

"I wasn't expecting thee to bring home another slave," Alice said, turning her attention back to John.

"Tami insists that she's a free woman," John said. "I'm not so sure."

He went on to recount the story the girl had told him earlier. Alice listened attentively. Cumby had set down the satchel. She stood with her hands clasped in front of her like a prisoner in the dock awaiting the verdict.

"I feel sorry for her," Alice said when he was finished, "but we can't make her a free woman. Only the man who owns her can do that."

"We can at least treat her as one."

"What about Ben? Are we to treat him as a free man?"

"I've thought about that since he ran off. Having Cumby here may prod me to decide."

Alice's expression softened as she studied the girl, who still stood with her hands clasped. "I could use some help," she said, "now that our fourth child is on the way."

A sob escaped John as he embraced his wife. "Are thou certain?"

"Quite certain."

Cumby too was smiling, a fact not lost upon Alice. "Are thou fond of children?" she asked the girl.

"Yes, ma'am. Young children very nice."

"Our oldest is eight."

"That a good age."

"Have thou given birth to a child?"

"No, ma'am." Cumby seemed not at all offended by the question.

"I suppose we could take her in," Alice said. "She can sleep with the children. Then I won't have to worry about them when the new one arrives."

"Wait," John said. "As a free woman Cumby has a say in this."

Alice looked at the girl. "Do thou agree?" she asked.

"I do what you say. I happy stay here."

"Then come inside, and I'll introduce thee to the children."

Alice spotted them just inside the door, where they had evidently been watching Crumby's arrival, sensing perhaps that their future was at stake. She motioned for them to come forward.

"This is Mary. She's the oldest. As I said, she's eight. Catherine is next. She's going on five. And Tiddeman, our youngest, is three."

Each child in turn got a hug from Cumby.

"I'll leave thee to get better acquainted," John said.

He went outside, where Ben had unhitched the horse.

"Cumby will be staying to help Alice care for the children," he said.

"She pretty woman," Ben said.

* * *

Following Paine's victory over the French privateers at Block Island, the waters off Newport became relatively safe. John took advantage of this respite to resume his trade with London. While there he visited the house in Horsleydown. Tidddeman's primary concern was the health of Alice and the children. Word had reached London of a smallpox outbreak in the colonies. John hastened to set his mind at ease.

"It lasted almost a year, but it was chiefly in Newport. Jamestown had but a single case."

Tiddeman also expressed some concern for those in Salem accused of witchcraft. John was glad to recount the story of Cumby and to assure him that Rhode Island had not succumbed to that mania.

For his part Tiddeman related news that King William had solidified his claim to the throne and turned his attention to the war on the continent.

"He wants to keep Louis XIV from exerting undue influence on the succession to the Spanish throne. The King of Spain is childless, and Louis wants a hand in appointing his successor. Opposing him seems hypocritical, considering the manner in which we treated King James. But who are we to question decisions made by royalty?"

"That day may come," John said. "The colonists in Boston cheered when Andros was arrested."

"They still have a royal governor, William Phips," Tiddeman said.

"Phips seems intent on warring against the French in Canada," John said. "He's asserted control over the Rhode Island militia for that purpose. That violates our charter. We've sent a man to England to plead our case."

"I take it thou are in favor of self-governance for the colonies."

"We're far from that," John said. "I need but consider the restrictions on trade and the taxes imposed on imports. The laws that govern us are made in England."

* * *

Cumby's previous experience with children made her a welcome and valuable addition to the household. Alice had a difficult time with her fourth pregnancy. She was glad to have someone to take over the domestic chores. The three children accepted Cumby at once. They went on hikes at the north end of the island. Cumby called them adventures. She appeared to be in tune with nature. Alice envied her for that. Born and raised in London, she was unaccustomed to life on a farm on a tiny island in the middle of a bay. An occasional trip to Newport was small compensation for the abundance of shops and goods readily available in London. She assured John that she was not unhappy. She just needed more time to adjust.

John too was well satisfied with the new arrangement. Heeding Alice's warning, he sought to forestall any problems with Ben by making him an indentured servant. He would be free in seven years, with four years to his credit already. Ben thanked him and appeared to be grateful.

All was serene on the Hull farm. Cumby cared for the house and the children. Ben worked in the fields and tended the animals. Alice gave birth at home to her fourth child, a daughter named Alice. So it went until one day, while nursing the baby, Alice made an observation.

"Cumby, are thou with child?"

The girl looked down as if ashamed, but she quickly recovered and met Alice's gaze. She seemed relieved to have her secret out in the open.

"Yes, ma'am," she said. "I mean to tell you."

"I gather that Ben is the father."

"Yes, ma'am. We much in love."

"Have thou made any plans for the future?"

"We not sure about that."

Alice continued to nurse, and Cumby went on with her housework.

John was less than surprised by the news. "We might have expected this," he said. "I've surprised them several times when their behavior made me think something was going on."

"Thou might have told me. Now that we know, what shall we do?"

"It seems to me that is largely up to them."

"Thou must speak to Ben," Alice said. "The poor girl has no idea what the future holds for her."

"I'll talk to him today," John said.

Ben was in the barn milking the cow. He paused in his labors when he saw John standing over him.

"Have thou something to tell me?" John asked.

A broad smile spread across Ben's face. "Cumby say you know about baby. We want marry and live together."

"That may be a problem," John said.

"Why you say that?" Ben asked.

"Officially thou are still a slave, and Cumby is a free woman in name only. I'm not sure whose approval is needed."

Ben forgot about the milking, and the cow expressed her displeasure by kicking over the bucket. He hastened to salvage what he could of the contents. When order was restored, he looked up at John.

"What can we do?" he asked.

"I'll speak to the minister. If he's willing to marry thee, I have no objection. Nor does Alice."

Ben's face lit up. "Then everything all right," he said.

"We shall see," John said.

The local minister was fashioned in the Puritan mold, a fact of which John was well aware. Nor was his own standing in the Society of Friends calculated to advance his petition. He presented his case, stating the facts as he knew them. The minister frowned repeatedly as he listened.

"Will thou consent to marry them?" John asked.

"Apart from religious concerns," the minister said, "both the man and the woman are still slaves in the eyes of the law. Your approval isn't enough, since it's doubtful that you own either one of them."

"I can't contact the family who owned Cumby without putting her life in jeopardy. And I have no idea who owned Ben before he came to me."

"What you ask is that I disregard the law. Slaves and their offspring are property. This couple is not free to marry without permission from their owner. I must refuse to perform the ceremony."

John struggled to control the anger that was rising within him. "Then I bid thee good day," he said.

Storming out of the house, he mounted his horse and gave it an extra stroke of the whip. Unaccustomed to such treatment, the animal bolted, nearly unseating him before it settled into a normal pace.

"What will thou do now?" Alice asked when she heard the story.

"An idea struck me on the ride home," John said. "As master of the *Ataquin* I think I'm entitled to perform marriages at sea. We can take a short voyage, and I'll marry them myself."

"Thou will need witnesses. I must stay home and care for the baby."

"Joseph and Experience have an interest in Ben. I'll ask them."

"Are thou sure such a marriage is legal?"

"Legal or not," John said, "it's better than no marriage at all."

John performed the ceremony on the navigation deck as the *Ataquin* sailed in calm seas off the shore of Block Island. Ben wore a borrowed suit that did not quite fit, but his face beamed as he repeated the vows. Cumby was radiant in a straight green dress she made herself from material provided by Alice. To all but a knowing eye it hid the fact that she was pregnant. Experience stood up for the bride, and Joseph for the groom. The crew of the *Ataquin,* gathered below on the main deck, cheered as the couple kissed.

John motioned for silence. "It is a longstanding custom for a newly married couple to receive a present. Since Ben and Cumby already have all they want in each other. I was at a loss for a suitable gift. Then I thought of one thing they don't have, something that is within my power to give them."

He paused to relish the looks of anticipation from the newlywed couple. "Be it known to all here assembled that from this day forward the Negro Ben is a free man. He shall earn a fair wage and support his wife and family by his own labor."

Turning to Ben, he asked, "What is thy first act as a free man?"

Ben's initial look of surprise evolved into a broad smile.

"I want to build house for my family," he said.

Sixteen

"Our son has chosen his own path and is lost to us."
(Rhode Island Colony, Autumn 1699)

A frost was on the ground when Joseph was confronted by one of his Indian laborers. The man was outwardly deferential, yet determined to say what was on his mind.

"Daughter have baby. She say your son Reuben is father."

"Are thou sure?" Joseph asked.

"Daughter not lie. Not know other man."

"What do thou want me to do about it?"

"You honest man. You do what is right."

"Surely thou don't expect Reuben to marry her."

Joseph sought to control his anger, which was directed at Reuben. The girl and her family were just victims of his son's unbridled lust.

"You do what is right," the Indian repeated.

"I'll have a talk with Reuben, and I'll see to it that thy daughter and the child are cared for."

"I tell daughter what you say."

With that the Indian returned to his labors.

"We might have expected something like this," Experience said when she heard the news. "Reuben is a strange boy. He has no friends that I know of. His sister Mary is the only one who can talk to him."

"He'll listen to me," Joseph said.

"What can we do for the girl?" Experience asked.

"I told the man we'd care for his daughter, but the only thing we can do is give him some money. That should pacify him."

"I can have a talk with the girl's mother."

"What will thou say to her?"

"I'll simply assure her of our support."

"Let me speak to Reuben first. I want to hear what he has to say."

"Don't be too hard on the boy. He's only sixteen."

"I just want to impress on him that he can't marry an Indian."

* * *

Reuben knew from his father's expression that all was not well. He suspected it was about the Indian girl.

"I'm told thou have been intimate with a woman who is neither a Friend nor one of our kind, but a heathen Indian," Joseph said.

He stood by the hearth. He was slightly taller than his third son, and his muscles were from years of labor. He spoke with parental authority, but also from the vantage of maturity and strength.

Reuben was seated at the table. He feared this day might come and thought he was prepared for it, but his father's harsh words drove any defense from his mind. He looked about for support. His mother was tidying up after a meal. The look she gave him said there would be no help in that quarter. His sister Mary was knitting squares for a blanket. She knew about the affair and had cautioned him against getting involved. She seemed now to be intent on her knitting.

"She's no different than the Indians who work in thy fields," Reuben said, recalling some of his defense. "I respect her beliefs."

"Thou dare speak of respect when thou have shown such disrespect for thy parents and all we have taught thee," Joseph said, raising his voice. "As for my laborers, that's their role in life. I pay them so they can provide for their families instead of getting drunk. They're free to marry their own kind, if that's what they call it."

"This girl taught me many things." The words were out before Reuben could stifle them.

"Things better learned in the marriage bed," Joseph said. "Are thou aware that the girl is with child?"

Stunned by the question, Reuben was speechless.

"I gave her father some money; and as far as I'm concerned, that's the end of it. I forbid thee to see the girl again."

"We love each other," Reuben said in a soft voice.

"Thou call it love! I call it unadulterated lust!"

"Peace, Joseph," Experience said. "Take a walk and calm thy spirit."

"Surely thou don't agree with him."

"Call it what thou will, it's part of growing up. We've all made mistakes in our youth. Reuben is no different."

Mary had set aside her knitting. "It's not all Reuben's fault," she said. "The girl was often nude at the swimming hole; and I saw her in the barn waiting for her father to finish work, or so she said. I think she had her eye set on Reuben."

Joseph glared at his daughter. "That doesn't excuse his weakness of character. He might have said something, and I would have put a stop to it."

Reuben rose and took up his coat. "I'm the one who needs a walk," he said as he headed toward the door.

"Go and ask thy squaw about the child she's carrying," Joseph said.

"Thou were too harsh on him," Experience said when Reuben was gone. "Thou might have settled this without rancor."

"He'll be back once he realizes the consequences of his actions," Joseph said.

* * *

When Experience forewent their customary embrace, Alice knew this was not an ordinary visit. Her first words were, "I need to speak to John."

"He's in the fields with Ben," Alice said. "Is something wrong?"

"Reuben has run off somewhere. He's been gone for three days. Joseph has knocked on every door in Kings Towne. No one has seen him."

"Thou should have told us. We could have helped."

"Joseph said it was our problem, and he would deal with it."

"I'll send Cumby out to fetch John back," Alice said.

"I can find him," Experience said as she set off.

John paid close attention to her account of events leading up to Reuben's disappearance.

"Joseph was rather hard on him," she concluded. "Reuben said he needed a walk, and we haven't seen him since. It's all the fault of that Indian girl who says she is bearing his child."

"That's hardly a reason to run away from home," John said.

"He's a strange boy. I often wonder what goes on in his head. He says he loves the girl, but he's too young to deal with this alone. We need to help him, not punish him. Have thou any idea where he might have gone?"

"He spoke not long ago about going to sea when he was older, but I didn't think he was serious," John said. "I'll ask around on the waterfront in Newport. Masters are often forced to recruit crewmen before they sail. Someone may know something."

"I'll go with thee," Experience said.

That afternoon they traversed the wharfs in Newport, but no one could tell them anything about the missing youth.

"We may find out more by visiting the taverns," Experience said.

John granted it was a good idea. "Thou can wait outside while I make inquiries within."

"Is that necessary?"

"It's best I speak to them alone. Apart from propriety they might not be as willing to talk in thy presence."

"Very well," Experience said. "I trust thee in this matter."

John appeared to know where the taverns were located. She stood in the street or an alley while he was occupied inside. Men passing paused to scrutinize her, but her forbidding look forestalled a closer approach. John's inquiries in three taverns yielded no results. His stern expression as he left the fourth told her the news was not good.

"A man I spoke to said he had a drink with a boy fitting Reuben's description. He said the boy was boasting about his first berth aboard a ship."

"Thank goodness he's safe," Experience said.

"The ship belongs to William Kidd," John hastened to add.

"The pirate?"

"The same. Kidded's ship is still in the bay. Rumor has it he's here to meet Thomas Paine, who has a house on Conanicut."

"Is that good or bad ?"

"I'm not sure. Paine became a local hero for preventing some French privateers from attacking Block Island. His wife is the daughter of former governor Caleb Carr. But before settling in Jamestown, he too was a pirate and had some association with Kidd."

"What does he do now?"

"He seems to be retired. His wife Mercy inherited a good fortune when her father died."

"Reuben wouldn't go willingly with a pirate," Experience said.

"Who knows what he was told to persuade him to sign with Kidd?"

"If I tell Joseph, I fear he'll go to Kidd and demand Reuben's release."

"Such an action might end badly," John said.

"What else can we do?"

"I can ask Paine to intercede with Kidd on our behalf."

"Will he agree to do that?"

"I can't say. I've had business dealings with him in the past, It's worth a try. I'll speak to him as soon as we get back to Jamestown."

"I can stay the night. I want to know the result of thy efforts."

"It's best that thou go home. I don't expect an immediate answer from Kidd, and Joseph will want to hear the news about Reuben."

"I won't mention Kidd," Experience said. "I'll say Reuben is at sea, and thou are trying to trace him."

"I'll let thee know when I have more news," John said.

Back home in Kings Towne, Experience approached her husband with some trepidation. She knew Joseph would not take kindly to the news about Reuben, but she hoped for some degree of patience and understanding.

Joseph showed little emotion as he listened to her account. "Our son has chosen his own path and is lost to us," he said when she was done.

"I'm sure he'll return soon," Experience said.

"Like the prodigal son," Joseph said. "Well, he'll find no fatted calf on his plate."

* * *

Apart from the French privateers, John's dealings with Thomas Paine were chiefly through their respective involvement in town affairs. He had never set foot inside Paine's home on the east shore of Conanicut, and he was not at all sure that Paine would take kindly to his request.

Mercy ushered him into the parlor. He accepted her offer of tea and biscuits while awaiting Paine's return from the village. No children were in evidence. John felt it advisable not to question their absence.

Paine evinced some surprise when he returned. "What brings you here, John?" he asked.

"My nephew Reuben has run away," John said. "I've come to ask for thy help in bringing him back."

Paine seemed puzzled by the request. "I'll do what I can, but I know nothing of your nephew."

"I have reason to believe he's signed on with William Kidd, whose ship is in the west bay. If I mistake not, thou have some dealings with Kidd."

"That's the talk in the village. His presence in the bay has nothing to do with me."

"I don't question thy business or his. I'm simply asking that thou use whatever influence thou have to bring about Reuben's return."

"What if he doesn't want to return?"

"He's too young to know what he wants," John said.

"Are you prepared to pay for his release?"

"If need be. Thou can tell Kidd that I might be of service to him."

"What kind of service?"

"I've heard of a warrant for his arrest. He stands a better chance of acquittal if someone pleads his case in England."

"I had no idea you were an attorney, John."

"Nor am I. But I could transport his emissary to London."

Paine stroked his beard. "I regard you as an honorable man. What I'm about to say is in confidence."

"Agreed," John said.

"You're right. Governor Bellomont has issued a warrant accusing Kidd of piracy. But Kidd has a valid license as a privateer. Bellomont has profited himself from some of the prizes Kidd took."

"Are thou saying that Kidd never engaged in piracy?"

Paine smiled. "I can hardly make such a claim. But his recent service to the Crown and the colonies outweighs any charges of piracy. Bellomont has assured him of a fair hearing and a King's pardon, if he discloses the location of a ship he captured in the Caribbean and of treasure he buried on Gardiners Island."

"Can Bellomont be trusted to keep his word?"

"Kidd has documents showing that all of the ships he seized as a privateer were French. But there is one thing you might do for him."

"What is that?" John asked.

"Kidd is prepared for whatever happens. If Bellomont breaks his promise or the courts rule against him, he wants to ensure that his wife is provided for. He's made arrangements to send her some treasure at regular intervals, but he needs someone to deliver it."

"Why would he trust me with his treasure?"

"I can't say he would. I can only suggest it to him."

"Thou can tell him I'll carry out his wishes," John said, "provided he releases Reuben from any contract he may have signed."

"I'll see to it that he gets your proposal," Paine said.

* * *

Paine was as good as his word. "Kidd considered your offer," he reported, "but he said it was up to your nephew to decide whether or not he wants to return home."

"Did thou see Reuben?" John asked.

"I did. The boy was adamant in his refusal. He said that nothing has changed since he left home, and he has no regrets. I tried to convince Kidd that he stood to benefit by tearing up the contract. He said he was satisfied with Bellomont's assurance of a pardon, and that getting treasure to his wife was no longer so important."

"I expected such an answer, but I hoped Reuben might reconsider."

"You did all you could," Paine said.

"That doesn't make it any easier to tell his mother that her son is lost to her," John said.

Experience appeared stoic when she heard the news, but John could tell she was taking it hard. Joseph was quick to deliver his verdict.

"The boy always had a rebellious streak in him. He's made his choice. Now he has to live with it."

"We must do something," Experience said. "Perhaps we can plead with Kidd ourselves."

"That is no longer possible," John said. "His ship left the bay this morning. I gather from what Paine said that he's on his way to Boston."

Experience stifled a sob. "I'm sure Reuben will soon come to regret his decision," she said.

"A lot depends on what happens to Kidd," John said.

Experience was silent, but he sensed that hope had been rekindled in her mind and her heart.

* * *

A fortnight later news arrived in Newport that Kidd had been arrested and was being held in prison for trial, but there was no word from or about Reuben. John held out little hope for his return.

"He's probably signed on another ship going who knows where."

Experience kept her composure as she listened; but she felt later that she had to do something, take some action related to her son. She decided to inquire into the welfare of the Indian girl. She had a stake in that baby. It was her grandchild.

When Joseph was away on business, she asked the girl's father to accompany her to his home so she could wish his daughter well. The Indian appeared somewhat flustered by her request but agreed to arrange a meeting. On their arrival in the village he summoned his wife to come out and meet Reuben's mother. Experience had prepared her opening statement.

"I've come to make sure thy daughter has all she needs."

"Daughter not well. She lose baby," the woman said.

"I'm sorry. May I see her?"

"You follow me."

She led the way to a communal hut, where several young women in various stages of pregnancy rested on mats. The woman addressed one of them in her native tongue. The girl smiled up at Experience. She appeared exhausted, as if she had survived a strenuous ordeal. It was clear that she was no longer pregnant.

"Are thou all right?" Experience asked.

The girl nodded. She looked down as if she were embarrassed.

"Is there anything I can do?"

"Tell Reuben I sorry I lose baby."

Experience frowned. The girl's father must know that Reuben had left home. "When did thou lose the baby?" she asked.

The girl had closed her eyes and did not reply.

"You come again when daughter feel better," the woman said.

"I shall. I hope she gets well soon."

The woman took Experience by the arm and led her out of the hut. The Indian laborer had little to say on the way back to the farm.

"Thy action was rash and foolhardy," Joseph said when he heard his wife's account of the meeting.

"I'm glad I saw the girl, even though they knew I was coming and were ready for me."

"What do thou mean?"

"The girl had been ill, but I doubt she was ever pregnant."

"Then it was all just a scheme to get money out of me," Joseph said.

"We may never know the answer to that," Experience said.

Seventeen

"Let him sleep in the stable with the horses."
(Rhode Island Colony, Summer 1701)

Piracy was often a topic of conversation when John visited the house in Horsleydown.

"Kidd stood trial in London," Tiddeman said after listening to his account of Reuben's disappearance. "He was hanged a month ago. I understand that Newport is still a friendly haven for pirates."

John laughed. "Samuel Cranston, our new governor, recently denied that charge before the Board of Trade. But what thou say is true in part. Rhode Island depends on the sea for trade and is liberal in issuing licenses to privateers. The authorities don't question their activities, as long as they obey the laws while they're in port."

"And as long as they contribute to the wealth of the community."

"That's the way of the world," John said. "Some years ago a pirate named Thomas Tew returned from the Red Sea with enough treasure to retire in fine style. He transformed himself into a respected citizen in Newport."

"Is he still enjoying the fruit of his ill-gotten gains?"

"Unfortunately, some of his crew squandered their share of the wealth and persuaded him to make another voyage. He never came back. Rumor has it that he spilled his guts on deck when struck by a Turkish cannonball."

"A cannonball or a gibbet," Tiddeman said. "Such is the fate of a pirate. I trust thy nephew will chart a different course."

"I'm always seeking news about him," John said. "One man thought he may have encountered Reuben on an island in the Caribbean, but that's all he could tell me."

"It must be hard on thy brother and his family."

"Experience is always eager for news," John said, "but Joseph seldom talks about him."

"Mothers are more inclined to forgive," Tiddeman said.

* * *

It took John a moment to recognize the young man at his door.

"Reuben!" he cried as they hugged each other.

Two years had elapsed since his nephew ran off and was lost to his family. Some sightings had made him question whether Reuben's seafaring career was completely legal, but he kept that news to himself. Looking now at the virtual stranger who stood before him, he felt that assessment was valid

Reuben was taller and heavier. A dark beard extended from ear to ear, but it failed to hide an ugly scar on his right cheek. To John's practiced eye such a scar was likely the result of a fight with sabers at sea or a brawl with knives in a waterfront tavern.

"Hello, Uncle John," Reuben said. "I've come back."

His soft deferential voice was more recognizable than his features.

"Thy parents will be glad to see thee," John said. "We've all been concerned for thy safety."

"I'm not sure I'll be welcome when I go home. That's why I'm here."

"Come inside. We can talk freely. Alice is out with the children."

Reuben took a seat at the table, but said nothing further.

"I know Kidd was arrested, tried in England, and hanged," John said. "I thought Lord Bellomont promised him a pardon. What went wrong when he got to Boston?"

"I'm not sure what happened," Reuben said. "I heard he couldn't produce the papers he needed for his defense."

"Paine said he had documents proving he was commissioned as a privateer and that all the ships he captured were French."

"I think Bellomont lied in order to get him to Boston."

"I suppose the authorities seized his ship."

"That's right," Reuben said. "Some of the crew were detained as witnesses, and others stayed to see how things would turn out. I signed on the first ship that had a berth. I wanted to get far away from him."

"Why were thou disillusioned with Kidd?"

"The crew were a rough lot. I know not if they were privateers or pirates, but their stories were all about actions that were outside the law."

"Surely thou knew about his reputation before thou signed on."

" My only thought was to get away from hone. Kidd claimed he would soon be in good favor with Bellomont and the King."

"I know why thou left," John said. "I can tell thee straight off that the Indian girl lost the child she was carrying. Thou are not a father."

"I suppose I should be glad of that."

"Where did thou ship out to after thou left Boston?"

"I've seen many ports and had a lot of experiences since then. I'm not proud of some of them. Now I just want to go home, but I don't know what to expect. Am I welcome, or have my parents disowned me?"

"Thy mother will open her arms," John said. "As for thy father, much will depend on what account thou can give of thy actions."

"I just want to be reconciled with them and with the community."

"To do that, thou must go to meeting and ask for a pardon."

Despite his reassurance, John felt a reconciliation between father and son was unlikely. Joseph was intransigent when it came to children obeying their parents. Experience said he blamed Reuben alone for the affair with the Indian girl and for signing with Kidd. He had refused to discuss the subject with John.

"I'll need some support at the meeting?" Reuben said.

"I'm favorably inclined," John said, "but I must reserve judgment until I hear what thou have done that needs to be forgiven."

"Maybe I should wait until I frame an acceptable story."

"Thy best course is to tell the truth to thy parents and at meeting," John said. "It may help if I go with thee. Thou can spend the night here with us, and we'll go to Kings Towne in the morning."

Reuben was silent, but John could tell that he appreciated the offer.

* * *

Experience greeted her son warmly, embracing Reuben and calling for the younger children to welcome their brother home. John was content to stand aside and observe the reunion.

"Where have thou been," she asked, "and what have thou been doing all this time?"

"Is Father here?" Reuben asked.

Before she could respond, Joseph entered from the back of the house. He stared long and hard at his son. "So thou have come back," he said. "Was the great world not to thy liking?"

"I made a mistake, and I'm sorry," Reuben said as John had coached him. "I want to apologize to everyone in the family for the trouble I caused."

"It's not thy only mistake. Thy escapade with that Indian whore caused thy mother a lot of grief and cost me a few pounds."

Reuben made no response. John sensed that he had almost given up hope and was withdrawing into himself.

"Thou would do well to follow the example of thy brother Tristram," Joseph went on. "Find and marry a good woman like Elizabeth Dyer whose grandmother Mary was hanged in Boston for being a Quaker."

"We've all heard about Mary Dyer," Reuben said. "I'm sorry I can't be more like Tristram, but"

"But no," Joseph cut him short. "Thou would rather consort with Indians and pirates."

"Peace, Joseph," Experience said. "We should be glad he's home."

Joseph ignored her. "My advice to thee is to reconcile thyself with the community of Friends. Maybe then thou will be welcome in this house."

"Where else should he go? This is his home," Experience said.

"Let him sleep in the stable with the horses," Joseph replied.

"Thy words are too harsh."

"I speak what is in my heart."

"He's welcome to stay with us in Jamestown," John said.

Joseph glared at him. "Stay out of it, John. This is a family matter."

"Am I not family?"

"I'm sorry. My quarrel is with my son, not with thee."

"I can ask my father to put Reuben up," Experience said. "Now I'm anxious to hear where he's been all this time."

"Let him tell his tale of woe at meeting," Joseph said.

When Experience was silent, John spoke up. "I trust thou will accept the decision of the community."

"So be it. I'll do my best to withhold judgment for the present."

"We'll alert Elder Matthews on the morrow," Experience said.

"Thou can speak to him," Joseph said.

"With thy approval," John said, "I should like to testify at meeting."

Joseph shrugged. "Suit thyself."

* * *

Elder Matthews rose, removed his hat, and faced the gathering of Friends. Standing there, he presented an imposing figure, six feet tall with broad shoulders and in the prime of life His voice resonated throughout the meeting house.

"We are here today to consider the case of our friend Reuben, son of Joseph and Experience Hull. His father claims that he ran away from home rather than face up to his responsibilities, and that he joined up with William Kidd, a man who was hanged for piracy. But before we render judgment on Reuben, it is right and fair that we allow him to answer to these charges."

Matthews paused to let his words sink in. His stern gaze lingered on each person in the room before he continued.

"Some here may be inclined to regard Reuben's homecoming as the return of a prodigal son. I would have thee consider that he left home at the tender age of sixteen and has been gone for two years. In a spirit of charity I admonish him to admit his transgressions and seek to be reconciled with this meeting. Those moved by the spirit to add to or detract from these charges, let them now speak."

Matthews took his seat on a bench facing the assembly. The men at meeting wore plain dark suits. The women had white dresses, kerchiefs, and caps of batiste with round plaits. The room was devoid of ornament. A single window was shuttered against worldly distractions, but a shaft of sunlight played with particles of dust suspended in the air.

Reuben was seated at the back on the visitor's bench. He bore a strained expression, as if he were wrestling with an inner demon. A strand of dark hair escaped from his cap. He had trimmed his beard, and the scar on his cheek was unmistakable.

The village schoolmaster was first to rise. A frayed jacket hung from his gaunt body. His gray eyes flashed as he spoke. He chose his words with care, gesticulating as if he were in a classroom.

"Not long ago Reuben was my pupil. He was quick to learn, diligent, and eager to help others who were slower than himself. Before school in the winter he split wood for the fire. I could always rely on him. I cannot speak to those actions for which he is charged. But I would have thee consider the old adage that, as the twig is bent, the tree shall grow. Before we consign this tree to the fire of our righteous indignation, we should ask ourselves whether his association with a pirate has warped his outlook on life.

Circumstances often lead us to make choices we later regret. His presence here today is an indication that he has reflected upon his actions. Let us hear him out and afford him a chance to regain his place in our community."

Some murmurs of sympathy were cut short by a stern glance from Elder Matthews. Reuben sat with his head cradled in his hands, his elbows resting on his knees. He appeared to be oblivious to his surroundings.

John rose as he had promised. "Reuben is my nephew," he said. "Whether he engaged in acts of piracy, I have no certain knowledge. But as master of a merchant ship I can testify to circumstances at sea that may oblige a man to accommodate his beliefs to the forces and conditions that face him. I grant that William Kidd was once a pirate, yet in later years he was licensed as a privateer to prey upon French shipping . He was vilified in some quarters and respected in others. Association with Kidd at this time in his life does not persuade me that my nephew engaged in acts of piracy. I shall reserve judgment until I hear his testimony and can better gauge whether or not he remained true to his beliefs. I urge all here gathered to do the same."

Silence followed John's witness. On the women's side Experience nodded in approval. Robert Harper was the next to address the meeting.

"Reuben is my grandson. He has been under my roof since his return, so I can speak to his present state of mind. He helped me to repair a shed, asking nothing in return but his bed and food. We talked about why he left home, and I can attest that he regrets his decision. I do not excuse his actions, but I urge thee to consider his age then and now in rendering judgment. That is all I have to say."

Another silence fell on the meeting. The midwife, a middle-aged woman known and respected in the community, rose. Instead of the usual smile that lit her face from within, she wore a pained expression.

"I cannot dispute those who have testified," she said. "I would only add what I heard from Reuben's mother while he was gone. She would speak for herself, but it's hard for a mother to chastise her children in public."

Experience sat with her eldest daughter Mary by the wood stove. It cast no heat at this season, but she claimed the seat through force of habit. If she knew what was coming, she gave no sign except to bow her head.

"Reuben left home against the wishes of his parents," the midwife continued. "His father needed him on the farm; and his mother was beset by anxiety, as thou may well imagine. Two years went by with no word from him. Adding to her worries was the fact that an Indian girl had lost the child fathered by her son. Since his return he has been ashamed to face his parents. I would urge him to make peace at home. Then let him ask our pardon."

Experience was silent, but Mary rose to her feet. Her voice was so soft it barely ruffled the still air in the room.

"My brother sits on the visitor's bench out of humility. It is not my place, but someone might offer him a seat in our midst that he may speak as one of us without constraint." That said, she sat down.

Elder Matthews stood and addressed Reuben.

"On behalf of this meeting I invite thee to come forward. As for speaking, that is for thee to decide."

Keeping his head down, Reuben walked to a bench near the front. After taking a seat, he appeared lost again in his own thoughts.

Joseph stood up. The muscles on his face were tense. All eyes were fastened upon him. Who was better qualified to shed light on this matter? He looked straight at Reuben, who seemed to shrink within himself.

"My son went away without a word of farewell to his mother or to me," he said. "After he left, I inquired into Kidded's background. I'm not as willing as my brother to excuse his actions, early or late. The courts in England have rendered judgment on his character. He was hanged a year ago for piracy. The fact is that my son ran away from home and joined a group of men who were or had once been pirates. He knew what he was doing. He had a chance to change his mind when Kidd was arrested, but he chose not to avail himself of that opportunity to admit his error. With regard to the Indian girl I suspect that her pregnancy was simply a scheme to get money out of me, but that is no excuse for fornicating with a heathen."

Joseph paused to collect his thoughts. "I thank those who testified to my son's character, but they do not know him as I do. He has been at odds with the world since he was born. I accept some of the blame for what he has become. I needed his help in my work and turned a deaf ear to his wishes. As for the rest I'm content to abide by the judgment of this community."

Elder Matthews rose and looked at Reuben. "If thou have anything to say for thyself, I invite thee to speak now."

Reuben got slowly to his feet. His head was down, and he appeared to be staring at the planks in the floor. A man seated behind him nudged him to remove his cap. He raised his eyes and looked at Elder Matthews, who had resumed his seat. When he spoke, his voice was strong and resolute.

"My uncle is right. After I left home, I tried to accommodate my beliefs to my actions. I didn't always succeed. I had been told that Kidd was once a pirate, but that's not the reason I signed aboard his ship; and I reaped little profit from the short time I was in his service. I look forward to being reconciled with my parents and this community."

Reuben paused. He glanced about warily, as if to gauge the reaction of those around him.

"If thou wish to be reconciled," Matthews said, "we must know more precisely what thou have done."

Reuben met the elder's gaze without flinching. "I own thy right to know my transgressions, that thou may better judge my guilt. While listening to the witness of others, I reviewed in my mind and heart all the events of the past two years. In the heat of youthful passion I did lie with an Indian girl. Rather than seeking to regain the trust and forgiveness of my father, I chose to leave home. Kidd's ship was in the bay, and I was told he was on his way to Boston to clear his name. After he was arrested, I did have a chance to reconsider my actions; but I was still loath to return home. I signed aboard a ship bound for Barbados. For a year or more I was back and forth to ports in the Caribbean. Then I faced up to my mistakes and came home."

"Tell us how far thou strayed from thy beliefs," Mathews said without standing. "That is more to the point."

Reuben looked down again at the floor. Several minutes passed before he spoke. "While at sea I conversed with men who had little respect for our beliefs. I was swayed by their talk and embraced a life they described as free. Along with my new companions I squandered what I earned on drink and women. They said that was what it meant to be free. They took delight in teaching me to be just like them.

When I came to realize that I wasn't one of them and refused to sign on for another voyage, they all turned against me. I felt isolated. That's why I decided to come home. I accept full responsibility for my actions and for any wrongdoing, and I ask forgiveness of all present at this meeting."

A hush fell over the gathering as Matthews conferred with the other elders on the bench. He rose to address the gathering.

"Reuben Hull, we bid thee to make peace with thy parents, that thou may once more be at peace with thyself. When that is done, thou are welcome to come again before this meeting. We look forward to that day."

Matthews and the other elders filed out of the building. Joseph took Experience by the arm and moved toward the door. She glanced back at Reuben, who sat with his head bowed. He rose and followed his parents.

Eighteen

"This, gentlemen, is Mr. Hull, my honored master."
(Rhode Island Colony, 1703-1710)

When Edmond Tiddeman died, John was not on hand for his funeral. On subsequent voyages to London he was keenly aware that he no longer had a ready source of information about the situation in England.

"I was quite attached to thy father," he confided to Alice. "I miss our long and comfortable talks at the house in Horsleydown."

"My strongest tie to England is broken," Alice said. "I regret that Father never saw his grandchildren when they were grown."

"I had planned to take Tiddeman to London on my next voyage," John said. "Thy father would have liked that, but it wasn't meant to be."

"Perhaps he'll visit London on his own accord when he's grown."

"I"ll see to it that he does," John said.

* * *

Three years later on a cold day in October the entire family gathered at the Friends cemetery in Kings Towne. Joseph had watched helplessly as Experience fought for breath and finally succumbed to a lung ailment the doctor called pleurisy. Their elder daughter Mary was married and had just given birth to her second child. Her sister Alice agreed to look after their father. Tristram and young Joseph were also married. Reuben was single; but he was seldom at home, and his whereabouts were often uncertain.

"I'm glad Alice is still at home," John commented to his wife.

"Not for long," she said. "She's engaged to a man from Newport."

"Then Joseph will be all alone in the house."

"Mary assured me that he'll be well cared for," Alice said. "I trust her to keep her word."

* * *

John was on his porch gazing out to the west, when his younger son burst out of the house.

"There's a man o' war in the east bay," young John cried.

The boy stood nearly as tall as his father. With his older brother Tiddeman he operated the north ferry to Newport. He was drawn to the sea and anticipated the day when he would sail with his father on the *Ataquin.* Tiddeman was more interested in restoring sick animals to health.

"Does this man 'o war have a name?" John asked.

"*HMS Falmouth,*" was the quick reply.

"I thank thee for the news," John said.

"Can I go aboard while she's in port?"

"If they accept visitors, I have no objection."

"Will thou arrange it."

"I can try, but I have little influence with the Royal Navy."

The boy ran off satisfied. John resumed his contemplation of the west bay. He couldn't see his brother's house, but in winter he fancied he could make out smoke from the chimney. Joseph was still active in the Society of Friends. His horses and his trade as a cooper had made him a prosperous man. He was grooming his three older sons to take over the business . Now in his mid-twenties, Reuben remained a problem. He had been fined for assault and was currently involved with a married woman. He displayed little interest in horses or trade.

John had no cause to be jealous of his brother. He had done quite well himself. He owned four hundred acres of land. His house was one of the grandest in town. The transatlantic trade had made him moderately wealthy. His children caused him no grief. He was active in town affairs, having served as assessor, councilman, deputy, and town clerk.

His thoughts turned to the warship in the bay. It was not a common occurrence, and he was curious. He resolved to inquire about it when he was in Newport, but he didn't have to wait that long. Later that morning a seaman in naval uniform arrived with a message.

It read: "Admiral Wager requests the honor of your presence aboard Her Majesty's ship *Falmouth* at your convenience."

He had encountered Wager only once since his apprentice accepted a post in the Royal Navy. In a London tavern they shared a bottle of fine Portuguese wine, while they recalled their voyages together on the *Ataquin*. Some years later he was surprised and pleased to receive a pipe of Madeira wine as a gift from Wager. That practice had continued at more or less yearly intervals.

"Tell the Admiral my son and I shall be pleased to come aboard," he told the messenger. "Is this afternoon too soon?"

"I have orders to wait upon your pleasure," the seaman said.

"Then thou shall join us for the noon meal," John said.

Young John was overjoyed at the swift realization of his dream. His brother Tiddeman also spoke up

"If thou have no objection, I'd like to go with thee."

"By all means," John said, mildly surprised by the request. "Forgive me for not asking. I felt thou would have little interest in a ship of the line."

"I'm more interested in meeting the admiral," Tiddeman said.

In the boat Wager had dispatched, John cautioned his younger son to control his eagerness. Tiddeman appeared more restrained. Once aboard the *Falmouth* they were escorted to the admiral's quarters, where Wager greeted them warmly.

"It's good to see you again, John. How have you been? You look hail and hearty. Are these your boys?"

"My sons Tiddeman and John. This is Admiral Charles Wager. Many years ago I agreed to take him on as an apprentice."

"Thou had an admiral as an apprentice!" young John exclaimed.

Wager laughed. "It takes a while to become an admiral. I was just a landlubber in London who thought he wanted to go to sea."

"What's it like to be an admiral?" the boy persisted.

"Most of my career was fairly dull," Wager said. "I spent several years off the French coast and in the Mediterranean. Then I was lucky enough to earn a knighthood by capturing a Spanish galleon in the Caribbean. Her cargo of silver made me fairly wealthy."

"That's enough," John told his son before he could pose any more questions. Turning to Wager, he asked, "What brings thee to Newport?" "The Crown has ordered an attack on the French fort at Port Royal in Canada. The Rhode Island Colony is to provide a hundred and eighty militia for the expedition. My mission is to recruit men and carry them to Boston."

"Didn't we attack Port Royal a few years ago?" John asked.

"This is our third attempt to capture the fort," Wager said. "We have a good chance for success this time. But enough of that. I know you're a man of peace. I trust you have prospered over the years, though I suspect this endless conflict with France interferes with your trade."

John granted that he had managed to prosper despite the wars and the navigation acts. "If thou have time," he concluded, "Alice and I would be pleased to have thee join us for one evening for dinner."

"I'd like to see Alice again. Please convey my greetings, and tell her I could can tomorrow, if that is convenient."

"Could thou ask one of thy men to show my son John about the ship? He's eager to pursue a life at sea."

"Of course. And what is Tiddeman's interest?"

"He can speak for himself."

"Will there be any doctors on this expedition?" Tiddeman asked.

Wager seemed surprised by the question. "As a matter of fact, we're a bit short of men qualified to care for the injured. Why do you ask?"

"I hope one day to call myself a doctor. I know men will be injured in the battle. I would welcome a chance to aid in their care."

"He already has a reputation on the island," John said. "He got much of his knowledge from a woman in Newport who deals in herbs and tonics."

"If it's experience you want," Wager said, "I can see to it that you're assigned to work on a hospital ship. But before you decide, perhaps you should talk with our ship surgeon. With your father's permission I'll ask him to join us tomorrow at dinner."

"That is no problem," John said.

Tiddeman's face lit in a broad smile. "I'd like that."

"Good! Now I'd like to introduce your father to my crew."

After ordering a seaman to take young John on a tour of the ship, Wager led the way to the command deck. With John at his side he addressed the assembled officers and crew.

"We have with us a distinguished citizen of the town of Jamestown. But he is more than that. This, gentlemen, is Mr. Hull, my honored master. He taught me the principles of seamanship and fostered my naval career. I'm indebted to him for all I have achieved."

John bowed his head in response to the cheers, while Tiddeman joined in the applause for his father.

* * *

The talk at dinner evoked in John pleasant memories of Wager's apprenticeship, along with a modest summary of his accomplishments in the Royal Navy and a discussion of the current state of affairs in England and the colonies. Alice had prepared a meal consisting of roast veal, potatoes, and green beans. Both Wager and the surgeon expressed their appreciation.

Tiddeman had persuaded his father to invite Reuben to join them at table. "He's having a hard time right now," he explained when John evinced some surprise. "It might be good for him, if he went to Port Royal."

"It's kind of thee to be concerned for him," John said.

"He's my cousin and my friend," Tiddeman said.

Reuben ate in silence but showed some interest when Alice referred to the expedition.

"I thank thee for giving Tiddeman an opportunity to advance his career," she said, "yet I can't help being concerned for his safety."

"I understand your concern," Wager said. "As I told John earlier, I'm confident that our expedition will be a success. We have a fleet consisting of five warships, two bomb galleys, and some thirty transports. The French will have no choice but to surrender in the face of our overwhelming force."

"What's a bomb galley?" Reuben asked.

"Don't interrupt," John chided him. "Let the admiral finish."

"I don't mind," Wager said. "It's a ship with a reinforced hull. Two mortars mounted on the bow can lob explosive shells on the target, in this case the fort at Port Royal."

"When I told Reuben about the expedition," Tiddeman said, "he asked if he could come along too."

"You're welcome to join us," Wager said. "Are your parents aware of your intention?"

"I'm old enough to make my own decisions," Reuben said.

Wager looked at John, who frowned as he nodded in agreement.

"Very well then," he said. "I'll be in port all week. You can present yourself to our recruiter in Newport."

"How long will the boys be gone?" Alice asked.

"Two or three months," Wager said. "We sail early in September. The actual fighting should be over in a week or so."

"Will we occupy Port Royal afterwards?" Reuben asked.

"We must until a permanent force arrives from England."

"I'd like to stay for the occupation?"

"I can't promise that, but I'm sure you'll have a chance."

"If you wish, I'll arrange for both of you to serve together on the hospital ship," the surgeon said.

"I want to be in the battle," Reuben said.

"Part of the battle is caring for the wounded," the surgeon said.

"Enough of this," John said, noting his wife's worried look. "I want to show the admiral about my property."

"I should like that," Wager said.

When Alice started to gather the plates. Reuben rose to help her

"Thy father will miss thee," Alice said. "He depends on thy help."

"'Father can manage without me. He'll be glad I'm gone. My sister Mary is the only one who understands me."

"Mary has her own family to think about," Alice said.

'She made a mistake when she married Hoxie," Reuben said.

"That's not for thee to judge," Alice said, turning away.

Reuben simply shrugged.

Tiddeman had listened in silence to this exchange. "Let's go for a walk," he said.

"That's a good idea," Reuben said. Pausing at the door, he called back to Alice. "Many thanks for the dinner."

Without waiting for a response, he joined his cousin on a path that led past the barn and into the woods beyond.

"What is thy grudge against Hoxie?" Tiddeman asked.

"What I've heard about him makes me wonder whether he'll be faithful to her. I tried to warn Mary, but she wouldn't listen."

"Thou are hardly one to advise anybody about marriage."

Reuben laughed. "You're right about that," he said.

"Is it thy wish to settle down and get married?" Tiddeman asked.

"I wouldn't mind," Reuben said. "Maybe I'll meet a nice French girl in Port Royal."

* * *

A colony of Indians had set up camp at the southern tip of Conanicut, an area known as Beavertail. Town officials put them to work on roads and placed them with farmers as bonded labor, but these efforts to help were not always successful. Many of them preferred drink to manual labor.

John viewed the Indians as free people who, justly or not, had been deprived of their land. Conanicut was their ancestral summer home. No doubt they felt an affinity for the island, but that was no excuse for drunkenness and disturbing the peace of the community. He had not offered to take an Indian on his farm. Ben and Cumby managed very well. No need to expose Alice and the children to needless risk.

But pressured by local officials, he finally agreed to let an Indian help him construct a cowshed. With Tiddeman in Canada, he was shorthanded for such a project. The Indian recommended to him was said to have experience in construction.

He thought often of Tiddeman. He had received no word from or about his son, nor about the expedition against Port Royal. A band of Indians loyal to the French had raided Deerfield in the

Massachusetts Colony, burning houses and taking captives. A certain unease pervaded New England as people waited for news that Port Royal had been captured and French influence was on the wane.

"I can't help but worry about Tiddeman," Alice said as John outlined plans for another voyage to England. "I fear something will happen to him. I couldn't deal with that alone. Can thou put off thy voyage until he returns?"

John regarded her with some surprise. "Nothing will happen to him," he assured her. "He's caring for those wounded in battle. Is anything else troubling thee?"

"There is something. That Indian makes me uneasy. It's nothing he's done. I just feel uncomfortable when he's around."

"I can't discharge him for no cause, but for thy sake I'll put off my voyage until the shed is finished."

"I feel much better, and I thank thee."

Alice made no further mention of the Indian, and John put their talk out of his mind. Every day he and Ben and the Indian labored to complete the shed. The framework and roof were complete, and planks for the siding and the floor were stacked up, ready to be installed. But one day on his return from the village he was surprised to find no one at work. His search for Ben and the Indian took him first to the barn. All was quiet as he entered.

Once inside he spotted Ben, a pitchfork in his hand, standing over the prostrate body of the Indian. Cumby, her clothing in disarray, cowered near the ladder that led to the hay loft.

"What have thou done?" John cried.

Ben turned abruptly to face him. His face was contorted with anger. He waved the pitchfork about as he spoke.

"Indian hurt Cumby. I kill him."

John looked more closely at Cumby, who crouched with her head down, both arms shielding her breasts. Her thin dress was hanging off one shoulder. She had a gash over her left eye, and blood was trickling down her cheek. A soft moan escaped her as he approached.

"Are thou all right?" he asked.

She looked up at him and tried to smile.

"Can thou tell me what happened?"

"I go to barn. See if chickens lay eggs. Indian have bottle. Tell me to drink. I say no. He hold my arms. Tear my dress. I scream. Ben come. Make him stop."

Cumby looked away, completely out of breath.

"I not sorry he dead," Ben said.

John knelt down and touched the inert body on the barn floor. The Indian made a futile effort to raise his right arm.

"Don't move," John said. Turning to Cumby, he ordered, "Tell Alice to bring some bandages and a pan of water."

He watched as Alice dressed a nasty looking wound just below the Indian's shoulder blade, where the pitchfork had penetrated. With Ben's help they loaded him onto a wagon and drove to the village. The man who called himself a doctor, though he tended more to animals than humans, allowed that Alice had done all she could. Reassured that the Indian would recover, John left him with the colony on Beavertail. On the way home he notified the town clerk about what had occurred.

That evening at home he sat with chin in hand, his elbows resting on the table. His eyes were shut as if in prayer. The food on his plate was untouched. Alice and the children cast sidelong glances at him as they ate.

"I can't let Ben just walk away from this," he muttered to himself. "That Indian might have died."

"He was defending his wife," Alice said softly.

John looked up, startled by her voice. "Why would the Indian assault Cumby?" he asked. "He must have known Ben was nearby."

"He was most likely drunk."

"Ben didn't have to use a pitchfork."

"He had no time to think. He used whatever was at hand."

"Thou may be right," John said.

He well knew that, called on to defend life or property, an otherwise peaceful man can act by instinct with no thought of the consequences. That night he went to bed, hoping that he had seen the end of the matter.

But the next morning a deputy named Barker was at his door. "I have a warrant for the arrest of your slave Ben," he said.

"He's not a slave," John said. "He's a free man."

"Whatever he is, he's charged with attacking an Indian with a pitchfork and causing him severe bodily harm."

"The Indian attacked Ben's wife. He was defending her."

"You can tell your story to the magistrate," Barker said. "I have my orders to conduct your slave to the town jail."

John sought to reassure a bewildered Ben and a distraught Cumby that everything would be all right. The next day he appeared before a magistrate, confident that liberating Ben was a straightforward matter. He need but explain what had happened, and the case would be dismissed.

The magistrate listened to John's account; but it was disputed by a man from the Indian colony, who asserted there was no valid reason for Ben's attack. The Indian was recovering from his injuries and unable to appear.

Barker was there to state the town's interest in the case. "In placing an Indian with a local farmer, the town assumes a certain responsibility for his welfare and safety. I suspect the slave Ben fancied his so-called wife was in some kind of danger. He resorted to violence without thinking, as might be expected from a Negro."

"Did you witness this attack on your servant woman?" the magistrate asked, turning to John.

"No, but I got there shortly afterward. Her face was covered with blood, and her dress was torn. She was half naked."

The magistrate looked toward Barker, but the deputy had nothing to add. Addressing Ben, who stood with eyes downcast, his hands clasped in front of him, he delivered his verdict.

"After considering the testimony, it is my opinion that the Negro Ben acted in defense of his fellow servant, saving her from an attack that possibly threatened her life. I find him therefore not guilty of assault. However, in light of what seems like excessive force and the severity of the wounds suffered by the Indian who was at that time a ward of the town, I order the Negro Ben to make restitution in the amount of five pounds."

John led a seemingly bewildered Ben out of the building. They got a sour look from Barker as they passed.

Alice listened to her husband's account of the hearing. "What do thou propose to do now?" she asked.

"I'll pay the five pounds and deduct it from Ben's wages," John said.

"I mean, how will thou go about delivering the money?"

"I'll let Barker deliver it. I want to be on record as having paid it."

"Better that thou visit the Indian's family thyself. Give them what is due for the man's labor, plus the five pounds. And take Ben with thee."

* * *

His trade with London curtailed by the perpetual warfare with France, John was ever on the alert for profitable enterprises closer to home. He had purchased the north ferry from Caleb Carr, an early settler on the island. It ran from the east shore of Conanicut to the long wharf in Newport. He kept his boat in good condition, and he personally trained his sons or others in the principles of seamanship. His ferry proved to be a profitable enterprise.

But when a sizeable village took root directly across the bay from Newport, another ferry was established. For a time both ferries had ample business. John soon come to realize that the future of Jamestown resided in the village. The franchise for this second ferry was originally awarded to Samuel Clarke. It passed through several hands until it was acquired by Robert Barker, the deputy who had arrested Ben.

When John heard of Barker's purchase, he confronted the town official who had approved the transfer. "Thou might have told me that the franchise was for sale. I would have placed a bid."

"Barker said you knew about it," the official said. "We liked the idea of a ferry that could carry livestock as well as people. Everyone at the hearing agreed to his proposal."

John went home convinced that Barker had acted out of revenge in gaining approval for his ferry. He made light of the competition, but farmers at the north end of the island were gravitating toward the village. Barker's ferry was better suited to their needs, and the passage took much less time. Business on the north ferry fell off sharply.

"I provide a service for people on this end of the island," he told Alice. "It doesn't matter whether or not I make a profit."

"I think thou just want to spite Barker," she said.

"Thou can think what thou like," John said.

Some time later Alice asked to go with him to the village. He allowed the horse pulling the wagon to set its own pace. Alice nudged him as they neared the end of their three-mile drive.

"Look, John! Barker's ferry is approaching the landing."

John gazed steadfastly toward the west as he replied. "I'll never look at his damned boat, not as long as I live."

And to Alice's knowledge he never did.

* * *

Toward the end of October John got word that the campaign against the French was successful. Port Royal was in British hands. It was December before Tiddeman returned home. He looked more mature, and he had lost some weight; but in voice and manner he was his former self.

"Where is Reuben?" John asked after greeting his son.

"He volunteered to stay on until a permanent force arrives from England to occupy the fort," Tiddeman said.

"I'll send word to Joseph tomorrow," John said.

"I'll be glad to tell him myself," Tiddeman said.

That evening the entire family, including Ben and Cumby, gathered to hear his account of the expedition.

"We sailed from Boston in mid-September. When the fleet reached Port Royal, one of the transports ran aground and was swept on the rocks. Twenty soldiers died along with the captain and some of the crew."

"Did thou see all that?" young John asked.

"Don't interrupt," Alice said. "Let thy brother tell it his way."

"I saw quite a lot of it," Tiddeman said. "Some soldiers were injured. I helped the surgeon set a number of broken arms and legs."

Young John was silent, but his looks showed that he was impressed.

"Once we got ashore, it went a little better. General Nicholson was in command of the expedition. He landed forces north and south of the town and the fort. I was with the southern force. We faced small arms fire from the French and their Indian allies. Three soldiers died on the first day, but we were able to establish a camp about four hundred yards from the fort. Over the next four days we brought up cannon and advanced to within a hundred yards. Nicholson sent a message demanding that the French surrender. Their commander signed an agreement the next day."

"Was it a formal surrender?" John asked.

"It was a sight to behold," Tiddeman said. "The French left the fort with drums beating and flags flying. They carried their arms and baggage. We stood at attention on either side of them as they marched to the ships that would take them back to France."

"Was Reuben also involved in the fighting?" Alice asked.

"He was with the force that landed north of the fort. I saw him briefly after the surrender. He didn't have much to say, but he was all right."

"I gather thou learned how to care for the wounded," John said.

"A surgeon on my ship taught me a lot. I cared for injured men during the siege, and I prescribed some of Tami's salves and tonics. I've decided that I want to learn all I can about medicine."

"It will be good to have a doctor in the family," John said.

"I may decide not to practice in Jamestown," Tiddeman said.

"Where else then?" John asked.

"This past summer I met a woman named Sarah Sands. She works in a milliner's shop in Newport. Her parents live on Block Island."

"When will we meet this Sarah?" Alice asked.

"It's still a bit early for that."

"I trust she's a member of our community."

"She is indeed," Tiddeman said.

Nineteen

"We find the defendant, Reuben Hull, guilty of murder."

(Rhode Island Colony, Spring 1719)

Following the expedition to Port Royal, Tiddeman pursued his medical studies whenever and wherever an opportunity presented. He assisted ship surgeons when they were in port. He pressed the local apothecary for information about treatments for common illnesses. After serving for two years as an apprentice to a physician in Newport who had a degree from Edinburgh, he was declared ready to call himself a doctor.

He had persuaded Tami to reveal the ingredients of many of her salves and potions. She was reluctant at first; but a progressive stomach ailment, for which Tiddeman was able to provide some relief, persuaded her to share the knowledge she had accumulated over a lifetime. She died at the age of seventy-four. Tiddeman procured a cemetery plot and, along with John and Alice, attended her burial. The populace of Newport, whom she had served for many years, took little or no heed of her passing.

Following his marriage to Sarah Sands, Tiddeman settled in the village of Jamestown, but he ministered to patients on Block Island as well as Conanicut. They had three children and were welcome visitors at the home of his parents on the north end of the island.

John was proud of his elder son, but he was also gratified that his other children were well settled. Young John had served an apprenticeship with a merchant sailing out of Newport and was mate on a ship plying the coastal trade. A third son, named Joseph after his great grandfather the minister, was eighteen and had yet to decide on a career. He seemed drawn to public office, exhibiting a keen interest in local government.

Two daughters, Mary and Alice, were happily married to men of means and bearing children. John and his wife still mourned the death of their second daughter Catherine, who had died two years earlier in childbirth. Their youngest girl, Hannah, was being courted by a man from Dartmouth in the Plymouth Colony.

"I really like him," she told her mother. "He hasn't proposed, but he's agreed to become a Friend, and he's taking lessons for my sake."

"That sounds familiar," Alice said.

* * *

Death struck Joseph's family again in the summer of 1718. His eldest son Tristram succumbed to a fever that swept through the colony. Tiddeman had no medicine in his bag to save his cousin. Tristram was laid to rest in the Friend's cemetery in Kings Towne. His wife Elizabeth and their ten children attended the services. The oldest girl was seventeen at the time, the youngest child only two.

Joseph was devastated by the loss of his favorite son. He had made no secret of his preference, which was due in large part to the fact that Tristram's wife Elizabeth was the daughter of Mary Dyer, whom the Society considered a martyr for their beliefs. He saw to it that the widow and her children were provided for. Elizabeth in turn dispatched her oldest daughter to keep house for Joseph, who was in his sixties.

Tristram had been groomed to take over his father's business. With his death two of his brothers, Joseph and John, assumed that role. Reuben showed no interest. He had yet to fasten upon a steadying influence in his life. He remained aloof from the family, save for his sister Mary who served as a point of contact.

Young Joseph, who had remarried following the death of his first wife, appeared to be content in his new role. But his second wife resented the influence Elizabeth and her daughter had over his father.

"He ought to be grateful for thy help," she told her husband, "but he treats thee more like a foreman than a son."

"I'm used to it," young Joseph said. "We have to look to the future."

* * *

John knew from his brother's look that something was terribly wrong.

"They say Reuben killed a woman," Joseph said.

His face was flushed from the row across the west bay and the trek up from the shore. He staggered as he spoke, grasping the side of a wagon that stood in the yard.

"Come inside and have some water," John said. "Then thou can tell us what happened."

Once in the house Joseph seemed to relax. "Two justices found her body early this morning," he said more calmly.

"Hold on!" John said. "Whose body?"

"Freelove Dolleware. I hear the name suits her. She has a reputation for being promiscuous."

"Where did this happen?"

"At the Hoxie house in Westerly. Thou wouldn't know the place."

"Why do they think Reuben did it?"

"They say there was a witness to the shooting."

"What does Reuben have to say about it?"

"The deputies are searching for him, and I couldn't find him," Joseph said, growing more agitated. "I thought he might have come to thee."

"We haven't seen him, but he may be hiding somewhere," John said. "We can search my property. I'll get Ben to help."

The three men searched the outbuildings and surrounding fields but found no trace of Reuben. Joseph appeared crestfallen.

"I may as well go home," he said. "Maybe there's some word of him."

"I can ask around on the island," John said.

"Perhaps he ran off to sea again," Alice said.

Joseph uttered a mirthless laugh. "He lost all interest in ships a long time ago. He's in hiding and afraid to show his face."

In the days that followed, John scoured Conanicut while Joseph searched the country around Kings Towne, but to no avail.

A warrant had been issued for Reuben's arrest. The victim's parents requested that a jury be impaneled. His trial was set for the next session of the General Court of Trials to be held in September in Newport.

During the summer Joseph was struck by yet another death in the family. Elizabeth, Tristram's widow, died in her sleep from an unexplained cause. Her older girls were quite capable of managing a household, and Joseph continued to aid the family financially. But having lost his eldest son a year earlier and with Reuben facing trial for murder, he now had to grieve for his favorite daughter-in-law.

Mary sent word to John that her father was in a dark mood. "He won't eat or tend to business. I know he's worried about Reuben, but he refuses to talk about him." Alice conveyed the message to her husband.

"I'll ask Tiddeman to have a look at him," John said.

When Joseph admitted that he had periodic chest pain, Tiddeman cautioned him against over exertion. He prescribed rest and an elixir made from hawthorn berries.

"Let me know if he has any more pain," he told Mary.

"I'm worried that the upcoming trial may upset him," she said.

"I'll attend the trial and keep an eye on him."

"Can they try Reuben if he's not there?"

"I'm afraid so. Of course, the sentence of the judges can't be carried out until they find Reuben."

"We may never see him again," Mary said.

"That's up to Reuben," Tiddeman said.

* * *

On a humid day toward the end of August John was at work in the barn when a familiar carriage drew up in the yard. The driver was Tiddeman, but there was another man with him. As John approached the carriage, he recognized Reuben. All his searches and inquiries during the spring and summer had been fruitless. Now the fugitive was on his doorstep. He called to Alice to come out and greet their lost nephew.

"We have many questions," John said when they had gathered in the parlor, "but we should let thee tell thy story in thy own manner."

Tiddeman spoke up. "I've known ever since April where Reuben was hiding. He told me he needed time to decide whether to turn himself in and stand trial. I knew he would do the right thing, and I felt it would benefit his father if Reuben were free rather than sitting in jail awaiting trial."

"So where was he?" John asked.

"In a shack on Block Island near Sarah's parents. I saw him whenever I was on the island in conjunction with my practice."

"I can't say I agree with thy reasoning," John said, "but I want to hear Reuben's account of what happened in April."

"She was seeing another man. I was jealous, and I shot her."

John waited for a further explanation, but none was forthcoming.

"Is that all thou have to say?" he asked.

"I've advised him not to talk about it," Tiddeman said. "Anything he says might be used against him at the trial."

"Are thou on thy way home?" Alice asked.

"I plan to give myself up, but I'd like to see my father first. Tiddeman says it will only upset him. We came to ask your opinion."

"I think seeing thee will be a comfort for him," Alice said.

"Rather a brief comfort, I'm afraid," Reuben said.

John thought for a moment before he replied. "Joseph will demand a full account of what happened. If thou are not prepared for that, thou would do better to take Tidddeman's advice."

"I don't expect him to forgive me," Reuben said. "I just want his support in what I'm about to do, what I have to do."

"It might help if John went with thee to see thy father," Alice said.

"I agree," Tiddeman said.

John regarded each of them in turn, then smiled. "I was about to suggest that myself," he said.

* * *

"So thou have decided to come back," Joseph said.

Reuben did not reply. He seemed hesitant to enter his father's house without permission.

"We can talk better inside," John said.

Joseph nodded and stood aside. In the house he began at once to question Reuben.

"Where have thou been? I searched everywhere for thee."

"I was on Block Island," Reuben said. "I needed time to think. Now I'm ready to stand trial for what I did."

"They claim thou murdered that woman."

Reuben nodded but said nothing.

"I can hire an attorney," Joseph said, clearly struggling to control his emotions.

"I won't need an attorney. I'm going to plead guilty."

"Thou admit that thou killed her! What made thee do such a thing?"

"I'm sorry. I wasn't thinking clearly."

"Then suppose thou tell me exactly what happened."

When Reuben was silent, John responded to his brother's demand. "Tiddeman advised him not to say anything before the trial."

"If he pleads guilty, what difference will it make?" Joseph asked.

"It could have some bearing on his sentence."

"Then go and give thyself up!" Joseph said, turning away from his son. "A murderer has no welcome in this house."

* * *

On a sunny day in September Joseph, accompanied by his daughter Mary and his son Joseph, joined John and Tiddeman at the courthouse in Newport, where Reuben was to be tried. Freelove's parents were already there, along with a considerable number of curious spectators. Joseph's anger had cooled somewhat, and he expressed the hope that his status in the colony might persuade the court to spare Reuben's life. John was less optimistic, but he kept that to himself.

The eight jurymen filed in and took their places. Reuben appeared calm, his head bowed, an attorney at his side. He had yielded to Tiddeman's argument that having an attorney would help to calm his father.

"Reuben plans to plead guilty," Mary said. "Why is there a jury?"

"Her parents requested it," John said. "I suppose they want to present all their evidence against Reuben."

"What evidence?"

"We'll have to wait and see."

A bailiff appeared at the door of the chamber. "On orders of Governor Samuel Cranston this court of trials at Newport is now in session. All rise."

The deputy governor and two assistants entered the courtroom and took their seats on the bench. One of the judges asked Reuben to stand.

"Reuben Hull, you are charged with the willful murder of Freelove Dolleware. How do you plead?"

"Guilty," Reuben said in a soft voice.

"May it please the court," his attorney said. "We have evidence that casts additional light on this case and may influence the sentence."

"You'll have your chance," the judge said.

The attorney for Freelove called Christopher Allen, one of the justices who found the body.

"Early in the morning of April twenty-third," Allen testified, "we were summoned to a house in Westerly. When we arrived, we found the body of a woman. She appeared to be dead ."

"In whose house did you find the body?" the attorney asked.

"The house was unoccupied. It used to belong to Joseph Hoxie."

"You say you were summoned. By whom?"

"Lawrence Vilett. He said there had been a shooting."

"Were you able to identify the body?"

"Her face and head were covered with blood, but we identified her as Freelove Dolleware."

"Did you see anything that would indicate the cause of death?"

"A window was broken. We figured that someone standing outside the house must have shot her through that window."

"Then what did you do?"

"I waited at the house while Rouse went to get the doctor," Allen said.

Rouse Helm corroborated the testimony given by his fellow justice. Reuben's attorney had no questions.

The doctor then testified that he had examined the body. "The woman was dead when I got there," he said.

"What was the cause of death?"

"She died of a gunshot wound to the head."

"How long had she been dead?"

"Several hours. I'd say she died around midnight."

Lawrence Vilett took the stand. His testimony from the initial hearing was read aloud. Joseph Sheffield, chairman of the jury, was at that hearing and certified that what was read was an accurate statement.

"You testified at a previous hearing that you saw Reuben Hull shoot the victim, Freelove Dolleware," the attorney said. "Please describe that event and tell the court how you came to witness it."

Vilett was about Reuben's age. He looked at the three judges seated on the bench, then fixed his gaze on the attorney. He mumbled something in a soft voice and was commanded to speak up.

"I was passing the Hoxie house that night, when I heard what sounded like a gunshot. Then I saw a man running away. He went right past me, so I had a good look at him. It was Reuben Hull."

"Then what did you do?"

"I went right away to tell a justice what I saw."

Reuben's attorney addressed the witness. "You say you were passing by the house when you heard the shot. Do you normally pass by that house at that hour of the night?"

Vilett appeared to consider the question. "I often take that route on my way home from the tavern."

"Were you at the tavern on the night in question?"

"I think I was. My memory is a bit foggy."

"Did you have a few drinks with the defendant?"

"I may have done. I don't remember."

"What was your relationship with Freelove Dolleware?"

"I knew her from the tavern. She works there, or she used to."

"Were you intimate with the victim?"

Vilett fidgeted in his chair before answering. "I liked her, but we weren't together in that way."

A murmur swept through the room as Reuben took the stand The presiding judge gaveled for order.

"You admit that you shot the victim, Freelove Dolleware," Reuben's attorney said. "Please tell the court how and why you committed that act."

Reuben spoke with his head down, but his voice carried clearly in a chamber that was suddenly quiet.

"I was in love with her. She led me to believe that she loved me. Then I heard someone at the tavern say she was meeting a man at that house in Westerly. I had to see if it was true. When I got there, she was with a man. He was on the floor, and she was on top of him. In a fit of jealousy I killed her."

"Are you sorry for what you did?"

"I was confused when I fired that shot. I was angry at her for being unfaithful and at him for taking her away from me."

Freelove's attorney rose to question Reuben. "Who was the other man in the house that night?"

"I didn't get a good look at him."

"Why did you run off and hide afterwards?"

"I needed time to think."

"What made you come back and stand trial?"

"I finally accepted what I did and blamed myself instead of them."

"You said you were confused. But were you thinking clearly when you went to the house to confirm your suspicions about the victim?"

"I suppose I was," Reuben said.

"And you had a gun. Was it your intention to use it, if your suspicions proved to be correct?"

"I had no clear idea what I would do. I always carry a gun when I go out alone at night."

"Even when you go to the tavern?"

"I don't remember being at the tavern. I might have been."

In summing up, Freelove's attorney stated that Reuben was in control of his actions prior to the murder, and that his flight afterwards was a rational decision. Reuben's attorney maintained that rage at the sight of Freelove with another man had affected Reuben's actions that night and long afterwards. The jury was instructed to retire to a side room and return with their verdict.

Joseph started to rise, then thought better of it and resumed his seat. Mary noted his action and pressed his hand reassuringly.

The jury deliberated less than an hour. Sheffield, the foreman, rose to deliver their verdict. "We find the defendant, Reuben Hull, guilty of murder."

The deputy governor thanked the jury. Without pause he announced, "Reuben Hull, I sentence you to be hanged by the neck until you are dead. To allow you time to settle your affairs, the date of your execution is set for the tenth of November next. This court is adjourned."

Joseph felt a tightness gripping his chest. He noted his daughter's look of concern, then slumped in his seat. Mary screamed. Amid the commotion that ensued, Tiddeman called for a straight-backed chair. Assisted by young Joseph, he carried his uncle from the room. Once outside Joseph regained consciousness. Tiddeman urged him to take deep breaths of fresh air. When Joseph was able to stand, Tiddeman secured a carriage.

"Take us to the ferry," he ordered the driver.

Twenty

"Some truths are best left unspoken."
(Rhode Island Colony, 1719-1720)

Confined to his jail cell, Reuben exhibited behavior that the jailer described as erratic. He would sit for hours preoccupied and unresponsive, as if in a trance. He often left his food untouched, and he called out in his sleep for his father and his dead mother.

"When I tried to rouse him," the jailer told Tiddeman, "he got angry and struck me and bloodied my nose."

"I can't help it," Reuben said when Tiddeman chided him for his actions. "I blame myself for what happened to Father."

"He's had these attacks before," Tiddeman said. "Thou aren't helping him by such outbursts. Thou are only hurting thyself."

"I've hurt others," Reuben said. "I deserve to be hurt."

As the date set for the execution approached, Joseph had a relapse. Based on Tiddeman's plea that hanging the son would kill the father, and on the jailer's report that Reuben's behavior often bordered on lunacy, the court put off the execution until the following spring. The magistrate also gave Reuben permission to visit his father, provided he was accompanied by a responsible person who could vouch for his return.

"That was the easy part," Tiddeman said, when John applauded him for his efforts. "I still have to convince Reuben to go to Kings Towne and persuade Joseph to let him in the house."

"They say he's a lunatic," John said. "What is thy opinion?"

"I can understand why a man in his position might exhibit strange behavior. If he's reconciled with his father, he may be better able to cope with his own future. At least that's my hope."

Tiddeman did arrange for a visit early in the winter; but Reuben declined to offer any further account of his actions, and Joseph was adamant in his refusal to accept an admitted murderer as his son. As Tiddeman prepared to leave, he was intercepted by Mary, who had listened to the heated exchange between father and son.

"Would being reconciled with Reuben really help Father ?" she asked. "Neither one seems to want it."

"I think it would benefit both of them," Tiddeman said.

"Perhaps I can find a way to soften his heart," Mary said.

"I doubt that thou can change his attitude, but it won't hurt to try."

Following the visit and despite Tidddeman's advice to rest, Joseph insisted on going out daily to oversee his Indian laborers.

"I want to be sure everything is going as it should," he said.

"Thy son Joseph can manage the business," Tiddeman said. "There's no need for thee to go on like this."

"This is the life I fashioned for myself, and I intend to live it out to the end," Joseph said.

* * *

There was nothing unusual in Mary's offer to prepare the evening meal, but Joseph was taken aback by the course of their conversation.

"Tiddeman thinks it would be good for thee and for Reuben if thou paid him a visit in jail," she said as they ate.

"Thou heard him when he was here," Joseph said. "I see nothing to be gained by such a visit."

"Not as long as thou regard him only as a murderer."

"That's what he is. How else would thou have me see him?"

"As thy son. He must have had a reason for what he did. I think he was protecting someone."

"What if he was? That's no excuse for murder."

"I think he wanted to protect me."

Joseph stared hard at his daughter. "I'm not sure what thou mean."

"The man he saw that night was my husband John."

"Is that what Reuben told thee?"

"No," Mary said, shaking her head, "but I had a feeling that John was seeing another woman. The pieces all fit together."

"Has he admitted being unfaithful?" Joseph asked.

"He denied it, but he hasn't been the same since the murder."

"I'll speak to him, if thou wish."

"We can work it out. I just want thee to know that Reuben may have had a motive other than jealousy for what he did."

Joseph appeared lost in thought. "I thank thee for thy honesty," he said at last. "As for visiting Reuben, I'll think about it."

* * *

"The next time thou visit Reuben," Joseph said, "I'd like to go along."

Tiddeman was mildly surprised by his uncle's request. He assumed Mary had spoken to her father; but the winter was well advanced, and he had given up hope that her efforts to bring about a reconciliation would bear fruit.

"He mustn't know, or he'll refuse to see me," Joseph added.

Tiddeman agreed that was the best course. They arrived unannounced at the jail in Newport.

"Hello, son," Joseph said when he saw Reuben.

Neither one of them made a move to shake hands or hug each other.

"Hello, Father," Reuben said.

Tiddeman broke the awkward silence. "I can leave and let thee talk in private."

"No need for that," Reuben said. "I have nothing more to say to him."

At these words Joseph found his voice. "I have something to say to thee. I was a bit harsh when last I saw thee. I'm sorry for that. I spoke to Mary afterward; or rather, she spoke to me. She made me see the reason for thy actions. I don't excuse them, but I think I understand."

Reuben frowned. "What did Mary have to say?" he asked.

"That thou wanted to protect her," Joseph said. "That the man thou saw at the house that night was her husband. At least that's what she thinks."

Reuben paced back and forth in the room where visitors spoke with those in jail. Pausing in front of his father, he said, "Tell Mary she's wrong."

"She'll be glad to hear it."

"Is there anything else?"

"I've said what I came to say."

Reuben's body appeared to shrink in upon itself as he sat down. "I'm sorry I caused everyone so much trouble," he said. "It will all be over soon."

"We've had too many deaths in the family," Joseph said. "I can't bear to witness another."

"I understand," Reuben said.

Joseph rose and walked to where his son was seated. Bending down, he hugged him as best he could. Reuben accepted the embrace but made no effort to get up. Tiddeman thought he heard a sob, but he wasn't sure which of them had uttered it.

"I'm glad that's over," Joseph said when they were outside the jail. "At least we learned that Mary's husband wasn't involved in this."

"I'm sure she'll be relieved," Tiddeman said, but he suspected that Reuben had not been completely honest.

* * *

With the advent of spring Joseph rode out to check the walls on his property. His horse was spooked by a wild animal, and he was thrown to the ground, injuring his neck and his back. Tiddeman did what he could to make him comfortable, but he had no remedies in his bag. Mary and young Joseph were at his bedside when he died.

The day of the funeral was dark and overcast. A brisk northwest wind whipped across the burial ground. After Joseph's body was lowered into the grave, his family along with other Friends and members of the community retired to the adjacent meeting house.

As a result of Tiddeman's efforts, Reuben was allowed to attend the funeral under guard. He watched the burial, standing apart, but declined to enter the meeting house.

"My presence would be a distraction." he told Tiddeman. "I'll pay my respects to Father at his grave."

Tiddeman agreed that was the best course. In the meeting house he joined his father on a bench at the front. His mother sat with Mary and her sister Alice. He had noted earlier that Mary's husband was not in attendance.

The elders took their place facing the gathering, men on their right and women on their left. One of them rose and addressed the gathering in a voice that was calm and clear.

"We gather today in a meeting for worship to give thanks for the grace of God as evidenced in the life of our friend, Joseph Hull. We invite anyone who is moved by the spirit to give voice to their feelings, but silence is equally meaningful as an expression of our sorrow."

A member of the Society recalled Joseph's contributions as a teacher and noted that he had made his home available until the meeting house was built. A local official spoke of how Joseph's life and work had benefitted the town and the colony.

A period of silence ensued before young Joseph rose and removed his hat. "I see several of father's Indian laborers here," he said. "Before I was born, he served as a militiaman in a war against the Narragansetts. The slaughter of women and children during a battle in a nearby swamp sickened him, and later in life he rescued a number of Indians from slavery. He put them to work in his fields, and he defended them and their property against exploitation by land companies. I promise to carry on the family heritage."

After another silence John rose. His voice cracked as he started to speak. Gathering his composure, he tried again with more success.

"Joseph was my brother and my friend. He went to war in my place. He enabled me to purchase my first ship. Moved by his example, I took a wife who is both a Friend and a loyal helpmate. Joseph was a loving husband and father, a success in business, a pillar in our Society. Our father Tristram and our grandfather, Reverend Joseph, would have been proud of him."

A murmur of approval greeted John as he resumed his seat. When no one else was moved to speak, an elder rose and shook hands with a man in the front row. Those gathered for the service heeded the signal that the meeting was over. Outside many of them offered condolences to the family.

Tiddeman looked about for Reuben. He spotted him standing as if transfixed by his father's grave. The constable guarding him stood nearby.

"Come and join the family," Tiddeman said, taking his arm.

Reuben allowed himself to be led away.

John and Alice presided over the gathering at the house Joseph had built for his wife and children some three decades earlier.

"What will become of this place?" John said, phrasing it more as a comment than a question.

"We'll make good use of it," young Joseph assured him.

"We've had too many funerals," Alice said, then looked away in confusion as all eyes turned toward Reuben.

"I intend to petition the court for another reprieve," Tiddeman said. "That will give everyone time to recover."

"We will recover with the help of our wives and children," John said.

Reuben had been silent and withdrawn. "A wife is a gift that we do nothing to merit," he said in a voice barely audible.

"The best we can do is seek to recognize the gift when it's presented to us," Mary said

"Some of us," Reuben said. "Father always said I looked in the wrong places. He was right."

"At least thou were reconciled before he died," Tiddeman said.

"I wouldn't call it that," Reuben said. "He never forgave me for what I did. I can't forgive myself. But we did reach some kind of understanding."

Tiddeman glanced toward Mary, but she averted her eyes.

"Joseph bore thee no ill will," John said.

"I wish I could believe that," Reuben said.

* * *

As the day set for the execution drew near, Tiddeman stopped by the jail whenever he was in Newport. On one of these visits Reuben appeared to be preoccupied, as if he were weighing a matter of great import. Tiddeman waited patiently for his cousin to speak.

"I've been asking myself why I acted as I did that night," he said at last. "It's all I have to think about."

Tiddeman refrained from asking whether he had an answer.

"I was jealous and a bit crazy," Reuben went on, "but I knew what I was doing."

Tiddeman nodded in agreement. "I never put much stock in the idea of lunacy, but it helped us get a delay in carrying out thy sentence."

Reuben continued as if he hadn't heard. "My mind was perfectly clear when I fired the shot that killed her."

Tiddeman did not reply. Better to let Reuben tell it his way.

"I waited years for a woman to say she loved me enough to marry me. Not that I considered myself any great prize, but men with a lot less to offer were happily married. I had a hundred and fifty acres in Westerly, a gift from Father; and I was building a house. I was aware of her reputation, but we talked more about the future. I was in love with her, and she made me believe she was the woman I was looking for."

Reuben stared for some time at the floor, as if he were uncertain how to proceed. "Everything was going well until I heard some men in the tavern talking about her. One of the men was Vilett. They said she was meeting a man at a house in Westerly. I knew the house they were talking about, so I followed her there. I had to find out if it was true."

He paused again. Tiddeman was silent.

"There was a light in the house, so I looked in the window. I wasn't thinking of killing anyone. I was going to confront her as she left the house. What I saw changed all that. The man was on the floor with his pants down, and she was on top of him. I was mad at both of them, but I knew what I had to do. I just raised my gun and fired. Then I panicked. I wanted to get as far away from that house as I could."

Tiddeman sensed that he had reached the end of his story. "Then thou did recognize the man," he said. "Was it Mary's husband?"

Reuben stared at him. His eyes were glazed, and he showed no sign of recognition. Tiddeman waited for him to return to the moment.

"I can't be sure," he said. "Whoever it was, I'll never forgive myself for what I did. I deserve to die."

Tiddeman realized that he had to be content with that explanation.

* * *

Although Reuben was little known in Newport, a crowd of men, women, and children gathered outside the jail to witness the execution. He declined the services of a minister. His brother Joseph along with Tiddeman and John were admitted to his cell for a private farewell and admonished to be quick about it.

Reuben had little to say. "I took a life, I'm ready to give mine."

Each of the men hugged him in turn, then joined the crowd outside the jail. Reuben emerged with his hands bound behind his back. He wore a white linen shirt over his clothes and a cap on his head. He was placed in a cart, his back to the horse. Two constables walked alongside the cart as it proceeded toward the long wharf. The crowd followed after. Tiddeman had arranged for a boatman to transport them across the inner harbor to Goat Island, where the gibbet was located. Others in the crowd did the same.

None of the three men had witnessed an execution, and they were unprepared for the scene that greeted them. A wide horsecart had drawn up beneath the gibbet. Reuben stood erect on the cart. The hangman was directly behind him. As they watched, he fastened a noose around Reuben's neck. That done, he stepped aside as the sheriff mounted the cart.

"The general court of trials for the colony of Rhode Island and Providence Plantations has found this man, Reuben Hull, guilty of murder and sentenced him to be hanged," he said in a voice devoid of emotion. "He has declined the services of a chaplain and has declared himself ready to die for his crime. I am not qualified to preach a proper execution sermon; but I admonish anyone here present, who may someday be tempted through anger or jealousy to take a human life, to reflect upon the consequences of such an action, and may the scene you're about to witness serve as a deterrent. Any relative of Reuben Hull who wishes to speak may now come forward."

Young Joseph mounted the cart.

A spasm wracked Reuben's body as he embraced his brother. "I'm sorry," he said, choking on his words. "Tell Mary that I love her."

The sheriff ushered Joseph off the cart and stepped down himself. The hangman pulled the cap down over Reuben's eyes. That done, he went to the front of the cart and picked up the reins. Raising the whip high over his head, he held it there. He seemed to be waiting for a signal.

A hush fell over the crowd. If there was a signal, neither Joseph nor Tiddeman nor John heard it. The hangman gave the horse a good lash. A gasp went up from the spectators as the cart lurched forward, leaving Reuben dangling from the gibbet. The sheriff tugged on his legs to hasten his death and prevent suffering.

The three men turned their eyes away from the scene as they waited for the crowd to disperse. They had paid to have Reuben's body delivered to them after the execution, sparing him the further indignity of public display usually accorded to a murderer. When the spectators were gone, they claimed the body, wrapped it in a clean sheet, and transported it back to Kings Towne.

* * *

Only family members were on hand to witness Reuben's burial in the Friends cemetery in Kings Towne. On the advice of the elders young Joseph decided to forego a memorial service. A light drizzle was falling as the family gathered at the grave site. As patriarch of the family, John spoke first.

"This is not the way we would have wished for Reuben's life to end. But this is the way he wanted it. He chose to settle accounts with his maker and society by giving up his life. It behooves all of us to respect his decision. We should not judge him solely on the basis of his final deed. We must look at the full canvas of his life. Troubled though it was at times, he remained a loyal son, brother, nephew, and cousin. I trust that we shall all remember him as one of the family."

Young Joseph was next to speak. "Reuben was four years my junior. We were never as close as brothers are meant to be. I regret that, now that he's gone. I couldn't understand why he made some of his decisions; but I liked him. I shall always remember him as my brother and my friend."

Mary started to speak, then stopped. When everyone at the grave turned to encourage her, she went on in a soft voice. "I was his older sister, but I often looked to Reuben for support. He protected me in any way he could. Sometimes I was able to help him. At least he was kind enough to say so. In recent years I've been fully occupied with my home and children. I was blind to Reuben's needs, and for that I ask his forgiveness."

With these last words she broke down and wept. When she had recovered, Tiddeman stepped forward. His voice was clear and strong.

"I'm gratified that I was able to gain Reuben's confidence toward the end of his life. I can testify that he served honorably in the campaign against the French at Port Royal. He wanted a wife and children, and he couldn't understand why fate denied him that boon. By taking responsibility for what he had done, he sought to make peace with himself and his family. May peace be with him."

As the gathering dispersed, Tiddeman took his mother aside. "Mary seemed quite upset," he said. "Perhaps thou should see what's troubling her. Father and I can wait for thee."

"I noticed it too," Alice said. "I'll speak to her."

Mary was standing apart from the family when Alice approached. "We all missed thy husband," she said.

"He had some urgent business," Mary said.

"He should be here to support thee at a time like this."

"I'll be all right. I was just a bit emotional at the grave."

"I felt really close to him," Alice said, "as if his spirit were lingering over us."

"I didn't realize thou cared that much about Reuben."

"He sought our advice, and Tiddeman often spoke of him."

Mary appeared more attentive. "I know, and I thank thee."

"I was moved by thy words at the grave," Alice said. "Reuben said thou were the only person who understood him. I didn't think he was close to anyone in his later years, except maybe Tiddeman."

"We were close friends as children, but in recent years we drifted apart. At least I did. It seems that Reuben stayed closer than I imagined. I blame myself for not realizing that he needed me. I might have saved him."

"What more could thou have done?" Alice asked.

"I could have listened to him."

Alice waited for a further explanation, but Mary was lost in her own thoughts. When it became obvious that nothing more was forthcoming, Alice took matters into her own hands. She had hoped it wouldn't come to that, but she saw no other way forward.

"Tiddeman told us what thy father said when he saw Reuben this past winter. Thou needn't talk unless thou wish, but I want thee to know that I'm aware of thy suspicions about thy husband."

"That is none of thy concern," Mary said.

In the silence that followed, her initial anger gradually gave way to an expression akin to relief. Alice waited for whatever was to come.

"I'm sorry," Mary said. "I know thou only want to help."

She was again silent, and Alice pressed on.

"Tiddeman said that Joseph asked Reuben if the man he saw that night at the house was thy husband, and that Reuben denied it. Have thou spoken to thy husband about this?"

"He refuses to talk about it. When I mention Reuben, he changes the subject. I want to believe Reuben, but I know he only said it to protect me. Just as he thought he was protecting me when he shot that woman. I don't deserve his loyalty."

Mary broke down and wept. Alice went to her, and they embraced.

"Allow me to give thee some advice," she said when Mary was calmer. "If thy mother were alive, I'm sure she would say the same thing."

"I know what thou are about to say."

Ignoring the comment, Alice pressed on. "If thou agonize over this in private, thou will make thyself sick. Speak to thy husband. Men are more inclined to tell the truth when confronted. Once thou know what thou are dealing with, thou can make a wiser decision on how to proceed."

"What if he admits it? Should I forgive him?"

"That is for thee to decide. Much will depend on what he has to say and how he says it. Thou must be willing to put all this behind thee, if thou are to go on with life together."

"I thank thee for thy advice," Mary replied. "As Father used to say, I'll think about it."

* * *

While he waited for Alice to return, John had a talk with his son.

"When thou last spoke to Reuben alone, did he tell thee anything more?" he asked.

Tiddeman was ready for the question. "He just repeated what he said at the trial. That he was overcome by anger and jealousy. That he loved her and felt he had finally found the right woman."

"Except she was seeing someone else. Did he say who the man was?"

Tiddeman had discussed Joseph's visit to the jail with his mother, thinking she might have occasion to speak to Mary. He saw no purpose to be served by telling his father about Mary's suspicions and Reuben's denial.

"He started to but thought better of it. I respect his decision. Some truths are best left unspoken."

"Quite right," John said. "It's none of our affair."

"That's not what I meant. Some of the blame lies on our shoulders. I for one might have done more to help him."

"What else could thou have done?"

"When he was hiding on Block Island, I saw that he was troubled."

"It was too late then," John said.

"True, but our talks made me realize that I might have done more to help him settle down in life. When we volunteered for the expedition against Port Royal, Reuben said he hoped to find a French woman who would marry him. I took it as a joke. I see now that he was very much in earnest."

"Thou are not to blame for thy youthful blindness."

"Perhaps not," Tiddeman said, "but if we had kept in contact, I would have been more aware of his problems."

"Thou were newly married and striving to become a doctor. Thou had no time for anything else."

"I could at least have listened and offered my support."

Both men were silent for a time.

"I too might have done more to help him," John said. "I did offer to take him on as an apprentice after his escapade with Captain Kidd. He said he'd had enough of the sea."

"I was nine when he ran away," Tiddeman said. "I remember thinking how exciting it must be to sail on a pirate ship. After he came home, I regarded him as someone who had experienced the world."

"What bothers me most," John said, "is that Reuben's death served no purpose."

"Perhaps it did," Tiddeman said. "As a doctor I had no training or experience with troubles of the mind. Thanks to Reuben, I'll be more alert to such problems in the future."

Alice approached them. "What are thou talking about?" she asked.

"I was just telling Father about a patient who died," Tiddeman said.